Top Cow Productions Presents

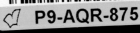

Sunstone

Created by Stjepan Sejic

Published by Top Cow Productions, Inc.
Los Angeles

Top Cow Productions Presents...

Stjepan Sejic
Creator, Artist, and Writer

Stjepan Sejic
Cover Art

Ryan Cady
Editor

Tricia Ramos
Book Design and Layout

For Top Cow Productions, Inc.

Marc Silvestri - *CEO* • Matt Hawkins - *President and COO*

Betsy Gonia - *Editor* • Bryan Hill - *Story Editor*

Elena Salcedo - *Operations Manager* • Ryan Cady - *Editorial Assistant*

Vincent Valentine - *Production Assistant*

To find the comic shop
nearest you, call:
1-888-COMICBOOK

Want more info? Check out:
www.topcow.com
for news & exclusive Top Cow merchandis

IMAGE COMICS, INC.
Robert Kirkman — Chief Operating Officer
Erik Larsen — Chief Financial Officer
Todd McFarlane — President
Marc Silvestri — Chief Executive Officer
Jim Valentino — Vice-President
Eric Stephenson — Publisher
Corey Murphy — Director of Sales
Jeff Boison — Director of Publishing Planning & Book Trade Sales
Jeremy Sullivan — Director of Digital Sales
Kat Salazar — Director of PR & Marketing
Emily Miller — Director of Operations
Branwyn Bigglestone — Senior Accounts Manager
Sarah Mello — Accounts Manager
Drew Gill — Art Director
Jonathan Chan — Production Manager
Meredith Wallace — Print Manager
Briah Skelly — Publicity Assistant
Sasha Head — Sales & Marketing Production Designer
Randy Okamura — Digital Marketing Designer
David Brothers — Branding Manager
Ally Power — Content Manager
Addison Duke — Production Artist
Vincent Kukua — Production Artist
Tricia Ramos — Production Artist
Jeff Stang — Direct Market Sales Representative
Emilio Bautista — Digital Sales Associate
Leanna Caunter — Accounting Assistant
Chloe Ramos-Peterson — Administrative Assistant
IMAGECOMICS.COM

Sunstone Volume 4 Trade Paperback.

February 2016. First Printing. ISBN: 978-1-63215-609-9. $14.99 USD. Published by Image Comics, Inc. Office of publicatic
2001 Center Street, Sixth Floor, Berkeley, CA 94704. Originally published on DeviantArt by Stjepan Sejic. Sunstone© 2016 Stjep
Sejic. All rights reserved. "Sunstone," its logos, and the likenesses of all characters (human or otherwise) featured herein are tradema
of Stjepan Sejic. "Image" and the Image Comics logos are registered trademarks of Image Comics, Inc. The characters, events, a
stories in this publication are entirely fictional. Any resemblance to actual persons, (living or dead) events, institutions, or local
without satiric intent, is coincidental. No portion of this publication may be reproduced or transmitted, in any form or by any mea
(except for short excerpts for journalistic or review purposes), without the express written permission of Stjepan Sejic. Printed in
USA. For information regarding the CPSIA on this printed material call: 203-595-3636 and provide reference #RICH–6585(

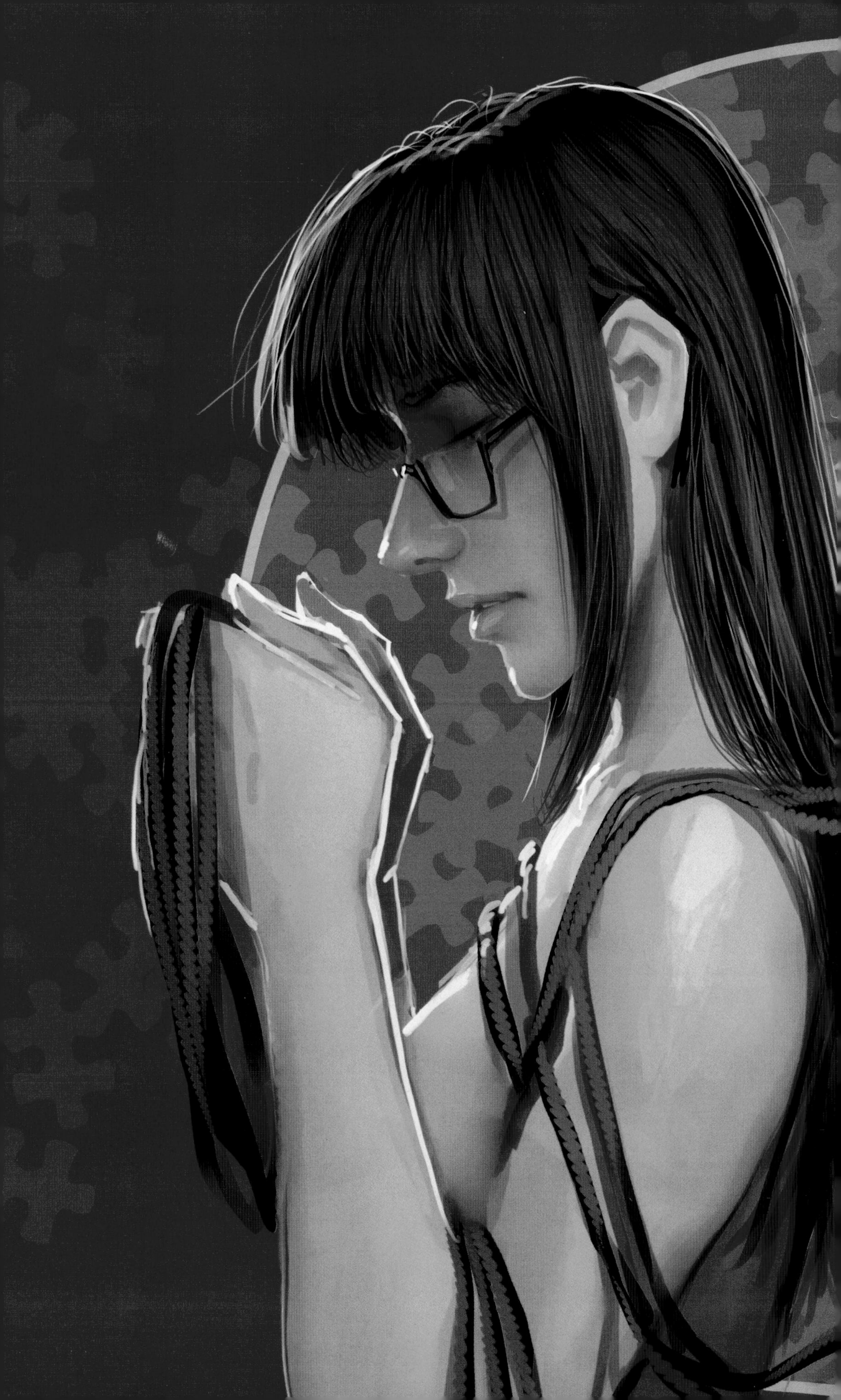

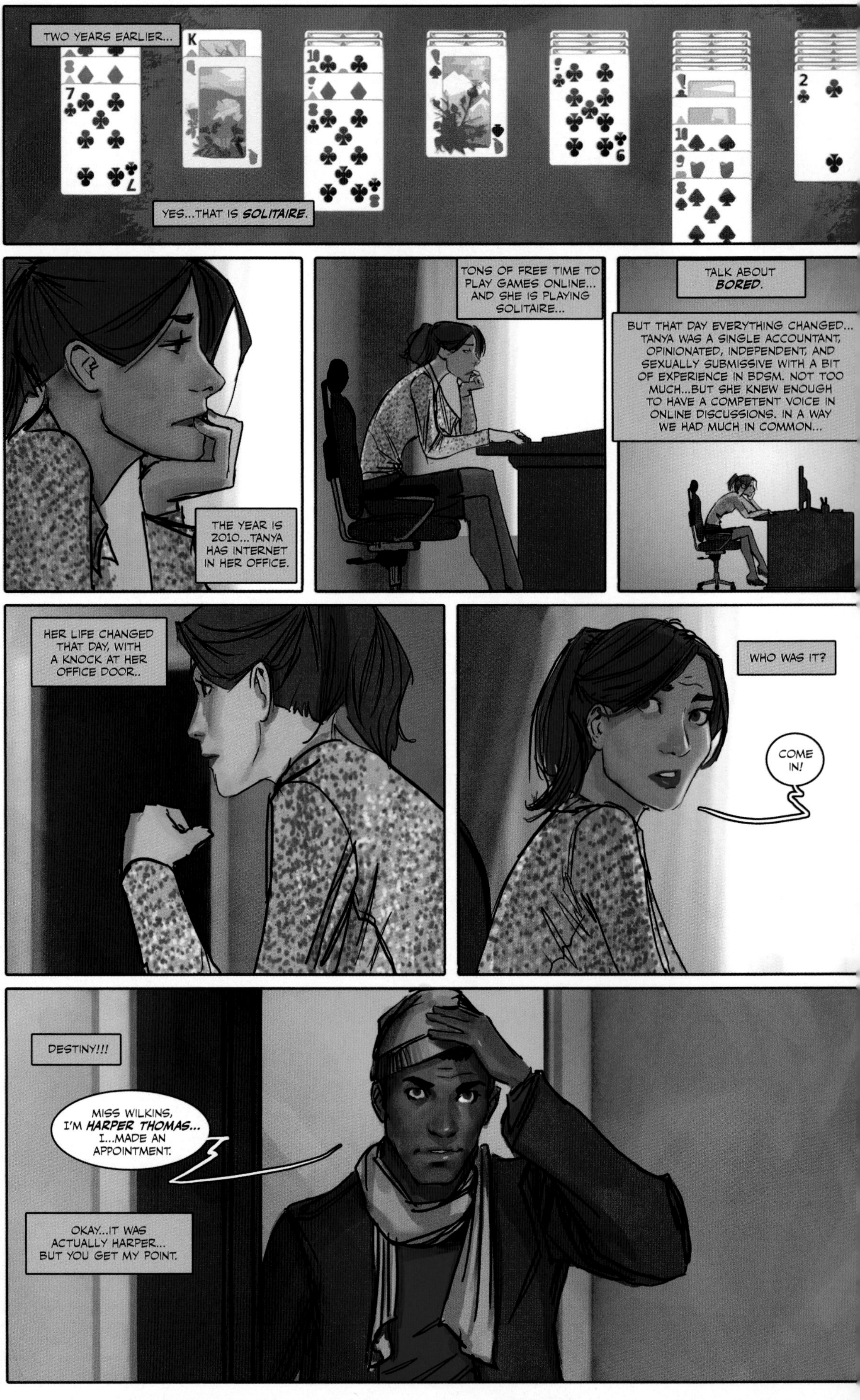

TWO YEARS EARLIER...
YES...THAT IS SOLITAIRE.
THE YEAR IS 2010...TANYA HAS INTERNET IN HER OFFICE.
TONS OF FREE TIME TO PLAY GAMES ONLINE... AND SHE IS PLAYING SOLITAIRE...
TALK ABOUT BORED.
BUT THAT DAY EVERYTHING CHANGED... TANYA WAS A SINGLE ACCOUNTANT, OPINIONATED, INDEPENDENT, AND SEXUALLY SUBMISSIVE WITH A BIT OF EXPERIENCE IN BDSM. NOT TOO MUCH...BUT SHE KNEW ENOUGH TO HAVE A COMPETENT VOICE IN ONLINE DISCUSSIONS. IN A WAY WE HAD MUCH IN COMMON...
HER LIFE CHANGED THAT DAY, WITH A KNOCK AT HER OFFICE DOOR..
WHO WAS IT?
COME IN!
DESTINY!!!
MISS WILKINS, I'M HARPER THOMAS... I...MADE AN APPOINTMENT.
OKAY...IT WAS ACTUALLY HARPER... BUT YOU GET MY POINT.

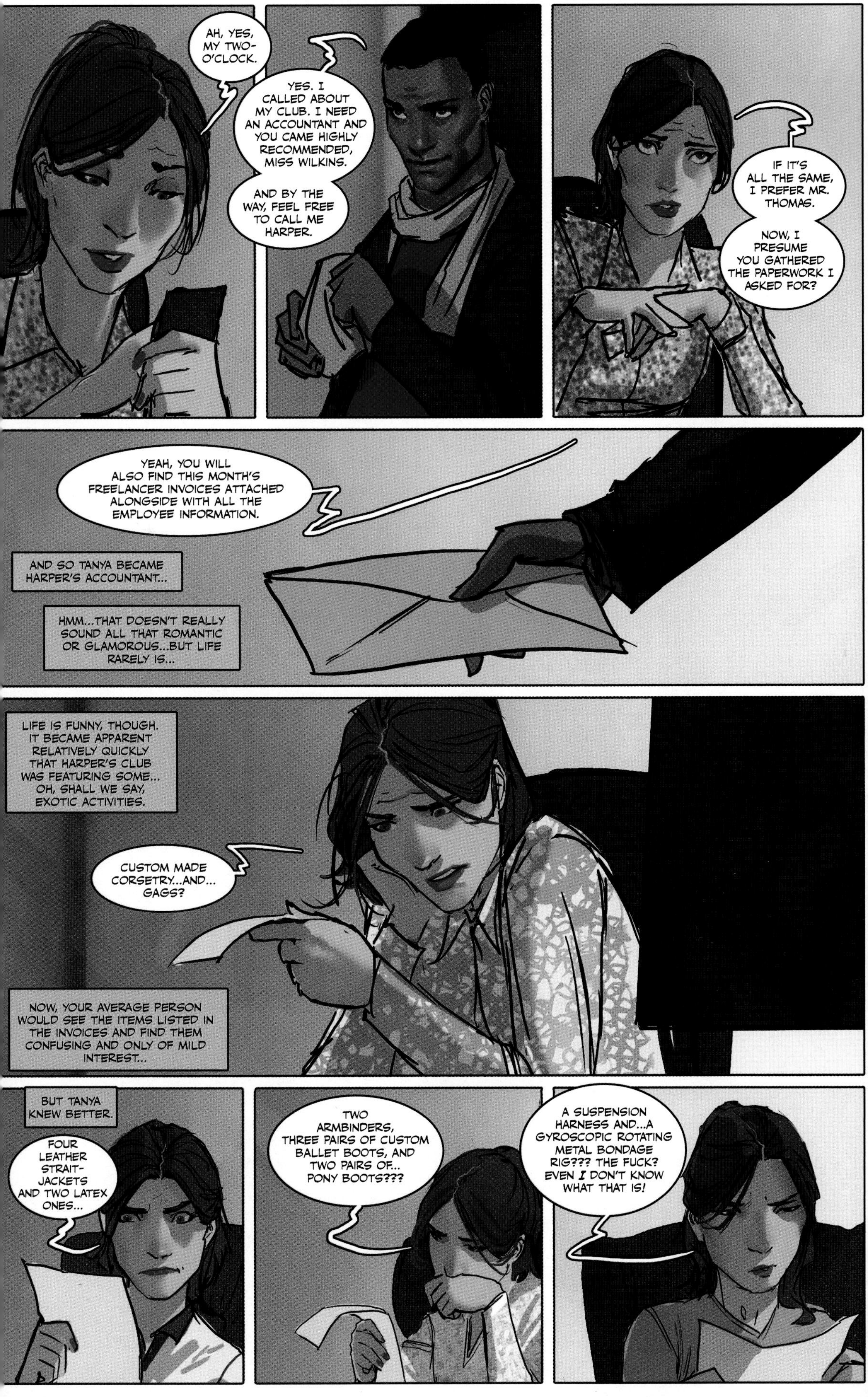
AH, YES, MY TWO-O'CLOCK.
YES. I CALLED ABOUT MY CLUB. I NEED AN ACCOUNTANT AND YOU CAME HIGHLY RECOMMENDED, MISS WILKINS.
AND BY THE WAY, FEEL FREE TO CALL ME HARPER.
IF IT'S ALL THE SAME, I PREFER MR. THOMAS.
NOW, I PRESUME YOU GATHERED THE PAPERWORK I ASKED FOR?
YEAH, YOU WILL ALSO FIND THIS MONTH'S FREELANCER INVOICES ATTACHED ALONGSIDE WITH ALL THE EMPLOYEE INFORMATION.
AND SO TANYA BECAME HARPER'S ACCOUNTANT...
HMM...THAT DOESN'T REALLY SOUND ALL THAT ROMANTIC OR GLAMOROUS...BUT LIFE RARELY IS...
LIFE IS FUNNY, THOUGH. IT BECAME APPARENT RELATIVELY QUICKLY THAT HARPER'S CLUB WAS FEATURING SOME... OH, SHALL WE SAY, EXOTIC ACTIVITIES.
CUSTOM MADE CORSETRY...AND... GAGS?
NOW, YOUR AVERAGE PERSON WOULD SEE THE ITEMS LISTED IN THE INVOICES AND FIND THEM CONFUSING AND ONLY OF MILD INTEREST...
BUT TANYA KNEW BETTER.
FOUR LEATHER STRAIT-JACKETS AND TWO LATEX ONES...
TWO ARMBINDERS, THREE PAIRS OF CUSTOM BALLET BOOTS, AND TWO PAIRS OF... PONY BOOTS???
A SUSPENSION HARNESS AND...A GYROSCOPIC ROTATING METAL BONDAGE RIG??? THE FUCK? EVEN I DON'T KNOW WHAT THAT IS!

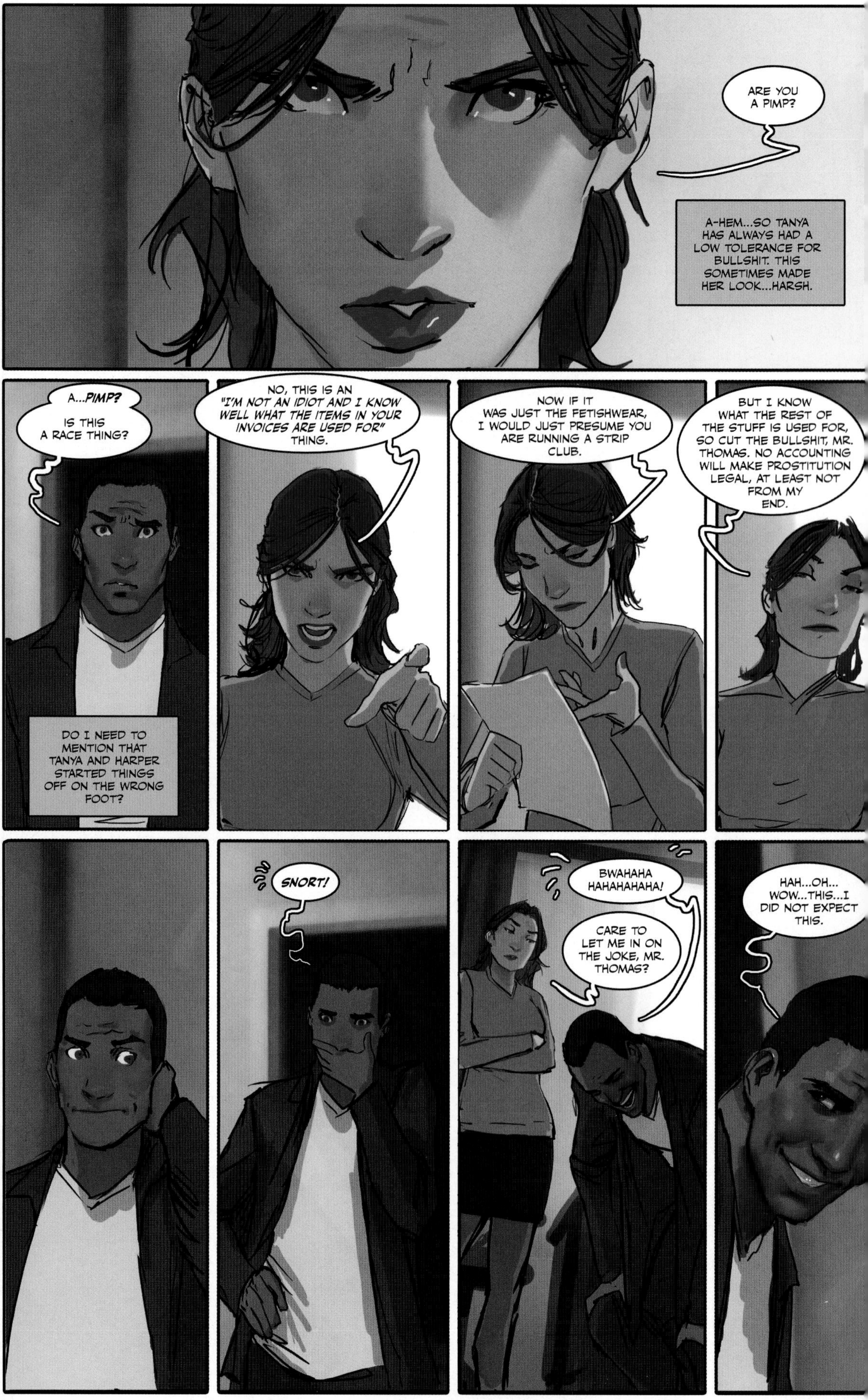
ARE YOU A PIMP?
A-HEM...SO TANYA HAS ALWAYS HAD A LOW TOLERANCE FOR BULLSHIT. THIS SOMETIMES MADE HER LOOK...HARSH.
A...PIMP? IS THIS A RACE THING?
DO I NEED TO MENTION THAT TANYA AND HARPER STARTED THINGS OFF ON THE WRONG FOOT?
NO, THIS IS AN "I'M NOT AN IDIOT AND I KNOW WELL WHAT THE ITEMS IN YOUR INVOICES ARE USED FOR" THING.
NOW IF IT WAS JUST THE FETISHWEAR, I WOULD JUST PRESUME YOU ARE RUNNING A STRIP CLUB.
BUT I KNOW WHAT THE REST OF THE STUFF IS USED FOR, SO CUT THE BULLSHIT, MR. THOMAS. NO ACCOUNTING WILL MAKE PROSTITUTION LEGAL, AT LEAST NOT FROM MY END.
SNORT!
BWAHAHA HAHAHAHAHA!
CARE TO LET ME IN ON THE JOKE, MR. THOMAS?
HAH...OH... WOW...THIS...I DID NOT EXPECT THIS.

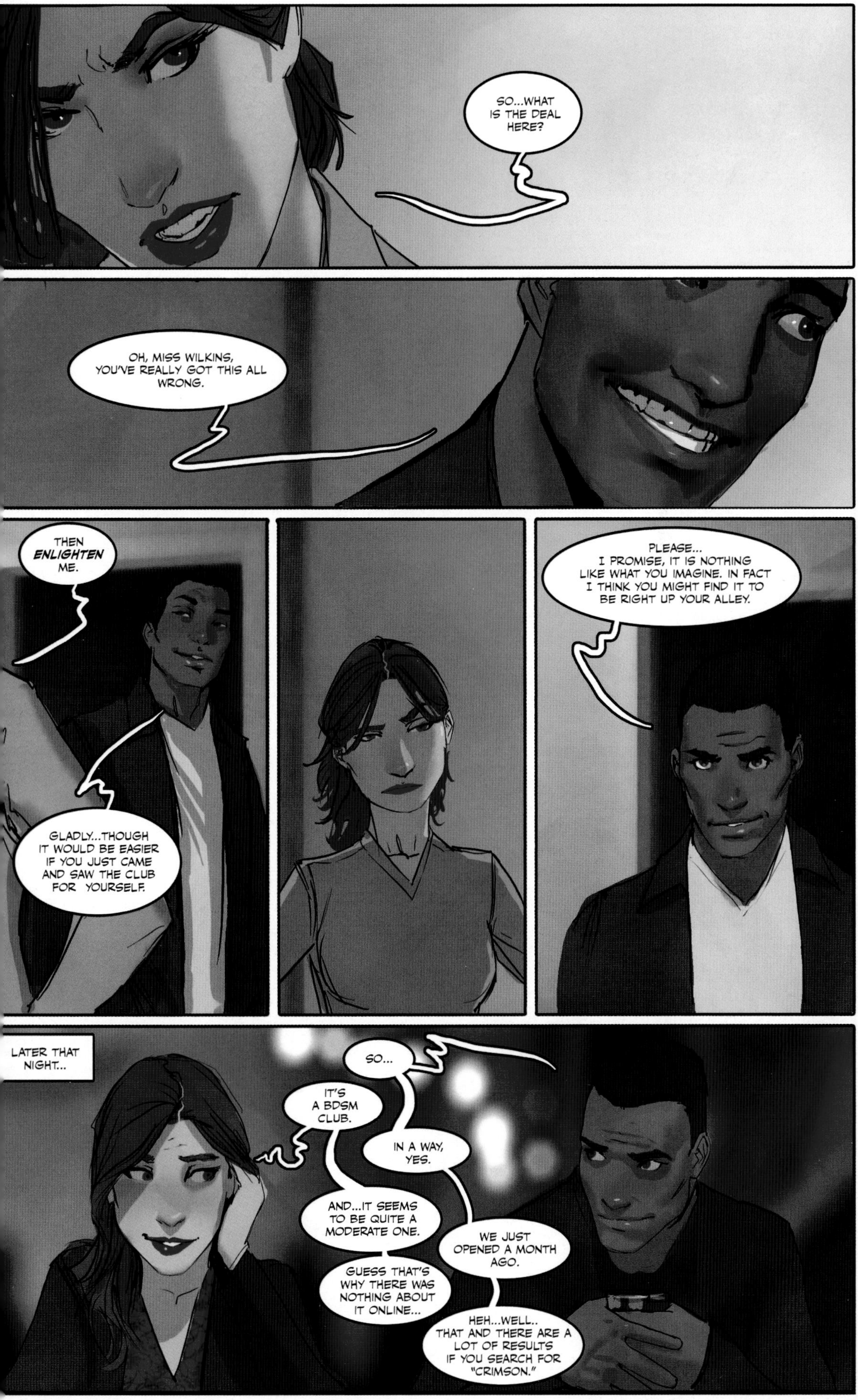
SO...WHAT IS THE DEAL HERE?
OH, MISS WILKINS, YOU'VE REALLY GOT THIS ALL WRONG.
THEN ***ENLIGHTEN*** ME.
GLADLY...THOUGH IT WOULD BE EASIER IF YOU JUST CAME AND SAW THE CLUB FOR YOURSELF.
PLEASE... I PROMISE, IT IS NOTHING LIKE WHAT YOU IMAGINE. IN FACT I THINK YOU MIGHT FIND IT TO BE RIGHT UP YOUR ALLEY.
LATER THAT NIGHT...
SO...
IT'S A BDSM CLUB.
IN A WAY, YES.
AND...IT SEEMS TO BE QUITE A MODERATE ONE.
WE JUST OPENED A MONTH AGO.
GUESS THAT'S WHY THERE WAS NOTHING ABOUT IT ONLINE...
HEH...WELL.. THAT AND THERE ARE A LOT OF RESULTS IF YOU SEARCH FOR "CRIMSON."

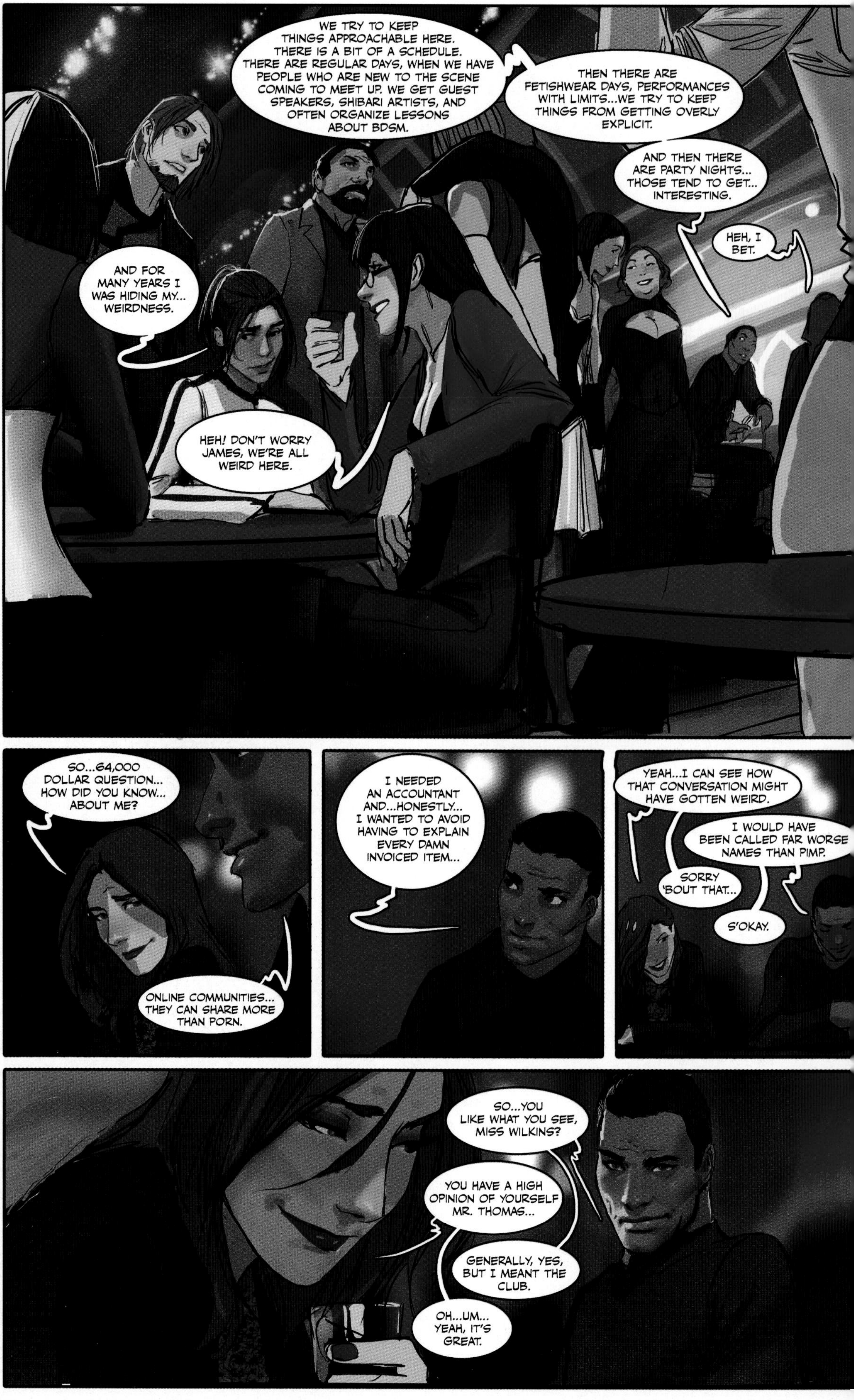
WE TRY TO KEEP THINGS APPROACHABLE HERE. THERE IS A BIT OF A SCHEDULE. THERE ARE REGULAR DAYS, WHEN WE HAVE PEOPLE WHO ARE NEW TO THE SCENE COMING TO MEET UP. WE GET GUEST SPEAKERS, SHIBARI ARTISTS, AND OFTEN ORGANIZE LESSONS ABOUT BDSM.
THEN THERE ARE FETISHWEAR DAYS, PERFORMANCES WITH LIMITS...WE TRY TO KEEP THINGS FROM GETTING OVERLY EXPLICIT.
AND THEN THERE ARE PARTY NIGHTS... THOSE TEND TO GET... INTERESTING.
HEH, I BET.
AND FOR MANY YEARS I WAS HIDING MY... WEIRDNESS.
HEH! DON'T WORRY JAMES, WE'RE ALL WEIRD HERE.
SO...64,000 DOLLAR QUESTION... HOW DID YOU KNOW... ABOUT ME?
ONLINE COMMUNITIES... THEY CAN SHARE MORE THAN PORN.
I NEEDED AN ACCOUNTANT AND...HONESTLY... I WANTED TO AVOID HAVING TO EXPLAIN EVERY DAMN INVOICED ITEM...
YEAH...I CAN SEE HOW THAT CONVERSATION MIGHT HAVE GOTTEN WEIRD.
I WOULD HAVE BEEN CALLED FAR WORSE NAMES THAN PIMP.
SORRY 'BOUT THAT...
S'OKAY.
SO...YOU LIKE WHAT YOU SEE, MISS WILKINS?
YOU HAVE A HIGH OPINION OF YOURSELF MR. THOMAS...
GENERALLY, YES, BUT I MEANT THE CLUB.
OH...UM... YEAH, IT'S GREAT.

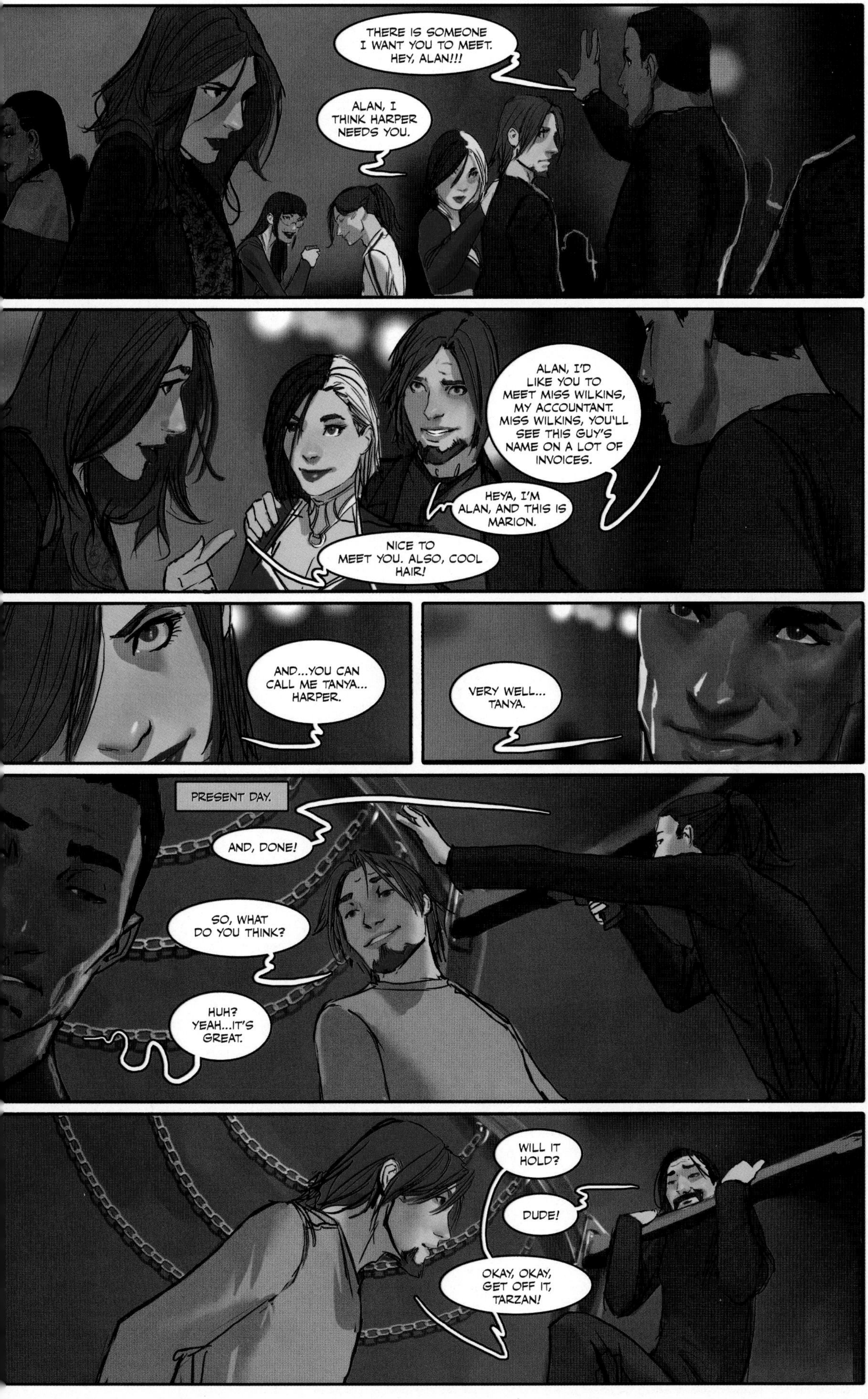
THERE IS SOMEONE I WANT YOU TO MEET. HEY, ALAN!!!
ALAN, I THINK HARPER NEEDS YOU.
ALAN, I'D LIKE YOU TO MEET MISS WILKINS, MY ACCOUNTANT. MISS WILKINS, YOU'LL SEE THIS GUY'S NAME ON A LOT OF INVOICES.
HEYA, I'M ALAN, AND THIS IS MARION.
NICE TO MEET YOU. ALSO, COOL HAIR!
AND...YOU CAN CALL ME TANYA... HARPER.
VERY WELL... TANYA.
PRESENT DAY.
AND, DONE!
SO, WHAT DO YOU THINK?
HUH? YEAH...IT'S GREAT.
WILL IT HOLD?
DUDE!
OKAY, OKAY, GET OFF IT, TARZAN!

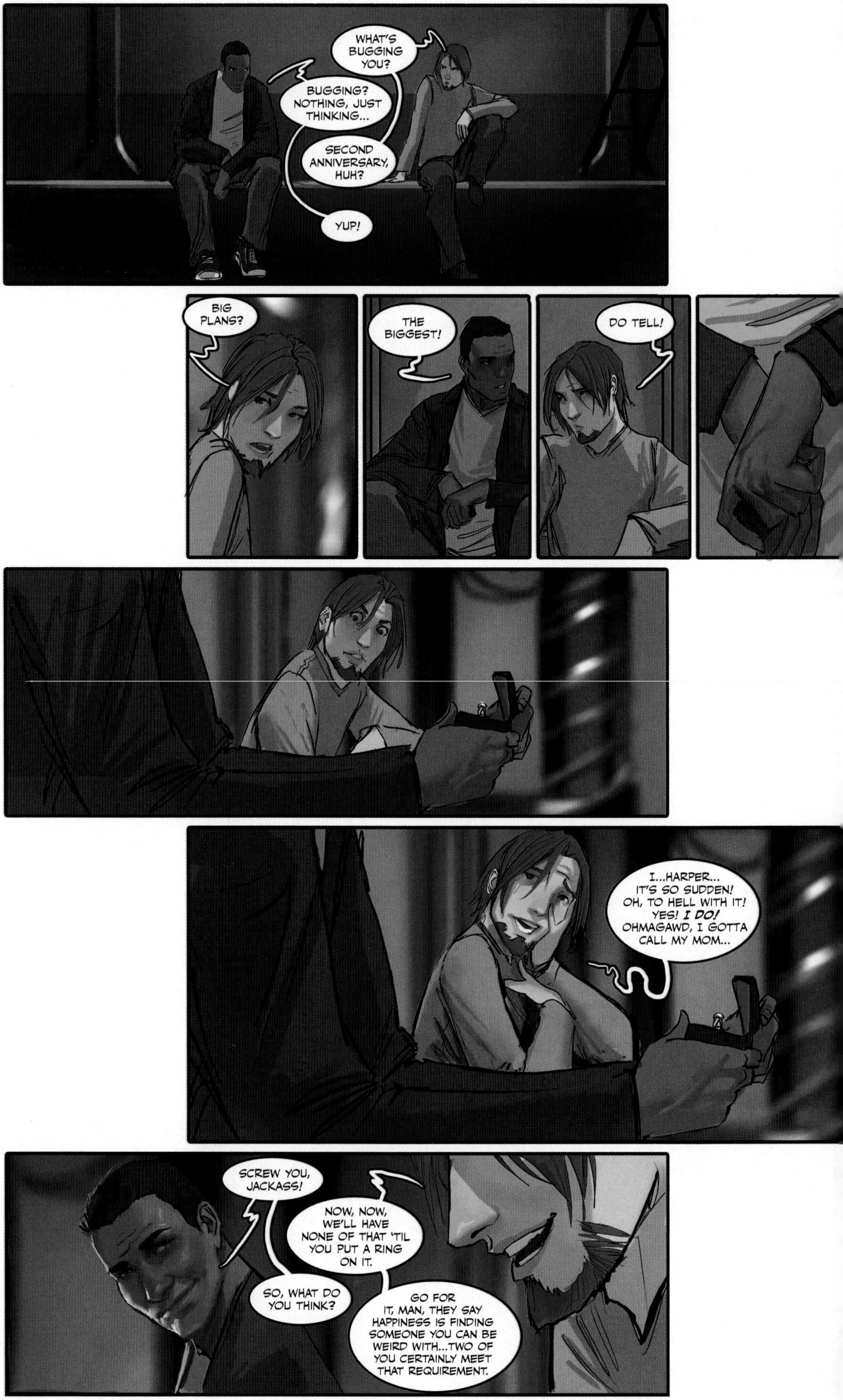
WHAT'S BUGGING YOU?
BUGGING? NOTHING, JUST THINKING...
SECOND ANNIVERSARY, HUH?
YUP!
BIG PLANS?
THE BIGGEST!
DO TELL!
I...HARPER... IT'S SO SUDDEN! OH, TO HELL WITH IT! YES! I DO! OHMAGAWD, I GOTTA CALL MY MOM...
SCREW YOU, JACKASS!
NOW, NOW, WE'LL HAVE NONE OF THAT 'TIL YOU PUT A RING ON IT.
SO, WHAT DO YOU THINK?
GO FOR IT, MAN, THEY SAY HAPPINESS IS FINDING SOMEONE YOU CAN BE WEIRD WITH...TWO OF YOU CERTAINLY MEET THAT REQUIREMENT.

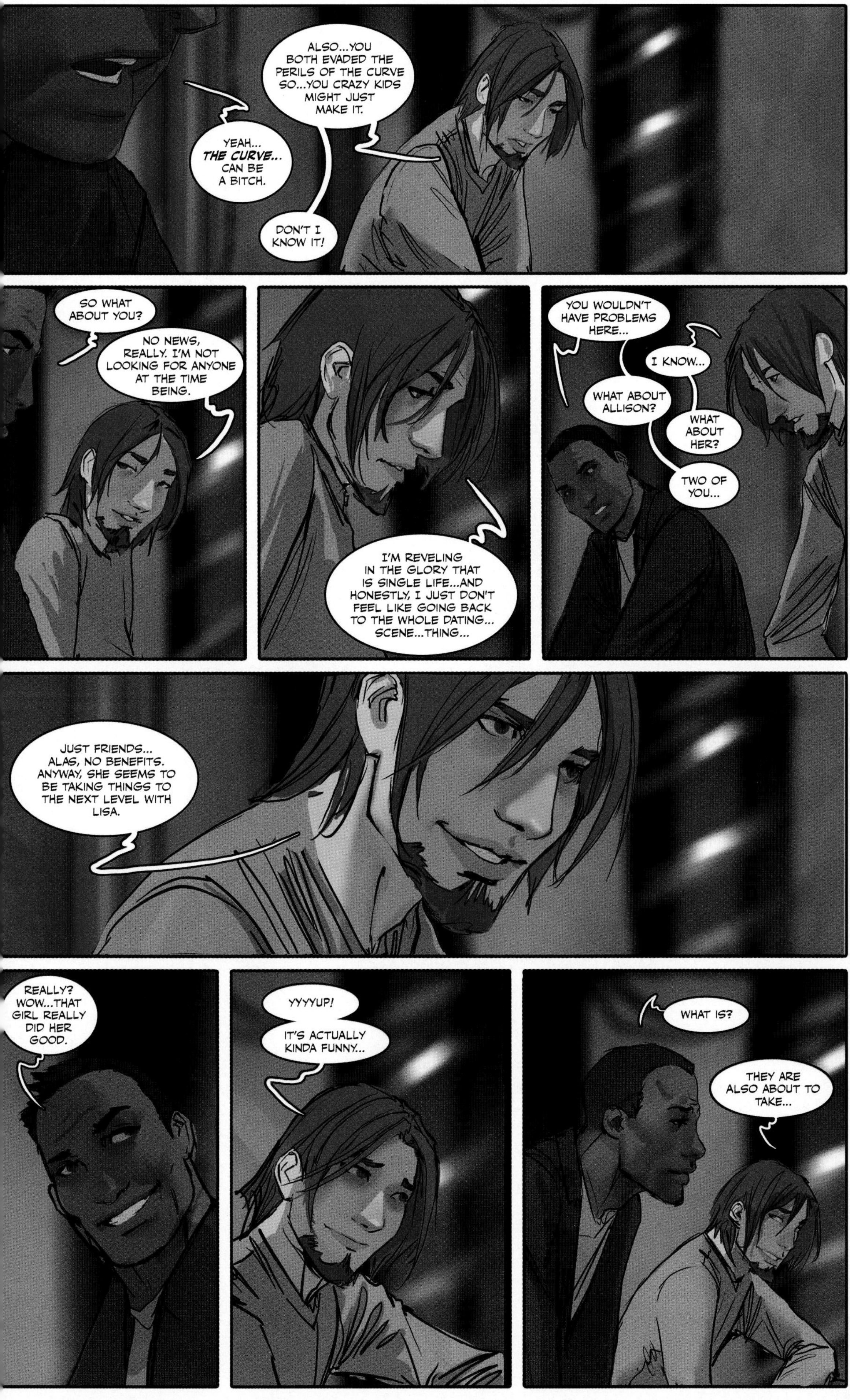
ALSO...YOU BOTH EVADED THE PERILS OF THE CURVE SO...YOU CRAZY KIDS MIGHT JUST MAKE IT.
YEAH... *THE CURVE...* CAN BE A BITCH.
DON'T I KNOW IT!
SO WHAT ABOUT YOU?
NO NEWS, REALLY. I'M NOT LOOKING FOR ANYONE AT THE TIME BEING.
I'M REVELING IN THE GLORY THAT IS SINGLE LIFE...AND HONESTLY, I JUST DON'T FEEL LIKE GOING BACK TO THE WHOLE DATING... SCENE...THING...
YOU WOULDN'T HAVE PROBLEMS HERE...
I KNOW...
WHAT ABOUT ALLISON?
WHAT ABOUT HER?
TWO OF YOU...
JUST FRIENDS... ALAS, NO BENEFITS. ANYWAY, SHE SEEMS TO BE TAKING THINGS TO THE NEXT LEVEL WITH LISA.
REALLY? WOW...THAT GIRL REALLY DID HER GOOD.
YYYYUP!
IT'S ACTUALLY KINDA FUNNY...
WHAT IS?
THEY ARE ALSO ABOUT TO TAKE...

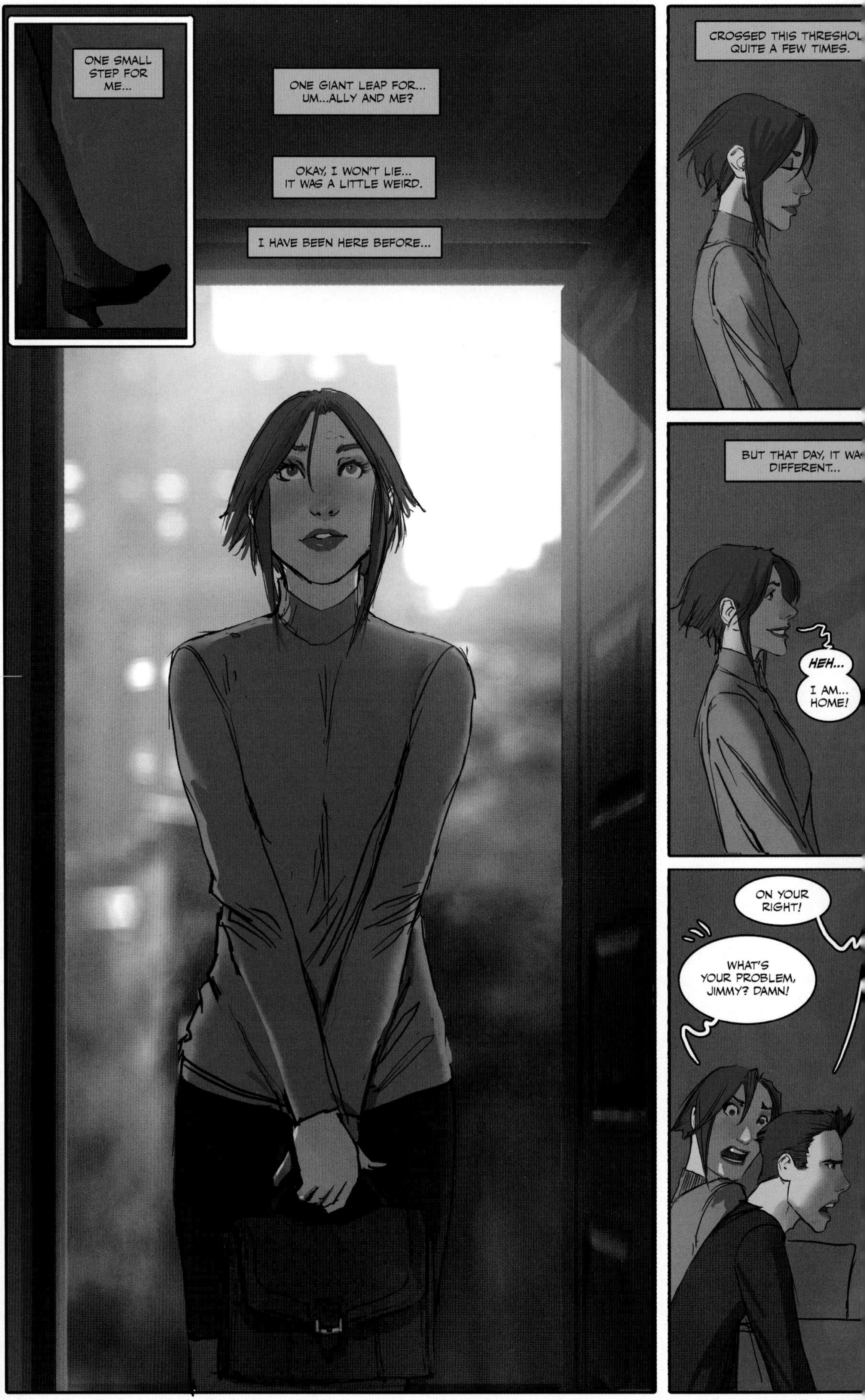

ONE SMALL STEP FOR ME...
ONE GIANT LEAP FOR... UM...ALLY AND ME?
OKAY, I WON'T LIE... IT WAS A LITTLE WEIRD.
I HAVE BEEN HERE BEFORE...
CROSSED THIS THRESHOL
QUITE A FEW TIMES.
BUT THAT DAY, IT WA
DIFFERENT...
HEH...
I AM... HOME!
ON YOUR RIGHT!
WHAT'S YOUR PROBLEM, JIMMY? DAMN!

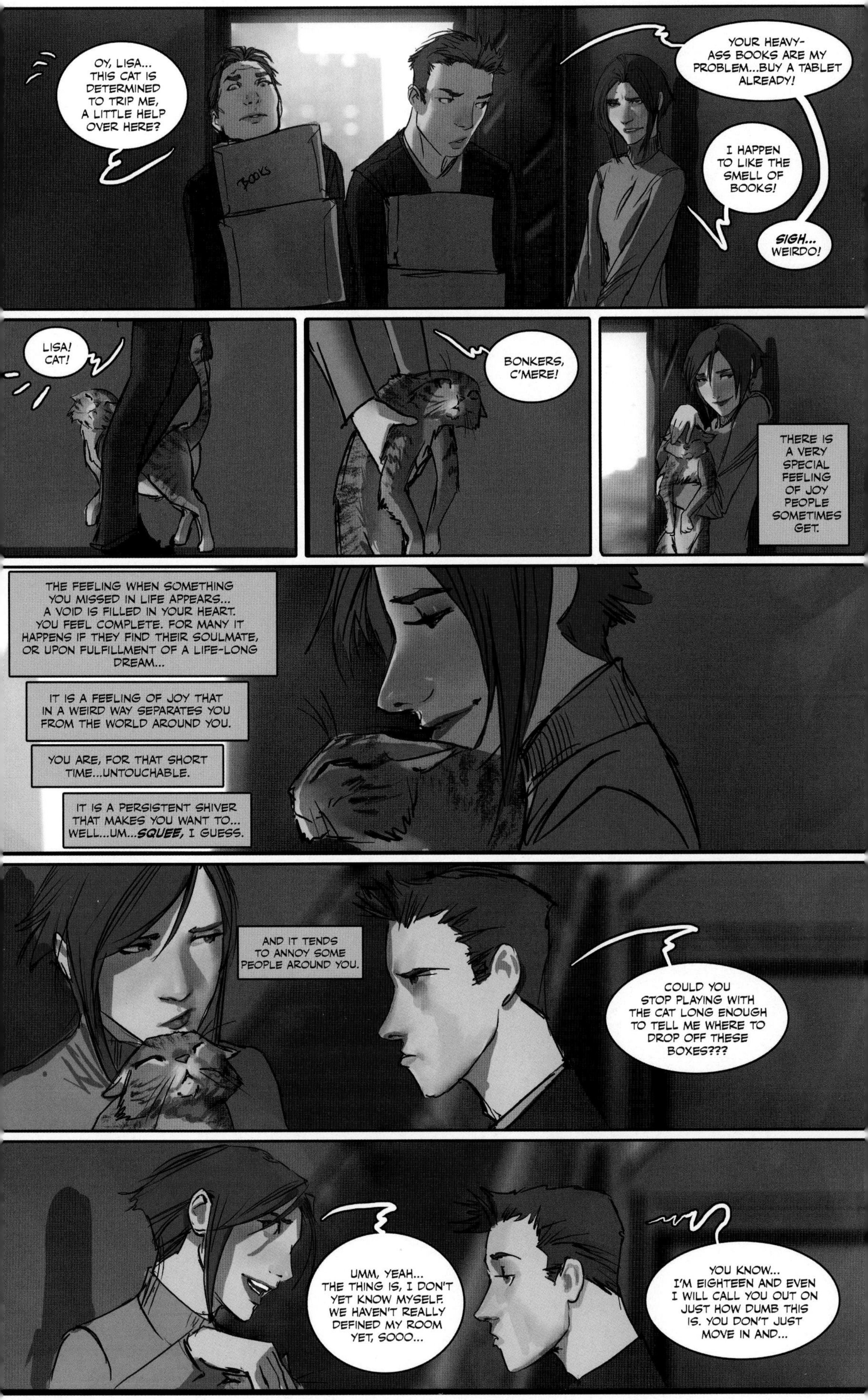

OY, LISA... THIS CAT IS DETERMINED TO TRIP ME, A LITTLE HELP OVER HERE?
BOOKS
YOUR HEAVY-ASS BOOKS ARE MY PROBLEM...BUY A TABLET ALREADY!
I HAPPEN TO LIKE THE SMELL OF BOOKS!
SIGH... WEIRDO!
LISA! CAT!
BONKERS, C'MERE!
THERE IS A VERY SPECIAL FEELING OF JOY PEOPLE SOMETIMES GET.
THE FEELING WHEN SOMETHING YOU MISSED IN LIFE APPEARS... A VOID IS FILLED IN YOUR HEART. YOU FEEL COMPLETE. FOR MANY IT HAPPENS IF THEY FIND THEIR SOULMATE, OR UPON FULFILLMENT OF A LIFE-LONG DREAM...
IT IS A FEELING OF JOY THAT IN A WEIRD WAY SEPARATES YOU FROM THE WORLD AROUND YOU.
YOU ARE, FOR THAT SHORT TIME...UNTOUCHABLE.
IT IS A PERSISTENT SHIVER THAT MAKES YOU WANT TO... WELL...UM...SQUEE, I GUESS.
AND IT TENDS TO ANNOY SOME PEOPLE AROUND YOU.
COULD YOU STOP PLAYING WITH THE CAT LONG ENOUGH TO TELL ME WHERE TO DROP OFF THESE BOXES???
UMM, YEAH... THE THING IS, I DON'T YET KNOW MYSELF. WE HAVEN'T REALLY DEFINED MY ROOM YET, SOOO...
YOU KNOW... I'M EIGHTEEN AND EVEN I WILL CALL YOU OUT ON JUST HOW DUMB THIS IS. YOU DON'T JUST MOVE IN AND...

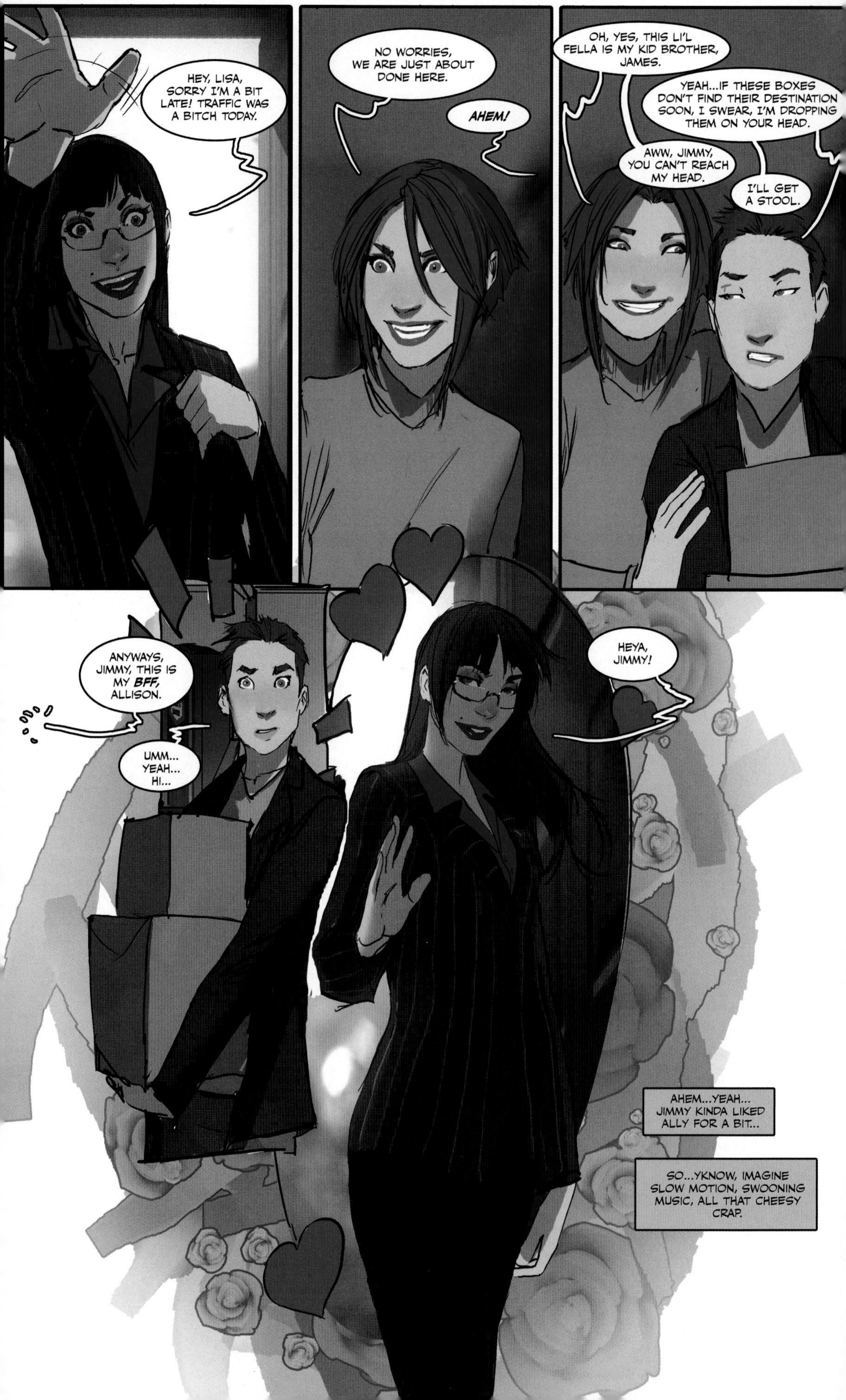
HEY, LISA, SORRY I'M A BIT LATE! TRAFFIC WAS A BITCH TODAY.
NO WORRIES, WE ARE JUST ABOUT DONE HERE.
AHEM!
OH, YES, THIS LI'L FELLA IS MY KID BROTHER, JAMES.
YEAH...IF THESE BOXES DON'T FIND THEIR DESTINATION SOON, I SWEAR, I'M DROPPING THEM ON YOUR HEAD.
AWW, JIMMY, YOU CAN'T REACH MY HEAD.
I'LL GET A STOOL.
ANYWAYS, JIMMY, THIS IS MY BFF, ALLISON.
HEYA, JIMMY!
UMM... YEAH... HI...
AHEM...YEAH... JIMMY KINDA LIKED ALLY FOR A BIT...
SO...YKNOW, IMAGINE SLOW MOTION, SWOONING MUSIC, ALL THAT CHEESY CRAP.

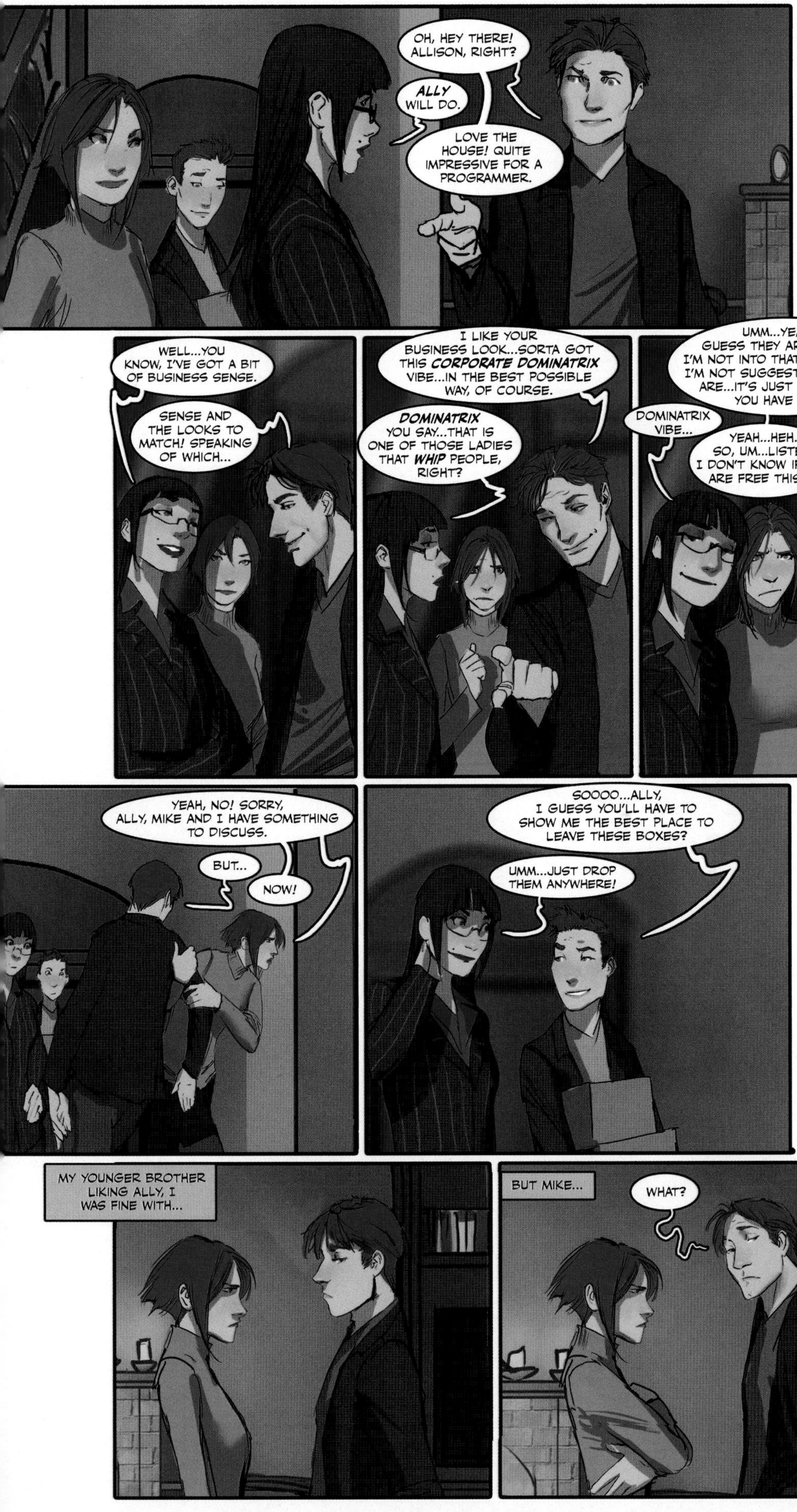
OH, HEY THERE! ALLISON, RIGHT?
ALLY WILL DO.
LOVE THE HOUSE! QUITE IMPRESSIVE FOR A PROGRAMMER.
WELL...YOU KNOW, I'VE GOT A BIT OF BUSINESS SENSE.
SENSE AND THE LOOKS TO MATCH! SPEAKING OF WHICH...
I LIKE YOUR BUSINESS LOOK...SORTA GOT THIS CORPORATE DOMINATRIX VIBE...IN THE BEST POSSIBLE WAY, OF COURSE.
DOMINATRIX YOU SAY...THAT IS ONE OF THOSE LADIES THAT WHIP PEOPLE, RIGHT?
UMM...YEAH...I GUESS THEY ARE...I MEAN, I'M NOT INTO THAT MYSELF...AND I'M NOT SUGGESTING THAT YOU ARE...IT'S JUST THAT...WELL, YOU HAVE THIS...
DOMINATRIX VIBE...
YEAH...HEH. SO, UM...LISTEN, I DON'T KNOW IF YOU ARE FREE THIS --
YEAH, NO! SORRY, ALLY, MIKE AND I HAVE SOMETHING TO DISCUSS.
BUT...
NOW!
SOOOO...ALLY, I GUESS YOU'LL HAVE TO SHOW ME THE BEST PLACE TO LEAVE THESE BOXES?
UMM...JUST DROP THEM ANYWHERE!
MY YOUNGER BROTHER LIKING ALLY, I WAS FINE WITH...
BUT MIKE...
WHAT?

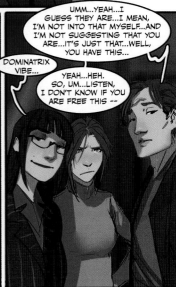

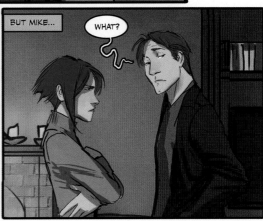

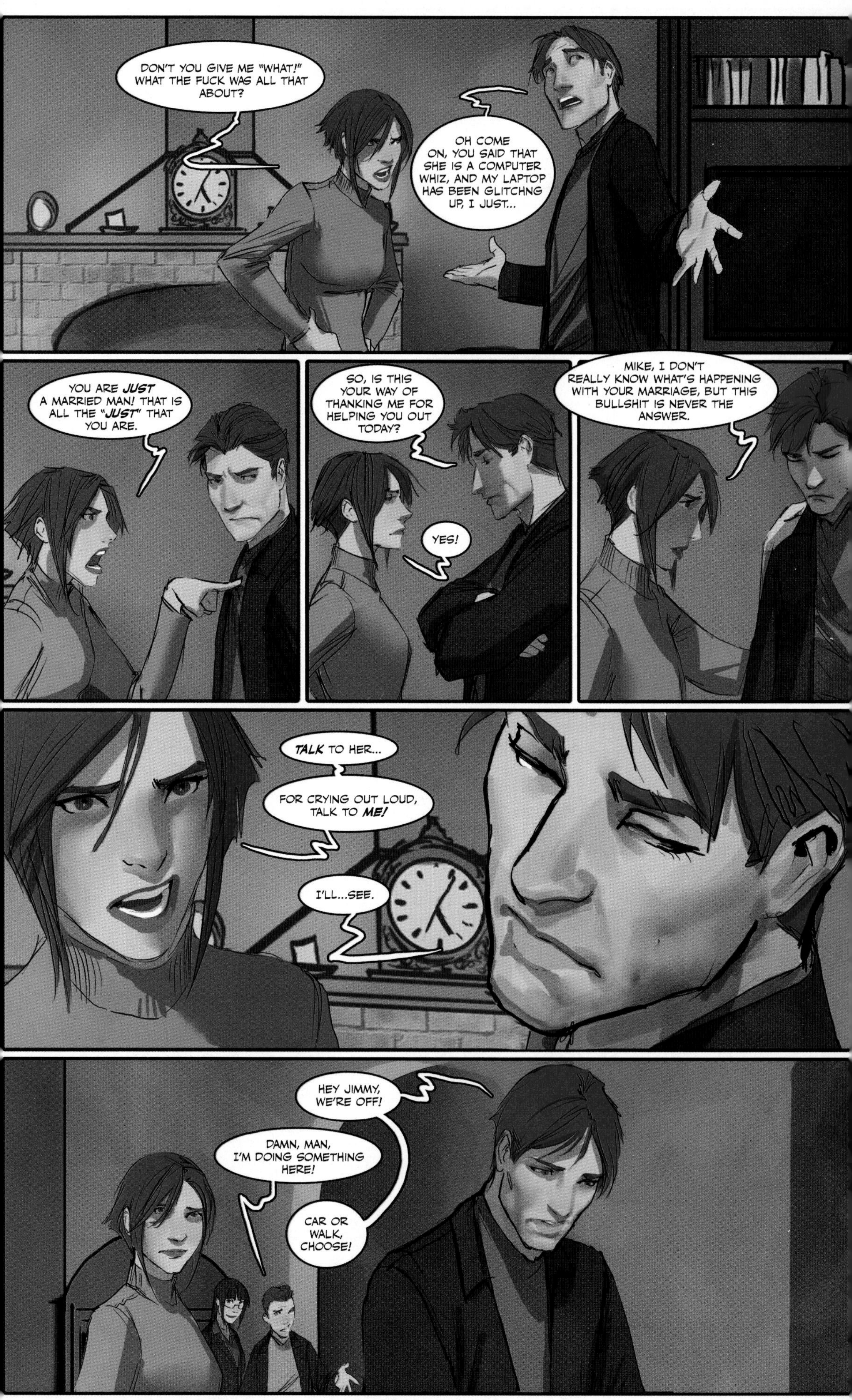
DON'T YOU GIVE ME "WHAT!" WHAT THE FUCK WAS ALL THAT ABOUT?
OH COME ON, YOU SAID THAT SHE IS A COMPUTER WHIZ, AND MY LAPTOP HAS BEEN GLITCHNG UP, I JUST...
YOU ARE *JUST* A MARRIED MAN! THAT IS ALL THE "*JUST*" THAT YOU ARE.
SO, IS THIS YOUR WAY OF THANKING ME FOR HELPING YOU OUT TODAY?
YES!
MIKE, I DON'T REALLY KNOW WHAT'S HAPPENING WITH YOUR MARRIAGE, BUT THIS BULLSHIT IS NEVER THE ANSWER.
TALK TO HER...
FOR CRYING OUT LOUD, TALK TO *ME!*
I'LL...SEE.
HEY JIMMY, WE'RE OFF!
DAMN, MAN, I'M DOING SOMETHING HERE!
CAR OR WALK, CHOOSE!

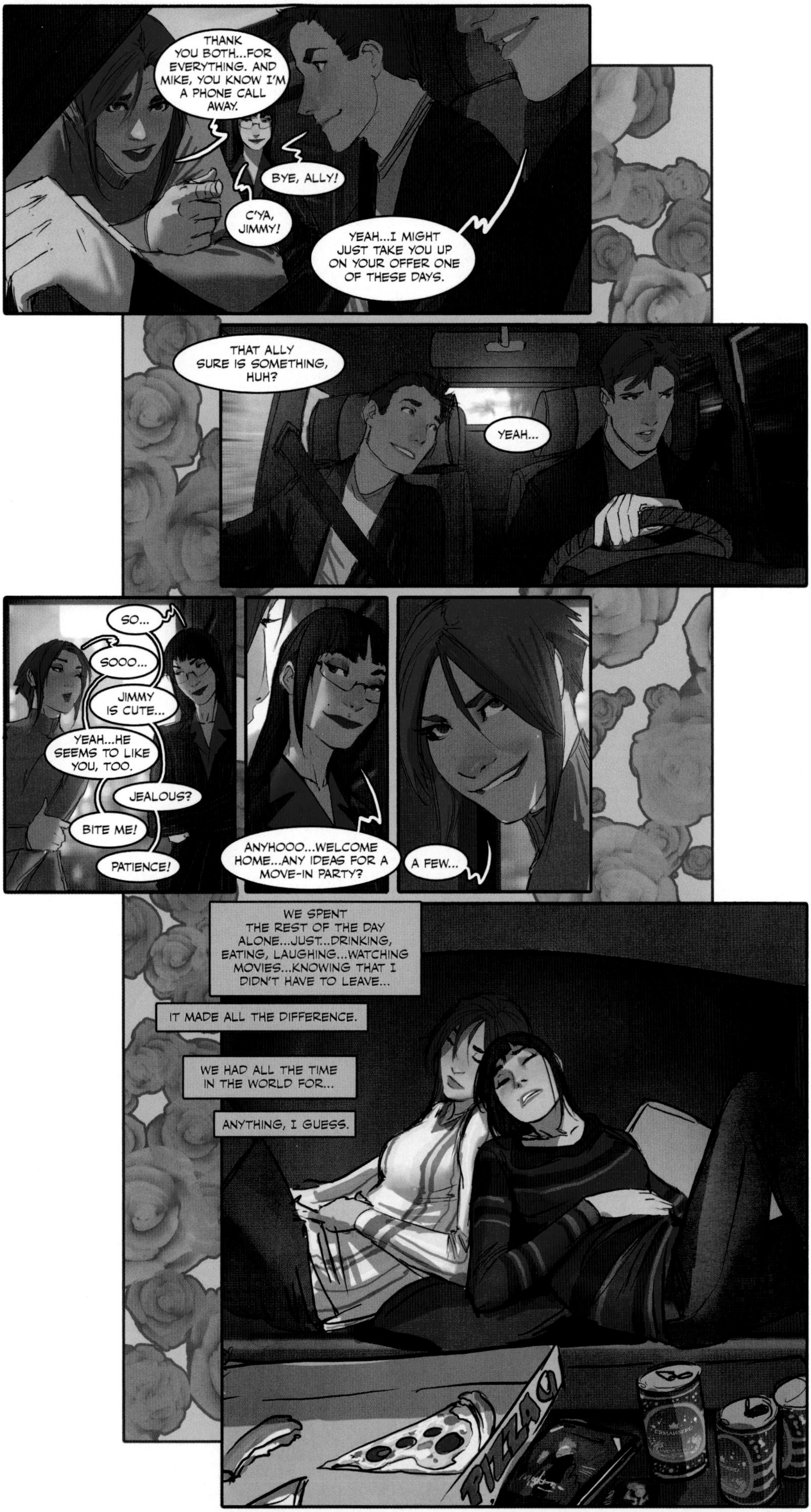
THANK YOU BOTH...FOR EVERYTHING. AND MIKE, YOU KNOW I'M A PHONE CALL AWAY.
BYE, ALLY!
C'YA, JIMMY!
YEAH...I MIGHT JUST TAKE YOU UP ON YOUR OFFER ONE OF THESE DAYS.
THAT ALLY SURE IS SOMETHING, HUH?
YEAH...
SO...
SOOO...
JIMMY IS CUTE...
YEAH...HE SEEMS TO LIKE YOU, TOO.
JEALOUS?
BITE ME!
PATIENCE!
ANYHOOO...WELCOME HOME...ANY IDEAS FOR A MOVE-IN PARTY?
A FEW...
WE SPENT THE REST OF THE DAY ALONE...JUST...DRINKING, EATING, LAUGHING...WATCHING MOVIES...KNOWING THAT I DIDN'T HAVE TO LEAVE...
IT MADE ALL THE DIFFERENCE.
WE HAD ALL THE TIME IN THE WORLD FOR...
ANYTHING, I GUESS.
PIZZA

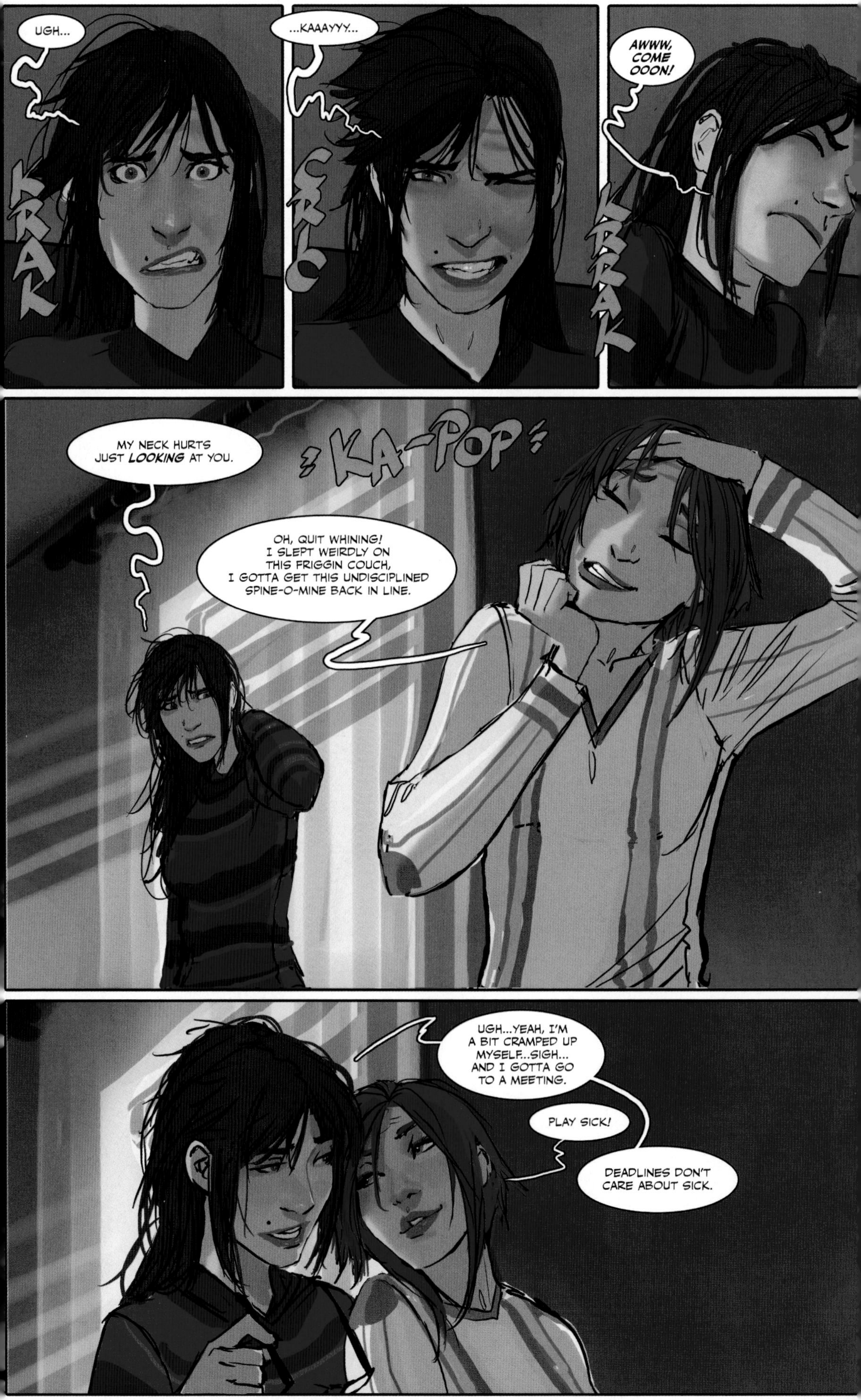
UGH...
KRAK
...KAAAYYY...
CRIC
AWWW, COME OOON!
KRRAK
MY NECK HURTS JUST **LOOKING** AT YOU.
KA-POP
OH, QUIT WHINING! I SLEPT WEIRDLY ON THIS FRIGGIN COUCH, I GOTTA GET THIS UNDISCIPLINED SPINE-O-MINE BACK IN LINE.
UGH...YEAH, I'M A BIT CRAMPED UP MYSELF...SIGH... AND I GOTTA GO TO A MEETING.
PLAY SICK!
DEADLINES DON'T CARE ABOUT SICK.

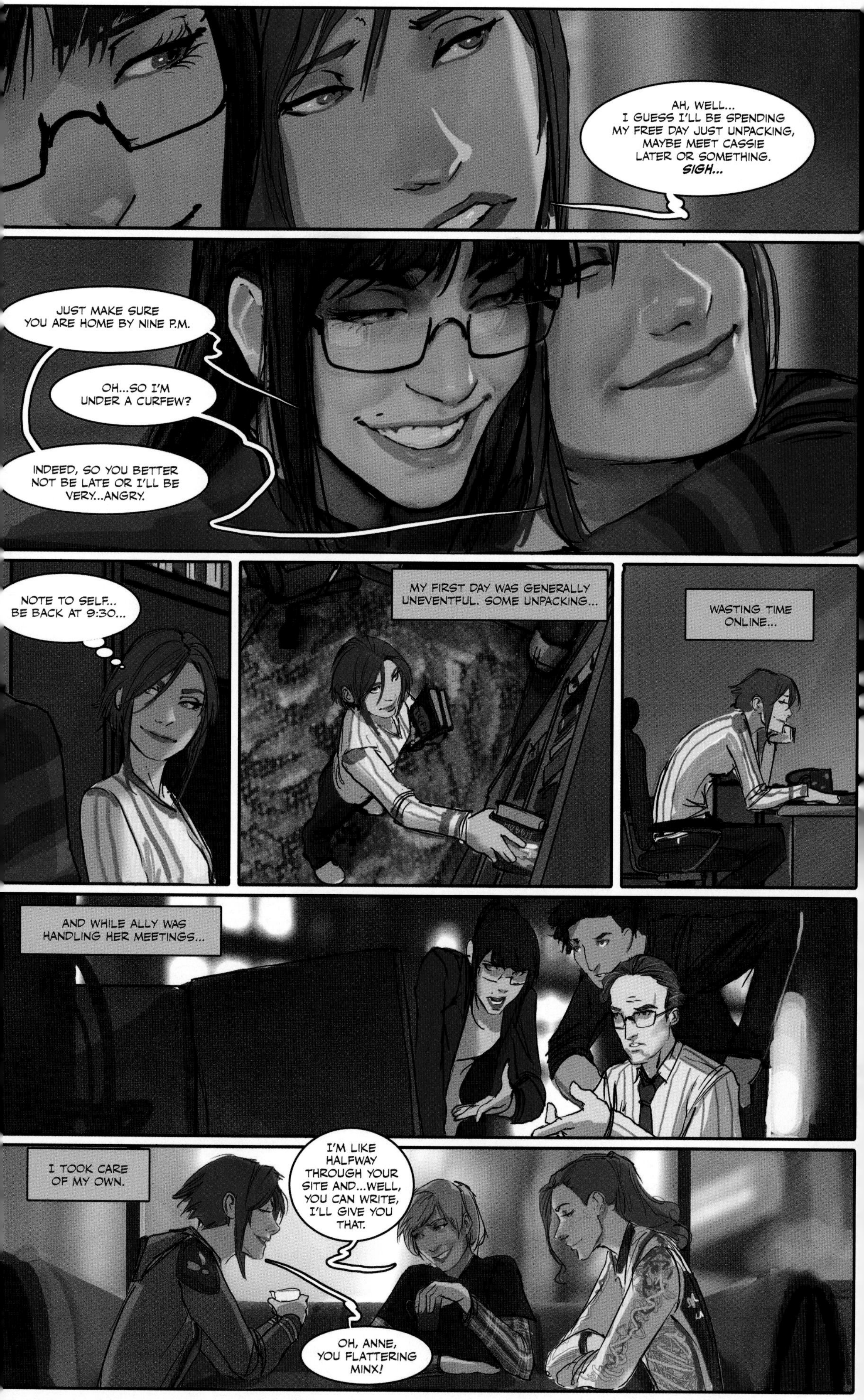
AH, WELL... I GUESS I'LL BE SPENDING MY FREE DAY JUST UNPACKING, MAYBE MEET CASSIE LATER OR SOMETHING. *SIGH...*
JUST MAKE SURE YOU ARE HOME BY NINE P.M.
OH...SO I'M UNDER A CURFEW?
INDEED, SO YOU BETTER NOT BE LATE OR I'LL BE VERY...ANGRY.
NOTE TO SELF... BE BACK AT 9:30...
MY FIRST DAY WAS GENERALLY UNEVENTFUL. SOME UNPACKING...
WASTING TIME ONLINE...
AND WHILE ALLY WAS HANDLING HER MEETINGS...
I TOOK CARE OF MY OWN.
I'M LIKE HALFWAY THROUGH YOUR SITE AND...WELL, YOU CAN WRITE, I'LL GIVE YOU THAT.
OH, ANNE, YOU FLATTERING MINX!

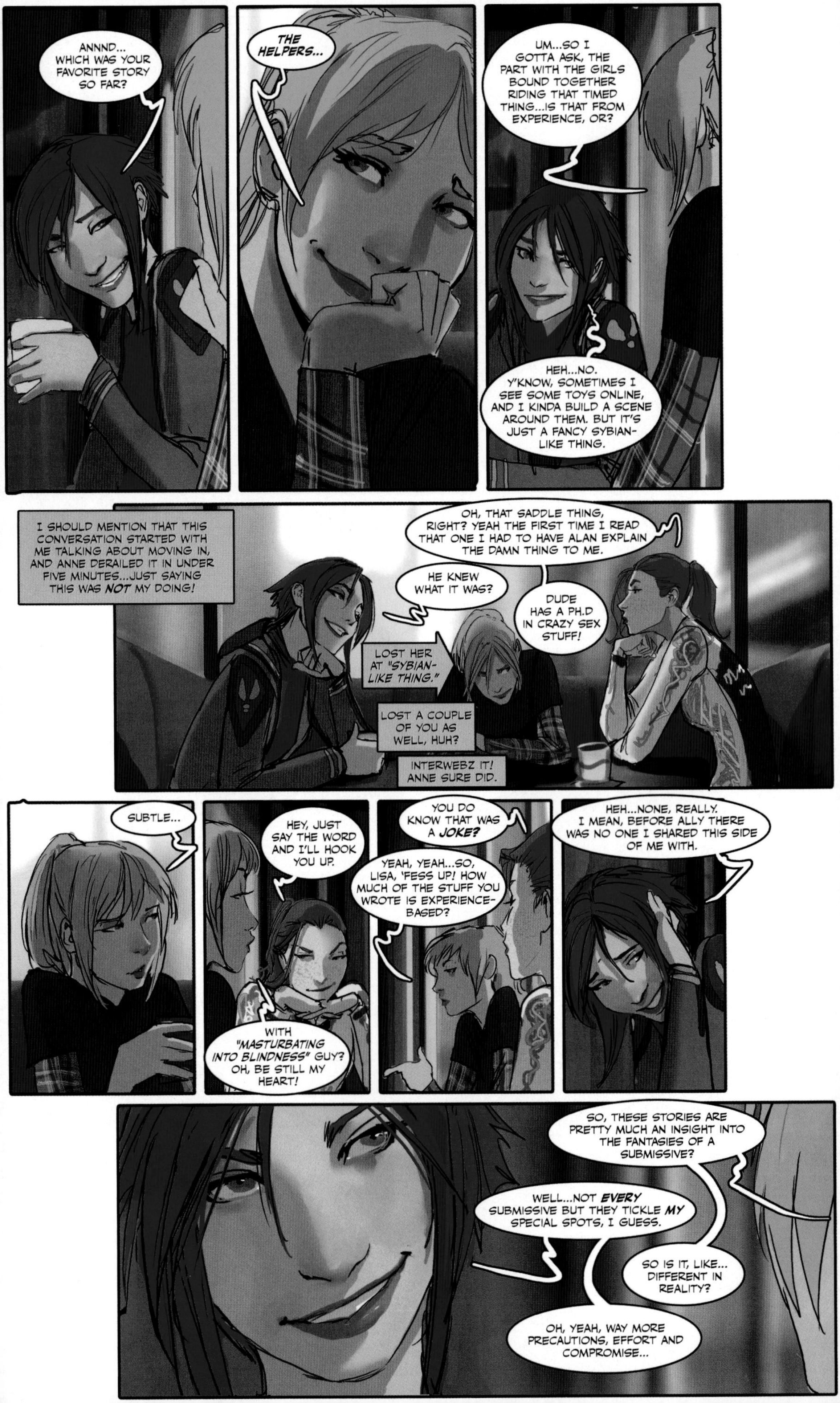
ANNND... WHICH WAS YOUR FAVORITE STORY SO FAR?
THE HELPERS...
UM...SO I GOTTA ASK, THE PART WITH THE GIRLS BOUND TOGETHER RIDING THAT TIMED THING...IS THAT FROM EXPERIENCE, OR?
HEH...NO. Y'KNOW, SOMETIMES I SEE SOME TOYS ONLINE, AND I KINDA BUILD A SCENE AROUND THEM. BUT IT'S JUST A FANCY SYBIAN-LIKE THING.
I SHOULD MENTION THAT THIS CONVERSATION STARTED WITH ME TALKING ABOUT MOVING IN, AND ANNE DERAILED IT IN UNDER FIVE MINUTES...JUST SAYING THIS WAS NOT MY DOING!
OH, THAT SADDLE THING, RIGHT? YEAH THE FIRST TIME I READ THAT ONE I HAD TO HAVE ALAN EXPLAIN THE DAMN THING TO ME.
HE KNEW WHAT IT WAS?
DUDE HAS A PH.D IN CRAZY SEX STUFF!
LOST HER AT "SYBIAN-LIKE THING."
LOST A COUPLE OF YOU AS WELL, HUH?
INTERWEBZ IT! ANNE SURE DID.
SUBTLE...
HEY, JUST SAY THE WORD AND I'LL HOOK YOU UP.
WITH "MASTURBATING INTO BLINDNESS" GUY? OH, BE STILL MY HEART!
YOU DO KNOW THAT WAS A JOKE?
YEAH, YEAH...SO, LISA, 'FESS UP! HOW MUCH OF THE STUFF YOU WROTE IS EXPERIENCE-BASED?
HEH...NONE, REALLY. I MEAN, BEFORE ALLY THERE WAS NO ONE I SHARED THIS SIDE OF ME WITH.
SO, THESE STORIES ARE PRETTY MUCH AN INSIGHT INTO THE FANTASIES OF A SUBMISSIVE?
WELL...NOT EVERY SUBMISSIVE BUT THEY TICKLE MY SPECIAL SPOTS, I GUESS.
SO IS IT, LIKE... DIFFERENT IN REALITY?
OH, YEAH, WAY MORE PRECAUTIONS, EFFORT AND COMPROMISE...

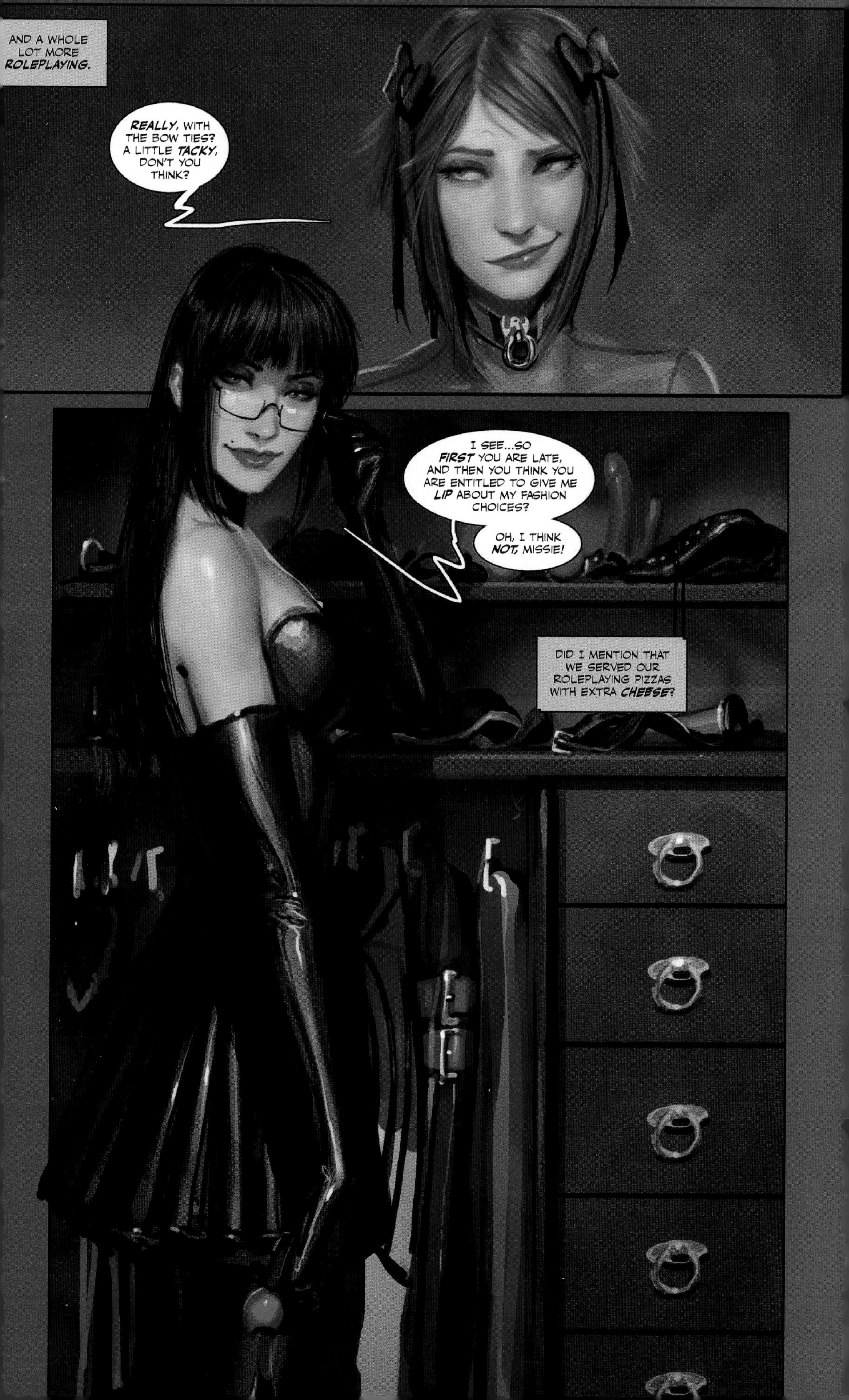
AND A WHOLE LOT MORE ROLEPLAYING.
REALLY, WITH THE BOW TIES? A LITTLE TACKY, DON'T YOU THINK?
I SEE...SO FIRST YOU ARE LATE, AND THEN YOU THINK YOU ARE ENTITLED TO GIVE ME LIP ABOUT MY FASHION CHOICES?
OH, I THINK NOT, MISSIE!
DID I MENTION THAT WE SERVED OUR ROLEPLAYING PIZZAS WITH EXTRA CHEESE?

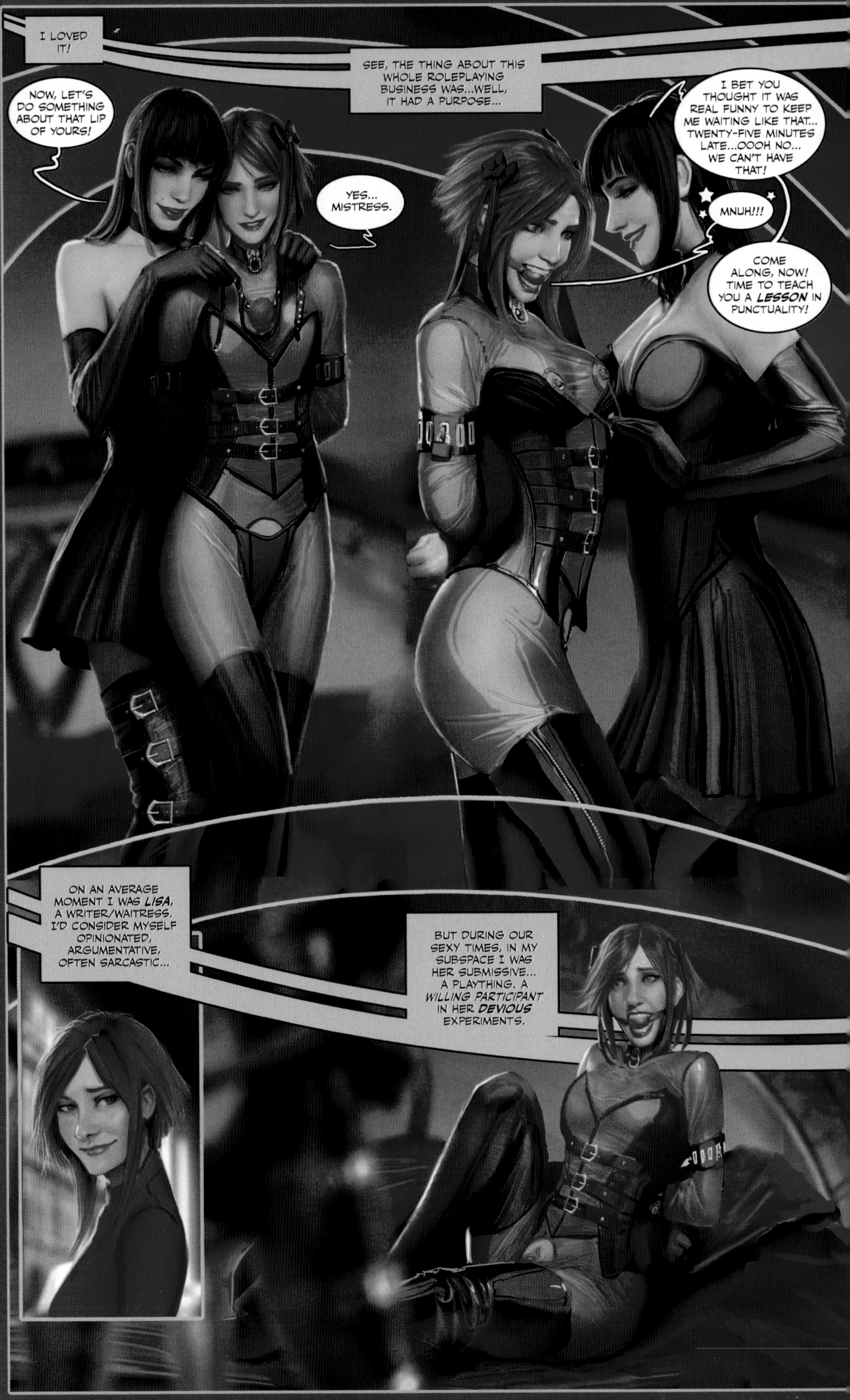

I LOVED IT!
NOW, LET'S DO SOMETHING ABOUT THAT LIP OF YOURS!
SEE, THE THING ABOUT THIS WHOLE ROLEPLAYING BUSINESS WAS...WELL, IT HAD A PURPOSE...
YES... MISTRESS.
I BET YOU THOUGHT IT WAS REAL FUNNY TO KEEP ME WAITING LIKE THAT... TWENTY-FIVE MINUTES LATE...OOOH NO... WE CAN'T HAVE THAT!
MNUH!!!
COME ALONG, NOW! TIME TO TEACH YOU A LESSON IN PUNCTUALITY!
ON AN AVERAGE MOMENT I WAS LISA, A WRITER/WAITRESS. I'D CONSIDER MYSELF OPINIONATED, ARGUMENTATIVE, OFTEN SARCASTIC...
BUT DURING OUR SEXY TIMES, IN MY SUBSPACE I WAS HER SUBMISSIVE... A PLAYTHING. A WILLING PARTICIPANT IN HER DEVIOUS EXPERIMENTS.

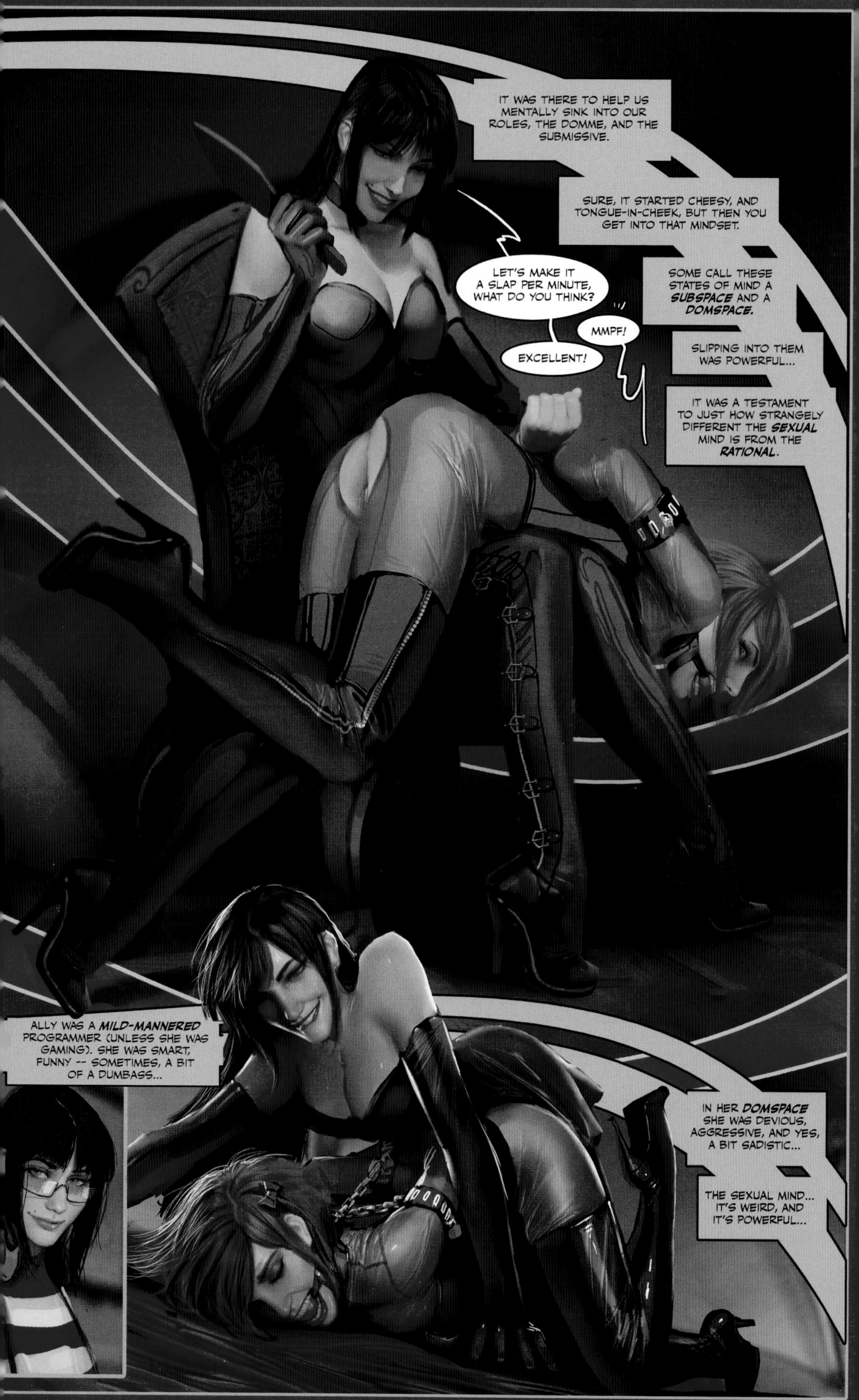

IT WAS THERE TO HELP US MENTALLY SINK INTO OUR ROLES, THE DOMME, AND THE SUBMISSIVE.
SURE, IT STARTED CHEESY, AND TONGUE-IN-CHEEK, BUT THEN YOU GET INTO THAT MINDSET.
LET'S MAKE IT A SLAP PER MINUTE, WHAT DO YOU THINK?
MMPF!
EXCELLENT!
SOME CALL THESE STATES OF MIND A **SUBSPACE** AND A **DOMSPACE.**
SLIPPING INTO THEM WAS POWERFUL...
IT WAS A TESTAMENT TO JUST HOW STRANGELY DIFFERENT THE **SEXUAL** MIND IS FROM THE **RATIONAL**.
ALLY WAS A **MILD-MANNERED** PROGRAMMER (UNLESS SHE WAS GAMING). SHE WAS SMART, FUNNY -- SOMETIMES, A BIT OF A DUMBASS...
IN HER **DOMSPACE** SHE WAS DEVIOUS, AGGRESSIVE, AND YES, A BIT SADISTIC...
THE SEXUAL MIND... IT'S WEIRD, AND IT'S POWERFUL...

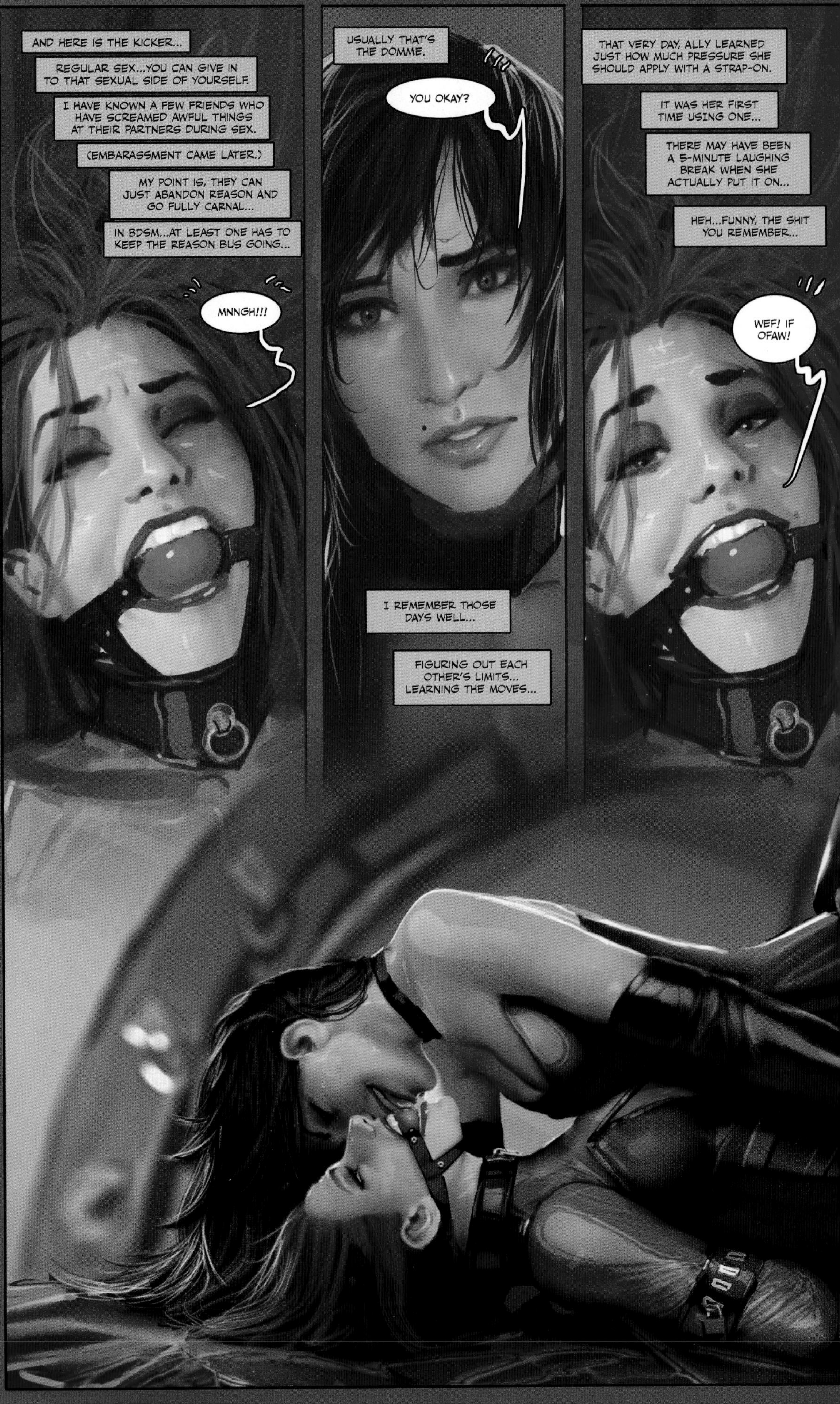
AND HERE IS THE KICKER...
REGULAR SEX...YOU CAN GIVE IN TO THAT SEXUAL SIDE OF YOURSELF.
I HAVE KNOWN A FEW FRIENDS WHO HAVE SCREAMED AWFUL THINGS AT THEIR PARTNERS DURING SEX.
(EMBARASSMENT CAME LATER.)
MY POINT IS, THEY CAN JUST ABANDON REASON AND GO FULLY CARNAL...
IN BDSM...AT LEAST ONE HAS TO KEEP THE REASON BUS GOING...
MNNGH!!!
USUALLY THAT'S THE DOMME.
YOU OKAY?
I REMEMBER THOSE DAYS WELL...
FIGURING OUT EACH OTHER'S LIMITS... LEARNING THE MOVES...
THAT VERY DAY, ALLY LEARNED JUST HOW MUCH PRESSURE SHE SHOULD APPLY WITH A STRAP-ON.
IT WAS HER FIRST TIME USING ONE...
THERE MAY HAVE BEEN A 5-MINUTE LAUGHING BREAK WHEN SHE ACTUALLY PUT IT ON...
HEH...FUNNY, THE SHIT YOU REMEMBER...
WEF! IF OFAW!

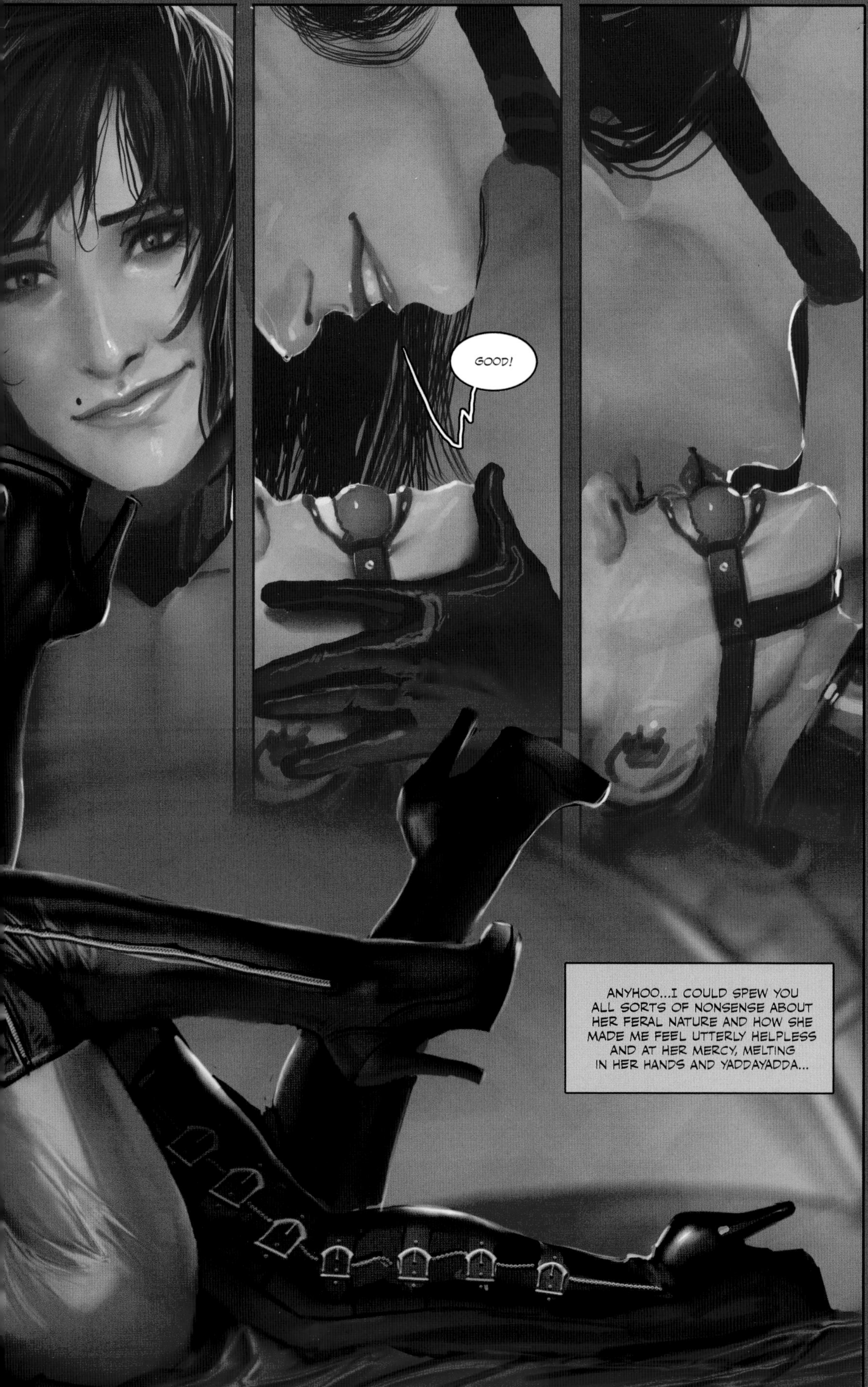
GOOD!
ANYHOO...I COULD SPEW YOU ALL SORTS OF NONSENSE ABOUT HER FERAL NATURE AND HOW SHE MADE ME FEEL UTTERLY HELPLESS AND AT HER MERCY, MELTING IN HER HANDS AND YADDAYADDA...

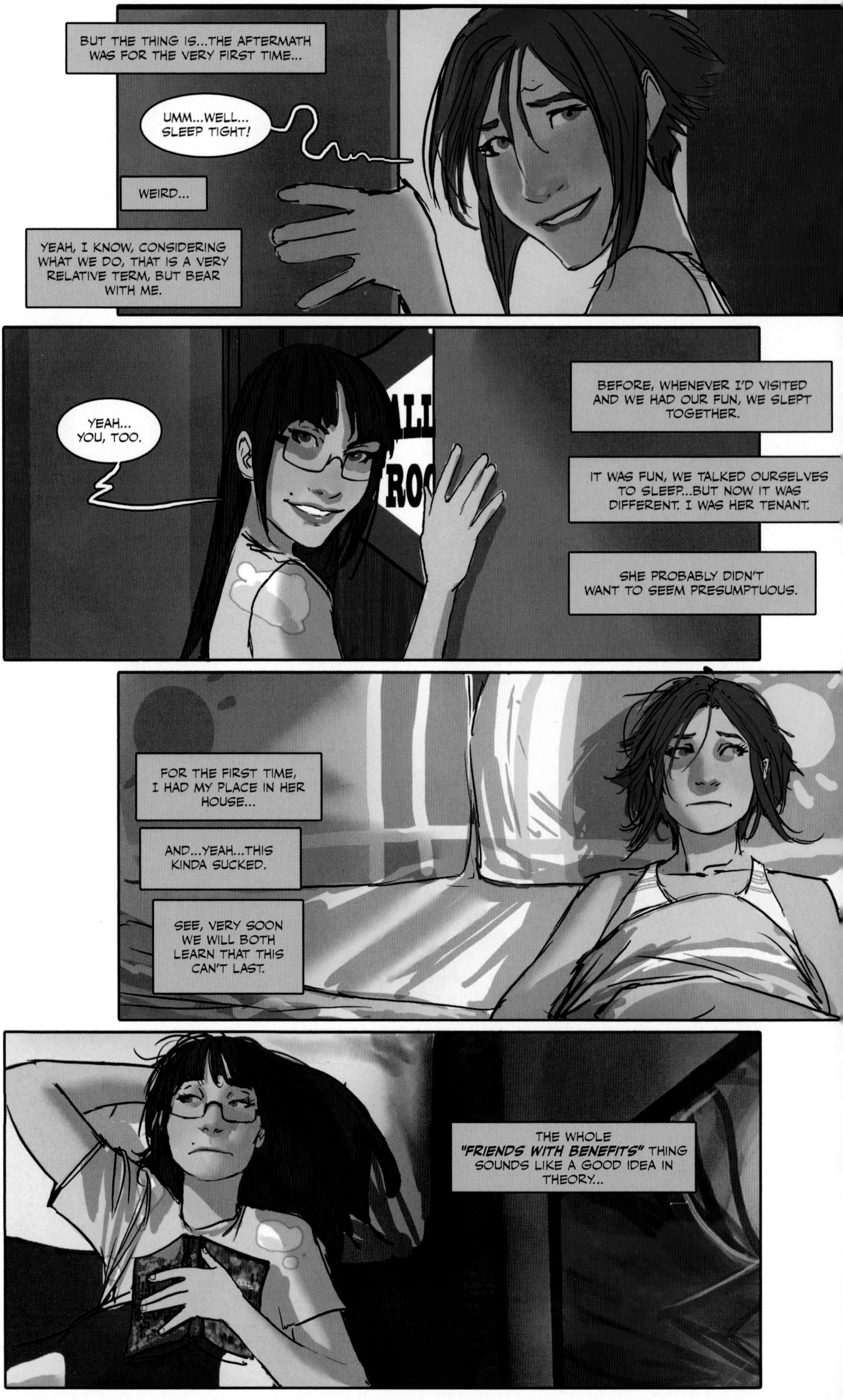
BUT THE THING IS...THE AFTERMATH WAS FOR THE VERY FIRST TIME...
UMM...WELL... SLEEP TIGHT!
WEIRD...
YEAH, I KNOW, CONSIDERING WHAT WE DO, THAT IS A VERY RELATIVE TERM, BUT BEAR WITH ME.
YEAH... YOU, TOO.
BEFORE, WHENEVER I'D VISITED AND WE HAD OUR FUN, WE SLEPT TOGETHER.
IT WAS FUN, WE TALKED OURSELVES TO SLEEP...BUT NOW IT WAS DIFFERENT. I WAS HER TENANT.
SHE PROBABLY DIDN'T WANT TO SEEM PRESUMPTUOUS.
FOR THE FIRST TIME, I HAD MY PLACE IN HER HOUSE...
AND...YEAH...THIS KINDA SUCKED.
SEE, VERY SOON WE WILL BOTH LEARN THAT THIS CAN'T LAST.
THE WHOLE ***"FRIENDS WITH BENEFITS"*** THING SOUNDS LIKE A GOOD IDEA IN THEORY...

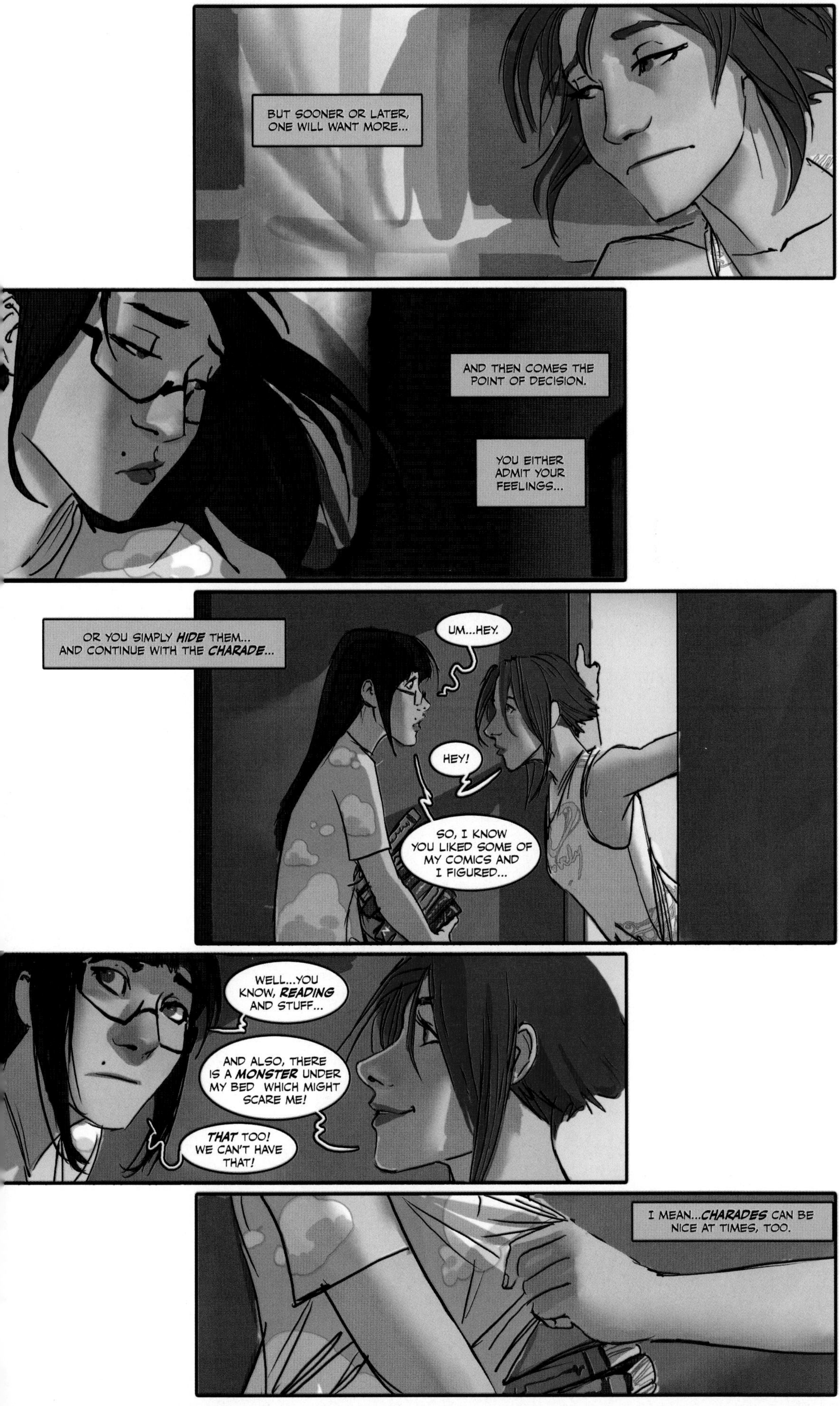

BUT SOONER OR LATER, ONE WILL WANT MORE...
AND THEN COMES THE POINT OF DECISION.
YOU EITHER ADMIT YOUR FEELINGS...
OR YOU SIMPLY HIDE THEM... AND CONTINUE WITH THE CHARADE...
UM...HEY.
HEY!
SO, I KNOW YOU LIKED SOME OF MY COMICS AND I FIGURED...
WELL...YOU KNOW, READING AND STUFF...
AND ALSO, THERE IS A MONSTER UNDER MY BED WHICH MIGHT SCARE ME!
THAT TOO! WE CAN'T HAVE THAT!
I MEAN...CHARADES CAN BE NICE AT TIMES, TOO.

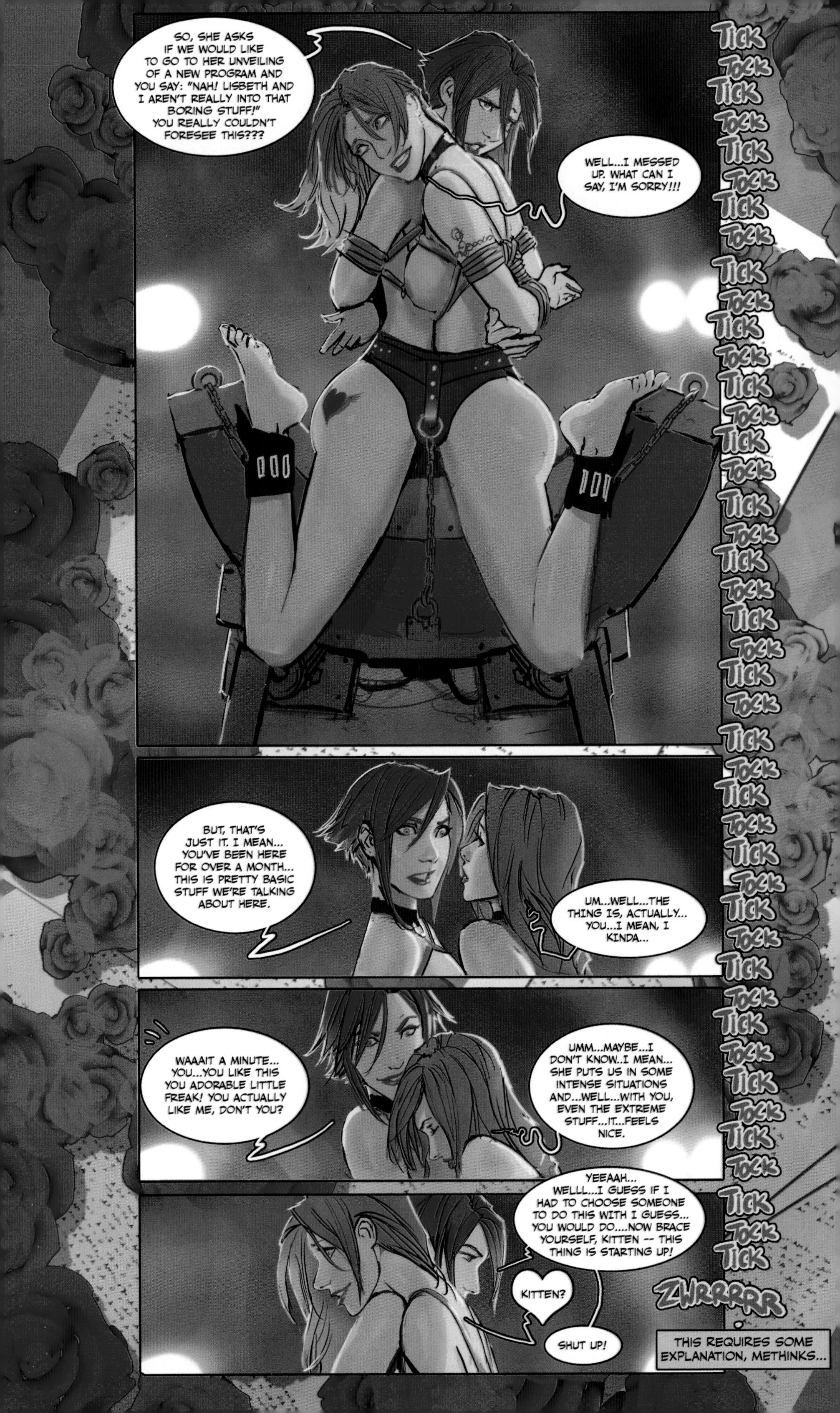
SO, SHE ASKS IF WE WOULD LIKE TO GO TO HER UNVEILING OF A NEW PROGRAM AND YOU SAY: "NAH! LISBETH AND I AREN'T REALLY INTO THAT BORING STUFF!" YOU REALLY COULDN'T FORESEE THIS???
WELL...I MESSED UP. WHAT CAN I SAY, I'M SORRY!!!
TICK TOCK TICK TOCK TICK TOCK TICK TOCK TICK TOCK TICK TOCK TICK TOCK TICK TOCK TICK TOCK TICK TOCK TICK TOCK TICK TOCK TICK TOCK TICK TOCK TICK TOCK TICK TOCK TICK TOCK TICK TOCK TICK TOCK TICK
BUT, THAT'S JUST IT. I MEAN... YOU'VE BEEN HERE FOR OVER A MONTH... THIS IS PRETTY BASIC STUFF WE'RE TALKING ABOUT HERE.
UM...WELL...THE THING IS, ACTUALLY... YOU...I MEAN, I KINDA...
WAAAIT A MINUTE... YOU...YOU LIKE THIS YOU ADORABLE LITTLE FREAK! YOU ACTUALLY LIKE ME, DON'T YOU?
UMM...MAYBE...I DON'T KNOW..I MEAN... SHE PUTS US IN SOME INTENSE SITUATIONS AND...WELL...WITH YOU, EVEN THE EXTREME STUFF...IT...FEELS NICE.
YEEAAH... WELLL...I GUESS IF I HAD TO CHOOSE SOMEONE TO DO THIS WITH I GUESS... YOU WOULD DO....NOW BRACE YOURSELF, KITTEN -- THIS THING IS STARTING UP!
KITTEN?
SHUT UP!
ZWRRRRR
THIS REQUIRES SOME EXPLANATION, METHINKS...

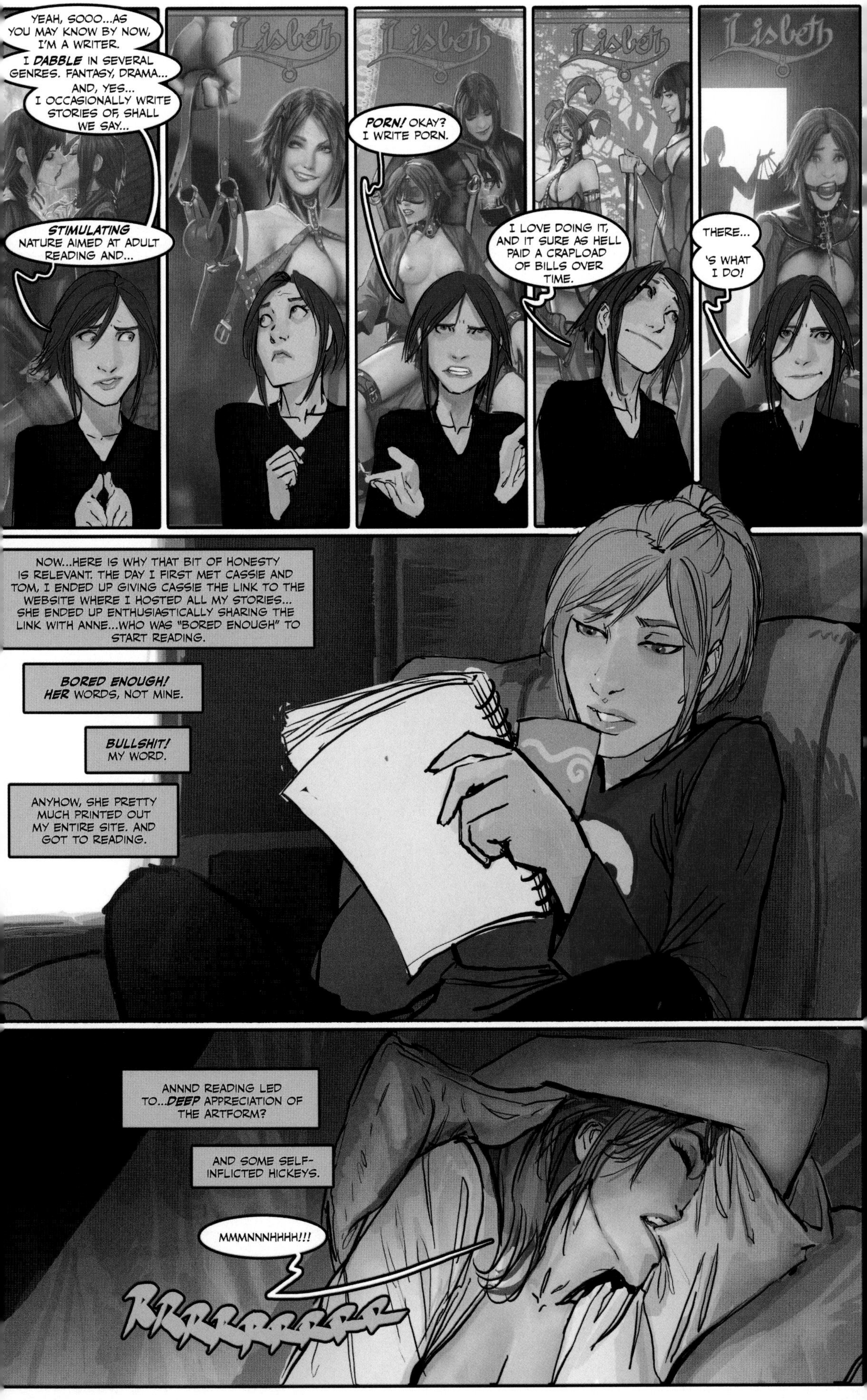
YEAH, SOOO...AS YOU MAY KNOW BY NOW, I'M A WRITER.
I DABBLE IN SEVERAL GENRES. FANTASY, DRAMA...
AND, YES... I OCCASIONALLY WRITE STORIES OF, SHALL WE SAY...
STIMULATING NATURE AIMED AT ADULT READING AND...
Lisbeth
Lisbeth
PORN! OKAY? I WRITE PORN.
Lisbeth
I LOVE DOING IT, AND IT SURE AS HELL PAID A CRAPLOAD OF BILLS OVER TIME.
Lisbeth
THERE...
'S WHAT I DO!
NOW...HERE IS WHY THAT BIT OF HONESTY IS RELEVANT. THE DAY I FIRST MET CASSIE AND TOM, I ENDED UP GIVING CASSIE THE LINK TO THE WEBSITE WHERE I HOSTED ALL MY STORIES... SHE ENDED UP ENTHUSIASTICALLY SHARING THE LINK WITH ANNE...WHO WAS "BORED ENOUGH" TO START READING.
BORED ENOUGH! HER WORDS, NOT MINE.
BULLSHIT! MY WORD.
ANYHOW, SHE PRETTY MUCH PRINTED OUT MY ENTIRE SITE. AND GOT TO READING.
ANNND READING LED TO...DEEP APPRECIATION OF THE ARTFORM?
AND SOME SELF-INFLICTED HICKEYS.
MMMNNNHHHH!!!
RRRRRRRRRR

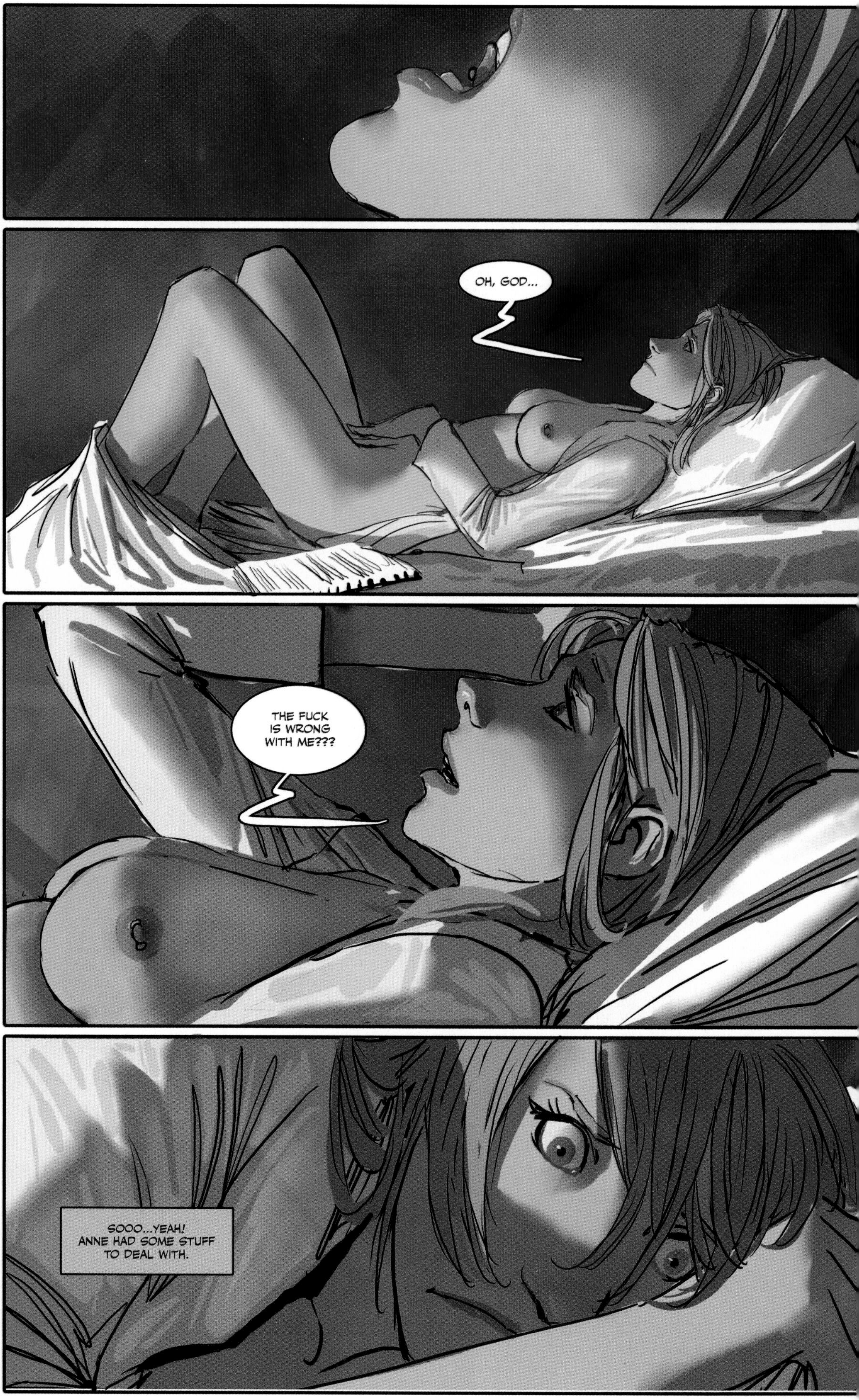
OH, GOD...
THE FUCK IS WRONG WITH ME???
SOOO...YEAH! ANNE HAD SOME STUFF TO DEAL WITH.

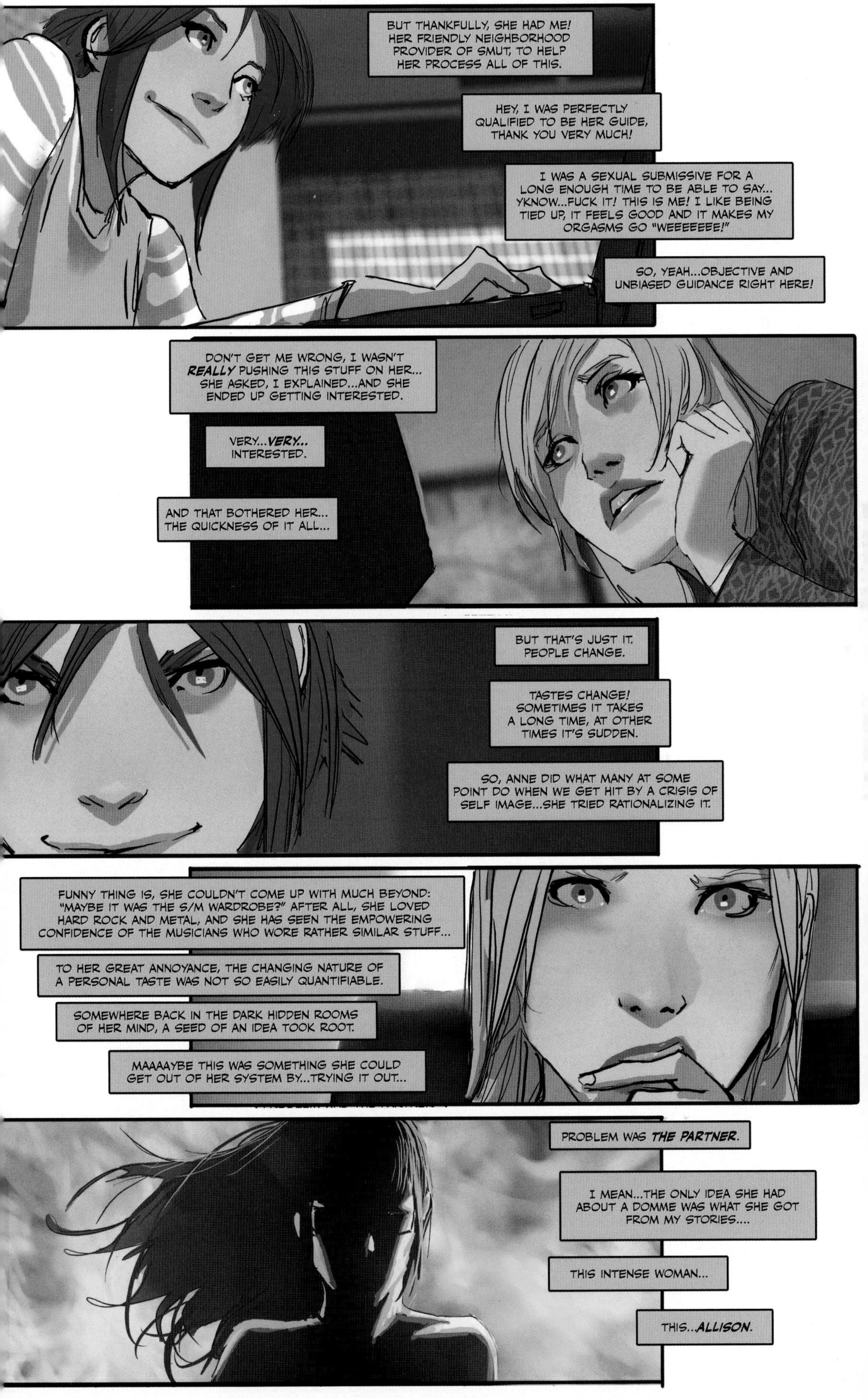
BUT THANKFULLY, SHE HAD ME! HER FRIENDLY NEIGHBORHOOD PROVIDER OF SMUT, TO HELP HER PROCESS ALL OF THIS.
HEY, I WAS PERFECTLY QUALIFIED TO BE HER GUIDE, THANK YOU VERY MUCH!
I WAS A SEXUAL SUBMISSIVE FOR A LONG ENOUGH TIME TO BE ABLE TO SAY... YKNOW...FUCK IT! THIS IS ME! I LIKE BEING TIED UP, IT FEELS GOOD AND IT MAKES MY ORGASMS GO "WEEEEEEE!"
SO, YEAH...OBJECTIVE AND UNBIASED GUIDANCE RIGHT HERE!
DON'T GET ME WRONG, I WASN'T ***REALLY*** PUSHING THIS STUFF ON HER... SHE ASKED, I EXPLAINED...AND SHE ENDED UP GETTING INTERESTED.
VERY...***VERY...*** INTERESTED.
AND THAT BOTHERED HER... THE QUICKNESS OF IT ALL...
BUT THAT'S JUST IT. PEOPLE CHANGE.
TASTES CHANGE! SOMETIMES IT TAKES A LONG TIME, AT OTHER TIMES IT'S SUDDEN.
SO, ANNE DID WHAT MANY AT SOME POINT DO WHEN WE GET HIT BY A CRISIS OF SELF IMAGE...SHE TRIED RATIONALIZING IT.
FUNNY THING IS, SHE COULDN'T COME UP WITH MUCH BEYOND: "MAYBE IT WAS THE S/M WARDROBE?" AFTER ALL, SHE LOVED HARD ROCK AND METAL, AND SHE HAS SEEN THE EMPOWERING CONFIDENCE OF THE MUSICIANS WHO WORE RATHER SIMILAR STUFF...
TO HER GREAT ANNOYANCE, THE CHANGING NATURE OF A PERSONAL TASTE WAS NOT SO EASILY QUANTIFIABLE.
SOMEWHERE BACK IN THE DARK HIDDEN ROOMS OF HER MIND, A SEED OF AN IDEA TOOK ROOT.
MAAAAYBE THIS WAS SOMETHING SHE COULD GET OUT OF HER SYSTEM BY...TRYING IT OUT...
PROBLEM WAS ***THE PARTNER***.
I MEAN...THE ONLY IDEA SHE HAD ABOUT A DOMME WAS WHAT SHE GOT FROM MY STORIES....
THIS INTENSE WOMAN...
THIS...***ALLISON***.

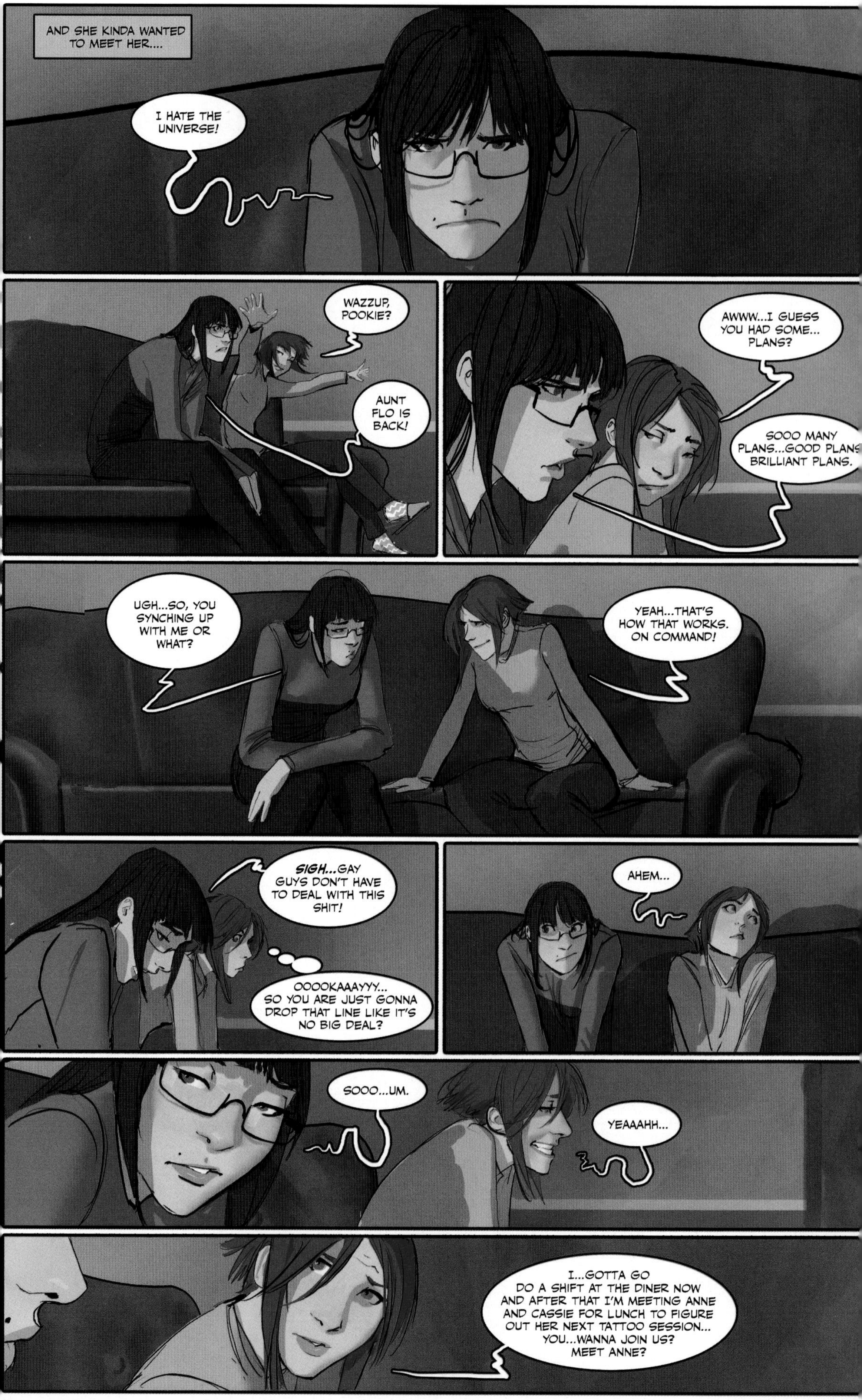
AND SHE KINDA WANTED TO MEET HER....
I HATE THE UNIVERSE!
WAZZUP, POOKIE?
AUNT FLO IS BACK!
AWWW...I GUESS YOU HAD SOME... PLANS?
SOOO MANY PLANS...GOOD PLANS BRILLIANT PLANS.
UGH...SO, YOU SYNCHING UP WITH ME OR WHAT?
YEAH...THAT'S HOW THAT WORKS. ON COMMAND!
SIGH...GAY GUYS DON'T HAVE TO DEAL WITH THIS SHIT!
OOOOKAAAYYY... SO YOU ARE JUST GONNA DROP THAT LINE LIKE IT'S NO BIG DEAL?
AHEM...
SOOO...UM.
YEAAAHH...
I...GOTTA GO DO A SHIFT AT THE DINER NOW AND AFTER THAT I'M MEETING ANNE AND CASSIE FOR LUNCH TO FIGURE OUT HER NEXT TATTOO SESSION... YOU...WANNA JOIN US? MEET ANNE?

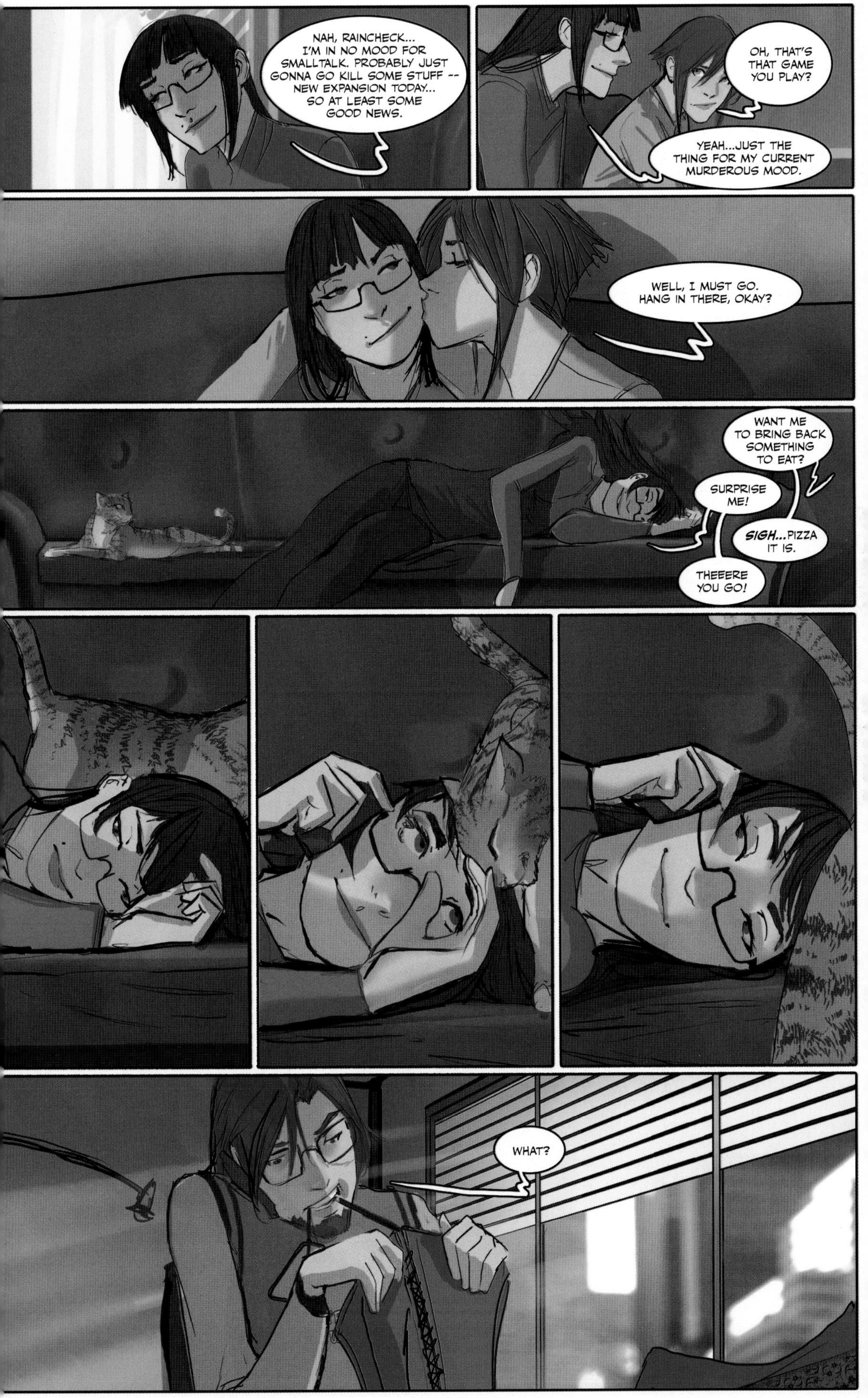
NAH, RAINCHECK... I'M IN NO MOOD FOR SMALLTALK. PROBABLY JUST GONNA GO KILL SOME STUFF -- NEW EXPANSION TODAY... SO AT LEAST SOME GOOD NEWS.
OH, THAT'S THAT GAME YOU PLAY?
YEAH...JUST THE THING FOR MY CURRENT MURDEROUS MOOD.
WELL, I MUST GO. HANG IN THERE, OKAY?
WANT ME TO BRING BACK SOMETHING TO EAT?
SURPRISE ME!
SIGH...PIZZA IT IS.
THEEERE YOU GO!
WHAT?

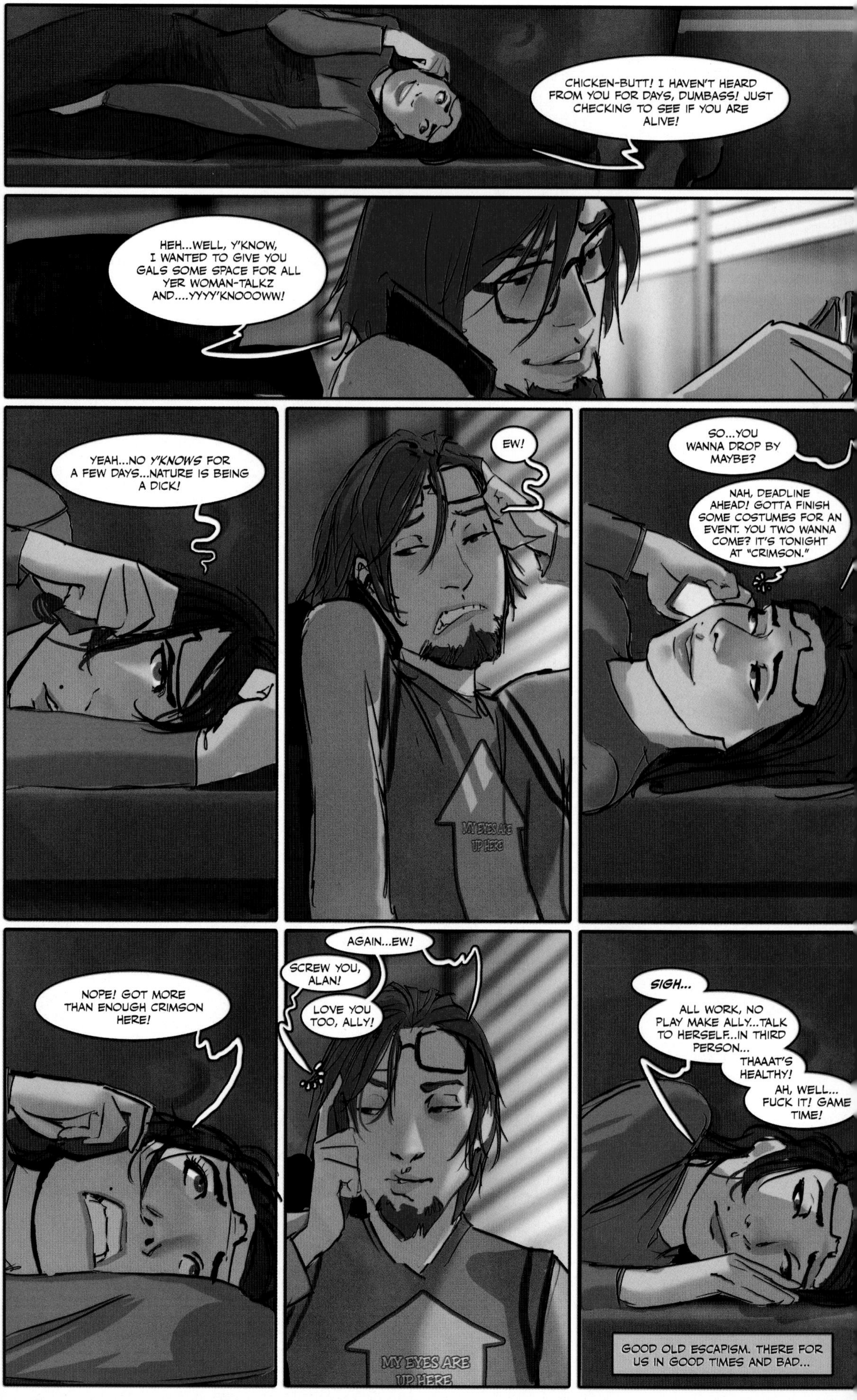

CHICKEN-BUTT! I HAVEN'T HEARD FROM YOU FOR DAYS, DUMBASS! JUST CHECKING TO SEE IF YOU ARE ALIVE!
HEH...WELL, Y'KNOW, I WANTED TO GIVE YOU GALS SOME SPACE FOR ALL YER WOMAN-TALKZ AND....YYYY'KNOOOWW!
YEAH...NO Y'KNOWS FOR A FEW DAYS...NATURE IS BEING A DICK!
EW!
MY EYES ARE UP HERE
SO...YOU WANNA DROP BY MAYBE?
NAH, DEADLINE AHEAD! GOTTA FINISH SOME COSTUMES FOR AN EVENT. YOU TWO WANNA COME? IT'S TONIGHT AT "CRIMSON."
NOPE! GOT MORE THAN ENOUGH CRIMSON HERE!
AGAIN...EW!
SCREW YOU, ALAN!
LOVE YOU TOO, ALLY!
MY EYES ARE UP HERE
SIGH...
ALL WORK, NO PLAY MAKE ALLY...TALK TO HERSELF...IN THIRD PERSON...
THAAAT'S HEALTHY!
AH, WELL... FUCK IT! GAME TIME!
GOOD OLD ESCAPISM. THERE FOR US IN GOOD TIMES AND BAD...

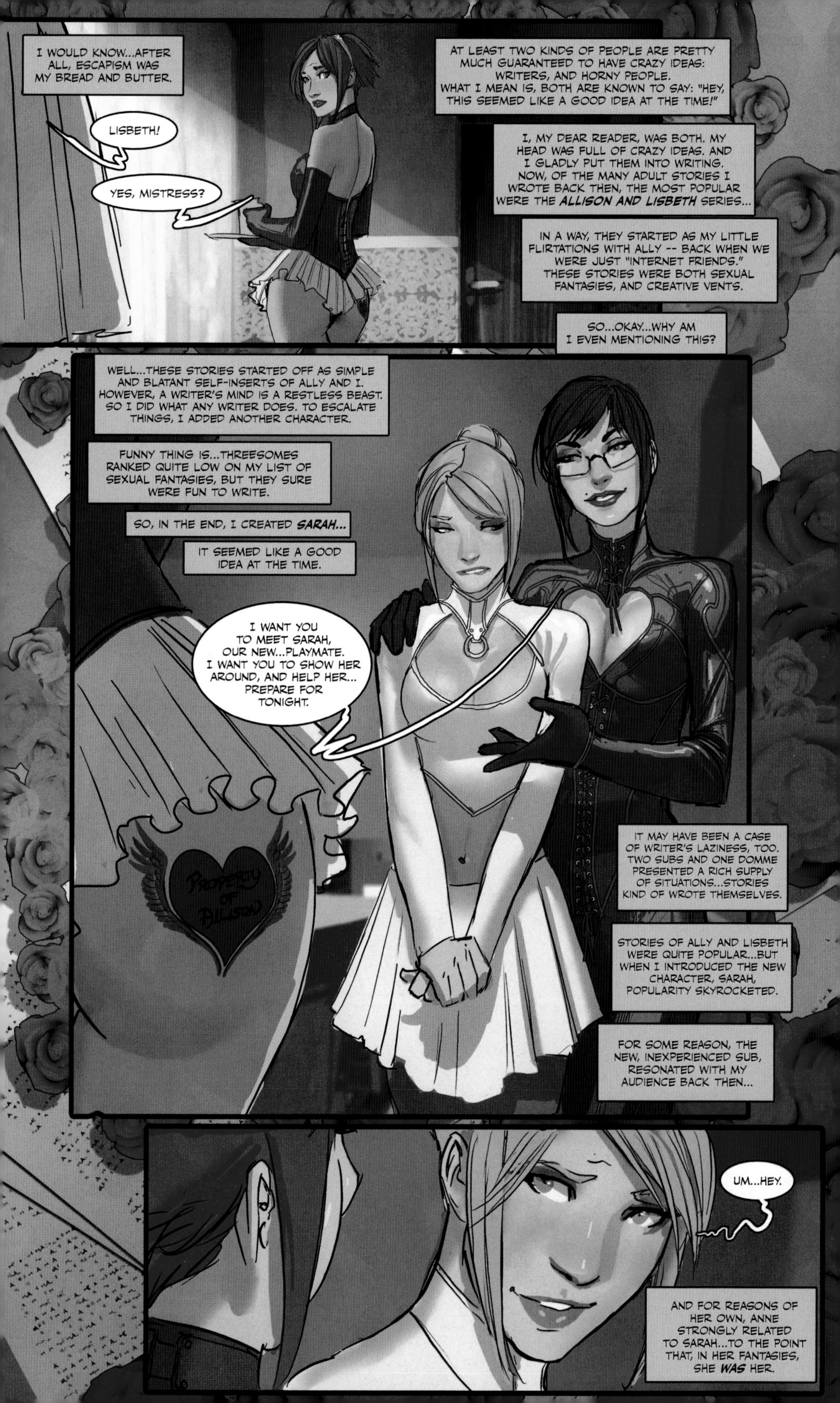
I WOULD KNOW...AFTER ALL, ESCAPISM WAS MY BREAD AND BUTTER.
AT LEAST TWO KINDS OF PEOPLE ARE PRETTY MUCH GUARANTEED TO HAVE CRAZY IDEAS: WRITERS, AND HORNY PEOPLE. WHAT I MEAN IS, BOTH ARE KNOWN TO SAY: "HEY, THIS SEEMED LIKE A GOOD IDEA AT THE TIME!"
LISBETH!
YES, MISTRESS?
I, MY DEAR READER, WAS BOTH. MY HEAD WAS FULL OF CRAZY IDEAS. AND I GLADLY PUT THEM INTO WRITING. NOW, OF THE MANY ADULT STORIES I WROTE BACK THEN, THE MOST POPULAR WERE THE ALLISON AND LISBETH SERIES...
IN A WAY, THEY STARTED AS MY LITTLE FLIRTATIONS WITH ALLY -- BACK WHEN WE WERE JUST "INTERNET FRIENDS." THESE STORIES WERE BOTH SEXUAL FANTASIES, AND CREATIVE VENTS.
SO...OKAY...WHY AM I EVEN MENTIONING THIS?
WELL...THESE STORIES STARTED OFF AS SIMPLE AND BLATANT SELF-INSERTS OF ALLY AND I. HOWEVER, A WRITER'S MIND IS A RESTLESS BEAST. SO I DID WHAT ANY WRITER DOES. TO ESCALATE THINGS, I ADDED ANOTHER CHARACTER.
FUNNY THING IS...THREESOMES RANKED QUITE LOW ON MY LIST OF SEXUAL FANTASIES, BUT THEY SURE WERE FUN TO WRITE.
SO, IN THE END, I CREATED SARAH...
IT SEEMED LIKE A GOOD IDEA AT THE TIME.
I WANT YOU TO MEET SARAH, OUR NEW...PLAYMATE. I WANT YOU TO SHOW HER AROUND, AND HELP HER... PREPARE FOR TONIGHT.
PROPERTY OF ALLISON
IT MAY HAVE BEEN A CASE OF WRITER'S LAZINESS, TOO. TWO SUBS AND ONE DOMME PRESENTED A RICH SUPPLY OF SITUATIONS...STORIES KIND OF WROTE THEMSELVES.
STORIES OF ALLY AND LISBETH WERE QUITE POPULAR...BUT WHEN I INTRODUCED THE NEW CHARACTER, SARAH, POPULARITY SKYROCKETED.
FOR SOME REASON, THE NEW, INEXPERIENCED SUB, RESONATED WITH MY AUDIENCE BACK THEN...
UM...HEY.
AND FOR REASONS OF HER OWN, ANNE STRONGLY RELATED TO SARAH...TO THE POINT THAT, IN HER FANTASIES, SHE WAS HER.

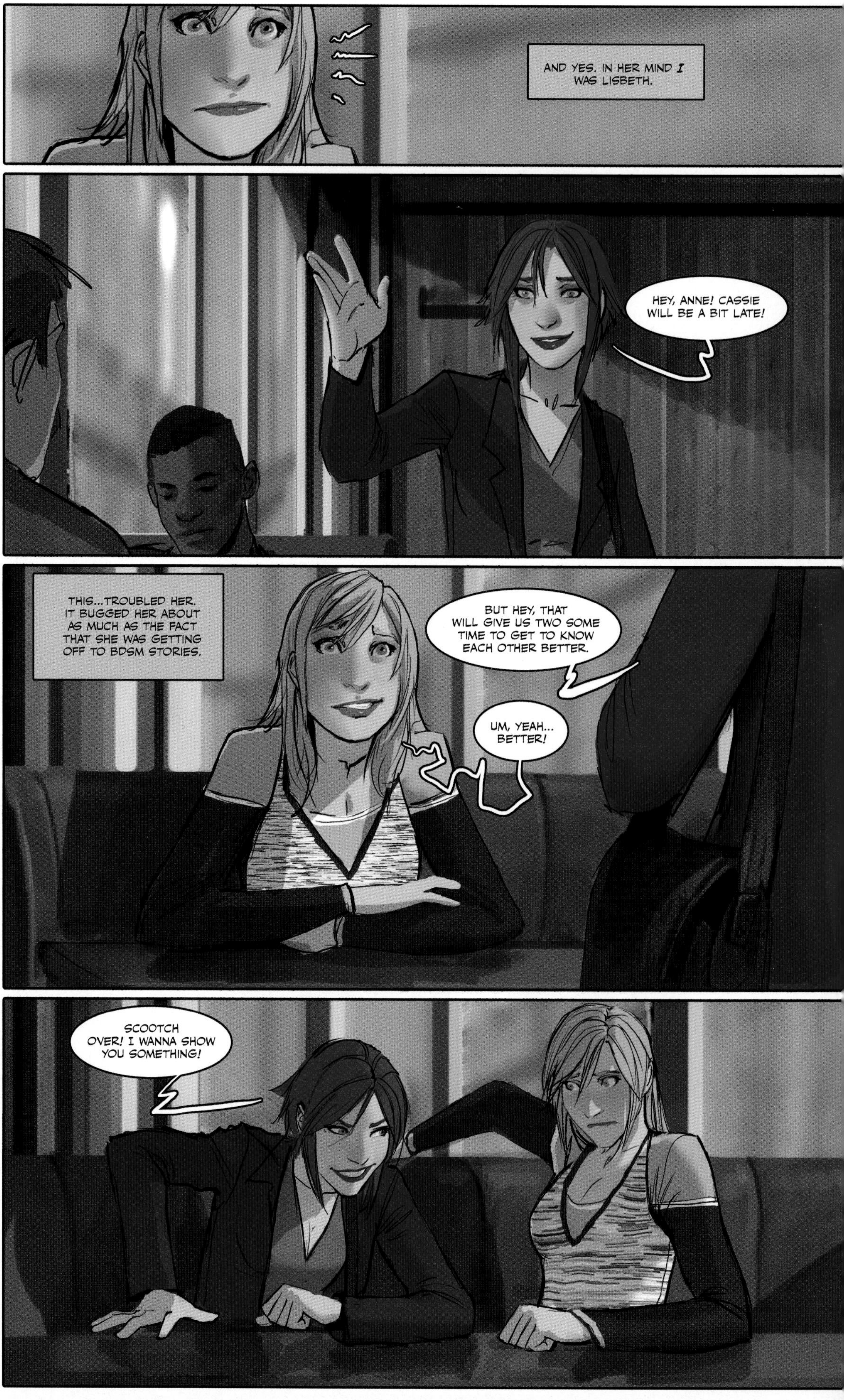
AND YES. IN HER MIND *I* WAS LISBETH.
HEY, ANNE! CASSIE WILL BE A BIT LATE!
THIS...TROUBLED HER. IT BUGGED HER ABOUT AS MUCH AS THE FACT THAT SHE WAS GETTING OFF TO BDSM STORIES.
BUT HEY, THAT WILL GIVE US TWO SOME TIME TO GET TO KNOW EACH OTHER BETTER.
UM, YEAH... BETTER!
SCOOTCH OVER! I WANNA SHOW YOU SOMETHING!

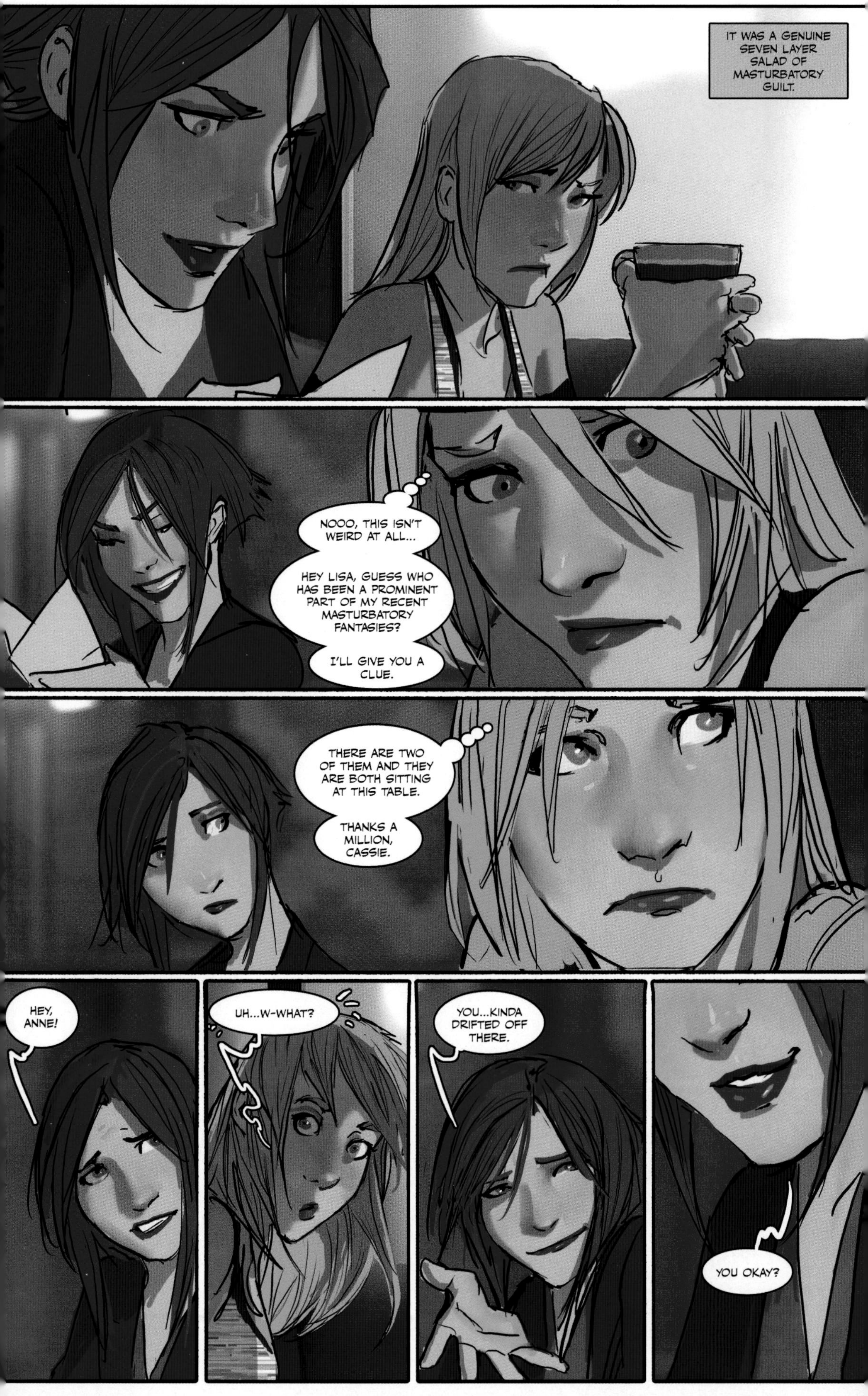
IT WAS A GENUINE SEVEN LAYER SALAD OF MASTURBATORY GUILT.
NOOO, THIS ISN'T WEIRD AT ALL...
HEY LISA, GUESS WHO HAS BEEN A PROMINENT PART OF MY RECENT MASTURBATORY FANTASIES?
I'LL GIVE YOU A CLUE.
THERE ARE TWO OF THEM AND THEY ARE BOTH SITTING AT THIS TABLE.
THANKS A MILLION, CASSIE.
HEY, ANNE!
UH...W-WHAT?
YOU...KINDA DRIFTED OFF THERE.
YOU OKAY?

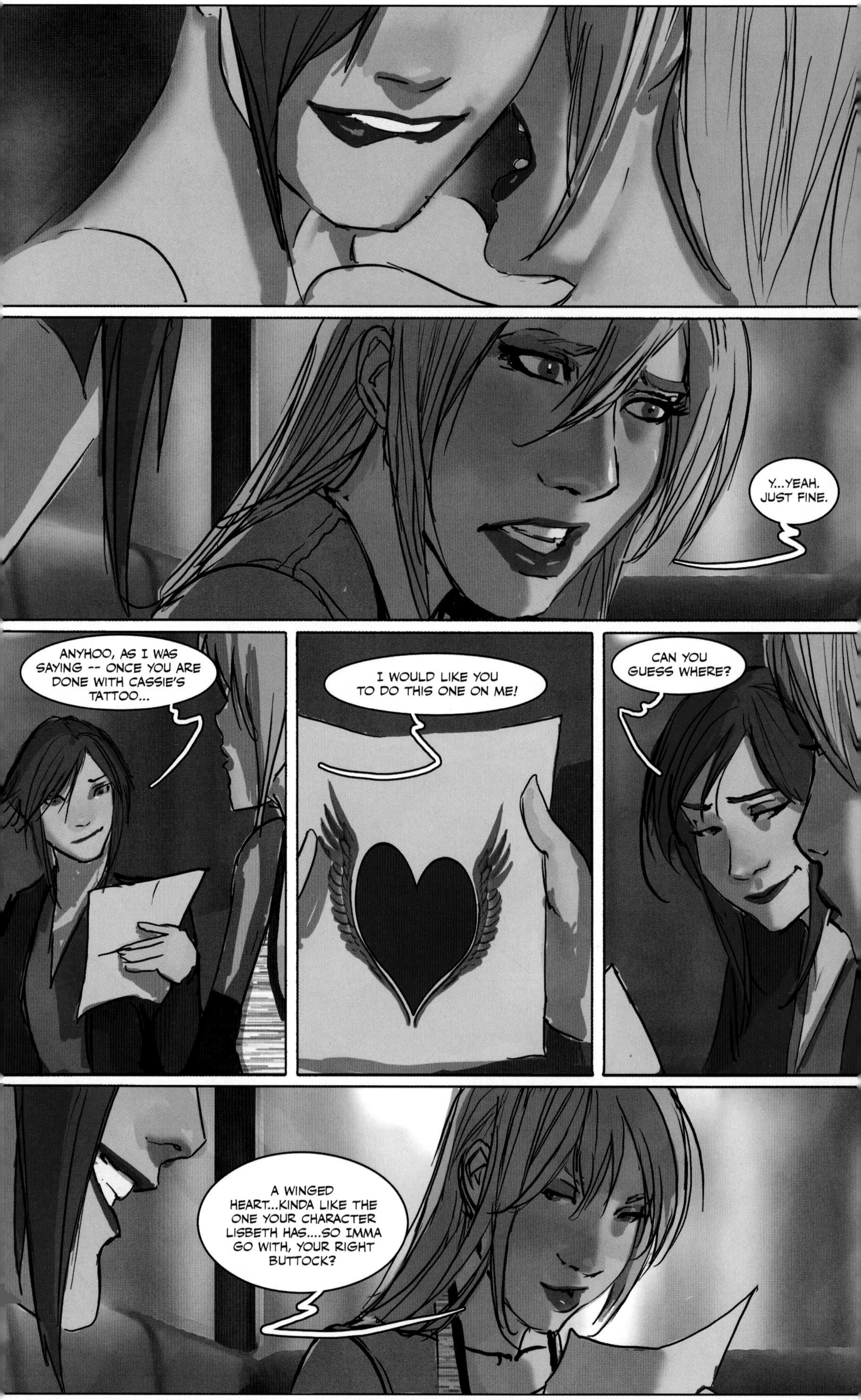

Y...YEAH. JUST FINE.
ANYHOO, AS I WAS SAYING -- ONCE YOU ARE DONE WITH CASSIE'S TATTOO...
I WOULD LIKE YOU TO DO THIS ONE ON ME!
CAN YOU GUESS WHERE?
A WINGED HEART...KINDA LIKE THE ONE YOUR CHARACTER LISBETH HAS....SO IMMA GO WITH, YOUR RIGHT BUTTOCK?

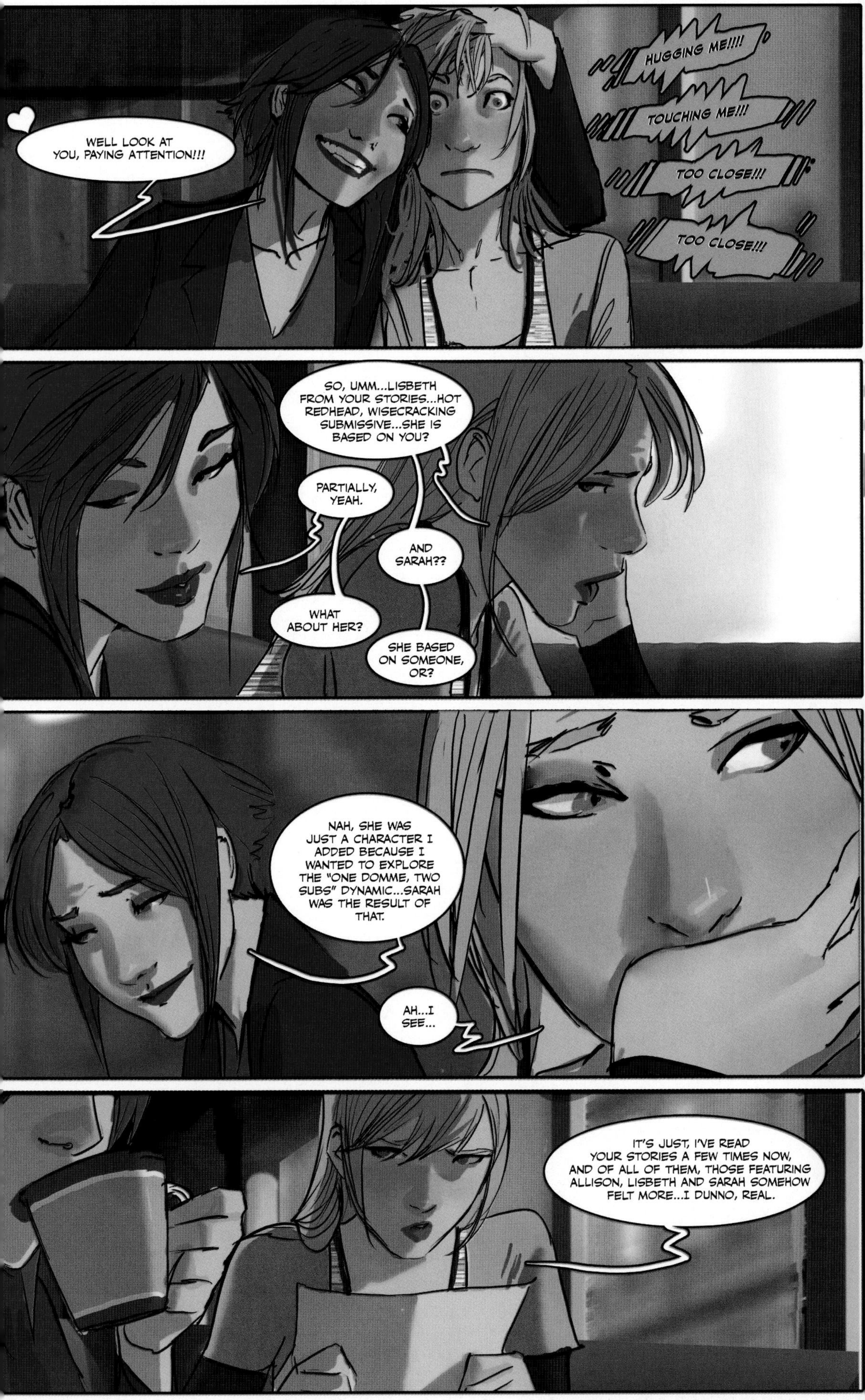
WELL LOOK AT YOU, PAYING ATTENTION!!!
HUGGING ME!!!!
TOUCHING ME!!!
TOO CLOSE!!!
TOO CLOSE!!!
SO, UMM...LISBETH FROM YOUR STORIES...HOT REDHEAD, WISECRACKING SUBMISSIVE...SHE IS BASED ON YOU?
PARTIALLY, YEAH.
AND SARAH??
WHAT ABOUT HER?
SHE BASED ON SOMEONE, OR?
NAH, SHE WAS JUST A CHARACTER I ADDED BECAUSE I WANTED TO EXPLORE THE "ONE DOMME, TWO SUBS" DYNAMIC...SARAH WAS THE RESULT OF THAT.
AH...I SEE...
IT'S JUST, I'VE READ YOUR STORIES A FEW TIMES NOW, AND OF ALL OF THEM, THOSE FEATURING ALLISON, LISBETH AND SARAH SOMEHOW FELT MORE...I DUNNO, REAL.

ALLISON IS BASED ON MY BEST FRIEND, ALLY, YOU KNOW.

YOUR DOMME?

YUP.

AND YOU ARE STILL BEST FRIENDS?

WHAT'S YOUR POINT?

I JUST DON'T THINK I COULD DO THAT... I MEAN IF CASSIE, FOR EXAMPLE... WELL...YOU KNOW...UM... DOESN'T IT GET WEIRD? LIKE... WHEN YOU ARE JUST HANGING OUT?

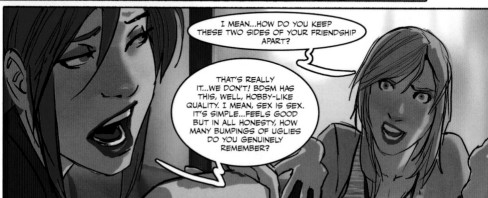

I MEAN...HOW DO YOU KEEP THESE TWO SIDES OF YOUR FRIENDSHIP APART?

THAT'S REALLY IT...WE DON'T! BDSM HAS THIS, WELL, HOBBY-LIKE QUALITY. I MEAN, SEX IS SEX. IT'S SIMPLE...FEELS GOOD BUT IN ALL HONESTY, HOW MANY BUMPINGS OF UGLIES DO YOU GENUINELY REMEMBER?

THIS...IS MUCH MORE LAYERED. MEMORIES ALONE ARE MORE THAN WORTH IT. THERE IS DISCUSSING RIGS, SCENARIOS, FANTASIES, WHAT MIGHT WORK AND WHAT WOULDN'T...IF YOU THINK ABOUT IT, IT'S MORE THAN SEX, IT'S A COMMON INTEREST.

SIGH....SO THE TWO OF YOU BASICALLY KNOW EACH OTHER BETTER THAN MY EX-BOYFRIEND AND I KNEW EACH OTHER. AIN'T THAT JUST A LITTLE BIT DEPRESSING...

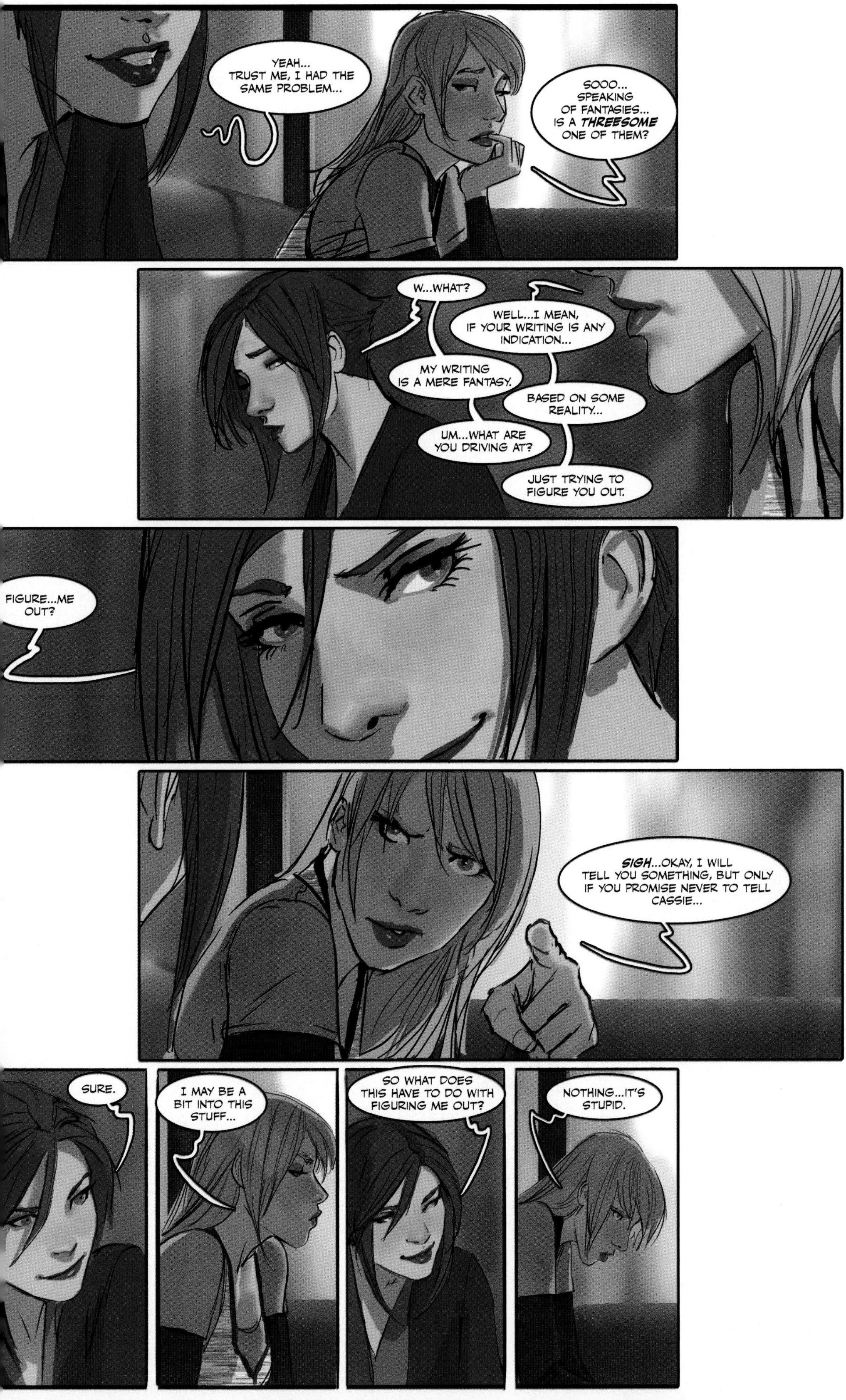
YEAH... TRUST ME, I HAD THE SAME PROBLEM...
SOOO... SPEAKING OF FANTASIES... IS A ***THREESOME*** ONE OF THEM?
W...WHAT?
WELL...I MEAN, IF YOUR WRITING IS ANY INDICATION...
MY WRITING IS A MERE FANTASY.
BASED ON SOME REALITY...
UM...WHAT ARE YOU DRIVING AT?
JUST TRYING TO FIGURE YOU OUT.
FIGURE...ME OUT?
SIGH...OKAY, I WILL TELL YOU SOMETHING, BUT ONLY IF YOU PROMISE NEVER TO TELL CASSIE...
SURE.
I MAY BE A BIT INTO THIS STUFF...
SO WHAT DOES THIS HAVE TO DO WITH FIGURING ME OUT?
NOTHING...IT'S STUPID.

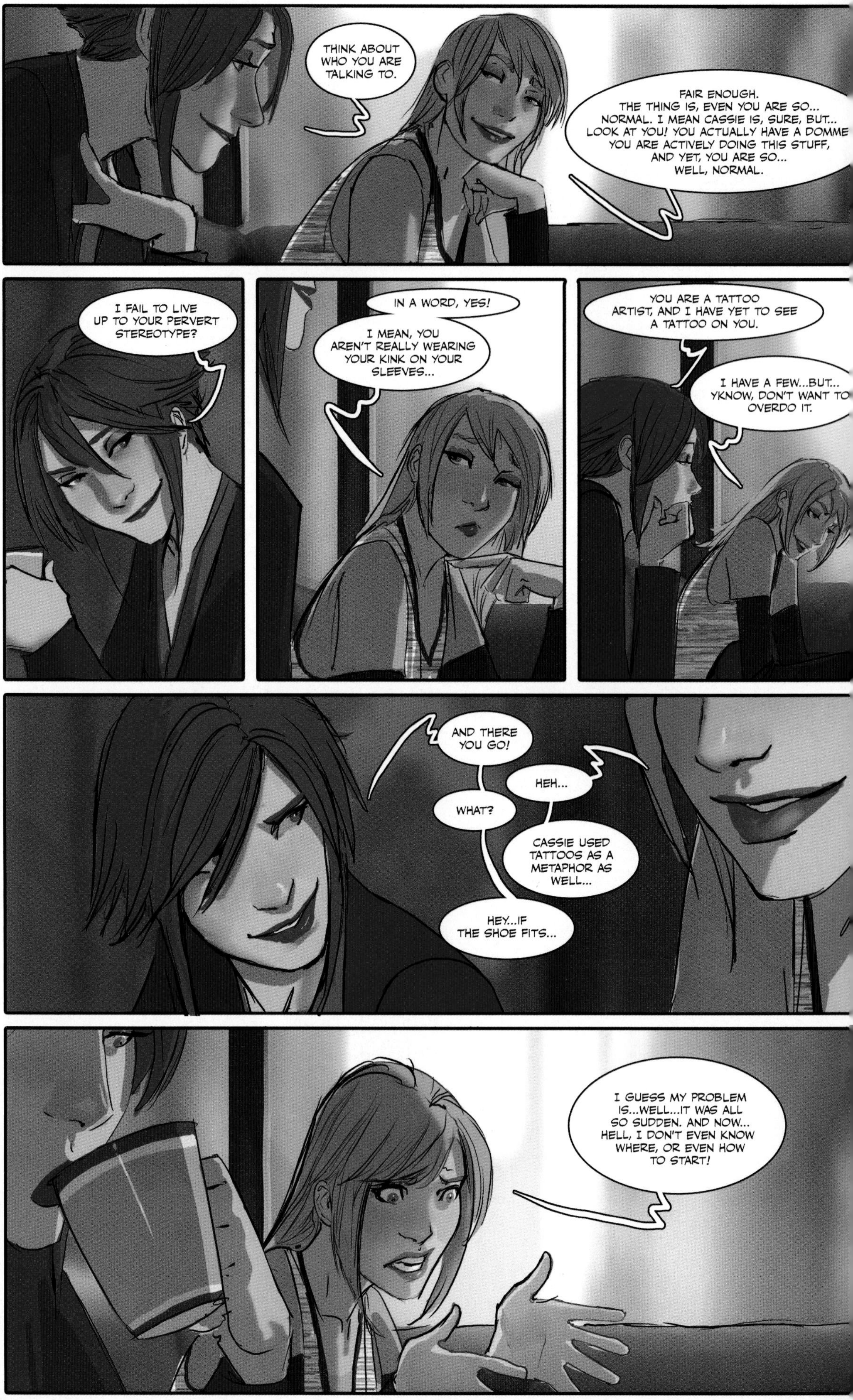

THINK ABOUT WHO YOU ARE TALKING TO.
FAIR ENOUGH. THE THING IS, EVEN YOU ARE SO... NORMAL. I MEAN CASSIE IS, SURE, BUT... LOOK AT YOU! YOU ACTUALLY HAVE A DOMME YOU ARE ACTIVELY DOING THIS STUFF, AND YET, YOU ARE SO... WELL, NORMAL.
I FAIL TO LIVE UP TO YOUR PERVERT STEREOTYPE?
IN A WORD, YES!
I MEAN, YOU AREN'T REALLY WEARING YOUR KINK ON YOUR SLEEVES...
YOU ARE A TATTOO ARTIST, AND I HAVE YET TO SEE A TATTOO ON YOU.
I HAVE A FEW...BUT... YKNOW, DON'T WANT TO OVERDO IT.
AND THERE YOU GO!
HEH...
WHAT?
CASSIE USED TATTOOS AS A METAPHOR AS WELL...
HEY...IF THE SHOE FITS...
I GUESS MY PROBLEM IS...WELL...IT WAS ALL SO SUDDEN. AND NOW... HELL, I DON'T EVEN KNOW WHERE, OR EVEN HOW TO START!

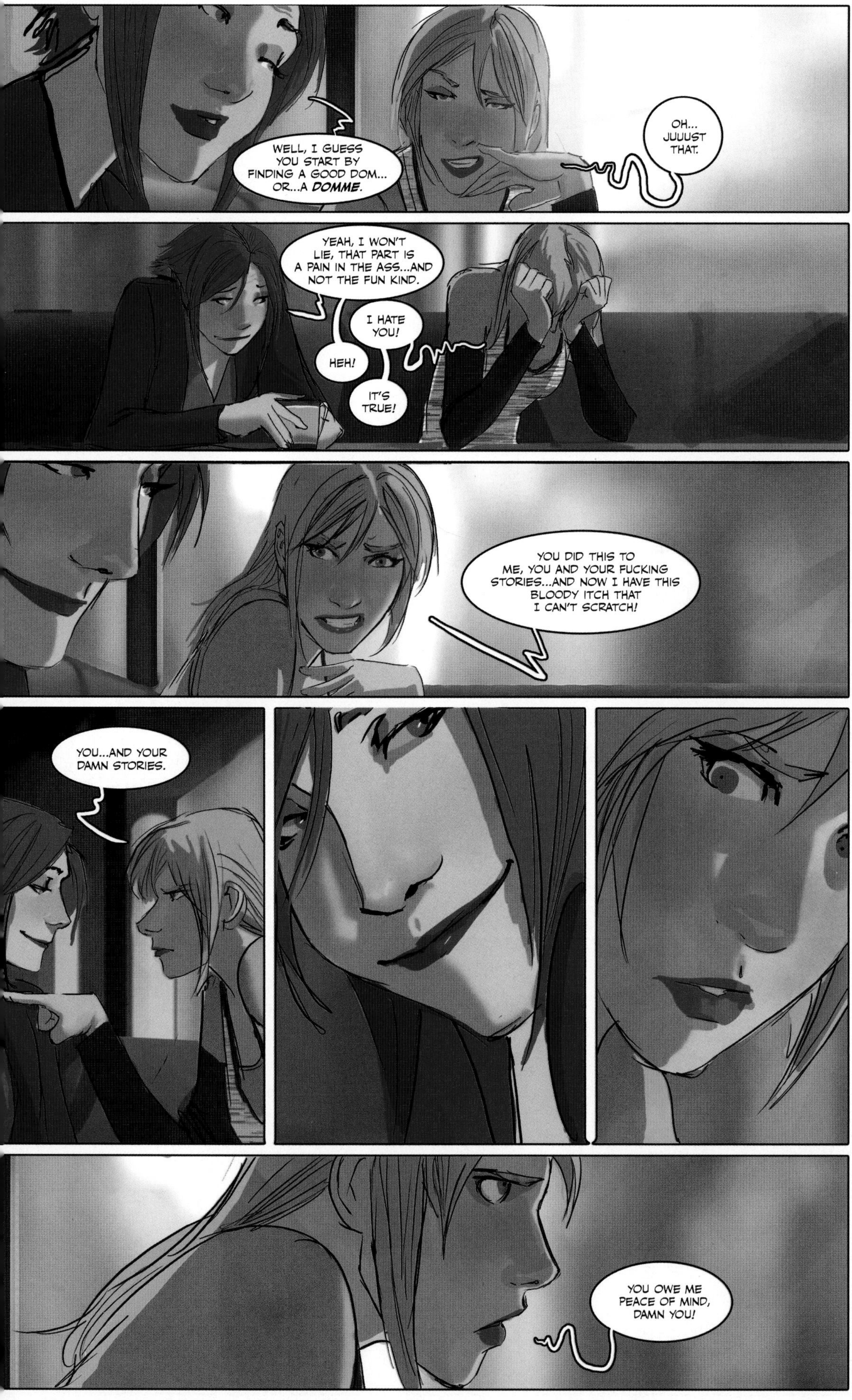
WELL, I GUESS YOU START BY FINDING A GOOD DOM... OR...A **DOMME**.
OH... JUUUST THAT.
YEAH, I WON'T LIE, THAT PART IS A PAIN IN THE ASS...AND NOT THE FUN KIND.
I HATE YOU!
HEH!
IT'S TRUE!
YOU DID THIS TO ME, YOU AND YOUR FUCKING STORIES...AND NOW I HAVE THIS BLOODY ITCH THAT I CAN'T SCRATCH!
YOU...AND YOUR DAMN STORIES.
YOU OWE ME PEACE OF MIND, DAMN YOU!

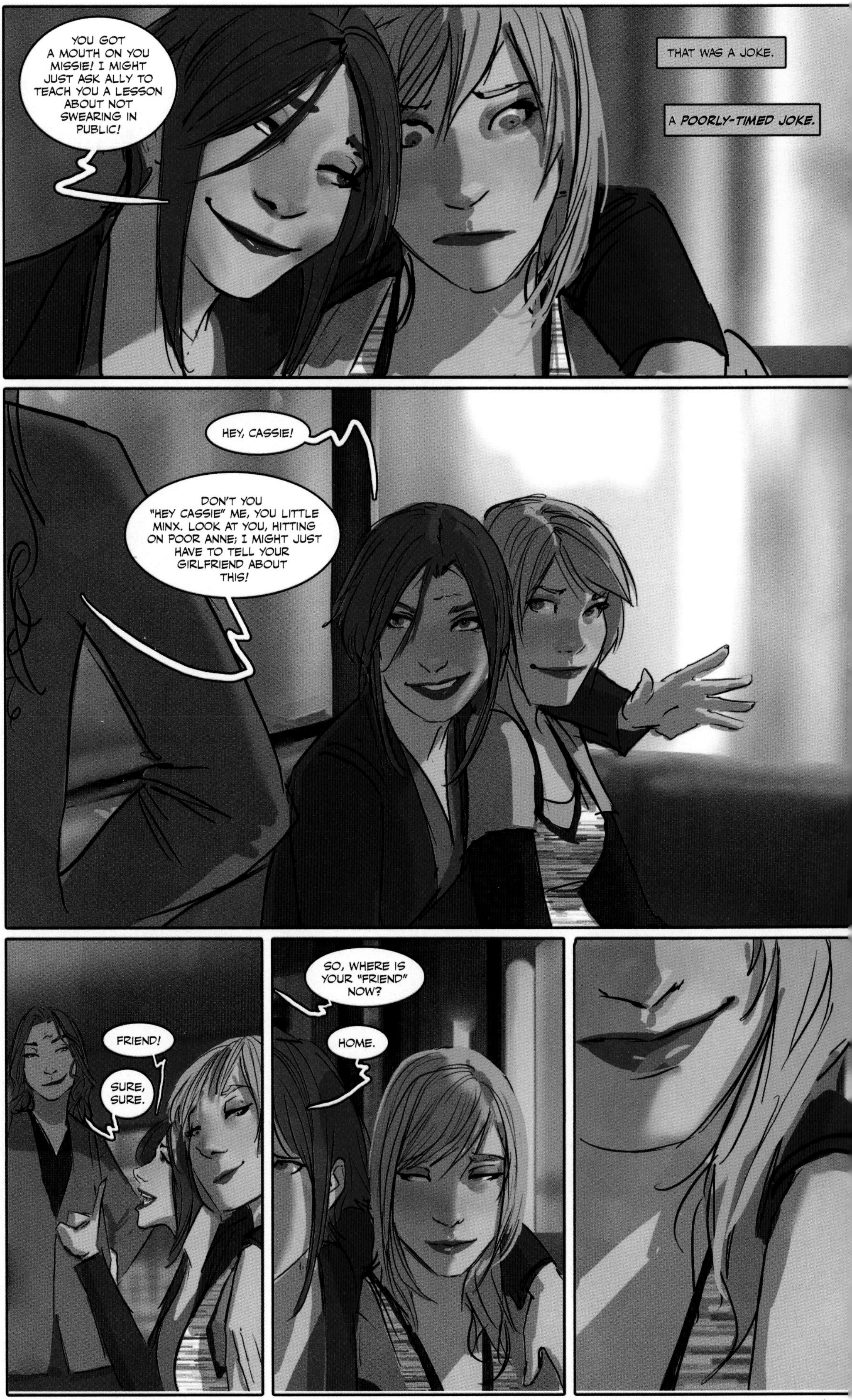
YOU GOT A MOUTH ON YOU MISSIE! I MIGHT JUST ASK ALLY TO TEACH YOU A LESSON ABOUT NOT SWEARING IN PUBLIC!
THAT WAS A JOKE.
A POORLY-TIMED JOKE.
HEY, CASSIE!
DON'T YOU "HEY CASSIE" ME, YOU LITTLE MINX. LOOK AT YOU, HITTING ON POOR ANNE; I MIGHT JUST HAVE TO TELL YOUR GIRLFRIEND ABOUT THIS!
FRIEND!
SURE, SURE.
SO, WHERE IS YOUR "FRIEND" NOW?
HOME.

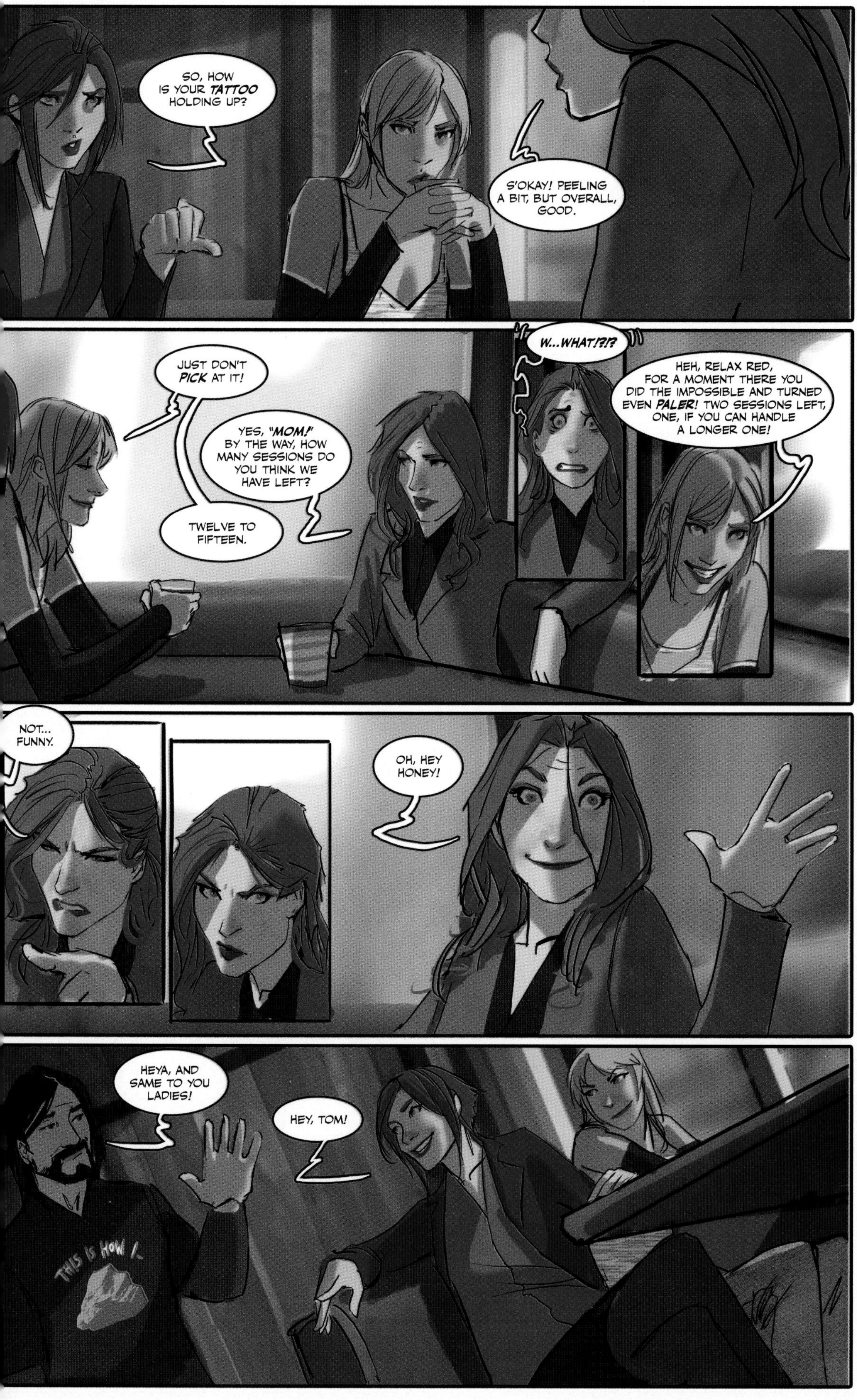
SO, HOW IS YOUR TATTOO HOLDING UP?
S'OKAY! PEELING A BIT, BUT OVERALL, GOOD.
JUST DON'T PICK AT IT!
YES, "MOM!" BY THE WAY, HOW MANY SESSIONS DO YOU THINK WE HAVE LEFT?
TWELVE TO FIFTEEN.
W...WHAT!?!?
HEH, RELAX RED, FOR A MOMENT THERE YOU DID THE IMPOSSIBLE AND TURNED EVEN PALER! TWO SESSIONS LEFT, ONE, IF YOU CAN HANDLE A LONGER ONE!
NOT... FUNNY.
OH, HEY HONEY!
HEYA, AND SAME TO YOU LADIES!
HEY, TOM!
THIS IS HOW I...

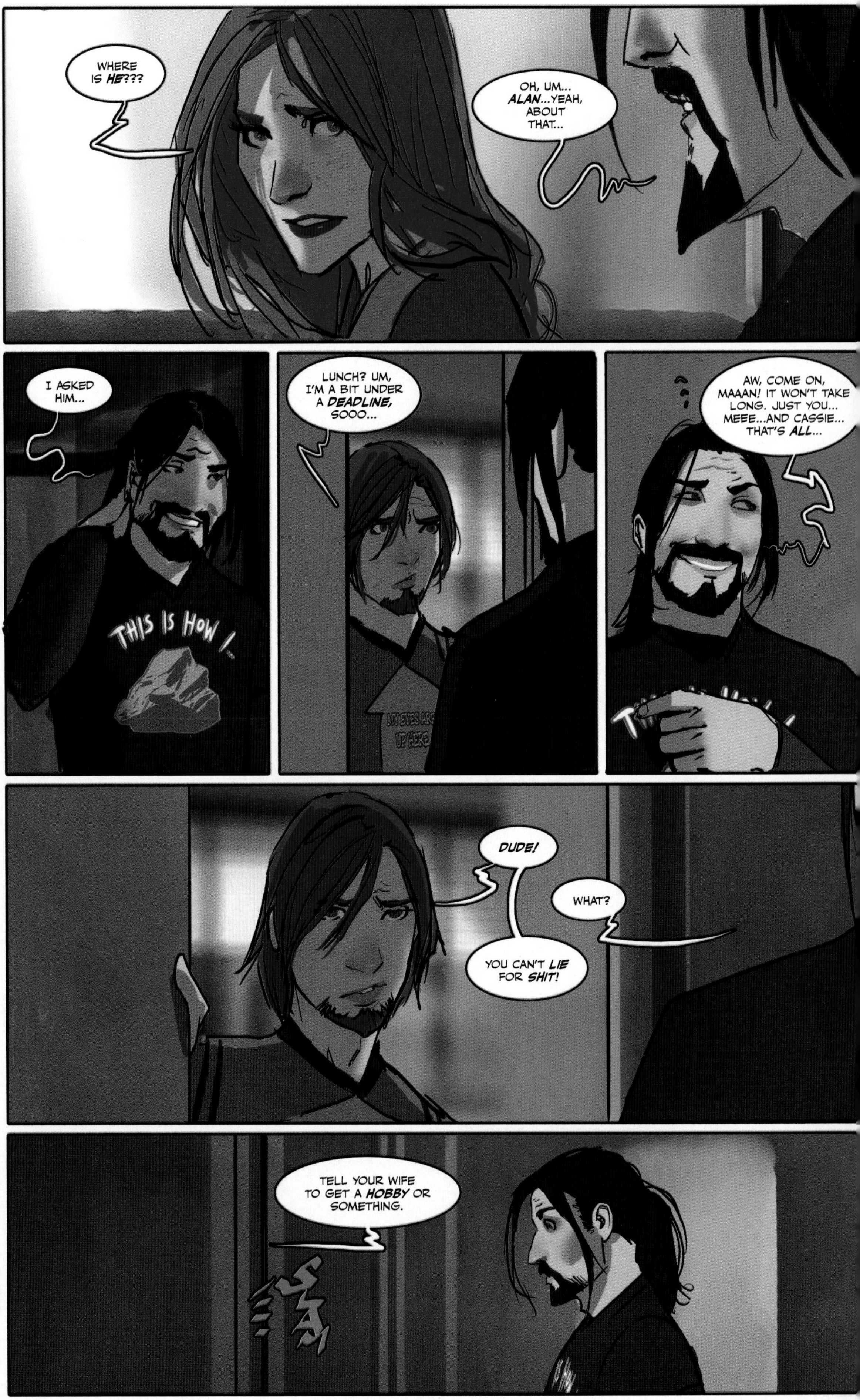
WHERE IS HE???
OH, UM... ALAN...YEAH, ABOUT THAT...
I ASKED HIM...
THIS IS HOW I...
LUNCH? UM, I'M A BIT UNDER A DEADLINE, SOOO...
AW, COME ON, MAAAN! IT WON'T TAKE LONG. JUST YOU... MEEE...AND CASSIE... THAT'S ALL...
DUDE!
WHAT?
YOU CAN'T LIE FOR SHIT!
TELL YOUR WIFE TO GET A HOBBY OR SOMETHING.
SLAM

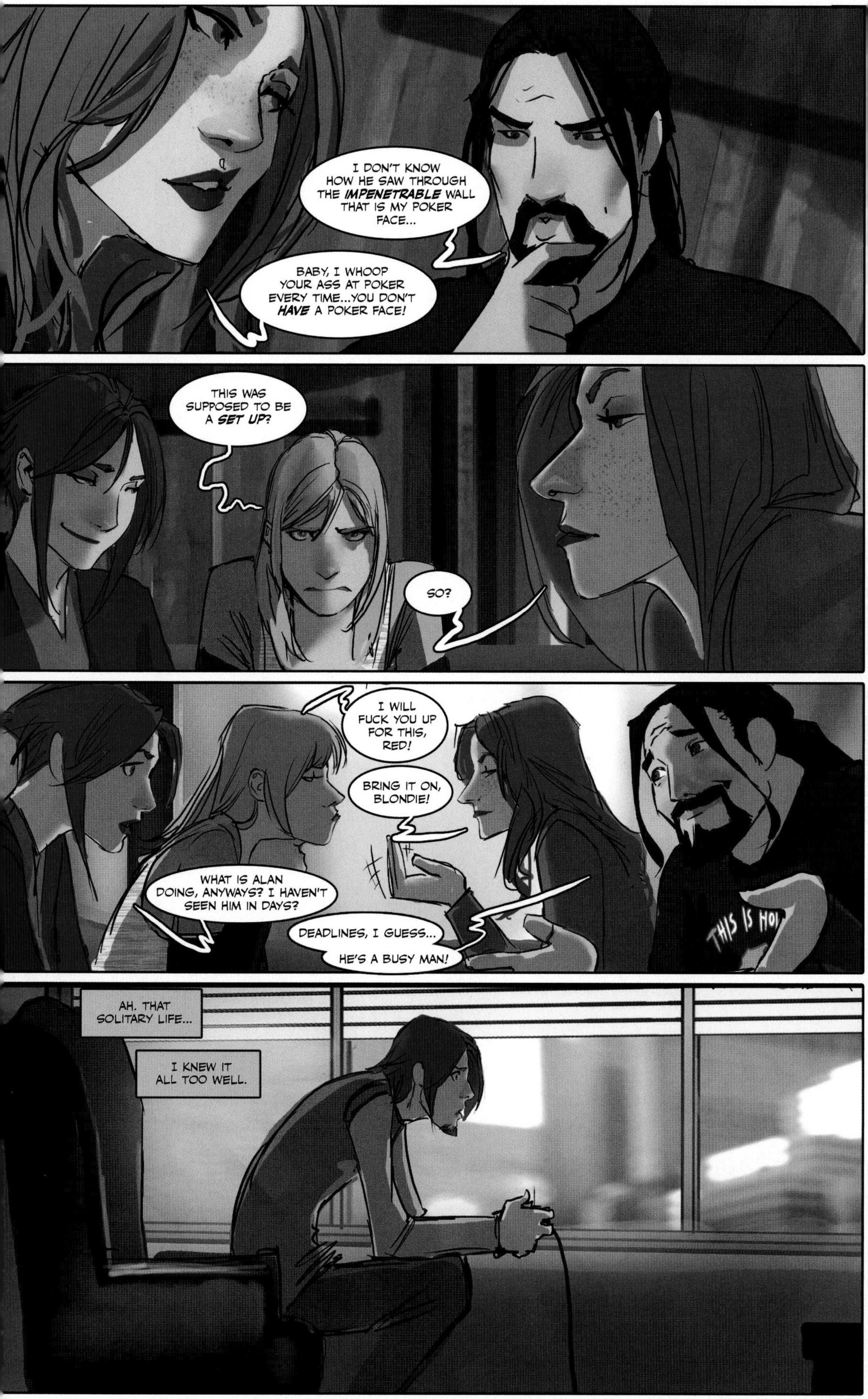
I DON'T KNOW HOW HE SAW THROUGH THE IMPENETRABLE WALL THAT IS MY POKER FACE...
BABY, I WHOOP YOUR ASS AT POKER EVERY TIME...YOU DON'T HAVE A POKER FACE!
THIS WAS SUPPOSED TO BE A SET UP?
SO?
I WILL FUCK YOU UP FOR THIS, RED!
BRING IT ON, BLONDIE!
WHAT IS ALAN DOING, ANYWAYS? I HAVEN'T SEEN HIM IN DAYS?
DEADLINES, I GUESS...
HE'S A BUSY MAN!
THIS IS HO
AH. THAT SOLITARY LIFE...
I KNEW IT ALL TOO WELL.

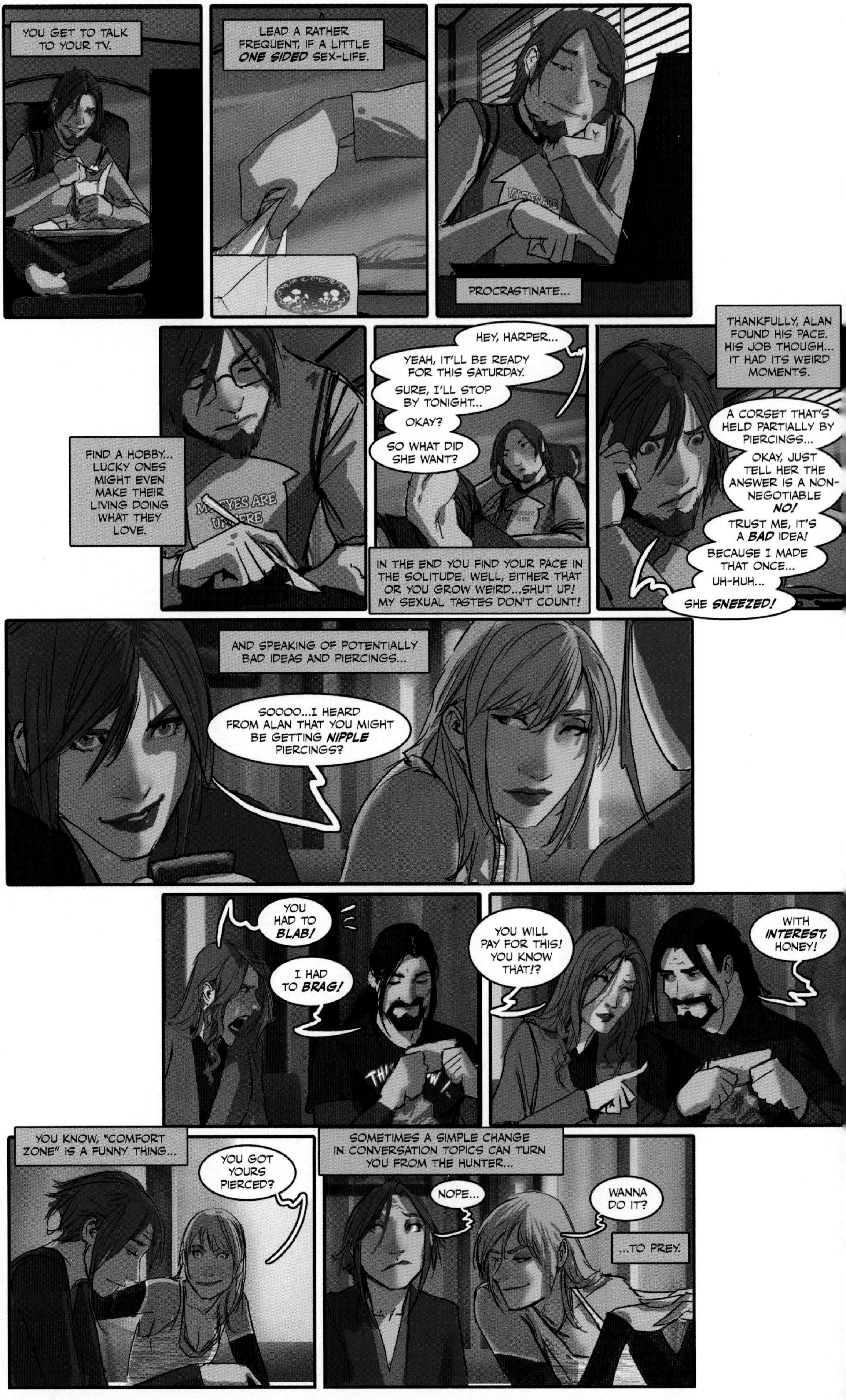

YOU GET TO TALK TO YOUR TV.
LEAD A RATHER FREQUENT, IF A LITTLE ONE SIDED SEX-LIFE.
MY EYES ARE
PROCRASTINATE...
FIND A HOBBY... LUCKY ONES MIGHT EVEN MAKE THEIR LIVING DOING WHAT THEY LOVE.
HEY, HARPER...
YEAH, IT'LL BE READY FOR THIS SATURDAY.
SURE, I'LL STOP BY TONIGHT...
OKAY?
SO WHAT DID SHE WANT?
IN THE END YOU FIND YOUR PACE IN THE SOLITUDE. WELL, EITHER THAT OR YOU GROW WEIRD...SHUT UP! MY SEXUAL TASTES DON'T COUNT!
THANKFULLY, ALAN FOUND HIS PACE. HIS JOB THOUGH... IT HAD ITS WEIRD MOMENTS.
A CORSET THAT'S HELD PARTIALLY BY PIERCINGS...
OKAY, JUST TELL HER THE ANSWER IS A NON-NEGOTIABLE NO!
TRUST ME, IT'S A BAD IDEA!
BECAUSE I MADE THAT ONCE...
UH-HUH...
SHE SNEEZED!
AND SPEAKING OF POTENTIALLY BAD IDEAS AND PIERCINGS...
SOOOO...I HEARD FROM ALAN THAT YOU MIGHT BE GETTING NIPPLE PIERCINGS?
YOU HAD TO BLAB!
I HAD TO BRAG!
YOU WILL PAY FOR THIS! YOU KNOW THAT!?
WITH INTEREST, HONEY!
YOU KNOW, "COMFORT ZONE" IS A FUNNY THING...
YOU GOT YOURS PIERCED?
SOMETIMES A SIMPLE CHANGE IN CONVERSATION TOPICS CAN TURN YOU FROM THE HUNTER...
NOPE...
WANNA DO IT?
...TO PREY.

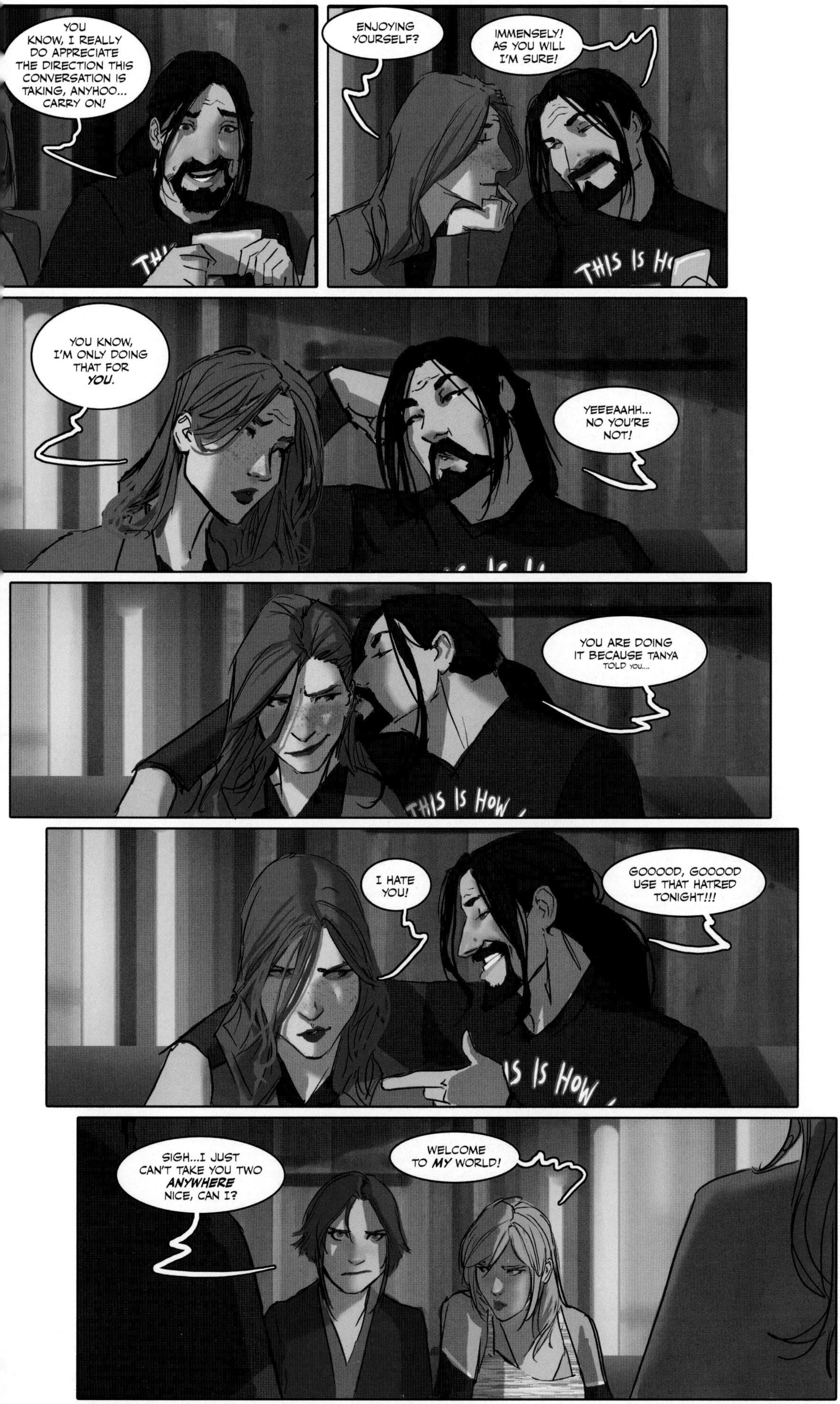

YOU KNOW, I REALLY DO APPRECIATE THE DIRECTION THIS CONVERSATION IS TAKING, ANYHOO... CARRY ON!
THIS
ENJOYING YOURSELF?
IMMENSELY! AS YOU WILL I'M SURE!
THIS IS H
YOU KNOW, I'M ONLY DOING THAT FOR *YOU*.
YEEEAAHH... NO YOU'RE NOT!
YOU ARE DOING IT BECAUSE TANYA TOLD YOU....
THIS IS HOW
I HATE YOU!
GOOOOD, GOOOOD USE THAT HATRED TONIGHT!!!
IS IS HOW
SIGH...I JUST CAN'T TAKE YOU TWO ***ANYWHERE*** NICE, CAN I?
WELCOME TO ***MY*** WORLD!

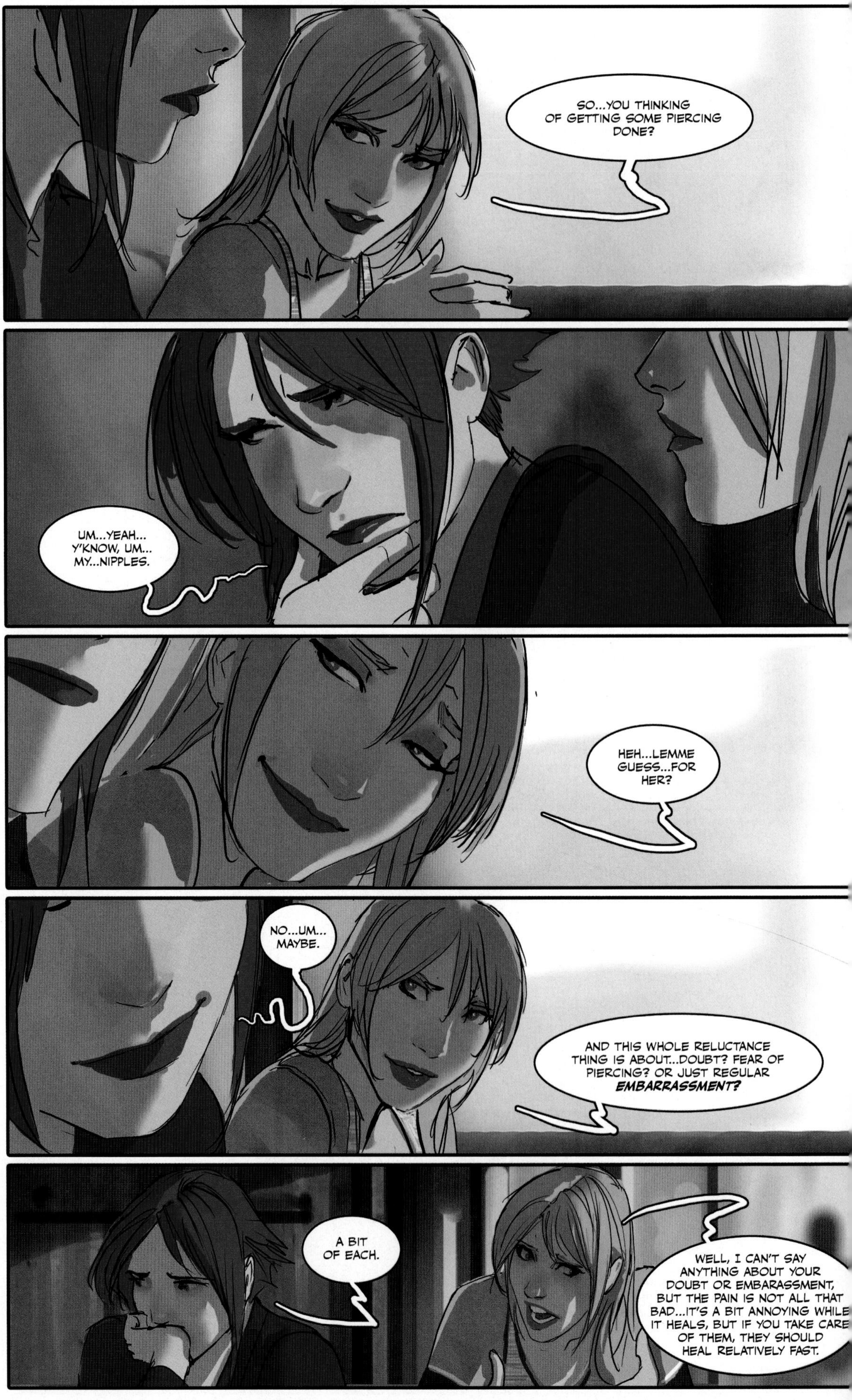
SO...YOU THINKING OF GETTING SOME PIERCING DONE?
UM...YEAH... Y'KNOW, UM... MY...NIPPLES.
HEH...LEMME GUESS...FOR HER?
NO...UM... MAYBE.
AND THIS WHOLE RELUCTANCE THING IS ABOUT...DOUBT? FEAR OF PIERCING? OR JUST REGULAR EMBARRASSMENT?
A BIT OF EACH.
WELL, I CAN'T SAY ANYTHING ABOUT YOUR DOUBT OR EMBARASSMENT, BUT THE PAIN IS NOT ALL THAT BAD...IT'S A BIT ANNOYING WHILE IT HEALS, BUT IF YOU TAKE CARE OF THEM, THEY SHOULD HEAL RELATIVELY FAST.

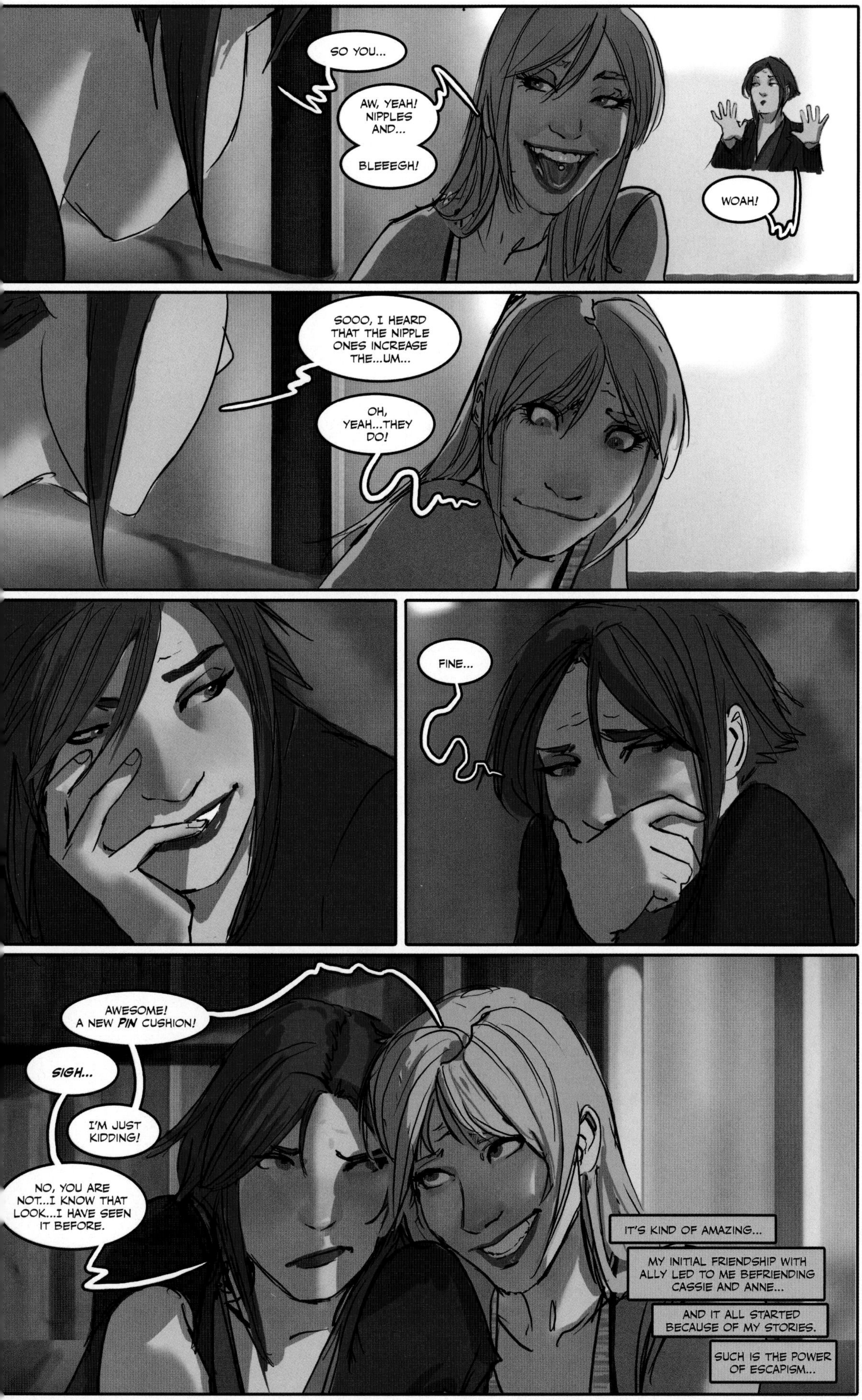
SO YOU...
AW, YEAH! NIPPLES AND...
BLEEEGH!
WOAH!
SOOO, I HEARD THAT THE NIPPLE ONES INCREASE THE...UM...
OH, YEAH...THEY DO!
FINE...
AWESOME! A NEW PIN CUSHION!
SIGH...
I'M JUST KIDDING!
NO, YOU ARE NOT...I KNOW THAT LOOK...I HAVE SEEN IT BEFORE.
IT'S KIND OF AMAZING...
MY INITIAL FRIENDSHIP WITH ALLY LED TO ME BEFRIENDING CASSIE AND ANNE...
AND IT ALL STARTED BECAUSE OF MY STORIES.
SUCH IS THE POWER OF ESCAPISM...

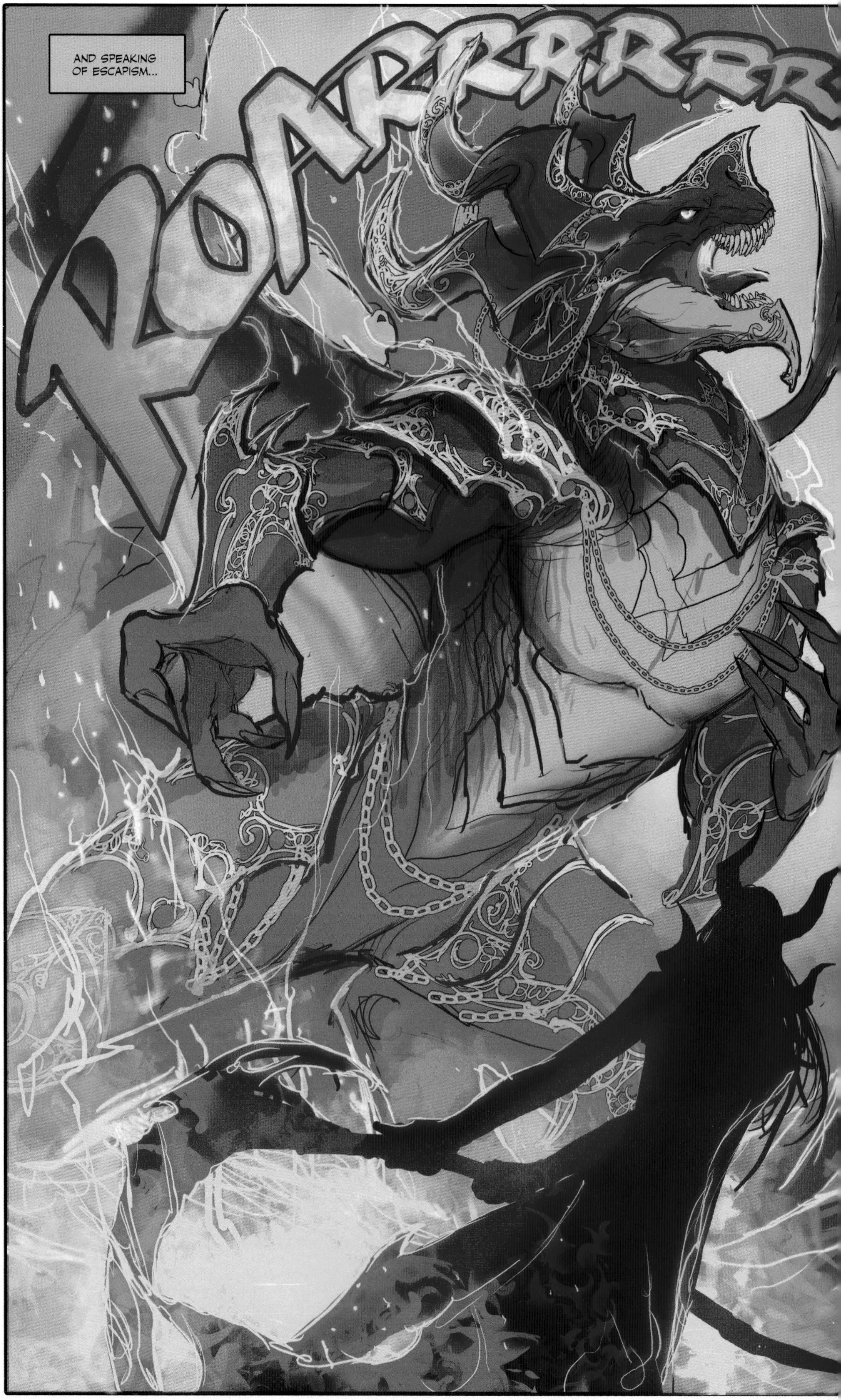
AND SPEAKING OF ESCAPISM...
ROARRRRRRR

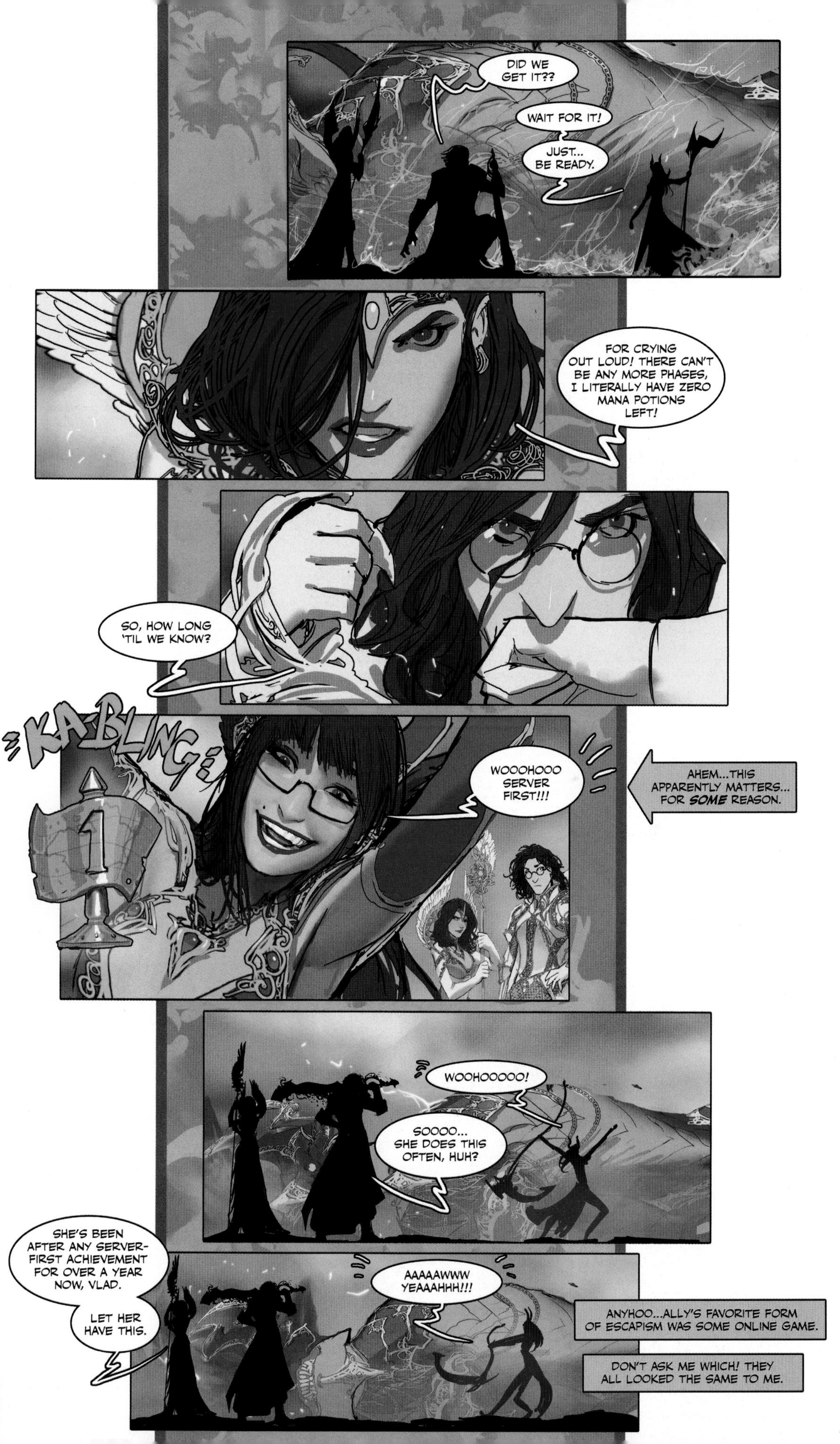
DID WE GET IT??
WAIT FOR IT!
JUST... BE READY.
FOR CRYING OUT LOUD! THERE CAN'T BE ANY MORE PHASES, I LITERALLY HAVE ZERO MANA POTIONS LEFT!
SO, HOW LONG 'TIL WE KNOW?
KA-BLING
1
WOOOHOOO SERVER FIRST!!!
AHEM...THIS APPARENTLY MATTERS... FOR *SOME* REASON.
WOOHOOOOO!
SOOOO... SHE DOES THIS OFTEN, HUH?
SHE'S BEEN AFTER ANY SERVER-FIRST ACHIEVEMENT FOR OVER A YEAR NOW, VLAD.
LET HER HAVE THIS.
AAAAAWWW YEAAAHHH!!!
ANYHOO...ALLY'S FAVORITE FORM OF ESCAPISM WAS SOME ONLINE GAME.
DON'T ASK ME WHICH! THEY ALL LOOKED THE SAME TO ME.

VIDEOGAMES MAY NOT BE MY THING, BUT I CERTAINLY UNDERSTOOD THE WAY THEY CONNECTED PEOPLE.

SURE, IT WAS DIFFERENT FROM MY PREFERED FORM OF ENTERTAINMENT...

BY THAT, I MEAN BOOKS...NOT TH SEX STUFF...

ARCANE DRAGON OF MAGIC

THIS PET WILL DRASTICALLY BOOST MAGE'S ELEMENTAL DAMAGE. OTHER CLASSES GAIN BOOST IN MAGIC RESISTANCE

ANYHOW...MY POINT IS, I GOT ITS APPEAL.

MEH... MIGHT AS WELL.

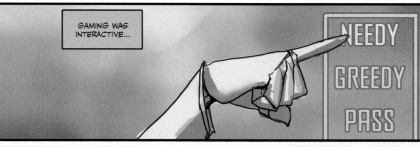

GAMING WAS INTERACTIVE...

NEEDY GREEDY PASS

NEEDY GREEDY PASS

EXCITING IN ITS OWN WAY...

WAIT, WHAT!?

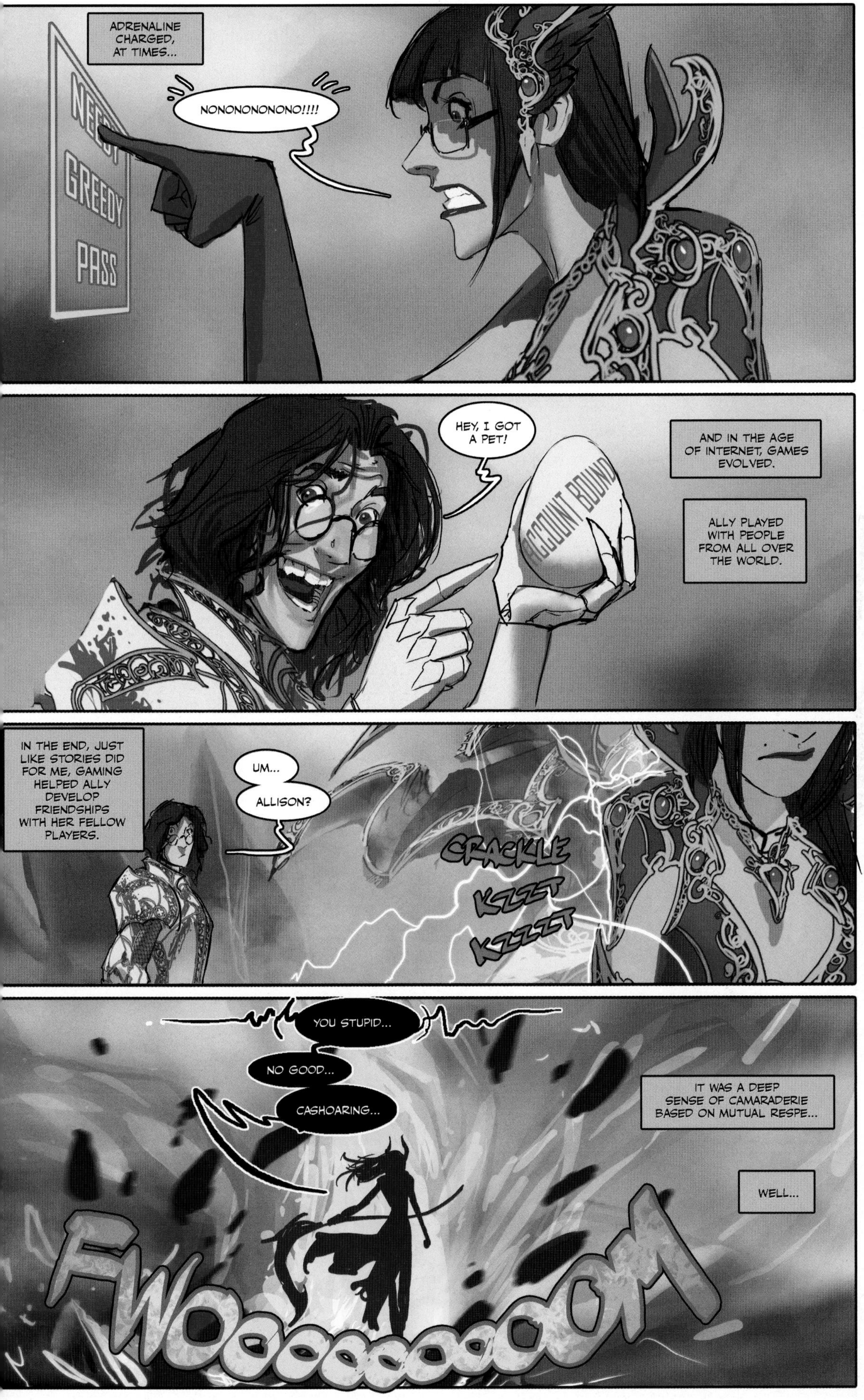
ADRENALINE CHARGED, AT TIMES...
NEED GREEDY PASS
NONONONONONO!!!!
HEY, I GOT A PET!
ACCOUNT BOUND
AND IN THE AGE OF INTERNET, GAMES EVOLVED.
ALLY PLAYED WITH PEOPLE FROM ALL OVER THE WORLD.
IN THE END, JUST LIKE STORIES DID FOR ME, GAMING HELPED ALLY DEVELOP FRIENDSHIPS WITH HER FELLOW PLAYERS.
UM...
ALLISON?
CRACKLE
KZZZT
KZZZZT
YOU STUPID...
NO GOOD...
CASHOARING...
IT WAS A DEEP SENSE OF CAMARADERIE BASED ON MUTUAL RESPE...
WELL...
FWOOOOOOOOOM

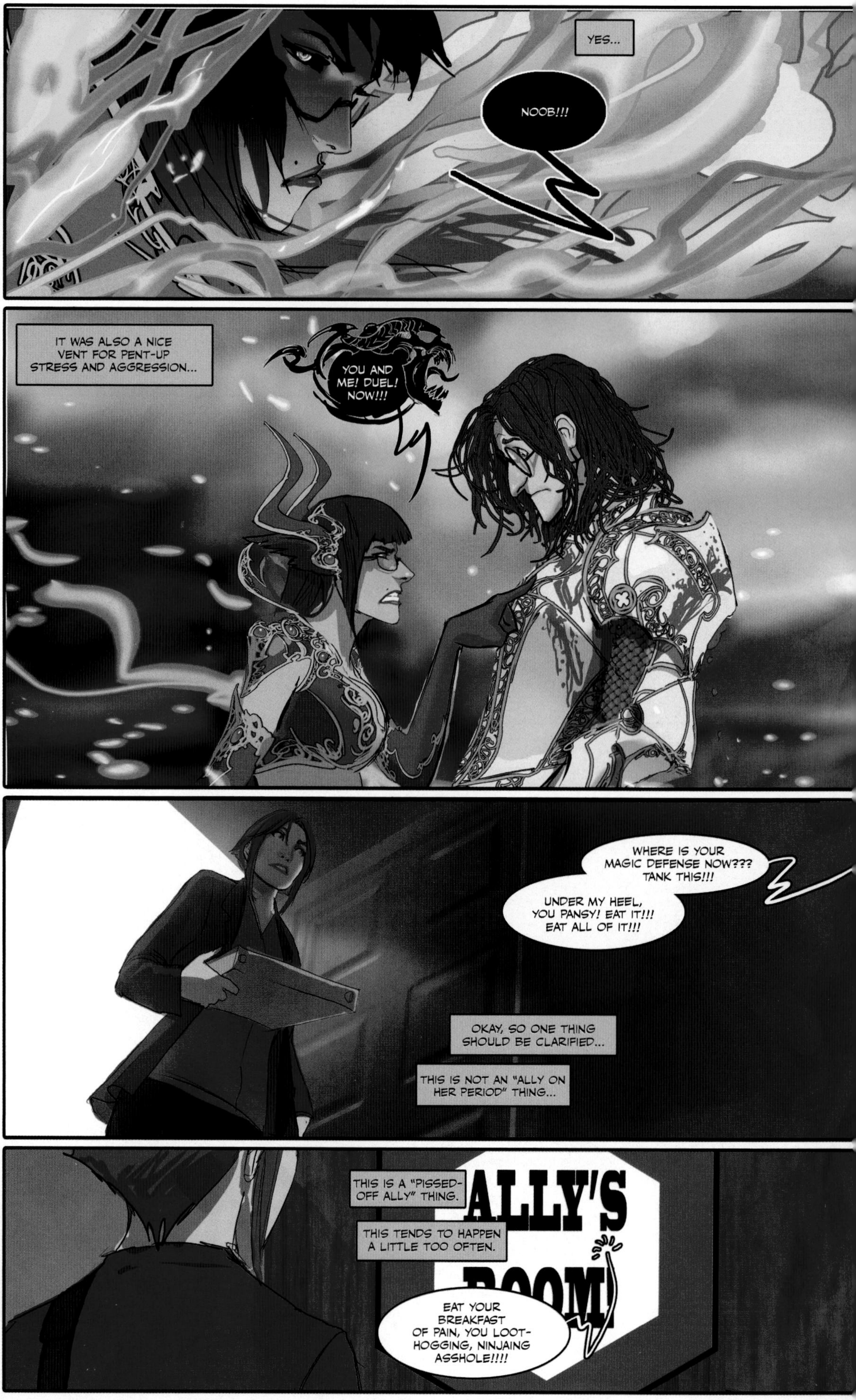
YES...
NOOB!!!
IT WAS ALSO A NICE VENT FOR PENT-UP STRESS AND AGGRESSION...
YOU AND ME! DUEL! NOW!!!
WHERE IS YOUR MAGIC DEFENSE NOW??? TANK THIS!!!
UNDER MY HEEL, YOU PANSY! EAT IT!!! EAT ALL OF IT!!!
OKAY, SO ONE THING SHOULD BE CLARIFIED...
THIS IS NOT AN "ALLY ON HER PERIOD" THING...
THIS IS A "PISSED-OFF ALLY" THING.
ALLY'S
THIS TENDS TO HAPPEN A LITTLE TOO OFTEN.
EAT YOUR BREAKFAST OF PAIN, YOU LOOT-HOGGING, NINJAING ASSHOLE!!!!

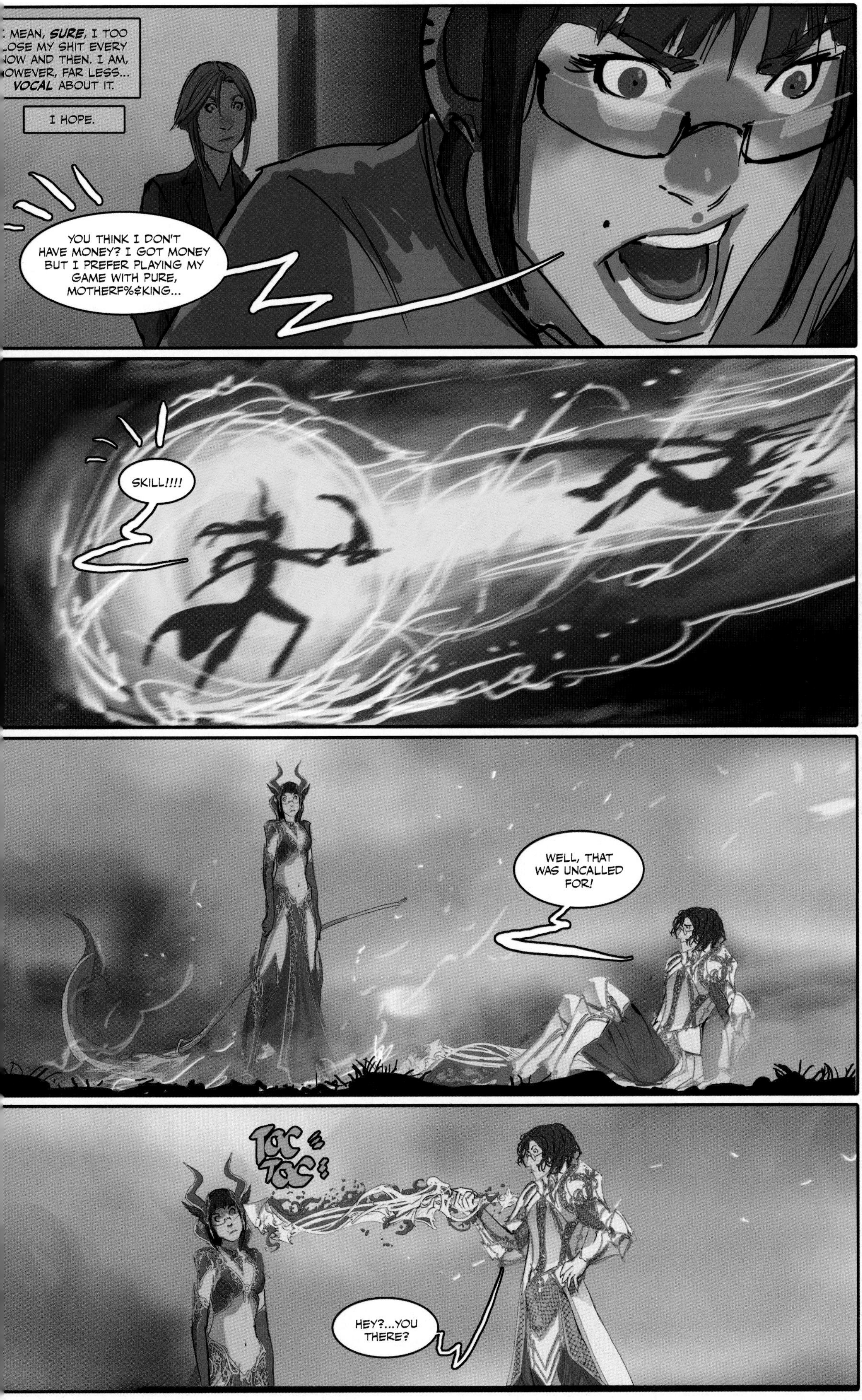
I MEAN, SURE, I TOO LOSE MY SHIT EVERY NOW AND THEN. I AM, HOWEVER, FAR LESS... VOCAL ABOUT IT.
I HOPE.
YOU THINK I DON'T HAVE MONEY? I GOT MONEY BUT I PREFER PLAYING MY GAME WITH PURE, MOTHERF%$KING...
SKILL!!!!
WELL, THAT WAS UNCALLED FOR!
TOC TOC
HEY?...YOU THERE?

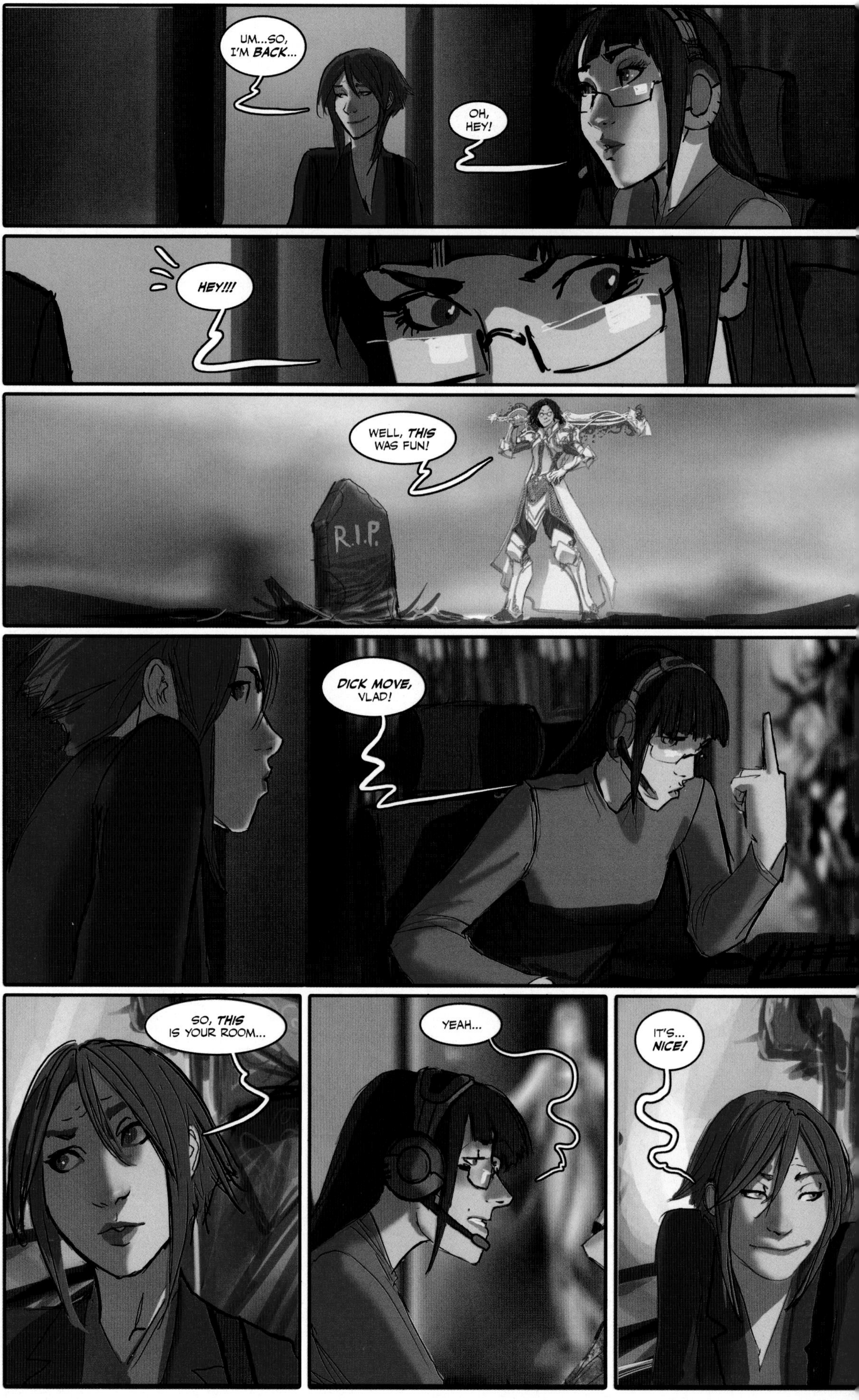
UM...SO, I'M BACK...
OH, HEY!
HEY!!!
WELL, THIS WAS FUN!
R.I.P.
DICK MOVE, VLAD!
SO, THIS IS YOUR ROOM...
YEAH...
IT'S... NICE!

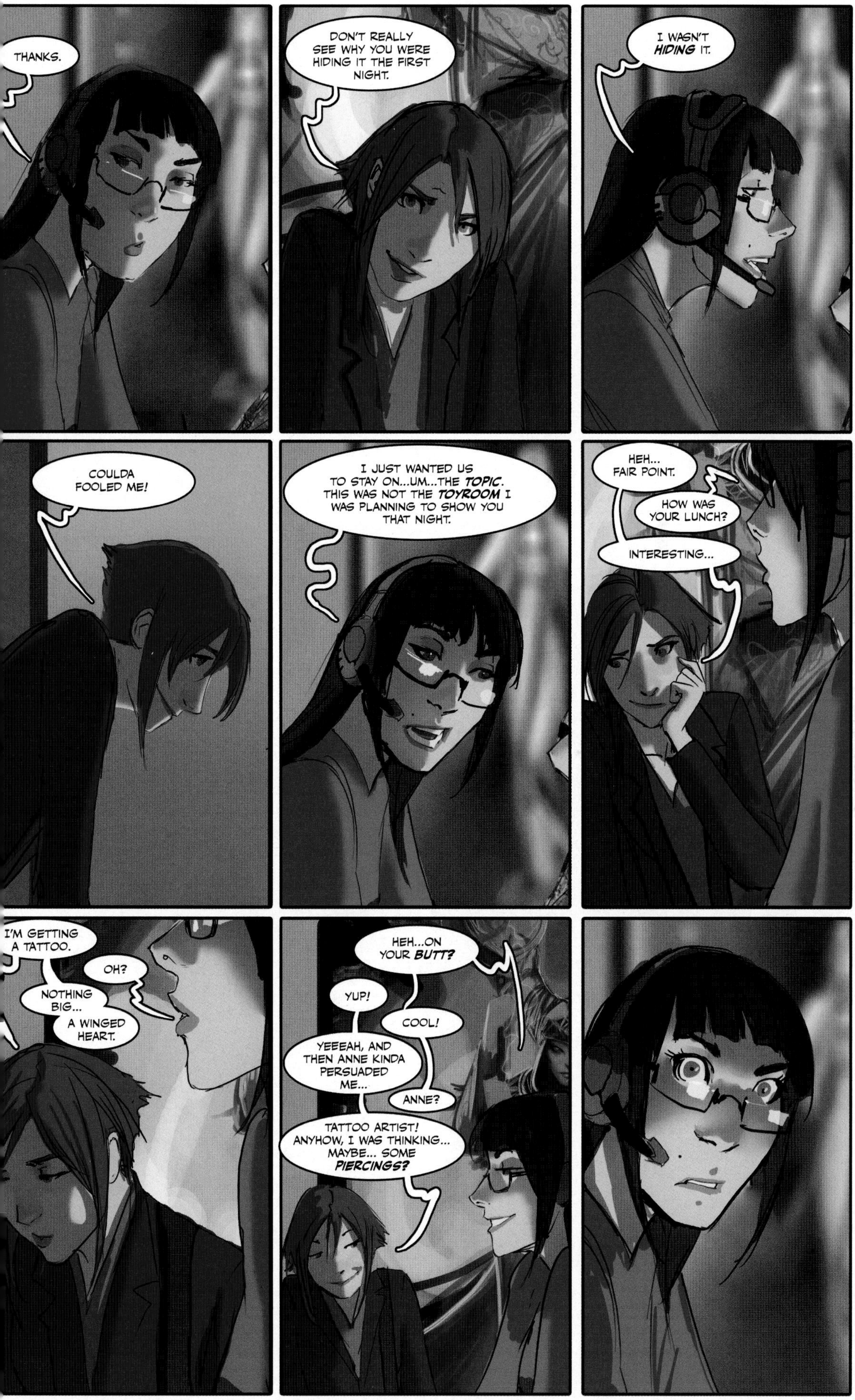
THANKS.
DON'T REALLY SEE WHY YOU WERE HIDING IT THE FIRST NIGHT.
I WASN'T HIDING IT.
COULDA FOOLED ME!
I JUST WANTED US TO STAY ON...UM...THE TOPIC. THIS WAS NOT THE TOYROOM I WAS PLANNING TO SHOW YOU THAT NIGHT.
HEH... FAIR POINT.
HOW WAS YOUR LUNCH?
INTERESTING...
I'M GETTING A TATTOO.
OH?
NOTHING BIG...
A WINGED HEART.
HEH...ON YOUR BUTT?
YUP!
COOL!
YEEEAH, AND THEN ANNE KINDA PERSUADED ME...
ANNE?
TATTOO ARTIST! ANYHOW, I WAS THINKING... MAYBE... SOME PIERCINGS?

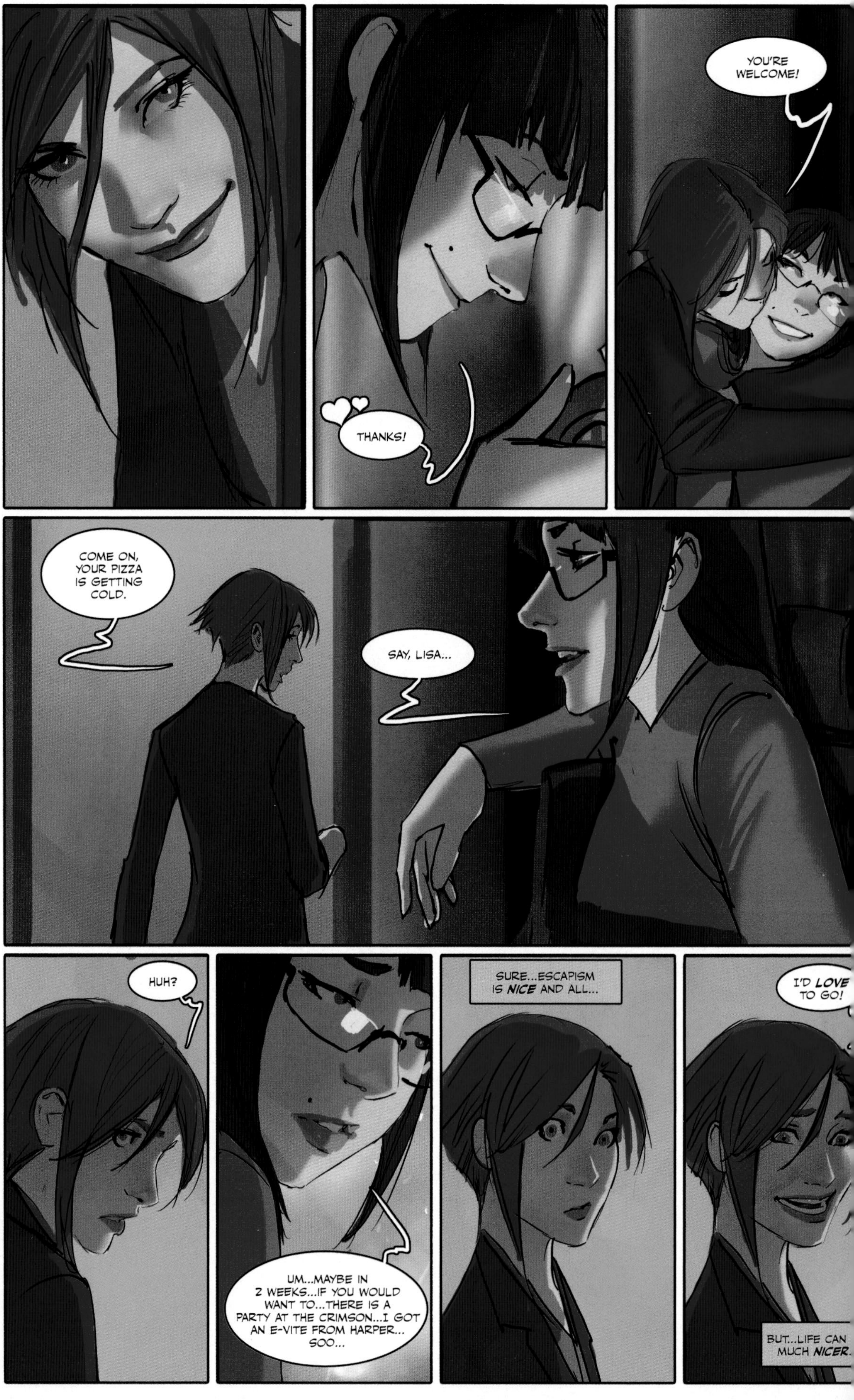

THANKS!
YOU'RE WELCOME!
COME ON, YOUR PIZZA IS GETTING COLD.
SAY, LISA...
HUH?
UM...MAYBE IN 2 WEEKS...IF YOU WOULD WANT TO...THERE IS A PARTY AT THE CRIMSON...I GOT AN E-VITE FROM HARPER... SOO...
SURE...ESCAPISM IS NICE AND ALL...
I'D LOVE TO GO!
BUT...LIFE CAN MUCH NICER.

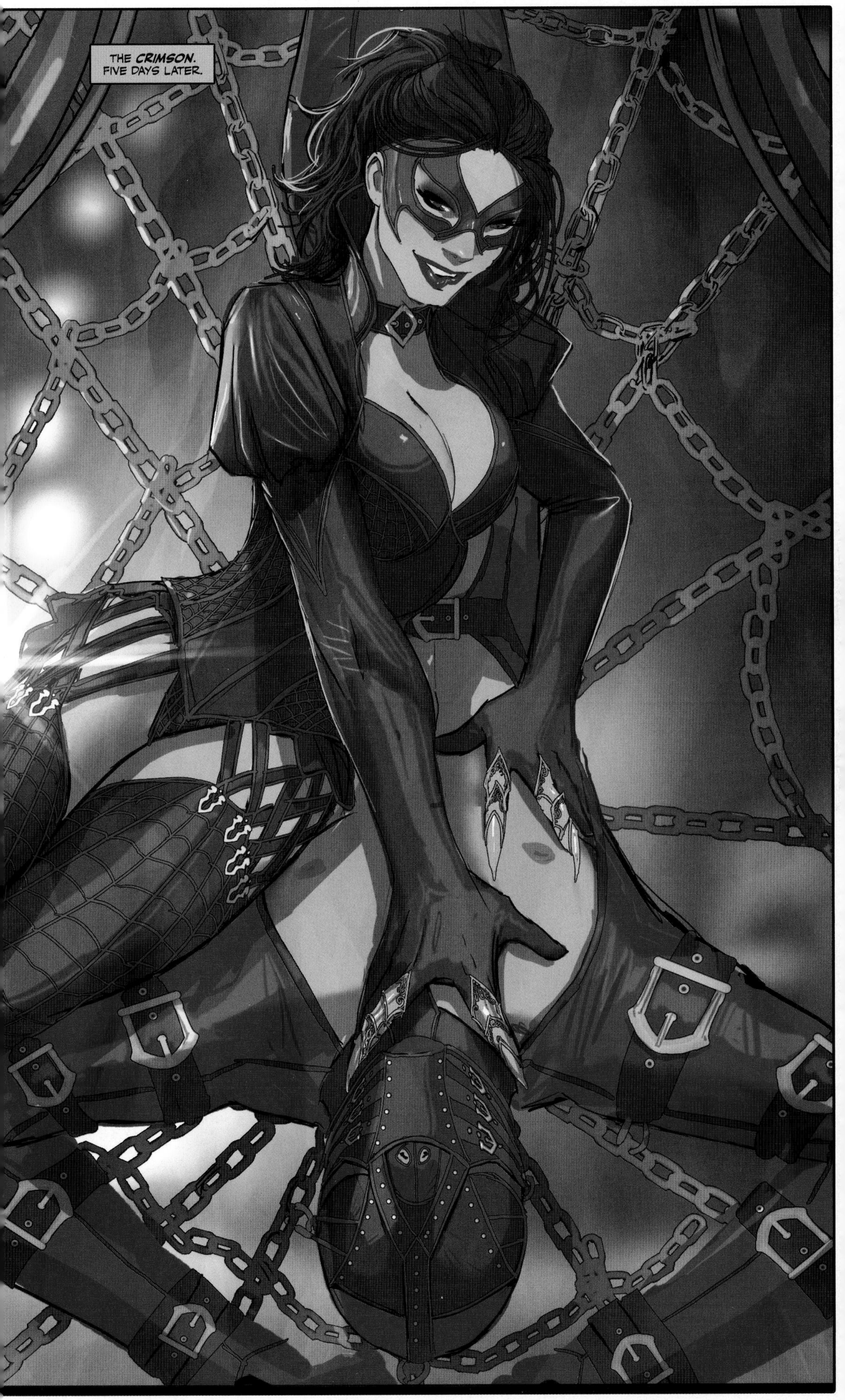
THE *CRIMSON*.
FIVE DAYS LATER.

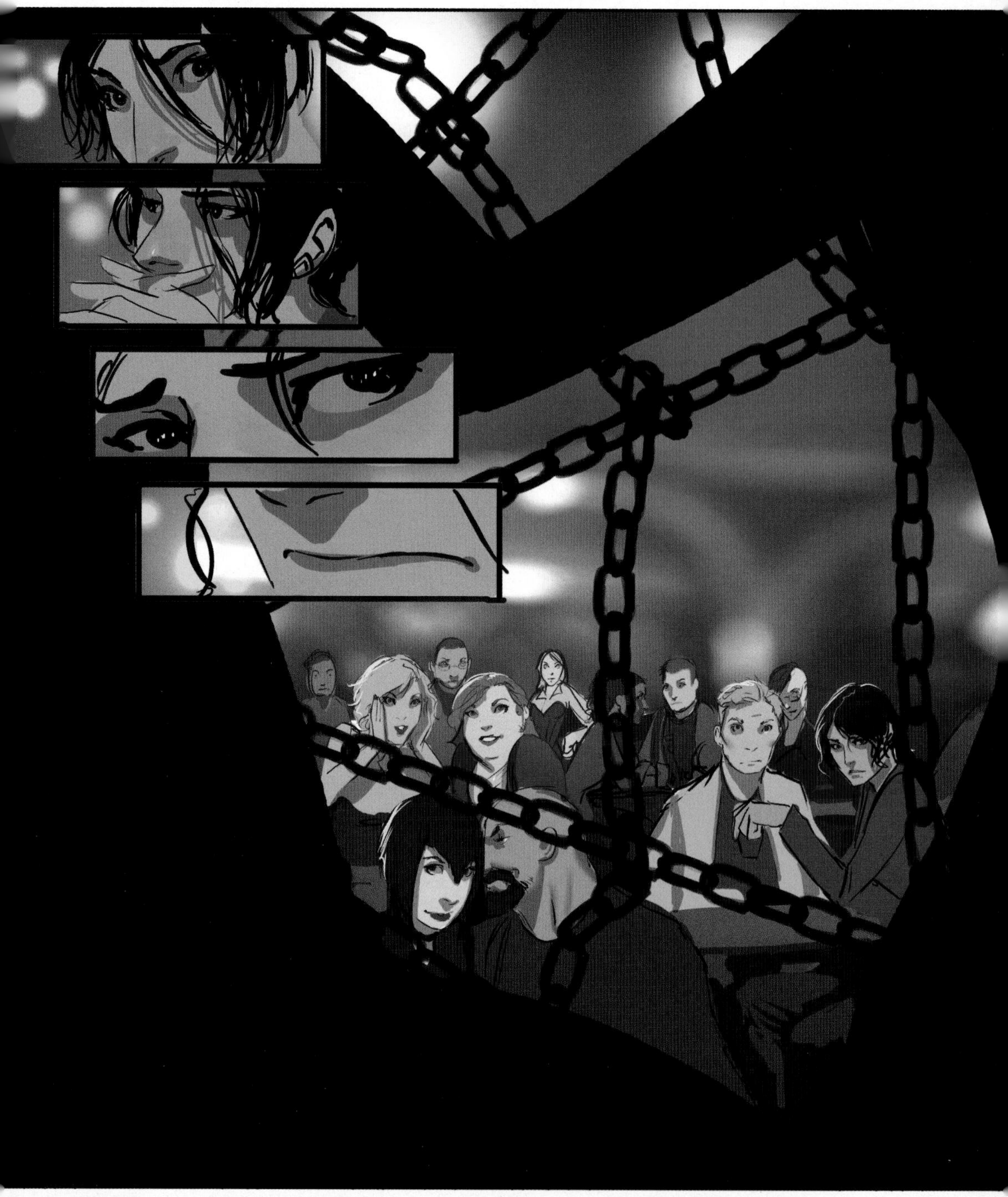

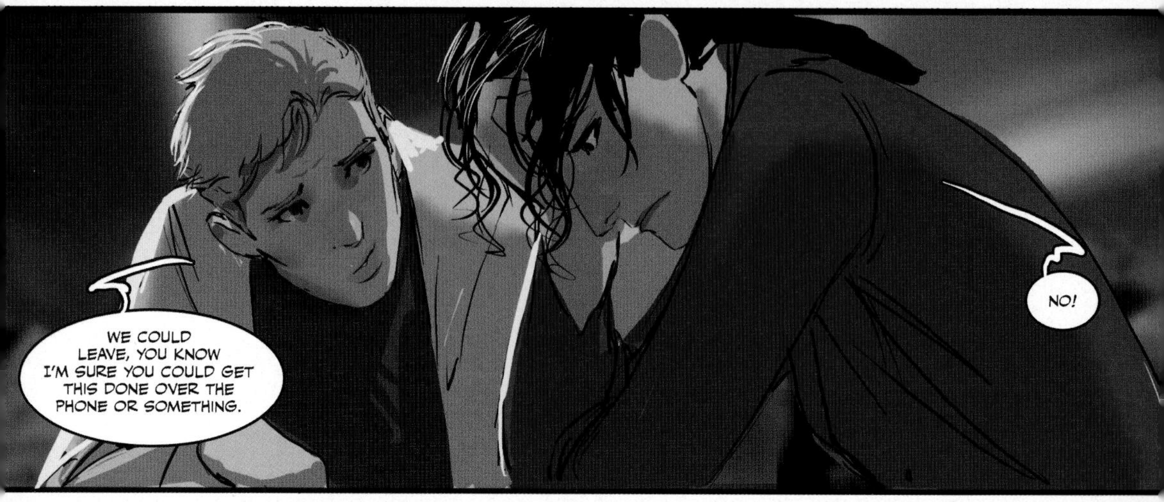
WE COULD LEAVE, YOU KNOW I'M SURE YOU COULD GET THIS DONE OVER THE PHONE OR SOMETHING.
NO!

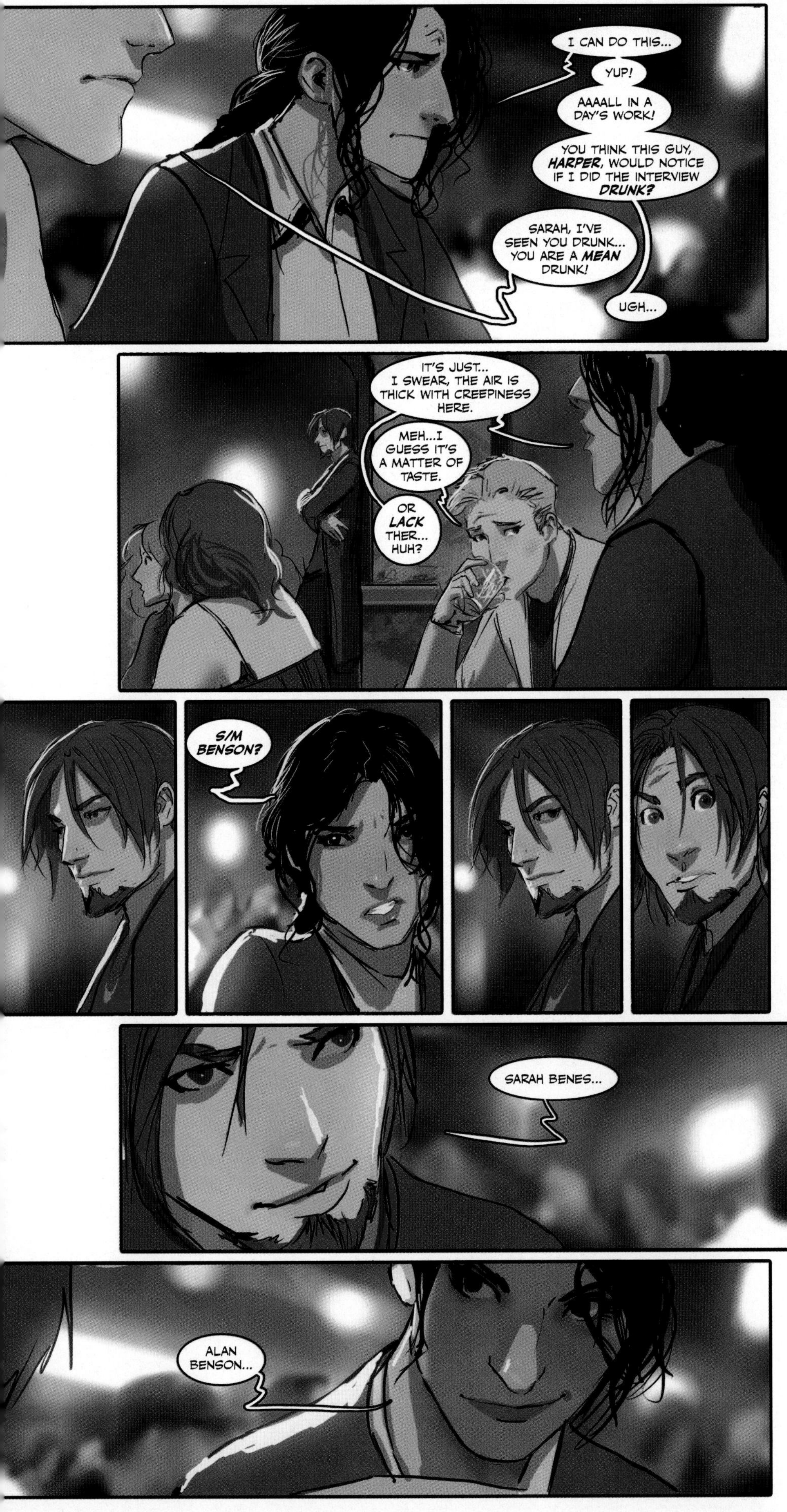

I CAN DO THIS...
YUP!
AAAALL IN A DAY'S WORK!
YOU THINK THIS GUY, **HARPER**, WOULD NOTICE IF I DID THE INTERVIEW ***DRUNK?***
SARAH, I'VE SEEN YOU DRUNK... YOU ARE A ***MEAN*** DRUNK!
UGH...
IT'S JUST... I SWEAR, THE AIR IS THICK WITH CREEPINESS HERE.
MEH...I GUESS IT'S A MATTER OF TASTE.
OR ***LACK*** THER... HUH?
S/M BENSON?
SARAH BENES...
ALAN BENSON...

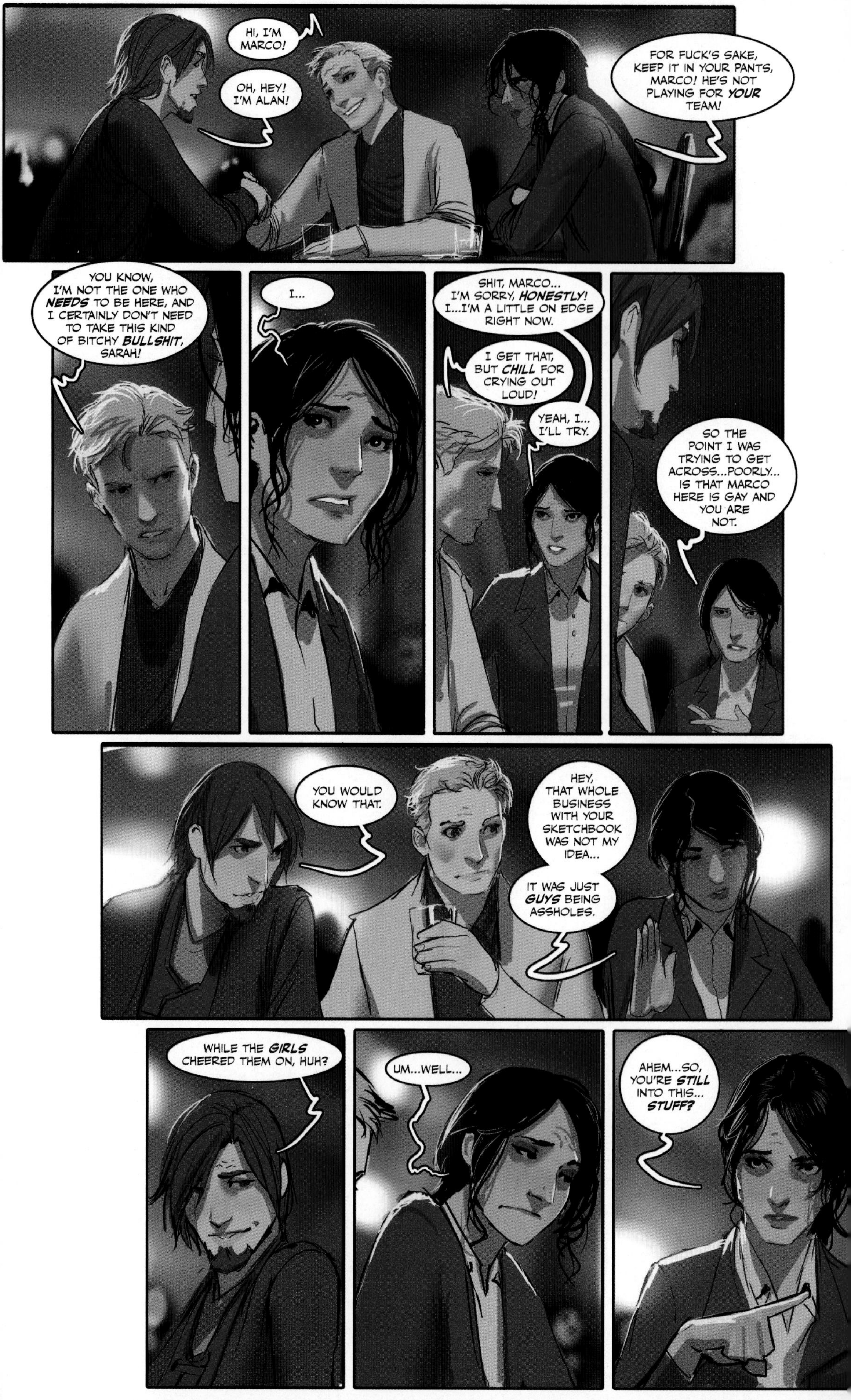

HI, I'M MARCO!
OH, HEY! I'M ALAN!
FOR FUCK'S SAKE, KEEP IT IN YOUR PANTS, MARCO! HE'S NOT PLAYING FOR YOUR TEAM!
YOU KNOW, I'M NOT THE ONE WHO NEEDS TO BE HERE, AND I CERTAINLY DON'T NEED TO TAKE THIS KIND OF BITCHY BULLSHIT, SARAH!
I...
SHIT, MARCO... I'M SORRY, HONESTLY! I...I'M A LITTLE ON EDGE RIGHT NOW.
I GET THAT, BUT CHILL FOR CRYING OUT LOUD!
YEAH, I... I'LL TRY.
SO THE POINT I WAS TRYING TO GET ACROSS...POORLY... IS THAT MARCO HERE IS GAY AND YOU ARE NOT.
YOU WOULD KNOW THAT.
HEY, THAT WHOLE BUSINESS WITH YOUR SKETCHBOOK WAS NOT MY IDEA...
IT WAS JUST GUYS BEING ASSHOLES.
WHILE THE GIRLS CHEERED THEM ON, HUH?
UM...WELL...
AHEM...SO, YOU'RE STILL INTO THIS... STUFF?

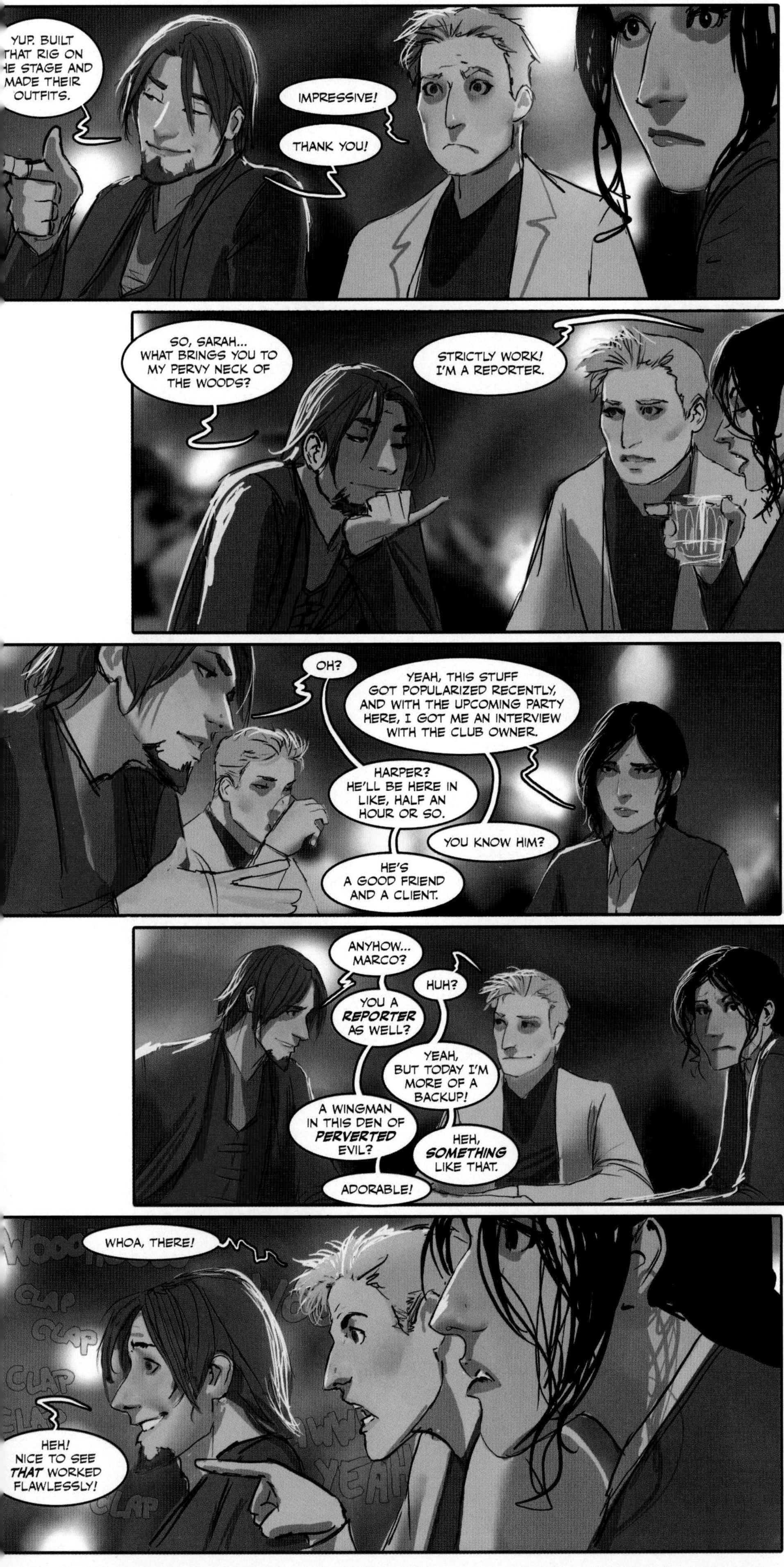
YUP. BUILT THAT RIG ON THE STAGE AND MADE THEIR OUTFITS.
IMPRESSIVE!
THANK YOU!
SO, SARAH... WHAT BRINGS YOU TO MY PERVY NECK OF THE WOODS?
STRICTLY WORK! I'M A REPORTER.
OH?
YEAH, THIS STUFF GOT POPULARIZED RECENTLY, AND WITH THE UPCOMING PARTY HERE, I GOT ME AN INTERVIEW WITH THE CLUB OWNER.
HARPER? HE'LL BE HERE IN LIKE, HALF AN HOUR OR SO.
YOU KNOW HIM?
HE'S A GOOD FRIEND AND A CLIENT.
ANYHOW... MARCO?
HUH?
YOU A REPORTER AS WELL?
YEAH, BUT TODAY I'M MORE OF A BACKUP!
A WINGMAN IN THIS DEN OF PERVERTED EVIL?
HEH, SOMETHING LIKE THAT.
ADORABLE!
WHOA, THERE!
CLAP
CLAP
CLAP
YEAH
HEH! NICE TO SEE THAT WORKED FLAWLESSLY!

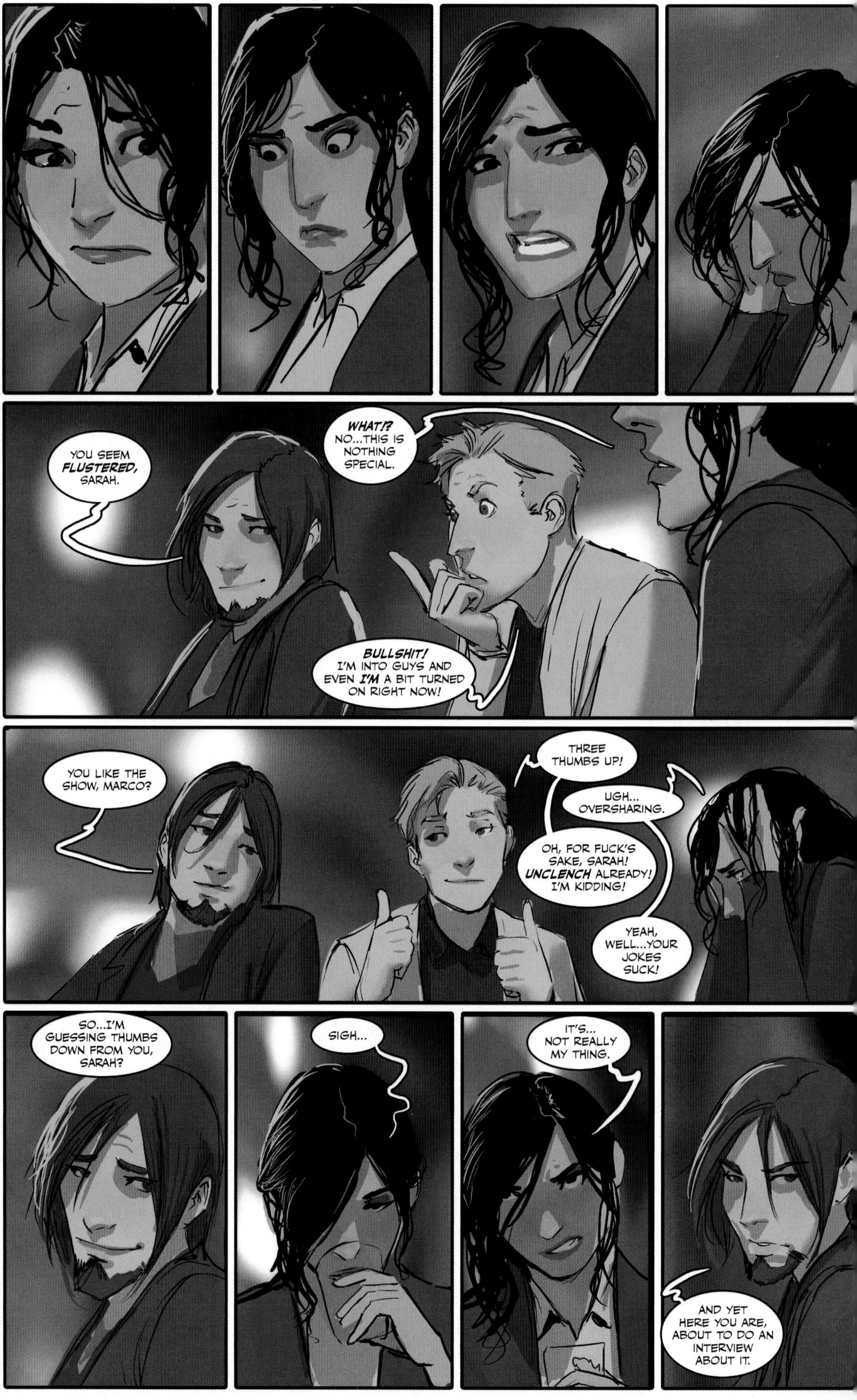
YOU SEEM FLUSTERED, SARAH.
WHAT!? NO...THIS IS NOTHING SPECIAL.
BULLSHIT! I'M INTO GUYS AND EVEN I'M A BIT TURNED ON RIGHT NOW!
YOU LIKE THE SHOW, MARCO?
THREE THUMBS UP!
UGH... OVERSHARING.
OH, FOR FUCK'S SAKE, SARAH! UNCLENCH ALREADY! I'M KIDDING!
YEAH, WELL...YOUR JOKES SUCK!
SO...I'M GUESSING THUMBS DOWN FROM YOU, SARAH?
SIGH...
IT'S... NOT REALLY MY THING.
AND YET HERE YOU ARE, ABOUT TO DO AN INTERVIEW ABOUT IT.

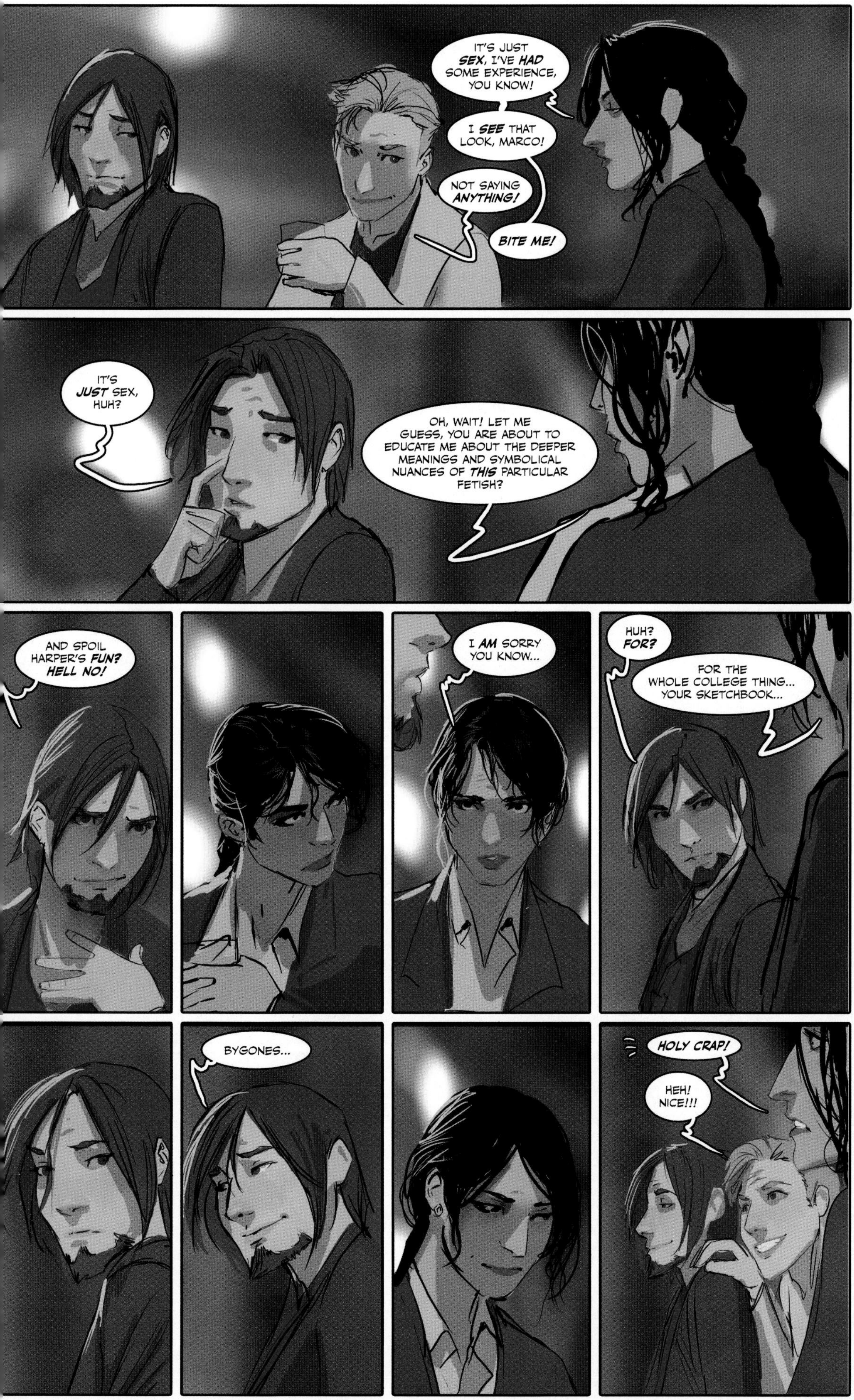

IT'S JUST SEX, I'VE HAD SOME EXPERIENCE, YOU KNOW!
I SEE THAT LOOK, MARCO!
NOT SAYING ANYTHING!
BITE ME!
IT'S JUST SEX, HUH?
OH, WAIT! LET ME GUESS, YOU ARE ABOUT TO EDUCATE ME ABOUT THE DEEPER MEANINGS AND SYMBOLICAL NUANCES OF THIS PARTICULAR FETISH?
AND SPOIL HARPER'S FUN? HELL NO!
I AM SORRY YOU KNOW...
HUH? FOR?
FOR THE WHOLE COLLEGE THING... YOUR SKETCHBOOK...
BYGONES...
HOLY CRAP!
HEH! NICE!!!

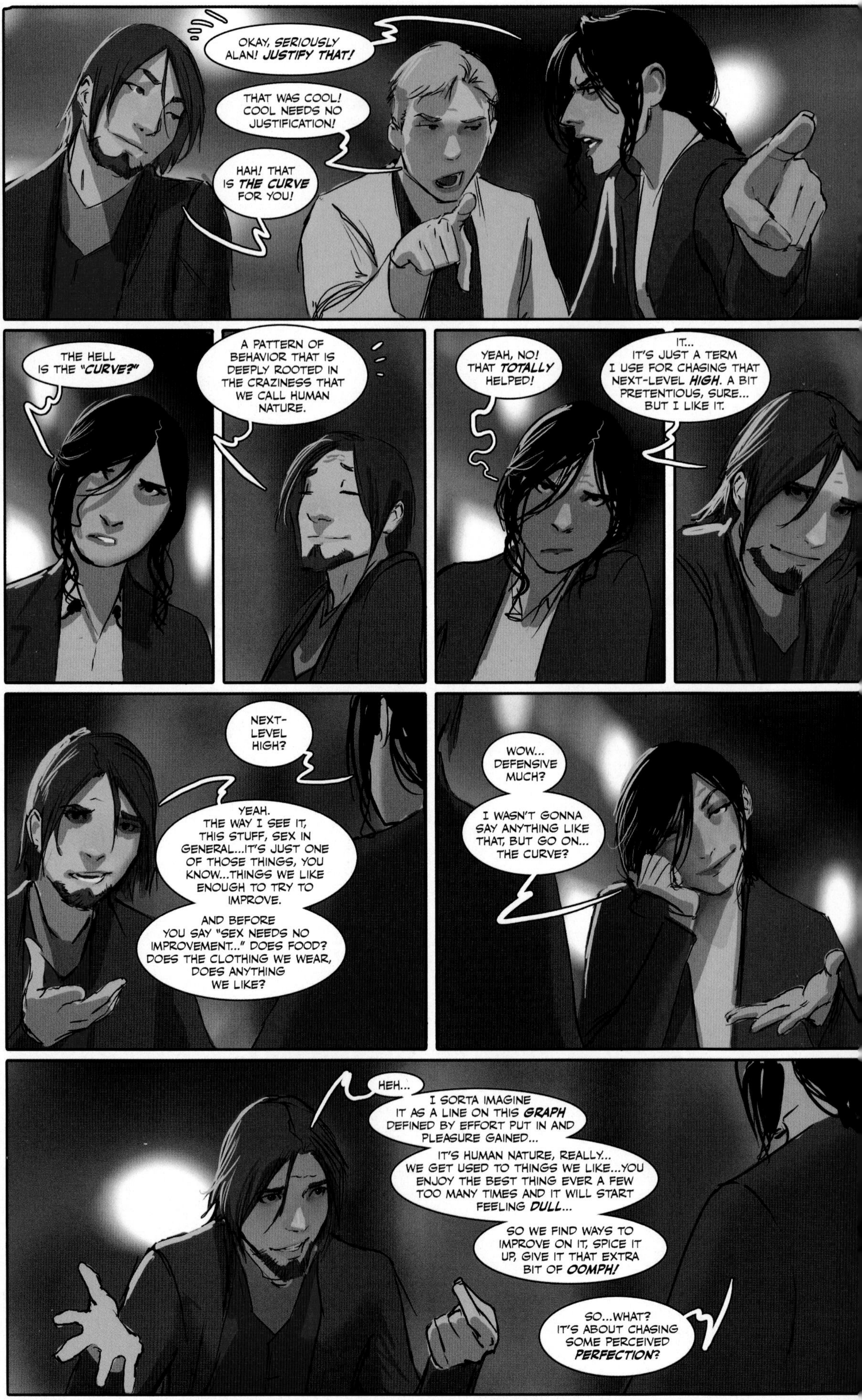
OKAY, SERIOUSLY ALAN! JUSTIFY THAT!
THAT WAS COOL! COOL NEEDS NO JUSTIFICATION!
HAH! THAT IS THE CURVE FOR YOU!
THE HELL IS THE "CURVE?"
A PATTERN OF BEHAVIOR THAT IS DEEPLY ROOTED IN THE CRAZINESS THAT WE CALL HUMAN NATURE.
YEAH, NO! THAT TOTALLY HELPED!
IT... IT'S JUST A TERM I USE FOR CHASING THAT NEXT-LEVEL HIGH. A BIT PRETENTIOUS, SURE... BUT I LIKE IT.
NEXT-LEVEL HIGH?
YEAH. THE WAY I SEE IT, THIS STUFF, SEX IN GENERAL...IT'S JUST ONE OF THOSE THINGS, YOU KNOW...THINGS WE LIKE ENOUGH TO TRY TO IMPROVE.
AND BEFORE YOU SAY "SEX NEEDS NO IMPROVEMENT..." DOES FOOD? DOES THE CLOTHING WE WEAR, DOES ANYTHING WE LIKE?
WOW... DEFENSIVE MUCH?
I WASN'T GONNA SAY ANYTHING LIKE THAT, BUT GO ON... THE CURVE?
HEH...
I SORTA IMAGINE IT AS A LINE ON THIS GRAPH DEFINED BY EFFORT PUT IN AND PLEASURE GAINED...
IT'S HUMAN NATURE, REALLY... WE GET USED TO THINGS WE LIKE...YOU ENJOY THE BEST THING EVER A FEW TOO MANY TIMES AND IT WILL START FEELING DULL...
SO WE FIND WAYS TO IMPROVE ON IT, SPICE IT UP, GIVE IT THAT EXTRA BIT OF OOMPH!
SO...WHAT? IT'S ABOUT CHASING SOME PERCEIVED PERFECTION?

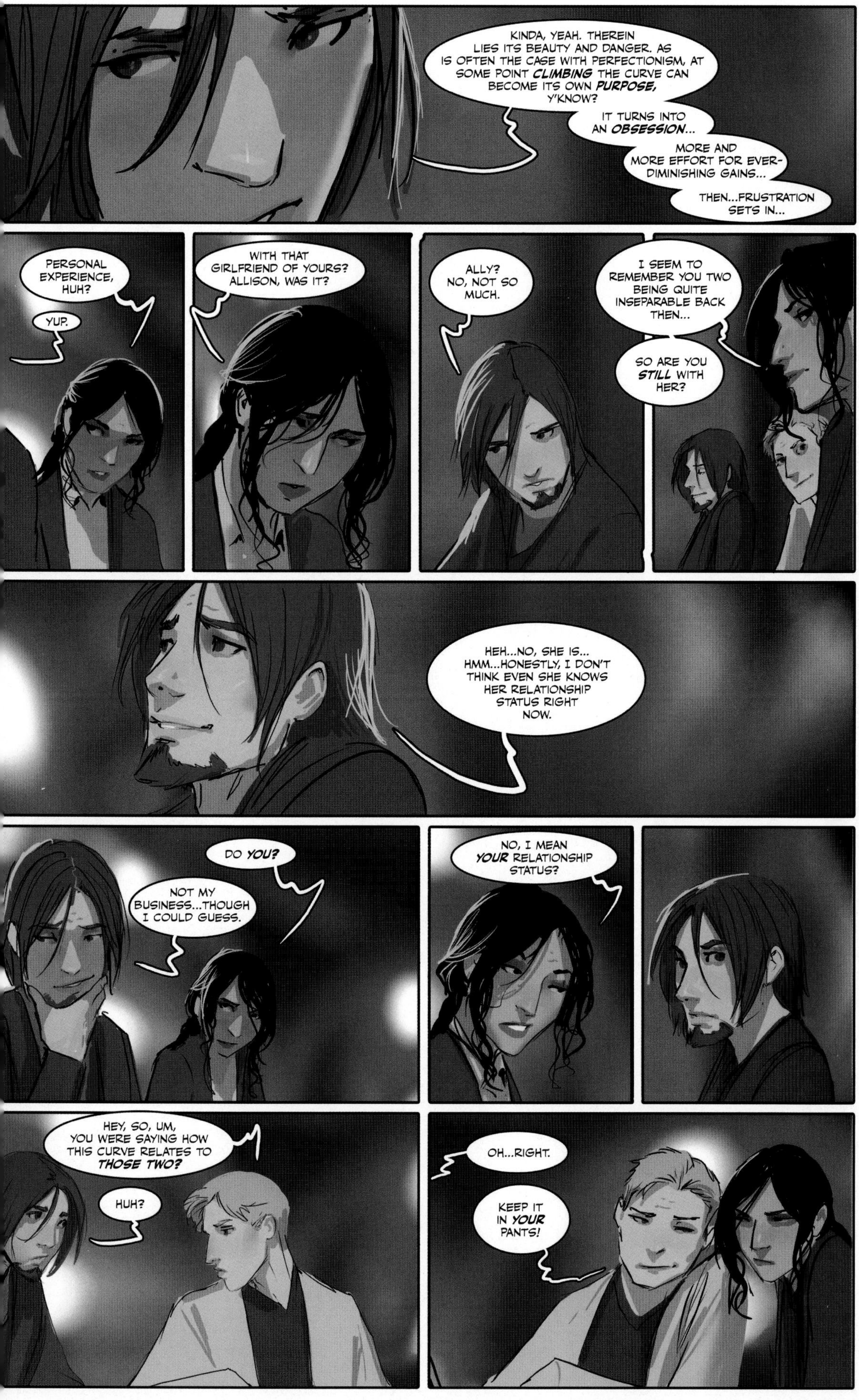
KINDA, YEAH. THEREIN LIES ITS BEAUTY AND DANGER. AS IS OFTEN THE CASE WITH PERFECTIONISM, AT SOME POINT *CLIMBING* THE CURVE CAN BECOME ITS OWN *PURPOSE,* Y'KNOW?
IT TURNS INTO AN *OBSESSION*...
MORE AND MORE EFFORT FOR EVER-DIMINISHING GAINS...
THEN...FRUSTRATION SETS IN...
PERSONAL EXPERIENCE, HUH?
YUP.
WITH THAT GIRLFRIEND OF YOURS? ALLISON, WAS IT?
ALLY? NO, NOT SO MUCH.
I SEEM TO REMEMBER YOU TWO BEING QUITE INSEPARABLE BACK THEN...
SO ARE YOU *STILL* WITH HER?
HEH...NO, SHE IS... HMM...HONESTLY, I DON'T THINK EVEN SHE KNOWS HER RELATIONSHIP STATUS RIGHT NOW.
DO *YOU?*
NOT MY BUSINESS...THOUGH I COULD GUESS.
NO, I MEAN *YOUR* RELATIONSHIP STATUS?
HEY, SO, UM, YOU WERE SAYING HOW THIS CURVE RELATES TO *THOSE TWO?*
HUH?
OH...RIGHT.
KEEP IT IN *YOUR* PANTS!

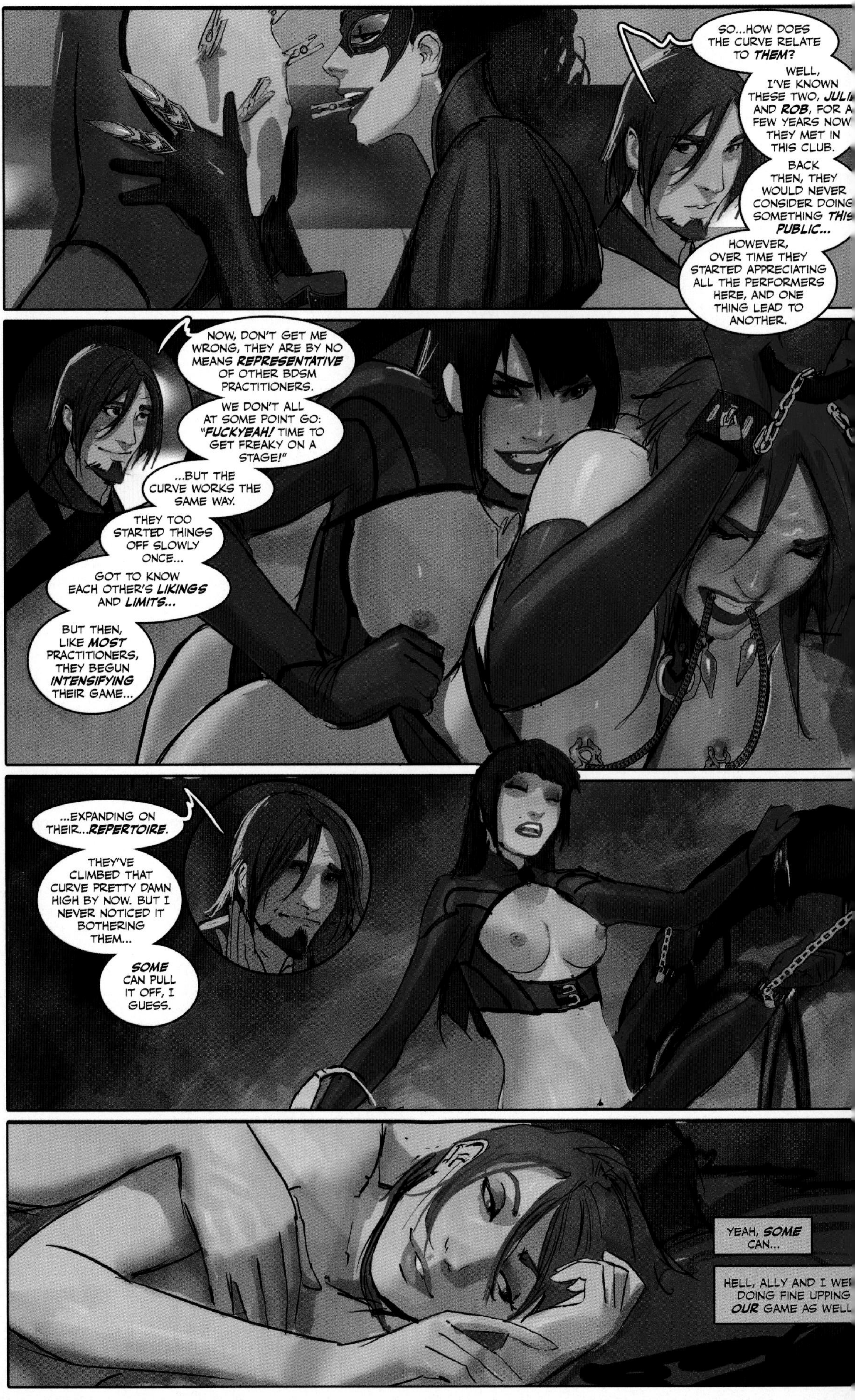
SO...HOW DOES THE CURVE RELATE TO *THEM*?
WELL, I'VE KNOWN THESE TWO, ***JULI*** AND ***ROB***, FOR A FEW YEARS NOW. THEY MET IN THIS CLUB.
BACK THEN, THEY WOULD NEVER CONSIDER DOING SOMETHING ***THI*** ***PUBLIC...***
HOWEVER, OVER TIME THEY STARTED APPRECIATING ALL THE PERFORMERS HERE, AND ONE THING LEAD TO ANOTHER.
NOW, DON'T GET ME WRONG, THEY ARE BY NO MEANS ***REPRESENTATIVE*** OF OTHER BDSM PRACTITIONERS.
WE DON'T ALL AT SOME POINT GO: "***FUCKYEAH!*** TIME TO GET FREAKY ON A STAGE!"
...BUT THE CURVE WORKS THE SAME WAY.
THEY TOO STARTED THINGS OFF SLOWLY ONCE...
GOT TO KNOW EACH OTHER'S ***LIKINGS*** AND ***LIMITS...***
BUT THEN, LIKE ***MOST*** PRACTITIONERS, THEY BEGUN ***INTENSIFYING*** THEIR GAME...
...EXPANDING ON THEIR...***REPERTOIRE***.
THEY'VE CLIMBED THAT CURVE PRETTY DAMN HIGH BY NOW. BUT I NEVER NOTICED IT BOTHERING THEM...
SOME CAN PULL IT OFF, I GUESS.
YEAH, ***SOME*** CAN...
HELL, ALLY AND I WE DOING FINE UPPING ***OUR*** GAME AS WELL

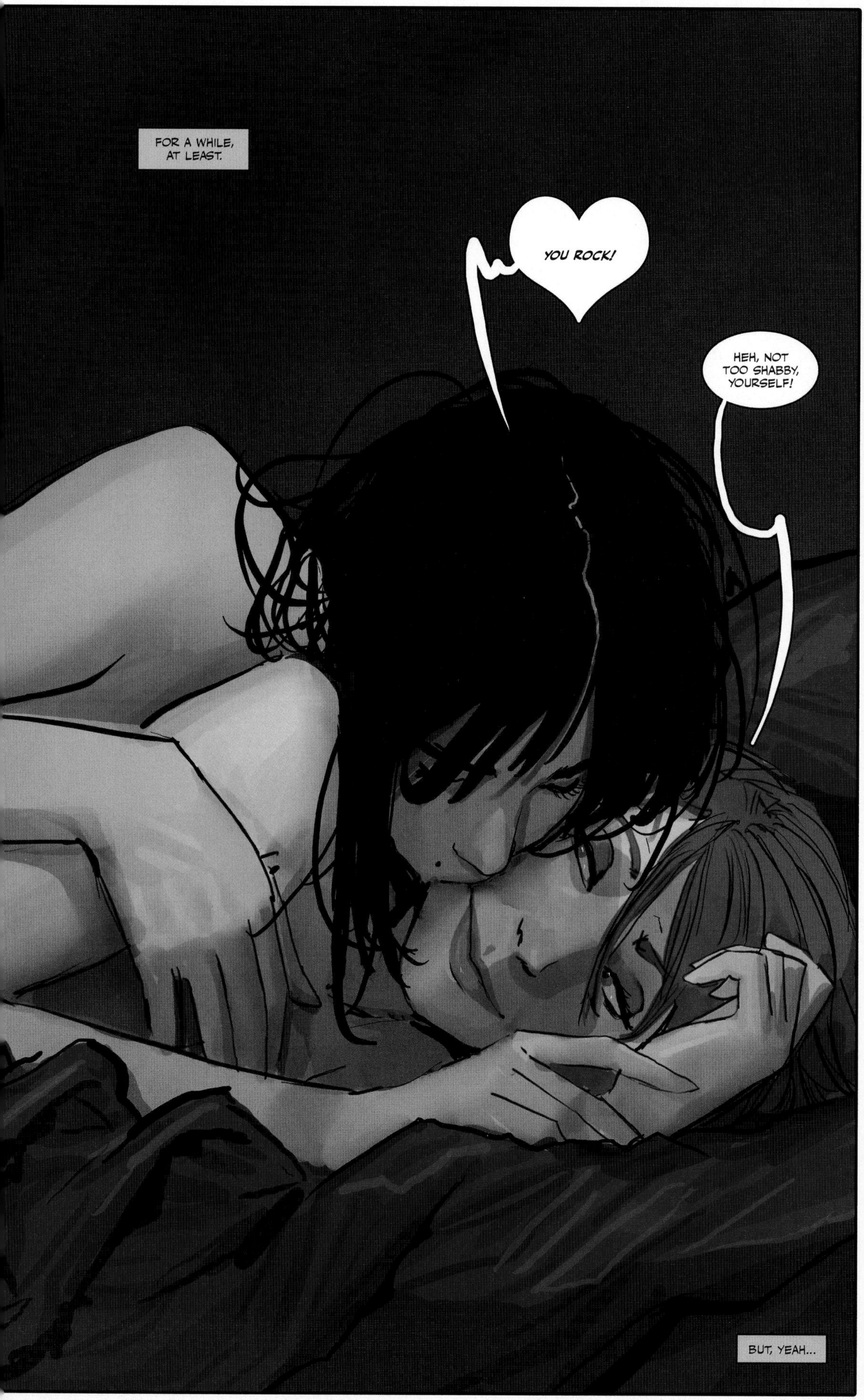
FOR A WHILE, AT LEAST.
YOU ROCK!
HEH, NOT TOO SHABBY, YOURSELF!
BUT, YEAH...

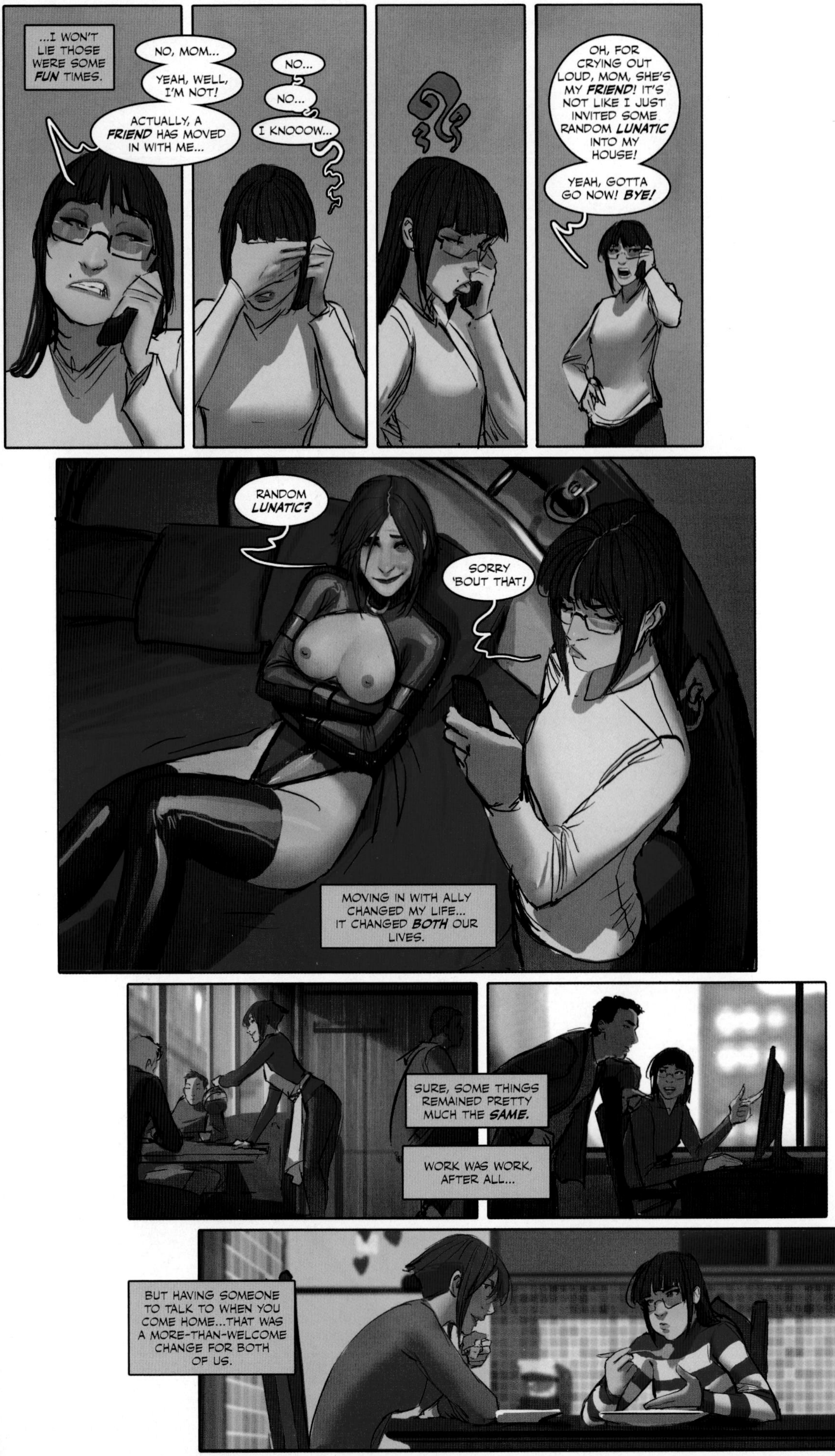

...I WON'T LIE THOSE WERE SOME FUN TIMES.
NO, MOM...
YEAH, WELL, I'M NOT!
ACTUALLY, A FRIEND HAS MOVED IN WITH ME...
NO...
NO...
I KNOOOW...
OH, FOR CRYING OUT LOUD, MOM, SHE'S MY FRIEND! IT'S NOT LIKE I JUST INVITED SOME RANDOM LUNATIC INTO MY HOUSE!
YEAH, GOTTA GO NOW! BYE!
RANDOM LUNATIC?
SORRY 'BOUT THAT!
MOVING IN WITH ALLY CHANGED MY LIFE... IT CHANGED BOTH OUR LIVES.
SURE, SOME THINGS REMAINED PRETTY MUCH THE SAME.
WORK WAS WORK, AFTER ALL...
BUT HAVING SOMEONE TO TALK TO WHEN YOU COME HOME...THAT WAS A MORE-THAN-WELCOME CHANGE FOR BOTH OF US.

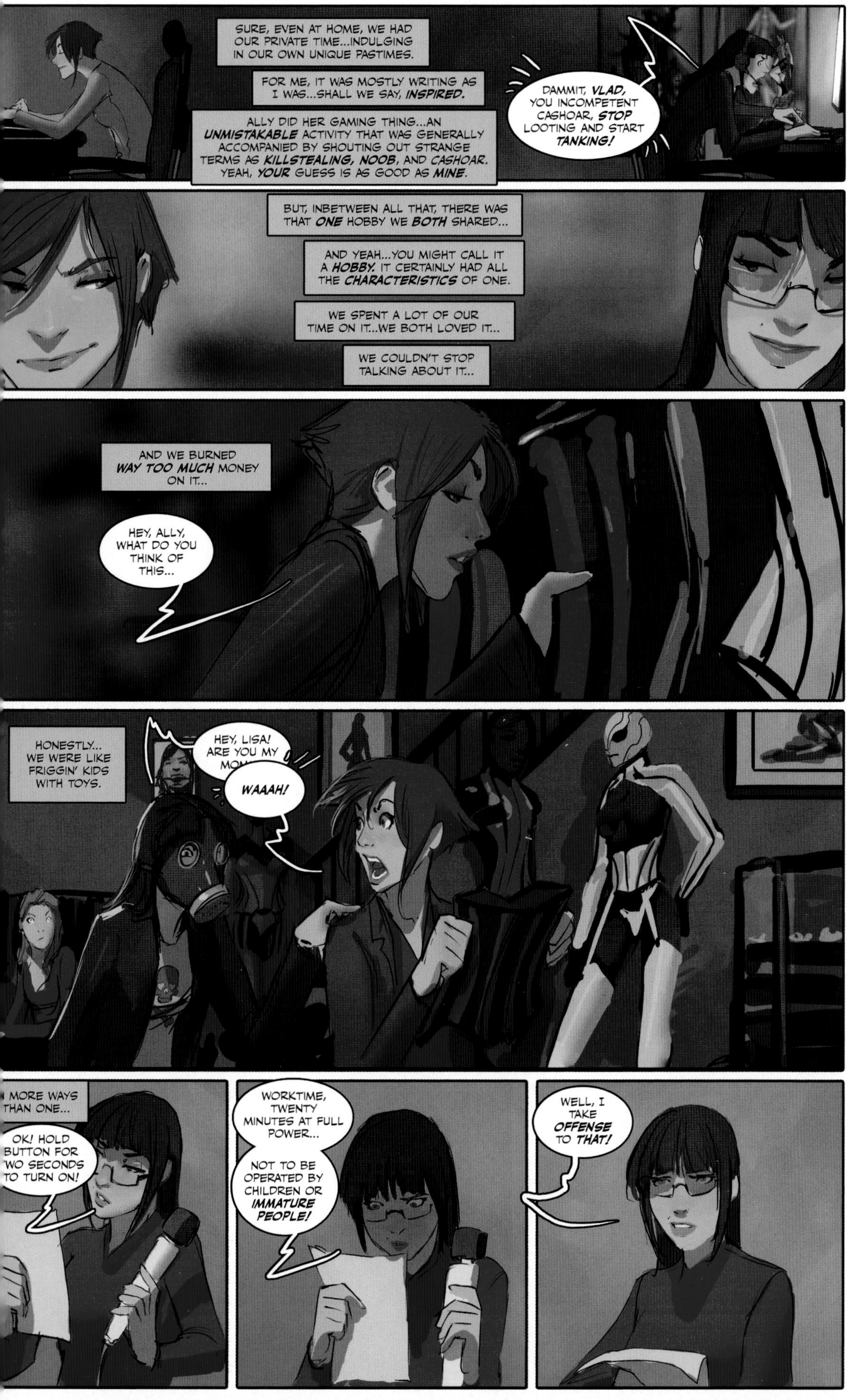
SURE, EVEN AT HOME, WE HAD OUR PRIVATE TIME...INDULGING IN OUR OWN UNIQUE PASTIMES.
FOR ME, IT WAS MOSTLY WRITING AS I WAS...SHALL WE SAY, INSPIRED.
ALLY DID HER GAMING THING...AN UNMISTAKABLE ACTIVITY THAT WAS GENERALLY ACCOMPANIED BY SHOUTING OUT STRANGE TERMS AS KILLSTEALING, NOOB, AND CASHOAR. YEAH, YOUR GUESS IS AS GOOD AS MINE.
DAMMIT, VLAD, YOU INCOMPETENT CASHOAR, STOP LOOTING AND START TANKING!
BUT, INBETWEEN ALL THAT, THERE WAS THAT ONE HOBBY WE BOTH SHARED...
AND YEAH...YOU MIGHT CALL IT A HOBBY. IT CERTAINLY HAD ALL THE CHARACTERISTICS OF ONE.
WE SPENT A LOT OF OUR TIME ON IT...WE BOTH LOVED IT...
WE COULDN'T STOP TALKING ABOUT IT...
AND WE BURNED WAY TOO MUCH MONEY ON IT...
HEY, ALLY, WHAT DO YOU THINK OF THIS...
HONESTLY... WE WERE LIKE FRIGGIN' KIDS WITH TOYS.
HEY, LISA! ARE YOU MY MOM
WAAAH!
MORE WAYS THAN ONE...
OK! HOLD BUTTON FOR TWO SECONDS TO TURN ON!
WORKTIME, TWENTY MINUTES AT FULL POWER...
NOT TO BE OPERATED BY CHILDREN OR IMMATURE PEOPLE!
WELL, I TAKE OFFENSE TO THAT!

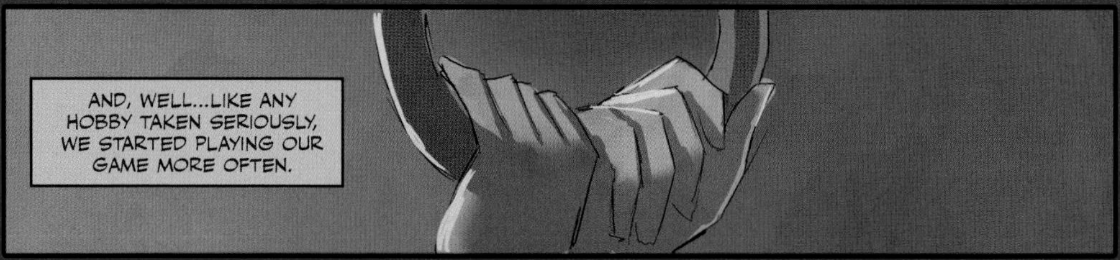
AND, WELL...LIKE ANY HOBBY TAKEN SERIOUSLY, WE STARTED PLAYING OUR GAME MORE OFTEN.

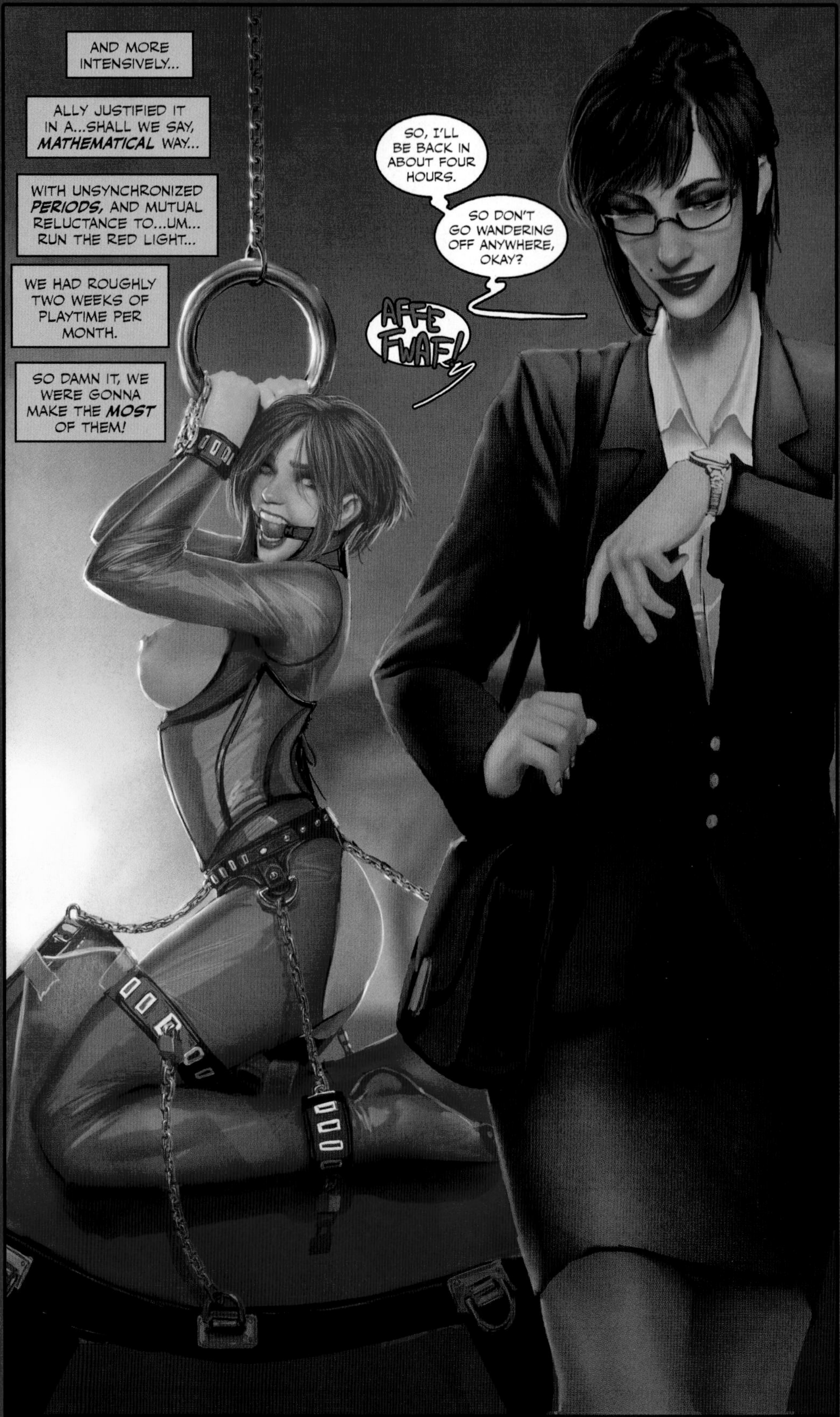
AND MORE INTENSIVELY...
ALLY JUSTIFIED IT IN A...SHALL WE SAY, *MATHEMATICAL* WAY...
WITH UNSYNCHRONIZED *PERIODS,* AND MUTUAL RELUCTANCE TO...UM... RUN THE RED LIGHT...
WE HAD ROUGHLY TWO WEEKS OF PLAYTIME PER MONTH.
SO DAMN IT, WE WERE GONNA MAKE THE *MOST* OF THEM!
SO, I'LL BE BACK IN ABOUT FOUR HOURS.
SO DON'T GO WANDERING OFF ANYWHERE, OKAY?
AFFE FWAF!

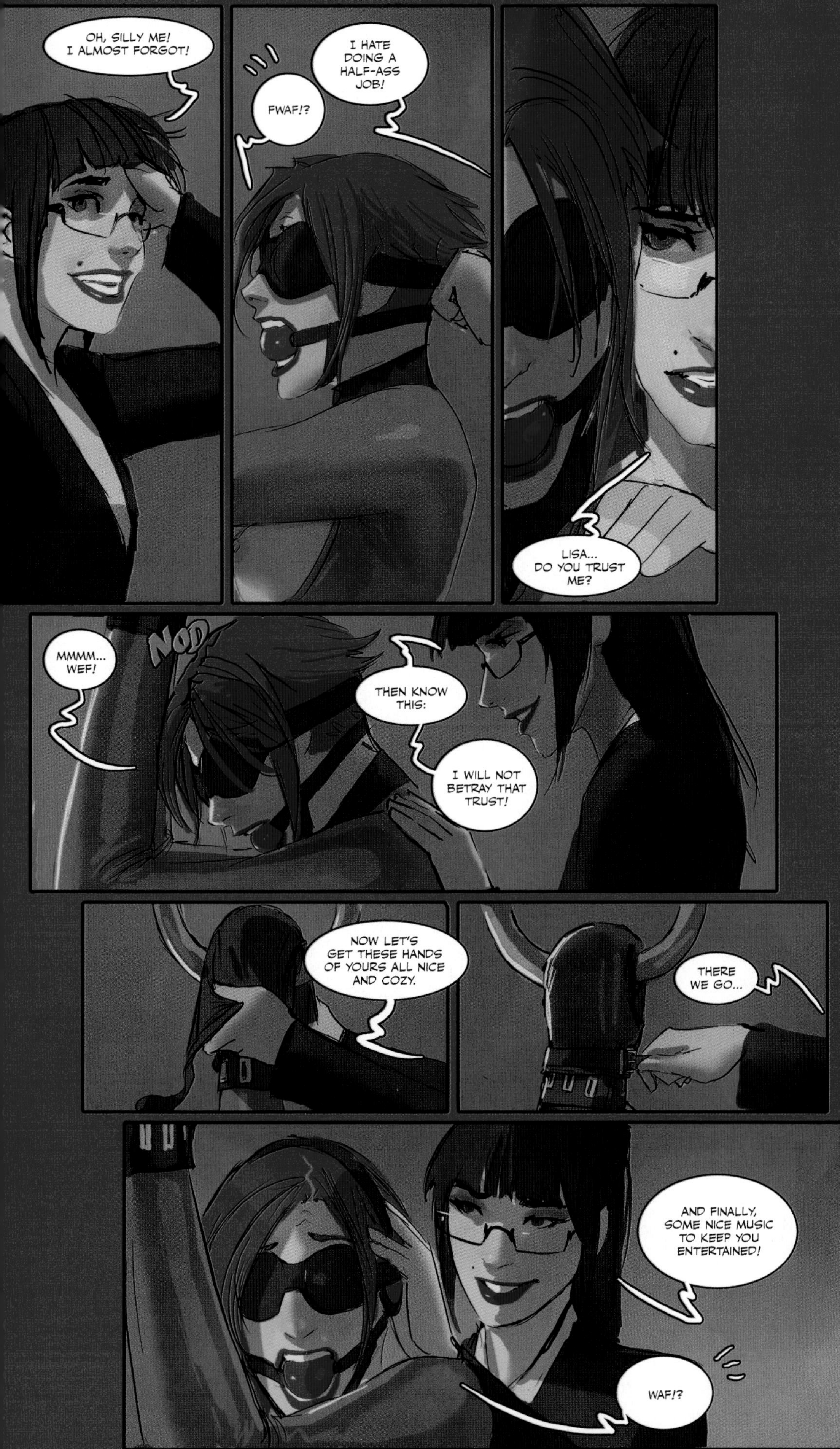
OH, SILLY ME! I ALMOST FORGOT!
I HATE DOING A HALF-ASS JOB!
FWAF!?
LISA... DO YOU TRUST ME?
NOD
MMMM... WEF!
THEN KNOW THIS:
I WILL NOT BETRAY THAT TRUST!
NOW LET'S GET THESE HANDS OF YOURS ALL NICE AND COZY.
THERE WE GO...
AND FINALLY, SOME NICE MUSIC TO KEEP YOU ENTERTAINED!
WAF!?

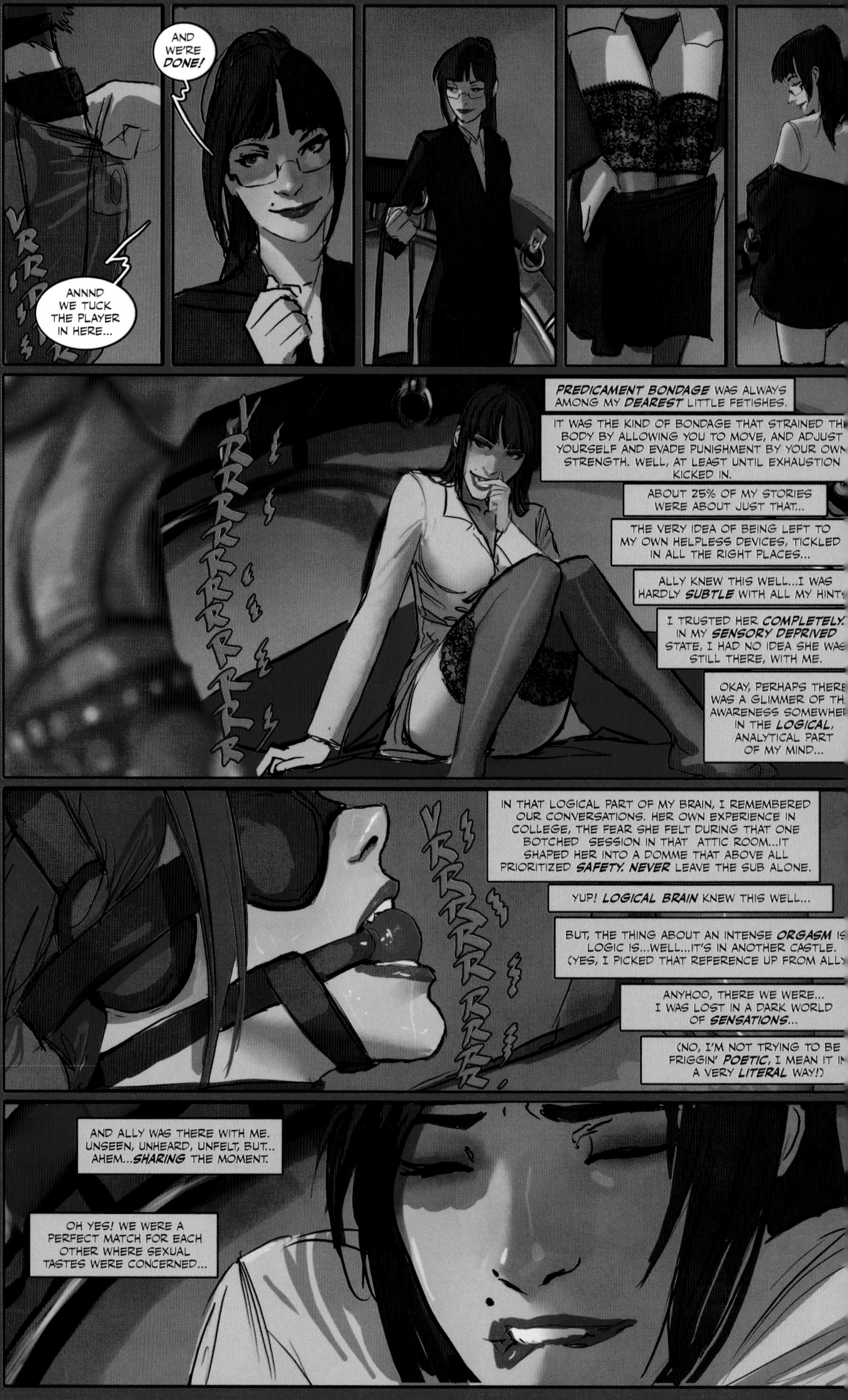

ANNND WE TUCK THE PLAYER IN HERE...
AND WE'RE DONE!
PREDICAMENT BONDAGE WAS ALWAYS AMONG MY DEAREST LITTLE FETISHES.
IT WAS THE KIND OF BONDAGE THAT STRAINED TH BODY BY ALLOWING YOU TO MOVE, AND ADJUST YOURSELF AND EVADE PUNISHMENT BY YOUR OWN STRENGTH. WELL, AT LEAST UNTIL EXHAUSTION KICKED IN.
ABOUT 25% OF MY STORIES WERE ABOUT JUST THAT...
THE VERY IDEA OF BEING LEFT TO MY OWN HELPLESS DEVICES, TICKLED IN ALL THE RIGHT PLACES...
ALLY KNEW THIS WELL...I WAS HARDLY SUBTLE WITH ALL MY HINTS
I TRUSTED HER COMPLETELY. IN MY SENSORY DEPRIVED STATE, I HAD NO IDEA SHE WAS STILL THERE, WITH ME.
OKAY, PERHAPS THERE WAS A GLIMMER OF TH AWARENESS SOMEWHE IN THE LOGICAL, ANALYTICAL PART OF MY MIND...
IN THAT LOGICAL PART OF MY BRAIN, I REMEMBERED OUR CONVERSATIONS. HER OWN EXPERIENCE IN COLLEGE, THE FEAR SHE FELT DURING THAT ONE BOTCHED SESSION IN THAT ATTIC ROOM...IT SHAPED HER INTO A DOMME THAT ABOVE ALL PRIORITIZED SAFETY. NEVER LEAVE THE SUB ALONE.
YUP! LOGICAL BRAIN KNEW THIS WELL...
BUT, THE THING ABOUT AN INTENSE ORGASM IS LOGIC IS...WELL...IT'S IN ANOTHER CASTLE. (YES, I PICKED THAT REFERENCE UP FROM ALLY
ANYHOO, THERE WE WERE... I WAS LOST IN A DARK WORLD OF SENSATIONS...
(NO, I'M NOT TRYING TO BE FRIGGIN' POETIC, I MEAN IT IN A VERY LITERAL WAY!)
AND ALLY WAS THERE WITH ME. UNSEEN, UNHEARD, UNFELT, BUT... AHEM...SHARING THE MOMENT.
OH YES! WE WERE A PERFECT MATCH FOR EACH OTHER WHERE SEXUAL TASTES WERE CONCERNED...

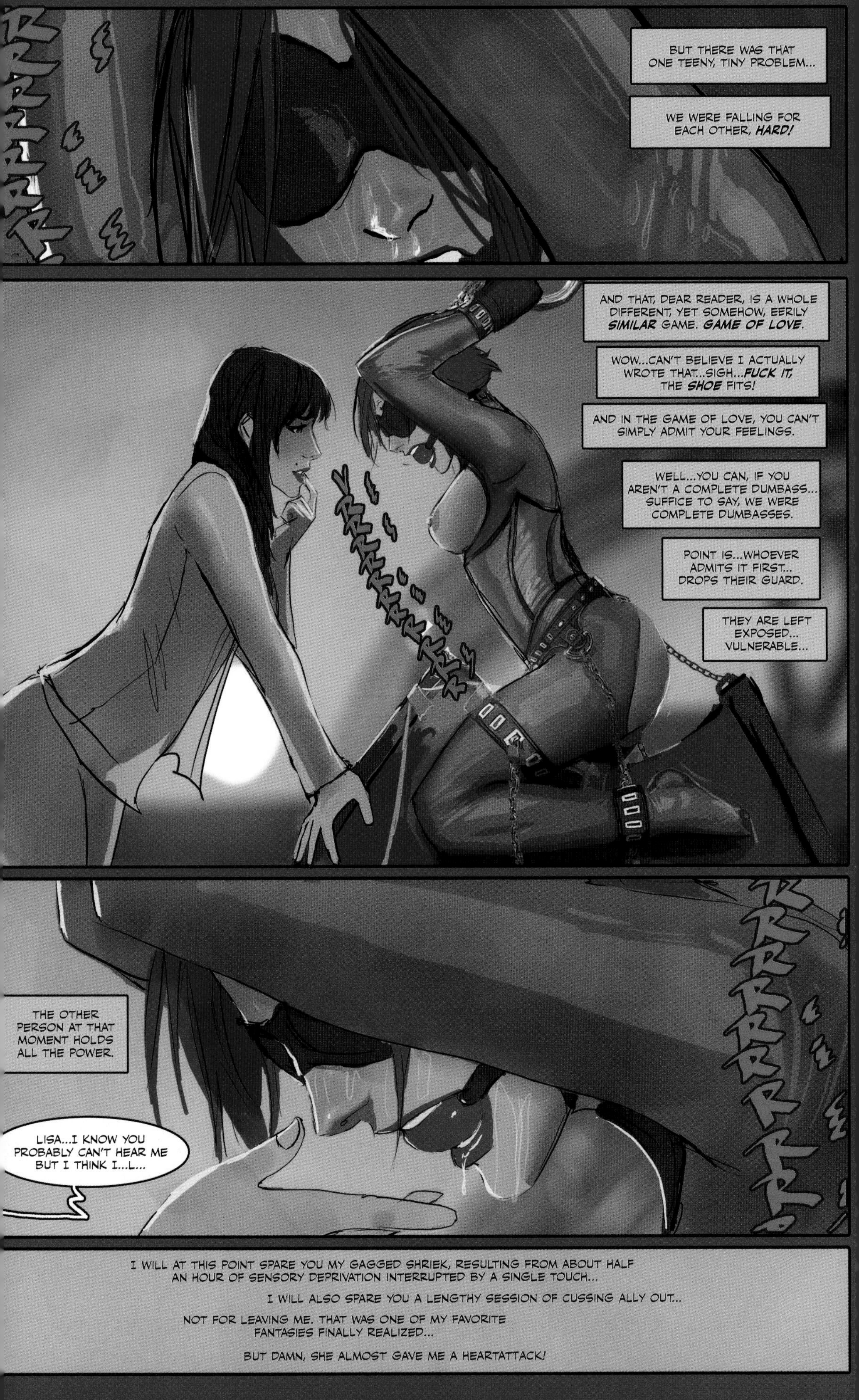
BUT THERE WAS THAT ONE TEENY, TINY PROBLEM...
WE WERE FALLING FOR EACH OTHER, *HARD!*
AND THAT, DEAR READER, IS A WHOLE DIFFERENT, YET SOMEHOW, EERILY *SIMILAR* GAME. *GAME OF LOVE*.
WOW...CAN'T BELIEVE I ACTUALLY WROTE THAT...SIGH...*FUCK IT,* THE *SHOE* FITS!
AND IN THE GAME OF LOVE, YOU CAN'T SIMPLY ADMIT YOUR FEELINGS.
WELL...YOU CAN, IF YOU AREN'T A COMPLETE DUMBASS... SUFFICE TO SAY, WE WERE COMPLETE DUMBASSES.
POINT IS...WHOEVER ADMITS IT FIRST... DROPS THEIR GUARD.
THEY ARE LEFT EXPOSED... VULNERABLE...
THE OTHER PERSON AT THAT MOMENT HOLDS ALL THE POWER.
LISA...I KNOW YOU PROBABLY CAN'T HEAR ME BUT I THINK I...L...
I WILL AT THIS POINT SPARE YOU MY GAGGED SHRIEK, RESULTING FROM ABOUT HALF AN HOUR OF SENSORY DEPRIVATION INTERRUPTED BY A SINGLE TOUCH...
I WILL ALSO SPARE YOU A LENGTHY SESSION OF CUSSING ALLY OUT...
NOT FOR LEAVING ME. THAT WAS ONE OF MY FAVORITE FANTASIES FINALLY REALIZED...
BUT DAMN, SHE ALMOST GAVE ME A HEARTATTACK!

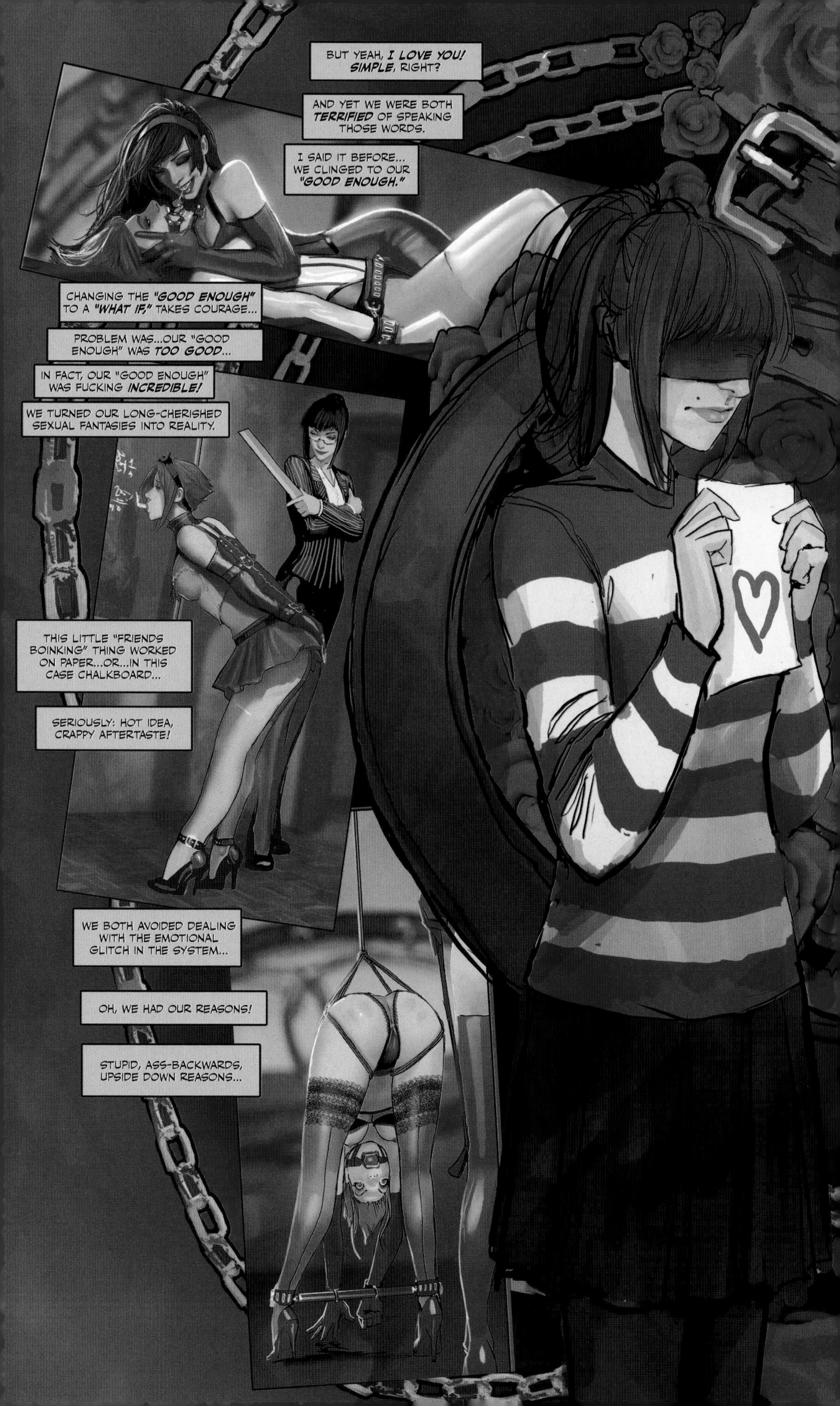

BUT YEAH, *I LOVE YOU! SIMPLE*, RIGHT?
AND YET WE WERE BOTH *TERRIFIED* OF SPEAKING THOSE WORDS.
I SAID IT BEFORE... WE CLINGED TO OUR *"GOOD ENOUGH."*
CHANGING THE *"GOOD ENOUGH"* TO A *"WHAT IF,"* TAKES COURAGE...
PROBLEM WAS...OUR "GOOD ENOUGH" WAS *TOO GOOD*...
IN FACT, OUR "GOOD ENOUGH" WAS FUCKING *INCREDIBLE!*
WE TURNED OUR LONG-CHERISHED SEXUAL FANTASIES INTO REALITY.
THIS LITTLE "FRIENDS BOINKING" THING WORKED ON PAPER...OR...IN THIS CASE CHALKBOARD...
SERIOUSLY: HOT IDEA, CRAPPY AFTERTASTE!
WE BOTH AVOIDED DEALING WITH THE EMOTIONAL GLITCH IN THE SYSTEM...
OH, WE HAD OUR REASONS!
STUPID, ASS-BACKWARDS, UPSIDE DOWN REASONS...

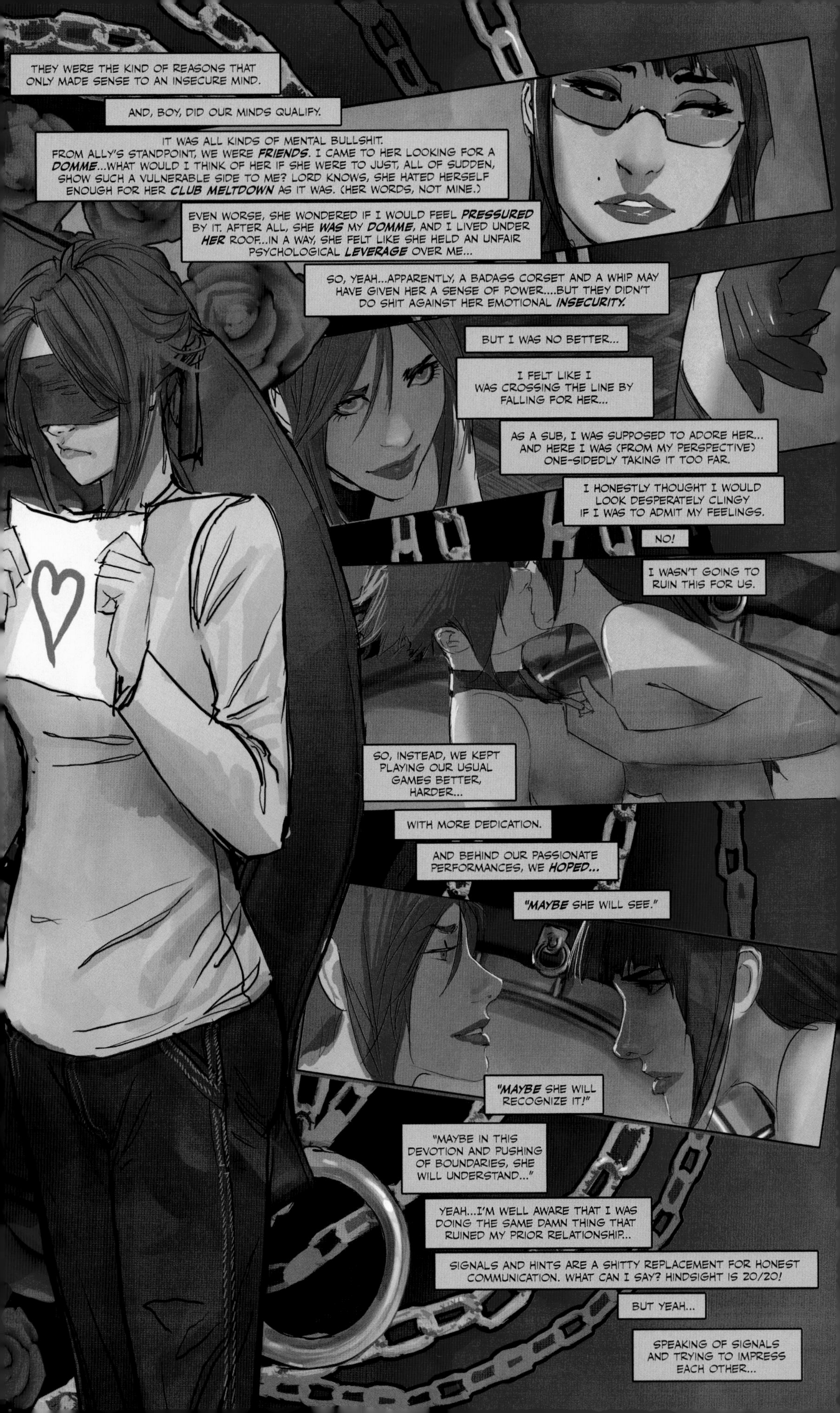
THEY WERE THE KIND OF REASONS THAT ONLY MADE SENSE TO AN INSECURE MIND.
AND, BOY, DID OUR MINDS QUALIFY.
IT WAS ALL KINDS OF MENTAL BULLSHIT. FROM ALLY'S STANDPOINT, WE WERE ***FRIENDS***. I CAME TO HER LOOKING FOR A ***DOMME***...WHAT WOULD I THINK OF HER IF SHE WERE TO JUST, ALL OF SUDDEN, SHOW SUCH A VULNERABLE SIDE TO ME? LORD KNOWS, SHE HATED HERSELF ENOUGH FOR HER ***CLUB MELTDOWN*** AS IT WAS. (HER WORDS, NOT MINE.)
EVEN WORSE, SHE WONDERED IF I WOULD FEEL ***PRESSURED*** BY IT. AFTER ALL, SHE ***WAS*** MY ***DOMME***, AND I LIVED UNDER ***HER*** ROOF...IN A WAY, SHE FELT LIKE SHE HELD AN UNFAIR PSYCHOLOGICAL ***LEVERAGE*** OVER ME...
SO, YEAH...APPARENTLY, A BADASS CORSET AND A WHIP MAY HAVE GIVEN HER A SENSE OF POWER....BUT THEY DIDN'T DO SHIT AGAINST HER EMOTIONAL ***INSECURITY.***
BUT I WAS NO BETTER...
I FELT LIKE I WAS CROSSING THE LINE BY FALLING FOR HER...
AS A SUB, I WAS SUPPOSED TO ADORE HER... AND HERE I WAS (FROM MY PERSPECTIVE) ONE-SIDEDLY TAKING IT TOO FAR.
I HONESTLY THOUGHT I WOULD LOOK DESPERATELY CLINGY IF I WAS TO ADMIT MY FEELINGS.
NO!
I WASN'T GOING TO RUIN THIS FOR US.
SO, INSTEAD, WE KEPT PLAYING OUR USUAL GAMES BETTER, HARDER...
WITH MORE DEDICATION.
AND BEHIND OUR PASSIONATE PERFORMANCES, WE ***HOPED...***
"***MAYBE*** SHE WILL SEE."
"***MAYBE*** SHE WILL RECOGNIZE IT!"
"MAYBE IN THIS DEVOTION AND PUSHING OF BOUNDARIES, SHE WILL UNDERSTAND..."
YEAH...I'M WELL AWARE THAT I WAS DOING THE SAME DAMN THING THAT RUINED MY PRIOR RELATIONSHIP...
SIGNALS AND HINTS ARE A SHITTY REPLACEMENT FOR HONEST COMMUNICATION. WHAT CAN I SAY? HINDSIGHT IS 20/20!
BUT YEAH...
SPEAKING OF SIGNALS AND TRYING TO IMPRESS EACH OTHER...

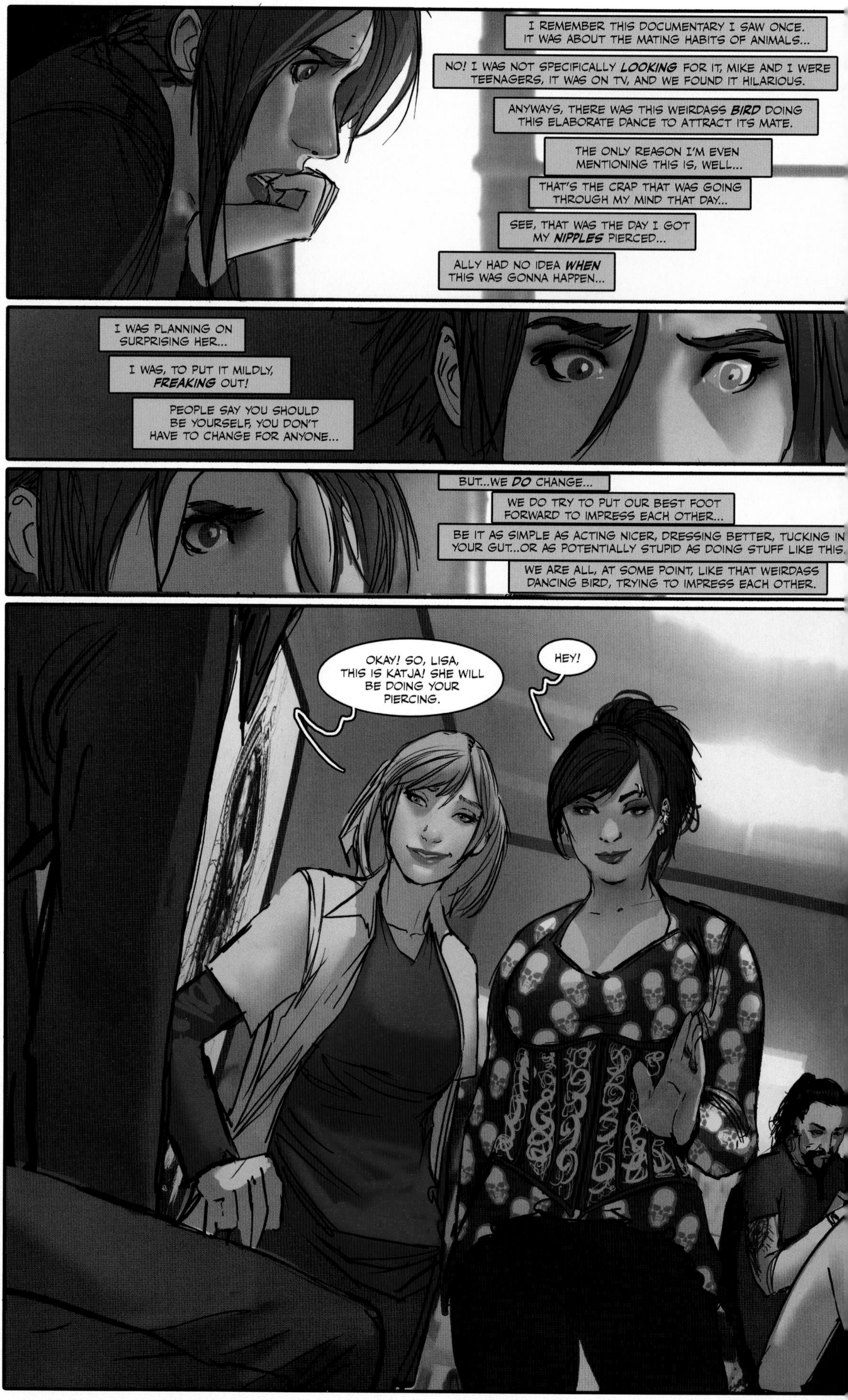
I REMEMBER THIS DOCUMENTARY I SAW ONCE. IT WAS ABOUT THE MATING HABITS OF ANIMALS...
NO! I WAS NOT SPECIFICALLY LOOKING FOR IT, MIKE AND I WERE TEENAGERS, IT WAS ON TV, AND WE FOUND IT HILARIOUS.
ANYWAYS, THERE WAS THIS WEIRDASS BIRD DOING THIS ELABORATE DANCE TO ATTRACT ITS MATE.
THE ONLY REASON I'M EVEN MENTIONING THIS IS, WELL...
THAT'S THE CRAP THAT WAS GOING THROUGH MY MIND THAT DAY...
SEE, THAT WAS THE DAY I GOT MY NIPPLES PIERCED...
ALLY HAD NO IDEA WHEN THIS WAS GONNA HAPPEN...
I WAS PLANNING ON SURPRISING HER...
I WAS, TO PUT IT MILDLY, FREAKING OUT!
PEOPLE SAY YOU SHOULD BE YOURSELF, YOU DON'T HAVE TO CHANGE FOR ANYONE...
BUT...WE DO CHANGE...
WE DO TRY TO PUT OUR BEST FOOT FORWARD TO IMPRESS EACH OTHER...
BE IT AS SIMPLE AS ACTING NICER, DRESSING BETTER, TUCKING IN YOUR GUT...OR AS POTENTIALLY STUPID AS DOING STUFF LIKE THIS.
WE ARE ALL, AT SOME POINT, LIKE THAT WEIRDASS DANCING BIRD, TRYING TO IMPRESS EACH OTHER.
OKAY! SO, LISA, THIS IS KATJA! SHE WILL BE DOING YOUR PIERCING.
HEY!

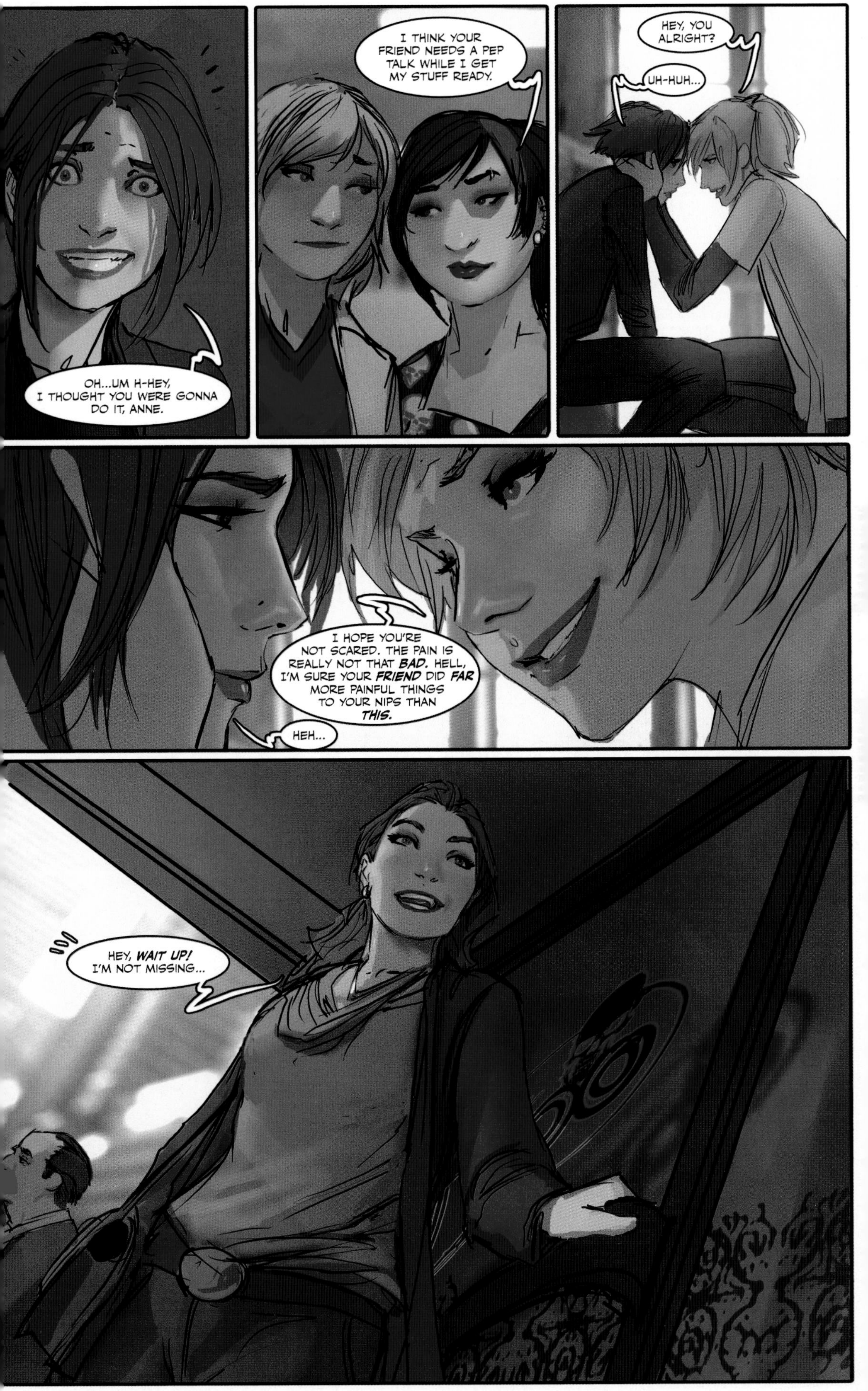
OH...UM H-HEY, I THOUGHT YOU WERE GONNA DO IT, ANNE.
I THINK YOUR FRIEND NEEDS A PEP TALK WHILE I GET MY STUFF READY.
HEY, YOU ALRIGHT?
UH-HUH...
I HOPE YOU'RE NOT SCARED. THE PAIN IS REALLY NOT THAT BAD. HELL, I'M SURE YOUR FRIEND DID FAR MORE PAINFUL THINGS TO YOUR NIPS THAN THIS.
HEH...
HEY, WAIT UP! I'M NOT MISSING...

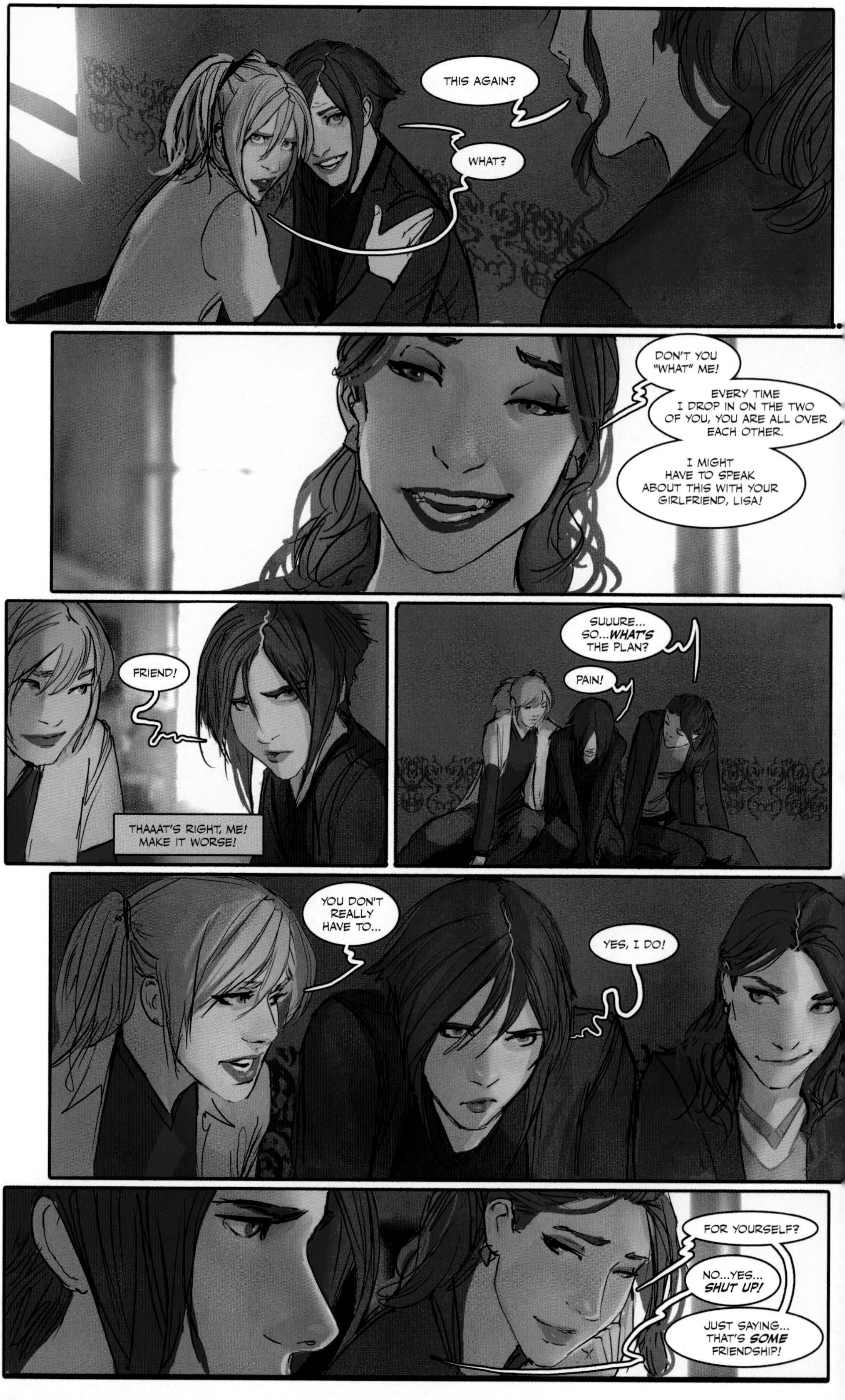
THIS AGAIN?
WHAT?
DON'T YOU "WHAT" ME!
EVERY TIME I DROP IN ON THE TWO OF YOU, YOU ARE ALL OVER EACH OTHER.
I MIGHT HAVE TO SPEAK ABOUT THIS WITH YOUR GIRLFRIEND, LISA!
FRIEND!
THAAAT'S RIGHT, ME! MAKE IT WORSE!
SUUURE... SO...WHAT'S THE PLAN?
PAIN!
YOU DON'T REALLY HAVE TO...
YES, I DO!
FOR YOURSELF?
NO...YES... SHUT UP!
JUST SAYING... THAT'S SOME FRIENDSHIP!

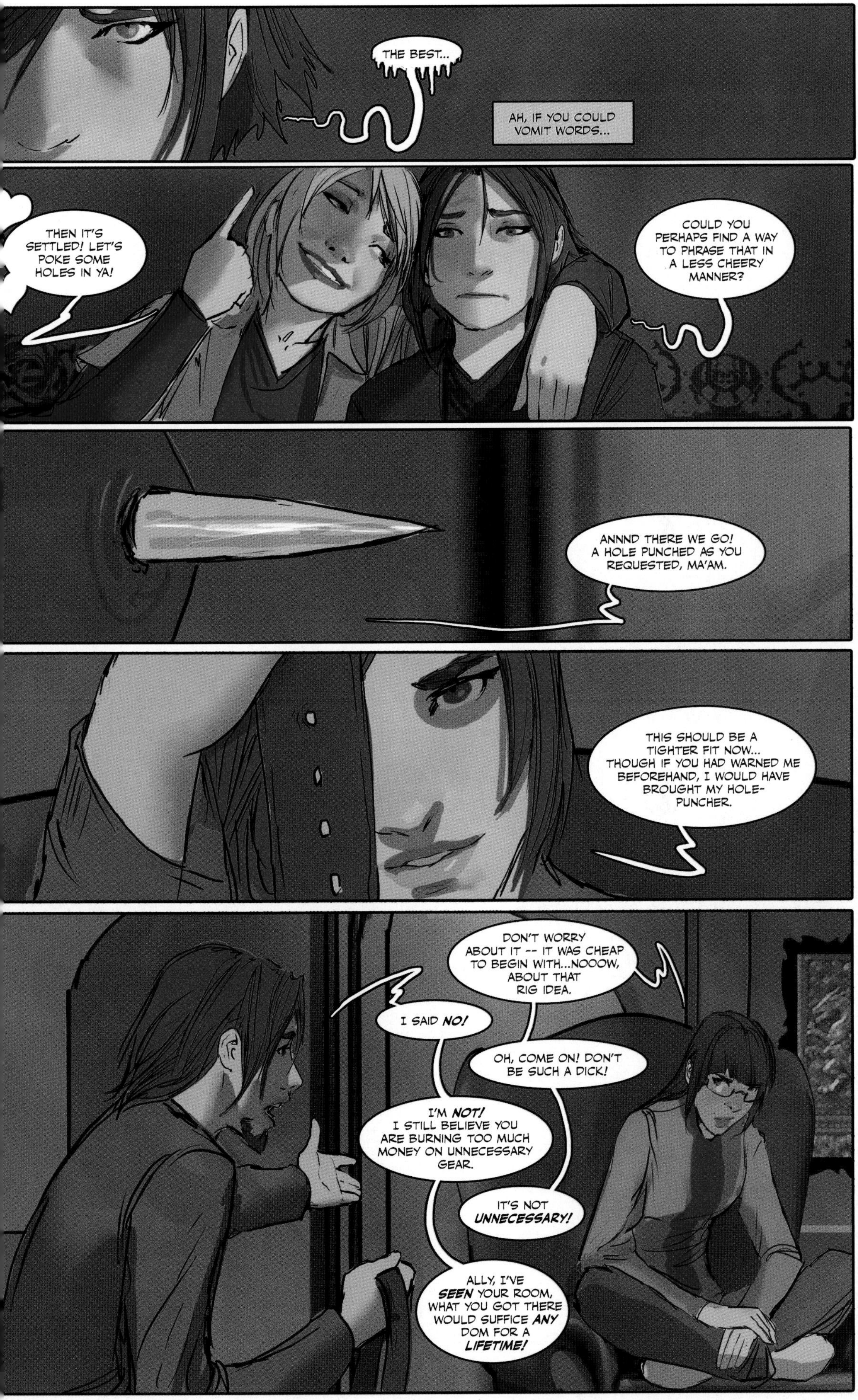
THE BEST...
AH, IF YOU COULD VOMIT WORDS...
THEN IT'S SETTLED! LET'S POKE SOME HOLES IN YA!
COULD YOU PERHAPS FIND A WAY TO PHRASE THAT IN A LESS CHEERY MANNER?
ANNND THERE WE GO! A HOLE PUNCHED AS YOU REQUESTED, MA'AM.
THIS SHOULD BE A TIGHTER FIT NOW... THOUGH IF YOU HAD WARNED ME BEFOREHAND, I WOULD HAVE BROUGHT MY HOLE-PUNCHER.
DON'T WORRY ABOUT IT -- IT WAS CHEAP TO BEGIN WITH...NOOOW, ABOUT THAT RIG IDEA.
I SAID NO!
OH, COME ON! DON'T BE SUCH A DICK!
I'M NOT! I STILL BELIEVE YOU ARE BURNING TOO MUCH MONEY ON UNNECESSARY GEAR.
IT'S NOT UNNECESSARY!
ALLY, I'VE SEEN YOUR ROOM, WHAT YOU GOT THERE WOULD SUFFICE ANY DOM FOR A LIFETIME!

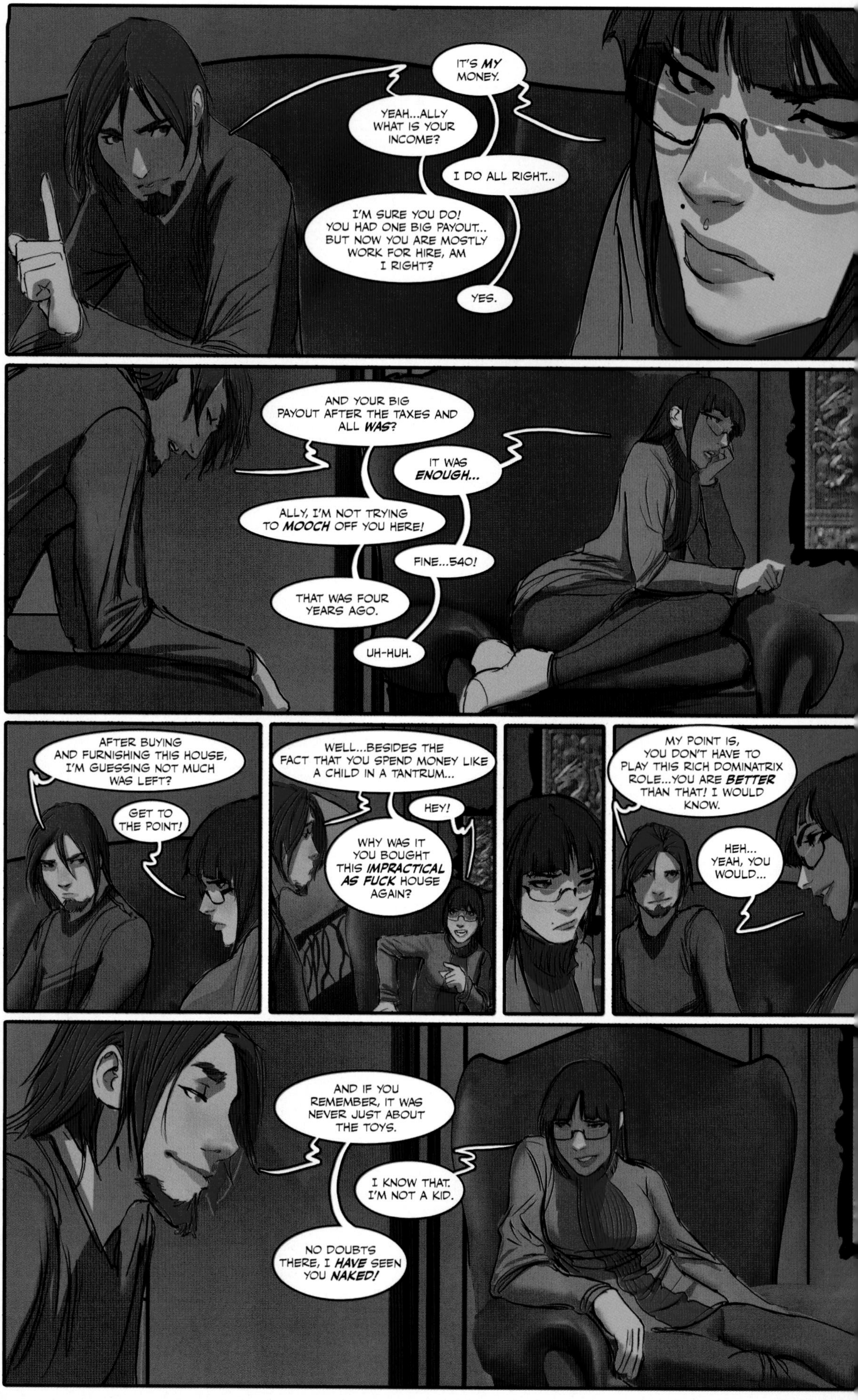

IT'S **MY** MONEY.
YEAH...ALLY WHAT IS YOUR INCOME?
I DO ALL RIGHT...
I'M SURE YOU DO! YOU HAD ONE BIG PAYOUT... BUT NOW YOU ARE MOSTLY WORK FOR HIRE, AM I RIGHT?
YES.
AND YOUR BIG PAYOUT AFTER THE TAXES AND ALL **WAS**?
IT WAS **ENOUGH...**
ALLY, I'M NOT TRYING TO **MOOCH** OFF YOU HERE!
FINE...540!
THAT WAS FOUR YEARS AGO.
UH-HUH.
AFTER BUYING AND FURNISHING THIS HOUSE, I'M GUESSING NOT MUCH WAS LEFT?
GET TO THE POINT!
WELL...BESIDES THE FACT THAT YOU SPEND MONEY LIKE A CHILD IN A TANTRUM...
HEY!
WHY WAS IT YOU BOUGHT THIS **IMPRACTICAL AS FUCK** HOUSE AGAIN?
MY POINT IS, YOU DON'T HAVE TO PLAY THIS RICH DOMINATRIX ROLE...YOU ARE **BETTER** THAN THAT! I WOULD KNOW.
HEH... YEAH, YOU WOULD...
AND IF YOU REMEMBER, IT WAS NEVER JUST ABOUT THE TOYS.
I KNOW THAT. I'M NOT A KID.
NO DOUBTS THERE, I **HAVE** SEEN YOU **NAKED!**

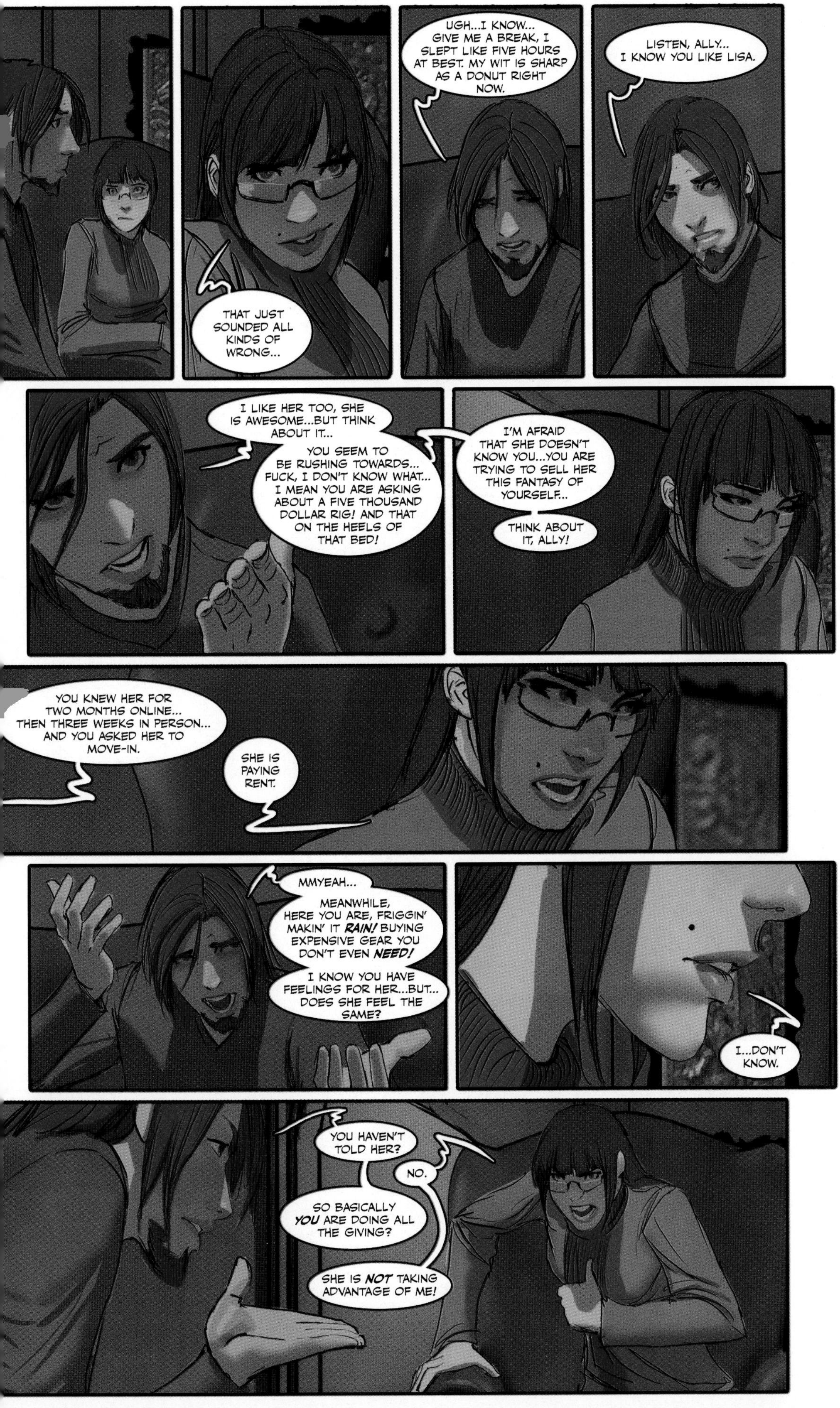
THAT JUST SOUNDED ALL KINDS OF WRONG...
UGH...I KNOW... GIVE ME A BREAK, I SLEPT LIKE FIVE HOURS AT BEST. MY WIT IS SHARP AS A DONUT RIGHT NOW.
LISTEN, ALLY... I KNOW YOU LIKE LISA.
I LIKE HER TOO, SHE IS AWESOME...BUT THINK ABOUT IT...
YOU SEEM TO BE RUSHING TOWARDS... FUCK, I DON'T KNOW WHAT... I MEAN YOU ARE ASKING ABOUT A FIVE THOUSAND DOLLAR RIG! AND THAT ON THE HEELS OF THAT BED!
I'M AFRAID THAT SHE DOESN'T KNOW YOU...YOU ARE TRYING TO SELL HER THIS FANTASY OF YOURSELF...
THINK ABOUT IT, ALLY!
YOU KNEW HER FOR TWO MONTHS ONLINE... THEN THREE WEEKS IN PERSON... AND YOU ASKED HER TO MOVE-IN.
SHE IS PAYING RENT.
MMYEAH...
MEANWHILE, HERE YOU ARE, FRIGGIN' MAKIN' IT *RAIN!* BUYING EXPENSIVE GEAR YOU DON'T EVEN *NEED!*
I KNOW YOU HAVE FEELINGS FOR HER...BUT... DOES SHE FEEL THE SAME?
I...DON'T KNOW.
YOU HAVEN'T TOLD HER?
NO.
SO BASICALLY *YOU* ARE DOING ALL THE GIVING?
SHE IS *NOT* TAKING ADVANTAGE OF ME!

OKAY THEN, *TELL ME!* WHAT HAS SHE DONE FOR YOU SPECIFICALLY?

SHE...

AND BEFORE YOU SAY IT, BEING A *SUB* DOESN'T COUNT!

UM...

YOU...DON'T KNOW HER AS I DO!

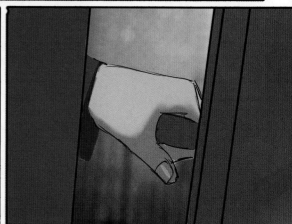

UM...HEY GUYS!

HI!

HEYA!

WHUT? OH, UMM...YEAH, FINE!

LISA? YOU *OKAY?*

SO, WHAT'S WI' THE *HUNCH?*

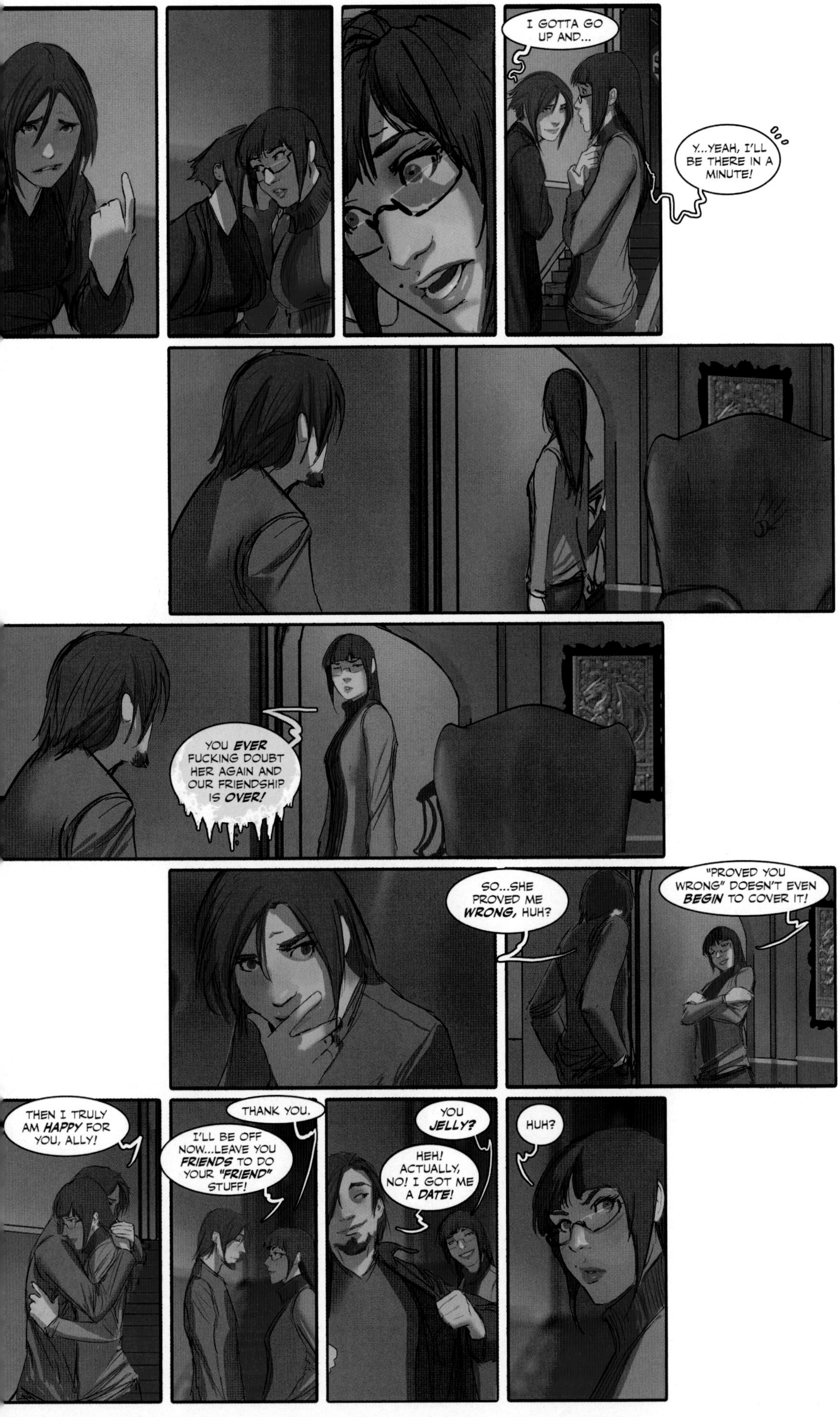
I GOTTA GO UP AND...
Y...YEAH, I'LL BE THERE IN A MINUTE!
YOU EVER FUCKING DOUBT HER AGAIN AND OUR FRIENDSHIP IS OVER!
SO...SHE PROVED ME WRONG, HUH?
"PROVED YOU WRONG" DOESN'T EVEN BEGIN TO COVER IT!
THEN I TRULY AM HAPPY FOR YOU, ALLY!
THANK YOU.
I'LL BE OFF NOW...LEAVE YOU FRIENDS TO DO YOUR "FRIEND" STUFF!
YOU JELLY?
HEH! ACTUALLY, NO! I GOT ME A DATE!
HUH?

NO PLAYING WITH THEM!

I...WASN'T GONNA!

WOW...CAN'T BELIEVE I'M ABOUT TO *SAY* THIS...

BUT MY *EYES* ARE UP HERE!

MEMORIES SURE ARE FUNNY...

THE WAY SOME OF THEM HAVE THIS WAY OF POSITIVELY *ENGRAVING* THEMSELVES IN YOUR MIND.

I REMEMBER THIS KISS *PERFECTLY*...

THE WAY SHE HUNCHED OVER ON HER TIPTOES TO AVOID HURTING ME...

I REMEMBER A FLEETING THOUGHT OF HER TAKING QUITE A BIT OF PLEASURE IN HURTING THOSE SAME NIPPLES ON OTHER OCCASIONS...

NOT *THAT* DAY.

EVEN THOUGH HER LITTLE PIERCED NIPPLE FETISH WAS SEXUAL IN NATUR

HER GRATITUDE THAT DAY WAS ANYTHING BUT.

I KNEW NOTHING OF HER TA WITH ALAN...OF HER FEARS AND DOUBTS...

I KNEW SHE WAS HAPPY JUST THEN...

AND THAT WAS ENOUGH.

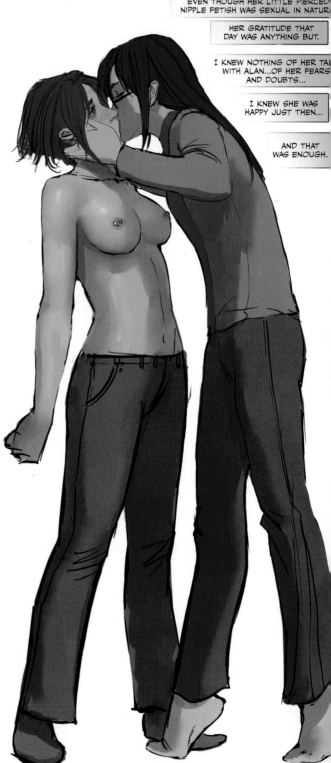

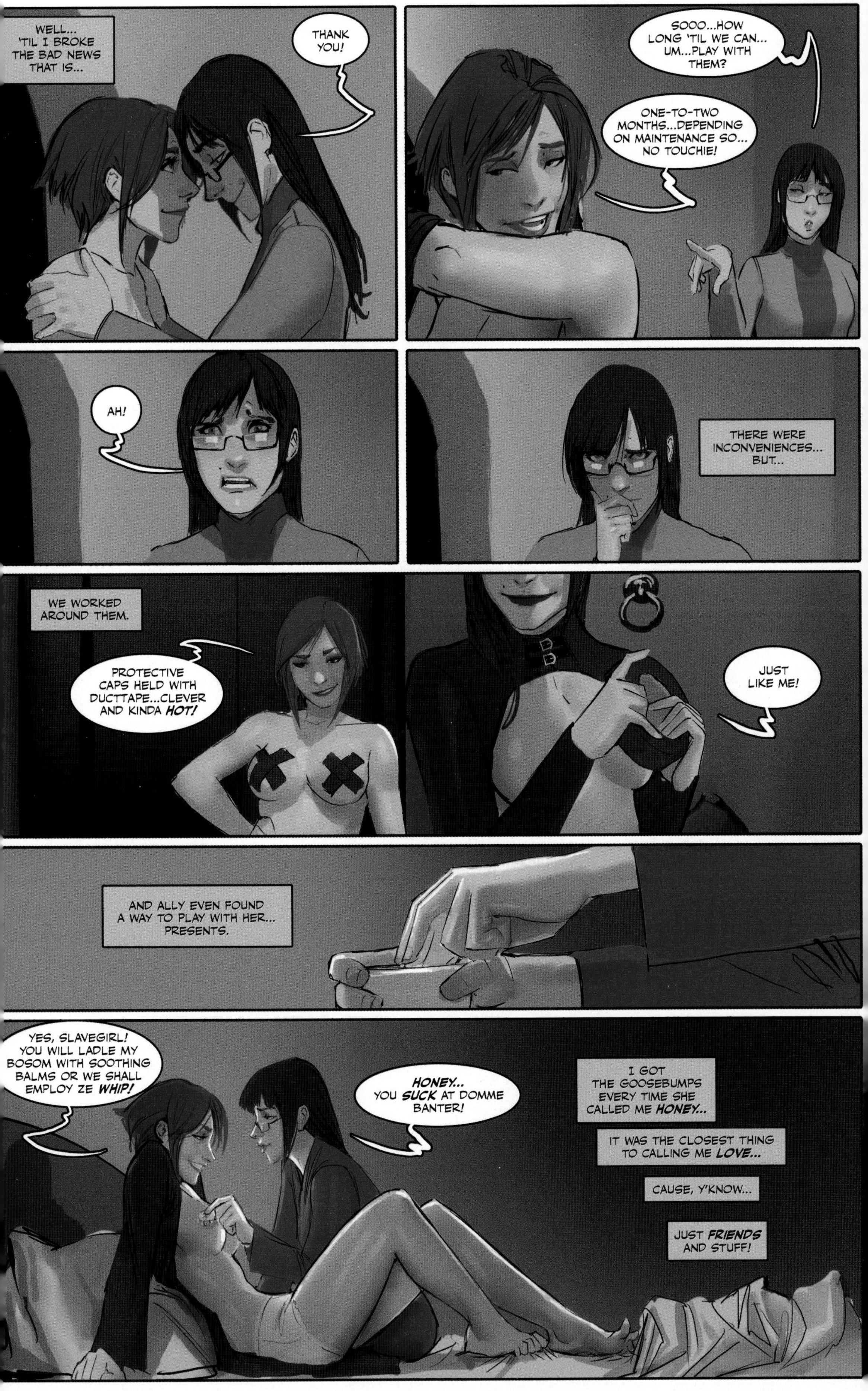

WELL... 'TIL I BROKE THE BAD NEWS THAT IS...
THANK YOU!
SOOO...HOW LONG 'TIL WE CAN... UM...PLAY WITH THEM?
ONE-TO-TWO MONTHS...DEPENDING ON MAINTENANCE SO... NO TOUCHIE!
AH!
THERE WERE INCONVENIENCES... BUT...
WE WORKED AROUND THEM.
PROTECTIVE CAPS HELD WITH DUCTTAPE...CLEVER AND KINDA *HOT!*
JUST LIKE ME!
AND ALLY EVEN FOUND A WAY TO PLAY WITH HER... PRESENTS.
YES, SLAVEGIRL! YOU WILL LADLE MY BOSOM WITH SOOTHING BALMS OR WE SHALL EMPLOY ZE *WHIP!*
HONEY... YOU *SUCK* AT DOMME BANTER!
I GOT THE GOOSEBUMPS EVERY TIME SHE CALLED ME *HONEY...*
IT WAS THE CLOSEST THING TO CALLING ME *LOVE...*
CAUSE, Y'KNOW...
JUST *FRIENDS* AND STUFF!

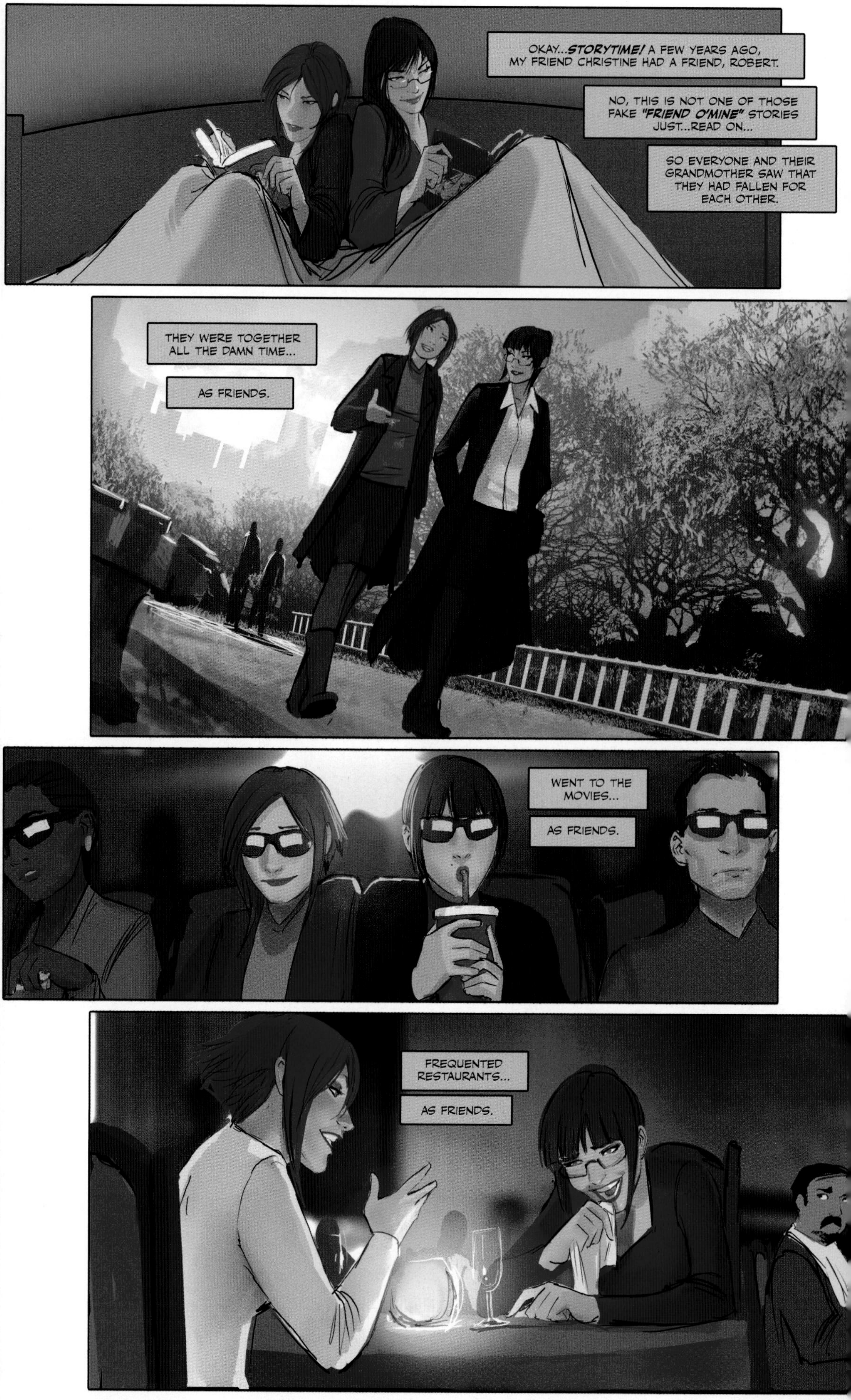

OKAY...**STORYTIME!** A FEW YEARS AGO, MY FRIEND CHRISTINE HAD A FRIEND, ROBERT.
NO, THIS IS NOT ONE OF THOSE FAKE ***"FRIEND O'MINE"*** STORIES JUST...READ ON...
SO EVERYONE AND THEIR GRANDMOTHER SAW THAT THEY HAD FALLEN FOR EACH OTHER.
THEY WERE TOGETHER ALL THE DAMN TIME...
AS FRIENDS.
WENT TO THE MOVIES...
AS FRIENDS.
FREQUENTED RESTAURANTS...
AS FRIENDS.

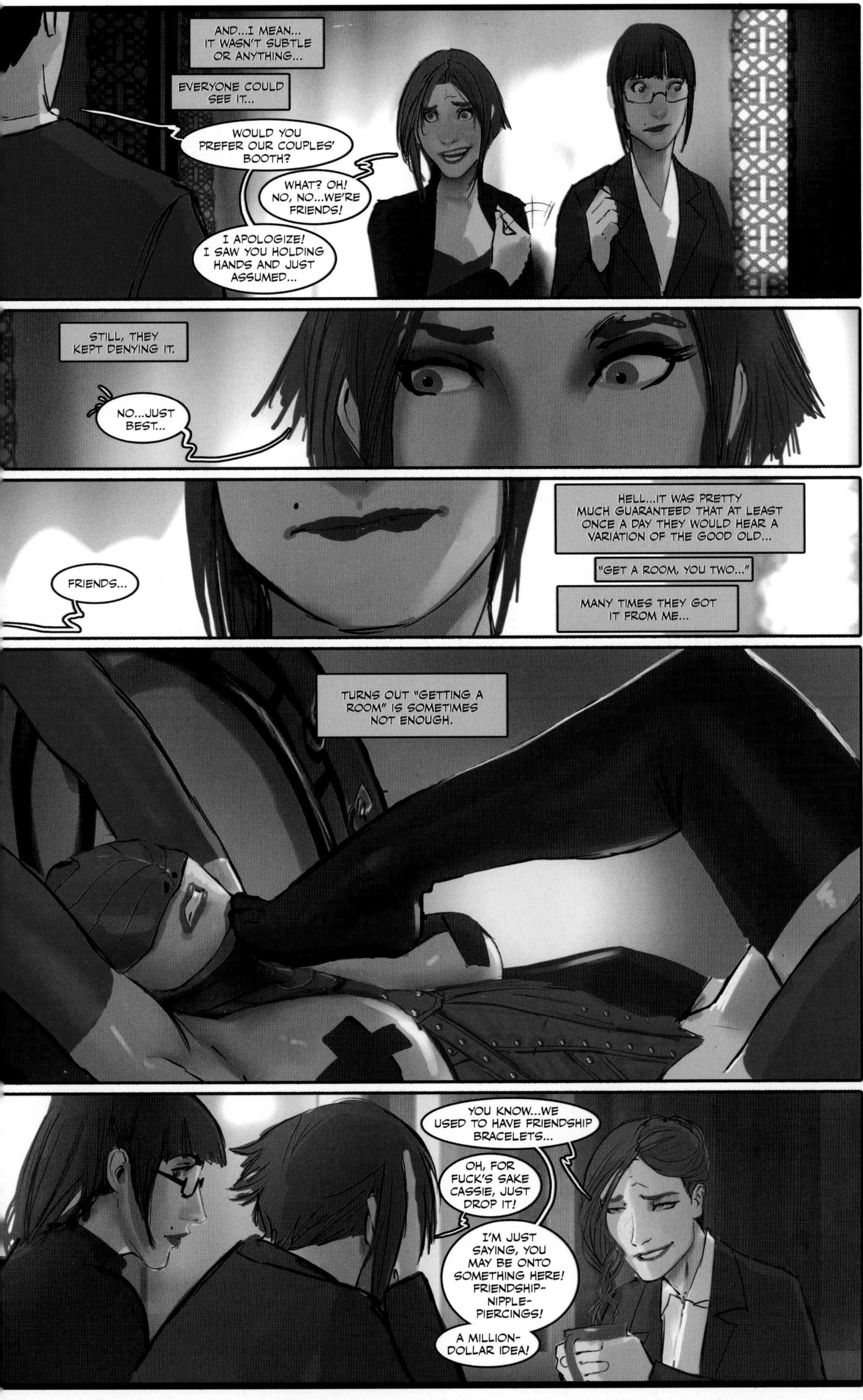
AND...I MEAN... IT WASN'T SUBTLE OR ANYTHING...
EVERYONE COULD SEE IT...
WOULD YOU PREFER OUR COUPLES' BOOTH?
WHAT? OH! NO, NO...WE'RE FRIENDS!
I APOLOGIZE! I SAW YOU HOLDING HANDS AND JUST ASSUMED...
STILL, THEY KEPT DENYING IT.
NO...JUST BEST...
FRIENDS...
HELL...IT WAS PRETTY MUCH GUARANTEED THAT AT LEAST ONCE A DAY THEY WOULD HEAR A VARIATION OF THE GOOD OLD...
"GET A ROOM, YOU TWO..."
MANY TIMES THEY GOT IT FROM ME...
TURNS OUT "GETTING A ROOM" IS SOMETIMES NOT ENOUGH.
YOU KNOW...WE USED TO HAVE FRIENDSHIP BRACELETS...
OH, FOR FUCK'S SAKE CASSIE, JUST DROP IT!
I'M JUST SAYING, YOU MAY BE ONTO SOMETHING HERE! FRIENDSHIP-NIPPLE-PIERCINGS!
A MILLION-DOLLAR IDEA!

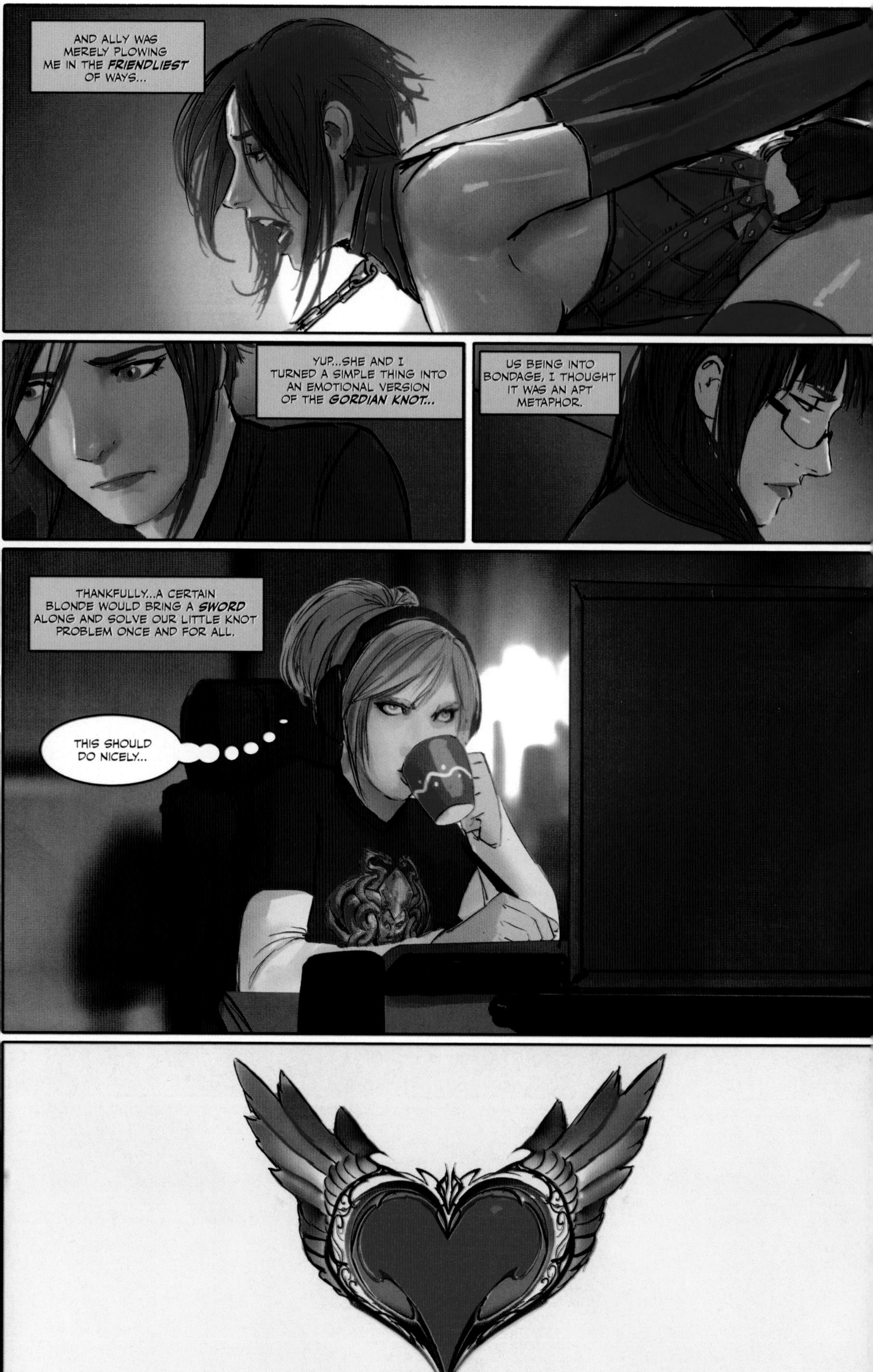
AND ALLY WAS MERELY PLOWING ME IN THE FRIENDLIEST OF WAYS...
YUP...SHE AND I TURNED A SIMPLE THING INTO AN EMOTIONAL VERSION OF THE GORDIAN KNOT...
US BEING INTO BONDAGE, I THOUGHT IT WAS AN APT METAPHOR.
THANKFULLY...A CERTAIN BLONDE WOULD BRING A SWORD ALONG AND SOLVE OUR LITTLE KNOT PROBLEM ONCE AND FOR ALL.
THIS SHOULD DO NICELY...

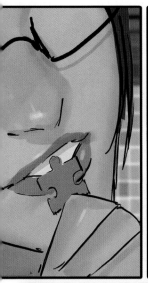

HEY!

YOU MIND NOT DROOLING ALL OVER MY PUZZLE?

DROOLING?

I'LL SHOW YOU DROOLING! I'LL LICK IT ALL OVER! MAKE IT NICE AND SOGGY!

GIVE IT HERE!

NO! MUST! LICK! PUZZLE!!!

BELELEP

TIME OUT!

Y'ELLO?

HEY ANNE!

NAH, JUST DOING A JIGSAW PUZZLE.

BLEEE!

WITH THE NEIGHBOR'S FIVE-YEAR-OLD APPARENTLY!

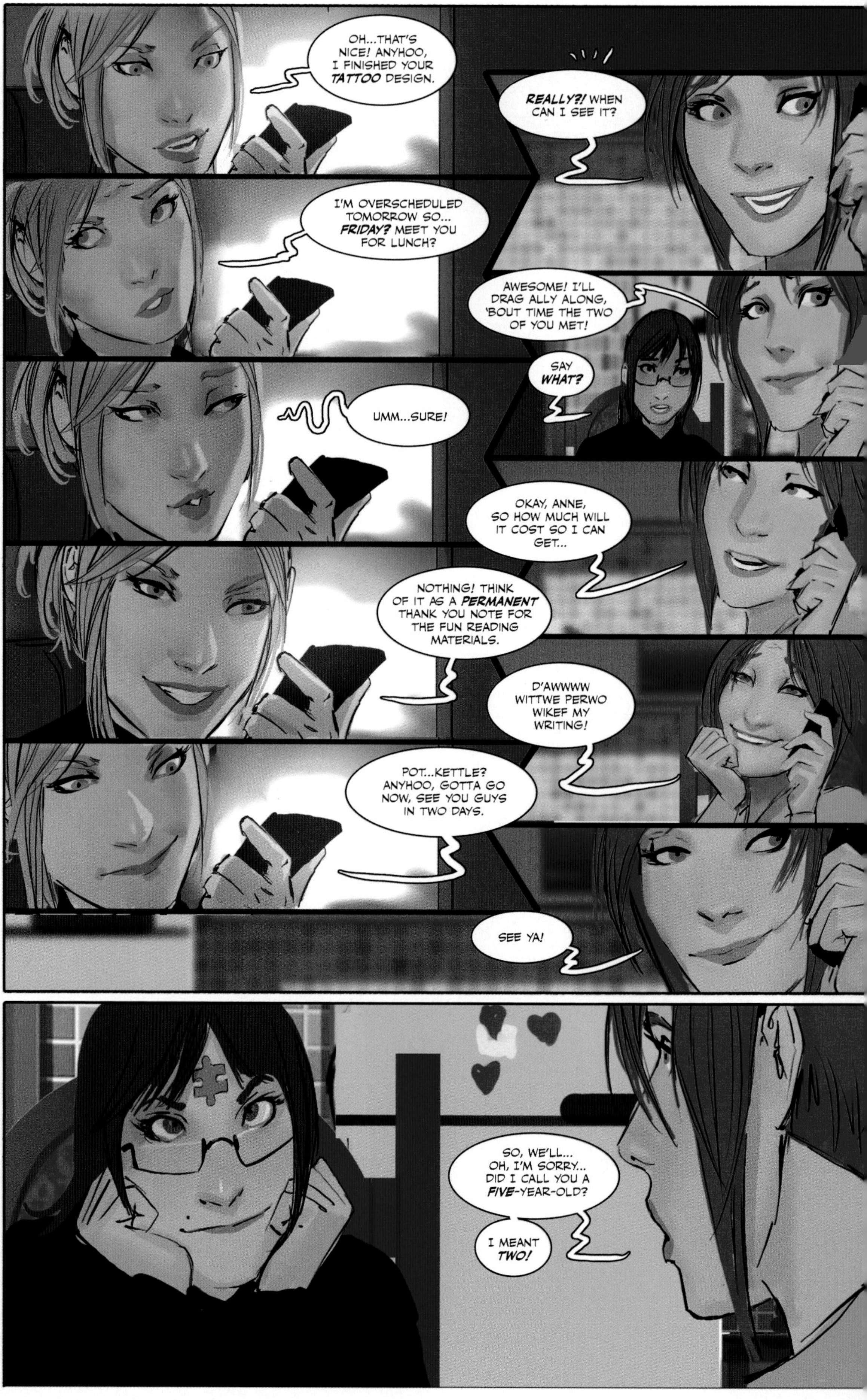

OH...THAT'S NICE! ANYHOO, I FINISHED YOUR TATTOO DESIGN.
REALLY?! WHEN CAN I SEE IT?
I'M OVERSCHEDULED TOMORROW SO... FRIDAY? MEET YOU FOR LUNCH?
AWESOME! I'LL DRAG ALLY ALONG, 'BOUT TIME THE TWO OF YOU MET!
SAY WHAT?
UMM...SURE!
OKAY, ANNE, SO HOW MUCH WILL IT COST SO I CAN GET...
NOTHING! THINK OF IT AS A PERMANENT THANK YOU NOTE FOR THE FUN READING MATERIALS.
D'AWWWW WITTWE PERWO WIKEF MY WRITING!
POT...KETTLE? ANYHOO, GOTTA GO NOW, SEE YOU GUYS IN TWO DAYS.
SEE YA!
SO, WE'LL... OH, I'M SORRY... DID I CALL YOU A FIVE-YEAR-OLD?
I MEANT TWO!

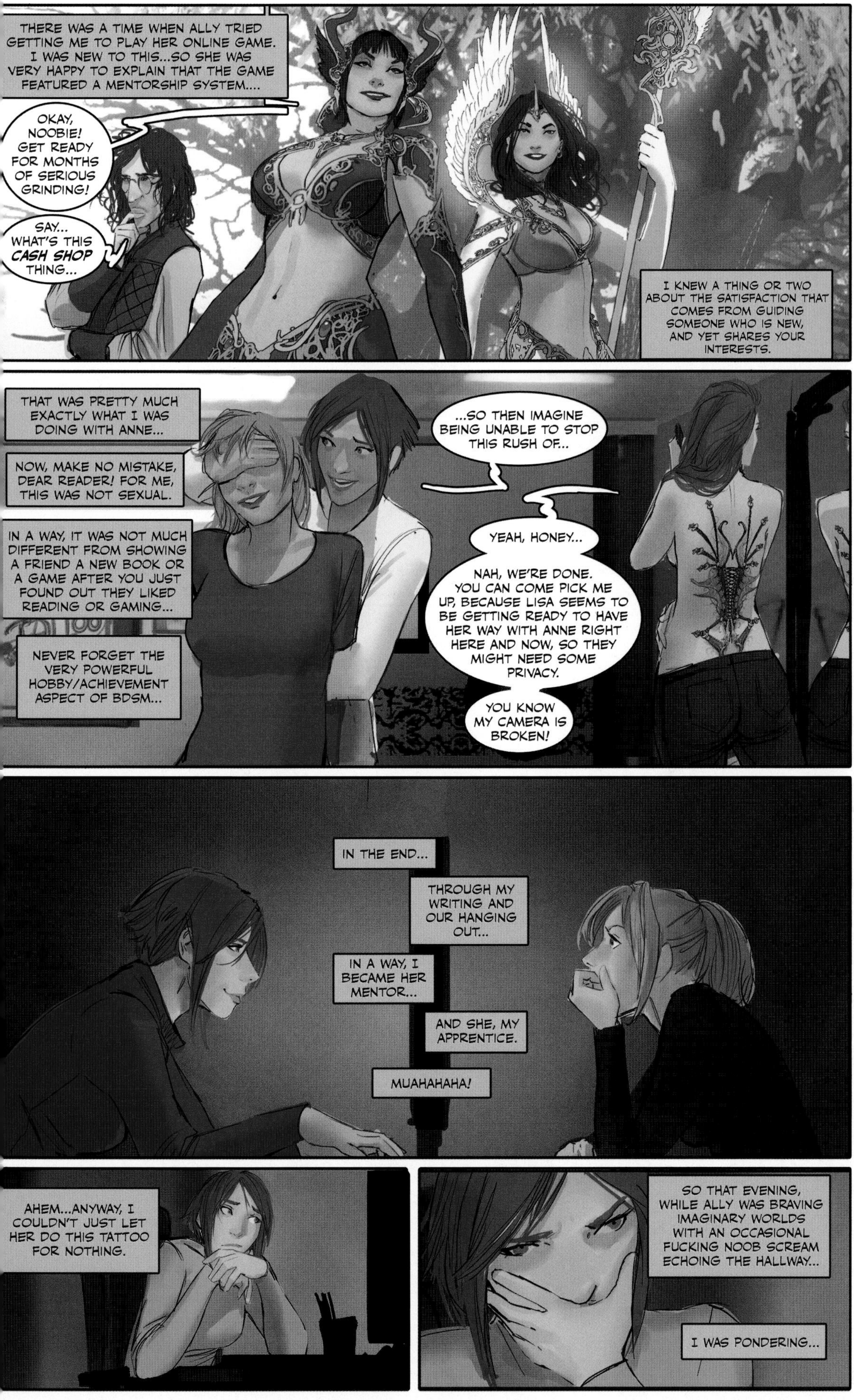
THERE WAS A TIME WHEN ALLY TRIED GETTING ME TO PLAY HER ONLINE GAME. I WAS NEW TO THIS...SO SHE WAS VERY HAPPY TO EXPLAIN THAT THE GAME FEATURED A MENTORSHIP SYSTEM....
OKAY, NOOBIE! GET READY FOR MONTHS OF SERIOUS GRINDING!
SAY... WHAT'S THIS CASH SHOP THING...
I KNEW A THING OR TWO ABOUT THE SATISFACTION THAT COMES FROM GUIDING SOMEONE WHO IS NEW, AND YET SHARES YOUR INTERESTS.
THAT WAS PRETTY MUCH EXACTLY WHAT I WAS DOING WITH ANNE...
NOW, MAKE NO MISTAKE, DEAR READER! FOR ME, THIS WAS NOT SEXUAL.
IN A WAY, IT WAS NOT MUCH DIFFERENT FROM SHOWING A FRIEND A NEW BOOK OR A GAME AFTER YOU JUST FOUND OUT THEY LIKED READING OR GAMING...
NEVER FORGET THE VERY POWERFUL HOBBY/ACHIEVEMENT ASPECT OF BDSM...
...SO THEN IMAGINE BEING UNABLE TO STOP THIS RUSH OF...
YEAH, HONEY...
NAH, WE'RE DONE. YOU CAN COME PICK ME UP, BECAUSE LISA SEEMS TO BE GETTING READY TO HAVE HER WAY WITH ANNE RIGHT HERE AND NOW, SO THEY MIGHT NEED SOME PRIVACY.
YOU KNOW MY CAMERA IS BROKEN!
IN THE END...
THROUGH MY WRITING AND OUR HANGING OUT...
IN A WAY, I BECAME HER MENTOR...
AND SHE, MY APPRENTICE.
MUAHAHAHA!
AHEM...ANYWAY, I COULDN'T JUST LET HER DO THIS TATTOO FOR NOTHING.
SO THAT EVENING, WHILE ALLY WAS BRAVING IMAGINARY WORLDS WITH AN OCCASIONAL FUCKING NOOB SCREAM ECHOING THE HALLWAY...
I WAS PONDERING...

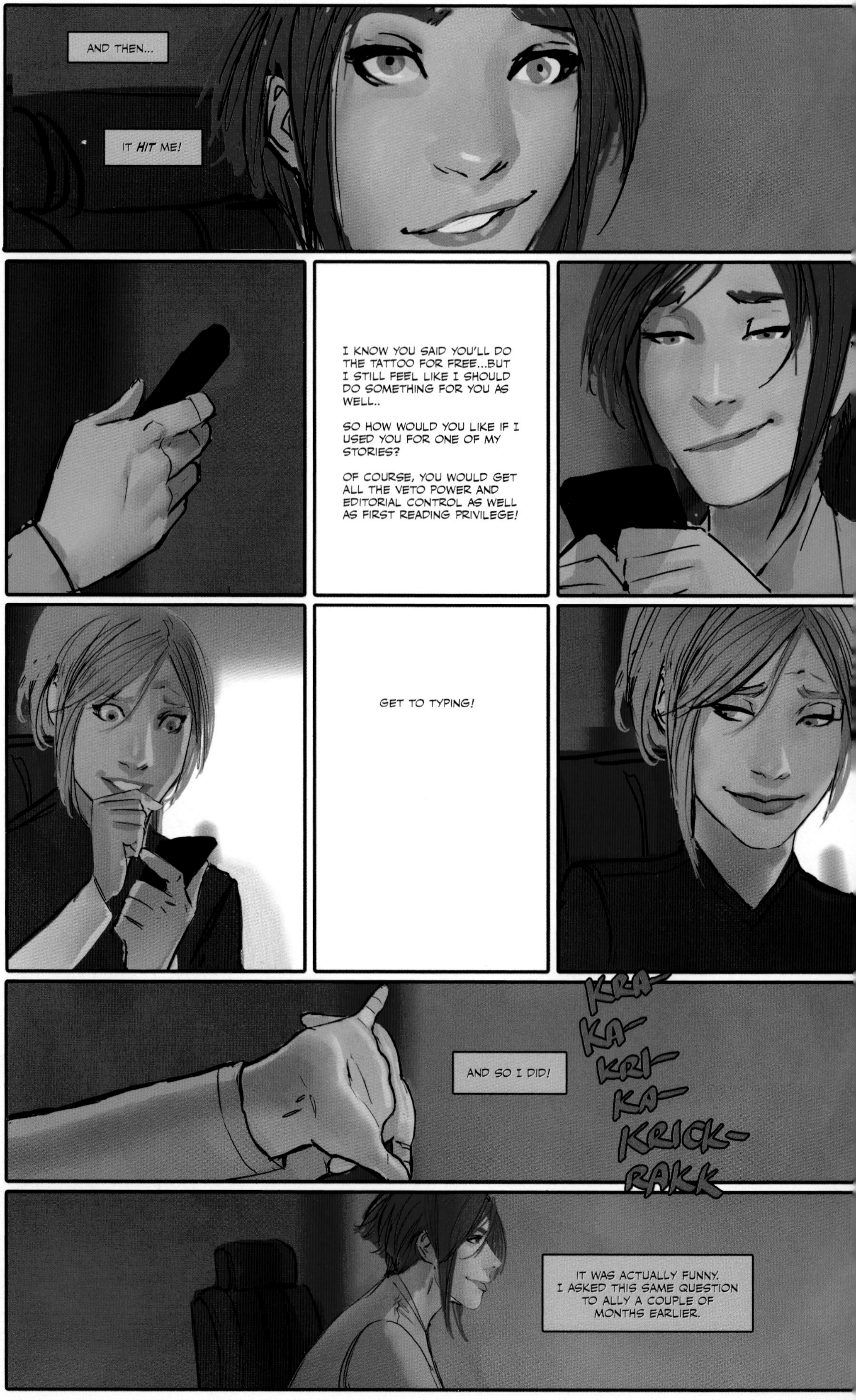
AND THEN...
IT HIT ME!
I KNOW YOU SAID YOU'LL DO THE TATTOO FOR FREE...BUT I STILL FEEL LIKE I SHOULD DO SOMETHING FOR YOU AS WELL..
SO HOW WOULD YOU LIKE IF I USED YOU FOR ONE OF MY STORIES?
OF COURSE, YOU WOULD GET ALL THE VETO POWER AND EDITORIAL CONTROL AS WELL AS FIRST READING PRIVILEGE!
GET TO TYPING!
AND SO I DID!
KRA KA-KRI-KA-KRICK-RAKK
IT WAS ACTUALLY FUNNY. I ASKED THIS SAME QUESTION TO ALLY A COUPLE OF MONTHS EARLIER.

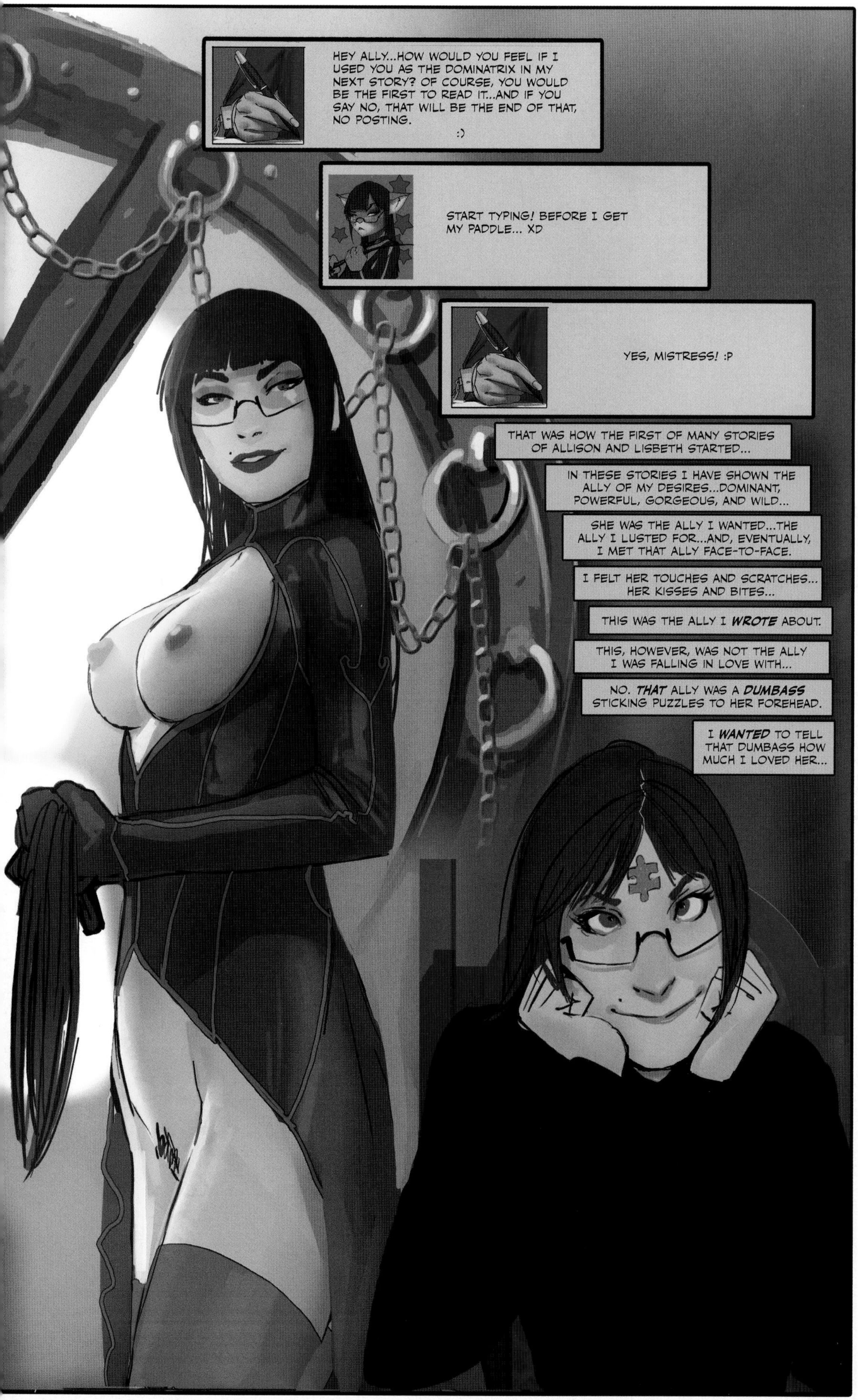
HEY ALLY...HOW WOULD YOU FEEL IF I USED YOU AS THE DOMINATRIX IN MY NEXT STORY? OF COURSE, YOU WOULD BE THE FIRST TO READ IT...AND IF YOU SAY NO, THAT WILL BE THE END OF THAT, NO POSTING.
:)
START TYPING! BEFORE I GET MY PADDLE... XD
YES, MISTRESS! :P
THAT WAS HOW THE FIRST OF MANY STORIES OF ALLISON AND LISBETH STARTED...
IN THESE STORIES I HAVE SHOWN THE ALLY OF MY DESIRES...DOMINANT, POWERFUL, GORGEOUS, AND WILD...
SHE WAS THE ALLY I WANTED...THE ALLY I LUSTED FOR...AND, EVENTUALLY, I MET THAT ALLY FACE-TO-FACE.
I FELT HER TOUCHES AND SCRATCHES... HER KISSES AND BITES...
THIS WAS THE ALLY I WROTE ABOUT.
THIS, HOWEVER, WAS NOT THE ALLY I WAS FALLING IN LOVE WITH...
NO. THAT ALLY WAS A DUMBASS STICKING PUZZLES TO HER FOREHEAD.
I WANTED TO TELL THAT DUMBASS HOW MUCH I LOVED HER...

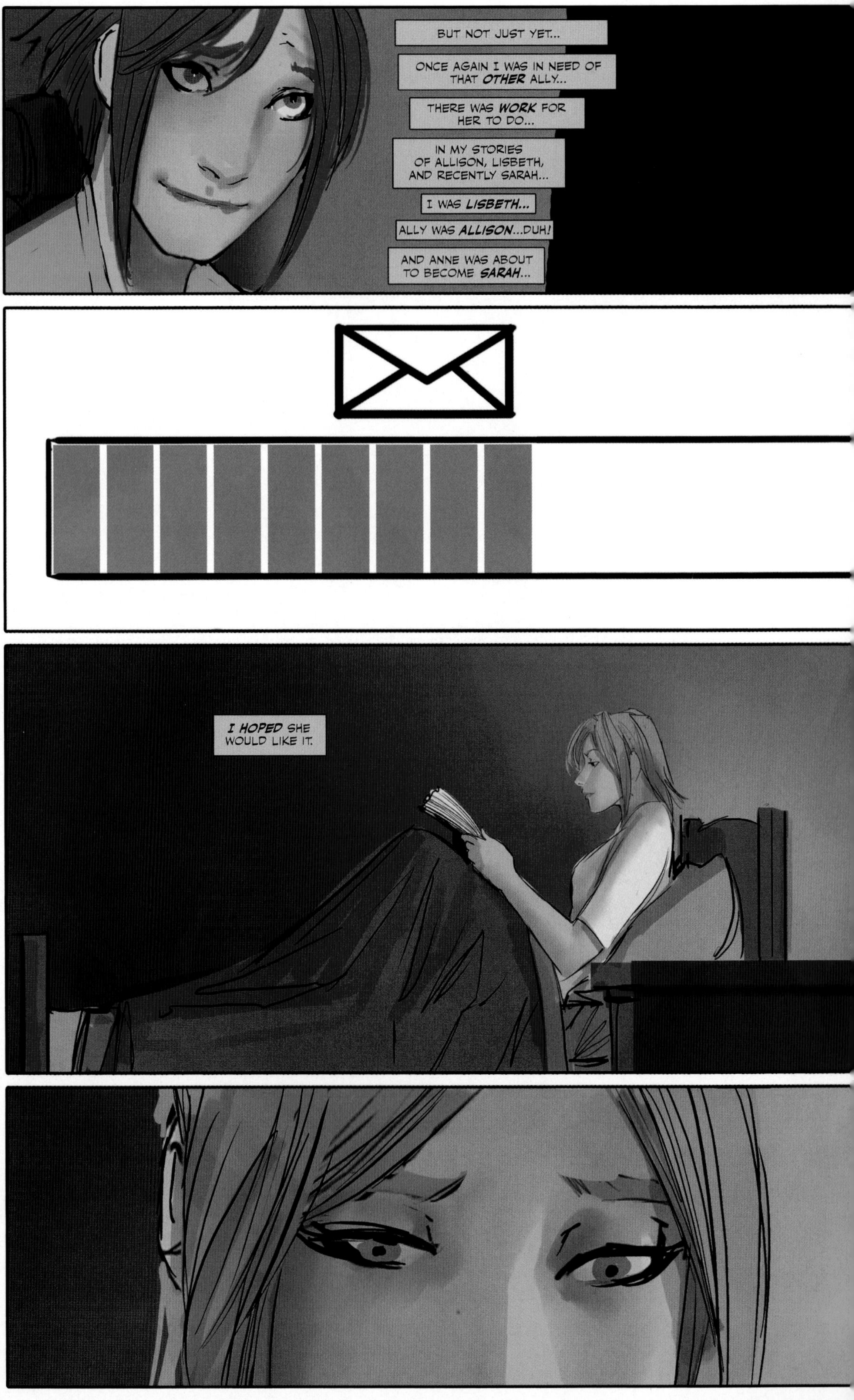
BUT NOT JUST YET...
ONCE AGAIN I WAS IN NEED OF THAT *OTHER* ALLY...
THERE WAS *WORK* FOR HER TO DO...
IN MY STORIES OF ALLISON, LISBETH, AND RECENTLY SARAH...
I WAS *LISBETH...*
ALLY WAS *ALLISON*...DUH!
AND ANNE WAS ABOUT TO BECOME *SARAH*...
I HOPED SHE WOULD LIKE IT.

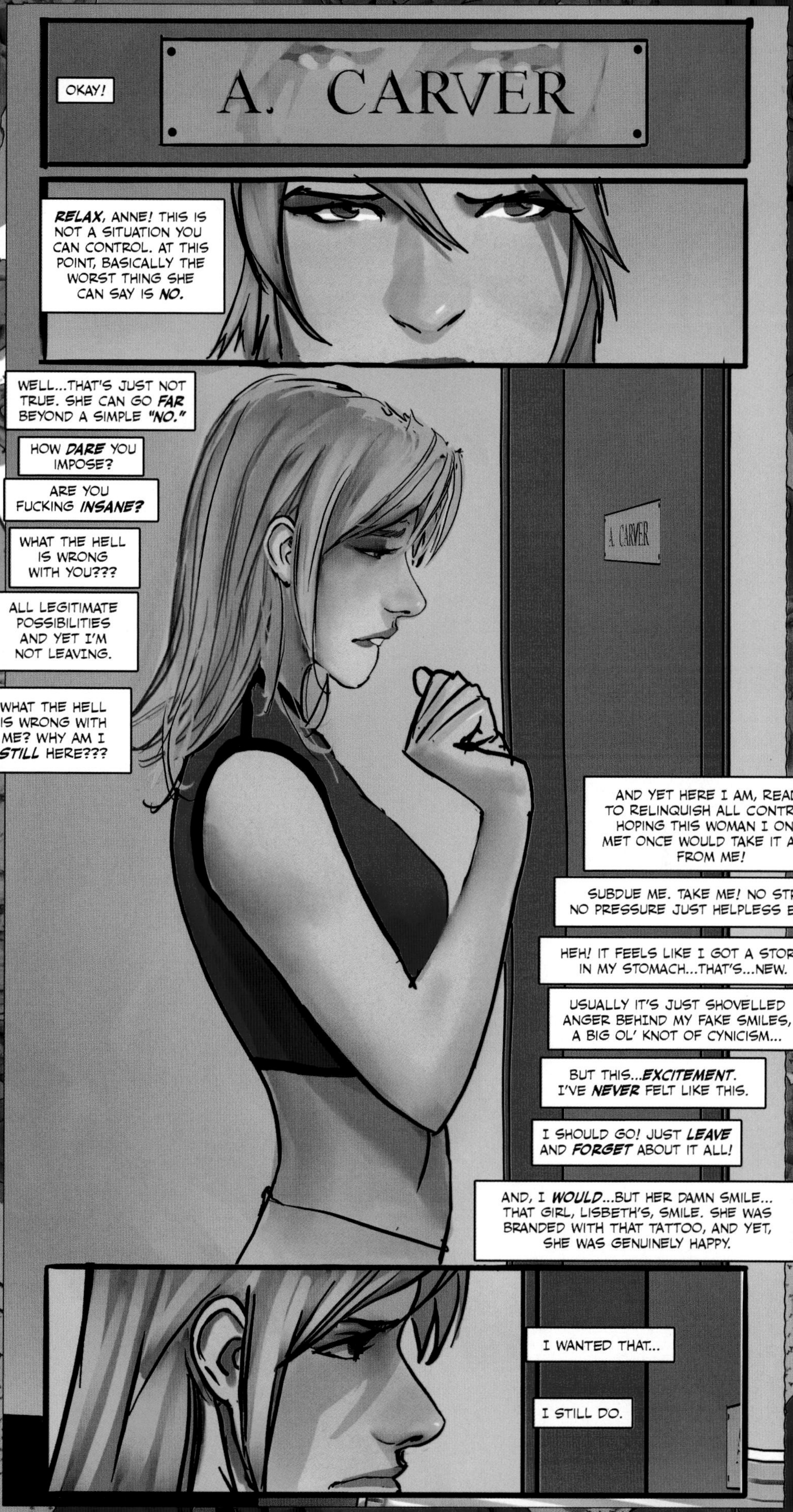
OKAY!
A. CARVER
RELAX, ANNE! THIS IS NOT A SITUATION YOU CAN CONTROL. AT THIS POINT, BASICALLY THE WORST THING SHE CAN SAY IS NO.
WELL...THAT'S JUST NOT TRUE. SHE CAN GO FAR BEYOND A SIMPLE "NO."
HOW DARE YOU IMPOSE?
ARE YOU FUCKING INSANE?
WHAT THE HELL IS WRONG WITH YOU???
ALL LEGITIMATE POSSIBILITIES AND YET I'M NOT LEAVING.
WHAT THE HELL IS WRONG WITH ME? WHY AM I STILL HERE???
A. CARVER
AND YET HERE I AM, READY TO RELINQUISH ALL CONTROL. HOPING THIS WOMAN I ONLY MET ONCE WOULD TAKE IT AWAY FROM ME!
SUBDUE ME. TAKE ME! NO STRESS, NO PRESSURE JUST HELPLESS ECSTASY.
HEH! IT FEELS LIKE I GOT A STORM IN MY STOMACH...THAT'S...NEW.
USUALLY IT'S JUST SHOVELLED ANGER BEHIND MY FAKE SMILES, A BIG OL' KNOT OF CYNICISM...
BUT THIS...EXCITEMENT. I'VE NEVER FELT LIKE THIS.
I SHOULD GO! JUST LEAVE AND FORGET ABOUT IT ALL!
AND, I WOULD...BUT HER DAMN SMILE... THAT GIRL, LISBETH'S, SMILE. SHE WAS BRANDED WITH THAT TATTOO, AND YET, SHE WAS GENUINELY HAPPY.
I WANTED THAT...
I STILL DO.

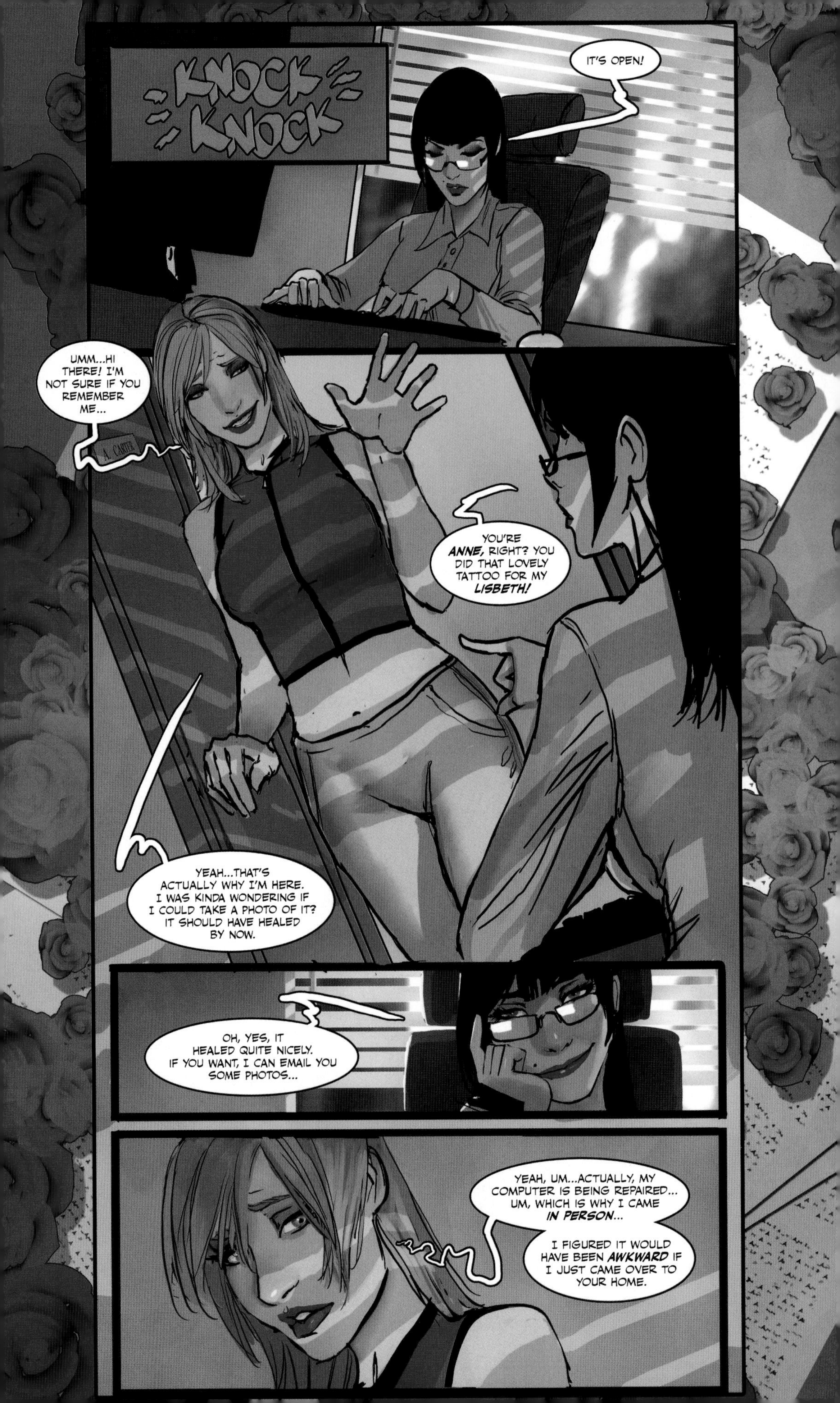
KNOCK KNOCK
IT'S OPEN!
UMM...HI THERE! I'M NOT SURE IF YOU REMEMBER ME...
YOU'RE ANNE, RIGHT? YOU DID THAT LOVELY TATTOO FOR MY LISBETH!
YEAH...THAT'S ACTUALLY WHY I'M HERE. I WAS KINDA WONDERING IF I COULD TAKE A PHOTO OF IT? IT SHOULD HAVE HEALED BY NOW.
OH, YES, IT HEALED QUITE NICELY. IF YOU WANT, I CAN EMAIL YOU SOME PHOTOS...
YEAH, UM...ACTUALLY, MY COMPUTER IS BEING REPAIRED... UM, WHICH IS WHY I CAME IN PERSON...
I FIGURED IT WOULD HAVE BEEN AWKWARD IF I JUST CAME OVER TO YOUR HOME.

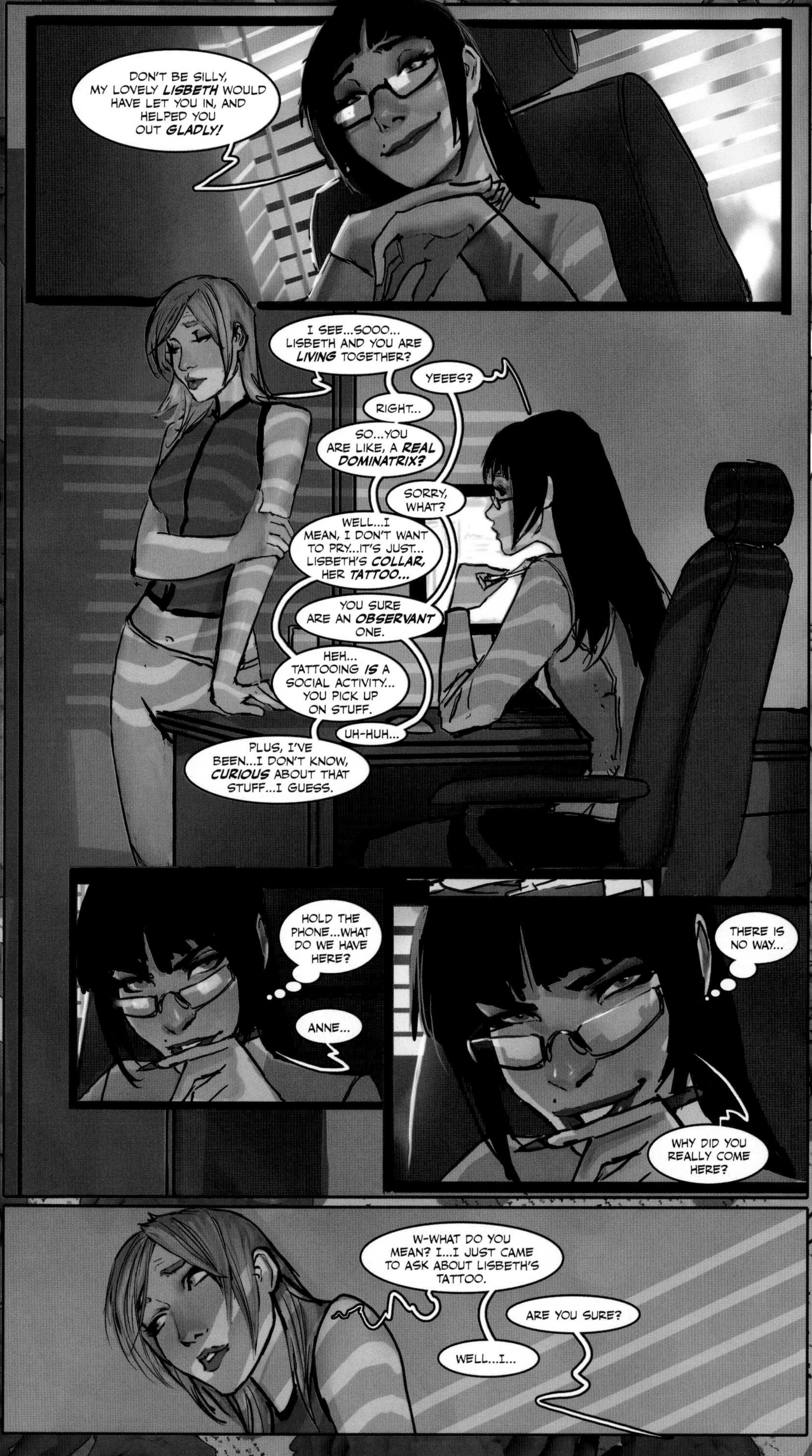

DON'T BE SILLY, MY LOVELY LISBETH WOULD HAVE LET YOU IN, AND HELPED YOU OUT GLADLY!
I SEE...SOOO... LISBETH AND YOU ARE LIVING TOGETHER?
YEEES?
RIGHT...
SO...YOU ARE LIKE, A REAL DOMINATRIX?
SORRY, WHAT?
WELL...I MEAN, I DON'T WANT TO PRY...IT'S JUST... LISBETH'S COLLAR, HER TATTOO...
YOU SURE ARE AN OBSERVANT ONE.
HEH... TATTOOING IS A SOCIAL ACTIVITY... YOU PICK UP ON STUFF.
UH-HUH...
PLUS, I'VE BEEN...I DON'T KNOW, CURIOUS ABOUT THAT STUFF...I GUESS.
HOLD THE PHONE...WHAT DO WE HAVE HERE?
ANNE...
THERE IS NO WAY...
WHY DID YOU REALLY COME HERE?
W-WHAT DO YOU MEAN? I...I JUST CAME TO ASK ABOUT LISBETH'S TATTOO.
ARE YOU SURE?
WELL...I...

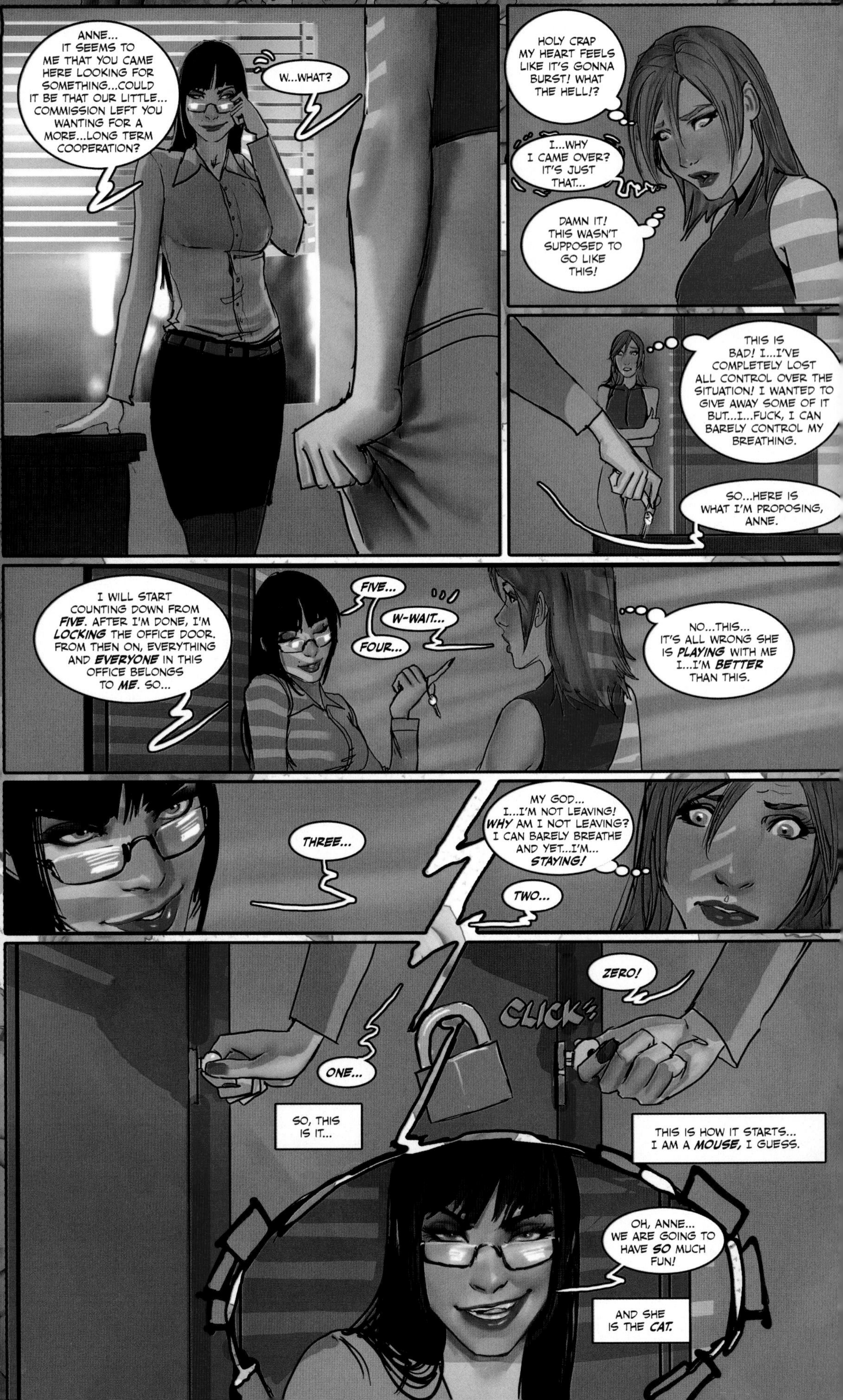
ANNE... IT SEEMS TO ME THAT YOU CAME HERE LOOKING FOR SOMETHING...COULD IT BE THAT OUR LITTLE... COMMISSION LEFT YOU WANTING FOR A MORE...LONG TERM COOPERATION?
W...WHAT?
HOLY CRAP MY HEART FEELS LIKE IT'S GONNA BURST! WHAT THE HELL!?
I...WHY I CAME OVER? IT'S JUST THAT...
DAMN IT! THIS WASN'T SUPPOSED TO GO LIKE THIS!
THIS IS BAD! I...I'VE COMPLETELY LOST ALL CONTROL OVER THE SITUATION! I WANTED TO GIVE AWAY SOME OF IT BUT...I...FUCK, I CAN BARELY CONTROL MY BREATHING.
SO...HERE IS WHAT I'M PROPOSING, ANNE.
I WILL START COUNTING DOWN FROM FIVE. AFTER I'M DONE, I'M LOCKING THE OFFICE DOOR. FROM THEN ON, EVERYTHING AND EVERYONE IN THIS OFFICE BELONGS TO ME. SO...
FIVE...
W-WAIT...
FOUR...
NO...THIS... IT'S ALL WRONG SHE IS PLAYING WITH ME I...I'M BETTER THAN THIS.
THREE...
MY GOD... I...I'M NOT LEAVING! WHY AM I NOT LEAVING? I CAN BARELY BREATHE AND YET...I'M... STAYING!
TWO...
ONE...
ZERO!
CLICK
SO, THIS IS IT...
THIS IS HOW IT STARTS... I AM A MOUSE, I GUESS.
OH, ANNE... WE ARE GOING TO HAVE SO MUCH FUN!
AND SHE IS THE CAT.

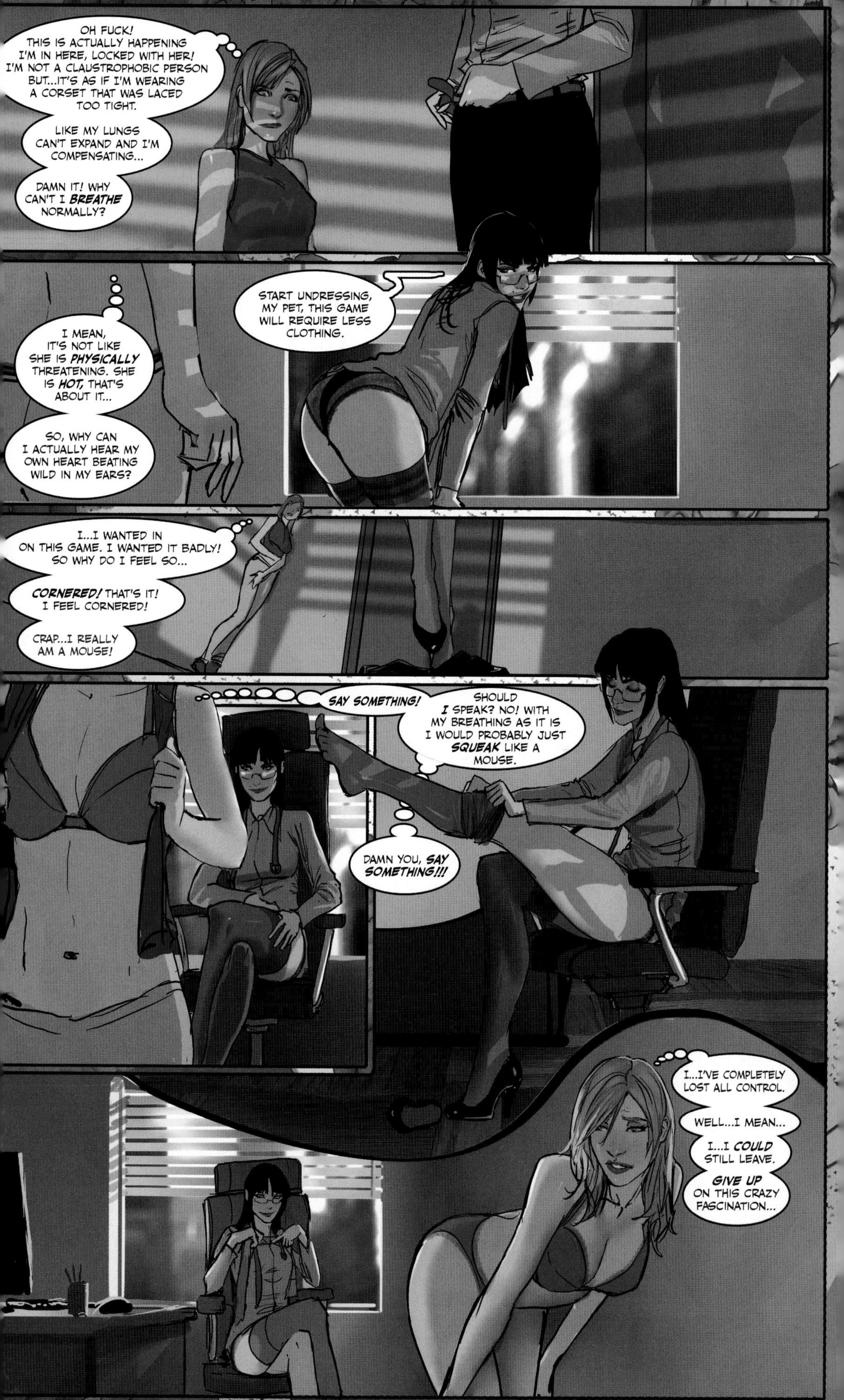
OH FUCK! THIS IS ACTUALLY HAPPENING I'M IN HERE, LOCKED WITH HER! I'M NOT A CLAUSTROPHOBIC PERSON BUT...IT'S AS IF I'M WEARING A CORSET THAT WAS LACED TOO TIGHT.
LIKE MY LUNGS CAN'T EXPAND AND I'M COMPENSATING...
DAMN IT! WHY CAN'T I BREATHE NORMALLY?
START UNDRESSING, MY PET, THIS GAME WILL REQUIRE LESS CLOTHING.
I MEAN, IT'S NOT LIKE SHE IS PHYSICALLY THREATENING. SHE IS HOT, THAT'S ABOUT IT...
SO, WHY CAN I ACTUALLY HEAR MY OWN HEART BEATING WILD IN MY EARS?
I...I WANTED IN ON THIS GAME. I WANTED IT BADLY! SO WHY DO I FEEL SO...
CORNERED! THAT'S IT! I FEEL CORNERED!
CRAP...I REALLY AM A MOUSE!
SAY SOMETHING!
SHOULD I SPEAK? NO! WITH MY BREATHING AS IT IS I WOULD PROBABLY JUST SQUEAK LIKE A MOUSE.
DAMN YOU, SAY SOMETHING!!!
I...I'VE COMPLETELY LOST ALL CONTROL.
WELL...I MEAN...
I...I COULD STILL LEAVE.
GIVE UP ON THIS CRAZY FASCINATION...

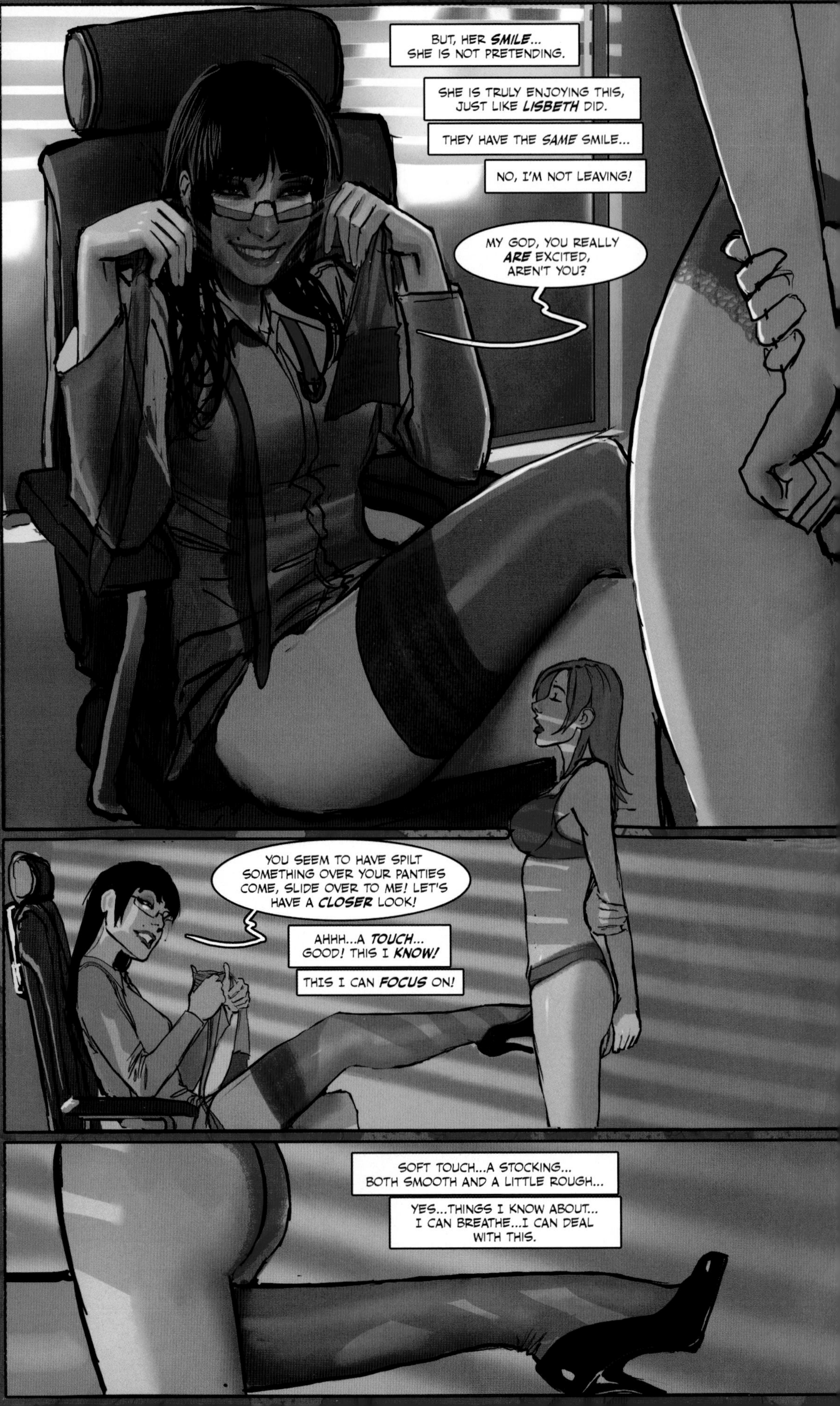

BUT, HER SMILE... SHE IS NOT PRETENDING.
SHE IS TRULY ENJOYING THIS, JUST LIKE LISBETH DID.
THEY HAVE THE SAME SMILE...
NO, I'M NOT LEAVING!
MY GOD, YOU REALLY ARE EXCITED, AREN'T YOU?
YOU SEEM TO HAVE SPILT SOMETHING OVER YOUR PANTIES COME, SLIDE OVER TO ME! LET'S HAVE A CLOSER LOOK!
AHHH...A TOUCH... GOOD! THIS I KNOW!
THIS I CAN FOCUS ON!
SOFT TOUCH...A STOCKING... BOTH SMOOTH AND A LITTLE ROUGH...
YES...THINGS I KNOW ABOUT... I CAN BREATHE...I CAN DEAL WITH THIS.

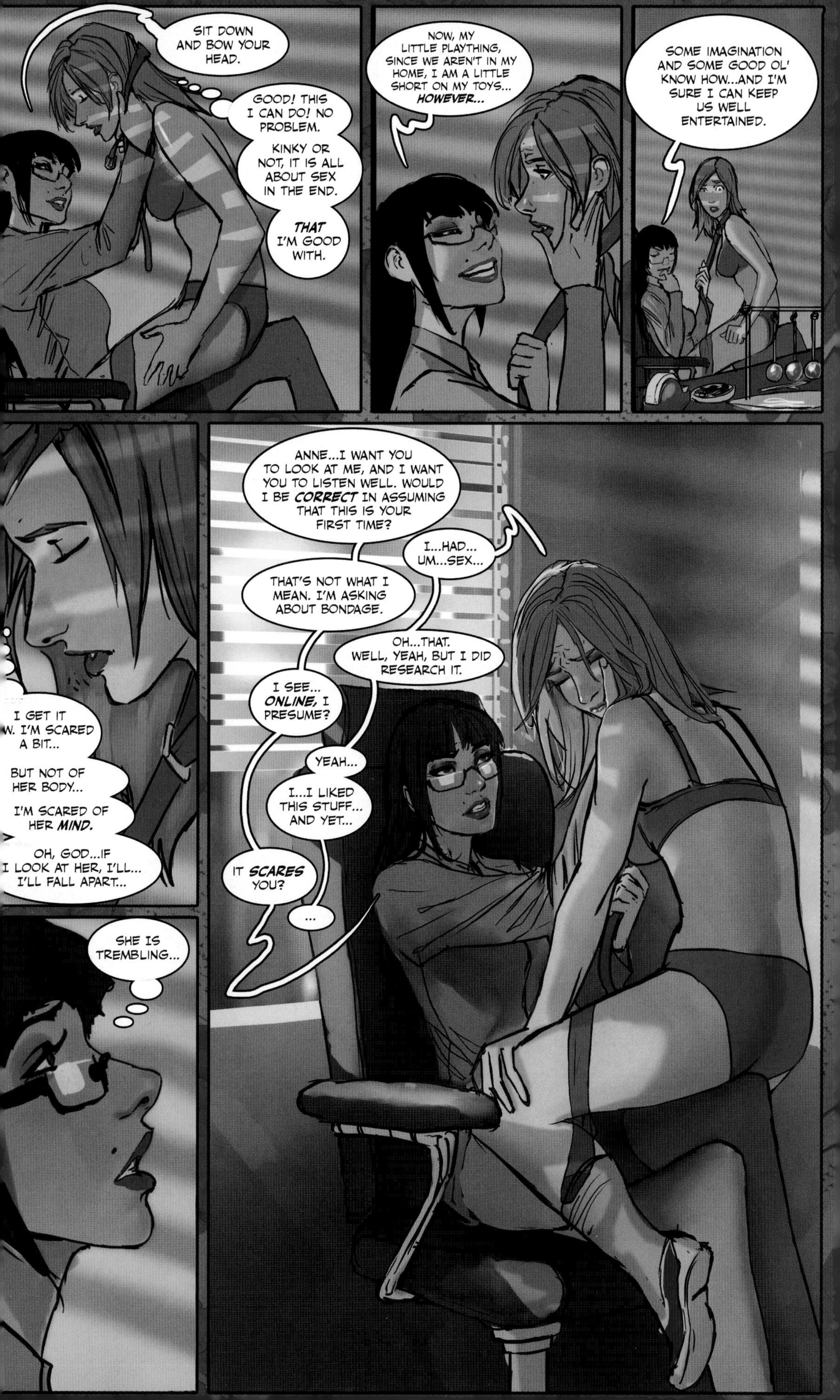

SIT DOWN AND BOW YOUR HEAD.
GOOD! THIS I CAN DO! NO PROBLEM.
KINKY OR NOT, IT IS ALL ABOUT SEX IN THE END.
THAT I'M GOOD WITH.
NOW, MY LITTLE PLAYTHING, SINCE WE AREN'T IN MY HOME, I AM A LITTLE SHORT ON MY TOYS... HOWEVER...
SOME IMAGINATION AND SOME GOOD OL' KNOW HOW...AND I'M SURE I CAN KEEP US WELL ENTERTAINED.
I GET IT
W. I'M SCARED A BIT...
BUT NOT OF HER BODY...
I'M SCARED OF HER MIND.
OH, GOD...IF I LOOK AT HER, I'LL... I'LL FALL APART...
SHE IS TREMBLING...
ANNE...I WANT YOU TO LOOK AT ME, AND I WANT YOU TO LISTEN WELL. WOULD I BE CORRECT IN ASSUMING THAT THIS IS YOUR FIRST TIME?
I...HAD... UM...SEX...
THAT'S NOT WHAT I MEAN. I'M ASKING ABOUT BONDAGE.
OH...THAT. WELL, YEAH, BUT I DID RESEARCH IT.
I SEE... ONLINE, I PRESUME?
YEAH...
I...I LIKED THIS STUFF... AND YET...
IT SCARES YOU?
...

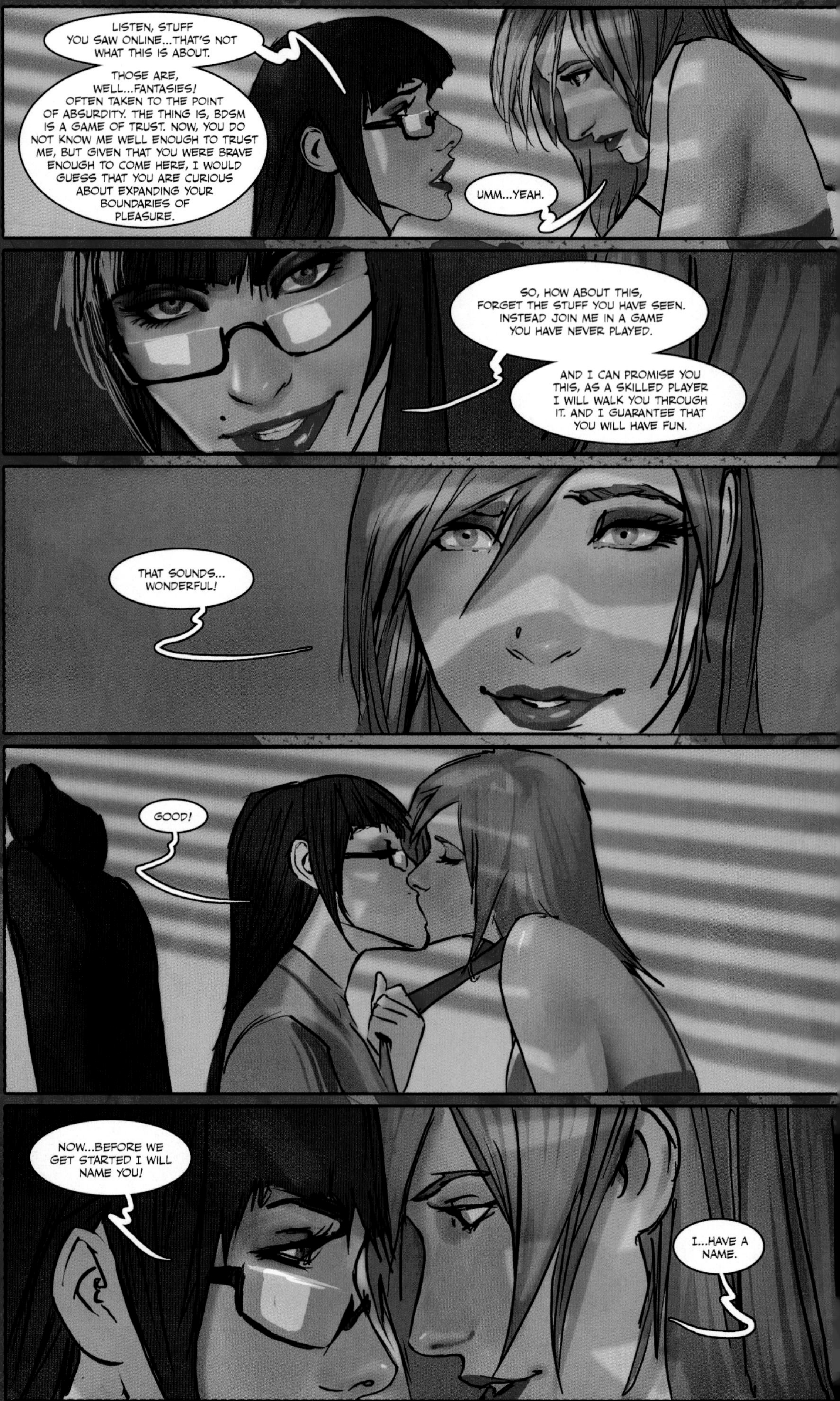
LISTEN, STUFF YOU SAW ONLINE...THAT'S NOT WHAT THIS IS ABOUT.
THOSE ARE, WELL...FANTASIES! OFTEN TAKEN TO THE POINT OF ABSURDITY. THE THING IS, BDSM IS A GAME OF TRUST. NOW, YOU DO NOT KNOW ME WELL ENOUGH TO TRUST ME, BUT GIVEN THAT YOU WERE BRAVE ENOUGH TO COME HERE, I WOULD GUESS THAT YOU ARE CURIOUS ABOUT EXPANDING YOUR BOUNDARIES OF PLEASURE.
UMM...YEAH.
SO, HOW ABOUT THIS, FORGET THE STUFF YOU HAVE SEEN. INSTEAD JOIN ME IN A GAME YOU HAVE NEVER PLAYED.
AND I CAN PROMISE YOU THIS, AS A SKILLED PLAYER I WILL WALK YOU THROUGH IT. AND I GUARANTEE THAT YOU WILL HAVE FUN.
THAT SOUNDS... WONDERFUL!
GOOD!
NOW...BEFORE WE GET STARTED I WILL NAME YOU!
I...HAVE A NAME.

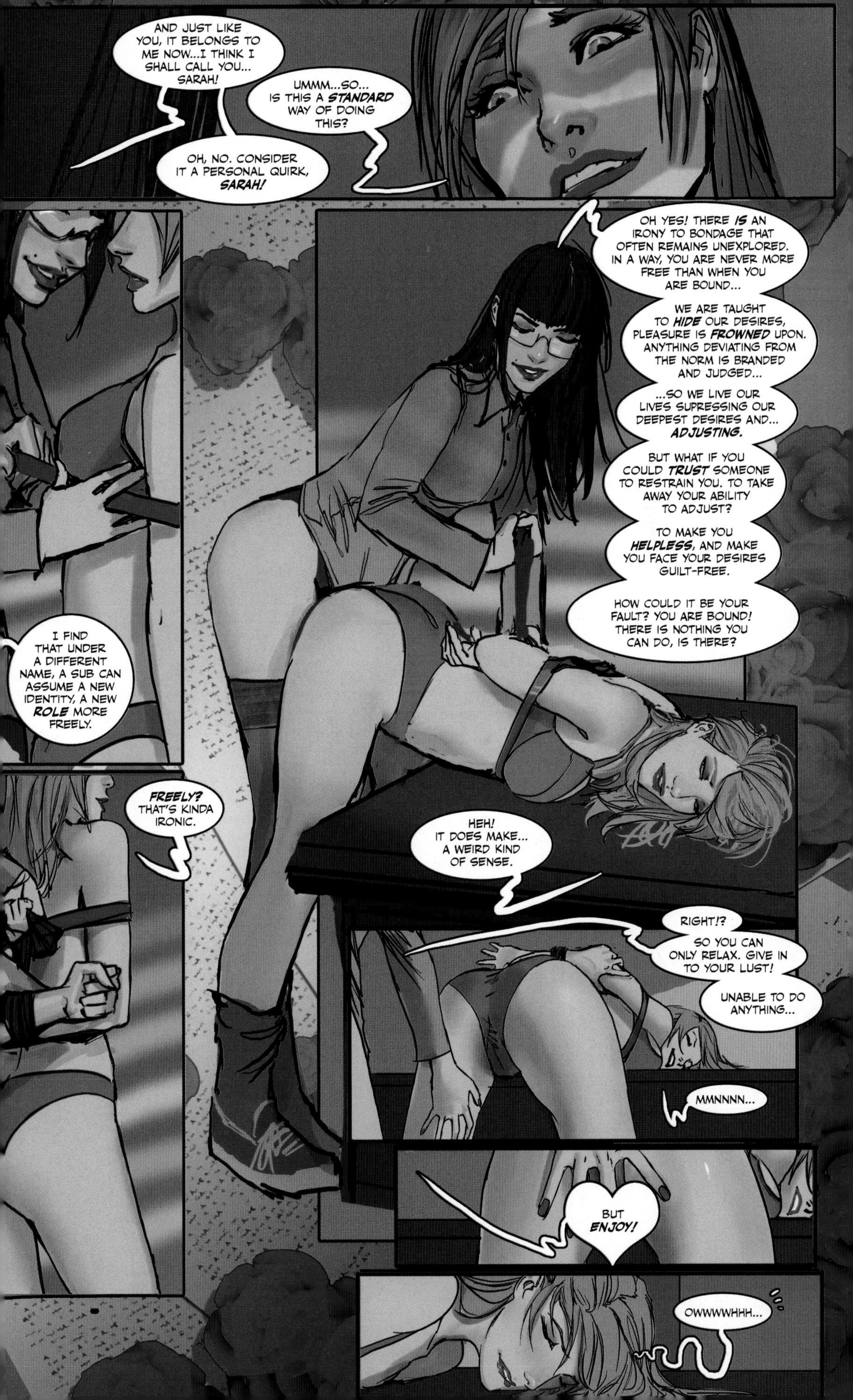

AND JUST LIKE YOU, IT BELONGS TO ME NOW...I THINK I SHALL CALL YOU... SARAH!
UMMM...SO... IS THIS A STANDARD WAY OF DOING THIS?
OH, NO. CONSIDER IT A PERSONAL QUIRK, SARAH!
I FIND THAT UNDER A DIFFERENT NAME, A SUB CAN ASSUME A NEW IDENTITY, A NEW ROLE MORE FREELY.
FREELY? THAT'S KINDA IRONIC.
OH YES! THERE IS AN IRONY TO BONDAGE THAT OFTEN REMAINS UNEXPLORED. IN A WAY, YOU ARE NEVER MORE FREE THAN WHEN YOU ARE BOUND...
WE ARE TAUGHT TO HIDE OUR DESIRES, PLEASURE IS FROWNED UPON. ANYTHING DEVIATING FROM THE NORM IS BRANDED AND JUDGED...
...SO WE LIVE OUR LIVES SUPRESSING OUR DEEPEST DESIRES AND... ADJUSTING.
BUT WHAT IF YOU COULD TRUST SOMEONE TO RESTRAIN YOU. TO TAKE AWAY YOUR ABILITY TO ADJUST?
TO MAKE YOU HELPLESS, AND MAKE YOU FACE YOUR DESIRES GUILT-FREE.
HOW COULD IT BE YOUR FAULT? YOU ARE BOUND! THERE IS NOTHING YOU CAN DO, IS THERE?
HEH! IT DOES MAKE... A WEIRD KIND OF SENSE.
RIGHT!?
SO YOU CAN ONLY RELAX. GIVE IN TO YOUR LUST!
UNABLE TO DO ANYTHING...
MMNNNN...
BUT ENJOY!
OWWWWHHH...

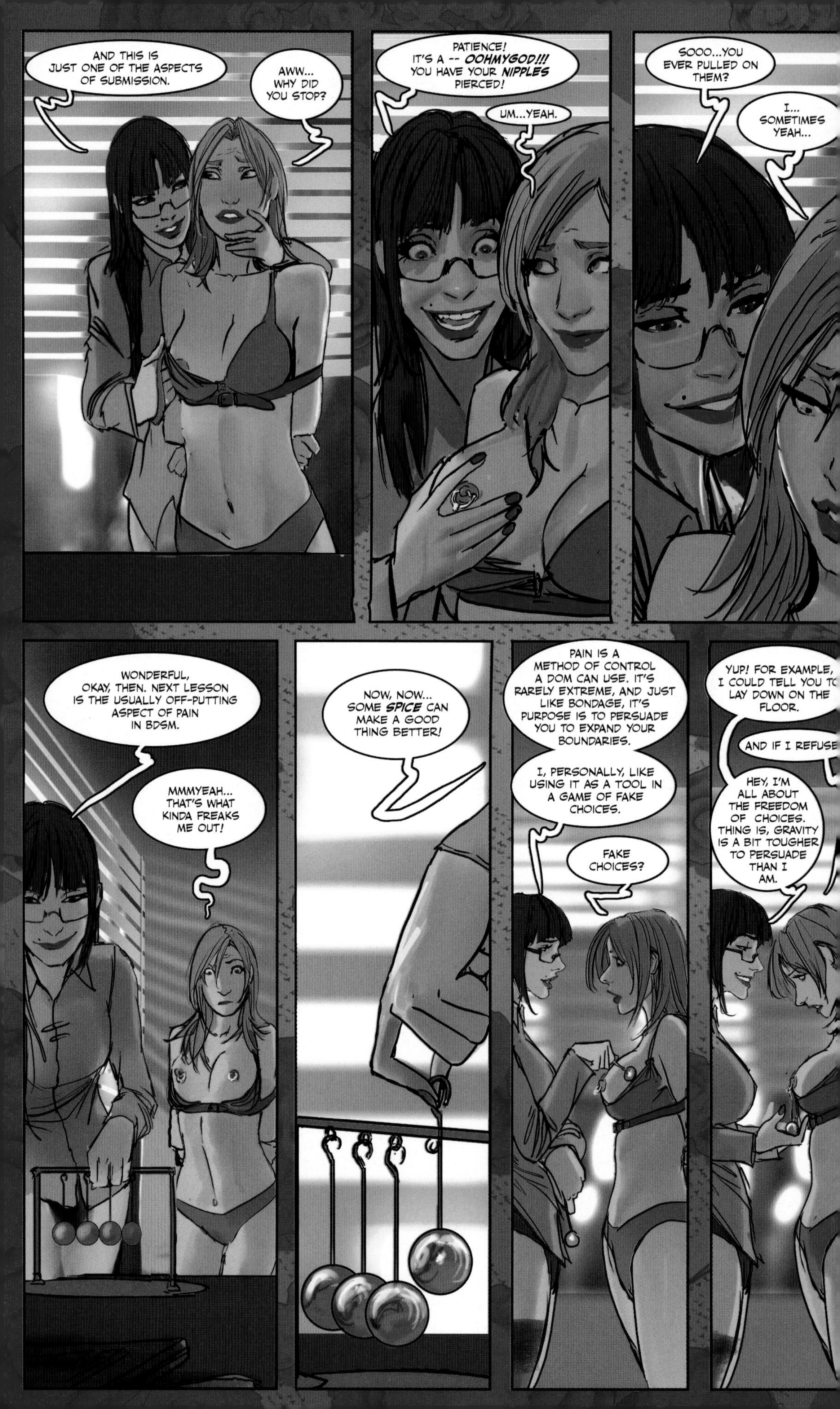

AND THIS IS JUST ONE OF THE ASPECTS OF SUBMISSION.
AWW... WHY DID YOU STOP?
PATIENCE! IT'S A -- OOHMYGOD!!! YOU HAVE YOUR NIPPLES PIERCED!
UM...YEAH.
SOOO...YOU EVER PULLED ON THEM?
I... SOMETIMES YEAH...
WONDERFUL, OKAY, THEN. NEXT LESSON IS THE USUALLY OFF-PUTTING ASPECT OF PAIN IN BDSM.
MMMYEAH... THAT'S WHAT KINDA FREAKS ME OUT!
NOW, NOW... SOME SPICE CAN MAKE A GOOD THING BETTER!
PAIN IS A METHOD OF CONTROL A DOM CAN USE. IT'S RARELY EXTREME, AND JUST LIKE BONDAGE, IT'S PURPOSE IS TO PERSUADE YOU TO EXPAND YOUR BOUNDARIES.
I, PERSONALLY, LIKE USING IT AS A TOOL IN A GAME OF FAKE CHOICES.
FAKE CHOICES?
YUP! FOR EXAMPLE, I COULD TELL YOU TO LAY DOWN ON THE FLOOR.
AND IF I REFUSE
HEY, I'M ALL ABOUT THE FREEDOM OF CHOICES. THING IS, GRAVITY IS A BIT TOUGHER TO PERSUADE THAN I AM.

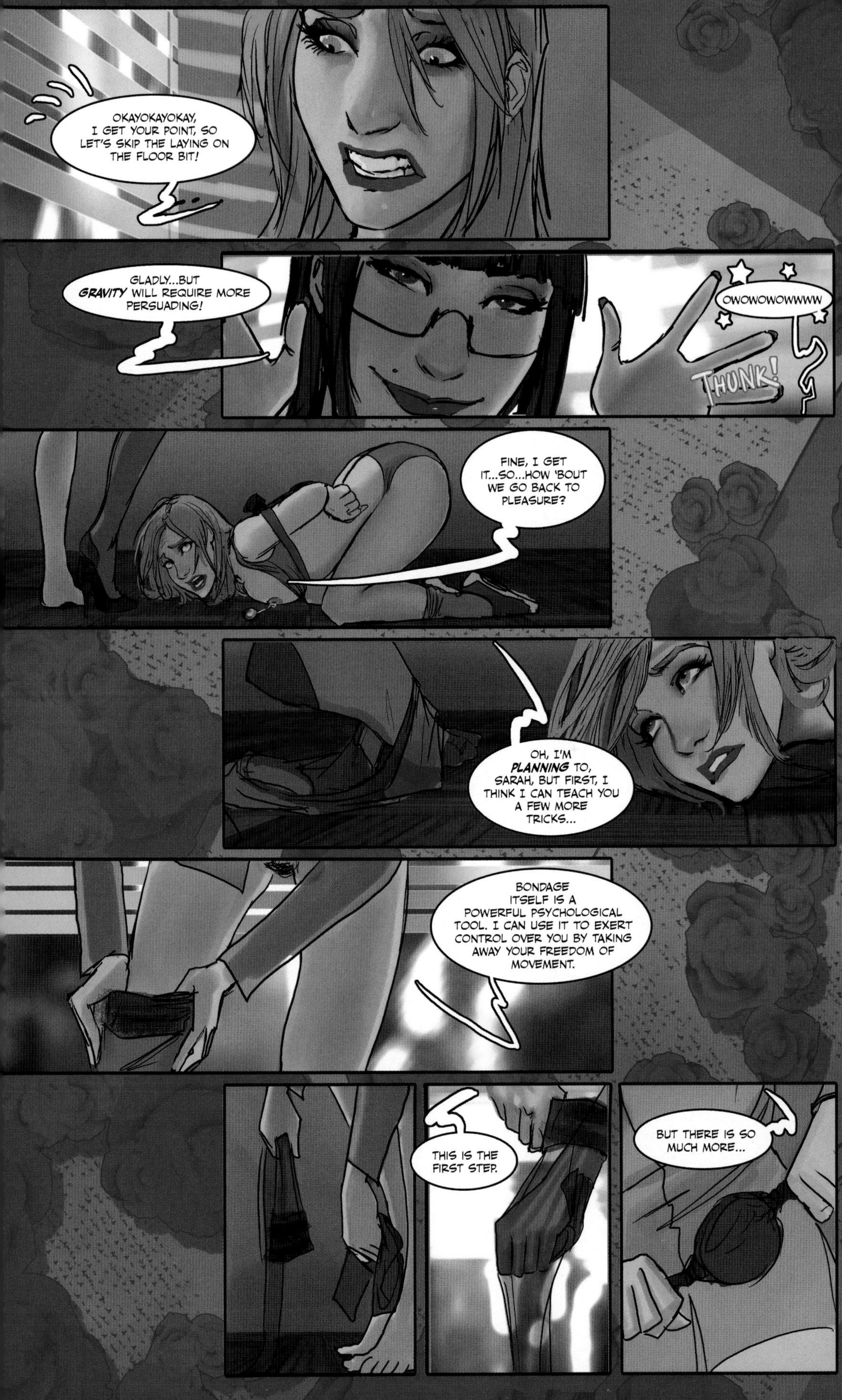
OKAYOKAYOKAY, I GET YOUR POINT, SO LET'S SKIP THE LAYING ON THE FLOOR BIT!
GLADLY...BUT GRAVITY WILL REQUIRE MORE PERSUADING!
THUNK!
OWOWOWOWWWW
FINE, I GET IT...SO...HOW 'BOUT WE GO BACK TO PLEASURE?
OH, I'M PLANNING TO, SARAH, BUT FIRST, I THINK I CAN TEACH YOU A FEW MORE TRICKS...
BONDAGE ITSELF IS A POWERFUL PSYCHOLOGICAL TOOL. I CAN USE IT TO EXERT CONTROL OVER YOU BY TAKING AWAY YOUR FREEDOM OF MOVEMENT.
THIS IS THE FIRST STEP.
BUT THERE IS SO MUCH MORE...

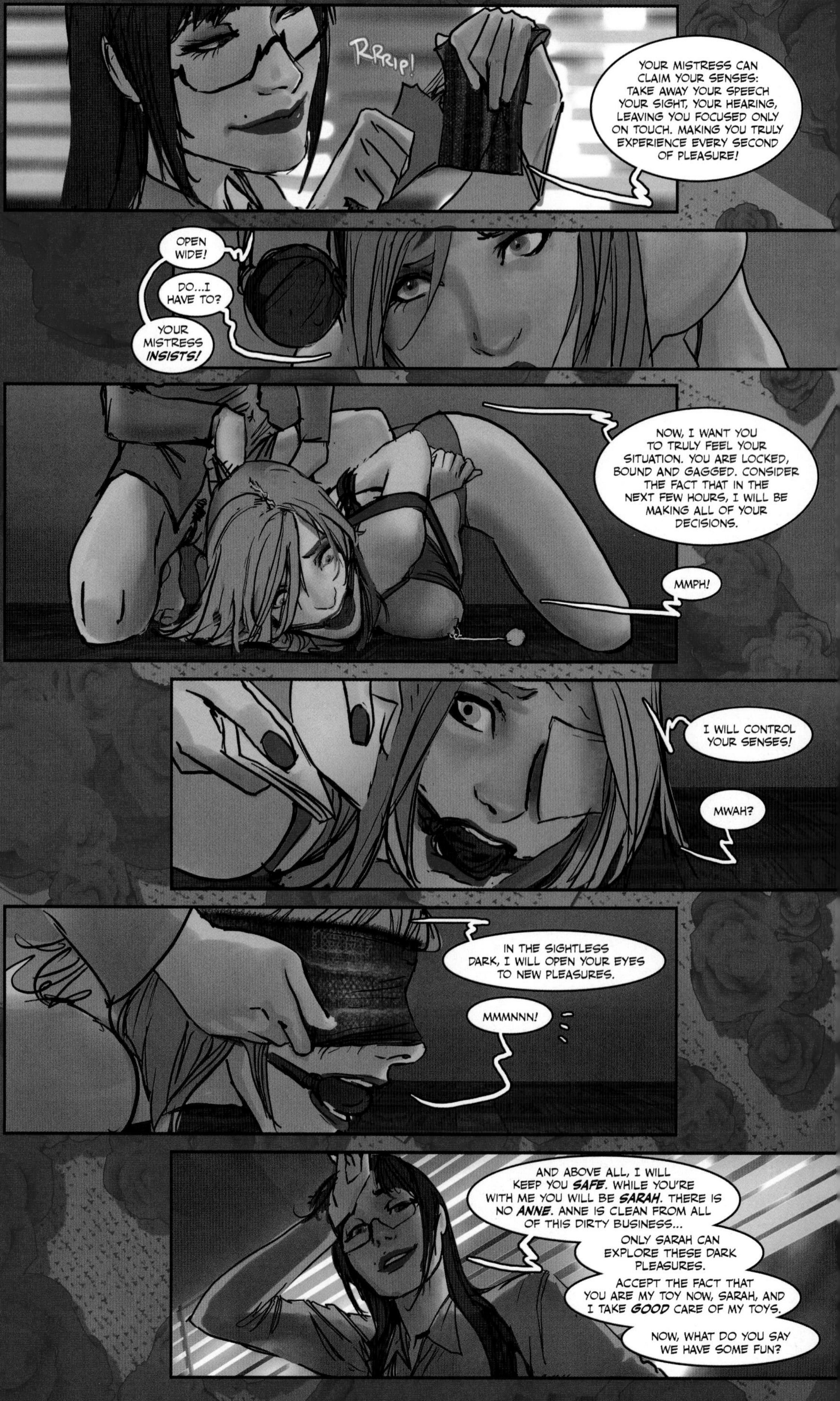
RRRIP!
YOUR MISTRESS CAN CLAIM YOUR SENSES: TAKE AWAY YOUR SPEECH YOUR SIGHT, YOUR HEARING, LEAVING YOU FOCUSED ONLY ON TOUCH. MAKING YOU TRULY EXPERIENCE EVERY SECOND OF PLEASURE!
OPEN WIDE!
DO...I HAVE TO?
YOUR MISTRESS INSISTS!
NOW, I WANT YOU TO TRULY FEEL YOUR SITUATION. YOU ARE LOCKED, BOUND AND GAGGED. CONSIDER THE FACT THAT IN THE NEXT FEW HOURS, I WILL BE MAKING ALL OF YOUR DECISIONS.
MMPH!
I WILL CONTROL YOUR SENSES!
MWAH?
IN THE SIGHTLESS DARK, I WILL OPEN YOUR EYES TO NEW PLEASURES.
MMMNNN!
AND ABOVE ALL, I WILL KEEP YOU SAFE. WHILE YOU'RE WITH ME YOU WILL BE SARAH. THERE IS NO ANNE. ANNE IS CLEAN FROM ALL OF THIS DIRTY BUSINESS...
ONLY SARAH CAN EXPLORE THESE DARK PLEASURES.
ACCEPT THE FACT THAT YOU ARE MY TOY NOW, SARAH, AND I TAKE GOOD CARE OF MY TOYS.
NOW, WHAT DO YOU SAY WE HAVE SOME FUN?

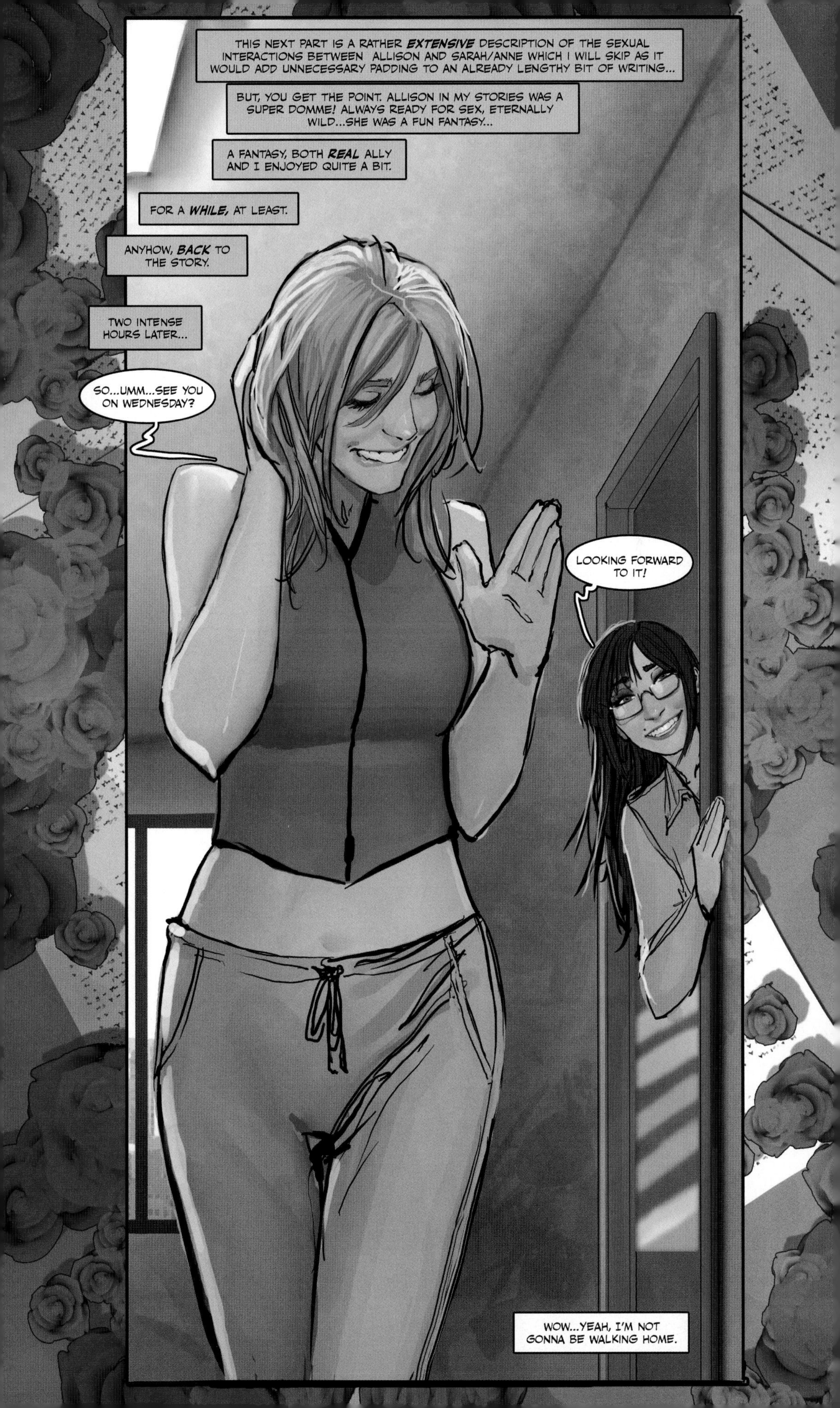
THIS NEXT PART IS A RATHER EXTENSIVE DESCRIPTION OF THE SEXUAL INTERACTIONS BETWEEN ALLISON AND SARAH/ANNE WHICH I WILL SKIP AS IT WOULD ADD UNNECESSARY PADDING TO AN ALREADY LENGTHY BIT OF WRITING...
BUT, YOU GET THE POINT. ALLISON IN MY STORIES WAS A SUPER DOMME! ALWAYS READY FOR SEX, ETERNALLY WILD...SHE WAS A FUN FANTASY...
A FANTASY, BOTH REAL ALLY AND I ENJOYED QUITE A BIT.
FOR A WHILE, AT LEAST.
ANYHOW, BACK TO THE STORY.
TWO INTENSE HOURS LATER...
SO...UMM...SEE YOU ON WEDNESDAY?
LOOKING FORWARD TO IT!
WOW...YEAH, I'M NOT GONNA BE WALKING HOME.

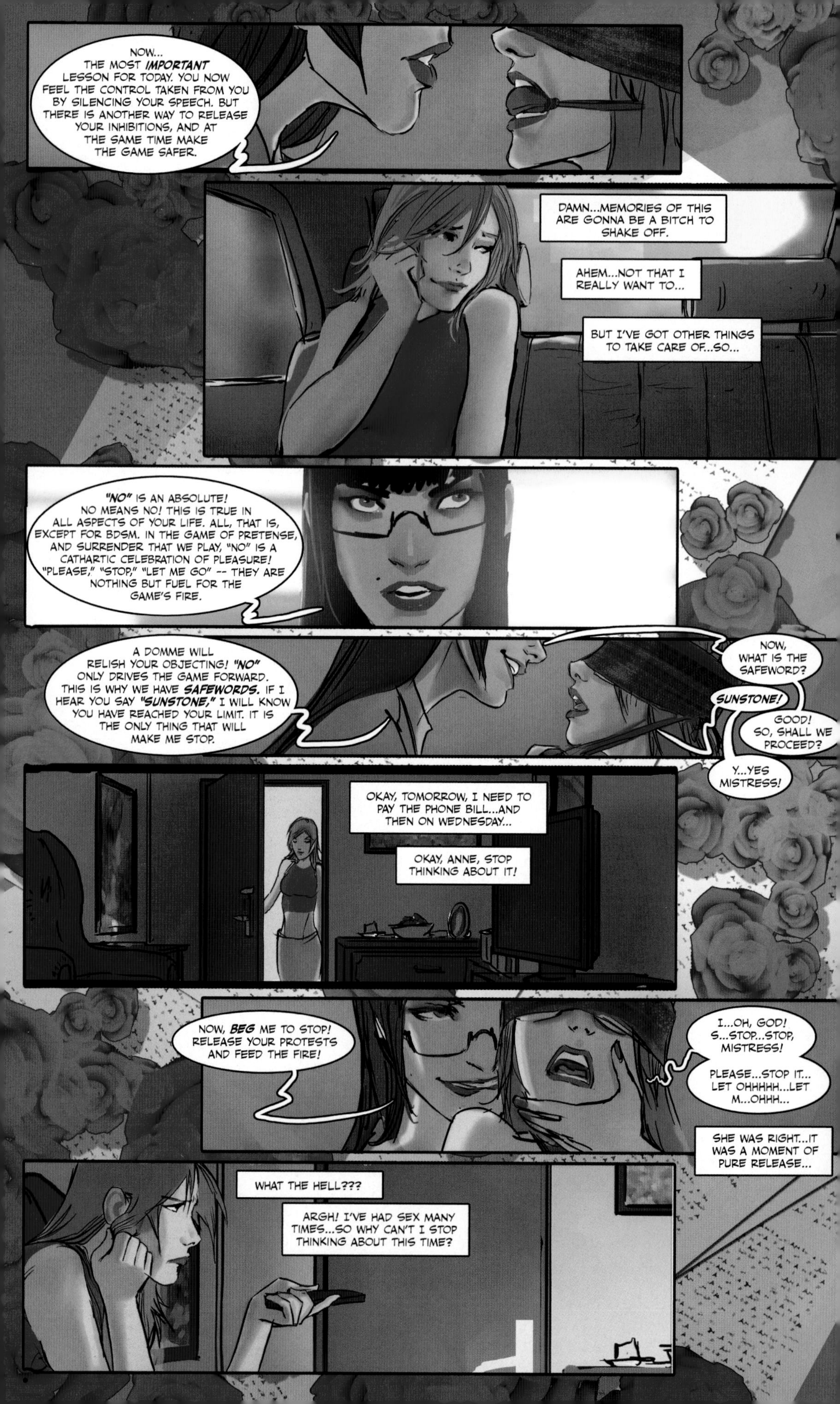
NOW... THE MOST *IMPORTANT* LESSON FOR TODAY. YOU NOW FEEL THE CONTROL TAKEN FROM YOU BY SILENCING YOUR SPEECH. BUT THERE IS ANOTHER WAY TO RELEASE YOUR INHIBITIONS, AND AT THE SAME TIME MAKE THE GAME SAFER.
DAMN...MEMORIES OF THIS ARE GONNA BE A BITCH TO SHAKE OFF.
AHEM...NOT THAT I REALLY WANT TO...
BUT I'VE GOT OTHER THINGS TO TAKE CARE OF...SO...
"NO" IS AN ABSOLUTE! NO MEANS NO! THIS IS TRUE IN ALL ASPECTS OF YOUR LIFE. ALL, THAT IS, EXCEPT FOR BDSM. IN THE GAME OF PRETENSE, AND SURRENDER THAT WE PLAY, "NO" IS A CATHARTIC CELEBRATION OF PLEASURE! "PLEASE," "STOP," "LET ME GO" -- THEY ARE NOTHING BUT FUEL FOR THE GAME'S FIRE.
A DOMME WILL RELISH YOUR OBJECTING! *"NO"* ONLY DRIVES THE GAME FORWARD. THIS IS WHY WE HAVE *SAFEWORDS.* IF I HEAR YOU SAY *"SUNSTONE,"* I WILL KNOW YOU HAVE REACHED YOUR LIMIT. IT IS THE ONLY THING THAT WILL MAKE ME STOP.
NOW, WHAT IS THE SAFEWORD?
SUNSTONE!
GOOD! SO, SHALL WE PROCEED?
Y...YES MISTRESS!
OKAY, TOMORROW, I NEED TO PAY THE PHONE BILL...AND THEN ON WEDNESDAY...
OKAY, ANNE, STOP THINKING ABOUT IT!
NOW, *BEG* ME TO STOP! RELEASE YOUR PROTESTS AND FEED THE FIRE!
I...OH, GOD! S...STOP...STOP, MISTRESS!
PLEASE...STOP IT... LET OHHHHH...LET M...OHHH...
SHE WAS RIGHT...IT WAS A MOMENT OF PURE RELEASE...
WHAT THE HELL???
ARGH! I'VE HAD SEX MANY TIMES...SO WHY CAN'T I STOP THINKING ABOUT THIS TIME?

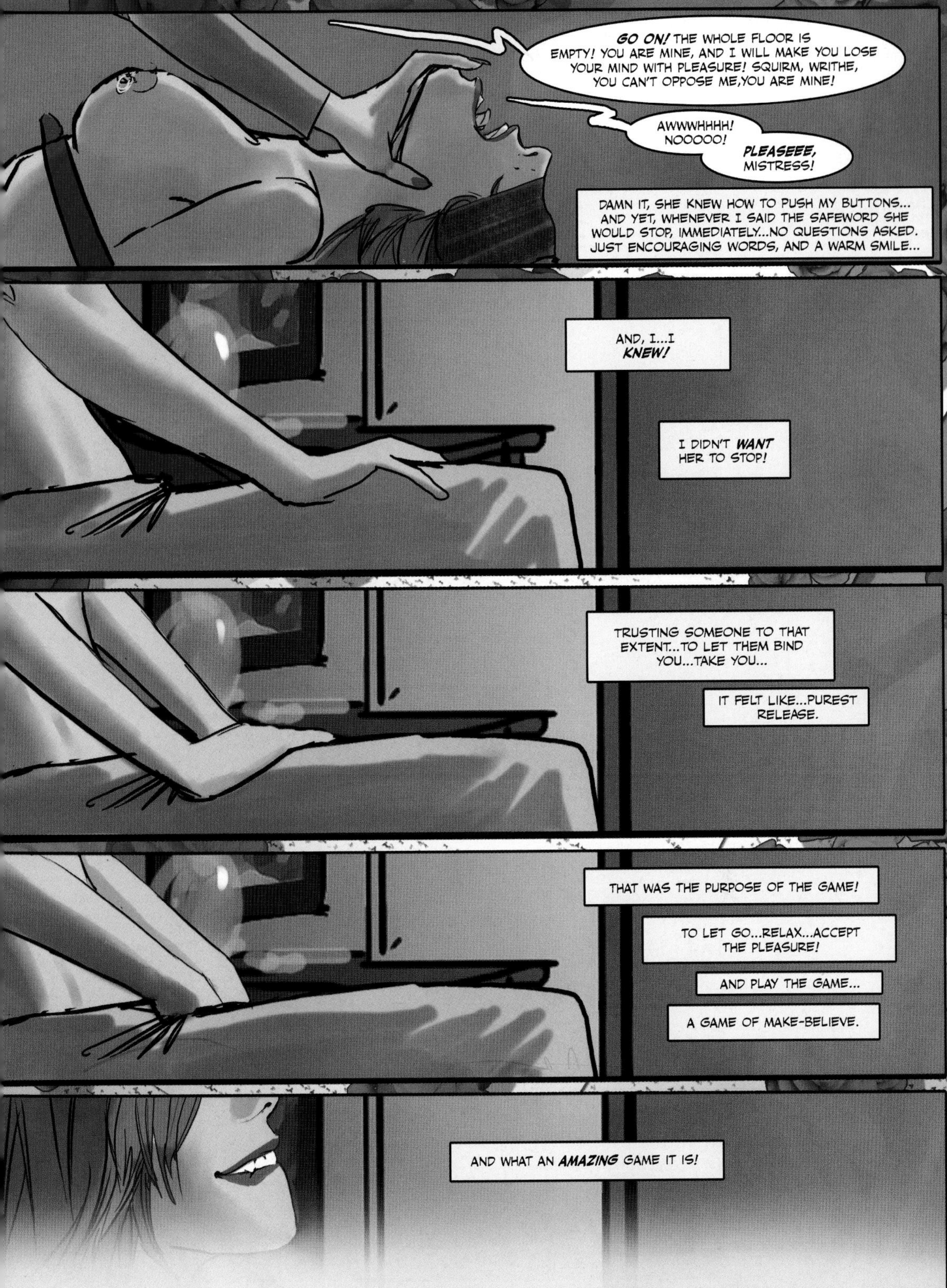
GO ON! THE WHOLE FLOOR IS EMPTY! YOU ARE MINE, AND I WILL MAKE YOU LOSE YOUR MIND WITH PLEASURE! SQUIRM, WRITHE, YOU CAN'T OPPOSE ME,YOU ARE MINE!
AWWWHHHH! NOOOOO! PLEASEEE, MISTRESS!
DAMN IT, SHE KNEW HOW TO PUSH MY BUTTONS... AND YET, WHENEVER I SAID THE SAFEWORD SHE WOULD STOP, IMMEDIATELY...NO QUESTIONS ASKED. JUST ENCOURAGING WORDS, AND A WARM SMILE...
AND, I...I KNEW!
I DIDN'T WANT HER TO STOP!
TRUSTING SOMEONE TO THAT EXTENT...TO LET THEM BIND YOU...TAKE YOU...
IT FELT LIKE...PUREST RELEASE.
THAT WAS THE PURPOSE OF THE GAME!
TO LET GO...RELAX...ACCEPT THE PLEASURE!
AND PLAY THE GAME...
A GAME OF MAKE-BELIEVE.
AND WHAT AN AMAZING GAME IT IS!

As her hands started mischievously moving in, Anne felt that warm sensation of sinking back into a wonderful world of secret pleasures.

At that moment, a small, still-rational part of her chuckled at the simple brilliance of Allison's idea of taking away her name. In a way, she was not the same person in these secret times of carnal release... Be it alone or with a partner, in these moments she was a wild, untamed creature of lust and desire.

Truth was...Allison hadn't taken her name. She had in fact given a name to that secret person she would become.

She was Sarah, and she was finally free.

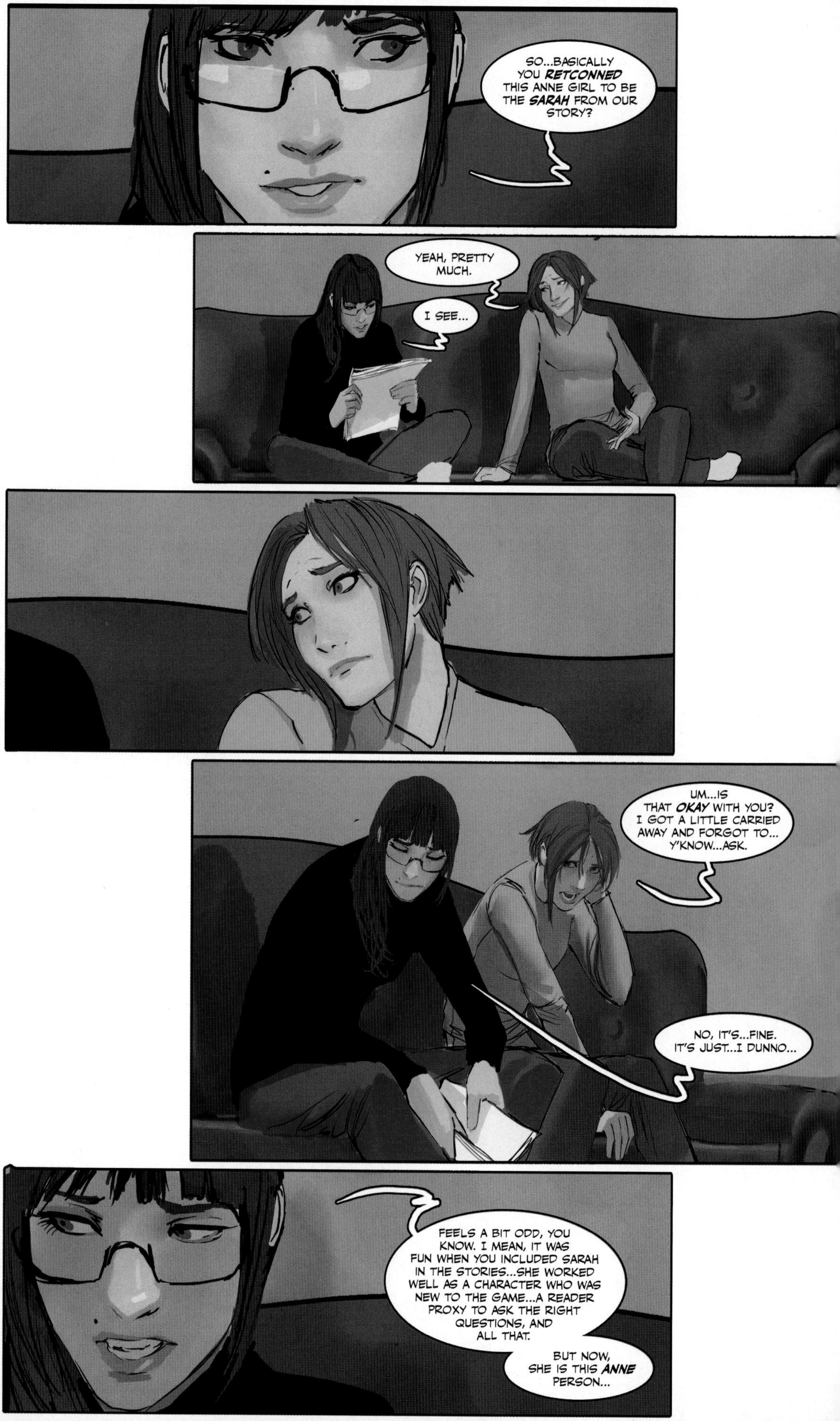
SO...BASICALLY YOU RETCONNED THIS ANNE GIRL TO BE THE SARAH FROM OUR STORY?
YEAH, PRETTY MUCH.
I SEE...
UM...IS THAT OKAY WITH YOU? I GOT A LITTLE CARRIED AWAY AND FORGOT TO... Y'KNOW...ASK.
NO, IT'S...FINE. IT'S JUST...I DUNNO...
FEELS A BIT ODD, YOU KNOW. I MEAN, IT WAS FUN WHEN YOU INCLUDED SARAH IN THE STORIES...SHE WORKED WELL AS A CHARACTER WHO WAS NEW TO THE GAME...A READER PROXY TO ASK THE RIGHT QUESTIONS, AND ALL THAT.
BUT NOW, SHE IS THIS ANNE PERSON...

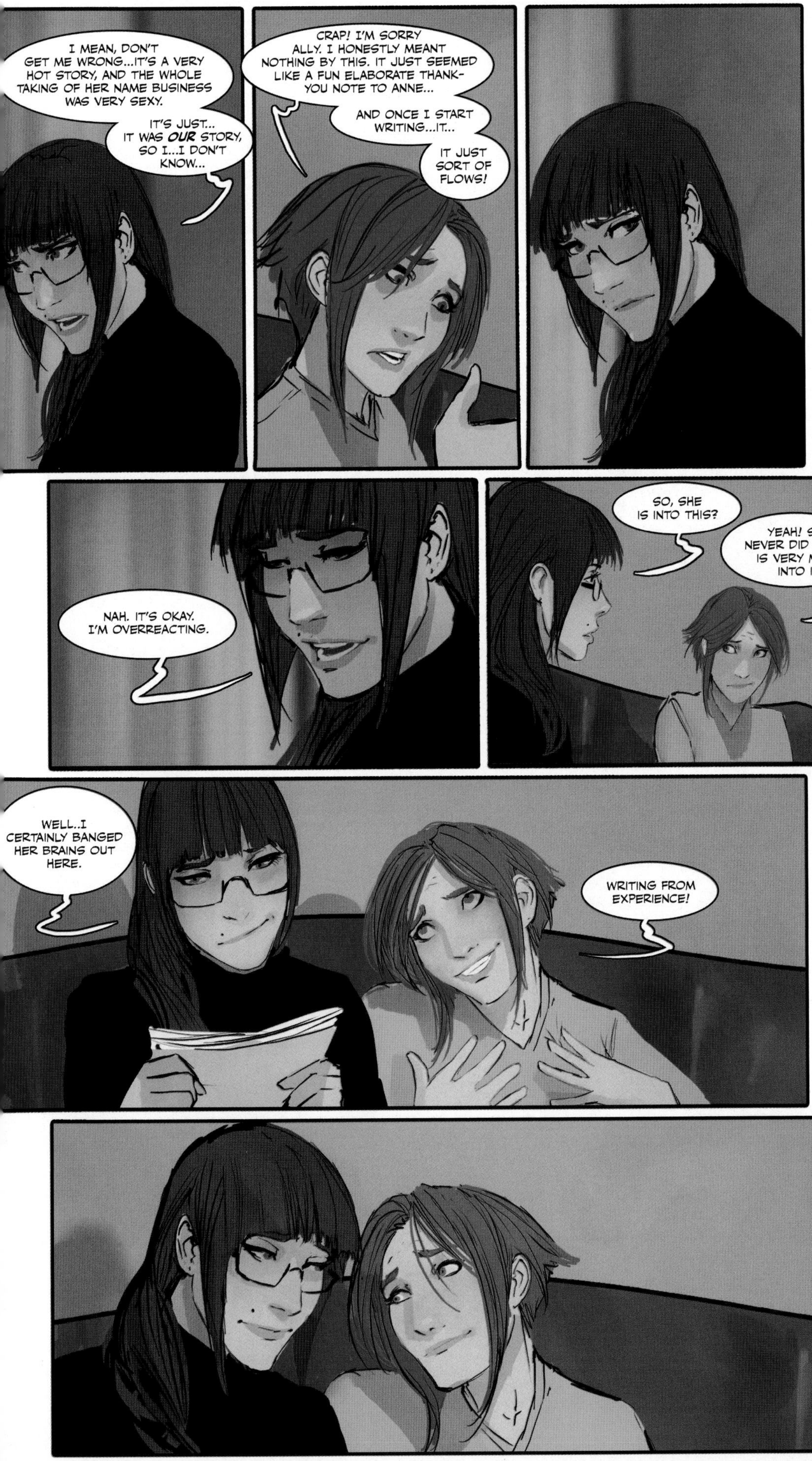
I MEAN, DON'T GET ME WRONG...IT'S A VERY HOT STORY, AND THE WHOLE TAKING OF HER NAME BUSINESS WAS VERY SEXY.
IT'S JUST... IT WAS *OUR* STORY, SO I...I DON'T KNOW...
CRAP! I'M SORRY ALLY. I HONESTLY MEANT NOTHING BY THIS. IT JUST SEEMED LIKE A FUN ELABORATE THANK-YOU NOTE TO ANNE...
AND ONCE I START WRITING...IT...
IT JUST SORT OF FLOWS!
NAH. IT'S OKAY. I'M OVERREACTING.
SO, SHE IS INTO THIS?
YEAH! SHE NEVER DID IT, BUT IS VERY MUCH INTO IT.
WELL..I CERTAINLY BANGED HER BRAINS OUT HERE.
WRITING FROM EXPERIENCE!

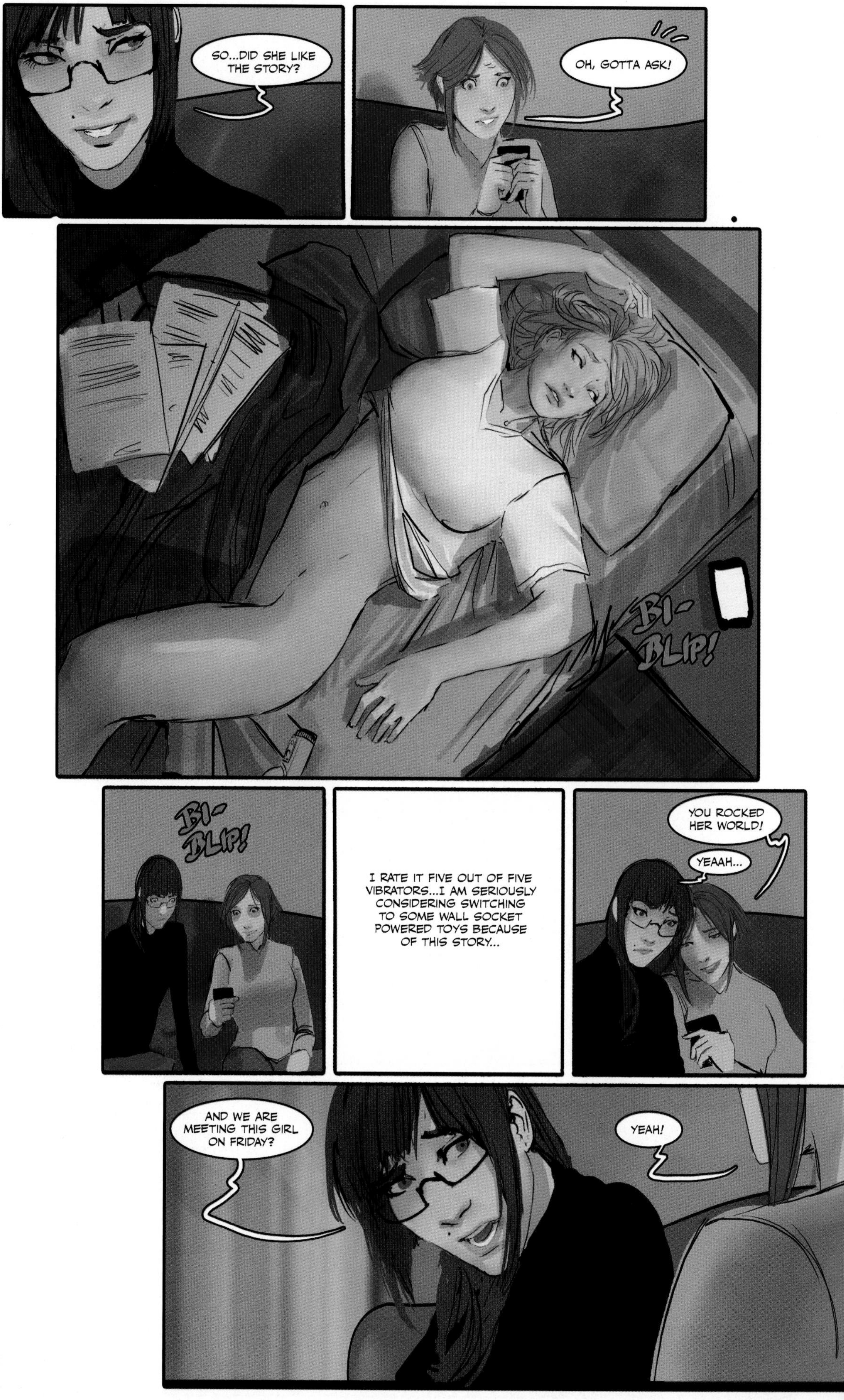
SO...DID SHE LIKE THE STORY?
OH, GOTTA ASK!
BI-BLIP!
BI-BLIP!
I RATE IT FIVE OUT OF FIVE VIBRATORS...I AM SERIOUSLY CONSIDERING SWITCHING TO SOME WALL SOCKET POWERED TOYS BECAUSE OF THIS STORY...
YOU ROCKED HER WORLD!
YEAAH...
AND WE ARE MEETING THIS GIRL ON FRIDAY?
YEAH!

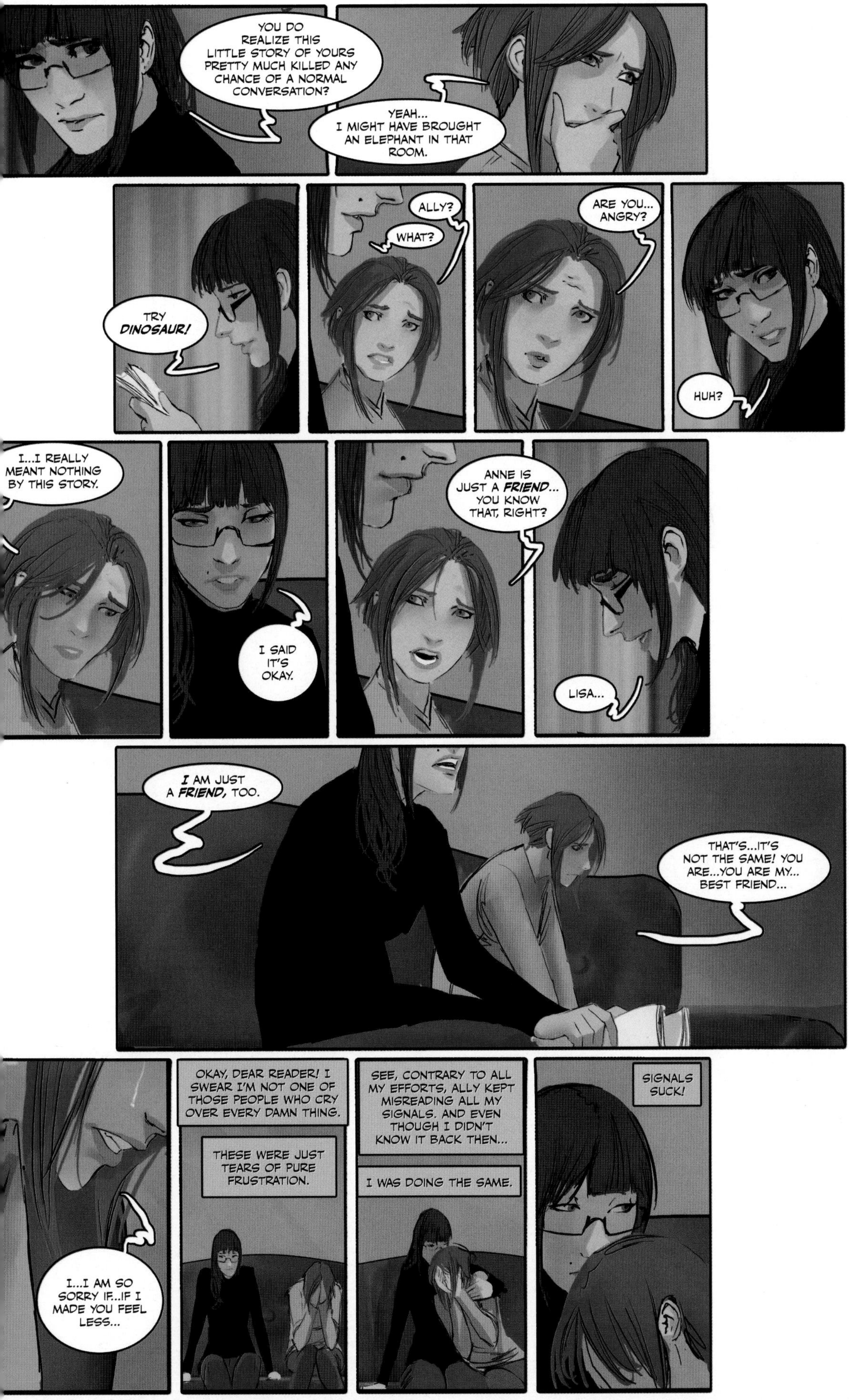
YOU DO REALIZE THIS LITTLE STORY OF YOURS PRETTY MUCH KILLED ANY CHANCE OF A NORMAL CONVERSATION?
YEAH... I MIGHT HAVE BROUGHT AN ELEPHANT IN THAT ROOM.
TRY DINOSAUR!
ALLY?
WHAT?
ARE YOU... ANGRY?
HUH?
I...I REALLY MEANT NOTHING BY THIS STORY.
I SAID IT'S OKAY.
ANNE IS JUST A FRIEND... YOU KNOW THAT, RIGHT?
LISA...
I AM JUST A FRIEND, TOO.
THAT'S...IT'S NOT THE SAME! YOU ARE...YOU ARE MY... BEST FRIEND...
I...I AM SO SORRY IF...IF I MADE YOU FEEL LESS...
OKAY, DEAR READER! I SWEAR I'M NOT ONE OF THOSE PEOPLE WHO CRY OVER EVERY DAMN THING.
THESE WERE JUST TEARS OF PURE FRUSTRATION.
SEE, CONTRARY TO ALL MY EFFORTS, ALLY KEPT MISREADING ALL MY SIGNALS. AND EVEN THOUGH I DIDN'T KNOW IT BACK THEN...
I WAS DOING THE SAME.
SIGNALS SUCK!

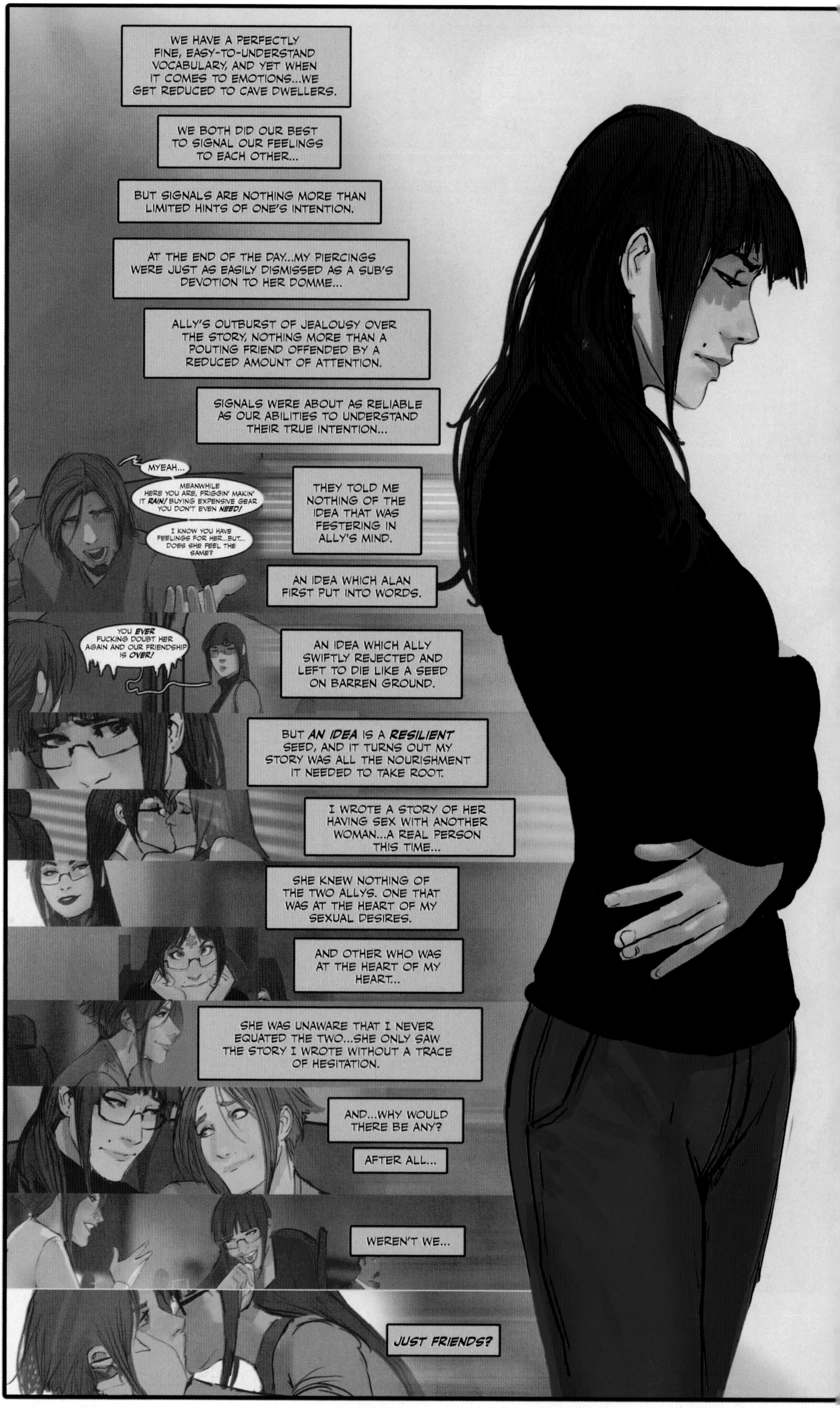
WE HAVE A PERFECTLY FINE, EASY-TO-UNDERSTAND VOCABULARY, AND YET WHEN IT COMES TO EMOTIONS...WE GET REDUCED TO CAVE DWELLERS.
WE BOTH DID OUR BEST TO SIGNAL OUR FEELINGS TO EACH OTHER...
BUT SIGNALS ARE NOTHING MORE THAN LIMITED HINTS OF ONE'S INTENTION.
AT THE END OF THE DAY...MY PIERCINGS WERE JUST AS EASILY DISMISSED AS A SUB'S DEVOTION TO HER DOMME...
ALLY'S OUTBURST OF JEALOUSY OVER THE STORY, NOTHING MORE THAN A POUTING FRIEND OFFENDED BY A REDUCED AMOUNT OF ATTENTION.
SIGNALS WERE ABOUT AS RELIABLE AS OUR ABILITIES TO UNDERSTAND THEIR TRUE INTENTION...
MYEAH...
MEANWHILE HERE YOU ARE, FRIGGIN' MAKIN' IT *RAIN!* BUYING EXPENSIVE GEAR YOU DON'T EVEN *NEED!*
I KNOW YOU HAVE FEELINGS FOR HER...BUT... DOES SHE FEEL THE SAME?
THEY TOLD ME NOTHING OF THE IDEA THAT WAS FESTERING IN ALLY'S MIND.
AN IDEA WHICH ALAN FIRST PUT INTO WORDS.
YOU *EVER* FUCKING DOUBT HER AGAIN AND OUR FRIENDSHIP IS *OVER!*
AN IDEA WHICH ALLY SWIFTLY REJECTED AND LEFT TO DIE LIKE A SEED ON BARREN GROUND.
BUT ***AN IDEA*** IS A ***RESILIENT*** SEED, AND IT TURNS OUT MY STORY WAS ALL THE NOURISHMENT IT NEEDED TO TAKE ROOT.
I WROTE A STORY OF HER HAVING SEX WITH ANOTHER WOMAN...A REAL PERSON THIS TIME...
SHE KNEW NOTHING OF THE TWO ALLYS. ONE THAT WAS AT THE HEART OF MY SEXUAL DESIRES.
AND OTHER WHO WAS AT THE HEART OF MY HEART...
SHE WAS UNAWARE THAT I NEVER EQUATED THE TWO...SHE ONLY SAW THE STORY I WROTE WITHOUT A TRACE OF HESITATION.
AND...WHY WOULD THERE BE ANY?
AFTER ALL...
WEREN'T WE...
JUST FRIENDS?

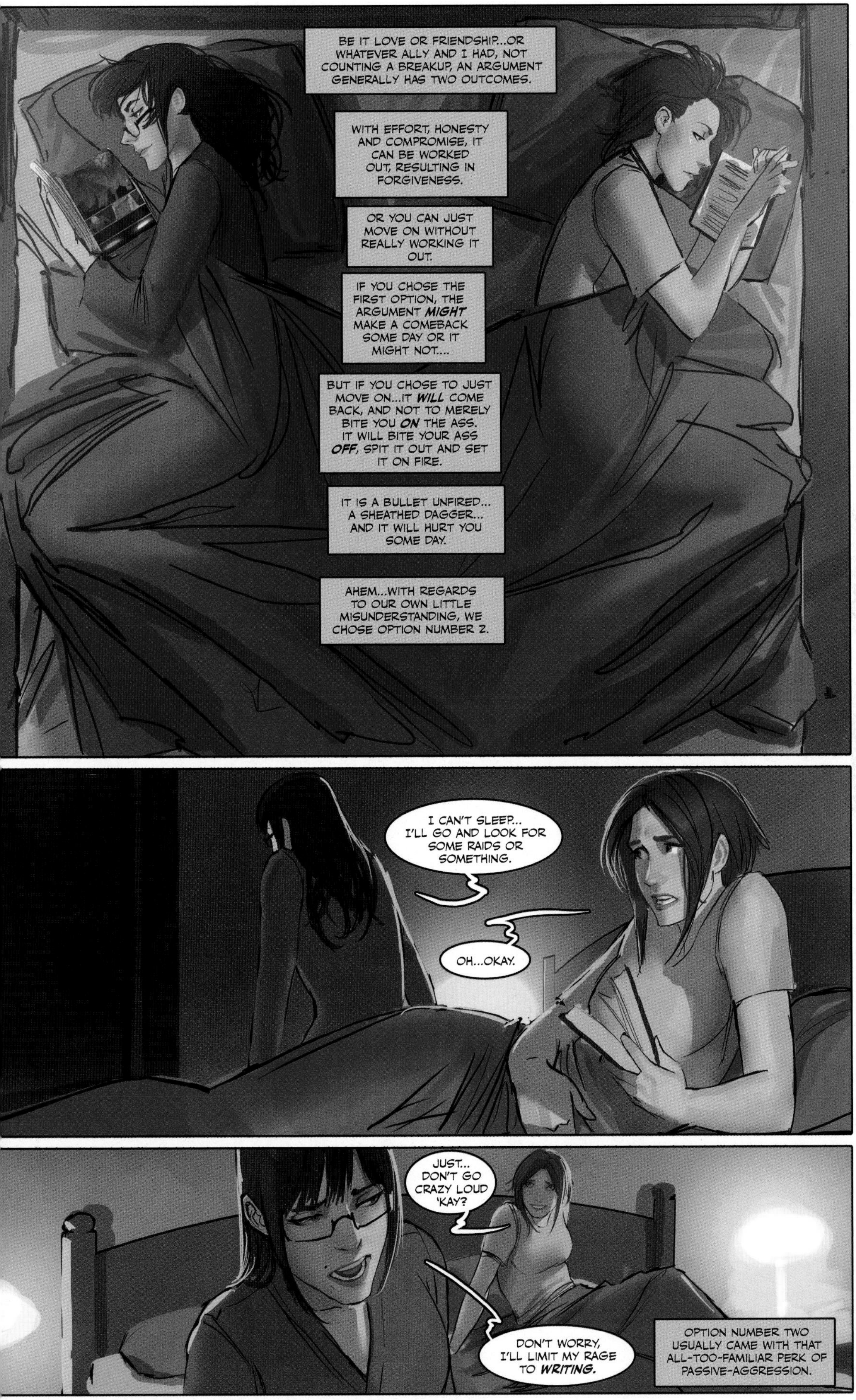
BE IT LOVE OR FRIENDSHIP...OR WHATEVER ALLY AND I HAD, NOT COUNTING A BREAKUP, AN ARGUMENT GENERALLY HAS TWO OUTCOMES.
WITH EFFORT, HONESTY AND COMPROMISE, IT CAN BE WORKED OUT, RESULTING IN FORGIVENESS.
OR YOU CAN JUST MOVE ON WITHOUT REALLY WORKING IT OUT.
IF YOU CHOSE THE FIRST OPTION, THE ARGUMENT *MIGHT* MAKE A COMEBACK SOME DAY OR IT MIGHT NOT....
BUT IF YOU CHOSE TO JUST MOVE ON...IT *WILL* COME BACK, AND NOT TO MERELY BITE YOU *ON* THE ASS. IT WILL BITE YOUR ASS *OFF*, SPIT IT OUT AND SET IT ON FIRE.
IT IS A BULLET UNFIRED... A SHEATHED DAGGER... AND IT WILL HURT YOU SOME DAY.
AHEM...WITH REGARDS TO OUR OWN LITTLE MISUNDERSTANDING, WE CHOSE OPTION NUMBER 2.
I CAN'T SLEEP... I'LL GO AND LOOK FOR SOME RAIDS OR SOMETHING.
OH...OKAY.
JUST... DON'T GO CRAZY LOUD 'KAY?
DON'T WORRY, I'LL LIMIT MY RAGE TO *WRITING.*
OPTION NUMBER TWO USUALLY CAME WITH THAT ALL-TOO-FAMILIAR PERK OF PASSIVE-AGGRESSION.

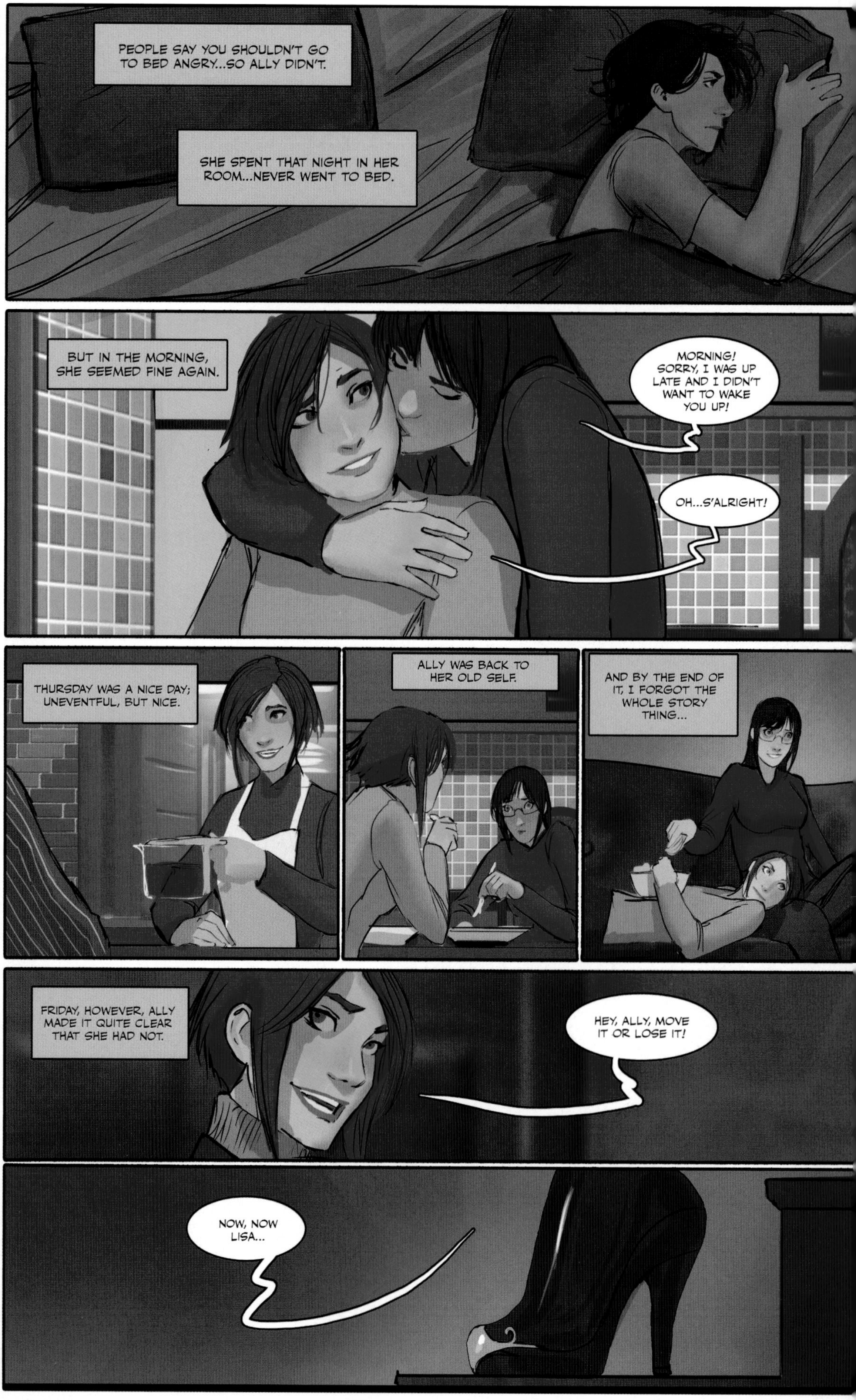
PEOPLE SAY YOU SHOULDN'T GO TO BED ANGRY...SO ALLY DIDN'T.
SHE SPENT THAT NIGHT IN HER ROOM...NEVER WENT TO BED.
BUT IN THE MORNING, SHE SEEMED FINE AGAIN.
MORNING! SORRY, I WAS UP LATE AND I DIDN'T WANT TO WAKE YOU UP!
OH...S'ALRIGHT!
THURSDAY WAS A NICE DAY; UNEVENTFUL, BUT NICE.
ALLY WAS BACK TO HER OLD SELF.
AND BY THE END OF IT, I FORGOT THE WHOLE STORY THING...
FRIDAY, HOWEVER, ALLY MADE IT QUITE CLEAR THAT SHE HAD NOT.
HEY, ALLY, MOVE IT OR LOSE IT!
NOW, NOW LISA...

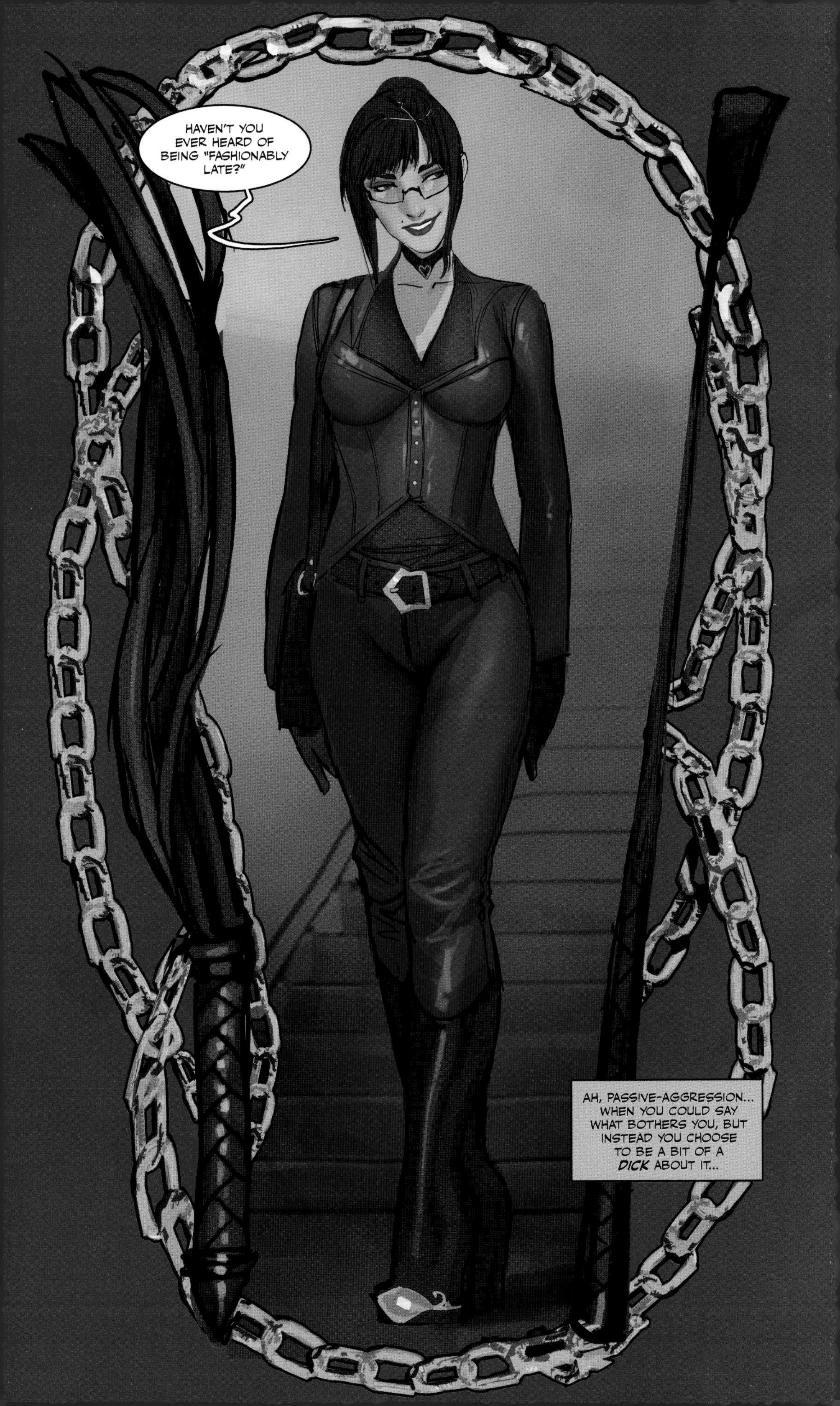

HAVEN'T YOU EVER HEARD OF BEING "FASHIONABLY LATE?"
AH, PASSIVE-AGGRESSION... WHEN YOU COULD SAY WHAT BOTHERS YOU, BUT INSTEAD YOU CHOOSE TO BE A BIT OF A DICK ABOUT IT...

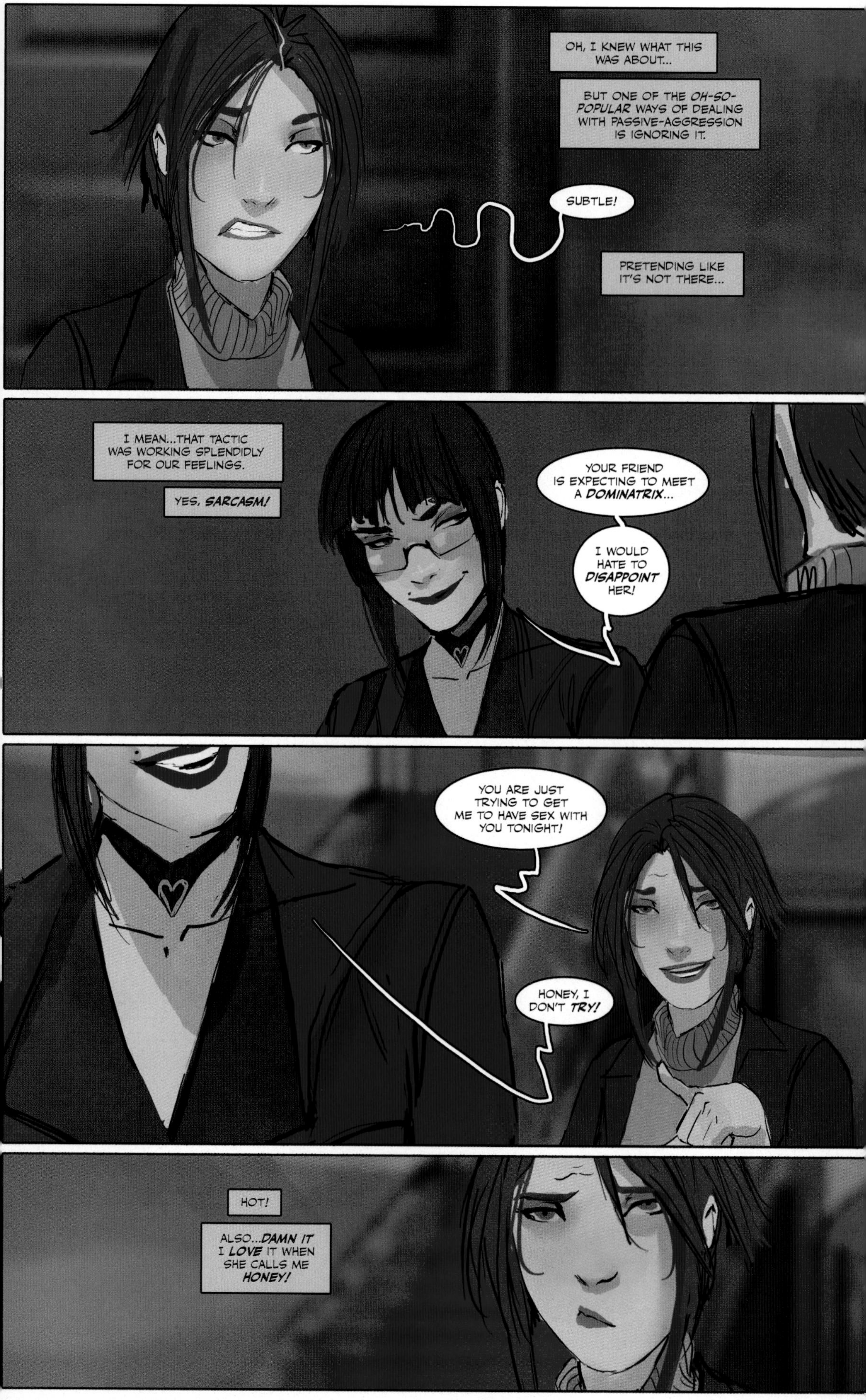
OH, I KNEW WHAT THIS WAS ABOUT...
BUT ONE OF THE *OH-SO-POPULAR* WAYS OF DEALING WITH PASSIVE-AGGRESSION IS IGNORING IT.
SUBTLE!
PRETENDING LIKE IT'S NOT THERE...
I MEAN...THAT TACTIC WAS WORKING SPLENDIDLY FOR OUR FEELINGS.
YES, ***SARCASM!***
YOUR FRIEND IS EXPECTING TO MEET A ***DOMINATRIX***...
I WOULD HATE TO ***DISAPPOINT*** HER!
YOU ARE JUST TRYING TO GET ME TO HAVE SEX WITH YOU TONIGHT!
HONEY, I DON'T ***TRY!***
HOT!
ALSO...***DAMN IT*** I ***LOVE*** IT WHEN SHE CALLS ME ***HONEY!***

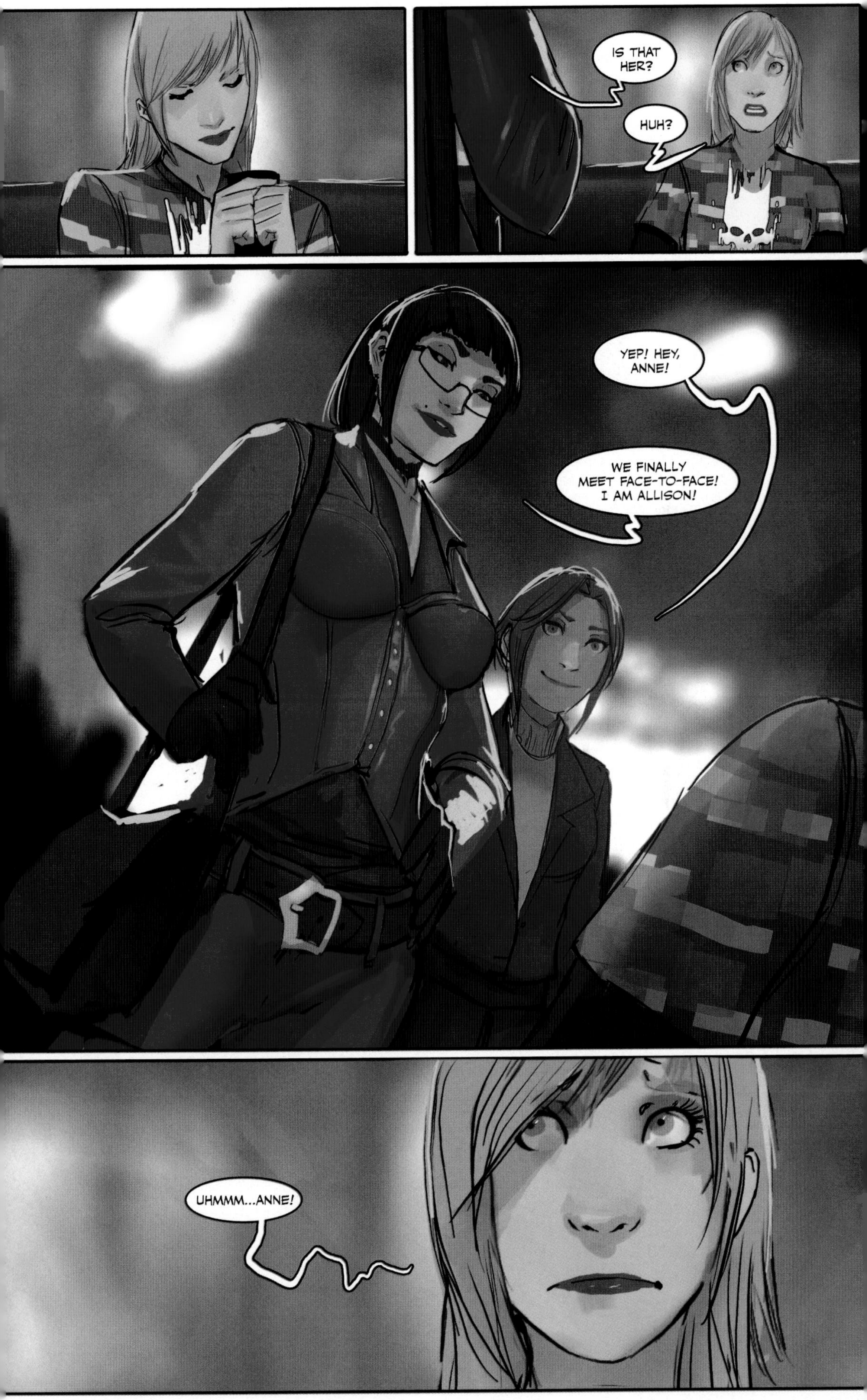
IS THAT HER?
HUH?
YEP! HEY, ANNE!
WE FINALLY MEET FACE-TO-FACE! I AM ALLISON!
UHMMM...ANNE!

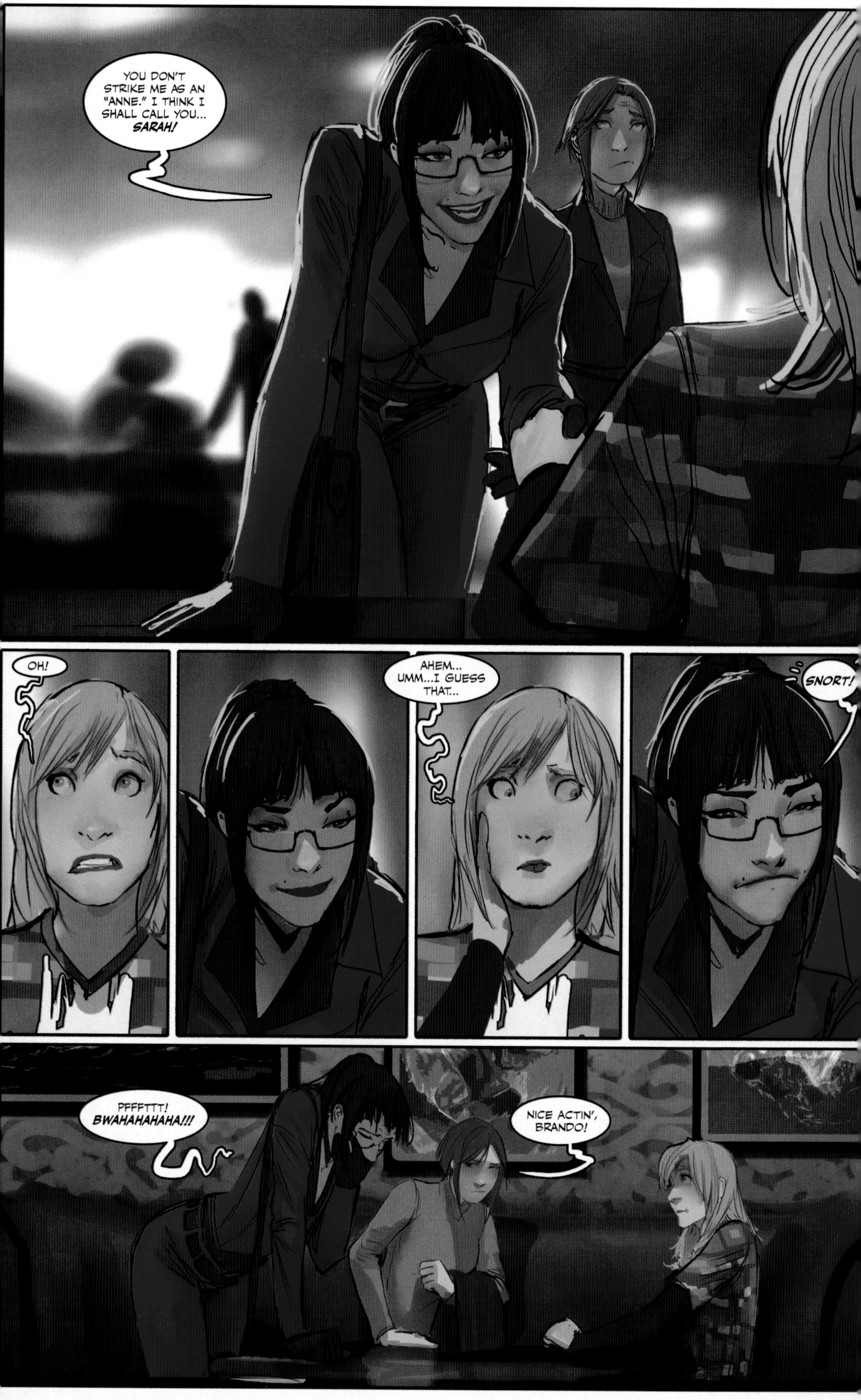
YOU DON'T STRIKE ME AS AN "ANNE." I THINK I SHALL CALL YOU... SARAH!
OH!
AHEM... UMM...I GUESS THAT...
SNORT!
PFFFTTT! BWAHAHAHAHA!!!
NICE ACTIN', BRANDO!

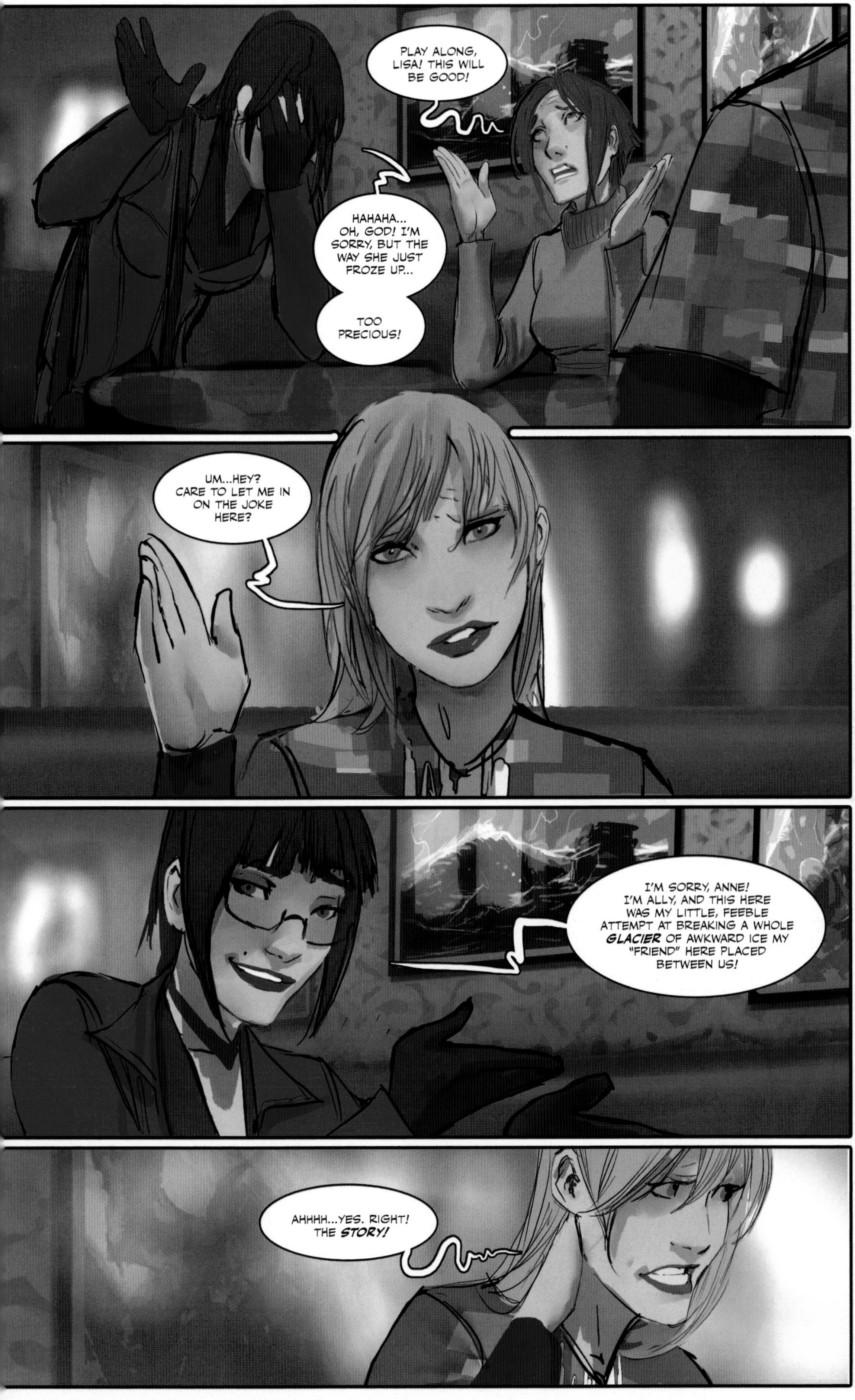
PLAY ALONG, LISA! THIS WILL BE GOOD!
HAHAHA... OH, GOD! I'M SORRY, BUT THE WAY SHE JUST FROZE UP...
TOO PRECIOUS!
UM...HEY? CARE TO LET ME IN ON THE JOKE HERE?
I'M SORRY, ANNE! I'M ALLY, AND THIS HERE WAS MY LITTLE, FEEBLE ATTEMPT AT BREAKING A WHOLE GLACIER OF AWKWARD ICE MY "FRIEND" HERE PLACED BETWEEN US!
AHHHH...YES. RIGHT! THE STORY!

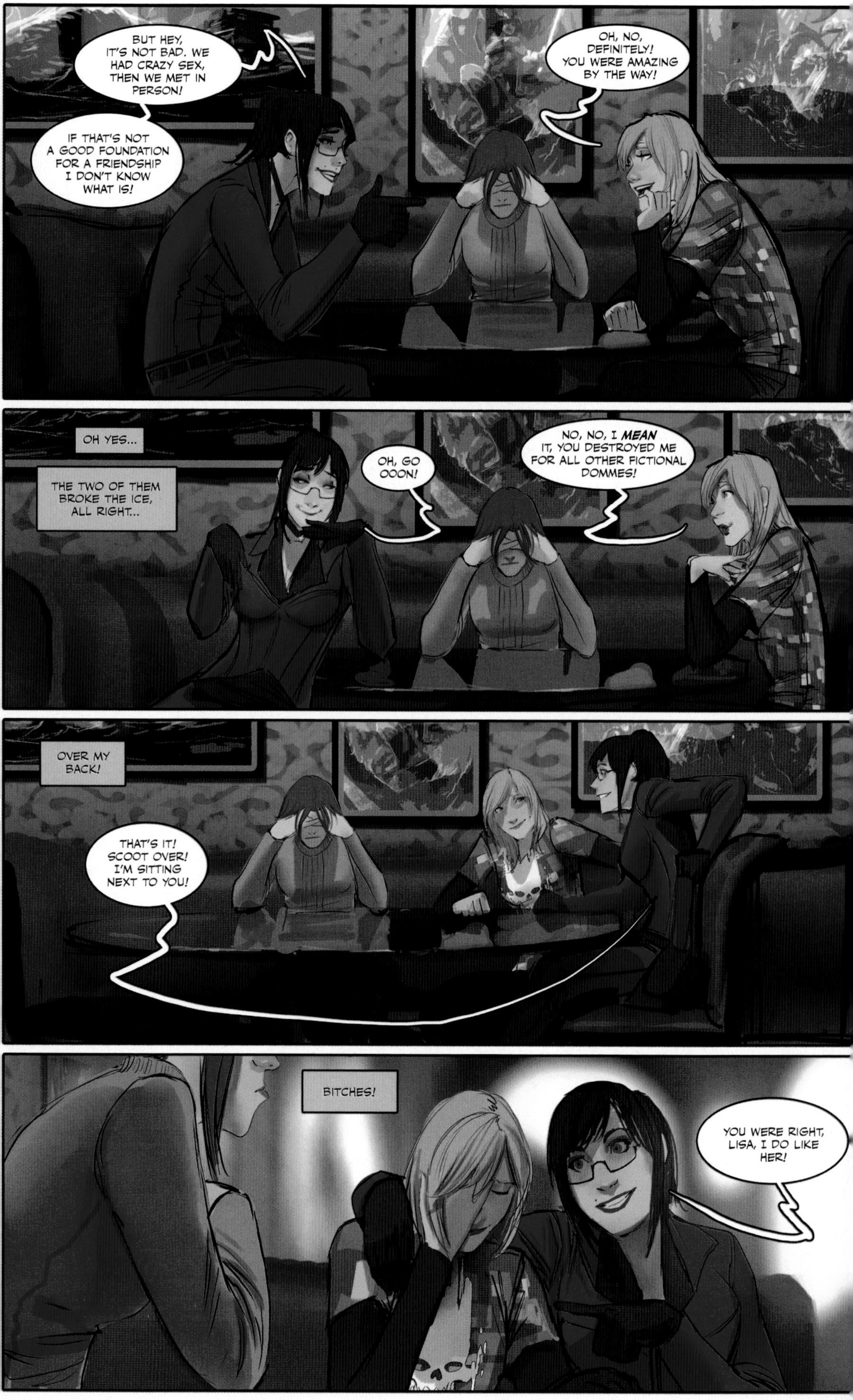
BUT HEY, IT'S NOT BAD. WE HAD CRAZY SEX, THEN WE MET IN PERSON!
IF THAT'S NOT A GOOD FOUNDATION FOR A FRIENDSHIP I DON'T KNOW WHAT IS!
OH, NO, DEFINITELY! YOU WERE AMAZING BY THE WAY!
OH YES...
THE TWO OF THEM BROKE THE ICE, ALL RIGHT...
OH, GO OOON!
NO, NO, I *MEAN* IT, YOU DESTROYED ME FOR ALL OTHER FICTIONAL DOMMES!
OVER MY BACK!
THAT'S IT! SCOOT OVER! I'M SITTING NEXT TO YOU!
BITCHES!
YOU WERE RIGHT, LISA, I DO LIKE HER!

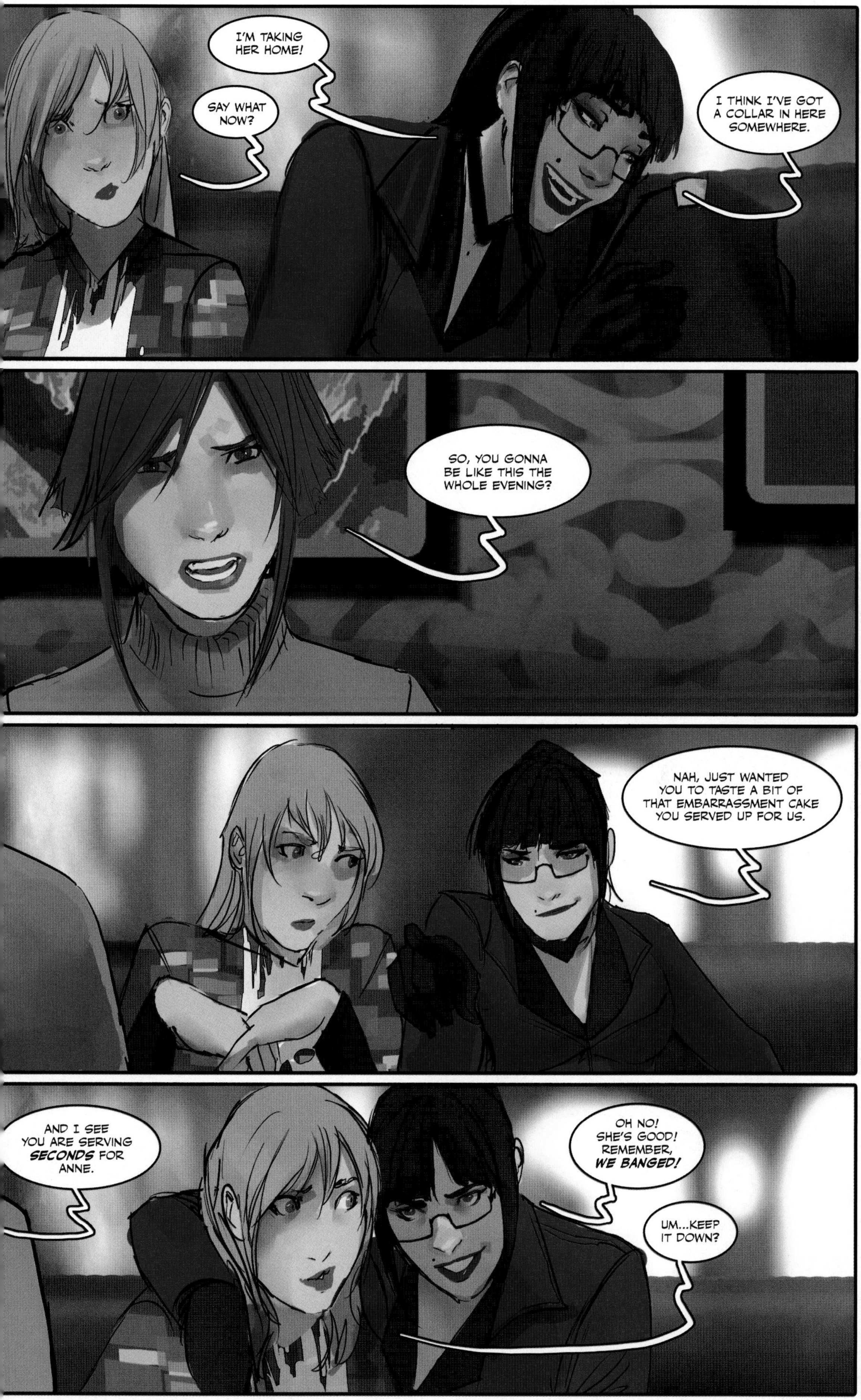
I'M TAKING HER HOME!
SAY WHAT NOW?
I THINK I'VE GOT A COLLAR IN HERE SOMEWHERE.
SO, YOU GONNA BE LIKE THIS THE WHOLE EVENING?
NAH, JUST WANTED YOU TO TASTE A BIT OF THAT EMBARRASSMENT CAKE YOU SERVED UP FOR US.
AND I SEE YOU ARE SERVING *SECONDS* FOR ANNE.
OH NO! SHE'S GOOD! REMEMBER, *WE BANGED!*
UM...KEEP IT DOWN?

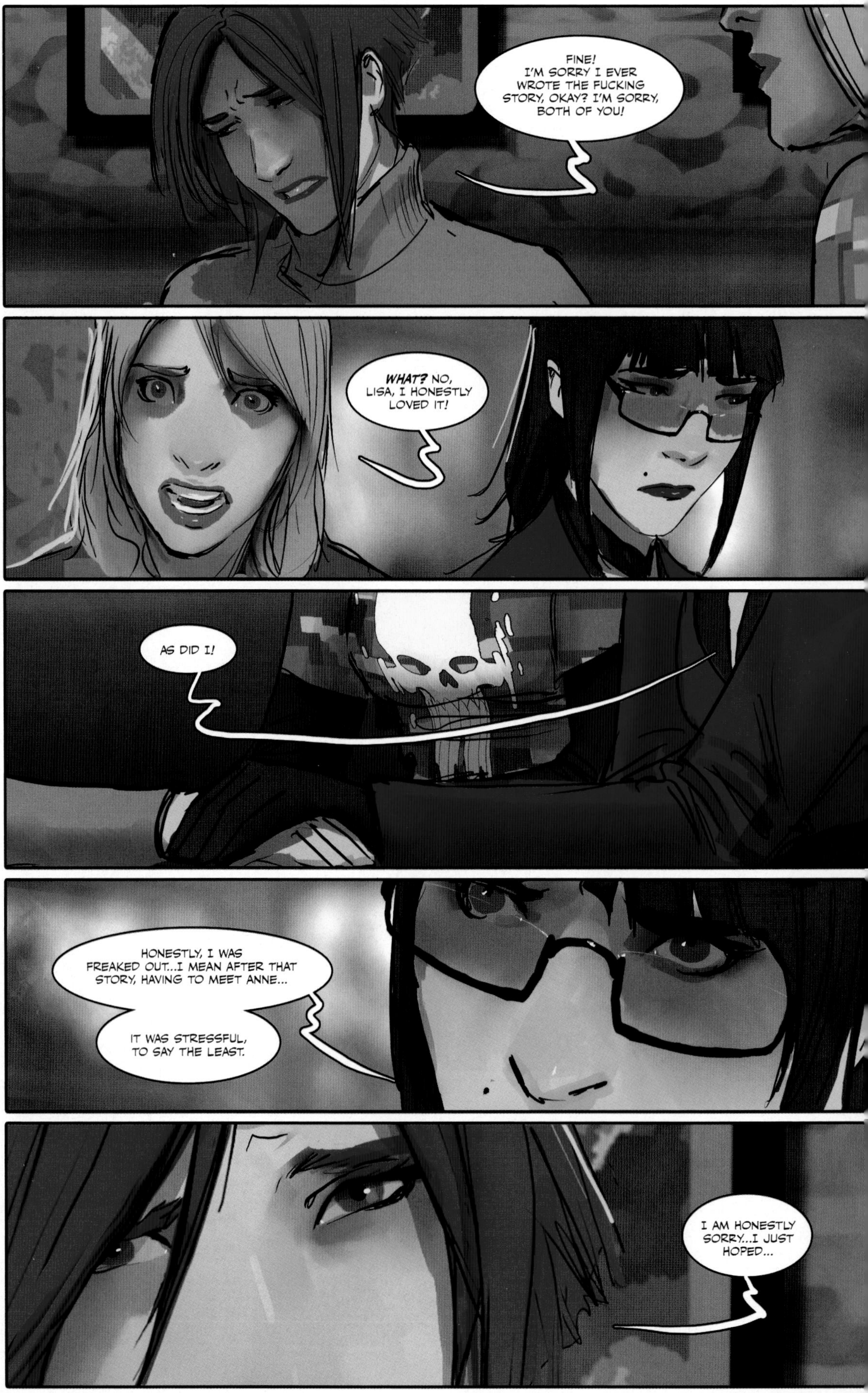
FINE! I'M SORRY I EVER WROTE THE FUCKING STORY, OKAY? I'M SORRY, BOTH OF YOU!
WHAT? NO, LISA, I HONESTLY LOVED IT!
AS DID I!
HONESTLY, I WAS FREAKED OUT...I MEAN AFTER THAT STORY, HAVING TO MEET ANNE...
IT WAS STRESSFUL, TO SAY THE LEAST.
I AM HONESTLY SORRY...I JUST HOPED...

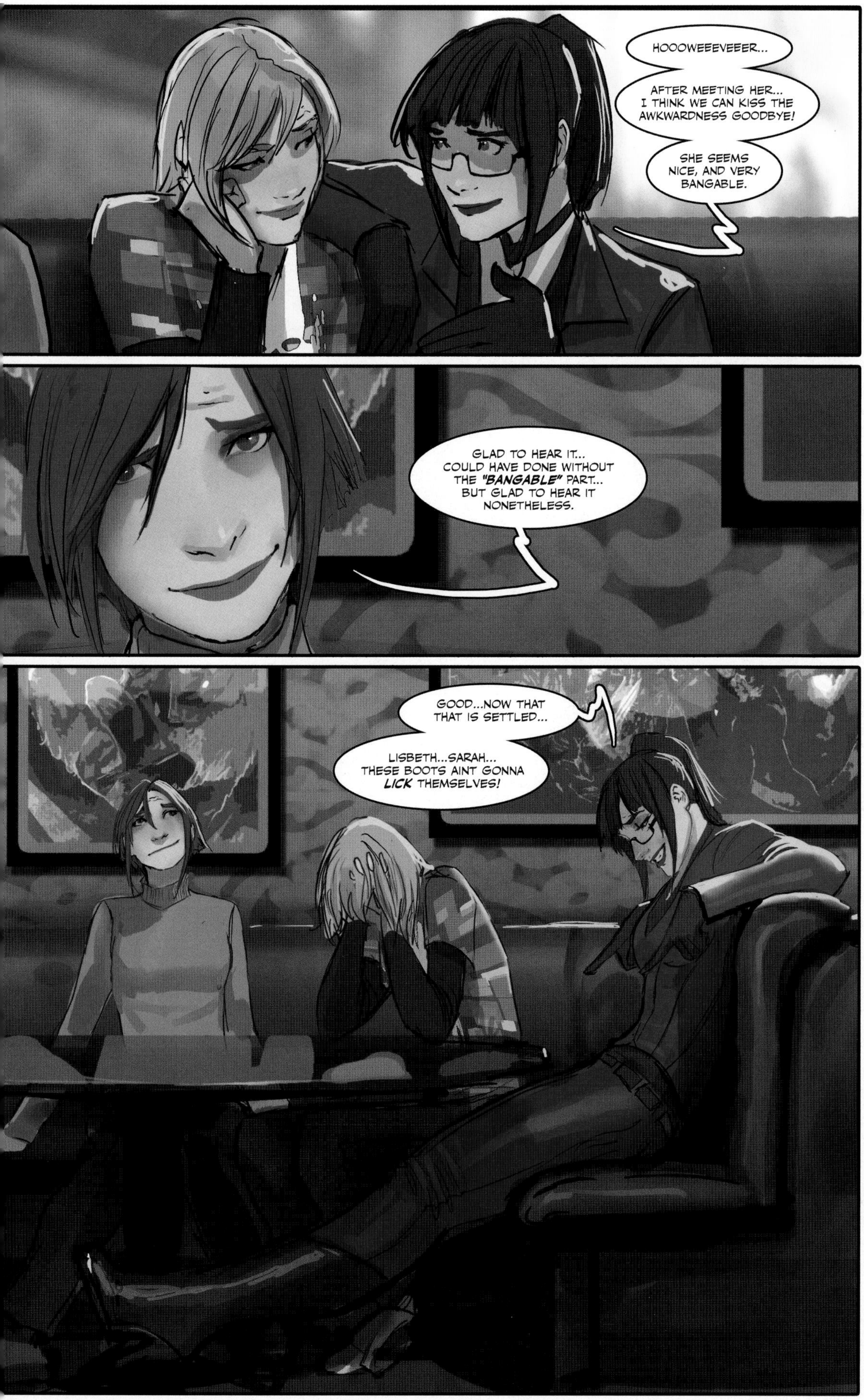
HOOOWEEEVEEER...
AFTER MEETING HER... I THINK WE CAN KISS THE AWKWARDNESS GOODBYE!
SHE SEEMS NICE, AND VERY BANGABLE.
GLAD TO HEAR IT... COULD HAVE DONE WITHOUT THE "BANGABLE" PART... BUT GLAD TO HEAR IT NONETHELESS.
GOOD...NOW THAT THAT IS SETTLED...
LISBETH...SARAH... THESE BOOTS AINT GONNA LICK THEMSELVES!

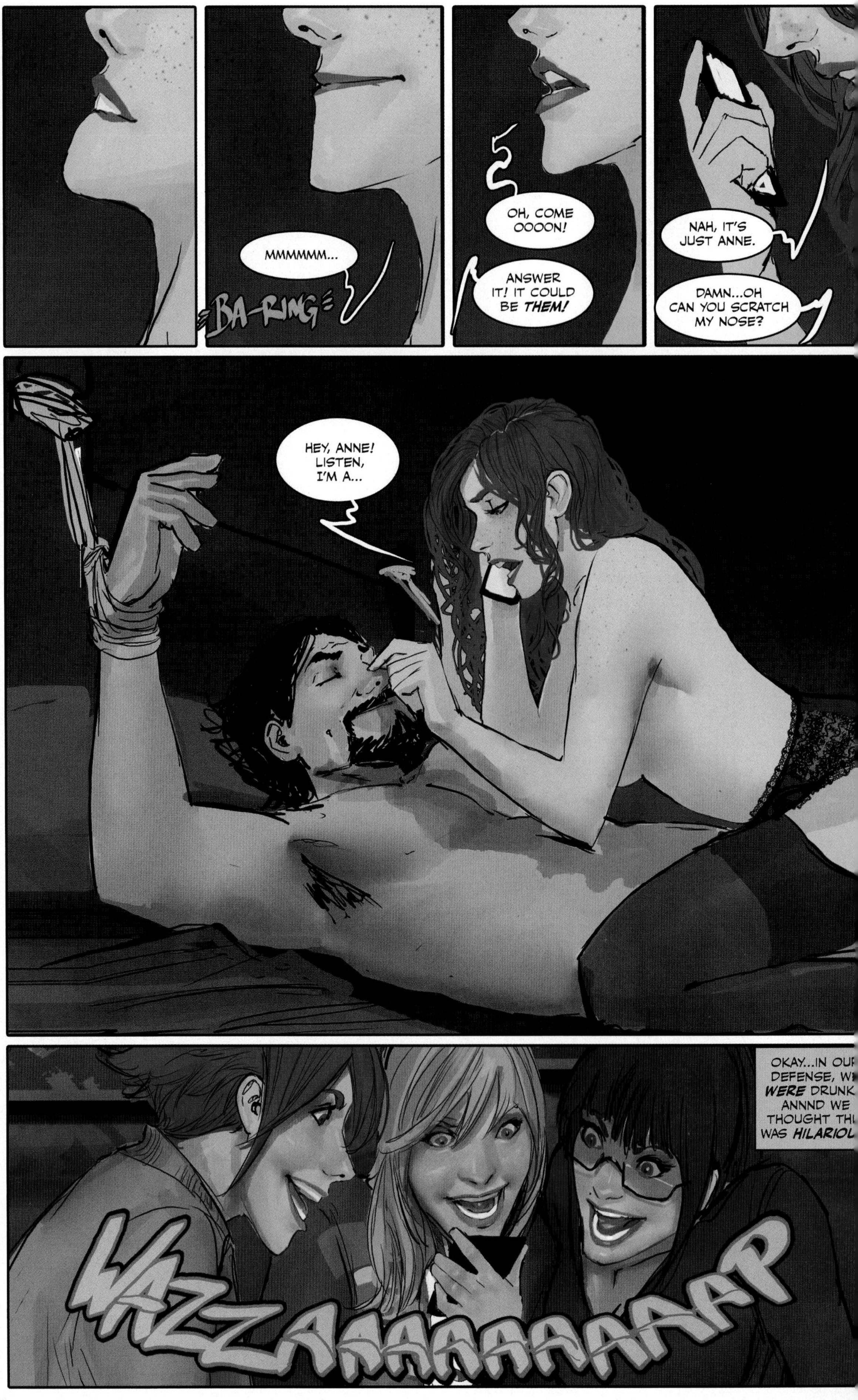
MMMMMM...
BA-RING
OH, COME OOOON!
ANSWER IT! IT COULD BE *THEM!*
NAH, IT'S JUST ANNE.
DAMN...OH CAN YOU SCRATCH MY NOSE?
HEY, ANNE! LISTEN, I'M A...
OKAY...IN OU
DEFENSE, W
WERE DRUNK
ANNND WE
THOUGHT THI
WAS *HILARIOU*
WAZZAAAAAAAAAP

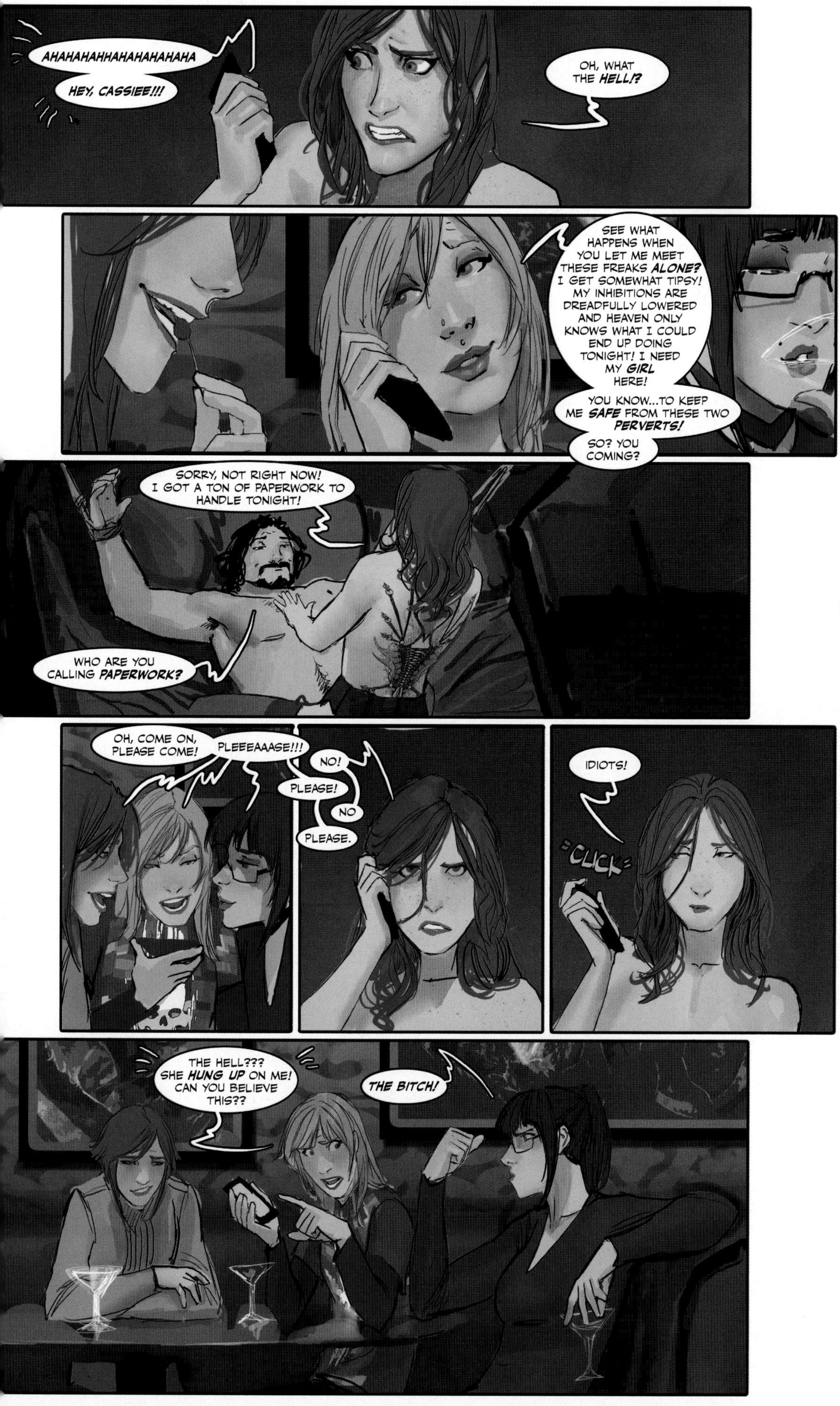
AHAHAHAHHAHAHAHAHAHA
HEY, CASSIEE!!!
OH, WHAT THE HELL!?
SEE WHAT HAPPENS WHEN YOU LET ME MEET THESE FREAKS ALONE? I GET SOMEWHAT TIPSY! MY INHIBITIONS ARE DREADFULLY LOWERED AND HEAVEN ONLY KNOWS WHAT I COULD END UP DOING TONIGHT! I NEED MY GIRL HERE!
YOU KNOW...TO KEEP ME SAFE FROM THESE TWO PERVERTS!
SO? YOU COMING?
SORRY, NOT RIGHT NOW! I GOT A TON OF PAPERWORK TO HANDLE TONIGHT!
WHO ARE YOU CALLING PAPERWORK?
OH, COME ON, PLEASE COME!
PLEEEAAAASE!!!
NO!
PLEASE!
NO
PLEASE.
IDIOTS!
CLICK
THE HELL??? SHE HUNG UP ON ME! CAN YOU BELIEVE THIS??
THE BITCH!

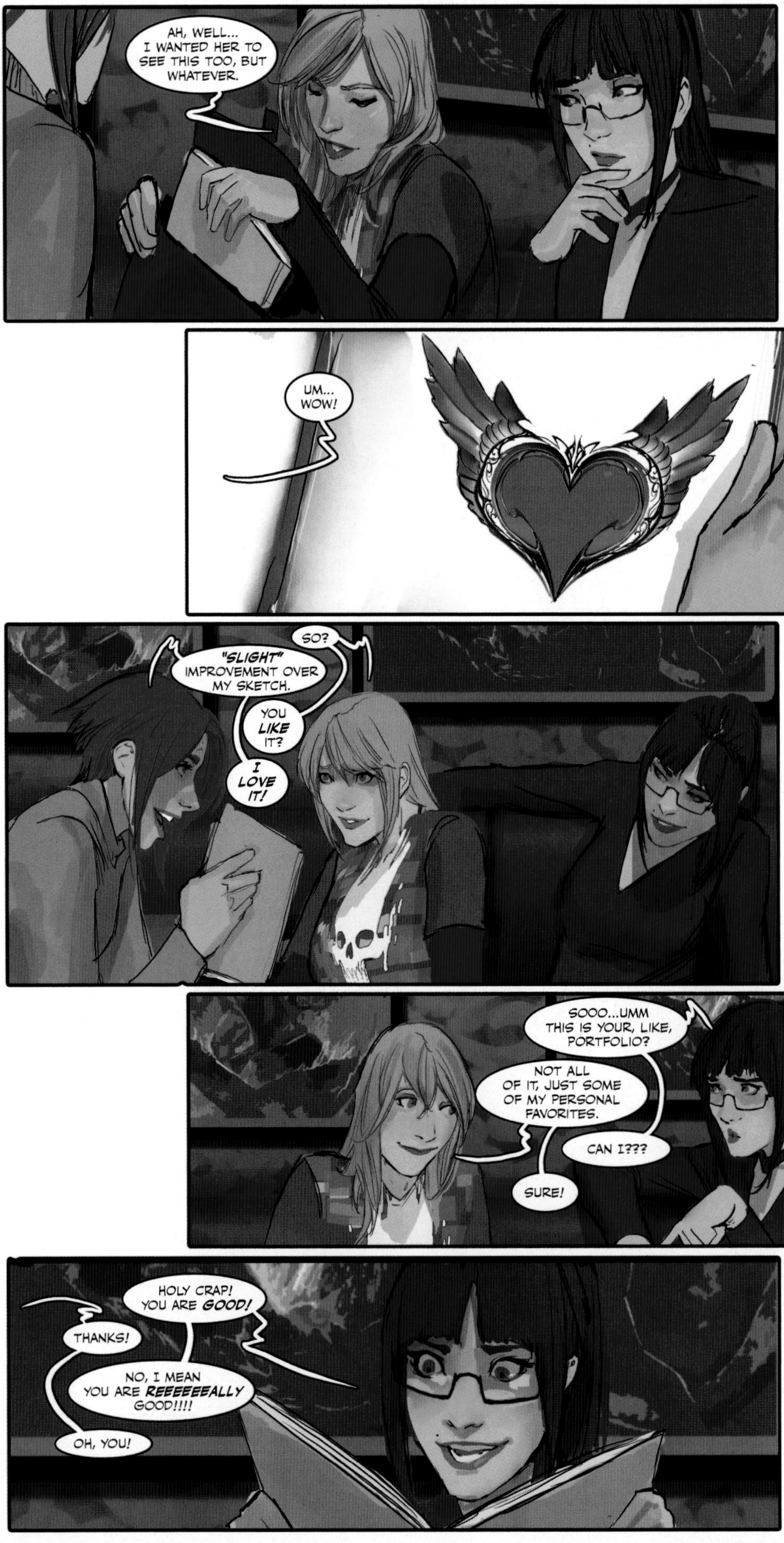

AH, WELL... I WANTED HER TO SEE THIS TOO, BUT WHATEVER.
UM... WOW!
"SLIGHT" IMPROVEMENT OVER MY SKETCH.
SO?
YOU LIKE IT?
I LOVE IT!
SOOO...UMM THIS IS YOUR, LIKE, PORTFOLIO?
NOT ALL OF IT, JUST SOME OF MY PERSONAL FAVORITES.
CAN I???
SURE!
HOLY CRAP! YOU ARE GOOD!
THANKS!
NO, I MEAN YOU ARE REEEEEEALLY GOOD!!!!
OH, YOU!

HEY! I *KNOW* THIS COMIC!!!

YEAH, I GET A BUTTLOAD OF ORDERS TO TATTOO HER.

HEH. I BET! YOU *READ* IT?

NAH, I MEAN, I TRIED. I WAS CURIOUS TO SEE WHAT THE DEAL WAS... Y'KNOW, *BEYOND* THE LOOKS.

YEAH, THERE WAS NEVER MUCH SUBSTANCE IN THAT COMIC...BUT THE ARTWORK WAS *GORGEOUS* IN THE FIRST FEW ARCS.

NERD!

NOPE! JUST AN ART AFICIONADO!

BUT IF YOU WANT TO READ SOME GOOD COMICS WITH STORY TO GO ALONGSIDE ART...

IT'S KINDA FUNNY...

ONE OF THE THINGS I REMEMBER ABOUT THAT NIGHT WAS A DEEP SENSE OF UNEASE.

I GUESS, WHEN YOU ARE TRYING TO GET INVOLVED WITH SOMEONE ROMANTICALLY, THE LAST THING YOU WANT IS THE COMPANY OF SOMEONE WHO HAS MORE IN COMMON WITH THAT PERSON.

AND ANNE CERTAINLY QUALIFIED.

SHE WAS BOTH INTO BDSM, FUN, AND AMAZINGLY ARTISTIC.

AND ALLY OBVIOUSLY ENJOYED HER COMPANY.

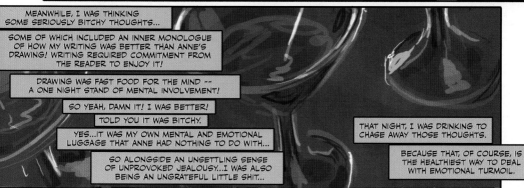

MEANWHILE, I WAS THINKING SOME SERIOUSLY BITCHY THOUGHTS...

SOME OF WHICH INCLUDED AN INNER MONOLOGUE OF HOW MY WRITING WAS BETTER THAN ANNE'S DRAWING! WRITING REQUIRED COMMITMENT FROM THE READER TO ENJOY IT!

DRAWING WAS FAST FOOD FOR THE MIND -- A ONE NIGHT STAND OF MENTAL INVOLVEMENT!

SO YEAH, DAMN IT! I WAS BETTER!

TOLD YOU IT WAS BITCHY.

YES...IT WAS MY OWN MENTAL AND EMOTIONAL LUGGAGE THAT ANNE HAD NOTHING TO DO WITH...

SO ALONGSIDE AN UNSETTLING SENSE OF UNPROVOKED JEALOUSY...I WAS ALSO BEING AN UNGRATEFUL LITTLE SHIT...

THAT NIGHT, I WAS DRINKING TO CHASE AWAY THOSE THOUGHTS.

BECAUSE THAT, OF COURSE, IS THE HEALTHIEST WAY TO DEAL WITH EMOTIONAL TURMOIL.

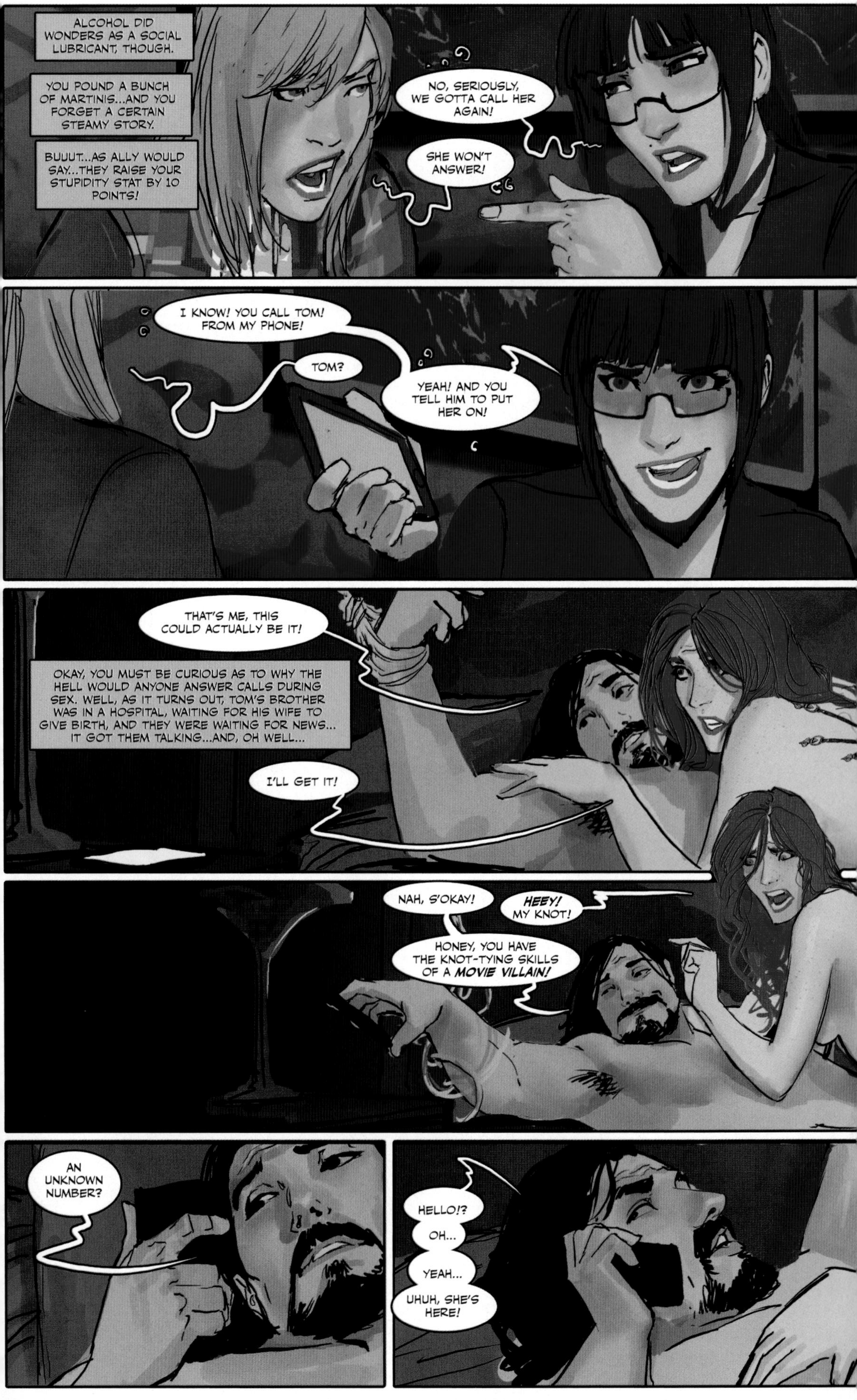
ALCOHOL DID WONDERS AS A SOCIAL LUBRICANT, THOUGH.
YOU POUND A BUNCH OF MARTINIS...AND YOU FORGET A CERTAIN STEAMY STORY.
BUUUT...AS ALLY WOULD SAY...THEY RAISE YOUR STUPIDITY STAT BY 10 POINTS!
NO, SERIOUSLY, WE GOTTA CALL HER AGAIN!
SHE WON'T ANSWER!
I KNOW! YOU CALL TOM! FROM MY PHONE!
TOM?
YEAH! AND YOU TELL HIM TO PUT HER ON!
THAT'S ME, THIS COULD ACTUALLY BE IT!
OKAY, YOU MUST BE CURIOUS AS TO WHY THE HELL WOULD ANYONE ANSWER CALLS DURING SEX. WELL, AS IT TURNS OUT, TOM'S BROTHER WAS IN A HOSPITAL, WAITING FOR HIS WIFE TO GIVE BIRTH, AND THEY WERE WAITING FOR NEWS... IT GOT THEM TALKING...AND, OH WELL...
I'LL GET IT!
NAH, S'OKAY!
HEEY! MY KNOT!
HONEY, YOU HAVE THE KNOT-TYING SKILLS OF A MOVIE VILLAIN!
AN UNKNOWN NUMBER?
HELLO!?
OH...
YEAH...
UHUH, SHE'S HERE!

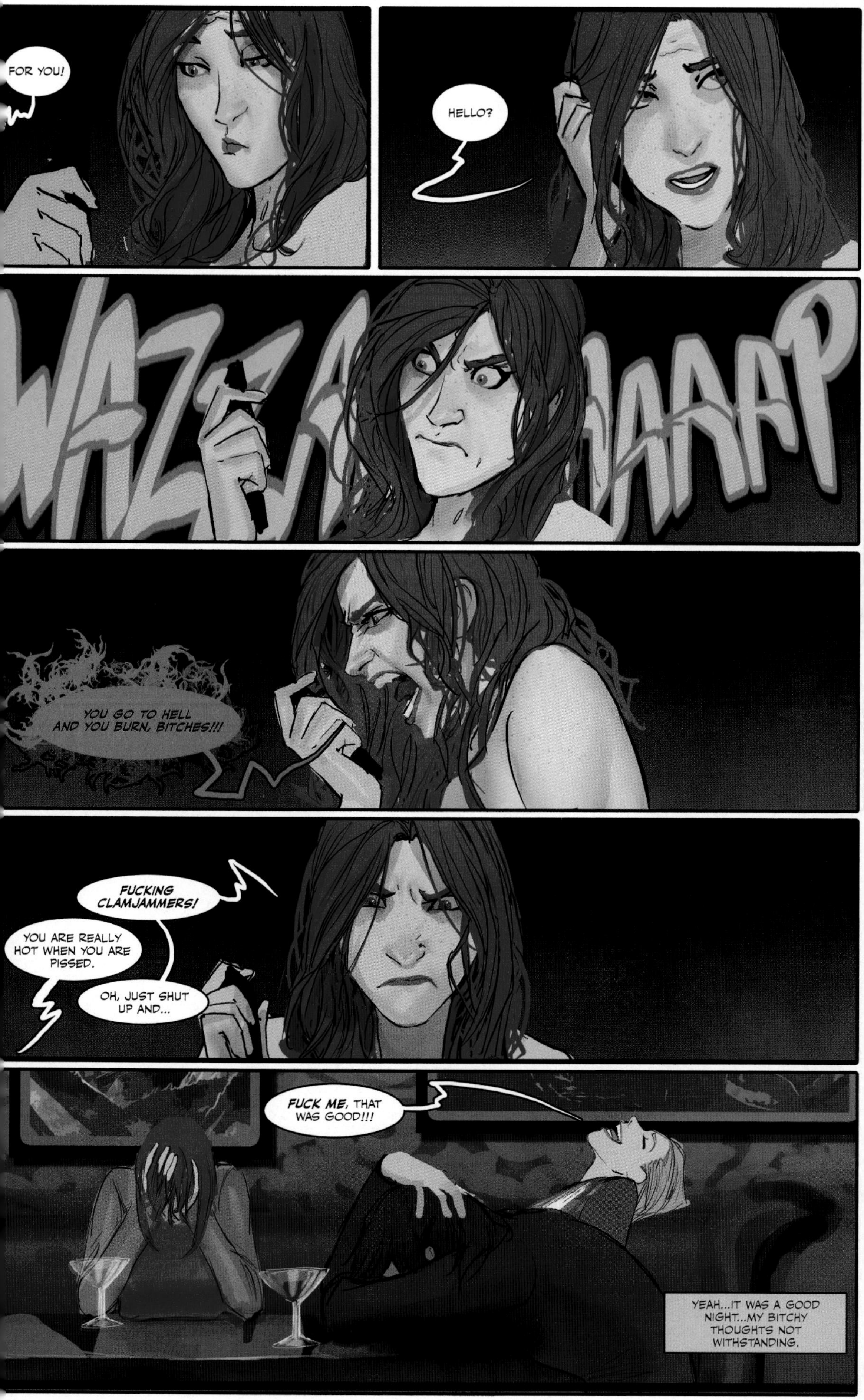
FOR YOU!
HELLO?
WAZZAAAAP
YOU GO TO HELL AND YOU BURN, BITCHES!!!
FUCKING CLAMJAMMERS!
YOU ARE REALLY HOT WHEN YOU ARE PISSED.
OH, JUST SHUT UP AND...
FUCK ME, THAT WAS GOOD!!!
YEAH...IT WAS A GOOD NIGHT...MY BITCHY THOUGHTS NOT WITHSTANDING.

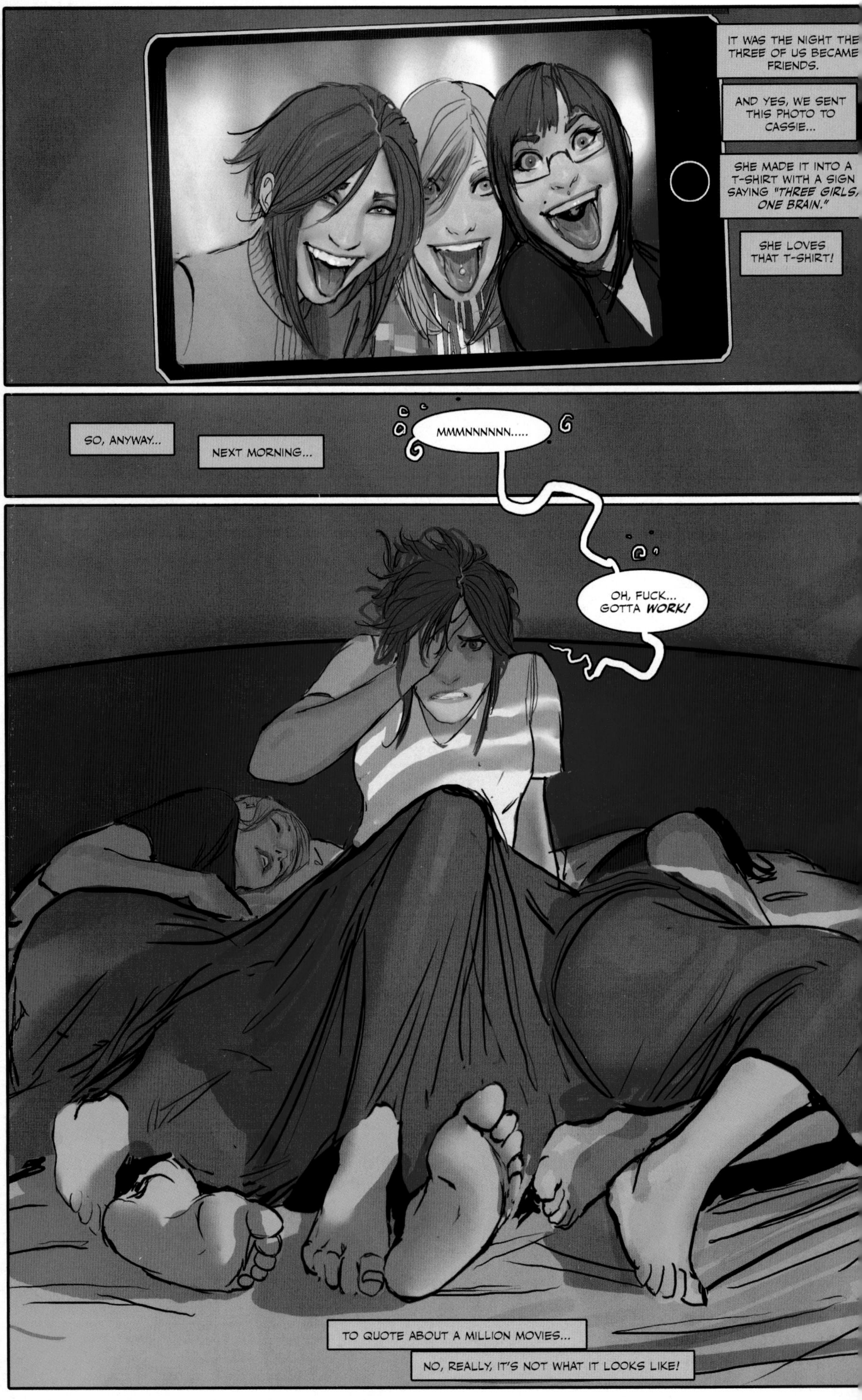

IT WAS THE NIGHT THE THREE OF US BECAME FRIENDS.
AND YES, WE SENT THIS PHOTO TO CASSIE...
SHE MADE IT INTO A T-SHIRT WITH A SIGN SAYING "THREE GIRLS, ONE BRAIN."
SHE LOVES THAT T-SHIRT!
SO, ANYWAY...
NEXT MORNING...
MMMNNNNNN.....
OH, FUCK... GOTTA WORK!
TO QUOTE ABOUT A MILLION MOVIES...
NO, REALLY, IT'S NOT WHAT IT LOOKS LIKE!

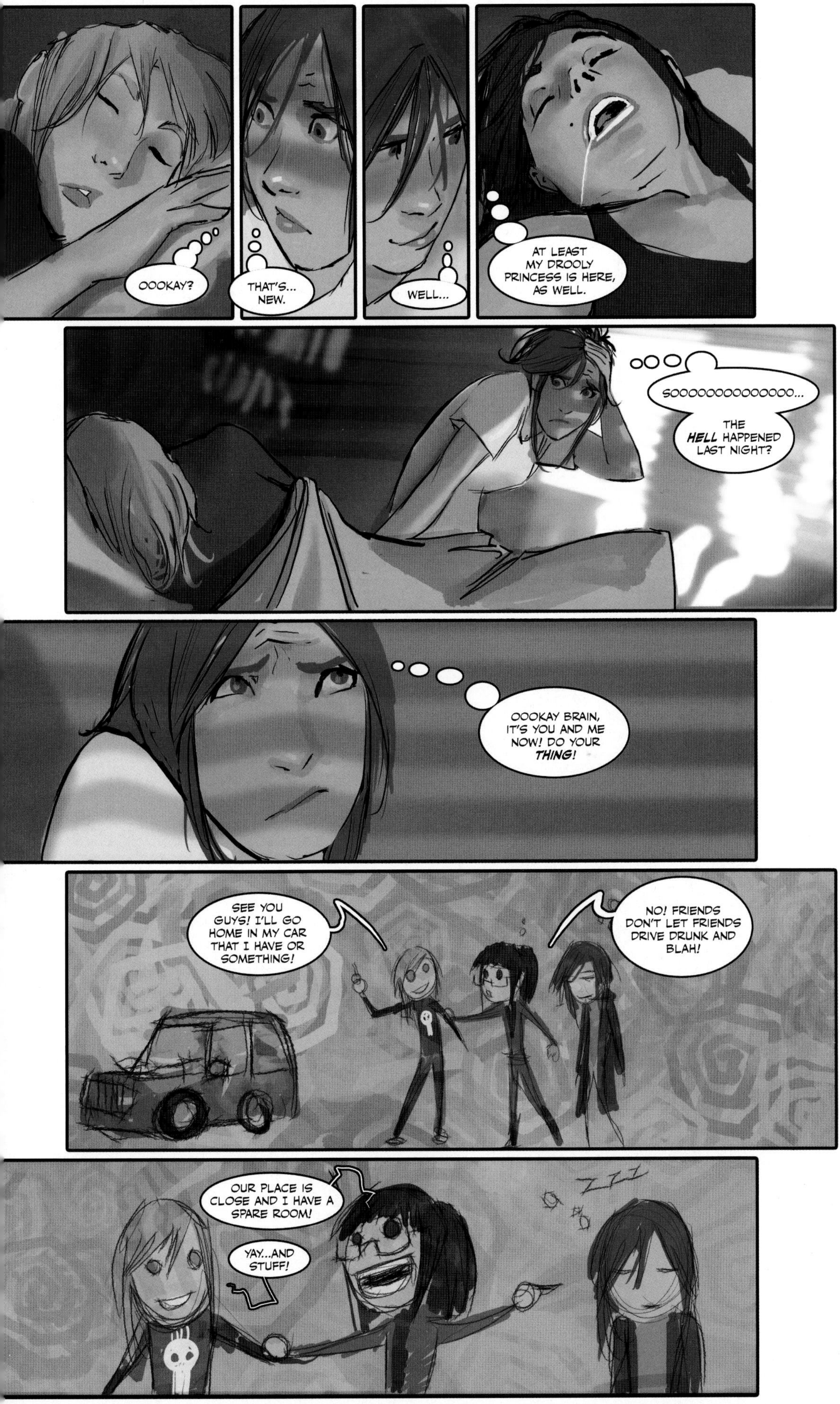

OOOKAY?
THAT'S... NEW.
WELL...
AT LEAST MY DROOLY PRINCESS IS HERE, AS WELL.
SOOOOOOOOOOOOOO...
THE HELL HAPPENED LAST NIGHT?
OOOKAY BRAIN, IT'S YOU AND ME NOW! DO YOUR THING!
SEE YOU GUYS! I'LL GO HOME IN MY CAR THAT I HAVE OR SOMETHING!
NO! FRIENDS DON'T LET FRIENDS DRIVE DRUNK AND BLAH!
OUR PLACE IS CLOSE AND I HAVE A SPARE ROOM!
YAY...AND STUFF!

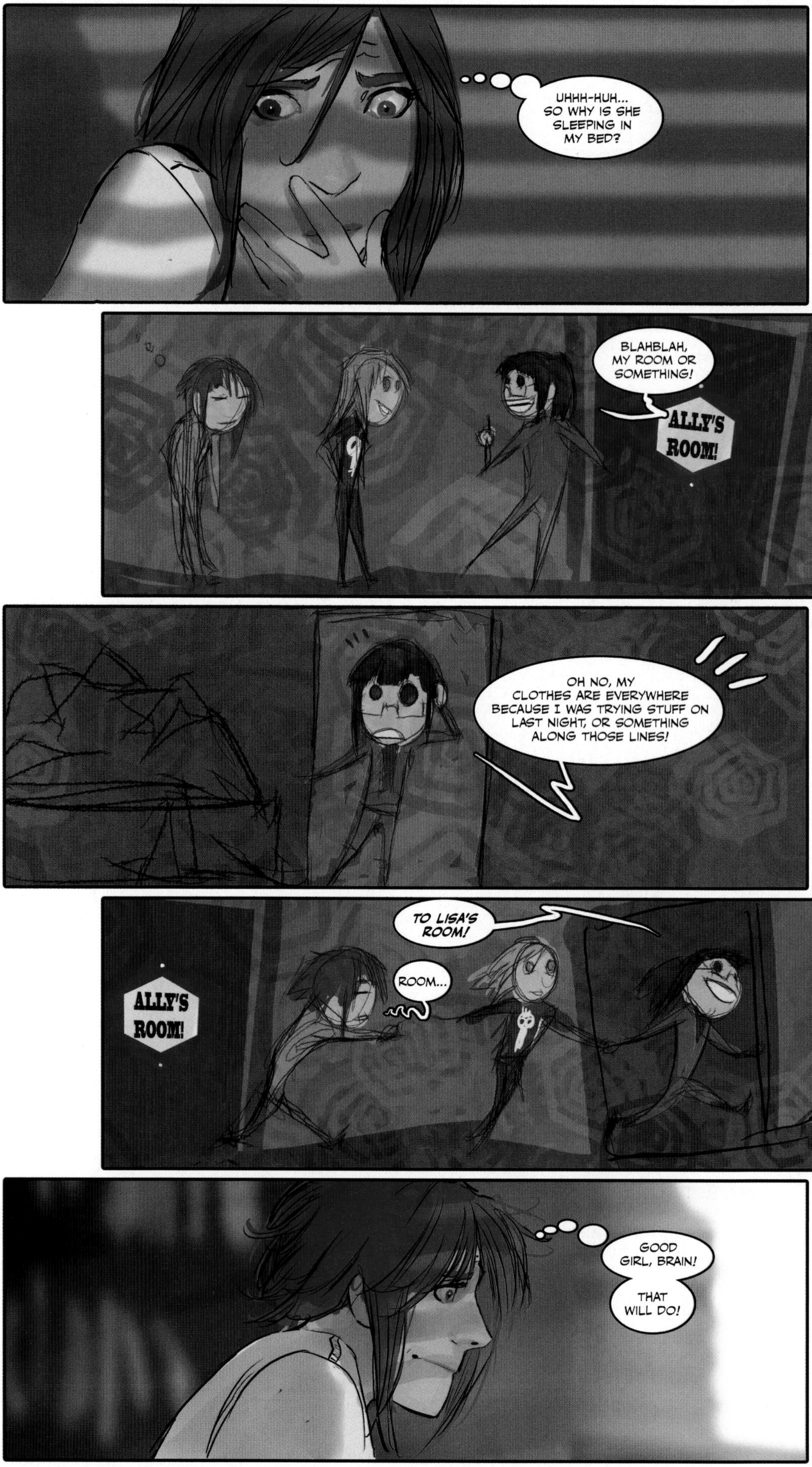
UHHH-HUH... SO WHY IS SHE SLEEPING IN MY BED?
BLAHBLAH, MY ROOM OR SOMETHING!
ALLY'S ROOM!
OH NO, MY CLOTHES ARE EVERYWHERE BECAUSE I WAS TRYING STUFF ON LAST NIGHT, OR SOMETHING ALONG THOSE LINES!
TO LISA'S ROOM!
ALLY'S ROOM!
ROOM...
GOOD GIRL, BRAIN!
THAT WILL DO!

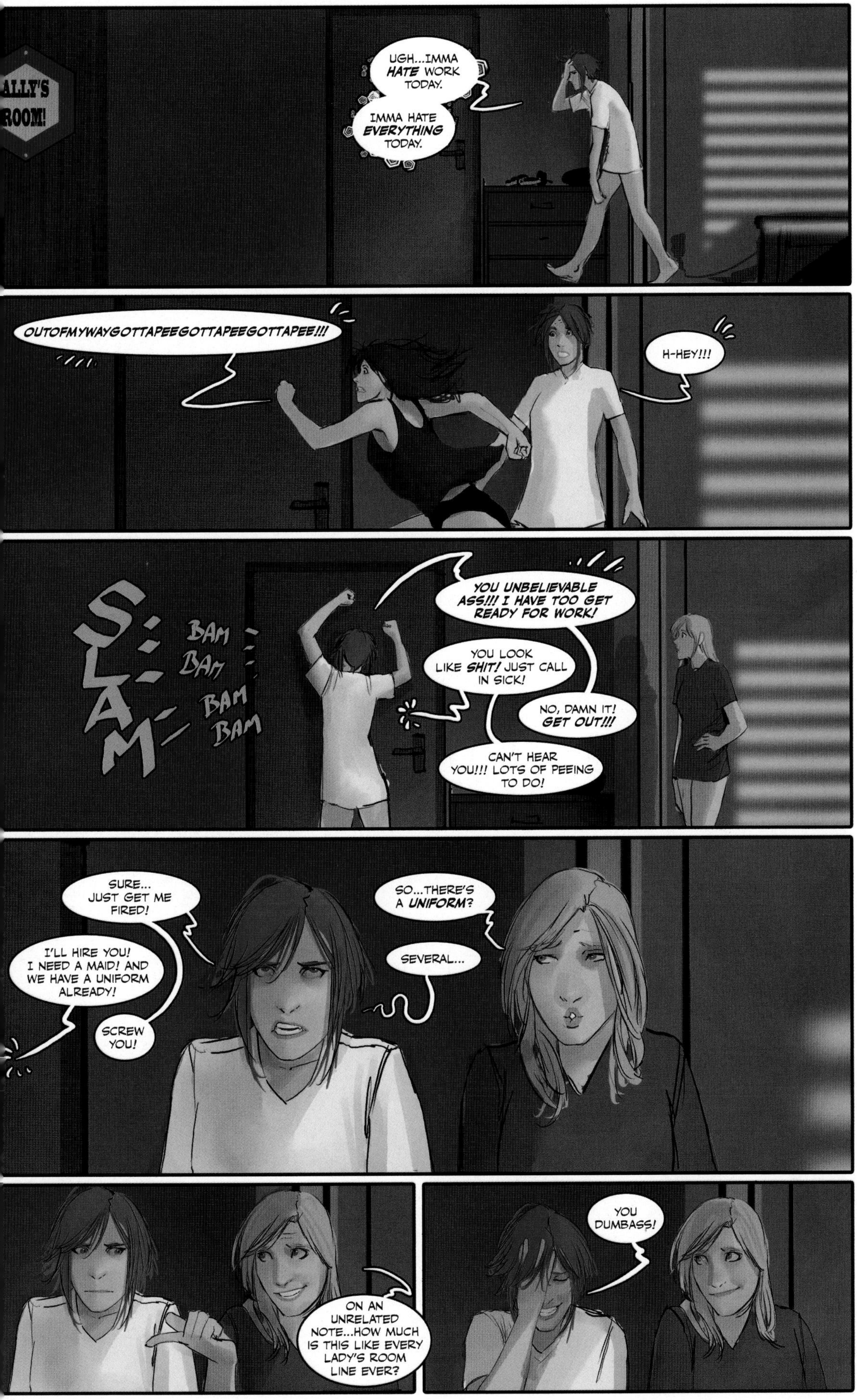
ALLY'S ROOM!
UGH...IMMA HATE WORK TODAY.
IMMA HATE EVERYTHING TODAY.
OUTOFMYWAYGOTTAPEEGOTTAPEEGOTTAPEE!!!
H-HEY!!!
SLAM
BAM BAM BAM BAM
YOU UNBELIEVABLE ASS!!! I HAVE TOO GET READY FOR WORK!
YOU LOOK LIKE SHIT! JUST CALL IN SICK!
NO, DAMN IT! GET OUT!!!
CAN'T HEAR YOU!!! LOTS OF PEEING TO DO!
SURE... JUST GET ME FIRED!
I'LL HIRE YOU! I NEED A MAID! AND WE HAVE A UNIFORM ALREADY!
SCREW YOU!
SO...THERE'S A UNIFORM?
SEVERAL...
ON AN UNRELATED NOTE...HOW MUCH IS THIS LIKE EVERY LADY'S ROOM LINE EVER?
YOU DUMBASS!

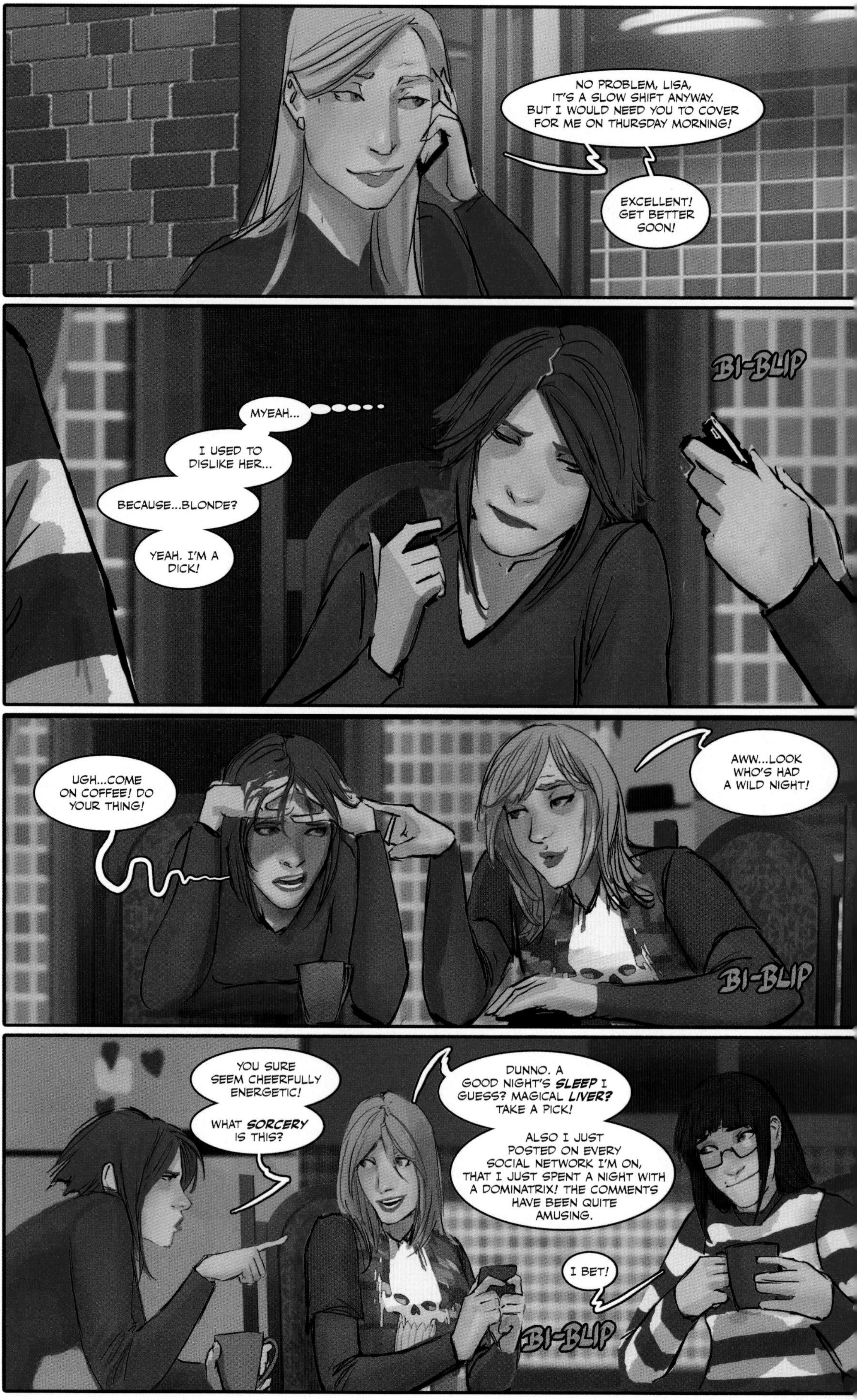
NO PROBLEM, LISA, IT'S A SLOW SHIFT ANYWAY. BUT I WOULD NEED YOU TO COVER FOR ME ON THURSDAY MORNING!
EXCELLENT! GET BETTER SOON!
BI-BLIP
MYEAH...
I USED TO DISLIKE HER...
BECAUSE...BLONDE?
YEAH. I'M A DICK!
UGH...COME ON COFFEE! DO YOUR THING!
AWW...LOOK WHO'S HAD A WILD NIGHT!
BI-BLIP
YOU SURE SEEM CHEERFULLY ENERGETIC!
WHAT SORCERY IS THIS?
DUNNO. A GOOD NIGHT'S SLEEP I GUESS? MAGICAL LIVER? TAKE A PICK!
ALSO I JUST POSTED ON EVERY SOCIAL NETWORK I'M ON, THAT I JUST SPENT A NIGHT WITH A DOMINATRIX! THE COMMENTS HAVE BEEN QUITE AMUSING.
I BET!
BI-BLIP

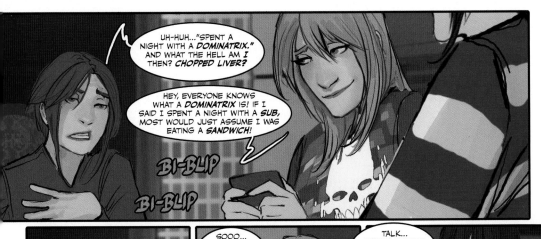

UH-HUH..."SPENT A NIGHT WITH A *DOMINATRIX.*" AND WHAT THE HELL AM *I* THEN? *CHOPPED LIVER?*

HEY, EVERYONE KNOWS WHAT A *DOMINATRIX* IS! IF I SAID I SPENT A NIGHT WITH A *SUB,* MOST WOULD JUST ASSUME I WAS EATING A *SANDWICH!*

BI-BLIP

BI-BLIP

FAIR POINT.

SOOO... WHAT IS IT THE TWO OF YOU USUALLY DO?

TALK... WATCH MOVIES READ...JUST... USUAL STUFF.

WE HAVE OUR OWN HOBBIES AS WELL.

I DO JIGSAW PUZZLES AT TIMES...

I PLAY SOME VIDEOGAMES... AND, *OH!* YOU MIGHT FIND THIS INTERESTING, ANNE!

YEAH?

I HAVE A SMALL COLLECTION OF SKETCHES FROM SOME COMIC ARTISTS.

YOU DO?

IT'S...NOT MUCH. JUST SEVERAL PIECES.

I NEVER KNEW THAT.

I DUNNO... DIDN'T THINK YOU WOULD FIND IT INTERESTING.

WWWWOW, I AM GETTING SPAMMED HERE!

WHAT ARE THEY SAYING?

BI-BLIP

BI-BLIP

BI-BLIP

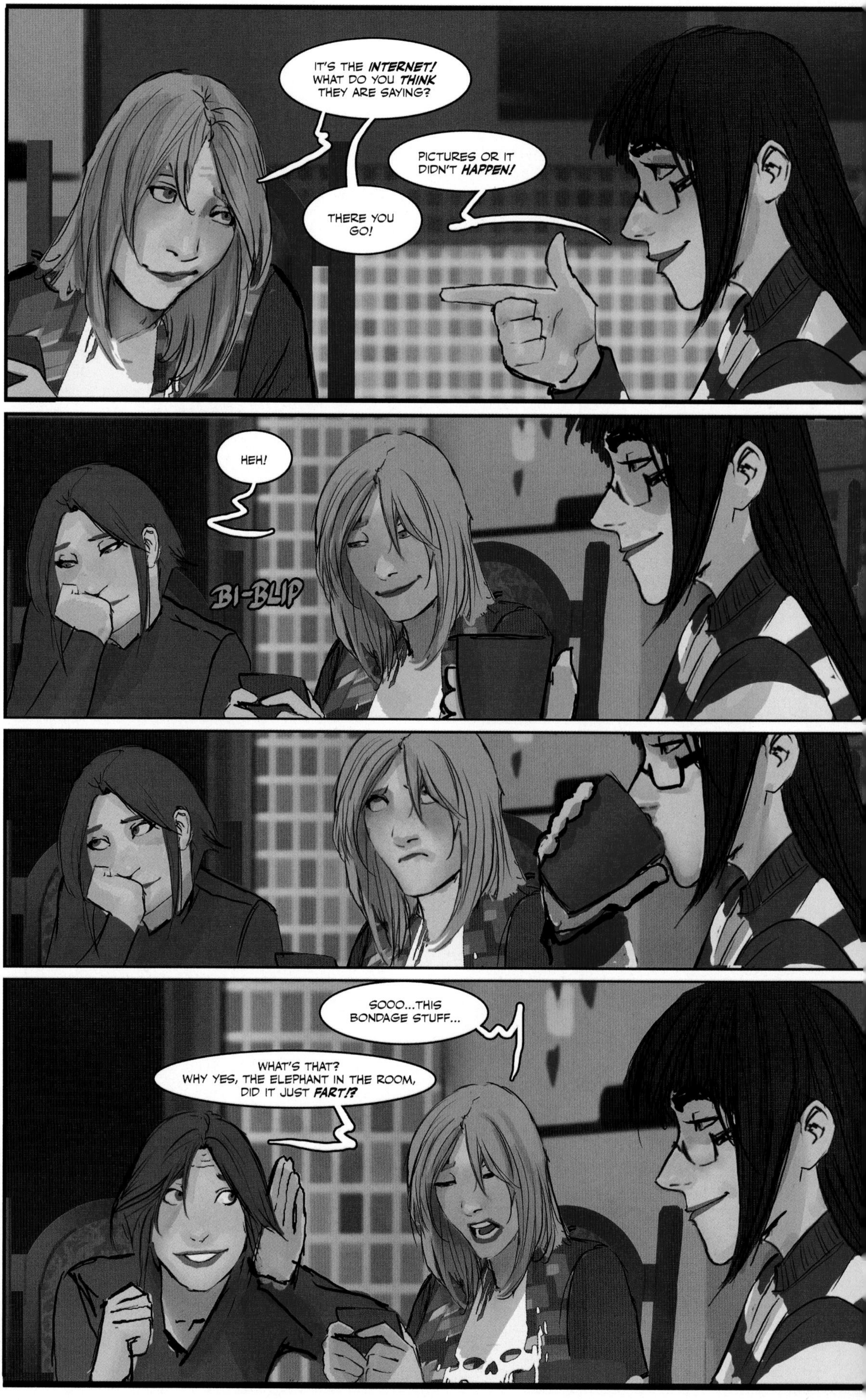
IT'S THE INTERNET! WHAT DO YOU THINK THEY ARE SAYING?
PICTURES OR IT DIDN'T HAPPEN!
THERE YOU GO!
HEH!
BI-BLIP
SOOO...THIS BONDAGE STUFF...
WHAT'S THAT? WHY YES, THE ELEPHANT IN THE ROOM, DID IT JUST FART!?

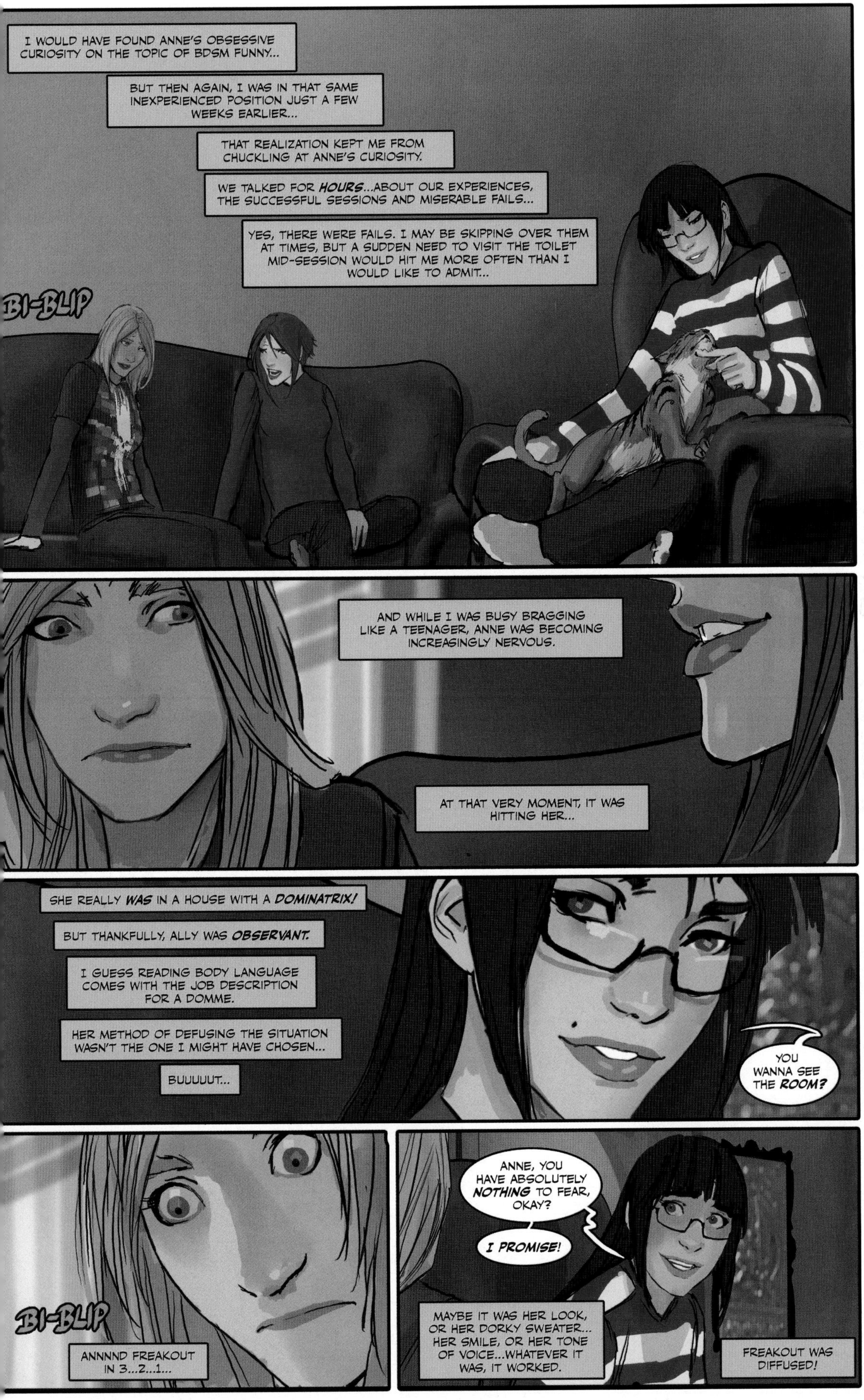
I WOULD HAVE FOUND ANNE'S OBSESSIVE CURIOSITY ON THE TOPIC OF BDSM FUNNY...
BUT THEN AGAIN, I WAS IN THAT SAME INEXPERIENCED POSITION JUST A FEW WEEKS EARLIER...
THAT REALIZATION KEPT ME FROM CHUCKLING AT ANNE'S CURIOSITY.
WE TALKED FOR HOURS...ABOUT OUR EXPERIENCES, THE SUCCESSFUL SESSIONS AND MISERABLE FAILS...
YES, THERE WERE FAILS. I MAY BE SKIPPING OVER THEM AT TIMES, BUT A SUDDEN NEED TO VISIT THE TOILET MID-SESSION WOULD HIT ME MORE OFTEN THAN I WOULD LIKE TO ADMIT...
BI-BLIP
AND WHILE I WAS BUSY BRAGGING LIKE A TEENAGER, ANNE WAS BECOMING INCREASINGLY NERVOUS.
AT THAT VERY MOMENT, IT WAS HITTING HER...
SHE REALLY WAS IN A HOUSE WITH A DOMINATRIX!
BUT THANKFULLY, ALLY WAS OBSERVANT.
I GUESS READING BODY LANGUAGE COMES WITH THE JOB DESCRIPTION FOR A DOMME.
HER METHOD OF DEFUSING THE SITUATION WASN'T THE ONE I MIGHT HAVE CHOSEN...
BUUUUUT...
YOU WANNA SEE THE ROOM?
BI-BLIP
ANNNND FREAKOUT IN 3...2...1...
ANNE, YOU HAVE ABSOLUTELY NOTHING TO FEAR, OKAY?
I PROMISE!
MAYBE IT WAS HER LOOK, OR HER DORKY SWEATER... HER SMILE, OR HER TONE OF VOICE...WHATEVER IT WAS, IT WORKED.
FREAKOUT WAS DIFFUSED!

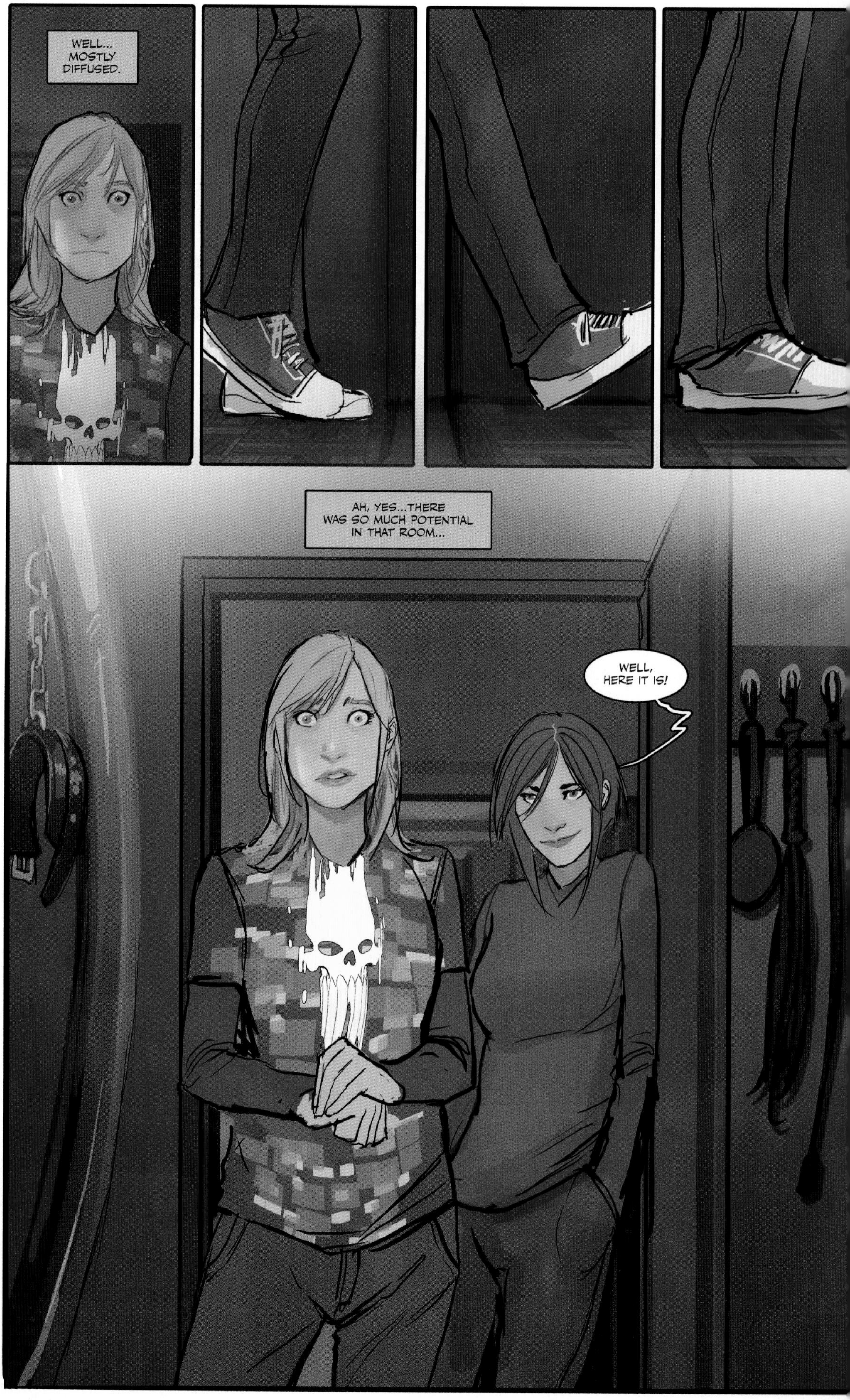
WELL... MOSTLY DIFFUSED.
AH, YES...THERE WAS SO MUCH POTENTIAL IN THAT ROOM...
WELL, HERE IT IS!

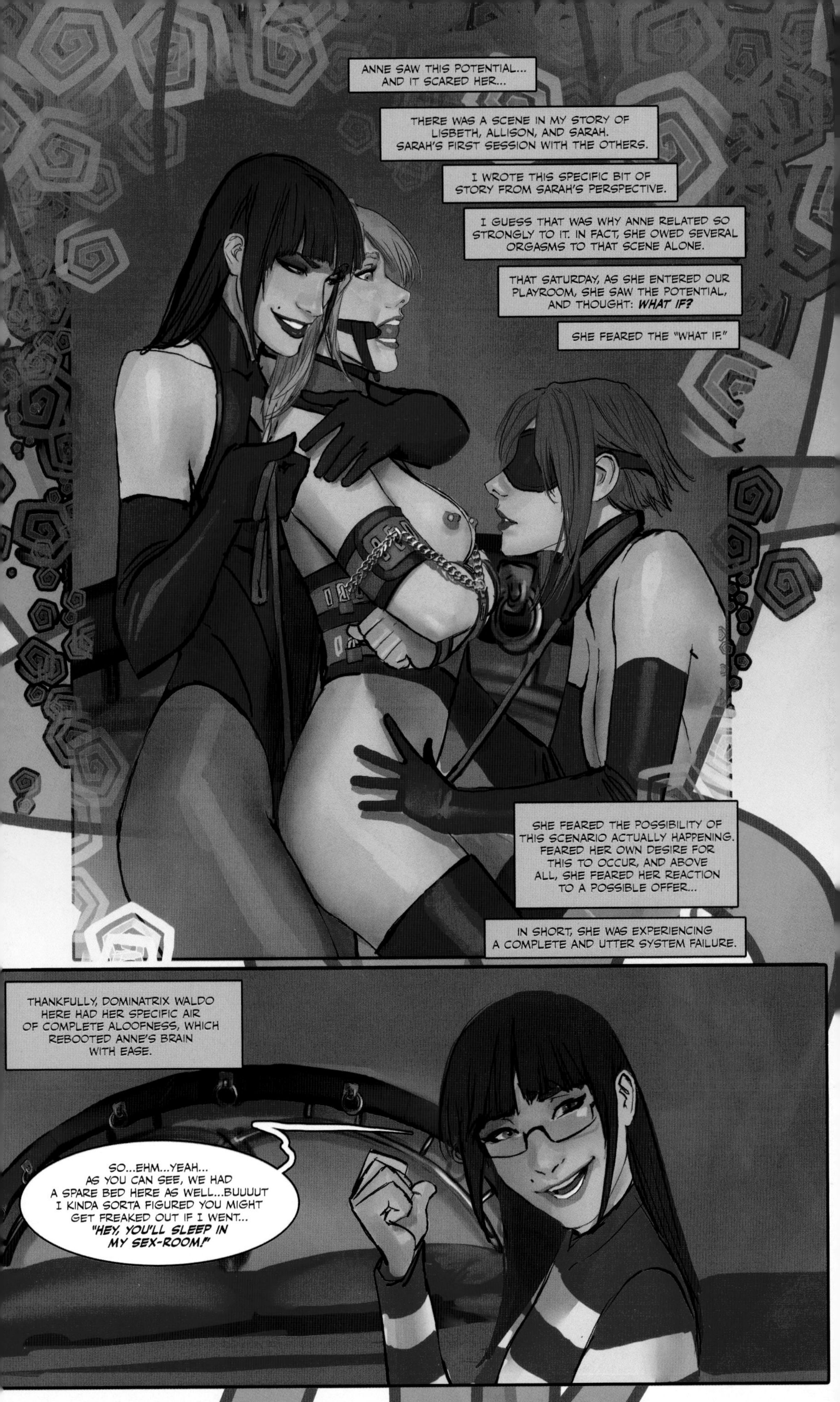
ANNE SAW THIS POTENTIAL... AND IT SCARED HER...
THERE WAS A SCENE IN MY STORY OF LISBETH, ALLISON, AND SARAH. SARAH'S FIRST SESSION WITH THE OTHERS.
I WROTE THIS SPECIFIC BIT OF STORY FROM SARAH'S PERSPECTIVE.
I GUESS THAT WAS WHY ANNE RELATED SO STRONGLY TO IT. IN FACT, SHE OWED SEVERAL ORGASMS TO THAT SCENE ALONE.
THAT SATURDAY, AS SHE ENTERED OUR PLAYROOM, SHE SAW THE POTENTIAL, AND THOUGHT: ***WHAT IF?***
SHE FEARED THE "WHAT IF."
SHE FEARED THE POSSIBILITY OF THIS SCENARIO ACTUALLY HAPPENING. FEARED HER OWN DESIRE FOR THIS TO OCCUR, AND ABOVE ALL, SHE FEARED HER REACTION TO A POSSIBLE OFFER...
IN SHORT, SHE WAS EXPERIENCING A COMPLETE AND UTTER SYSTEM FAILURE.
THANKFULLY, DOMINATRIX WALDO HERE HAD HER SPECIFIC AIR OF COMPLETE ALOOFNESS, WHICH REBOOTED ANNE'S BRAIN WITH EASE.
SO...EHM...YEAH... AS YOU CAN SEE, WE HAD A SPARE BED HERE AS WELL...BUUUUT I KINDA SORTA FIGURED YOU MIGHT GET FREAKED OUT IF I WENT... ***"HEY, YOU'LL SLEEP IN MY SEX-ROOM!"***

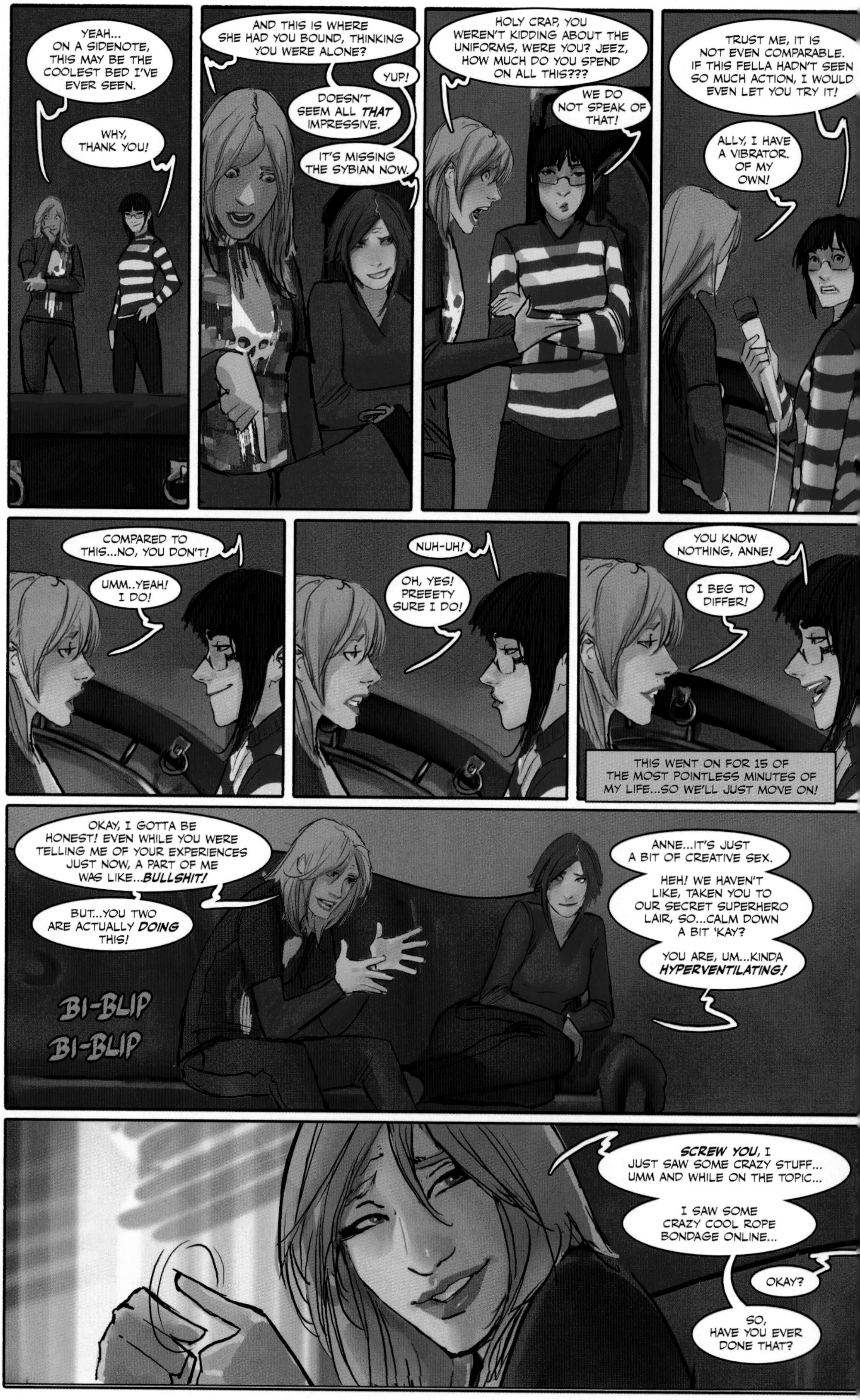

YEAH... ON A SIDENOTE, THIS MAY BE THE COOLEST BED I'VE EVER SEEN.
WHY, THANK YOU!
AND THIS IS WHERE SHE HAD YOU BOUND, THINKING YOU WERE ALONE?
YUP!
DOESN'T SEEM ALL THAT IMPRESSIVE.
IT'S MISSING THE SYBIAN NOW.
HOLY CRAP, YOU WEREN'T KIDDING ABOUT THE UNIFORMS, WERE YOU? JEEZ, HOW MUCH DO YOU SPEND ON ALL THIS???
WE DO NOT SPEAK OF THAT!
TRUST ME, IT IS NOT EVEN COMPARABLE. IF THIS FELLA HADN'T SEEN SO MUCH ACTION, I WOULD EVEN LET YOU TRY IT!
ALLY, I HAVE A VIBRATOR. OF MY OWN!
COMPARED TO THIS...NO, YOU DON'T!
UMM..YEAH! I DO!
NUH-UH!
OH, YES! PREEETY SURE I DO!
YOU KNOW NOTHING, ANNE!
I BEG TO DIFFER!
THIS WENT ON FOR 15 OF THE MOST POINTLESS MINUTES OF MY LIFE...SO WE'LL JUST MOVE ON!
OKAY, I GOTTA BE HONEST! EVEN WHILE YOU WERE TELLING ME OF YOUR EXPERIENCES JUST NOW, A PART OF ME WAS LIKE...BULLSHIT!
BUT...YOU TWO ARE ACTUALLY DOING THIS!
ANNE...IT'S JUST A BIT OF CREATIVE SEX.
HEH! WE HAVEN'T LIKE, TAKEN YOU TO OUR SECRET SUPERHERO LAIR, SO...CALM DOWN A BIT 'KAY?
YOU ARE, UM...KINDA HYPERVENTILATING!
BI-BLIP
BI-BLIP
SCREW YOU, I JUST SAW SOME CRAZY STUFF... UMM AND WHILE ON THE TOPIC...
I SAW SOME CRAZY COOL ROPE BONDAGE ONLINE...
OKAY?
SO, HAVE YOU EVER DONE THAT?

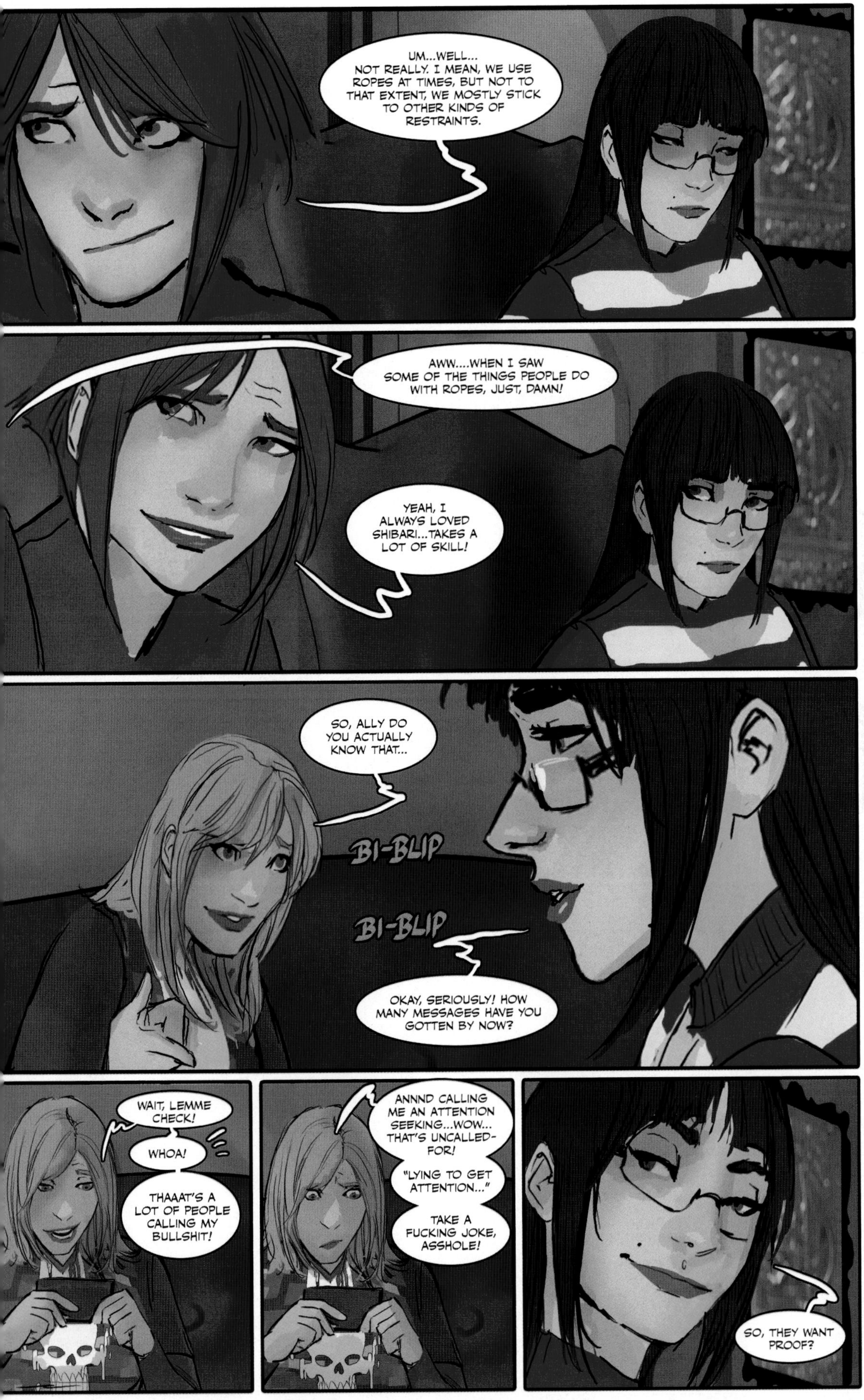
UM...WELL... NOT REALLY. I MEAN, WE USE ROPES AT TIMES, BUT NOT TO THAT EXTENT, WE MOSTLY STICK TO OTHER KINDS OF RESTRAINTS.
AWW....WHEN I SAW SOME OF THE THINGS PEOPLE DO WITH ROPES, JUST, DAMN!
YEAH, I ALWAYS LOVED SHIBARI...TAKES A LOT OF SKILL!
SO, ALLY DO YOU ACTUALLY KNOW THAT...
BI-BLIP
BI-BLIP
OKAY, SERIOUSLY! HOW MANY MESSAGES HAVE YOU GOTTEN BY NOW?
WAIT, LEMME CHECK!
WHOA!
THAAAT'S A LOT OF PEOPLE CALLING MY BULLSHIT!
ANNND CALLING ME AN ATTENTION SEEKING...WOW... THAT'S UNCALLED-FOR!
"LYING TO GET ATTENTION..."
TAKE A FUCKING JOKE, ASSHOLE!
SO, THEY WANT PROOF?

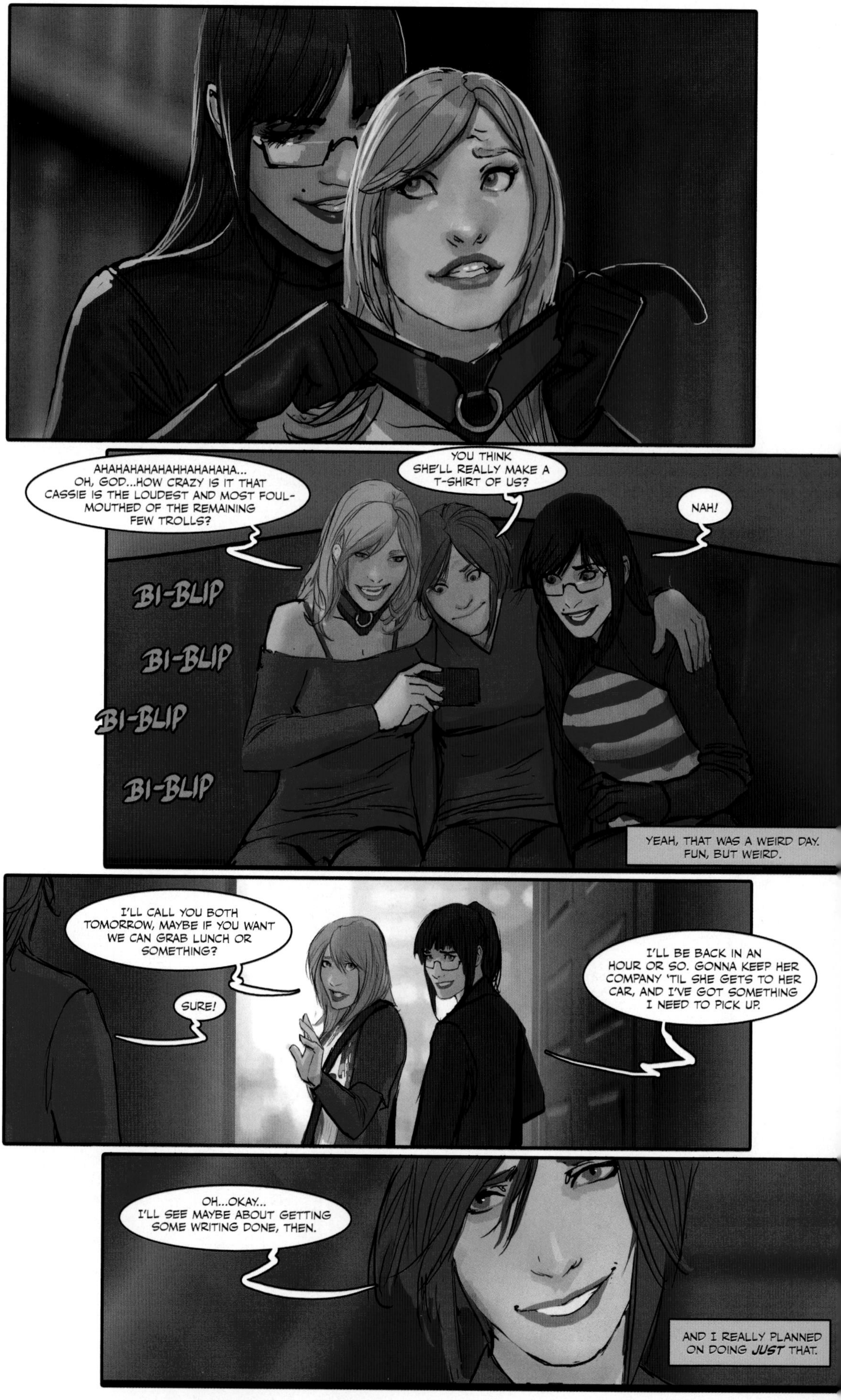
AHAHAHAHAHAHHAHAHAHA...
OH, GOD...HOW CRAZY IS IT THAT CASSIE IS THE LOUDEST AND MOST FOUL-MOUTHED OF THE REMAINING FEW TROLLS?
YOU THINK SHE'LL REALLY MAKE A T-SHIRT OF US?
NAH!
BI-BLIP
BI-BLIP
BI-BLIP
BI-BLIP
YEAH, THAT WAS A WEIRD DAY. FUN, BUT WEIRD.
I'LL CALL YOU BOTH TOMORROW, MAYBE IF YOU WANT WE CAN GRAB LUNCH OR SOMETHING?
SURE!
I'LL BE BACK IN AN HOUR OR SO. GONNA KEEP HER COMPANY 'TIL SHE GETS TO HER CAR, AND I'VE GOT SOMETHING I NEED TO PICK UP.
OH...OKAY...
I'LL SEE MAYBE ABOUT GETTING SOME WRITING DONE, THEN.
AND I REALLY PLANNED ON DOING *JUST* THAT.

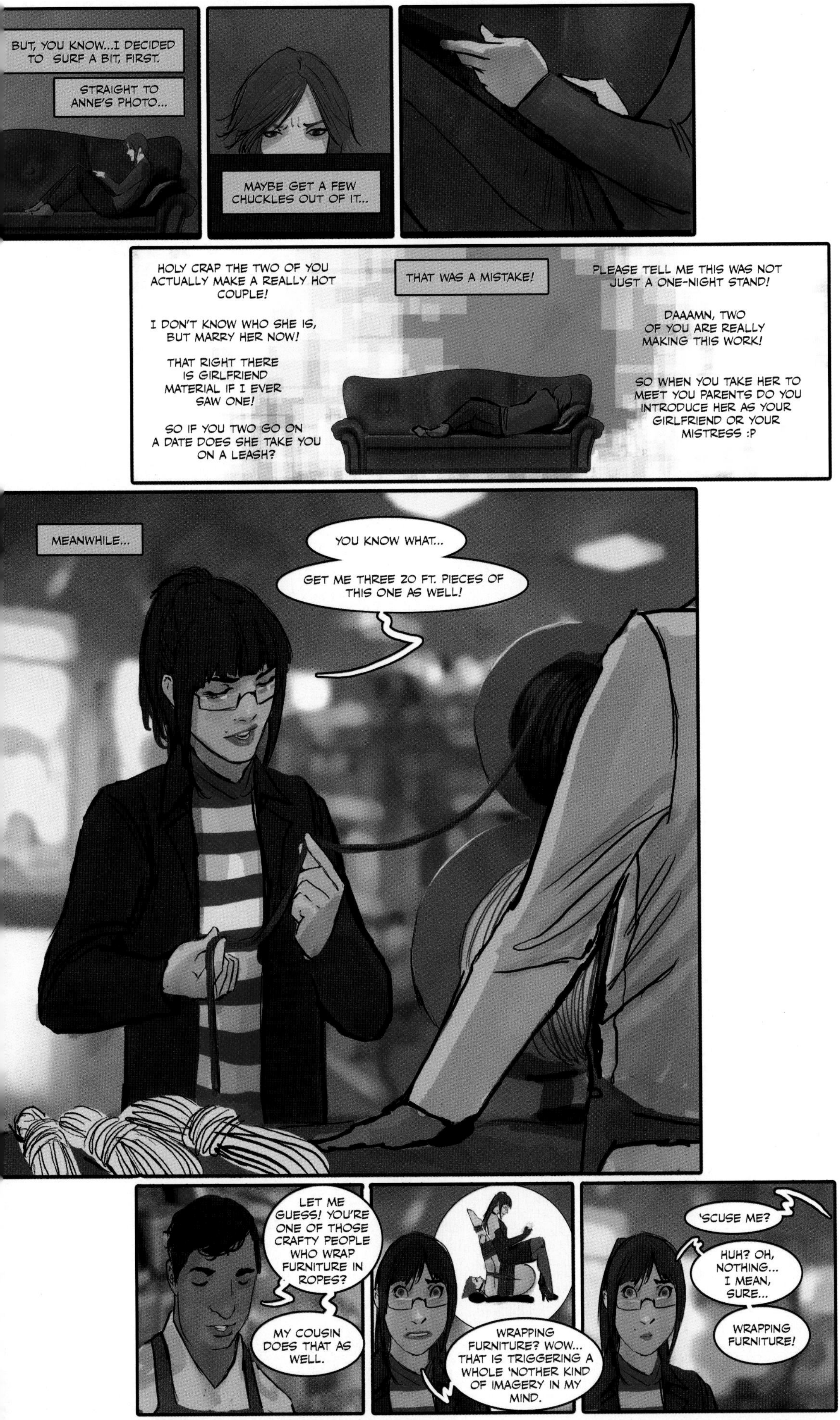

BUT, YOU KNOW...I DECIDED TO SURF A BIT, FIRST.
STRAIGHT TO ANNE'S PHOTO...
MAYBE GET A FEW CHUCKLES OUT OF IT...
HOLY CRAP THE TWO OF YOU ACTUALLY MAKE A REALLY HOT COUPLE!
I DON'T KNOW WHO SHE IS, BUT MARRY HER NOW!
THAT RIGHT THERE IS GIRLFRIEND MATERIAL IF I EVER SAW ONE!
SO IF YOU TWO GO ON A DATE DOES SHE TAKE YOU ON A LEASH?
THAT WAS A MISTAKE!
PLEASE TELL ME THIS WAS NOT JUST A ONE-NIGHT STAND!
DAAAMN, TWO OF YOU ARE REALLY MAKING THIS WORK!
SO WHEN YOU TAKE HER TO MEET YOU PARENTS DO YOU INTRODUCE HER AS YOUR GIRLFRIEND OR YOUR MISTRESS :P
MEANWHILE...
YOU KNOW WHAT...
GET ME THREE 20 FT. PIECES OF THIS ONE AS WELL!
LET ME GUESS! YOU'RE ONE OF THOSE CRAFTY PEOPLE WHO WRAP FURNITURE IN ROPES?
MY COUSIN DOES THAT AS WELL.
WRAPPING FURNITURE? WOW... THAT IS TRIGGERING A WHOLE 'NOTHER KIND OF IMAGERY IN MY MIND.
'SCUSE ME?
HUH? OH, NOTHING... I MEAN, SURE...
WRAPPING FURNITURE!

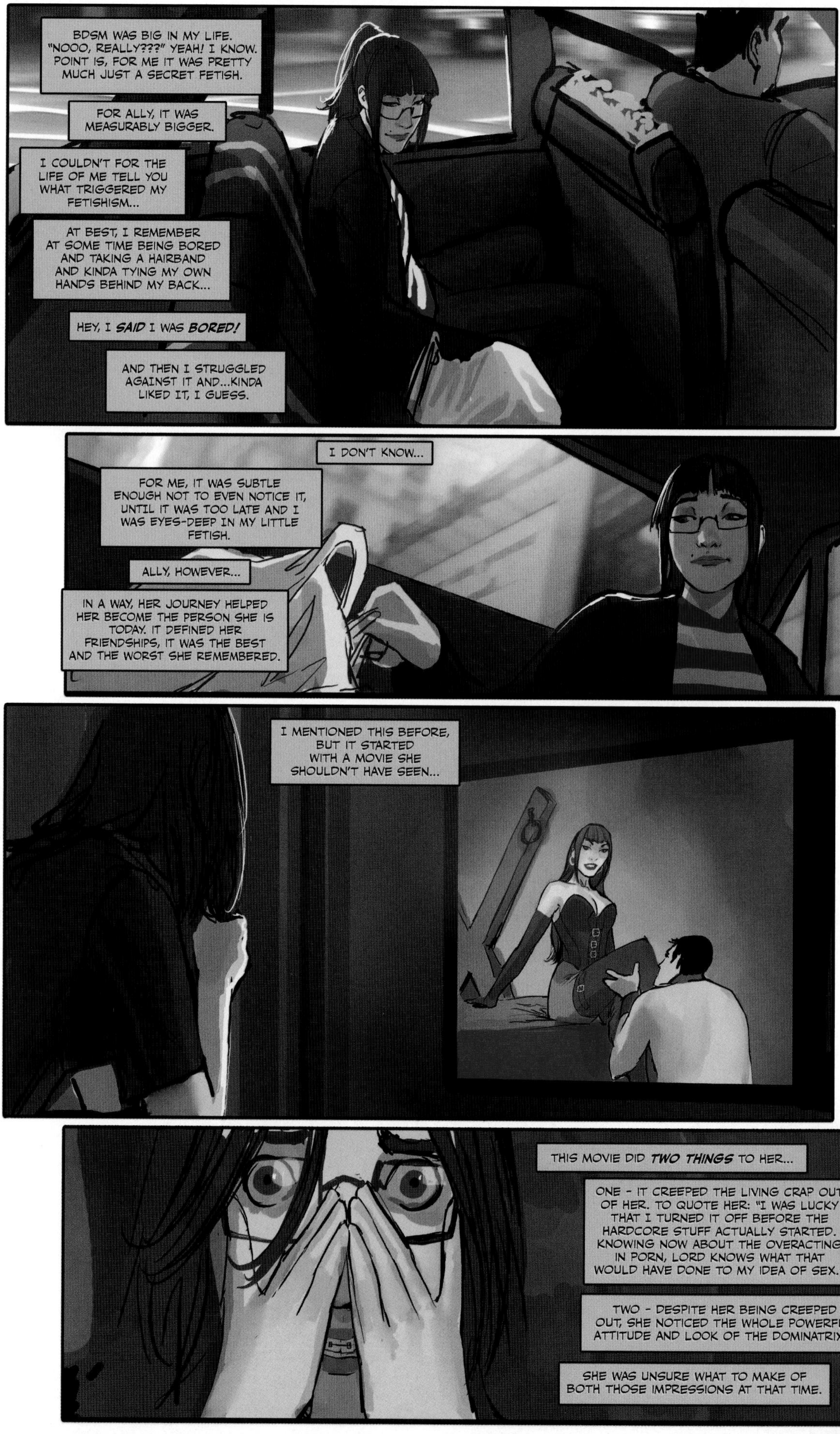

BDSM WAS BIG IN MY LIFE. "NOOO, REALLY???" YEAH! I KNOW. POINT IS, FOR ME IT WAS PRETTY MUCH JUST A SECRET FETISH.
FOR ALLY, IT WAS MEASURABLY BIGGER.
I COULDN'T FOR THE LIFE OF ME TELL YOU WHAT TRIGGERED MY FETISHISM...
AT BEST, I REMEMBER AT SOME TIME BEING BORED AND TAKING A HAIRBAND AND KINDA TYING MY OWN HANDS BEHIND MY BACK...
HEY, I *SAID* I WAS *BORED!*
AND THEN I STRUGGLED AGAINST IT AND...KINDA LIKED IT, I GUESS.
I DON'T KNOW...
FOR ME, IT WAS SUBTLE ENOUGH NOT TO EVEN NOTICE IT, UNTIL IT WAS TOO LATE AND I WAS EYES-DEEP IN MY LITTLE FETISH.
ALLY, HOWEVER...
IN A WAY, HER JOURNEY HELPED HER BECOME THE PERSON SHE IS TODAY. IT DEFINED HER FRIENDSHIPS, IT WAS THE BEST AND THE WORST SHE REMEMBERED.
I MENTIONED THIS BEFORE, BUT IT STARTED WITH A MOVIE SHE SHOULDN'T HAVE SEEN...
THIS MOVIE DID *TWO THINGS* TO HER...
ONE - IT CREEPED THE LIVING CRAP OUT OF HER. TO QUOTE HER: "I WAS LUCKY THAT I TURNED IT OFF BEFORE THE HARDCORE STUFF ACTUALLY STARTED. KNOWING NOW ABOUT THE OVERACTING IN PORN, LORD KNOWS WHAT THAT WOULD HAVE DONE TO MY IDEA OF SEX."
TWO - DESPITE HER BEING CREEPED OUT, SHE NOTICED THE WHOLE POWERFUL ATTITUDE AND LOOK OF THE DOMINATRIX...
SHE WAS UNSURE WHAT TO MAKE OF BOTH THOSE IMPRESSIONS AT THAT TIME.

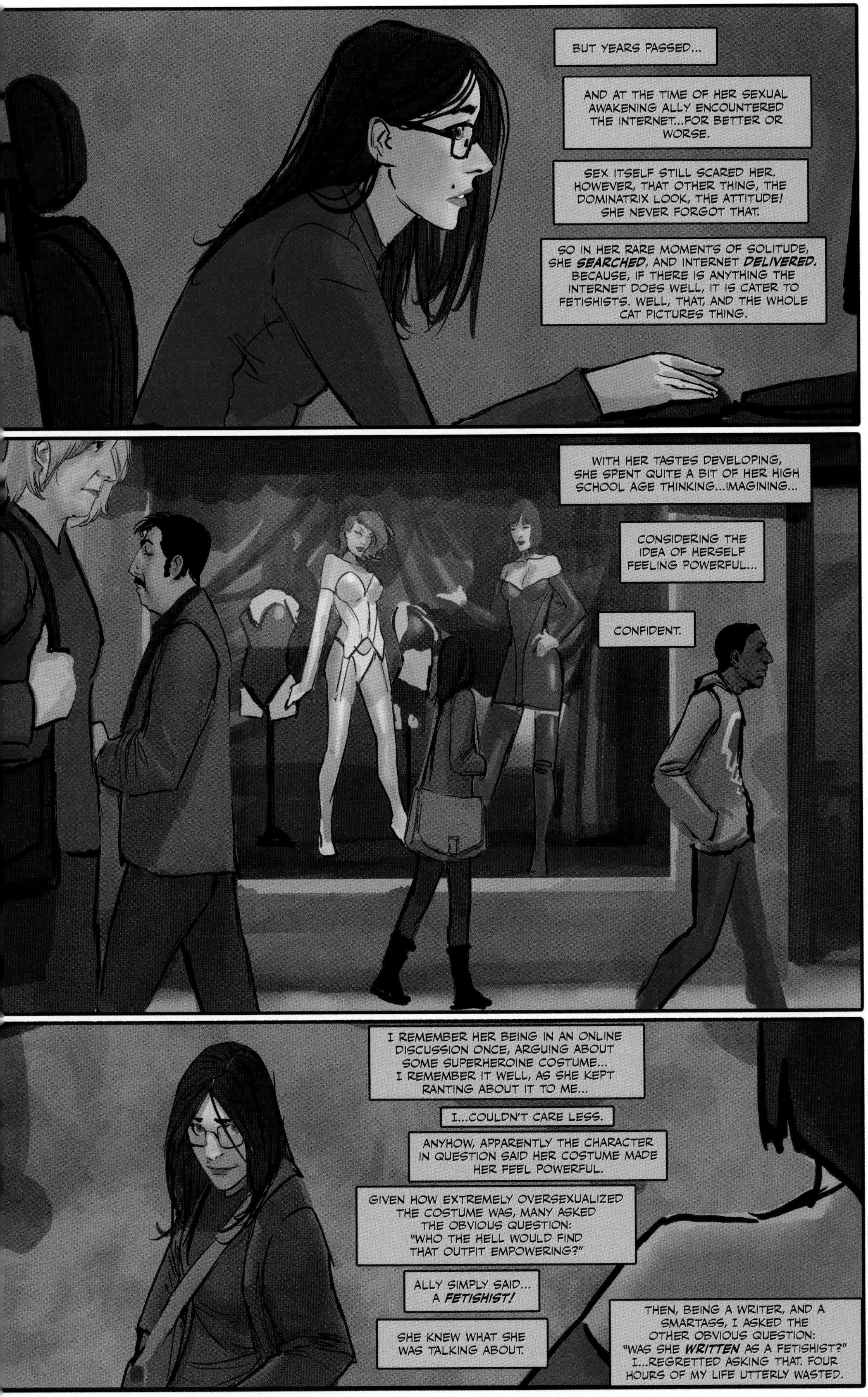
BUT YEARS PASSED...
AND AT THE TIME OF HER SEXUAL AWAKENING ALLY ENCOUNTERED THE INTERNET...FOR BETTER OR WORSE.
SEX ITSELF STILL SCARED HER. HOWEVER, THAT OTHER THING, THE DOMINATRIX LOOK, THE ATTITUDE! SHE NEVER FORGOT THAT.
SO IN HER RARE MOMENTS OF SOLITUDE, SHE ***SEARCHED***, AND INTERNET ***DELIVERED.*** BECAUSE, IF THERE IS ANYTHING THE INTERNET DOES WELL, IT IS CATER TO FETISHISTS. WELL, THAT, AND THE WHOLE CAT PICTURES THING.
WITH HER TASTES DEVELOPING, SHE SPENT QUITE A BIT OF HER HIGH SCHOOL AGE THINKING...IMAGINING...
CONSIDERING THE IDEA OF HERSELF FEELING POWERFUL...
CONFIDENT.
I REMEMBER HER BEING IN AN ONLINE DISCUSSION ONCE, ARGUING ABOUT SOME SUPERHEROINE COSTUME... I REMEMBER IT WELL, AS SHE KEPT RANTING ABOUT IT TO ME...
I...COULDN'T CARE LESS.
ANYHOW, APPARENTLY THE CHARACTER IN QUESTION SAID HER COSTUME MADE HER FEEL POWERFUL.
GIVEN HOW EXTREMELY OVERSEXUALIZED THE COSTUME WAS, MANY ASKED THE OBVIOUS QUESTION: "WHO THE HELL WOULD FIND THAT OUTFIT EMPOWERING?"
ALLY SIMPLY SAID... A ***FETISHIST!***
SHE KNEW WHAT SHE WAS TALKING ABOUT.
THEN, BEING A WRITER, AND A SMARTASS, I ASKED THE OTHER OBVIOUS QUESTION: "WAS SHE ***WRITTEN*** AS A FETISHIST?" I...REGRETTED ASKING THAT. FOUR HOURS OF MY LIFE UTTERLY WASTED.

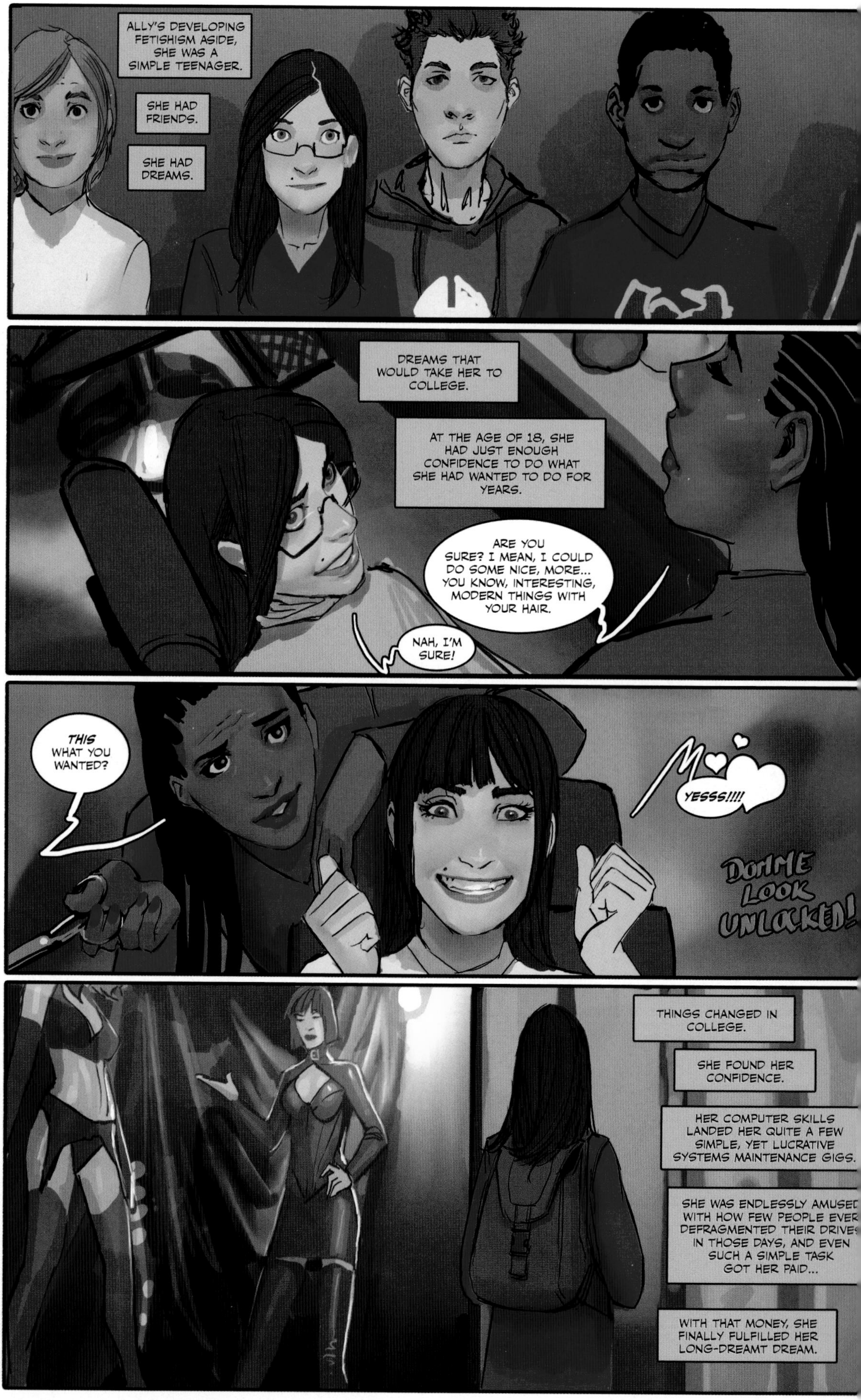
ALLY'S DEVELOPING FETISHISM ASIDE, SHE WAS A SIMPLE TEENAGER.
SHE HAD FRIENDS.
SHE HAD DREAMS.
DREAMS THAT WOULD TAKE HER TO COLLEGE.
AT THE AGE OF 18, SHE HAD JUST ENOUGH CONFIDENCE TO DO WHAT SHE HAD WANTED TO DO FOR YEARS.
ARE YOU SURE? I MEAN, I COULD DO SOME NICE, MORE... YOU KNOW, INTERESTING, MODERN THINGS WITH YOUR HAIR.
NAH, I'M SURE!
THIS WHAT YOU WANTED?
YESSS!!!!
DOMME LOOK UNLOCKED!
THINGS CHANGED IN COLLEGE.
SHE FOUND HER CONFIDENCE.
HER COMPUTER SKILLS LANDED HER QUITE A FEW SIMPLE, YET LUCRATIVE SYSTEMS MAINTENANCE GIGS.
SHE WAS ENDLESSLY AMUSED WITH HOW FEW PEOPLE EVER DEFRAGMENTED THEIR DRIVES IN THOSE DAYS, AND EVEN SUCH A SIMPLE TASK GOT HER PAID...
WITH THAT MONEY, SHE FINALLY FULFILLED HER LONG-DREAMT DREAM.

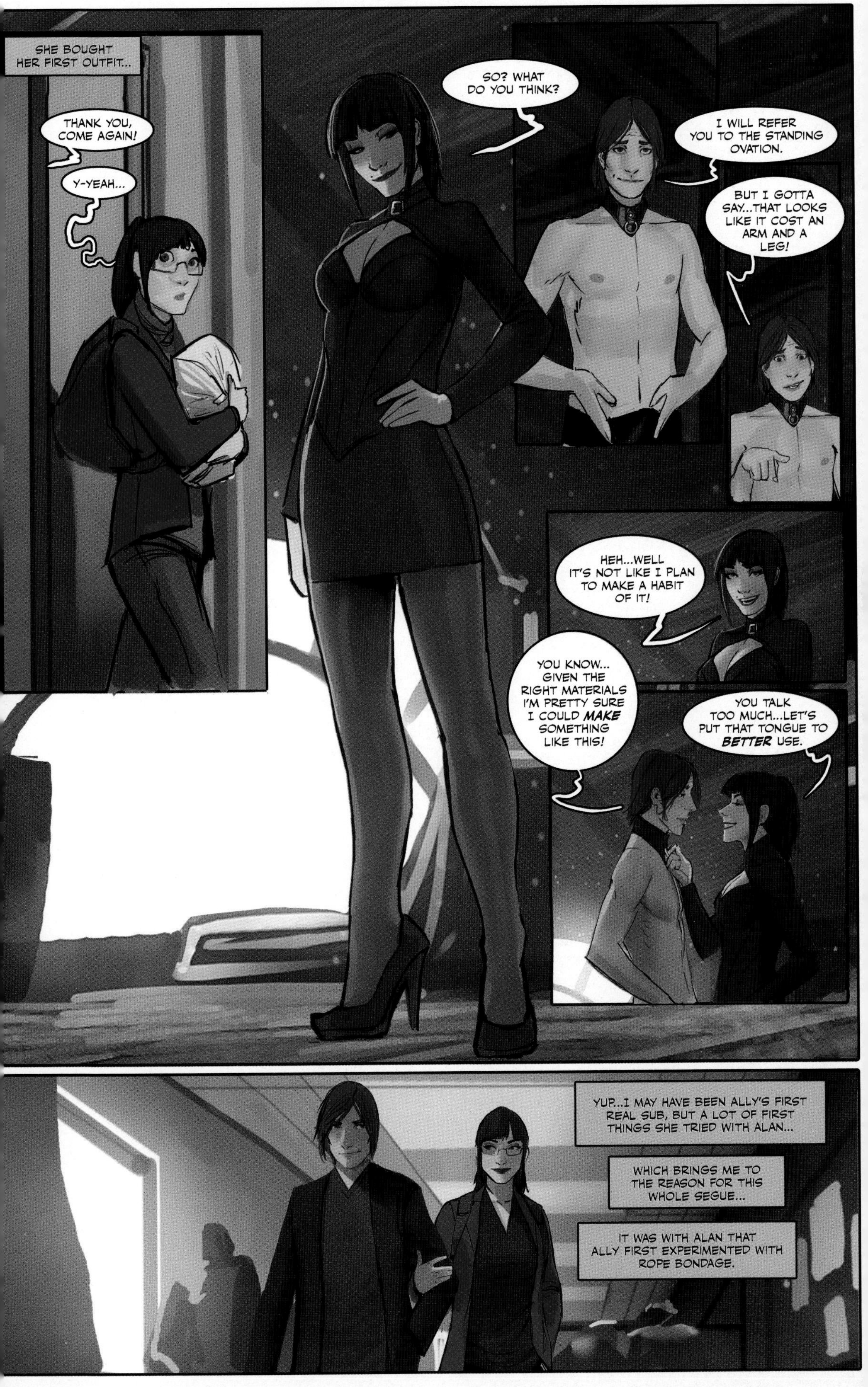

SHE BOUGHT HER FIRST OUTFIT...
THANK YOU, COME AGAIN!
Y-YEAH...
SO? WHAT DO YOU THINK?
I WILL REFER YOU TO THE STANDING OVATION.
BUT I GOTTA SAY...THAT LOOKS LIKE IT COST AN ARM AND A LEG!
HEH...WELL IT'S NOT LIKE I PLAN TO MAKE A HABIT OF IT!
YOU KNOW... GIVEN THE RIGHT MATERIALS I'M PRETTY SURE I COULD MAKE SOMETHING LIKE THIS!
YOU TALK TOO MUCH...LET'S PUT THAT TONGUE TO BETTER USE.
YUP...I MAY HAVE BEEN ALLY'S FIRST REAL SUB, BUT A LOT OF FIRST THINGS SHE TRIED WITH ALAN...
WHICH BRINGS ME TO THE REASON FOR THIS WHOLE SEGUE...
IT WAS WITH ALAN THAT ALLY FIRST EXPERIMENTED WITH ROPE BONDAGE.

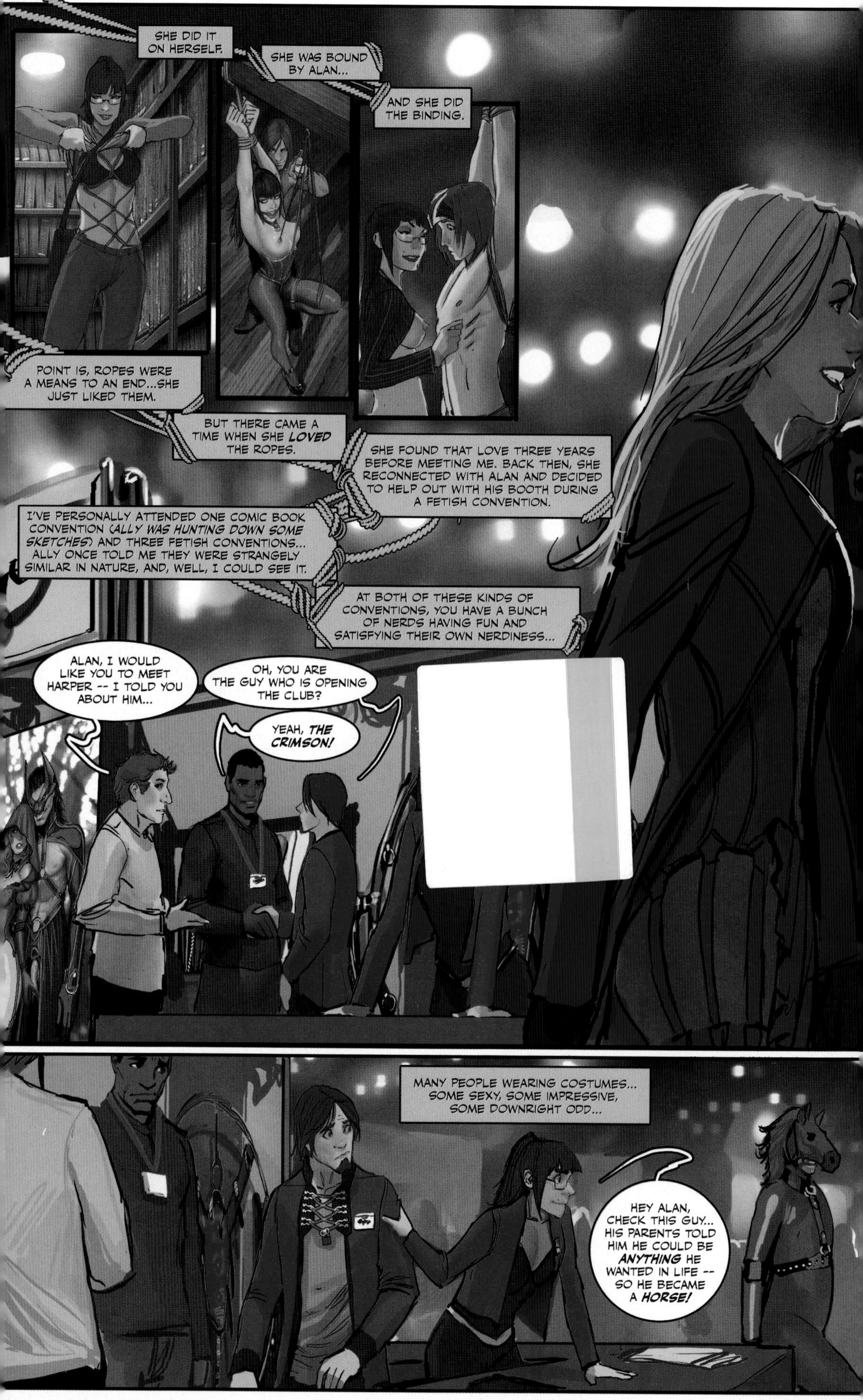
SHE DID IT ON HERSELF.
SHE WAS BOUND BY ALAN...
AND SHE DID THE BINDING.
POINT IS, ROPES WERE A MEANS TO AN END...SHE JUST LIKED THEM.
BUT THERE CAME A TIME WHEN SHE LOVED THE ROPES.
SHE FOUND THAT LOVE THREE YEARS BEFORE MEETING ME. BACK THEN, SHE RECONNECTED WITH ALAN AND DECIDED TO HELP OUT WITH HIS BOOTH DURING A FETISH CONVENTION.
I'VE PERSONALLY ATTENDED ONE COMIC BOOK CONVENTION (ALLY WAS HUNTING DOWN SOME SKETCHES) AND THREE FETISH CONVENTIONS... ALLY ONCE TOLD ME THEY WERE STRANGELY SIMILAR IN NATURE, AND, WELL, I COULD SEE IT.
AT BOTH OF THESE KINDS OF CONVENTIONS, YOU HAVE A BUNCH OF NERDS HAVING FUN AND SATISFYING THEIR OWN NERDINESS...
ALAN, I WOULD LIKE YOU TO MEET HARPER -- I TOLD YOU ABOUT HIM...
OH, YOU ARE THE GUY WHO IS OPENING THE CLUB?
YEAH, THE CRIMSON!
MANY PEOPLE WEARING COSTUMES... SOME SEXY, SOME IMPRESSIVE, SOME DOWNRIGHT ODD...
HEY ALAN, CHECK THIS GUY... HIS PARENTS TOLD HIM HE COULD BE ANYTHING HE WANTED IN LIFE -- SO HE BECAME A HORSE!

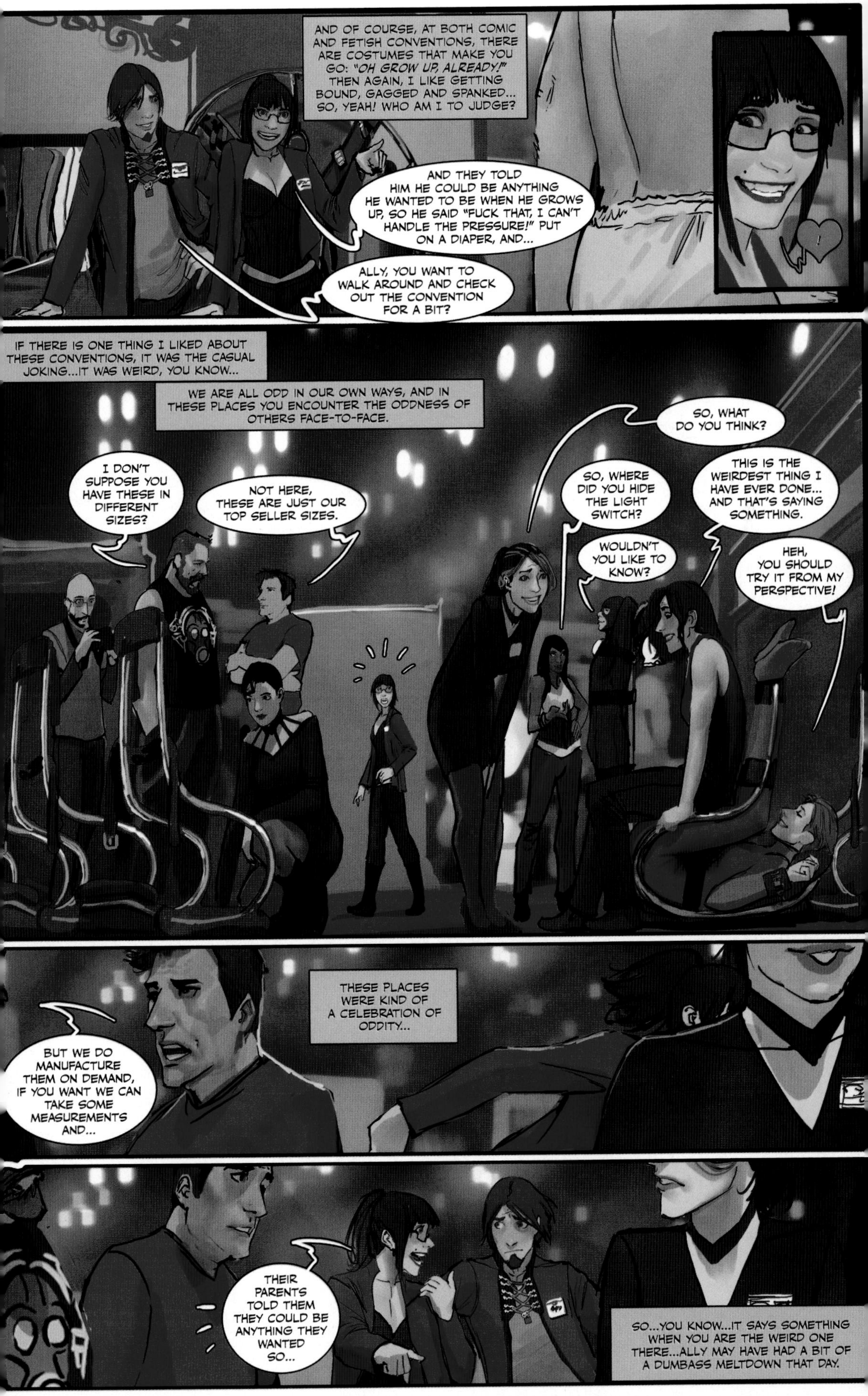

AND OF COURSE, AT BOTH COMIC AND FETISH CONVENTIONS, THERE ARE COSTUMES THAT MAKE YOU GO: "OH GROW UP, ALREADY!" THEN AGAIN, I LIKE GETTING BOUND, GAGGED AND SPANKED... SO, YEAH! WHO AM I TO JUDGE?
AND THEY TOLD HIM HE COULD BE ANYTHING HE WANTED TO BE WHEN HE GROWS UP, SO HE SAID "FUCK THAT, I CAN'T HANDLE THE PRESSURE!" PUT ON A DIAPER, AND...
ALLY, YOU WANT TO WALK AROUND AND CHECK OUT THE CONVENTION FOR A BIT?
IF THERE IS ONE THING I LIKED ABOUT THESE CONVENTIONS, IT WAS THE CASUAL JOKING...IT WAS WEIRD, YOU KNOW...
WE ARE ALL ODD IN OUR OWN WAYS, AND IN THESE PLACES YOU ENCOUNTER THE ODDNESS OF OTHERS FACE-TO-FACE.
I DON'T SUPPOSE YOU HAVE THESE IN DIFFERENT SIZES?
NOT HERE, THESE ARE JUST OUR TOP SELLER SIZES.
SO, WHAT DO YOU THINK?
SO, WHERE DID YOU HIDE THE LIGHT SWITCH?
WOULDN'T YOU LIKE TO KNOW?
THIS IS THE WEIRDEST THING I HAVE EVER DONE... AND THAT'S SAYING SOMETHING.
HEH, YOU SHOULD TRY IT FROM MY PERSPECTIVE!
THESE PLACES WERE KIND OF A CELEBRATION OF ODDITY...
BUT WE DO MANUFACTURE THEM ON DEMAND, IF YOU WANT WE CAN TAKE SOME MEASUREMENTS AND...
THEIR PARENTS TOLD THEM THEY COULD BE ANYTHING THEY WANTED SO...
SO...YOU KNOW...IT SAYS SOMETHING WHEN YOU ARE THE WEIRD ONE THERE...ALLY MAY HAVE HAD A BIT OF A DUMBASS MELTDOWN THAT DAY.

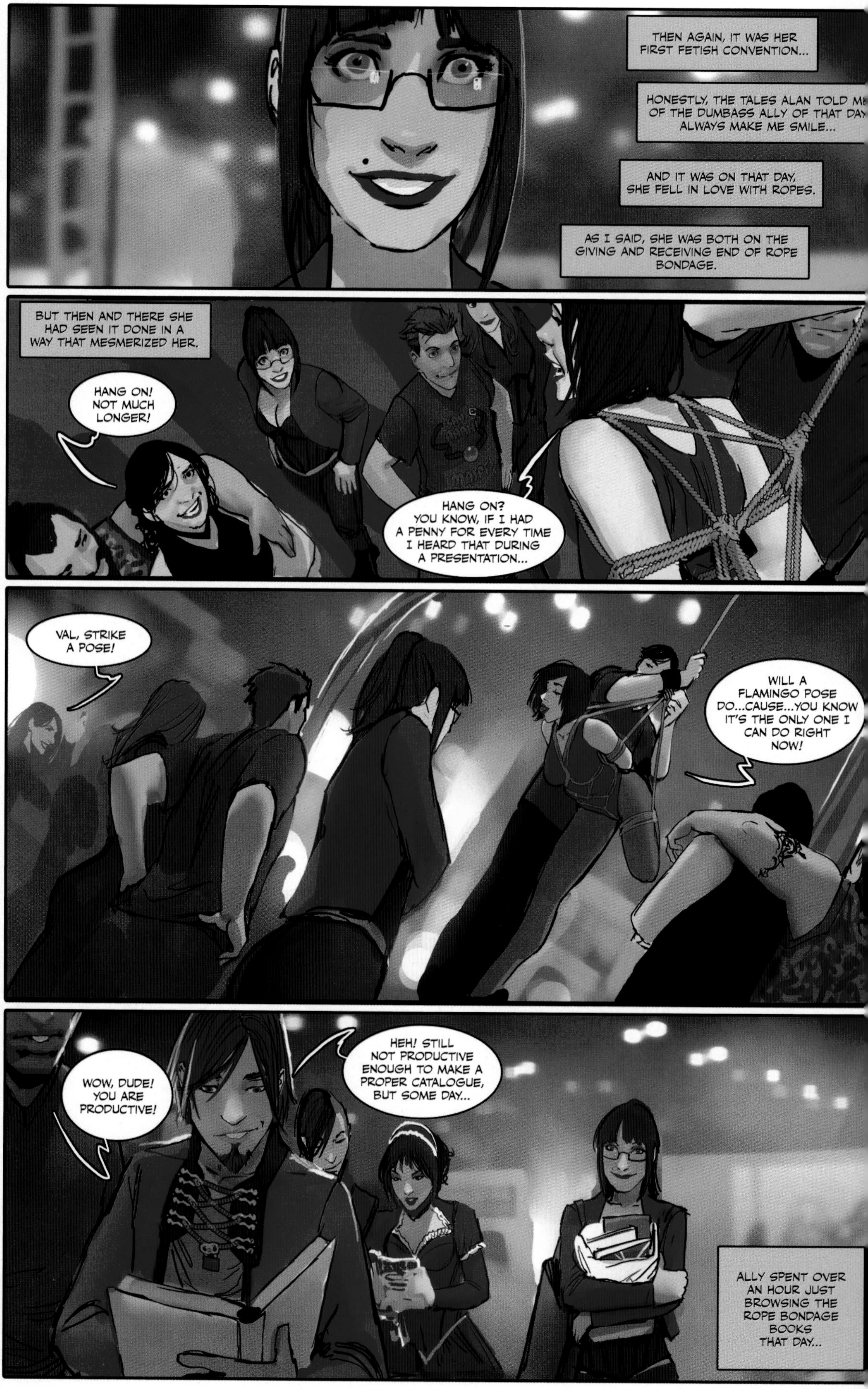
THEN AGAIN, IT WAS HER FIRST FETISH CONVENTION...
HONESTLY, THE TALES ALAN TOLD ME OF THE DUMBASS ALLY OF THAT DAY ALWAYS MAKE ME SMILE...
AND IT WAS ON THAT DAY, SHE FELL IN LOVE WITH ROPES.
AS I SAID, SHE WAS BOTH ON THE GIVING AND RECEIVING END OF ROPE BONDAGE.
BUT THEN AND THERE SHE HAD SEEN IT DONE IN A WAY THAT MESMERIZED HER.
HANG ON! NOT MUCH LONGER!
HANG ON? YOU KNOW, IF I HAD A PENNY FOR EVERY TIME I HEARD THAT DURING A PRESENTATION...
VAL, STRIKE A POSE!
WILL A FLAMINGO POSE DO...CAUSE...YOU KNOW IT'S THE ONLY ONE I CAN DO RIGHT NOW!
WOW, DUDE! YOU ARE PRODUCTIVE!
HEH! STILL NOT PRODUCTIVE ENOUGH TO MAKE A PROPER CATALOGUE, BUT SOME DAY...
ALLY SPENT OVER AN HOUR JUST BROWSING THE ROPE BONDAGE BOOKS THAT DAY...

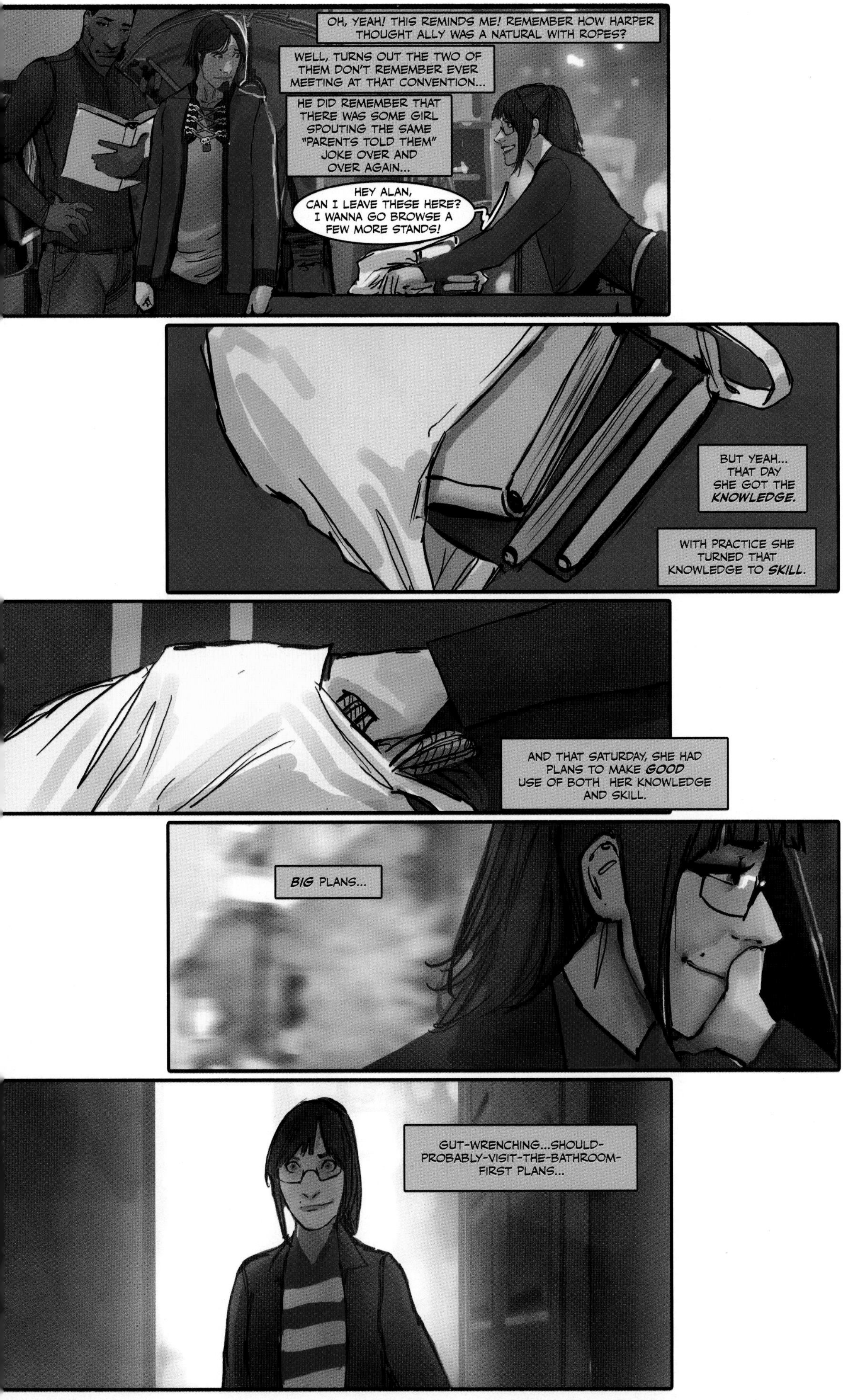
OH, YEAH! THIS REMINDS ME! REMEMBER HOW HARPER THOUGHT ALLY WAS A NATURAL WITH ROPES?
WELL, TURNS OUT THE TWO OF THEM DON'T REMEMBER EVER MEETING AT THAT CONVENTION...
HE DID REMEMBER THAT THERE WAS SOME GIRL SPOUTING THE SAME "PARENTS TOLD THEM" JOKE OVER AND OVER AGAIN...
HEY ALAN, CAN I LEAVE THESE HERE? I WANNA GO BROWSE A FEW MORE STANDS!
BUT YEAH... THAT DAY SHE GOT THE *KNOWLEDGE.*
WITH PRACTICE SHE TURNED THAT KNOWLEDGE TO *SKILL.*
AND THAT SATURDAY, SHE HAD PLANS TO MAKE *GOOD* USE OF BOTH HER KNOWLEDGE AND SKILL.
BIG PLANS...
GUT-WRENCHING...SHOULD-PROBABLY-VISIT-THE-BATHROOM-FIRST PLANS...

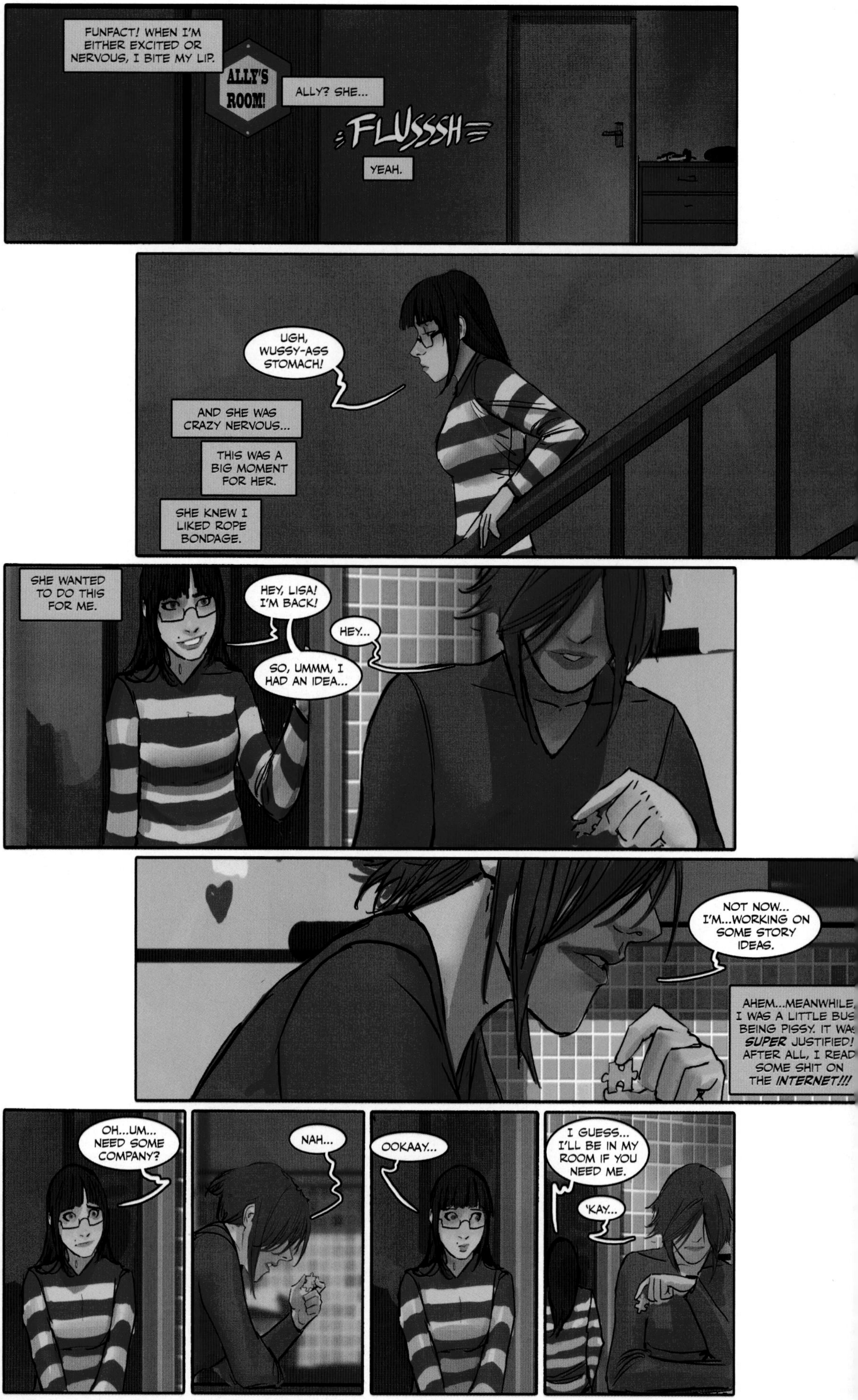
FUNFACT! WHEN I'M EITHER EXCITED OR NERVOUS, I BITE MY LIP.
ALLY'S ROOM!
ALLY? SHE...
FLUSSSH
YEAH.
UGH, WUSSY-ASS STOMACH!
AND SHE WAS CRAZY NERVOUS...
THIS WAS A BIG MOMENT FOR HER.
SHE KNEW I LIKED ROPE BONDAGE.
SHE WANTED TO DO THIS FOR ME.
HEY, LISA! I'M BACK!
HEY...
SO, UMMM, I HAD AN IDEA...
NOT NOW... I'M...WORKING ON SOME STORY IDEAS.
AHEM...MEANWHILE, I WAS A LITTLE BUS BEING PISSY. IT WAS SUPER JUSTIFIED! AFTER ALL, I READ SOME SHIT ON THE INTERNET!!!
OH...UM... NEED SOME COMPANY?
NAH...
OOKAAY...
I GUESS... I'LL BE IN MY ROOM IF YOU NEED ME.
'KAY...

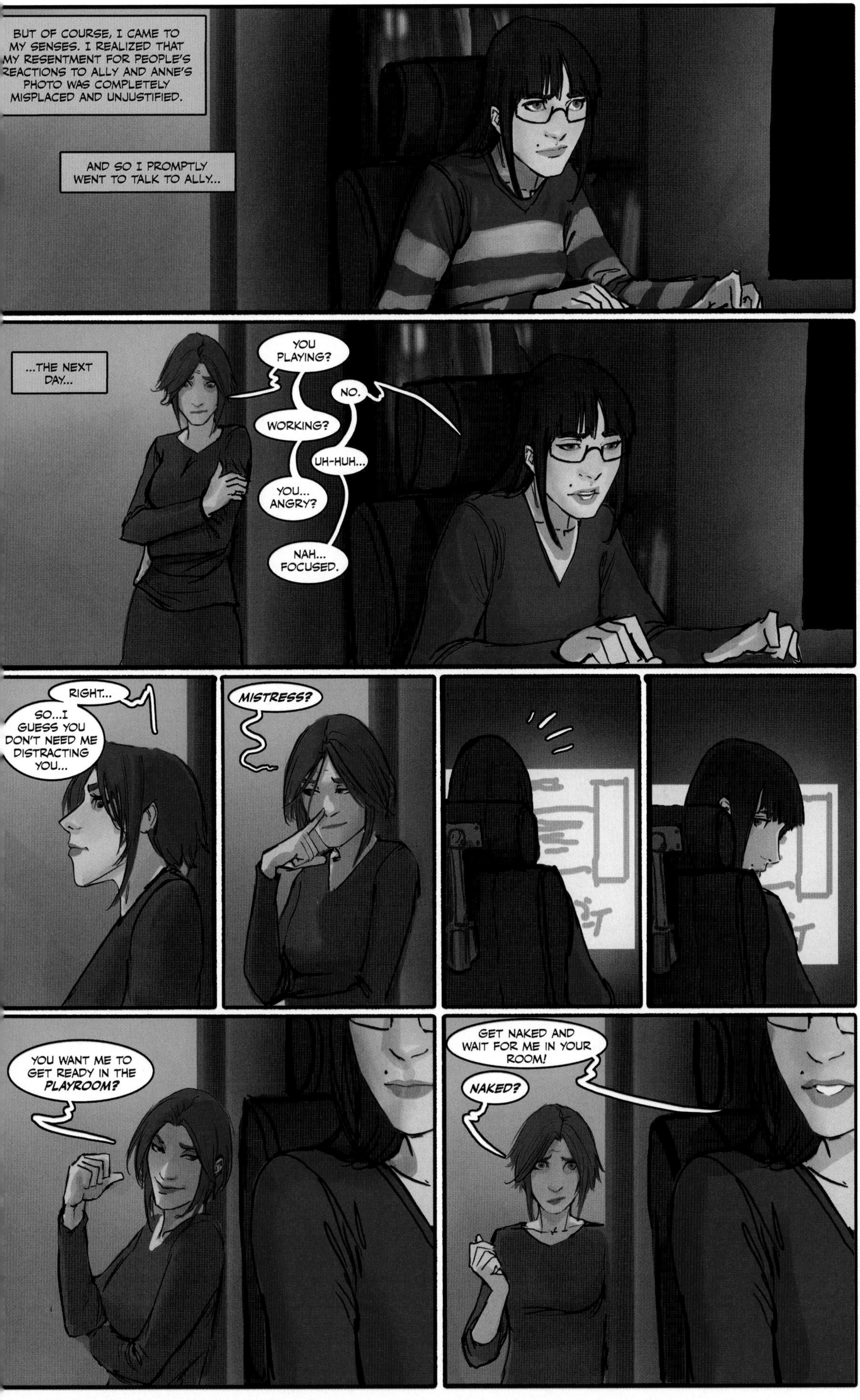
BUT OF COURSE, I CAME TO MY SENSES. I REALIZED THAT MY RESENTMENT FOR PEOPLE'S REACTIONS TO ALLY AND ANNE'S PHOTO WAS COMPLETELY MISPLACED AND UNJUSTIFIED.
AND SO I PROMPTLY WENT TO TALK TO ALLY...
...THE NEXT DAY...
YOU PLAYING?
NO.
WORKING?
UH-HUH...
YOU... ANGRY?
NAH... FOCUSED.
RIGHT...
SO...I GUESS YOU DON'T NEED ME DISTRACTING YOU...
MISTRESS?
YOU WANT ME TO GET READY IN THE PLAYROOM?
GET NAKED AND WAIT FOR ME IN YOUR ROOM!
NAKED?

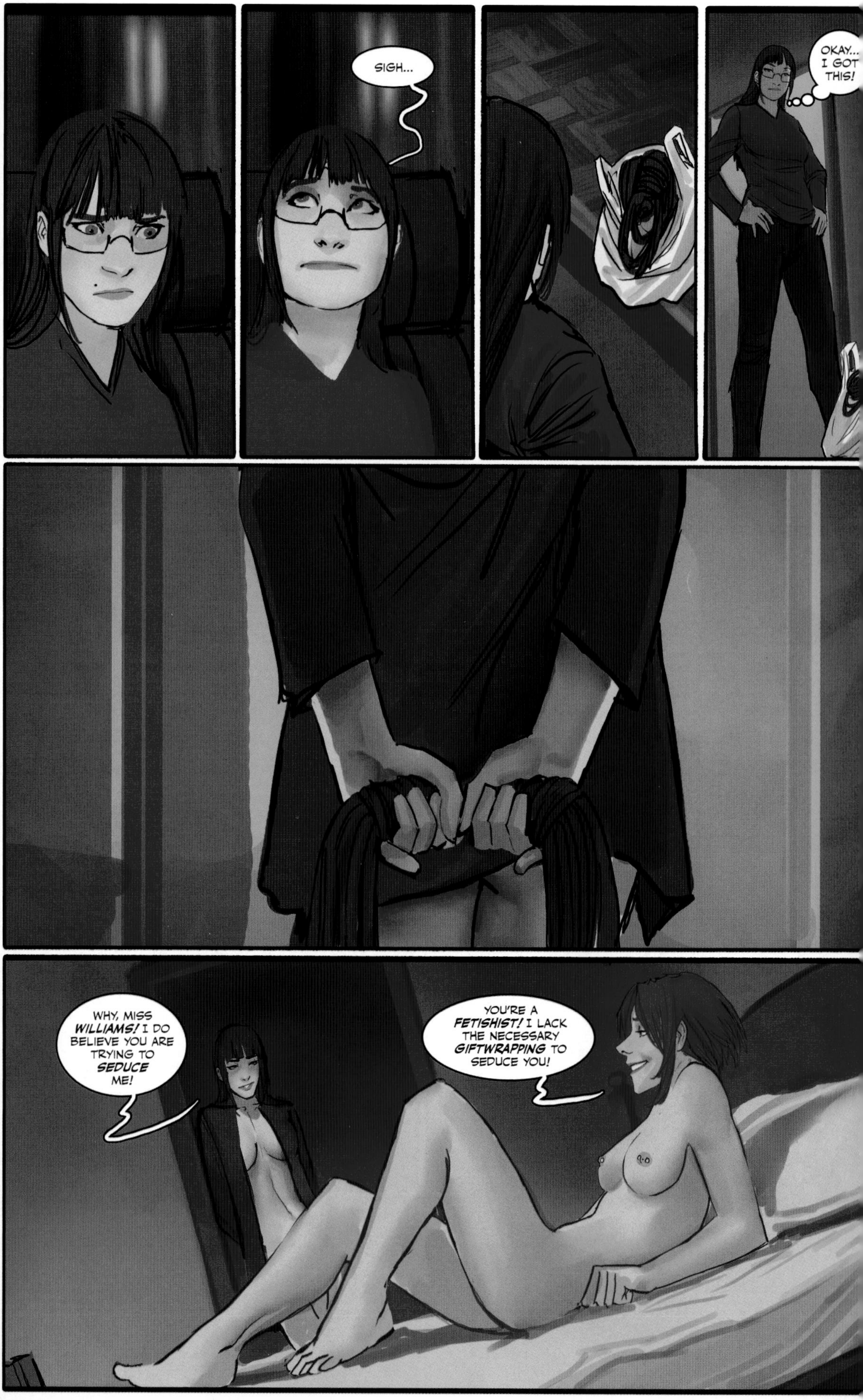
SIGH...
OKAY... I GOT THIS!
WHY, MISS WILLIAMS! I DO BELIEVE YOU ARE TRYING TO SEDUCE ME!
YOU'RE A FETISHIST! I LACK THE NECESSARY GIFTWRAPPING TO SEDUCE YOU!

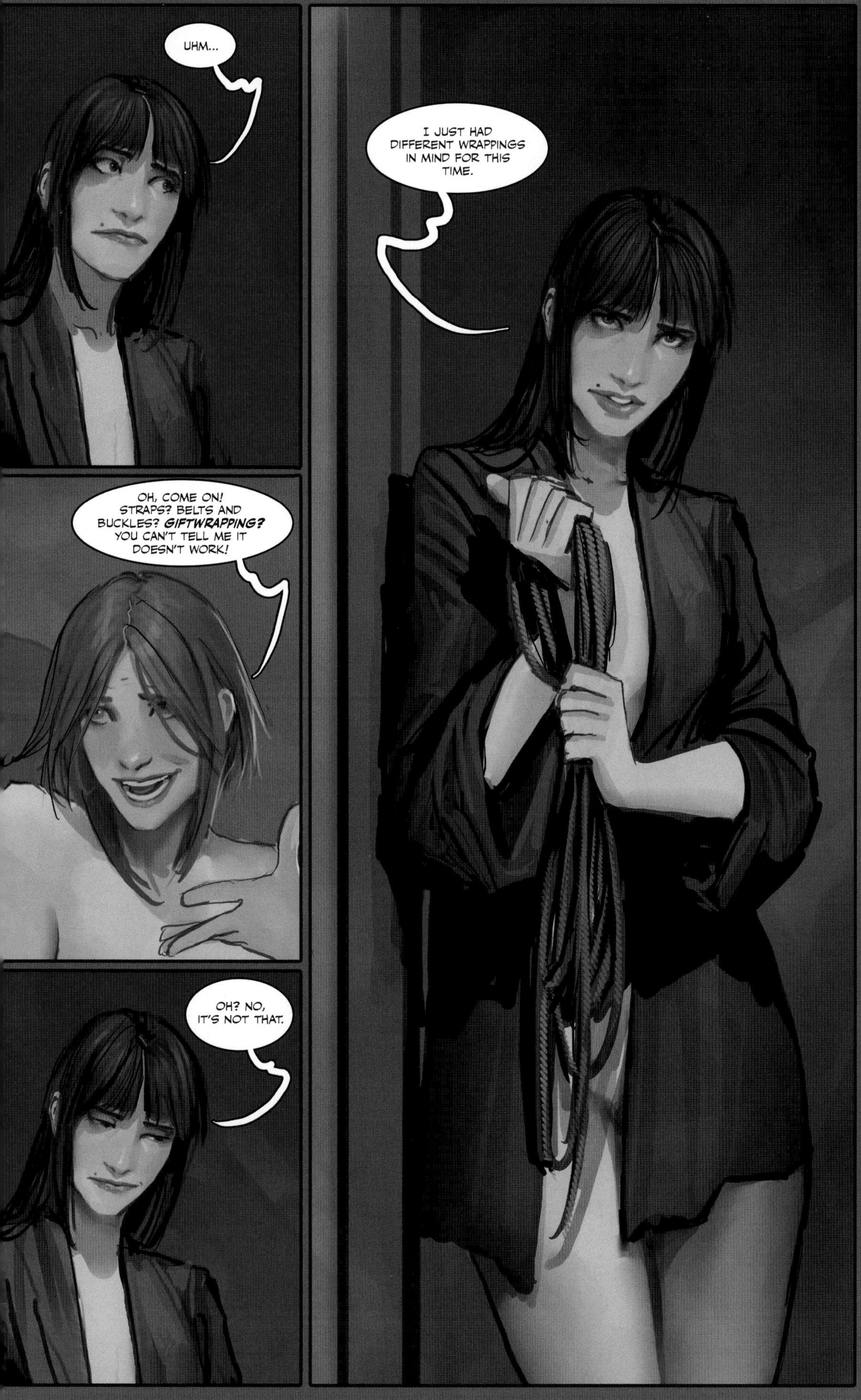
UHM...
OH, COME ON! STRAPS? BELTS AND BUCKLES? *GIFTWRAPPING?* YOU CAN'T TELL ME IT DOESN'T WORK!
OH? NO, IT'S NOT THAT.
I JUST HAD DIFFERENT WRAPPINGS IN MIND FOR THIS TIME.

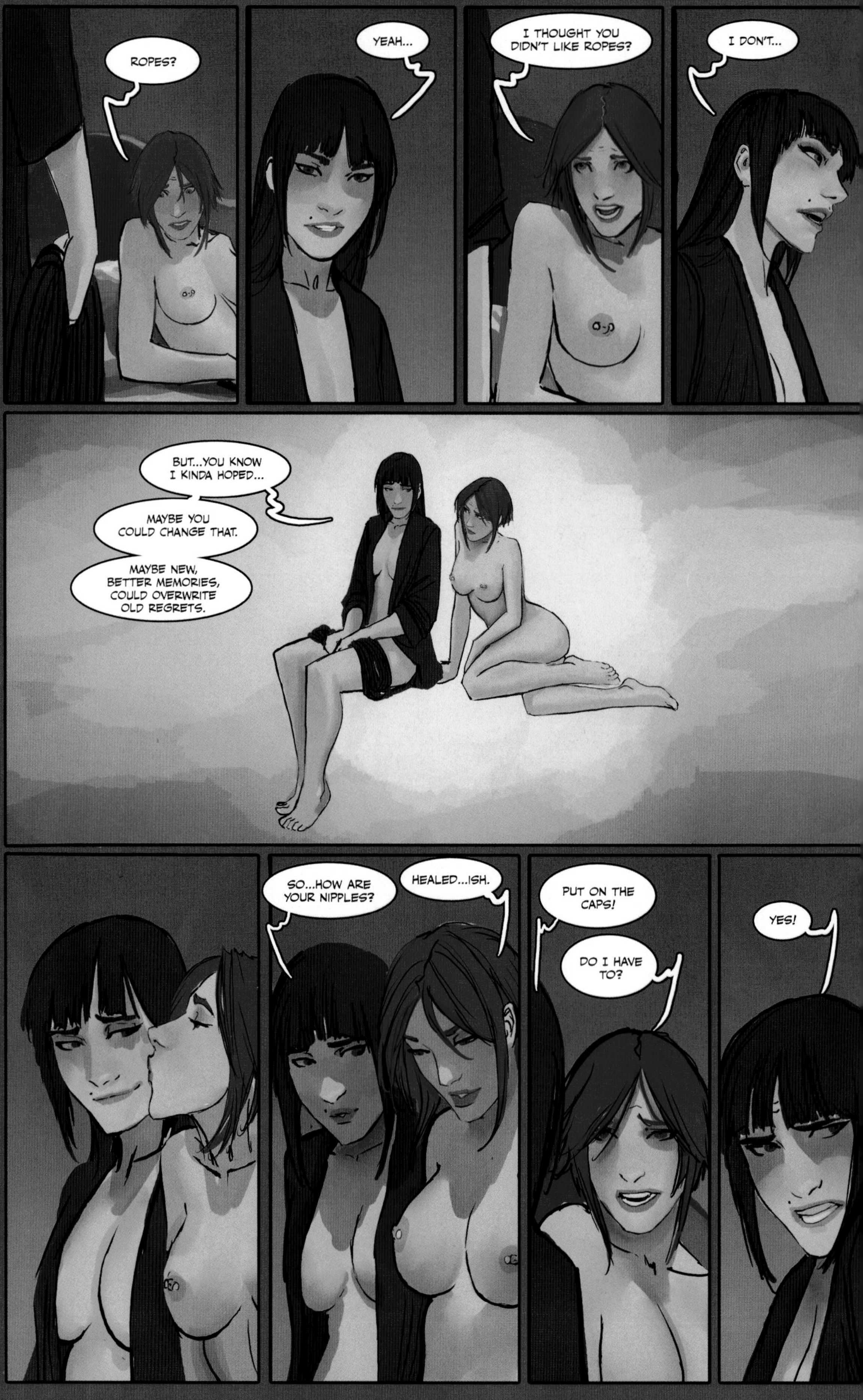
ROPES?
YEAH...
I THOUGHT YOU DIDN'T LIKE ROPES?
I DON'T...
BUT...YOU KNOW I KINDA HOPED...
MAYBE YOU COULD CHANGE THAT.
MAYBE NEW, BETTER MEMORIES, COULD OVERWRITE OLD REGRETS.
SO...HOW ARE YOUR NIPPLES?
HEALED...ISH.
PUT ON THE CAPS!
DO I HAVE TO?
YES!

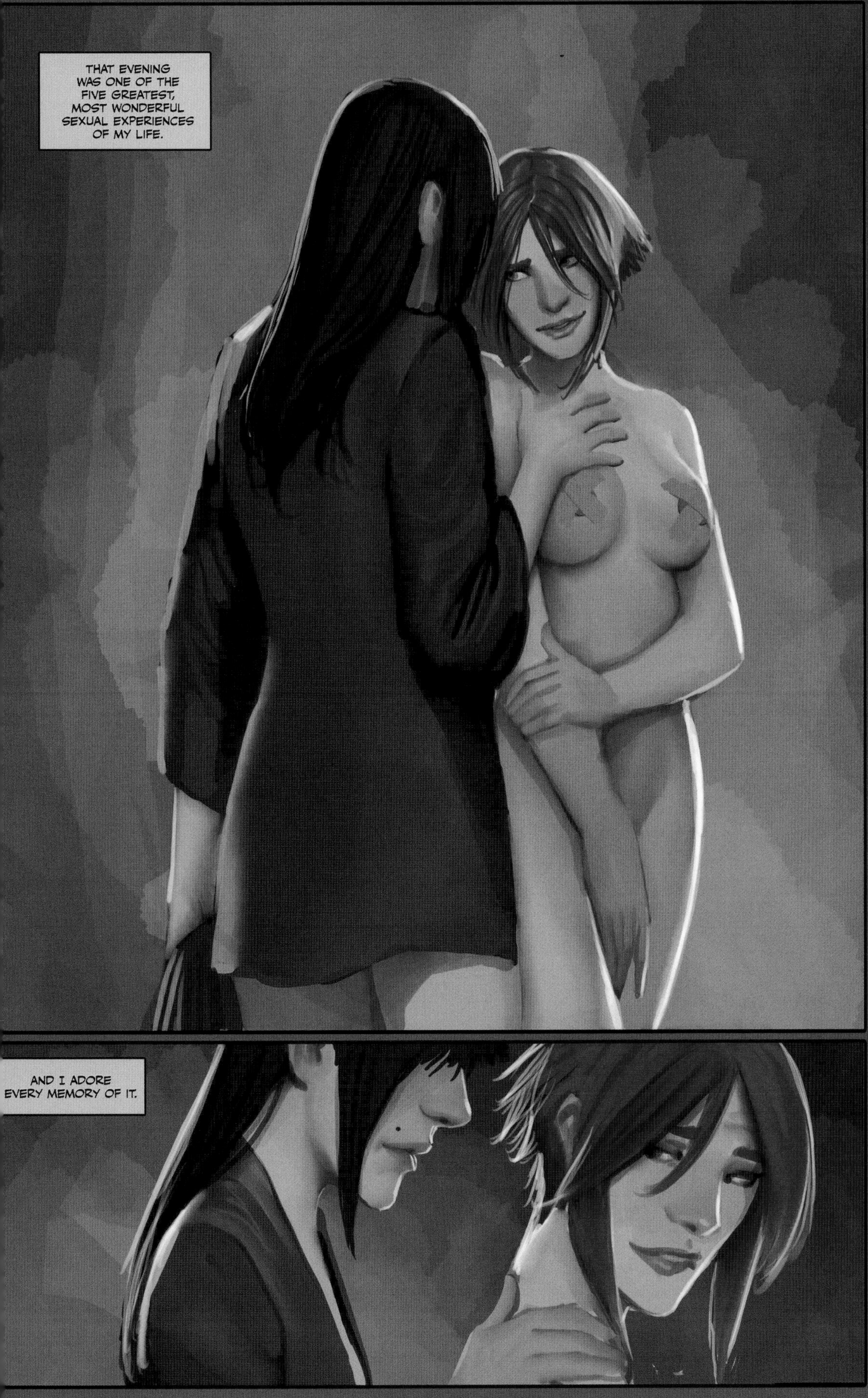
THAT EVENING WAS ONE OF THE FIVE GREATEST, MOST WONDERFUL SEXUAL EXPERIENCES OF MY LIFE.
AND I ADORE EVERY MEMORY OF IT.

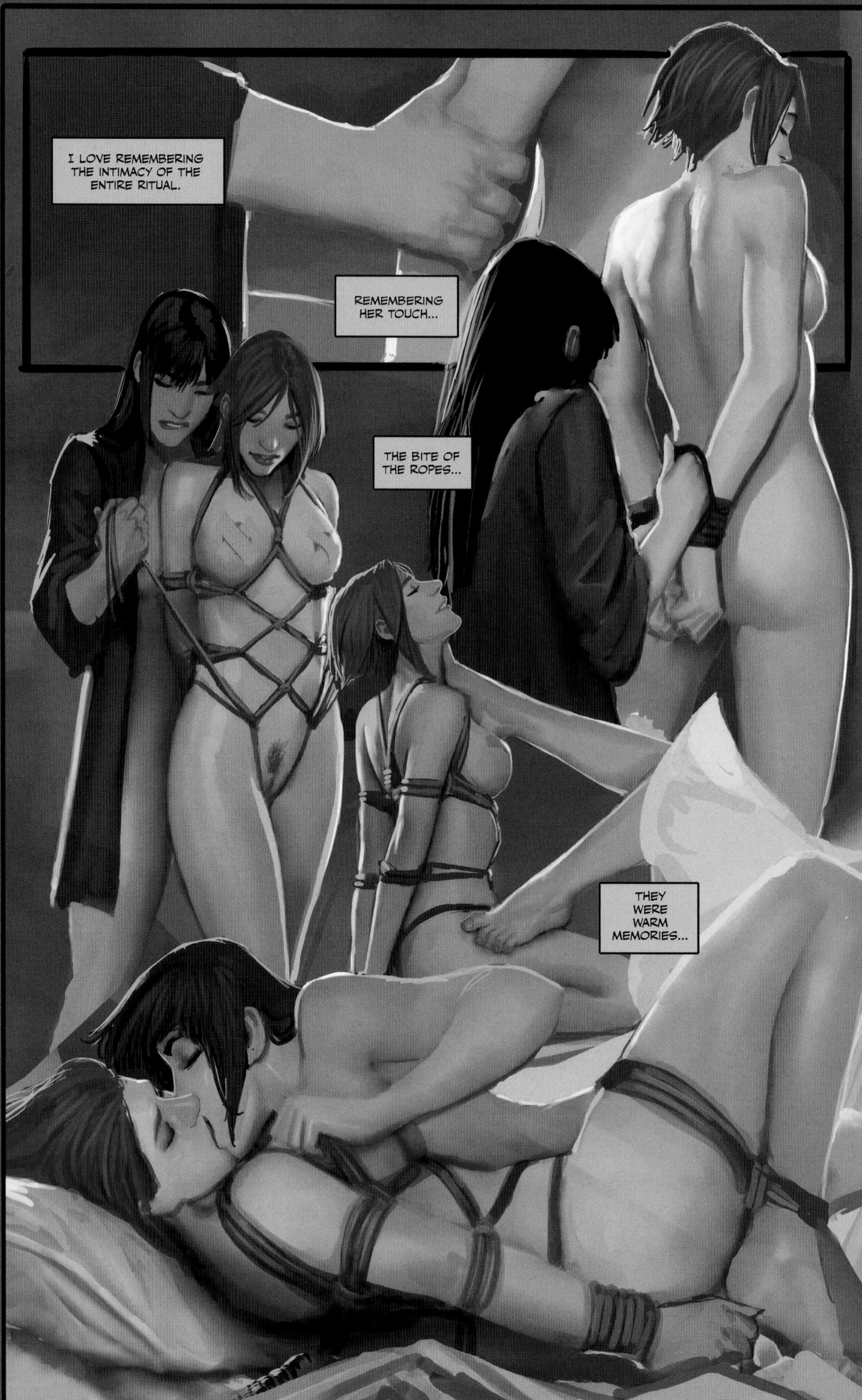
I LOVE REMEMBERING THE INTIMACY OF THE ENTIRE RITUAL.
REMEMBERING HER TOUCH...
THE BITE OF THE ROPES...
THEY WERE WARM MEMORIES...

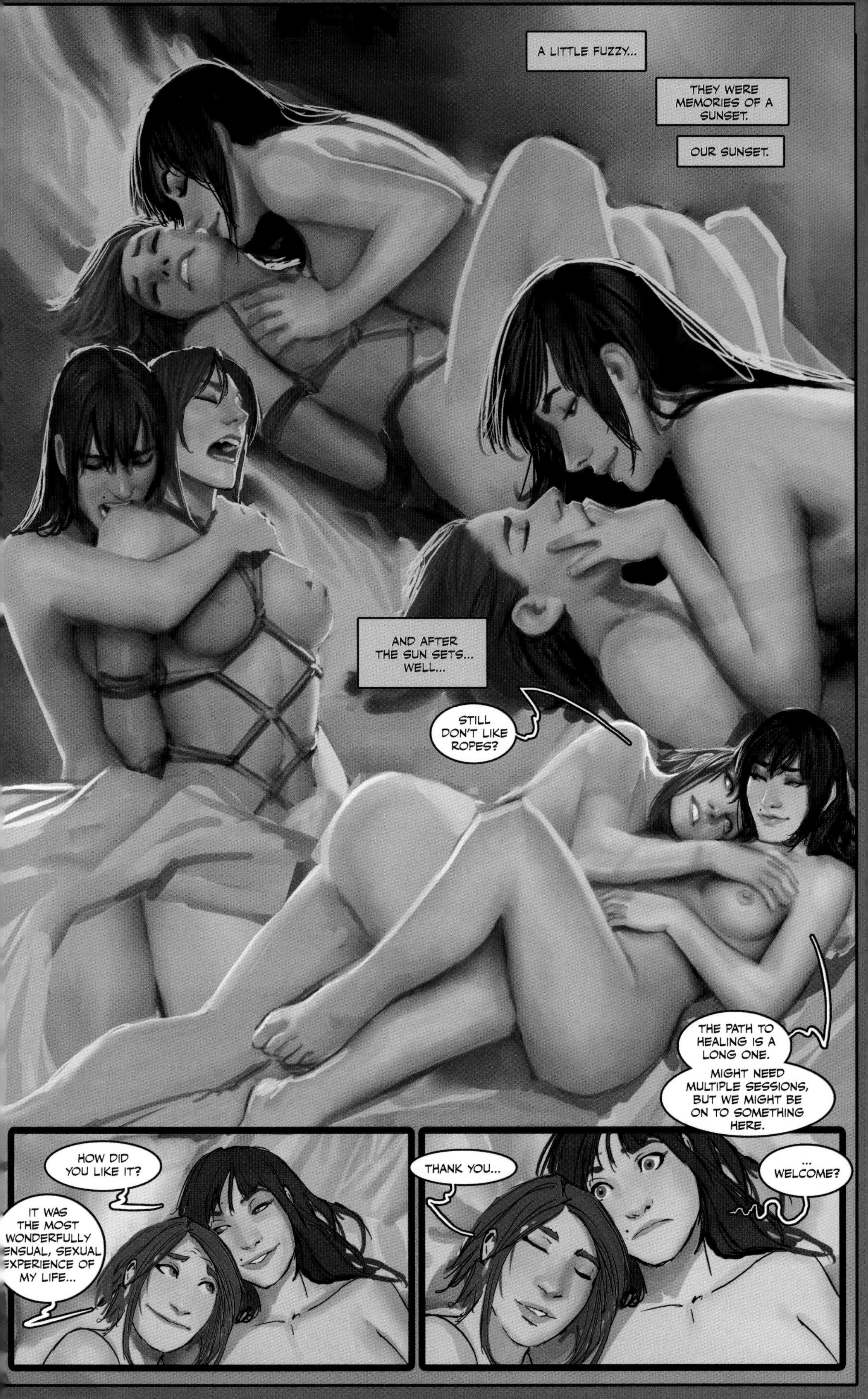
A LITTLE FUZZY...
THEY WERE MEMORIES OF A SUNSET.
OUR SUNSET.
AND AFTER THE SUN SETS... WELL...
STILL DON'T LIKE ROPES?
THE PATH TO HEALING IS A LONG ONE.
MIGHT NEED MULTIPLE SESSIONS, BUT WE MIGHT BE ON TO SOMETHING HERE.
HOW DID YOU LIKE IT?
IT WAS THE MOST WONDERFULLY ENSUAL, SEXUAL EXPERIENCE OF MY LIFE...
THANK YOU...
... WELCOME?

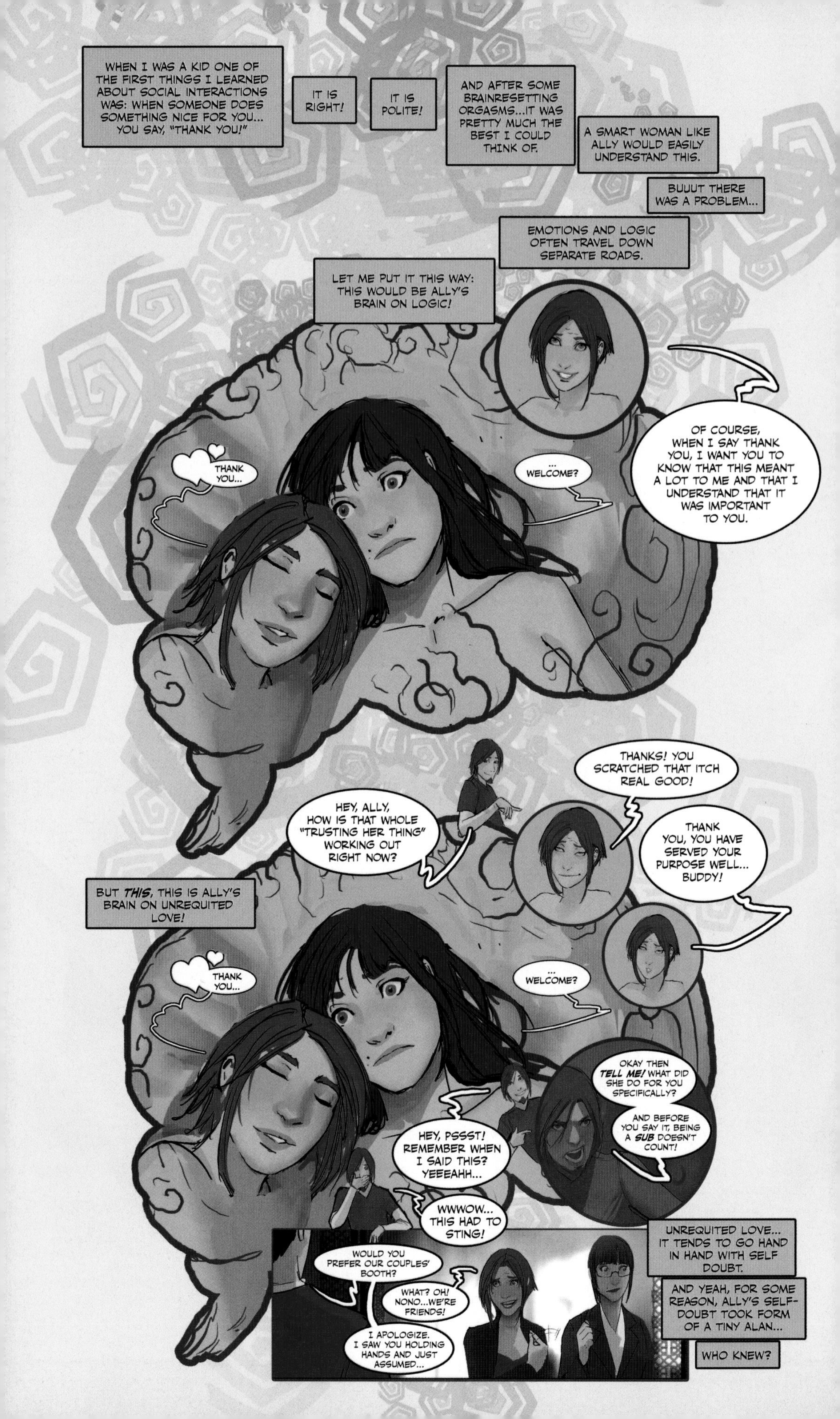
WHEN I WAS A KID ONE OF THE FIRST THINGS I LEARNED ABOUT SOCIAL INTERACTIONS WAS: WHEN SOMEONE DOES SOMETHING NICE FOR YOU... YOU SAY, "THANK YOU!"
IT IS RIGHT!
IT IS POLITE!
AND AFTER SOME BRAINRESETTING ORGASMS...IT WAS PRETTY MUCH THE BEST I COULD THINK OF.
A SMART WOMAN LIKE ALLY WOULD EASILY UNDERSTAND THIS.
BUUUT THERE WAS A PROBLEM...
EMOTIONS AND LOGIC OFTEN TRAVEL DOWN SEPARATE ROADS.
LET ME PUT IT THIS WAY: THIS WOULD BE ALLY'S BRAIN ON LOGIC!
THANK YOU...
... WELCOME?
OF COURSE, WHEN I SAY THANK YOU, I WANT YOU TO KNOW THAT THIS MEANT A LOT TO ME AND THAT I UNDERSTAND THAT IT WAS IMPORTANT TO YOU.
HEY, ALLY, HOW IS THAT WHOLE "TRUSTING HER THING" WORKING OUT RIGHT NOW?
THANKS! YOU SCRATCHED THAT ITCH REAL GOOD!
THANK YOU, YOU HAVE SERVED YOUR PURPOSE WELL... BUDDY!
BUT THIS, THIS IS ALLY'S BRAIN ON UNREQUITED LOVE!
THANK YOU...
... WELCOME?
OKAY THEN TELL ME! WHAT DID SHE DO FOR YOU SPECIFICALLY?
AND BEFORE YOU SAY IT, BEING A SUB DOESN'T COUNT!
HEY, PSSST! REMEMBER WHEN I SAID THIS? YEEEAHH...
WWWOW... THIS HAD TO STING!
WOULD YOU PREFER OUR COUPLES' BOOTH?
WHAT? OH! NONO...WE'RE FRIENDS!
I APOLOGIZE. I SAW YOU HOLDING HANDS AND JUST ASSUMED...
UNREQUITED LOVE... IT TENDS TO GO HAND IN HAND WITH SELF DOUBT.
AND YEAH, FOR SOME REASON, ALLY'S SELF-DOUBT TOOK FORM OF A TINY ALAN...
WHO KNEW?

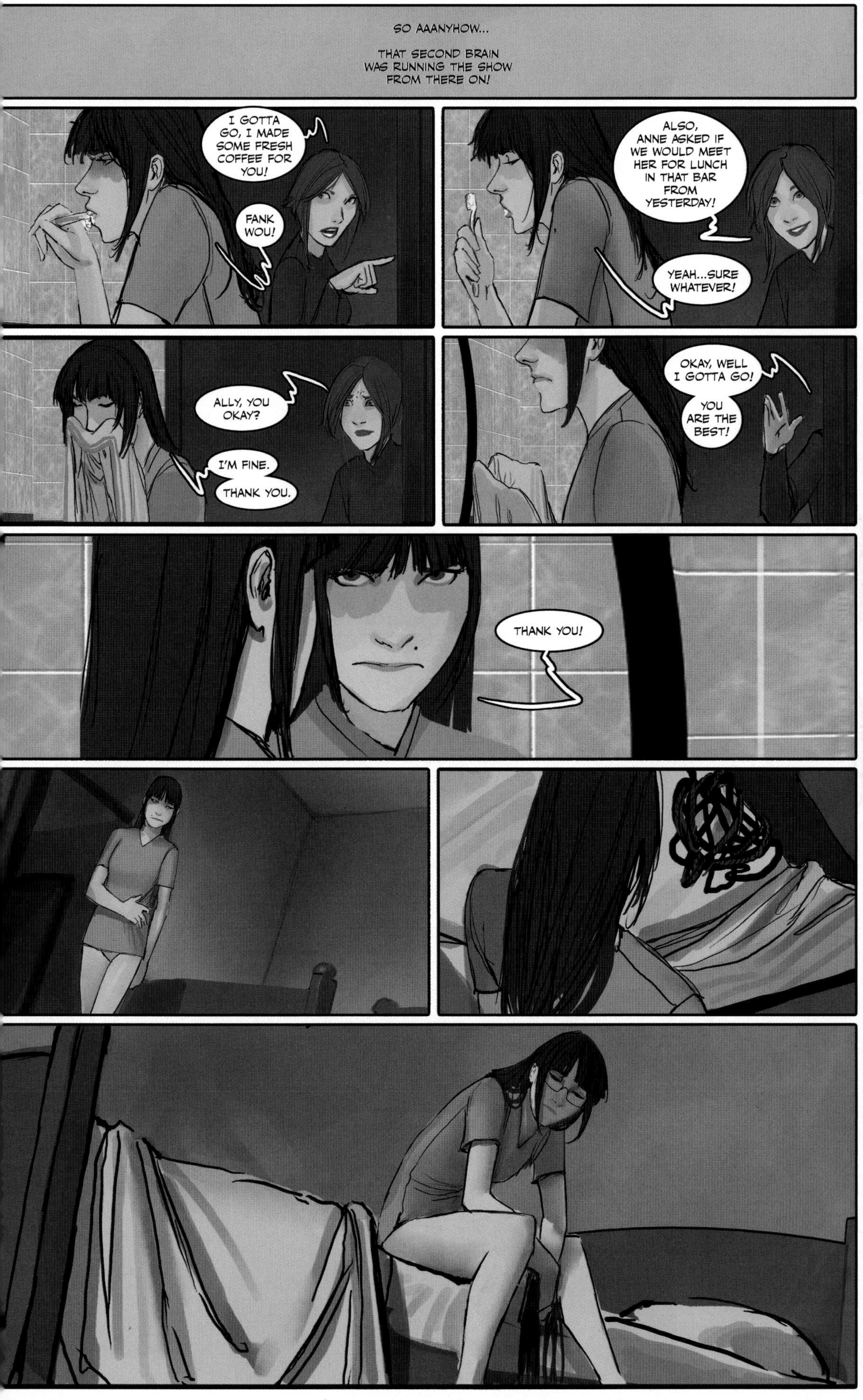
SO AAANYHOW...
THAT SECOND BRAIN WAS RUNNING THE SHOW FROM THERE ON!
I GOTTA GO, I MADE SOME FRESH COFFEE FOR YOU!
FANK WOU!
ALSO, ANNE ASKED IF WE WOULD MEET HER FOR LUNCH IN THAT BAR FROM YESTERDAY!
YEAH...SURE WHATEVER!
ALLY, YOU OKAY?
I'M FINE.
THANK YOU.
OKAY, WELL I GOTTA GO!
YOU ARE THE BEST!
THANK YOU!

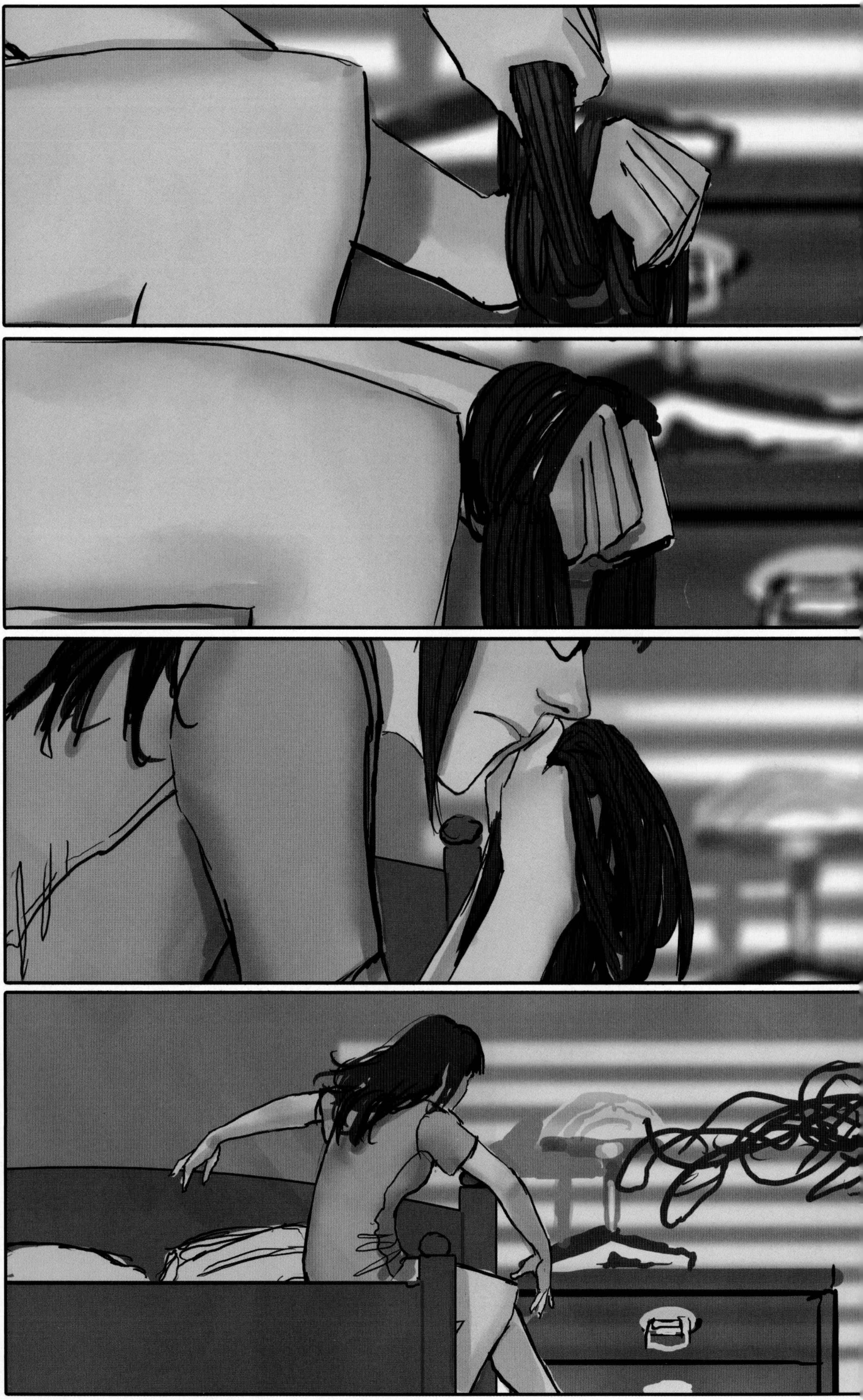

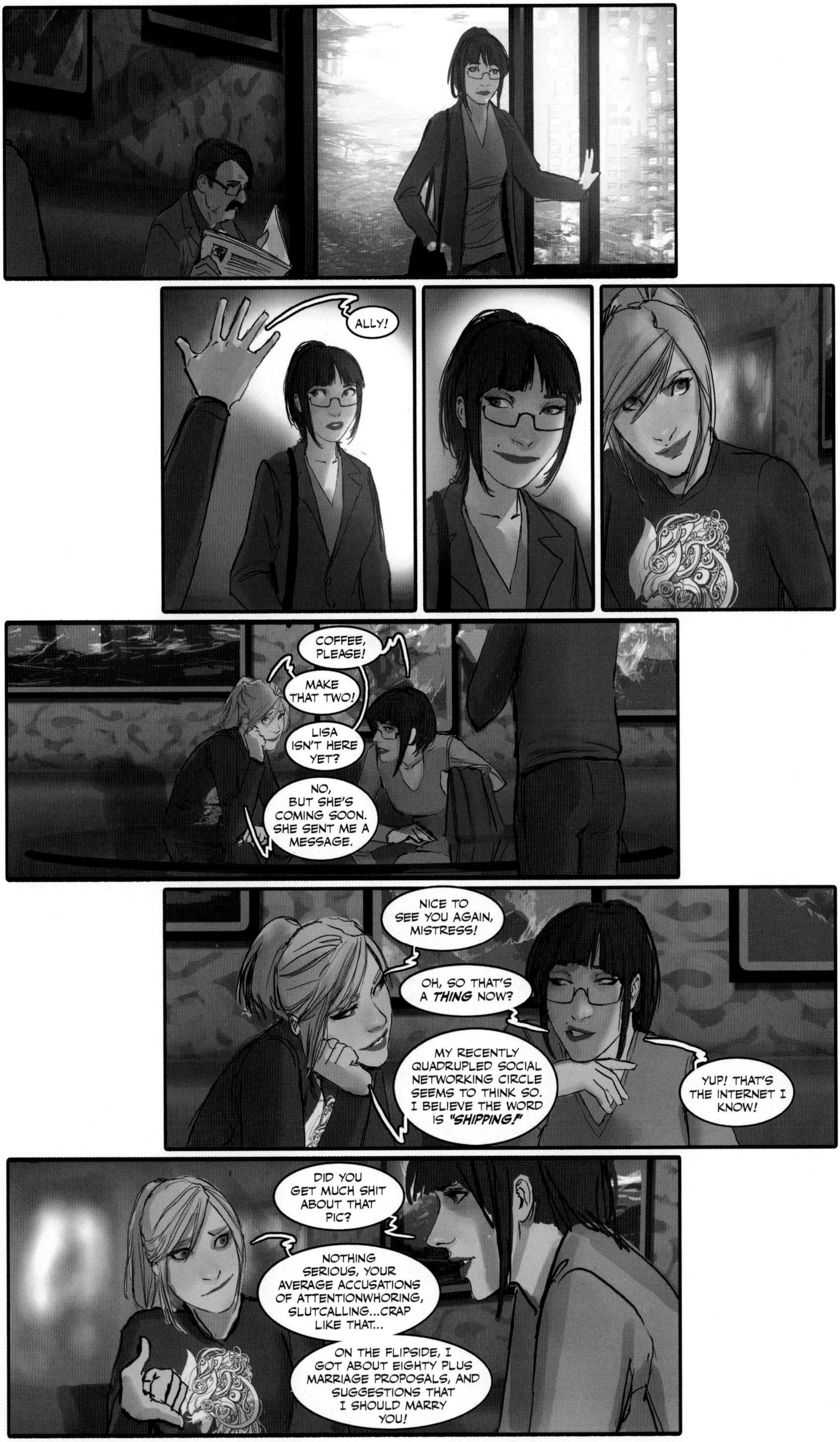
ALLY!
COFFEE, PLEASE!
MAKE THAT TWO!
LISA ISN'T HERE YET?
NO, BUT SHE'S COMING SOON. SHE SENT ME A MESSAGE.
NICE TO SEE YOU AGAIN, MISTRESS!
OH, SO THAT'S A *THING* NOW?
MY RECENTLY QUADRUPLED SOCIAL NETWORKING CIRCLE SEEMS TO THINK SO. I BELIEVE THE WORD IS *"SHIPPING!"*
YUP! THAT'S THE INTERNET I KNOW!
DID YOU GET MUCH SHIT ABOUT THAT PIC?
NOTHING SERIOUS, YOUR AVERAGE ACCUSATIONS OF ATTENTIONWHORING, SLUTCALLING...CRAP LIKE THAT...
ON THE FLIPSIDE, I GOT ABOUT EIGHTY PLUS MARRIAGE PROPOSALS, AND SUGGESTIONS THAT I SHOULD MARRY YOU!

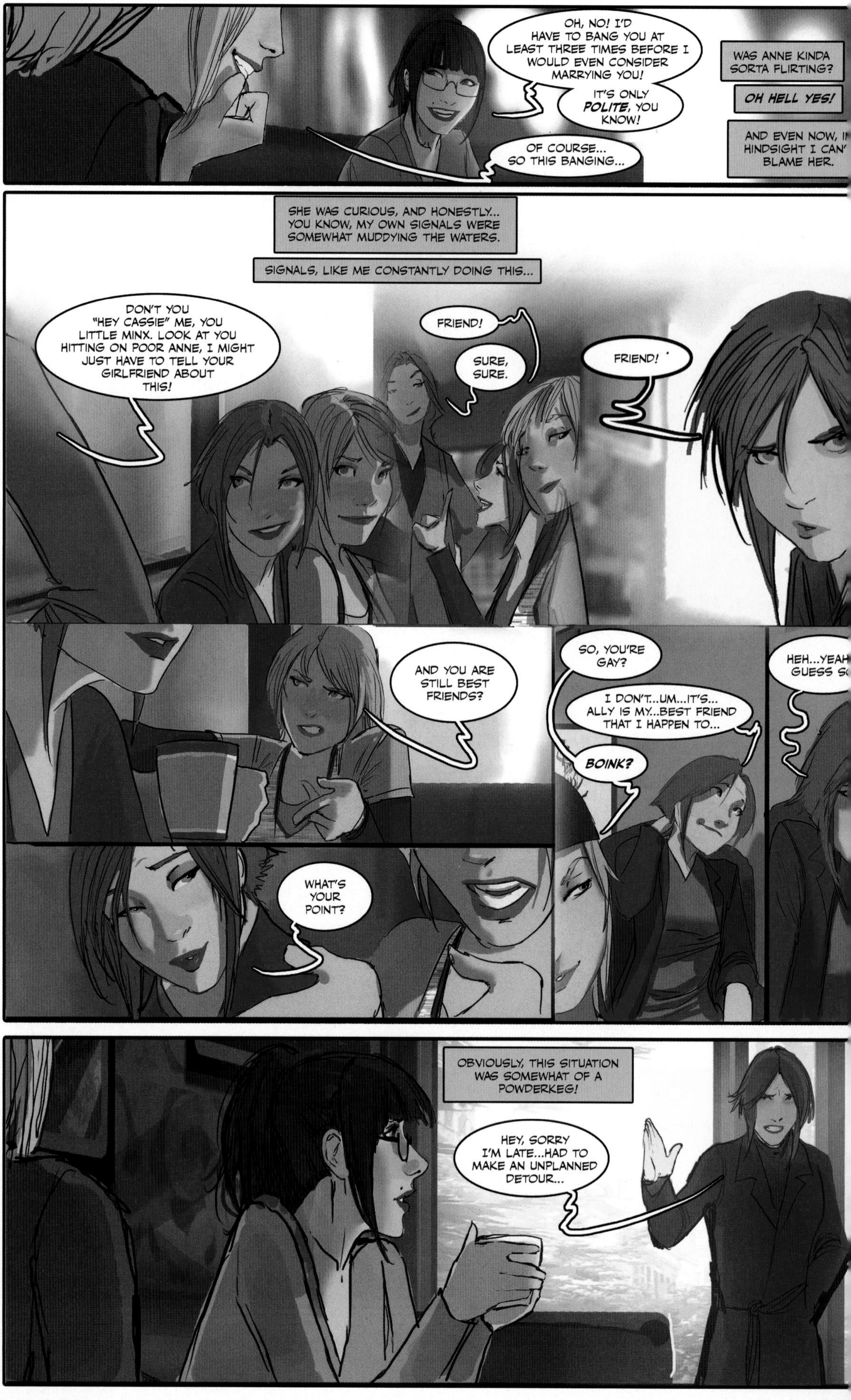
OH, NO! I'D HAVE TO BANG YOU AT LEAST THREE TIMES BEFORE I WOULD EVEN CONSIDER MARRYING YOU!
IT'S ONLY POLITE, YOU KNOW!
OF COURSE... SO THIS BANGING...
WAS ANNE KINDA SORTA FLIRTING?
OH HELL YES!
AND EVEN NOW, IN HINDSIGHT I CAN'T BLAME HER.
SHE WAS CURIOUS, AND HONESTLY... YOU KNOW, MY OWN SIGNALS WERE SOMEWHAT MUDDYING THE WATERS.
SIGNALS, LIKE ME CONSTANTLY DOING THIS...
DON'T YOU "HEY CASSIE" ME, YOU LITTLE MINX. LOOK AT YOU HITTING ON POOR ANNE, I MIGHT JUST HAVE TO TELL YOUR GIRLFRIEND ABOUT THIS!
FRIEND!
SURE, SURE.
FRIEND!
AND YOU ARE STILL BEST FRIENDS?
WHAT'S YOUR POINT?
SO, YOU'RE GAY?
I DON'T...UM...IT'S... ALLY IS MY...BEST FRIEND THAT I HAPPEN TO...
BOINK?
HEH...YEAH GUESS SO
OBVIOUSLY, THIS SITUATION WAS SOMEWHAT OF A POWDERKEG!
HEY, SORRY I'M LATE...HAD TO MAKE AN UNPLANNED DETOUR...

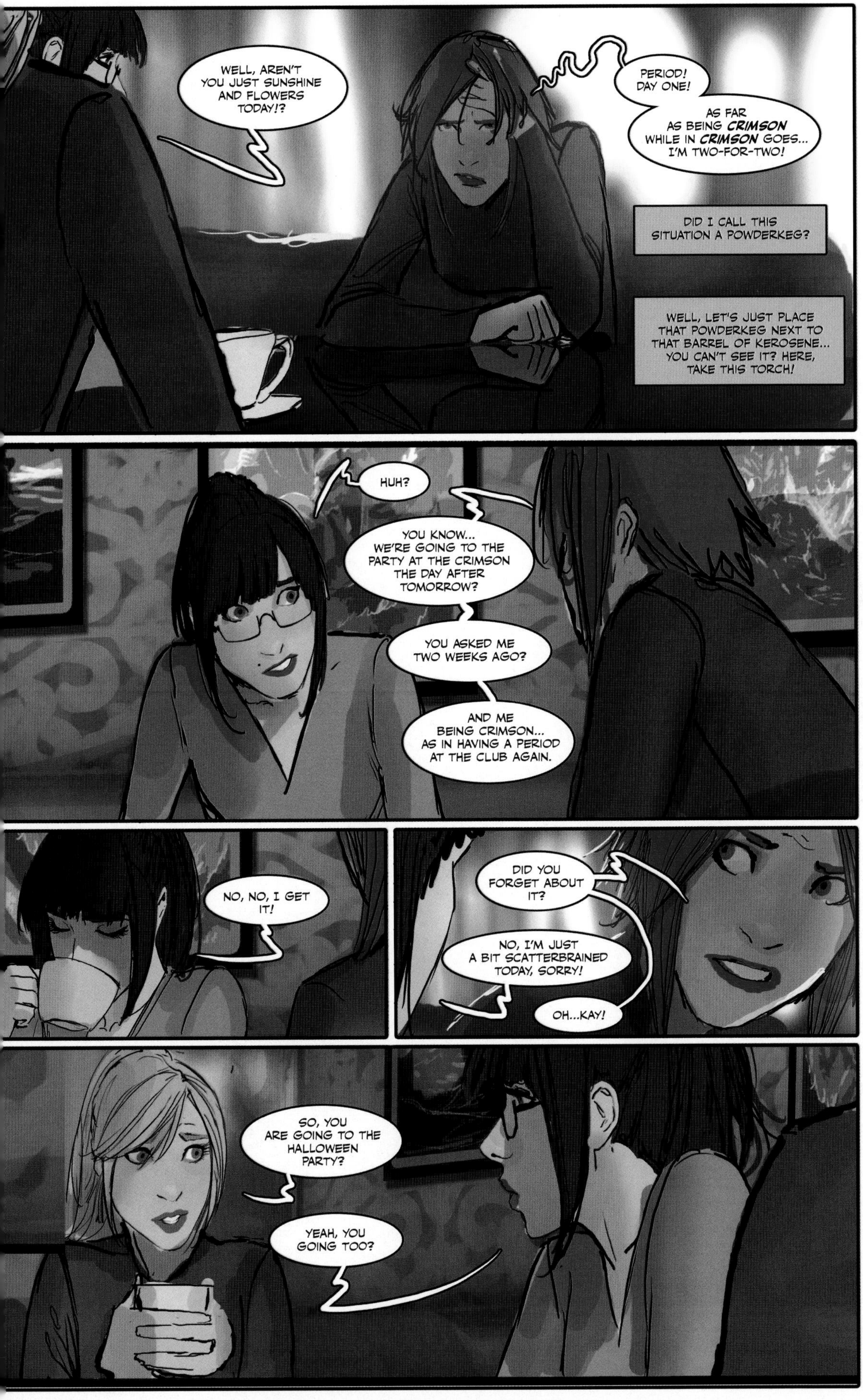
WELL, AREN'T YOU JUST SUNSHINE AND FLOWERS TODAY!?
PERIOD! DAY ONE!
AS FAR AS BEING **CRIMSON** WHILE IN **CRIMSON** GOES... I'M TWO-FOR-TWO!
DID I CALL THIS SITUATION A POWDERKEG?
WELL, LET'S JUST PLACE THAT POWDERKEG NEXT TO THAT BARREL OF KEROSENE... YOU CAN'T SEE IT? HERE, TAKE THIS TORCH!
HUH?
YOU KNOW... WE'RE GOING TO THE PARTY AT THE CRIMSON THE DAY AFTER TOMORROW?
YOU ASKED ME TWO WEEKS AGO?
AND ME BEING CRIMSON... AS IN HAVING A PERIOD AT THE CLUB AGAIN.
NO, NO, I GET IT!
DID YOU FORGET ABOUT IT?
NO, I'M JUST A BIT SCATTERBRAINED TODAY, SORRY!
OH...KAY!
SO, YOU ARE GOING TO THE HALLOWEEN PARTY?
YEAH, YOU GOING TOO?

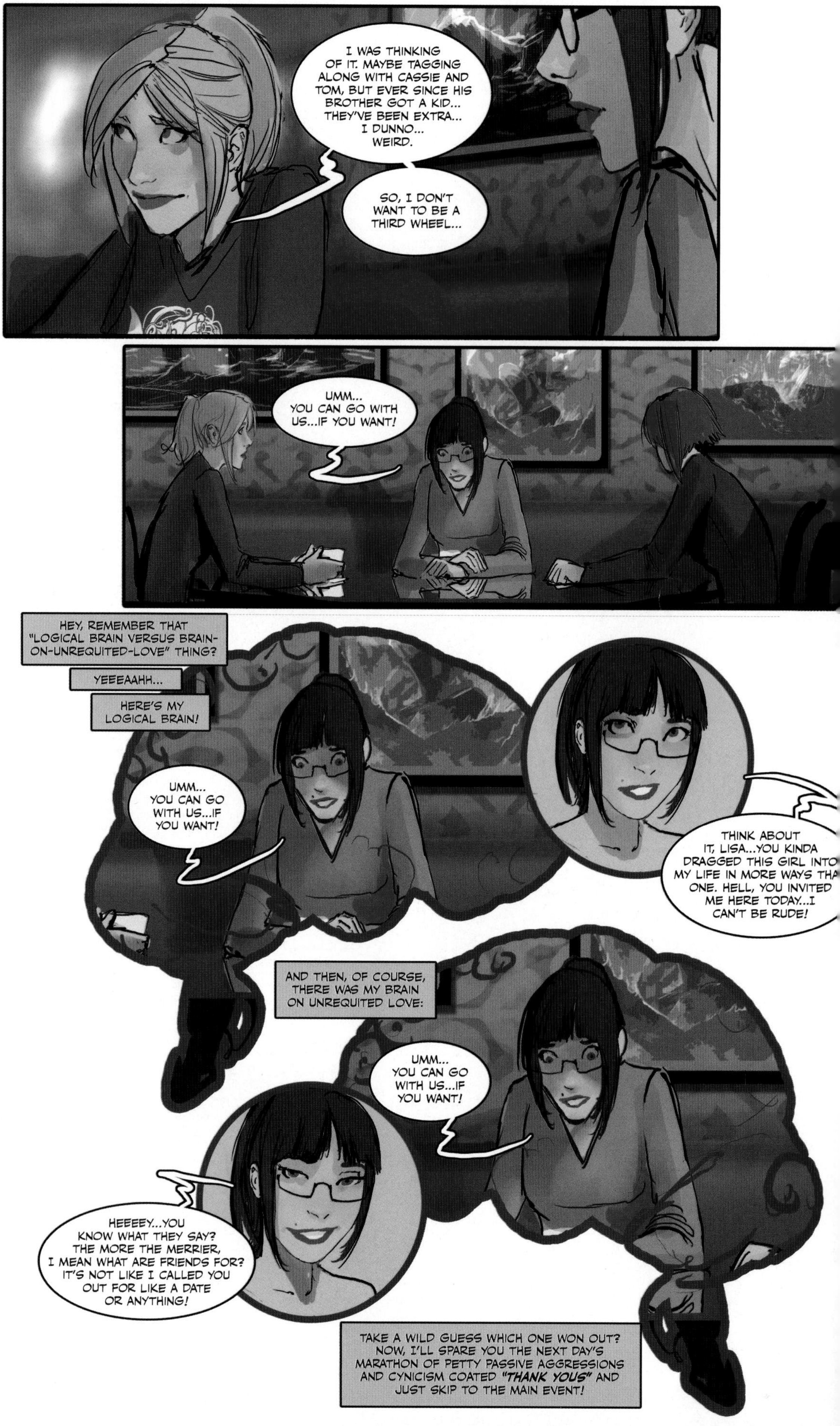

I WAS THINKING OF IT. MAYBE TAGGING ALONG WITH CASSIE AND TOM, BUT EVER SINCE HIS BROTHER GOT A KID... THEY'VE BEEN EXTRA... I DUNNO... WEIRD.
SO, I DON'T WANT TO BE A THIRD WHEEL...
UMM... YOU CAN GO WITH US...IF YOU WANT!
HEY, REMEMBER THAT "LOGICAL BRAIN VERSUS BRAIN-ON-UNREQUITED-LOVE" THING?
YEEEAAHH...
HERE'S MY LOGICAL BRAIN!
UMM... YOU CAN GO WITH US...IF YOU WANT!
THINK ABOUT IT, LISA...YOU KINDA DRAGGED THIS GIRL INTO MY LIFE IN MORE WAYS THA ONE. HELL, YOU INVITED ME HERE TODAY...I CAN'T BE RUDE!
AND THEN, OF COURSE, THERE WAS MY BRAIN ON UNREQUITED LOVE:
UMM... YOU CAN GO WITH US...IF YOU WANT!
HEEEEY...YOU KNOW WHAT THEY SAY? THE MORE THE MERRIER, I MEAN WHAT ARE FRIENDS FOR? IT'S NOT LIKE I CALLED YOU OUT FOR LIKE A DATE OR ANYTHING!
TAKE A WILD GUESS WHICH ONE WON OUT? NOW, I'LL SPARE YOU THE NEXT DAY'S MARATHON OF PETTY PASSIVE AGGRESSIONS AND CYNICISM COATED *"THANK YOUS"* AND JUST SKIP TO THE MAIN EVENT!

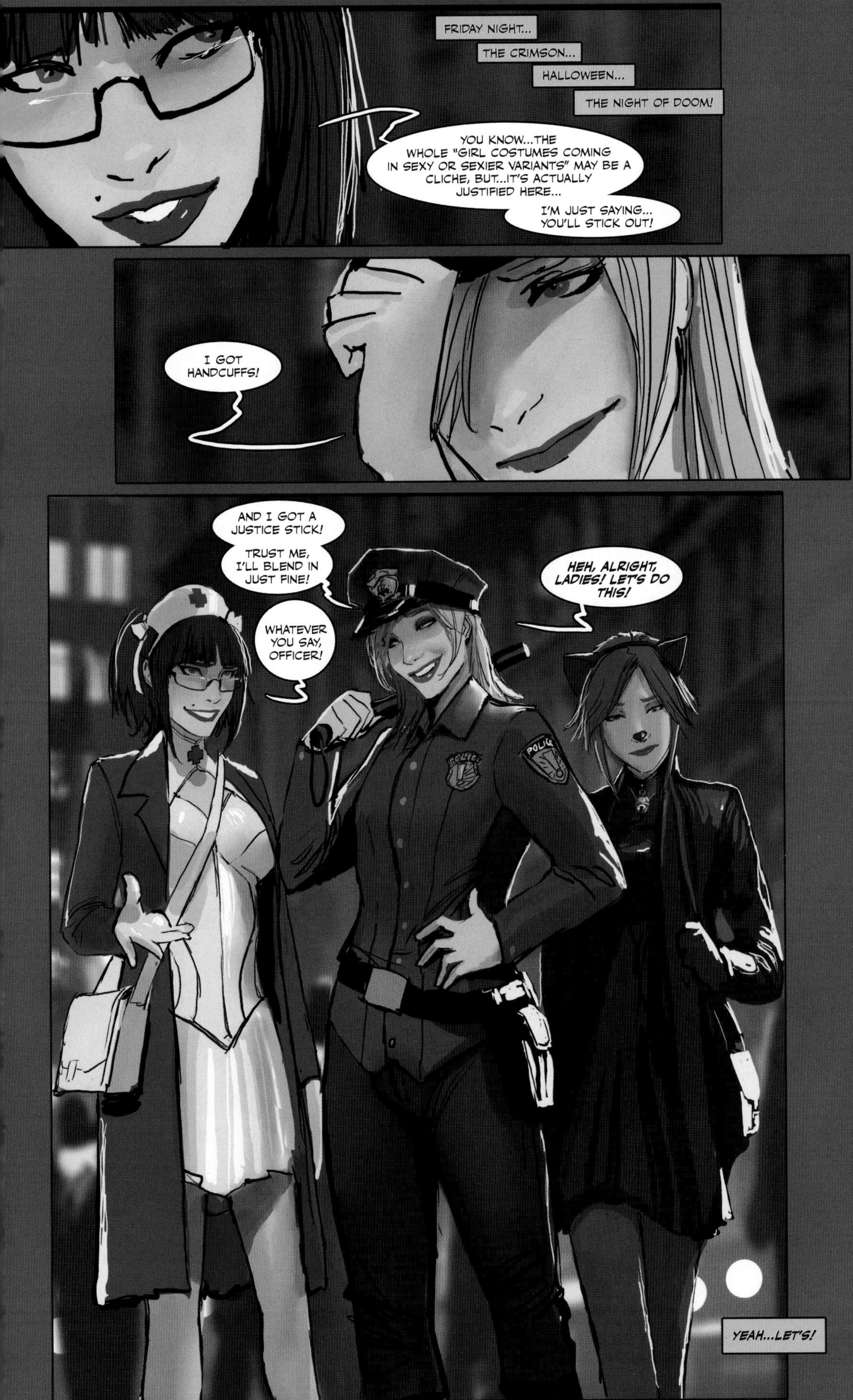
FRIDAY NIGHT...
THE CRIMSON...
HALLOWEEN...
THE NIGHT OF DOOM!
YOU KNOW...THE WHOLE "GIRL COSTUMES COMING IN SEXY OR SEXIER VARIANTS" MAY BE A CLICHE, BUT...IT'S ACTUALLY JUSTIFIED HERE...
I'M JUST SAYING... YOU'LL STICK OUT!
I GOT HANDCUFFS!
AND I GOT A JUSTICE STICK!
TRUST ME, I'LL BLEND IN JUST FINE!
WHATEVER YOU SAY, OFFICER!
HEH, ALRIGHT, LADIES! LET'S DO THIS!
YEAH...LET'S!

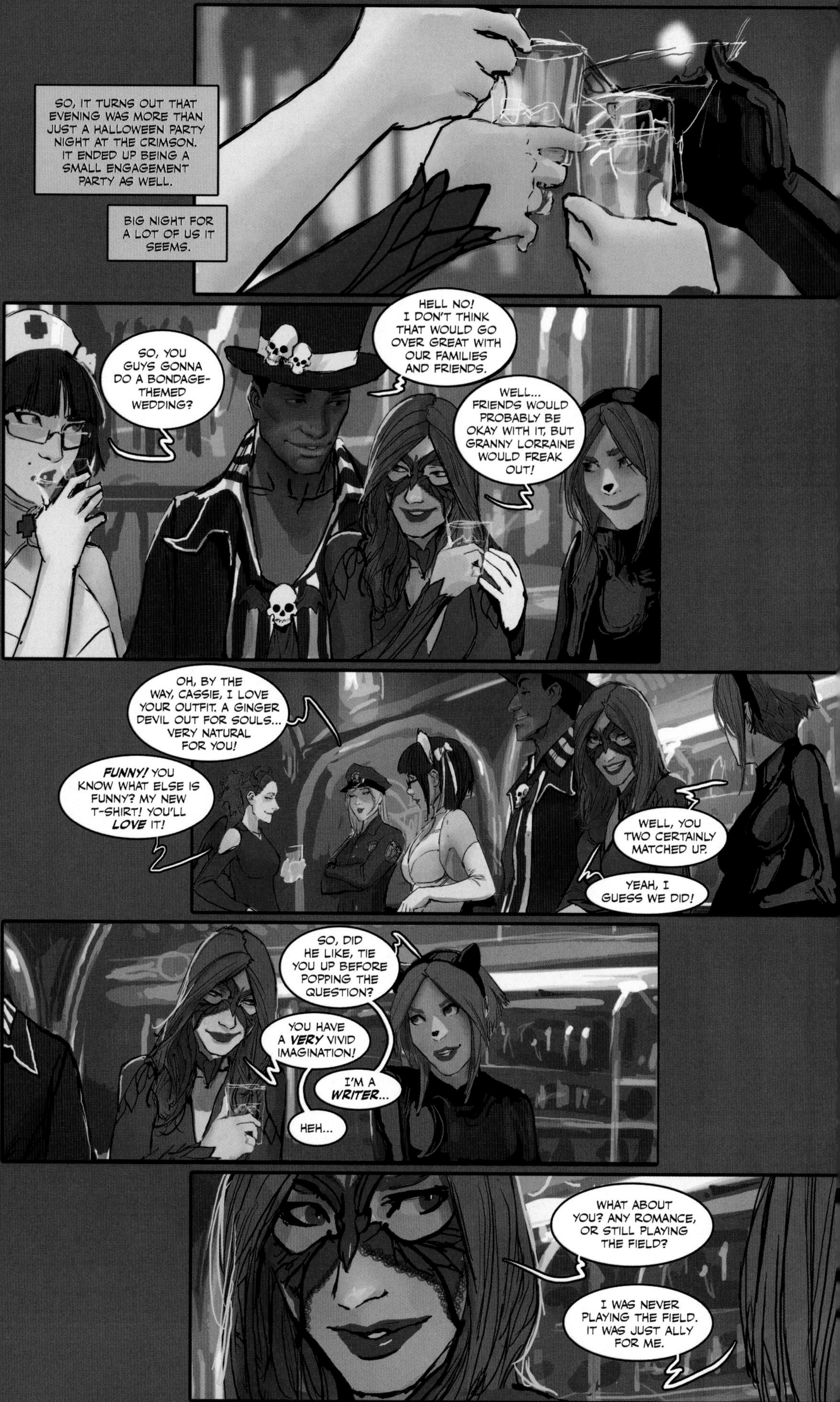
SO, IT TURNS OUT THAT EVENING WAS MORE THAN JUST A HALLOWEEN PARTY NIGHT AT THE CRIMSON. IT ENDED UP BEING A SMALL ENGAGEMENT PARTY AS WELL.
BIG NIGHT FOR A LOT OF US IT SEEMS.
SO, YOU GUYS GONNA DO A BONDAGE-THEMED WEDDING?
HELL NO! I DON'T THINK THAT WOULD GO OVER GREAT WITH OUR FAMILIES AND FRIENDS.
WELL... FRIENDS WOULD PROBABLY BE OKAY WITH IT, BUT GRANNY LORRAINE WOULD FREAK OUT!
OH, BY THE WAY, CASSIE, I LOVE YOUR OUTFIT. A GINGER DEVIL OUT FOR SOULS... VERY NATURAL FOR YOU!
FUNNY! YOU KNOW WHAT ELSE IS FUNNY? MY NEW T-SHIRT! YOU'LL LOVE IT!
WELL, YOU TWO CERTAINLY MATCHED UP.
YEAH, I GUESS WE DID!
SO, DID HE LIKE, TIE YOU UP BEFORE POPPING THE QUESTION?
YOU HAVE A VERY VIVID IMAGINATION!
I'M A WRITER...
HEH...
WHAT ABOUT YOU? ANY ROMANCE, OR STILL PLAYING THE FIELD?
I WAS NEVER PLAYING THE FIELD. IT WAS JUST ALLY FOR ME.

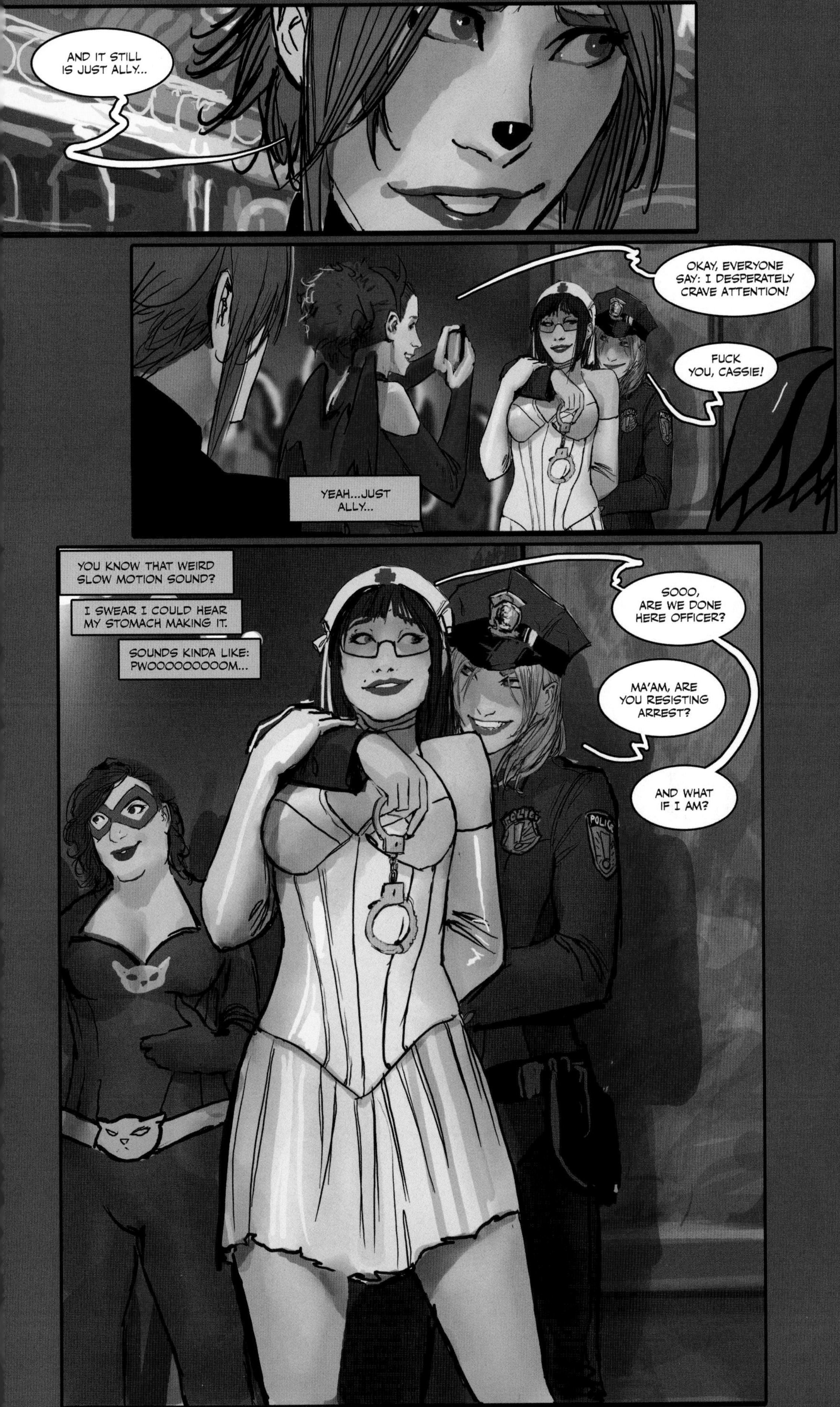
AND IT STILL IS JUST ALLY...
OKAY, EVERYONE SAY: I DESPERATELY CRAVE ATTENTION!
FUCK YOU, CASSIE!
YEAH...JUST ALLY...
YOU KNOW THAT WEIRD SLOW MOTION SOUND?
I SWEAR I COULD HEAR MY STOMACH MAKING IT.
SOUNDS KINDA LIKE: PWOOOOOOOOOM...
SOOO, ARE WE DONE HERE OFFICER?
MA'AM, ARE YOU RESISTING ARREST?
AND WHAT IF I AM?

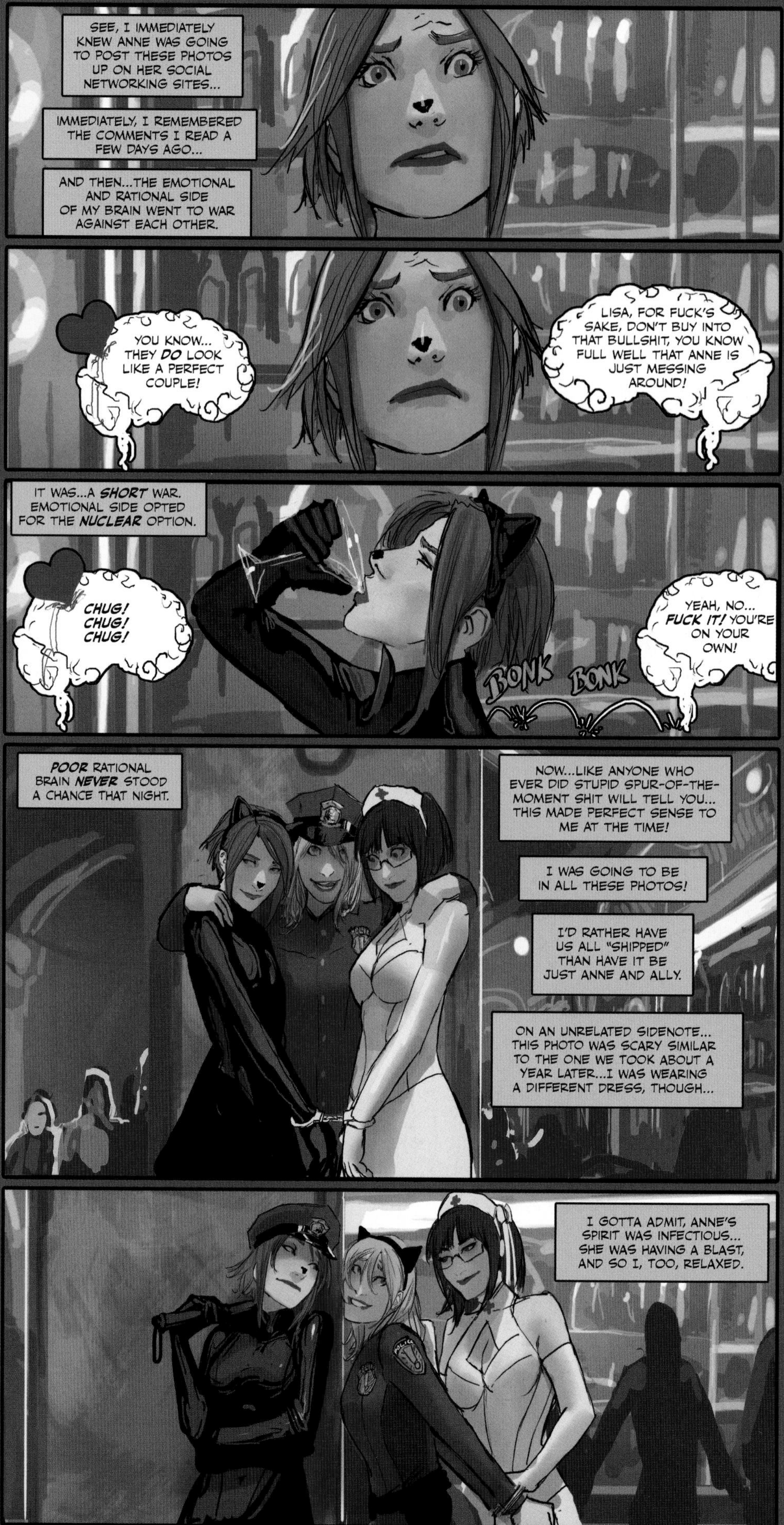
SEE, I IMMEDIATELY KNEW ANNE WAS GOING TO POST THESE PHOTOS UP ON HER SOCIAL NETWORKING SITES...
IMMEDIATELY, I REMEMBERED THE COMMENTS I READ A FEW DAYS AGO...
AND THEN...THE EMOTIONAL AND RATIONAL SIDE OF MY BRAIN WENT TO WAR AGAINST EACH OTHER.
YOU KNOW... THEY DO LOOK LIKE A PERFECT COUPLE!
LISA, FOR FUCK'S SAKE, DON'T BUY INTO THAT BULLSHIT, YOU KNOW FULL WELL THAT ANNE IS JUST MESSING AROUND!
IT WAS...A SHORT WAR. EMOTIONAL SIDE OPTED FOR THE NUCLEAR OPTION.
CHUG! CHUG! CHUG!
YEAH, NO... FUCK IT! YOU'RE ON YOUR OWN!
BONK BONK
POOR RATIONAL BRAIN NEVER STOOD A CHANCE THAT NIGHT.
NOW...LIKE ANYONE WHO EVER DID STUPID SPUR-OF-THE-MOMENT SHIT WILL TELL YOU... THIS MADE PERFECT SENSE TO ME AT THE TIME!
I WAS GOING TO BE IN ALL THESE PHOTOS!
I'D RATHER HAVE US ALL "SHIPPED" THAN HAVE IT BE JUST ANNE AND ALLY.
ON AN UNRELATED SIDENOTE... THIS PHOTO WAS SCARY SIMILAR TO THE ONE WE TOOK ABOUT A YEAR LATER...I WAS WEARING A DIFFERENT DRESS, THOUGH...
I GOTTA ADMIT, ANNE'S SPIRIT WAS INFECTIOUS... SHE WAS HAVING A BLAST, AND SO I, TOO, RELAXED.

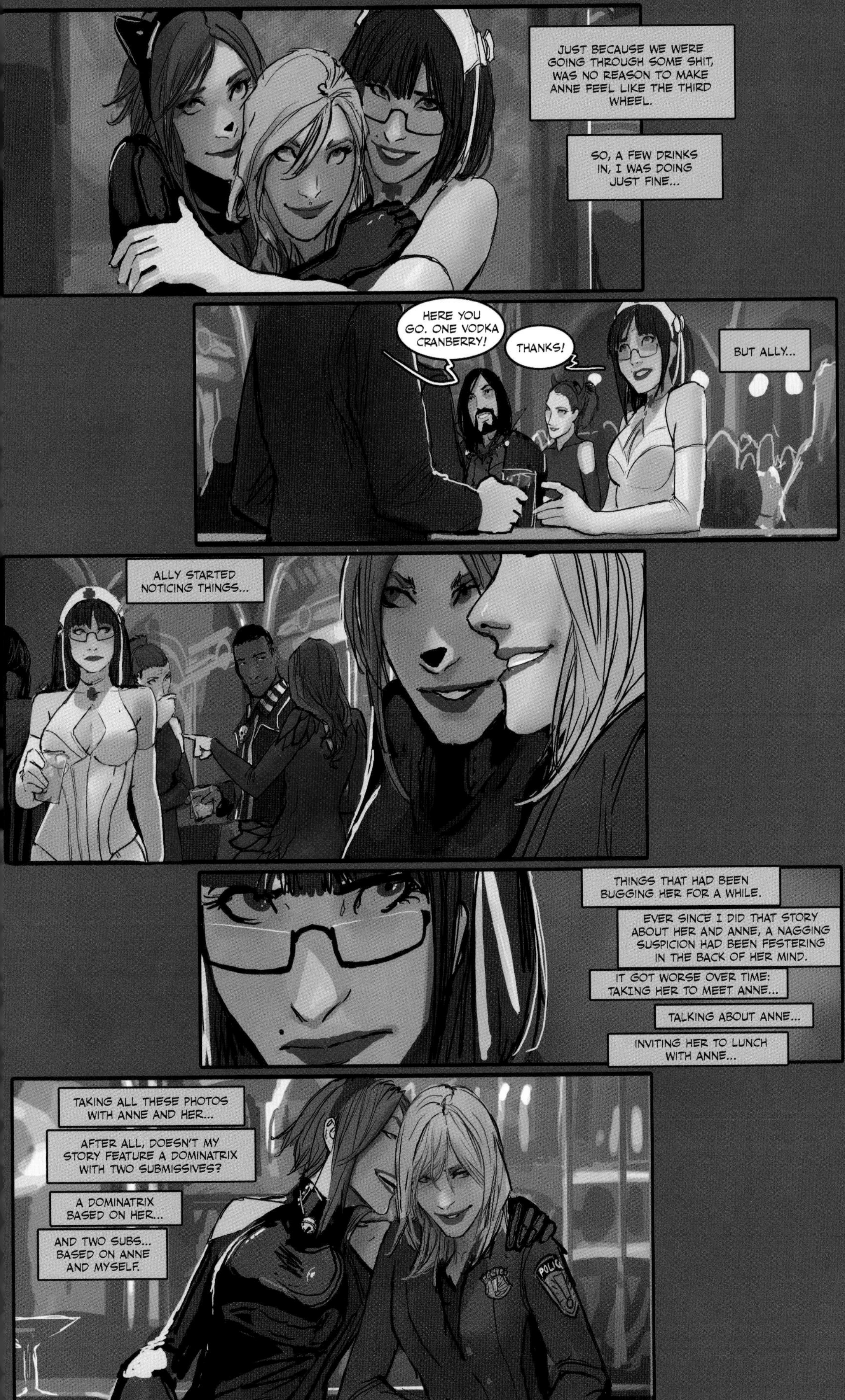
JUST BECAUSE WE WERE GOING THROUGH SOME SHIT, WAS NO REASON TO MAKE ANNE FEEL LIKE THE THIRD WHEEL.
SO, A FEW DRINKS IN, I WAS DOING JUST FINE...
HERE YOU GO. ONE VODKA CRANBERRY!
THANKS!
BUT ALLY...
ALLY STARTED NOTICING THINGS...
THINGS THAT HAD BEEN BUGGING HER FOR A WHILE.
EVER SINCE I DID THAT STORY ABOUT HER AND ANNE, A NAGGING SUSPICION HAD BEEN FESTERING IN THE BACK OF HER MIND.
IT GOT WORSE OVER TIME: TAKING HER TO MEET ANNE...
TALKING ABOUT ANNE...
INVITING HER TO LUNCH WITH ANNE...
TAKING ALL THESE PHOTOS WITH ANNE AND HER...
AFTER ALL, DOESN'T MY STORY FEATURE A DOMINATRIX WITH TWO SUBMISSIVES?
A DOMINATRIX BASED ON HER...
AND TWO SUBS... BASED ON ANNE AND MYSELF.
POLICE

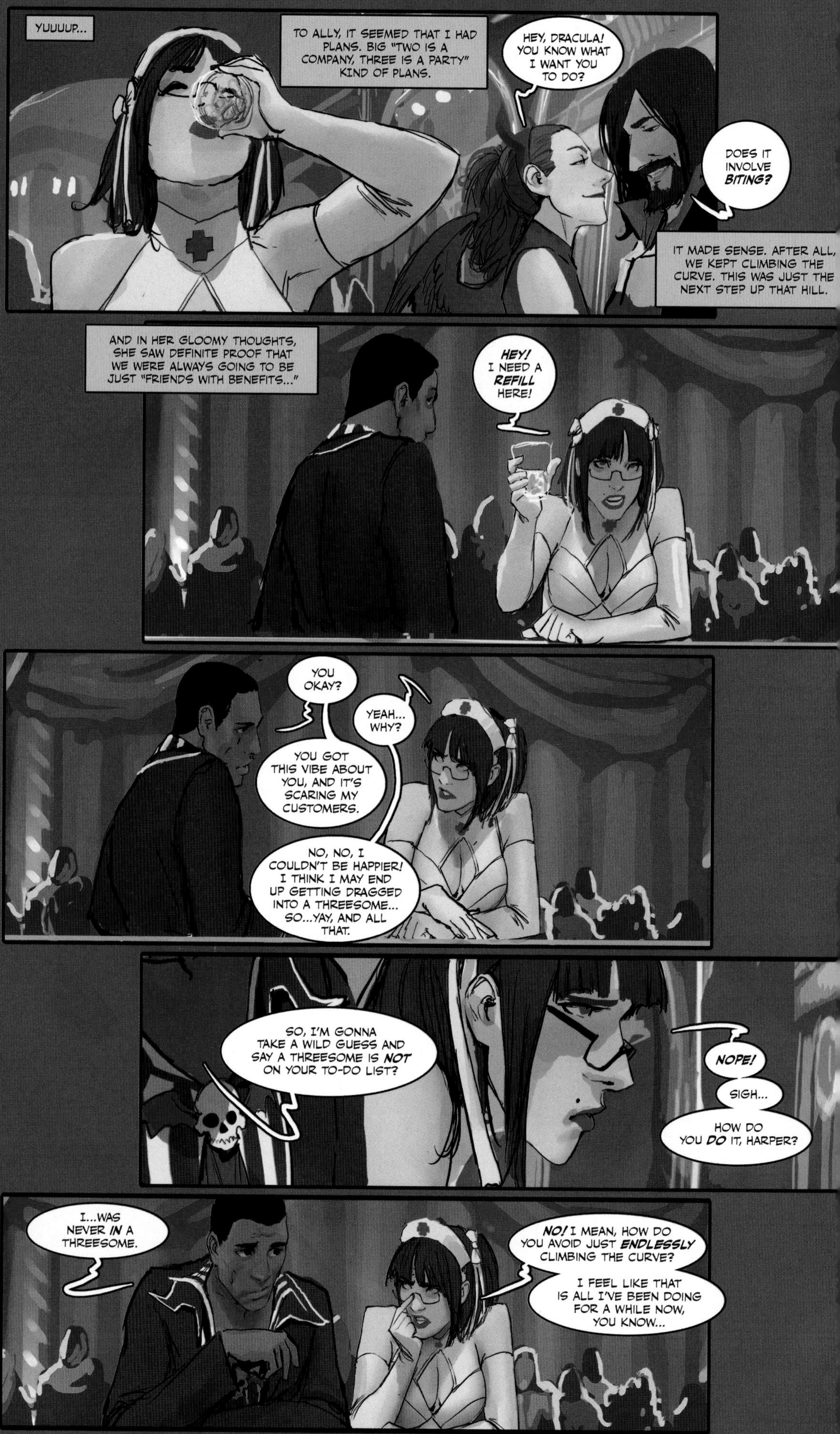
YUUUUP...
TO ALLY, IT SEEMED THAT I HAD PLANS. BIG "TWO IS A COMPANY, THREE IS A PARTY" KIND OF PLANS.
HEY, DRACULA! YOU KNOW WHAT I WANT YOU TO DO?
DOES IT INVOLVE BITING?
IT MADE SENSE. AFTER ALL, WE KEPT CLIMBING THE CURVE. THIS WAS JUST THE NEXT STEP UP THAT HILL.
AND IN HER GLOOMY THOUGHTS, SHE SAW DEFINITE PROOF THAT WE WERE ALWAYS GOING TO BE JUST "FRIENDS WITH BENEFITS..."
HEY! I NEED A REFILL HERE!
YOU OKAY?
YEAH... WHY?
YOU GOT THIS VIBE ABOUT YOU, AND IT'S SCARING MY CUSTOMERS.
NO, NO, I COULDN'T BE HAPPIER! I THINK I MAY END UP GETTING DRAGGED INTO A THREESOME... SO...YAY, AND ALL THAT.
SO, I'M GONNA TAKE A WILD GUESS AND SAY A THREESOME IS NOT ON YOUR TO-DO LIST?
NOPE!
SIGH...
HOW DO YOU DO IT, HARPER?
I...WAS NEVER IN A THREESOME.
NO! I MEAN, HOW DO YOU AVOID JUST ENDLESSLY CLIMBING THE CURVE?
I FEEL LIKE THAT IS ALL I'VE BEEN DOING FOR A WHILE NOW, YOU KNOW...

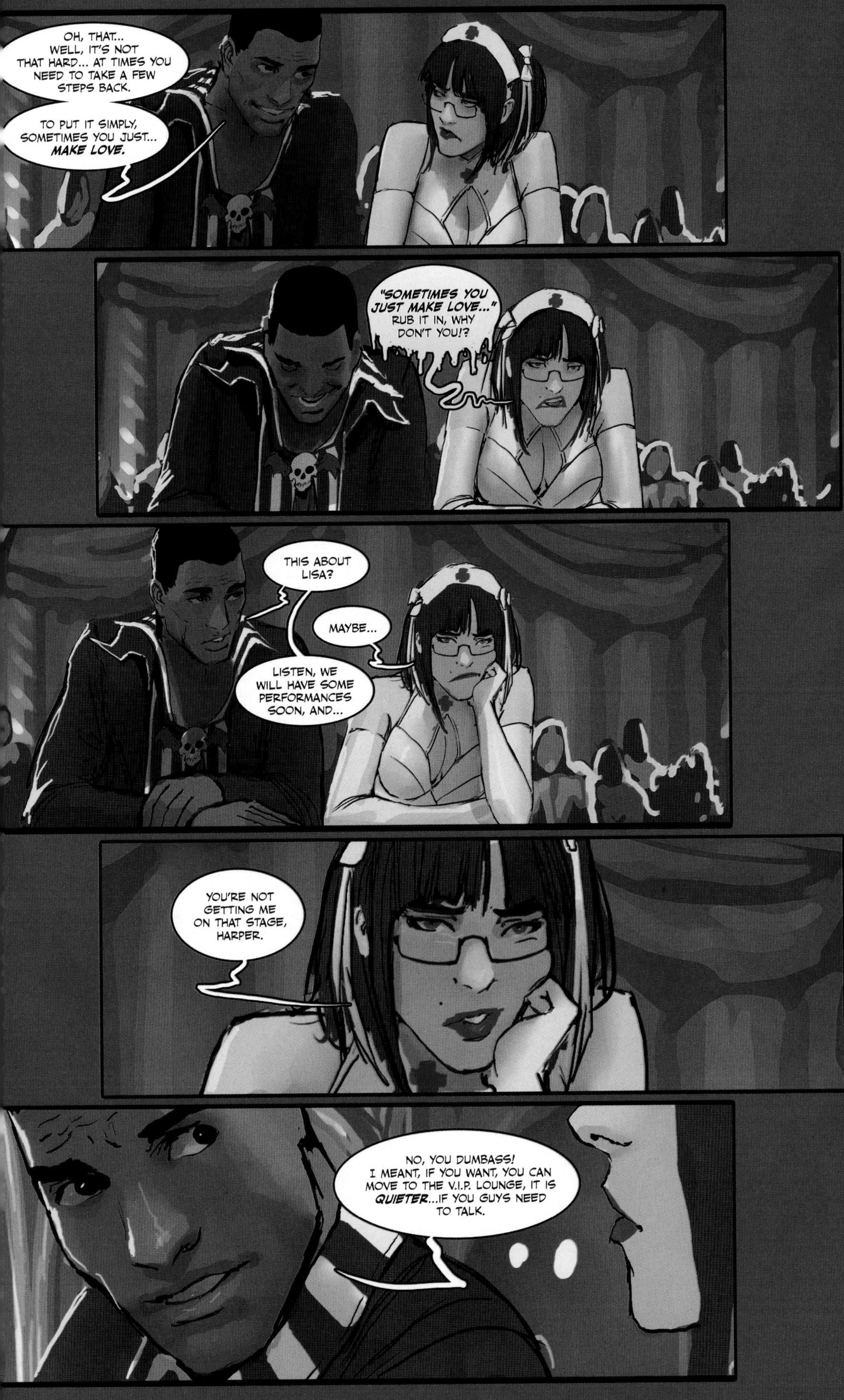
OH, THAT... WELL, IT'S NOT THAT HARD... AT TIMES YOU NEED TO TAKE A FEW STEPS BACK.
TO PUT IT SIMPLY, SOMETIMES YOU JUST... ***MAKE LOVE.***
"SOMETIMES YOU JUST MAKE LOVE..." RUB IT IN, WHY DON'T YOU!?
THIS ABOUT LISA?
MAYBE...
LISTEN, WE WILL HAVE SOME PERFORMANCES SOON, AND...
YOU'RE NOT GETTING ME ON THAT STAGE, HARPER.
NO, YOU DUMBASS! I MEANT, IF YOU WANT, YOU CAN MOVE TO THE V.I.P. LOUNGE, IT IS ***QUIETER***...IF YOU GUYS NEED TO TALK.

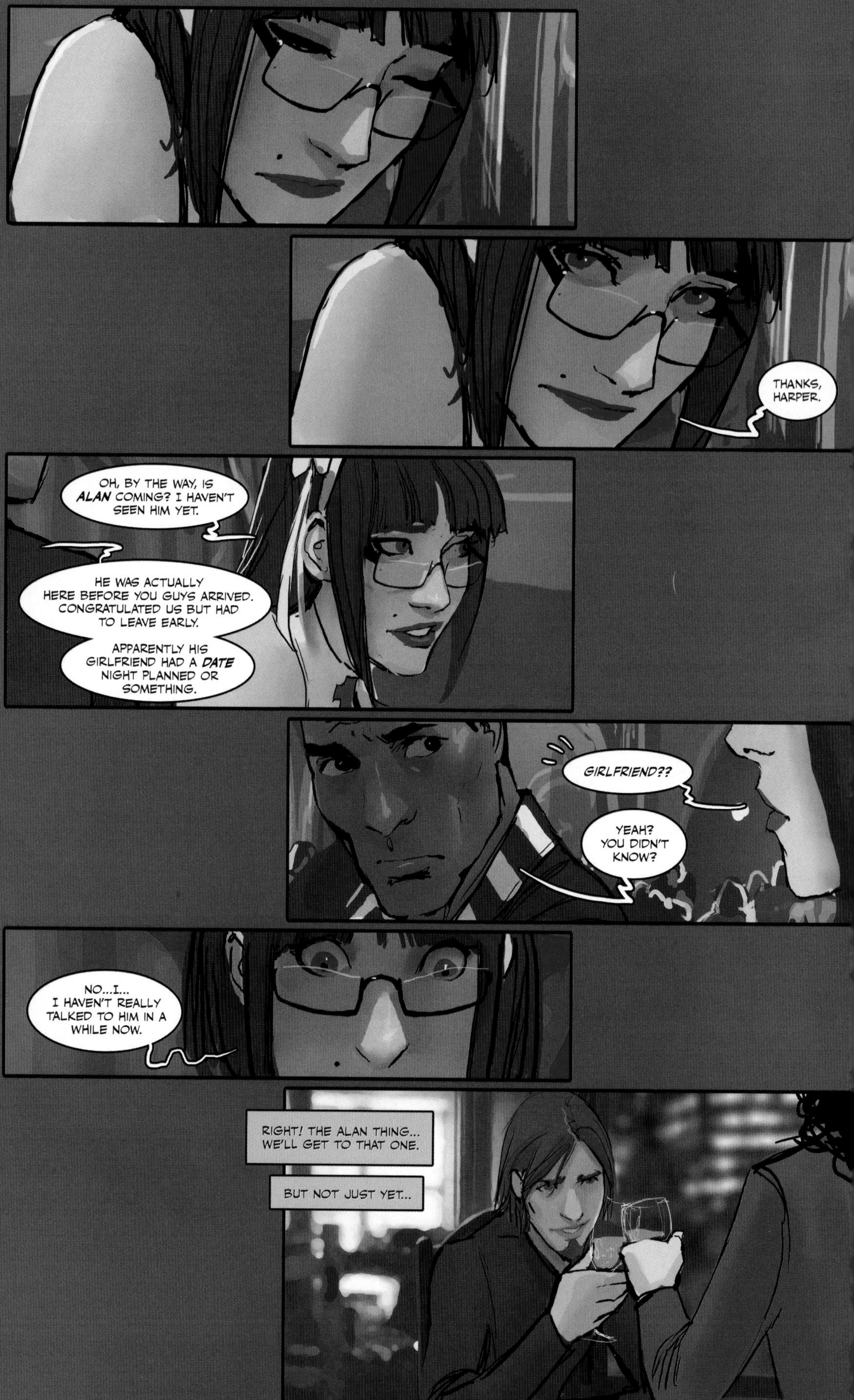
THANKS, HARPER.
OH, BY THE WAY, IS ALAN COMING? I HAVEN'T SEEN HIM YET.
HE WAS ACTUALLY HERE BEFORE YOU GUYS ARRIVED. CONGRATULATED US BUT HAD TO LEAVE EARLY.
APPARENTLY HIS GIRLFRIEND HAD A DATE NIGHT PLANNED OR SOMETHING.
GIRLFRIEND??
YEAH? YOU DIDN'T KNOW?
NO...I... I HAVEN'T REALLY TALKED TO HIM IN A WHILE NOW.
RIGHT! THE ALAN THING... WE'LL GET TO THAT ONE.
BUT NOT JUST YET...

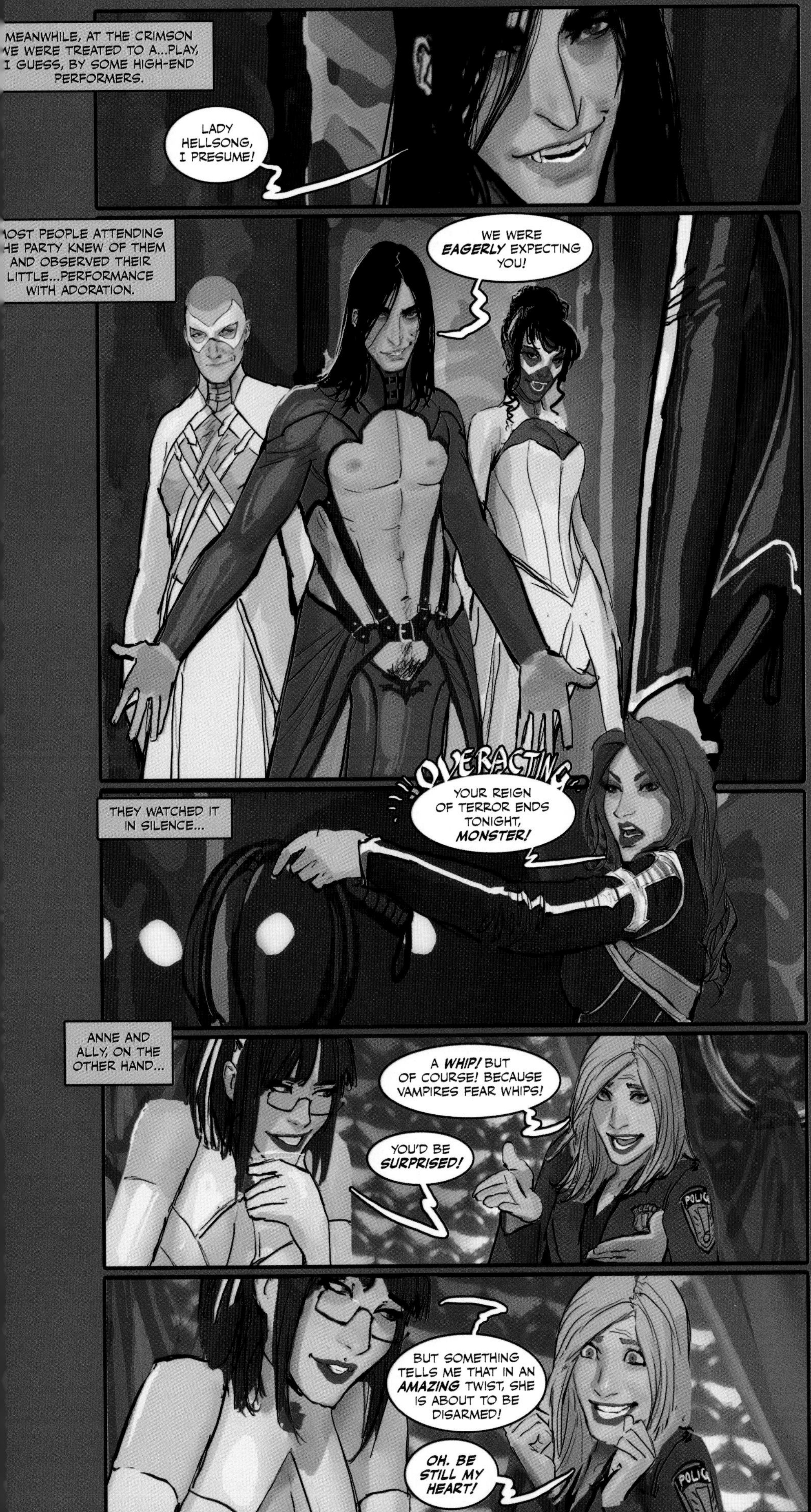
MEANWHILE, AT THE CRIMSON WE WERE TREATED TO A...PLAY, I GUESS, BY SOME HIGH-END PERFORMERS.
LADY HELLSONG, I PRESUME!
MOST PEOPLE ATTENDING THE PARTY KNEW OF THEM AND OBSERVED THEIR LITTLE...PERFORMANCE WITH ADORATION.
WE WERE EAGERLY EXPECTING YOU!
THEY WATCHED IT IN SILENCE...
OVERACTING
YOUR REIGN OF TERROR ENDS TONIGHT, MONSTER!
ANNE AND ALLY, ON THE OTHER HAND...
A WHIP! BUT OF COURSE! BECAUSE VAMPIRES FEAR WHIPS!
YOU'D BE SURPRISED!
BUT SOMETHING TELLS ME THAT IN AN AMAZING TWIST, SHE IS ABOUT TO BE DISARMED!
OH. BE STILL MY HEART!

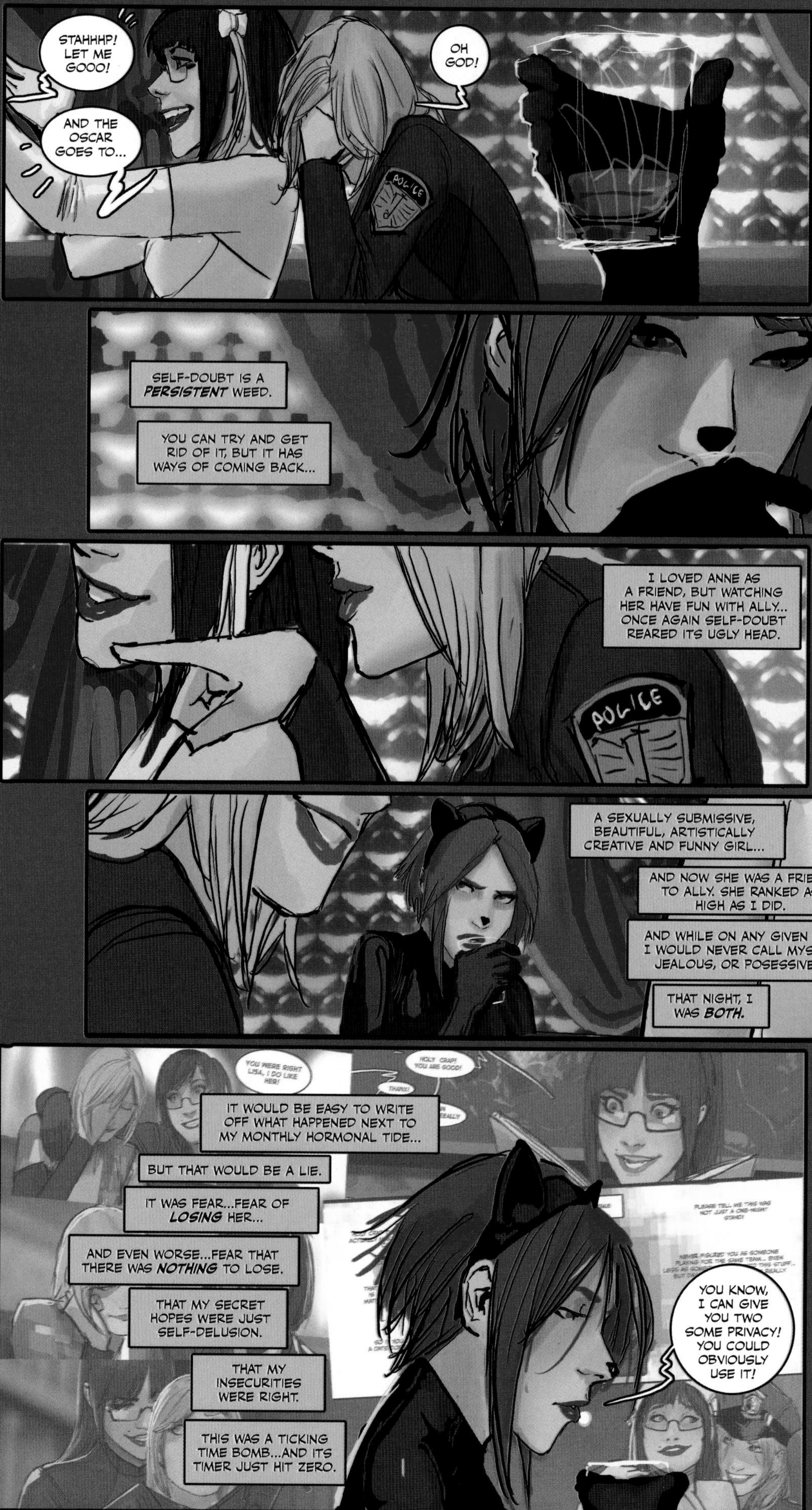
STAHHHP! LET ME GOOO!
AND THE OSCAR GOES TO...
OH GOD!
SELF-DOUBT IS A *PERSISTENT* WEED.
YOU CAN TRY AND GET RID OF IT, BUT IT HAS WAYS OF COMING BACK...
I LOVED ANNE AS A FRIEND, BUT WATCHING HER HAVE FUN WITH ALLY... ONCE AGAIN SELF-DOUBT REARED ITS UGLY HEAD.
A SEXUALLY SUBMISSIVE, BEAUTIFUL, ARTISTICALLY CREATIVE AND FUNNY GIRL...
AND NOW SHE WAS A FRIEND TO ALLY. SHE RANKED AS HIGH AS I DID.
AND WHILE ON ANY GIVEN DAY, I WOULD NEVER CALL MYSELF JEALOUS, OR POSESSIVE...
THAT NIGHT, I WAS **BOTH.**
YOU WERE RIGHT LISA, I DO LIKE HER!
HOLY CRAP! YOU ARE GOOD!
THANX!
IT WOULD BE EASY TO WRITE OFF WHAT HAPPENED NEXT TO MY MONTHLY HORMONAL TIDE...
BUT THAT WOULD BE A LIE.
IT WAS FEAR...FEAR OF *LOSING* HER...
AND EVEN WORSE...FEAR THAT THERE WAS *NOTHING* TO LOSE.
THAT MY SECRET HOPES WERE JUST SELF-DELUSION.
THAT MY INSECURITIES WERE RIGHT.
THIS WAS A TICKING TIME BOMB...AND ITS TIMER JUST HIT ZERO.
PLEASE TELL ME THIS WAS NOT JUST A ONE-NIGHT STAND!
YOU KNOW, I CAN GIVE YOU TWO SOME PRIVACY! YOU COULD OBVIOUSLY USE IT!

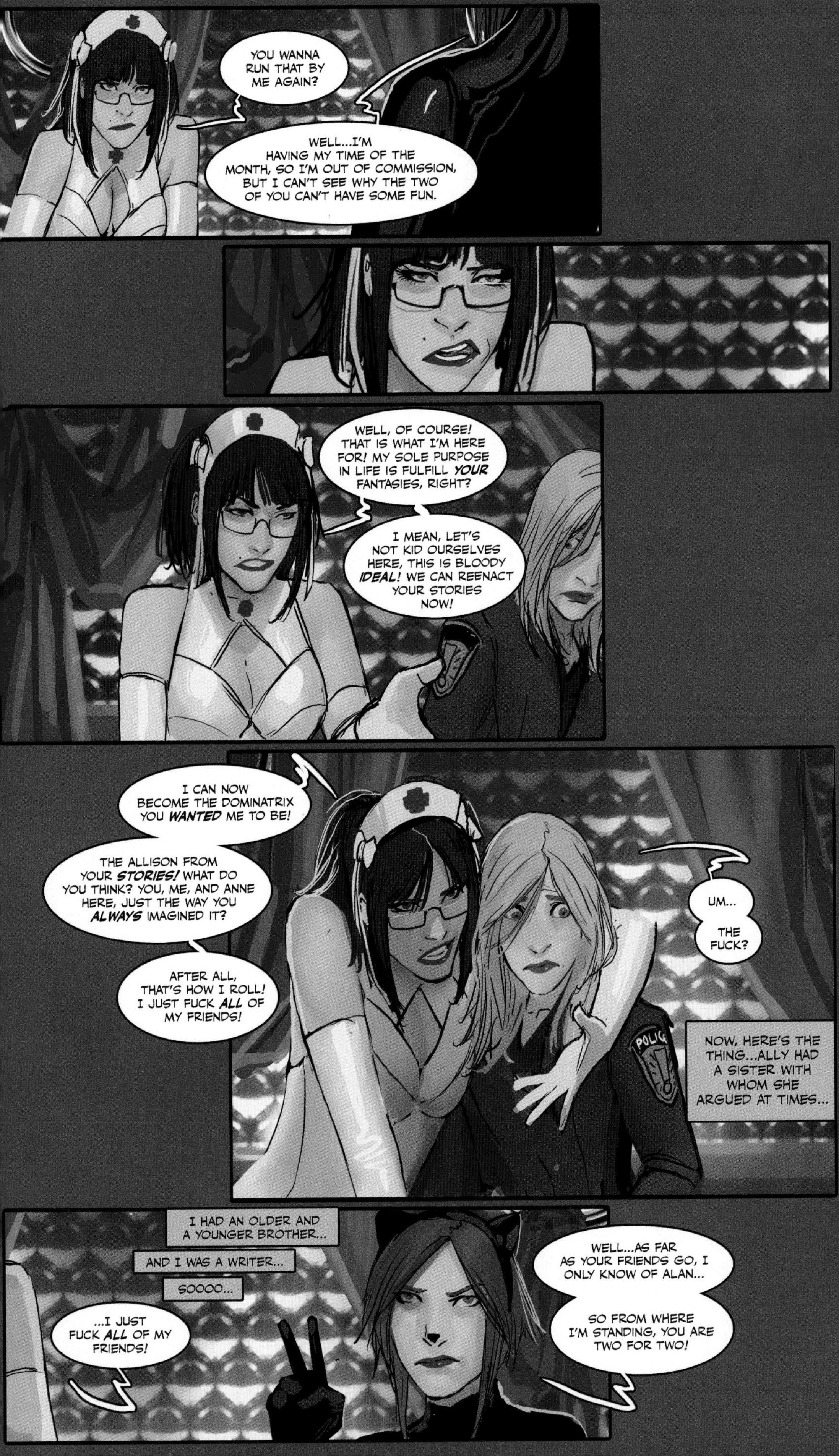
YOU WANNA RUN THAT BY ME AGAIN?
WELL...I'M HAVING MY TIME OF THE MONTH, SO I'M OUT OF COMMISSION, BUT I CAN'T SEE WHY THE TWO OF YOU CAN'T HAVE SOME FUN.
WELL, OF COURSE! THAT IS WHAT I'M HERE FOR! MY SOLE PURPOSE IN LIFE IS FULFILL *YOUR* FANTASIES, RIGHT?
I MEAN, LET'S NOT KID OURSELVES HERE, THIS IS BLOODY *IDEAL!* WE CAN REENACT YOUR STORIES NOW!
I CAN NOW BECOME THE DOMINATRIX YOU *WANTED* ME TO BE!
THE ALLISON FROM YOUR *STORIES!* WHAT DO YOU THINK? YOU, ME, AND ANNE HERE, JUST THE WAY YOU *ALWAYS* IMAGINED IT?
AFTER ALL, THAT'S HOW I ROLL! I JUST FUCK *ALL* OF MY FRIENDS!
UM...
THE FUCK?
NOW, HERE'S THE THING...ALLY HAD A SISTER WITH WHOM SHE ARGUED AT TIMES...
I HAD AN OLDER AND A YOUNGER BROTHER...
AND I WAS A WRITER...
SOOOO...
...I JUST FUCK *ALL* OF MY FRIENDS!
WELL...AS FAR AS YOUR FRIENDS GO, I ONLY KNOW OF ALAN...
SO FROM WHERE I'M STANDING, YOU ARE TWO FOR TWO!

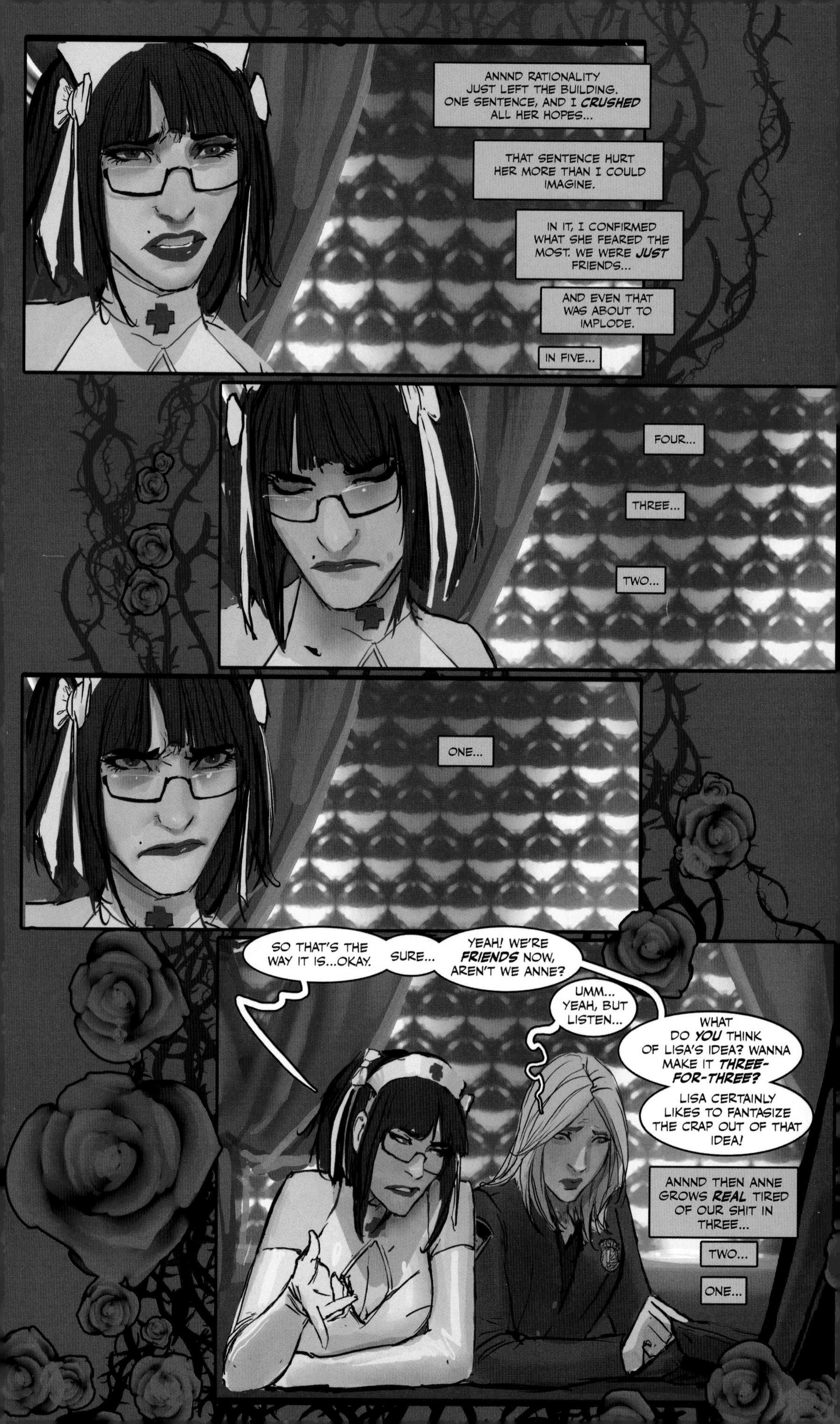
ANNND RATIONALITY JUST LEFT THE BUILDING. ONE SENTENCE, AND I *CRUSHED* ALL HER HOPES...
THAT SENTENCE HURT HER MORE THAN I COULD IMAGINE.
IN IT, I CONFIRMED WHAT SHE FEARED THE MOST. WE WERE *JUST* FRIENDS...
AND EVEN THAT WAS ABOUT TO IMPLODE.
IN FIVE...
FOUR...
THREE...
TWO...
ONE...
SO THAT'S THE WAY IT IS...OKAY.
SURE...
YEAH! WE'RE *FRIENDS* NOW, AREN'T WE ANNE?
UMM... YEAH, BUT LISTEN...
WHAT DO *YOU* THINK OF LISA'S IDEA? WANNA MAKE IT *THREE-FOR-THREE?*
LISA CERTAINLY LIKES TO FANTASIZE THE CRAP OUT OF THAT IDEA!
ANNND THEN ANNE GROWS *REAL* TIRED OF OUR SHIT IN THREE...
TWO...
ONE...

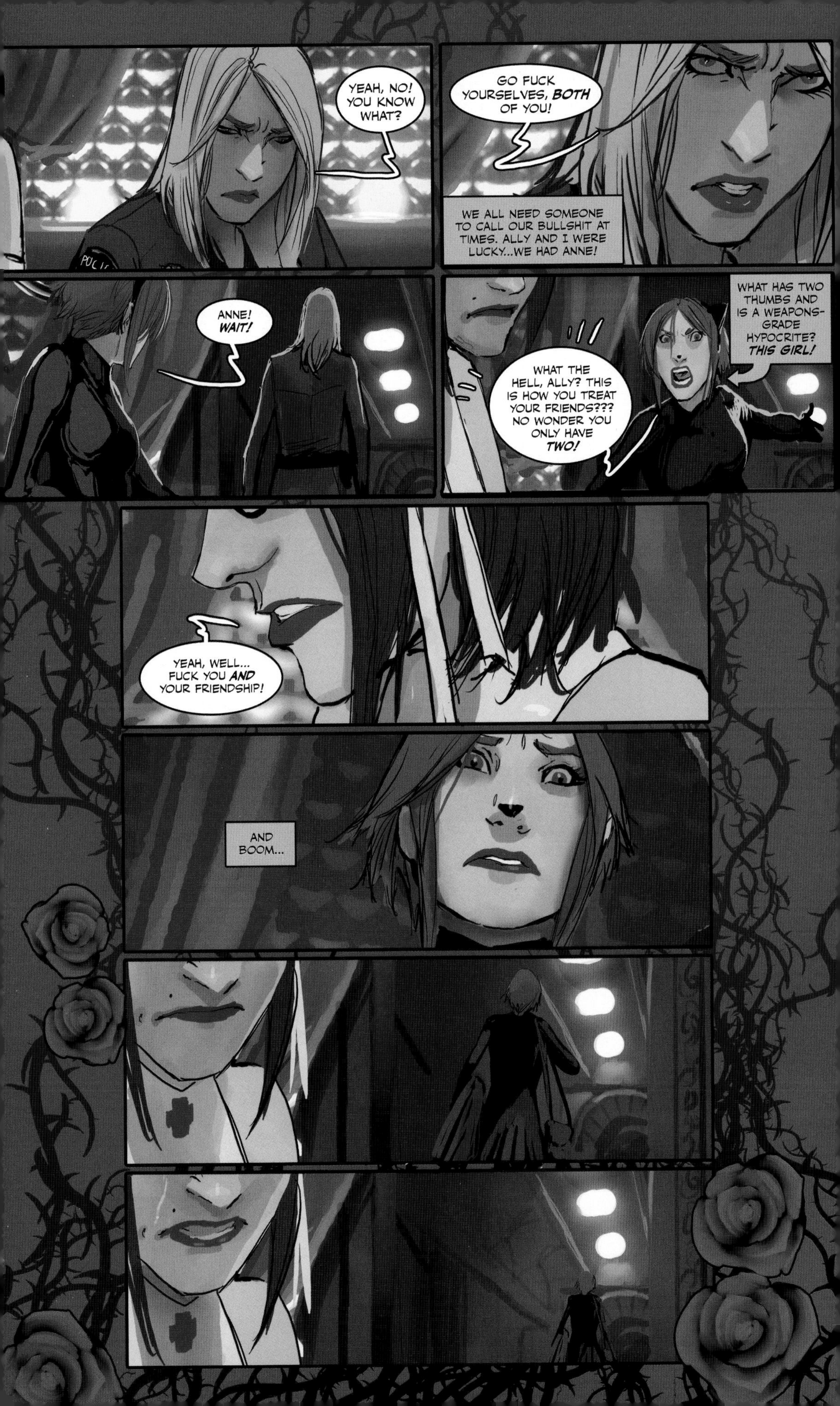
YEAH, NO! YOU KNOW WHAT?
GO FUCK YOURSELVES, BOTH OF YOU!
WE ALL NEED SOMEONE TO CALL OUR BULLSHIT AT TIMES. ALLY AND I WERE LUCKY...WE HAD ANNE!
ANNE! WAIT!
WHAT THE HELL, ALLY? THIS IS HOW YOU TREAT YOUR FRIENDS??? NO WONDER YOU ONLY HAVE TWO!
WHAT HAS TWO THUMBS AND IS A WEAPONS-GRADE HYPOCRITE? THIS GIRL!
YEAH, WELL... FUCK YOU AND YOUR FRIENDSHIP!
AND BOOM...

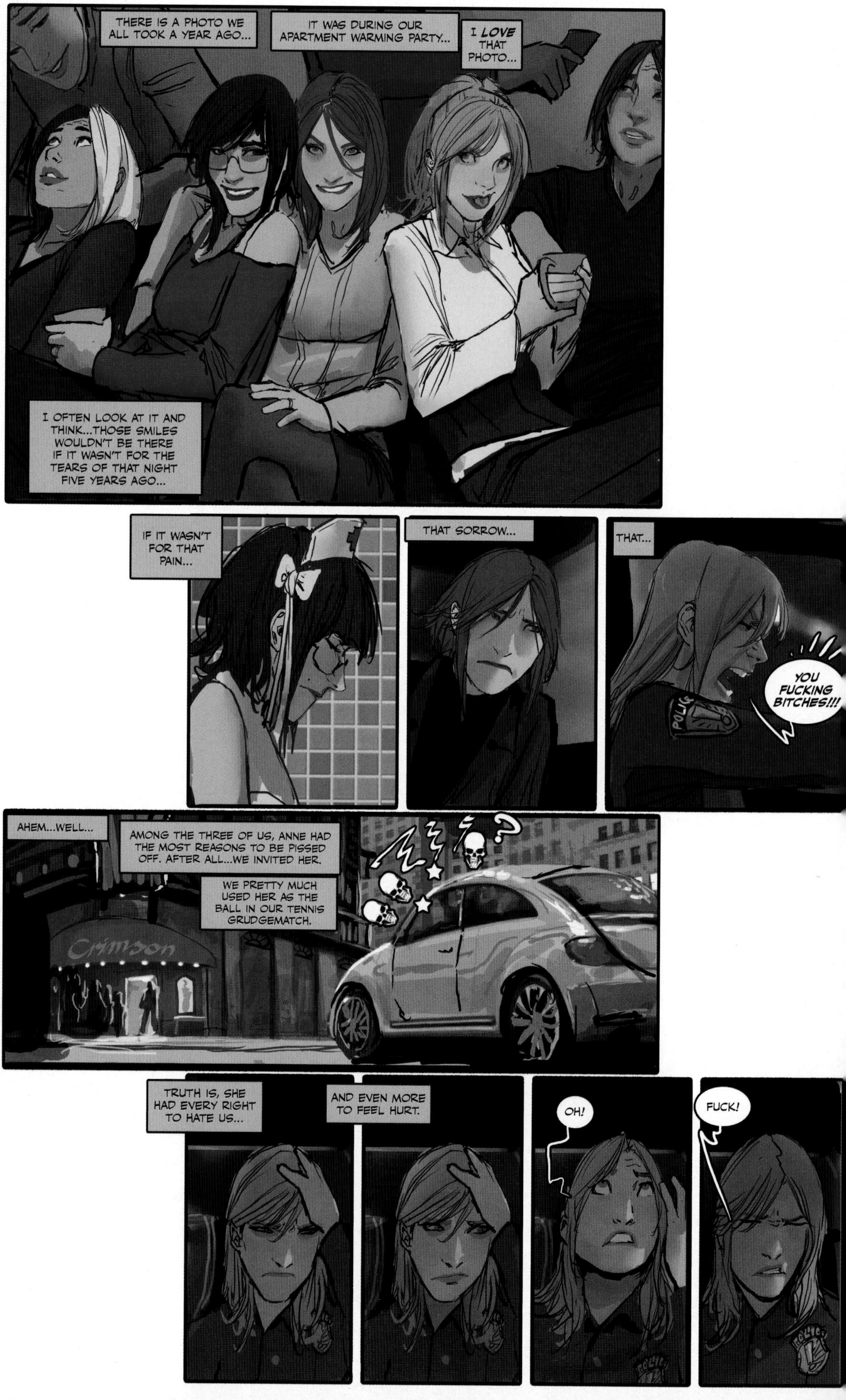
THERE IS A PHOTO WE ALL TOOK A YEAR AGO...
IT WAS DURING OUR APARTMENT WARMING PARTY...
I LOVE THAT PHOTO...
I OFTEN LOOK AT IT AND THINK...THOSE SMILES WOULDN'T BE THERE IF IT WASN'T FOR THE TEARS OF THAT NIGHT FIVE YEARS AGO...
IF IT WASN'T FOR THAT PAIN...
THAT SORROW...
THAT...
YOU FUCKING BITCHES!!!
AHEM...WELL...
AMONG THE THREE OF US, ANNE HAD THE MOST REASONS TO BE PISSED OFF. AFTER ALL...WE INVITED HER.
WE PRETTY MUCH USED HER AS THE BALL IN OUR TENNIS GRUDGEMATCH.
Crimson
TRUTH IS, SHE HAD EVERY RIGHT TO HATE US...
AND EVEN MORE TO FEEL HURT.
OH!
FUCK!

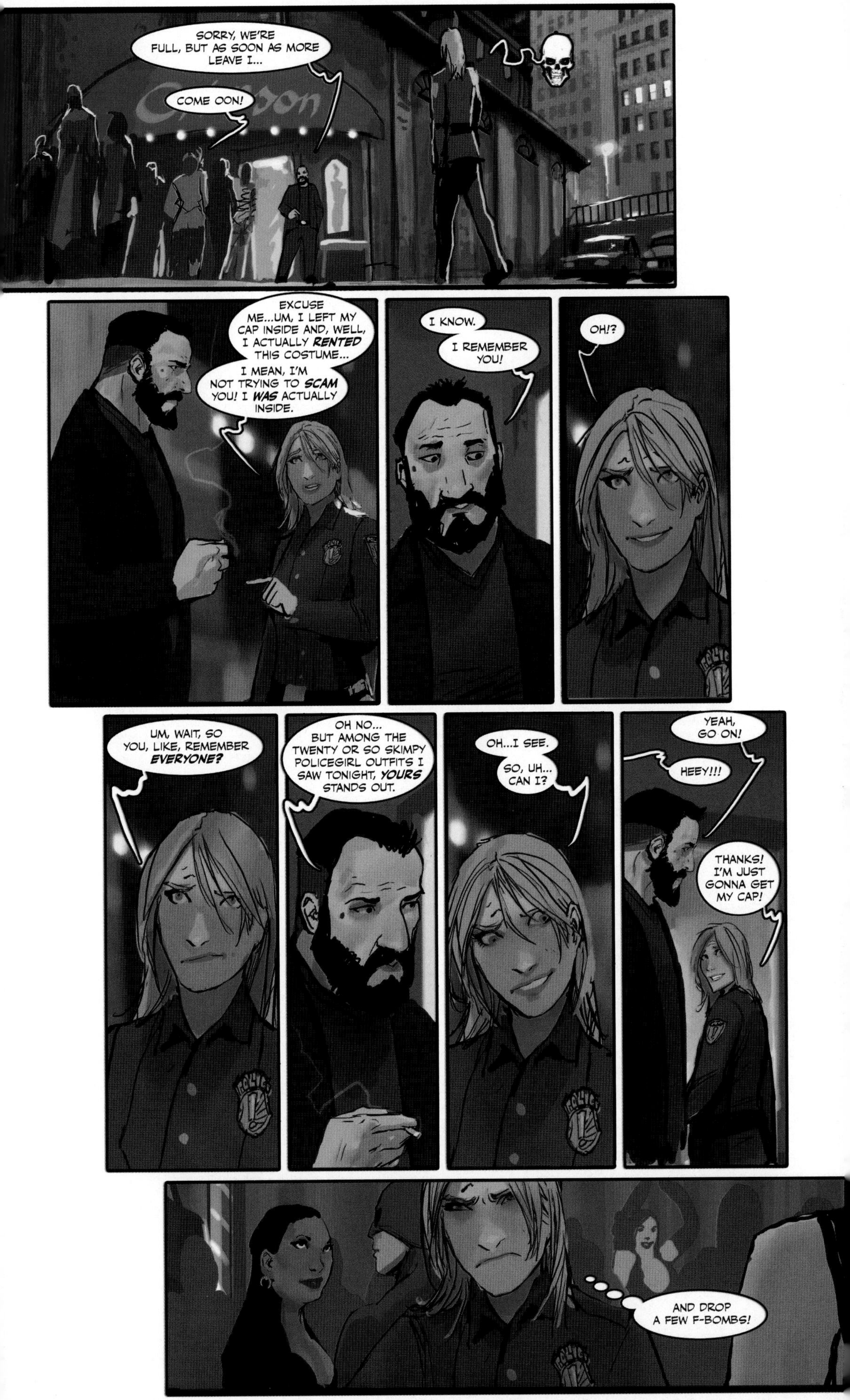
SORRY, WE'RE FULL, BUT AS SOON AS MORE LEAVE I...
COME OON!
EXCUSE ME...UM, I LEFT MY CAP INSIDE AND, WELL, I ACTUALLY **RENTED** THIS COSTUME...
I MEAN, I'M NOT TRYING TO **SCAM** YOU! I **WAS** ACTUALLY INSIDE.
I KNOW.
I REMEMBER YOU!
OH!?
UM, WAIT, SO YOU, LIKE, REMEMBER **EVERYONE?**
OH NO... BUT AMONG THE TWENTY OR SO SKIMPY POLICEGIRL OUTFITS I SAW TONIGHT, **YOURS** STANDS OUT.
OH...I SEE.
SO, UH... CAN I?
YEAH, GO ON!
HEEY!!!
THANKS! I'M JUST GONNA GET MY CAP!
AND DROP A FEW F-BOMBS!

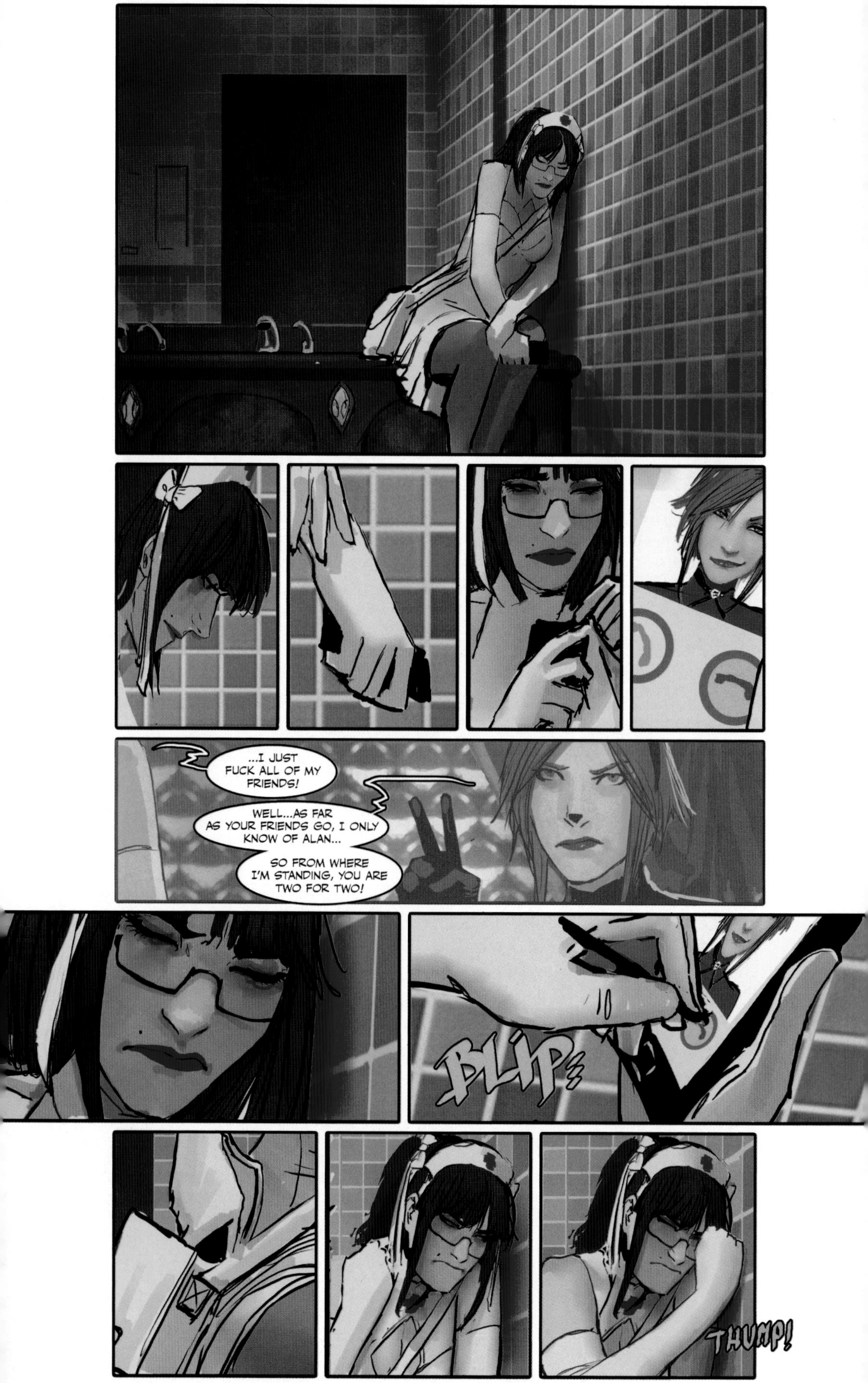
...I JUST FUCK ALL OF MY FRIENDS!
WELL...AS FAR AS YOUR FRIENDS GO, I ONLY KNOW OF ALAN...
SO FROM WHERE I'M STANDING, YOU ARE TWO FOR TWO!
BLIP
THUMP!

OKAY, STORYTIME!

WHEN I WAS A KID, MY BROTHER MIKE STARTED GOING TO TAEKWONDO...OF COURSE, BEING A CLINGY LITTLE SISTER, I WANTED TO GO AS WELL.

NOW, ONE OF THE FIRST THINGS I LEARNED THERE WAS...

WITH YOUR WRIST BENT LIKE THAT, LANDING A PUNCH WILL RESULT IN A LIKELY INJURY.

YOUR FIST NEEDS TO BE ALIGNED WITH YOUR ARM, OR WHEN YOU LAND A PUNCH, FORCE WILL END UP TEARING YOUR LIGAMENTS OR EVEN BREAKING A BONE.

SO, LOCK YOUR WRIST!

LIKE THIS?

EXCELLENT!

WHAP

SO, ALLY DIDN'T KNOW THAT, AND...

GMMMMPFF!

ANYHOO...WHILE ALLY WAS TRYING HER HARDEST TO SUPRESS A SCREAM, I WAS JUST ARRIVING HOME, COURTESY OF CASSIE AND TOM...WHO TO MY GREAT SURPRISE ASKED VERY FEW QUESTIONS.

ACCORDING TO CASSIE, I HAD A HUGE *"DON'T FUCKING ASK"* EXPRESSION ON MY FACE...

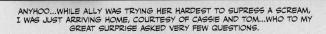

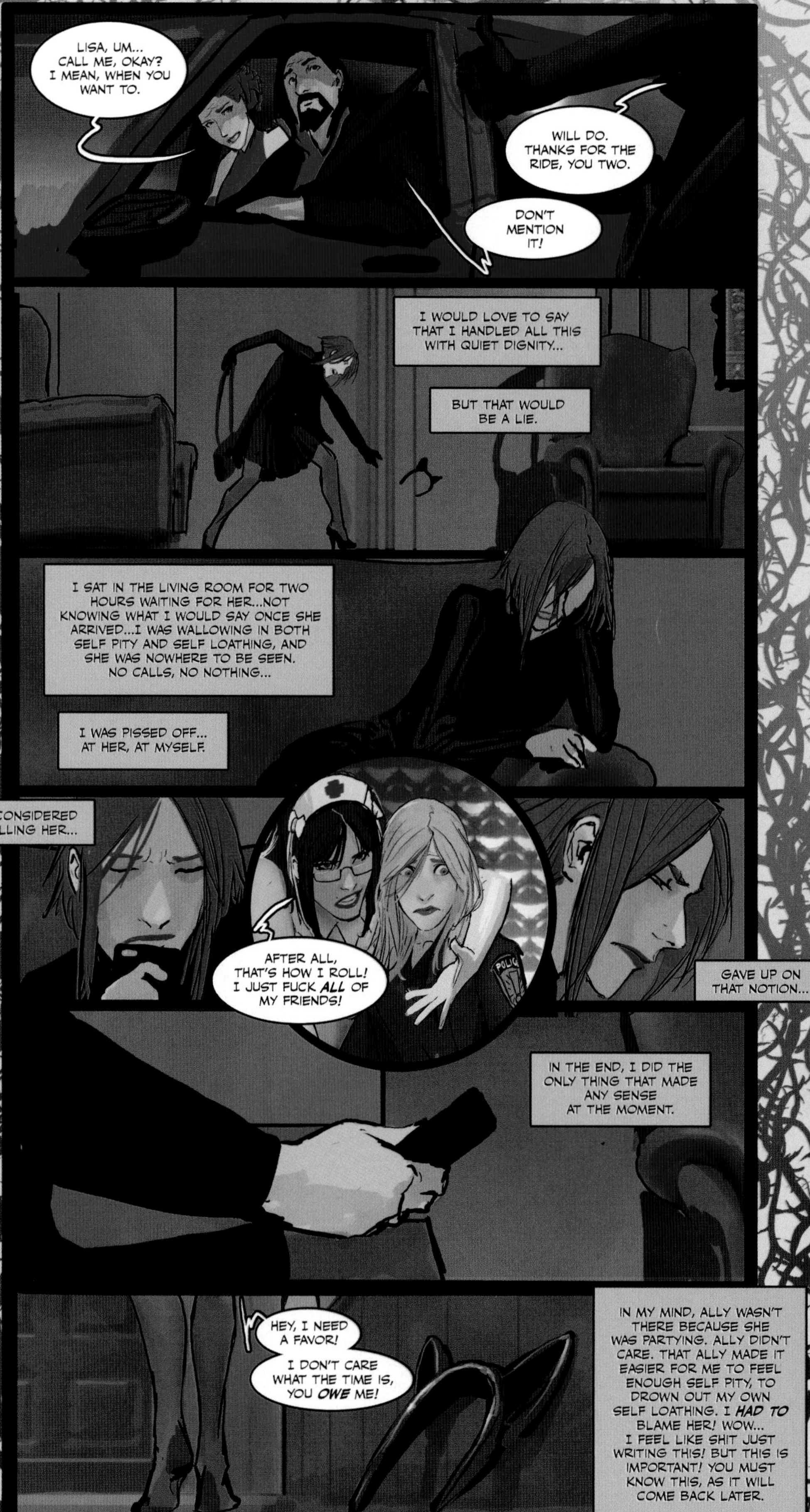
LISA, UM... CALL ME, OKAY? I MEAN, WHEN YOU WANT TO.
WILL DO. THANKS FOR THE RIDE, YOU TWO.
DON'T MENTION IT!
I WOULD LOVE TO SAY THAT I HANDLED ALL THIS WITH QUIET DIGNITY...
BUT THAT WOULD BE A LIE.
I SAT IN THE LIVING ROOM FOR TWO HOURS WAITING FOR HER...NOT KNOWING WHAT I WOULD SAY ONCE SHE ARRIVED...I WAS WALLOWING IN BOTH SELF PITY AND SELF LOATHING, AND SHE WAS NOWHERE TO BE SEEN. NO CALLS, NO NOTHING...
I WAS PISSED OFF... AT HER, AT MYSELF.
I CONSIDERED CALLING HER...
AFTER ALL, THAT'S HOW I ROLL! I JUST FUCK ALL OF MY FRIENDS!
GAVE UP ON THAT NOTION...
IN THE END, I DID THE ONLY THING THAT MADE ANY SENSE AT THE MOMENT.
HEY, I NEED A FAVOR!
I DON'T CARE WHAT THE TIME IS, YOU OWE ME!
IN MY MIND, ALLY WASN'T THERE BECAUSE SHE WAS PARTYING. ALLY DIDN'T CARE. THAT ALLY MADE IT EASIER FOR ME TO FEEL ENOUGH SELF PITY, TO DROWN OUT MY OWN SELF LOATHING. I HAD TO BLAME HER! WOW... I FEEL LIKE SHIT JUST WRITING THIS! BUT THIS IS IMPORTANT! YOU MUST KNOW THIS, AS IT WILL COME BACK LATER.

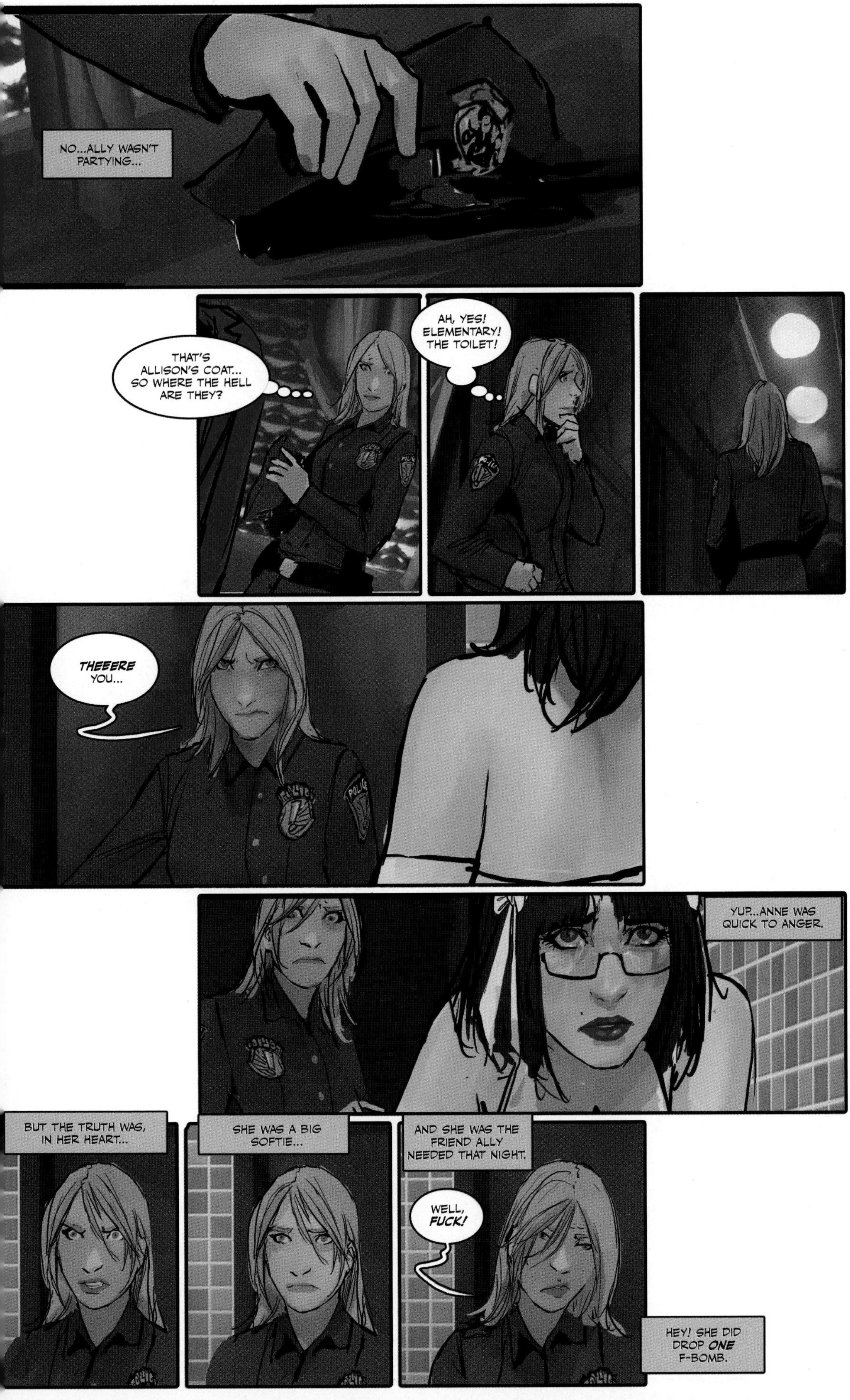
NO...ALLY WASN'T PARTYING...
THAT'S ALLISON'S COAT... SO WHERE THE HELL ARE THEY?
AH, YES! ELEMENTARY! THE TOILET!
THEEERE YOU...
YUP...ANNE WAS QUICK TO ANGER.
BUT THE TRUTH WAS, IN HER HEART...
SHE WAS A BIG SOFTIE...
AND SHE WAS THE FRIEND ALLY NEEDED THAT NIGHT.
WELL, FUCK!
HEY! SHE DID DROP ONE F-BOMB.

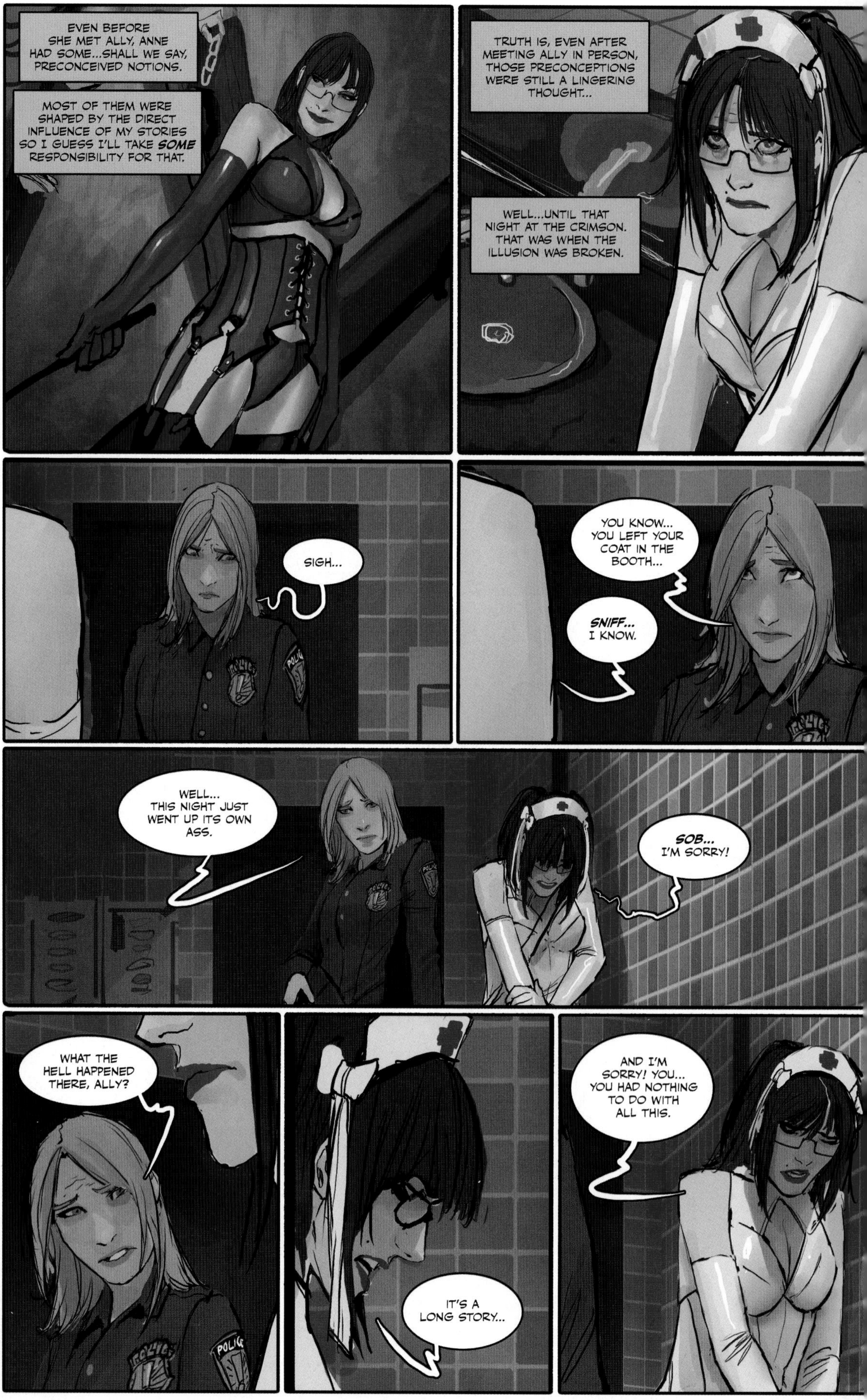
EVEN BEFORE SHE MET ALLY, ANNE HAD SOME...SHALL WE SAY, PRECONCEIVED NOTIONS.
MOST OF THEM WERE SHAPED BY THE DIRECT INFLUENCE OF MY STORIES SO I GUESS I'LL TAKE ***SOME*** RESPONSIBILITY FOR THAT.
TRUTH IS, EVEN AFTER MEETING ALLY IN PERSON, THOSE PRECONCEPTIONS WERE STILL A LINGERING THOUGHT...
WELL...UNTIL THAT NIGHT AT THE CRIMSON. THAT WAS WHEN THE ILLUSION WAS BROKEN.
SIGH...
YOU KNOW... YOU LEFT YOUR COAT IN THE BOOTH...
SNIFF... I KNOW.
WELL... THIS NIGHT JUST WENT UP ITS OWN ASS.
SOB... I'M SORRY!
WHAT THE HELL HAPPENED THERE, ALLY?
IT'S A LONG STORY...
AND I'M SORRY! YOU... YOU HAD NOTHING TO DO WITH ALL THIS.

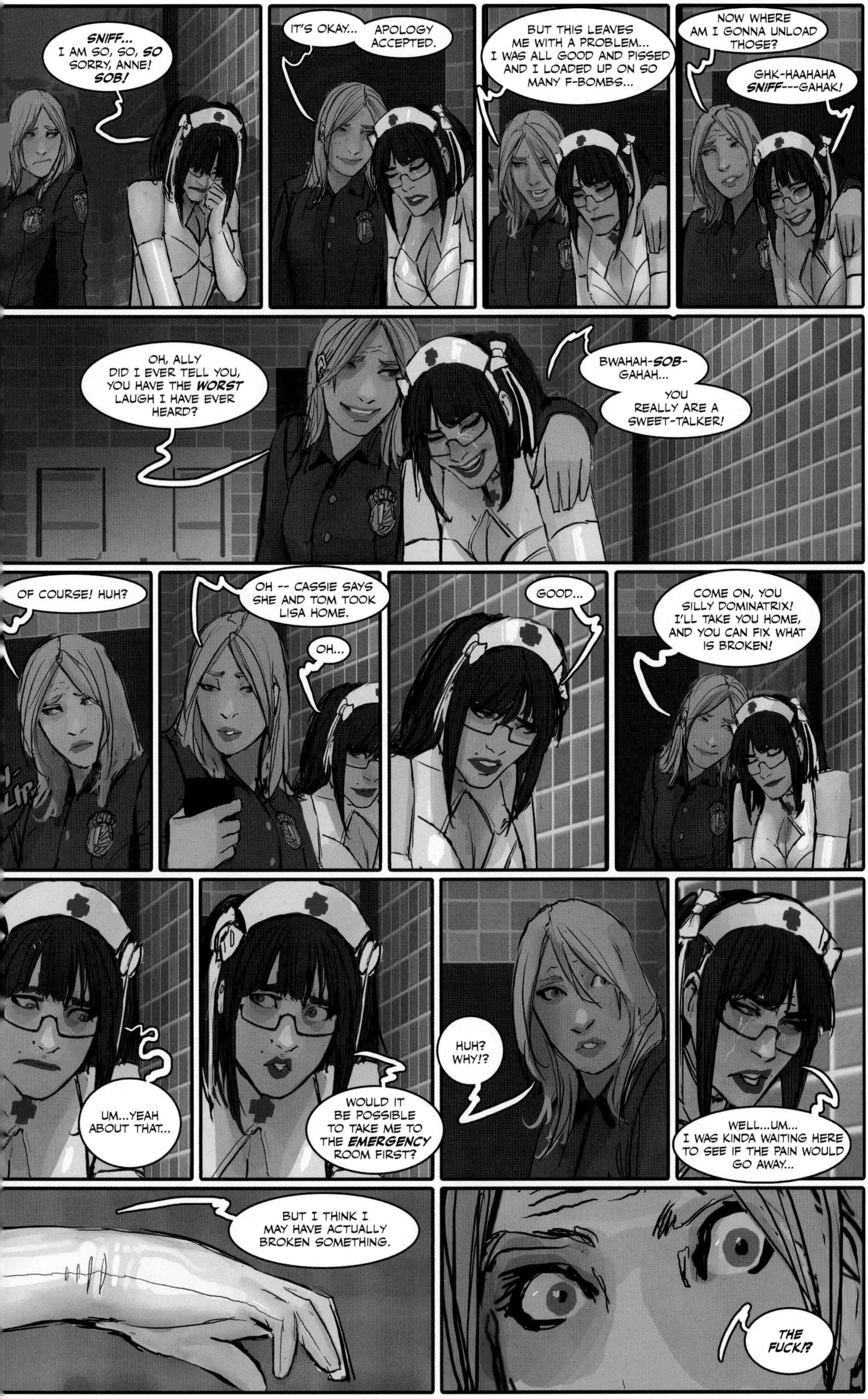
SNIFF... I AM SO, SO, SO SORRY, ANNE! SOB!
IT'S OKAY...
APOLOGY ACCEPTED.
BUT THIS LEAVES ME WITH A PROBLEM... I WAS ALL GOOD AND PISSED AND I LOADED UP ON SO MANY F-BOMBS...
NOW WHERE AM I GONNA UNLOAD THOSE?
GHK-HAAHAHA SNIFF---GAHAK!
OH, ALLY DID I EVER TELL YOU, YOU HAVE THE WORST LAUGH I HAVE EVER HEARD?
BWAHAH-SOB-GAHAH...
YOU REALLY ARE A SWEET-TALKER!
OF COURSE! HUH?
OH -- CASSIE SAYS SHE AND TOM TOOK LISA HOME.
OH...
GOOD...
COME ON, YOU SILLY DOMINATRIX! I'LL TAKE YOU HOME, AND YOU CAN FIX WHAT IS BROKEN!
UM...YEAH ABOUT THAT...
WOULD IT BE POSSIBLE TO TAKE ME TO THE EMERGENCY ROOM FIRST?
HUH? WHY!?
WELL...UM... I WAS KINDA WAITING HERE TO SEE IF THE PAIN WOULD GO AWAY...
BUT I THINK I MAY HAVE ACTUALLY BROKEN SOMETHING.
THE FUCK!?

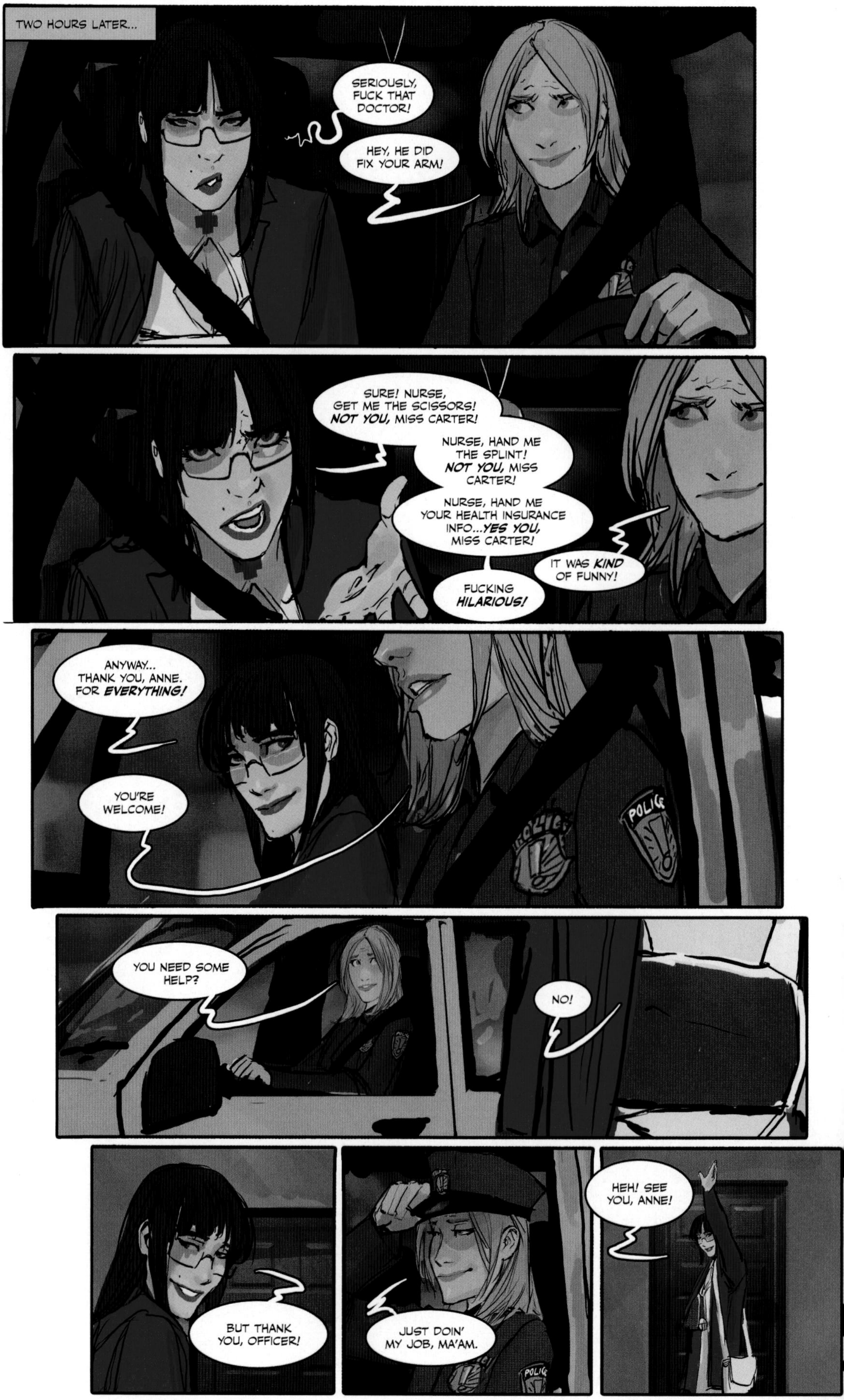
TWO HOURS LATER...
SERIOUSLY, FUCK THAT DOCTOR!
HEY, HE DID FIX YOUR ARM!
SURE! NURSE, GET ME THE SCISSORS! NOT YOU, MISS CARTER!
NURSE, HAND ME THE SPLINT! NOT YOU, MISS CARTER!
NURSE, HAND ME YOUR HEALTH INSURANCE INFO...YES YOU, MISS CARTER!
IT WAS KIND OF FUNNY!
FUCKING HILARIOUS!
ANYWAY... THANK YOU, ANNE. FOR EVERYTHING!
YOU'RE WELCOME!
POLICE
YOU NEED SOME HELP?
NO!
BUT THANK YOU, OFFICER!
JUST DOIN' MY JOB, MA'AM.
HEH! SEE YOU, ANNE!

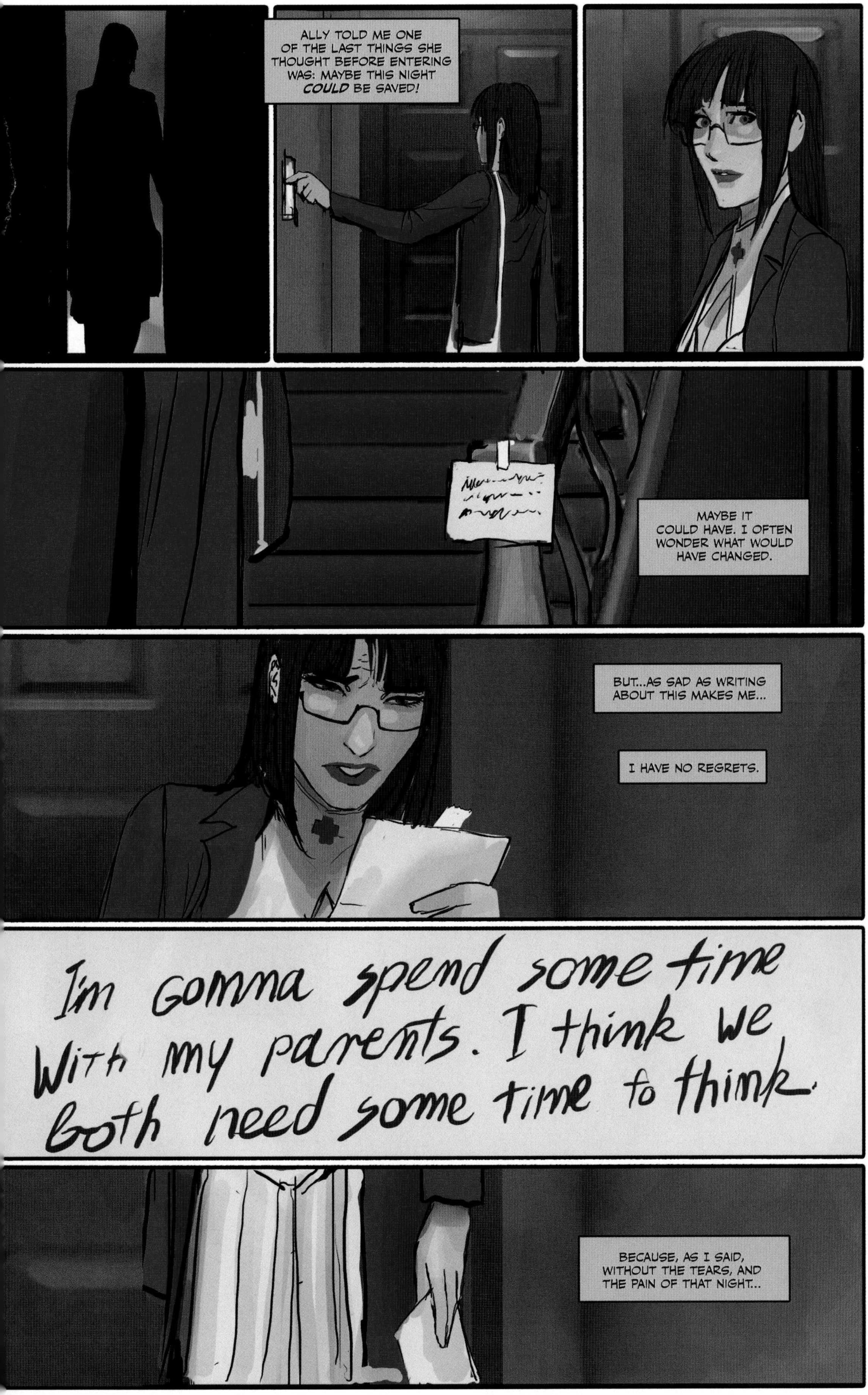
ALLY TOLD ME ONE OF THE LAST THINGS SHE THOUGHT BEFORE ENTERING WAS: MAYBE THIS NIGHT *COULD* BE SAVED!
MAYBE IT COULD HAVE. I OFTEN WONDER WHAT WOULD HAVE CHANGED.
BUT...AS SAD AS WRITING ABOUT THIS MAKES ME...
I HAVE NO REGRETS.
I'm gonna spend some time with my parents. I think we both need some time to think.
BECAUSE, AS I SAID, WITHOUT THE TEARS, AND THE PAIN OF THAT NIGHT...

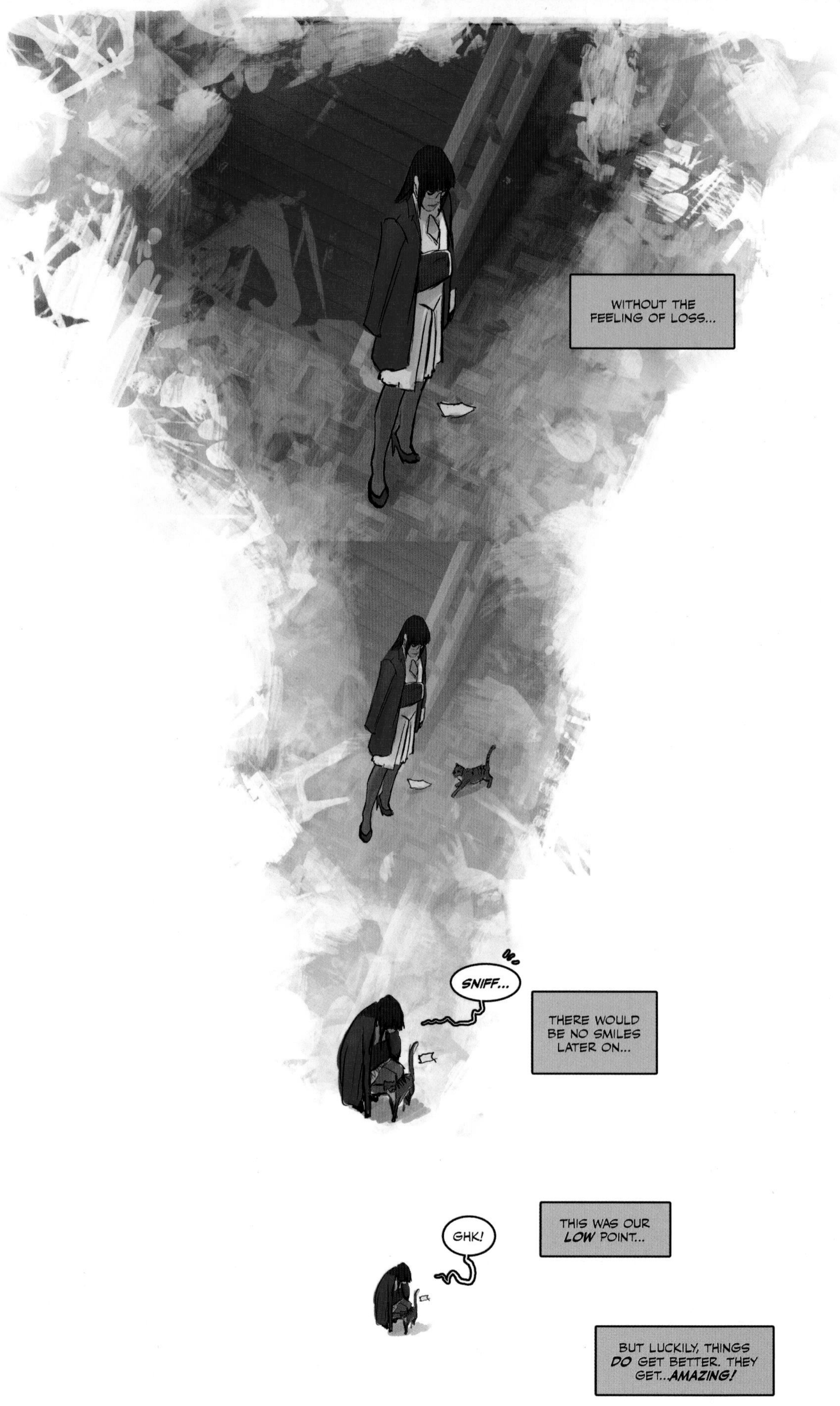
WITHOUT THE FEELING OF LOSS...
SNIFF...
THERE WOULD BE NO SMILES LATER ON...
GHK!
THIS WAS OUR LOW POINT...
BUT LUCKILY, THINGS DO GET BETTER. THEY GET...AMAZING!

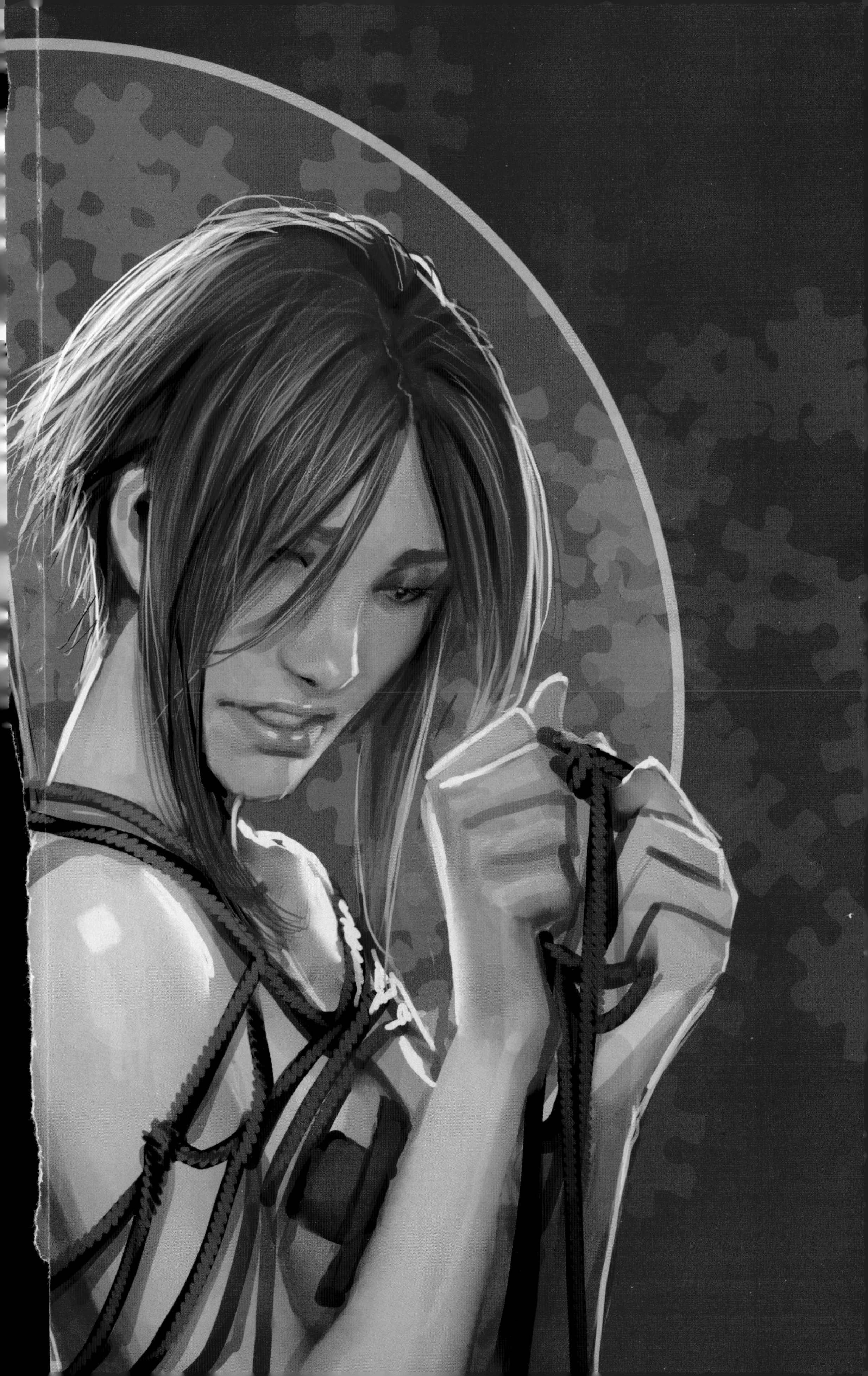

Read the Entire Seduction with...

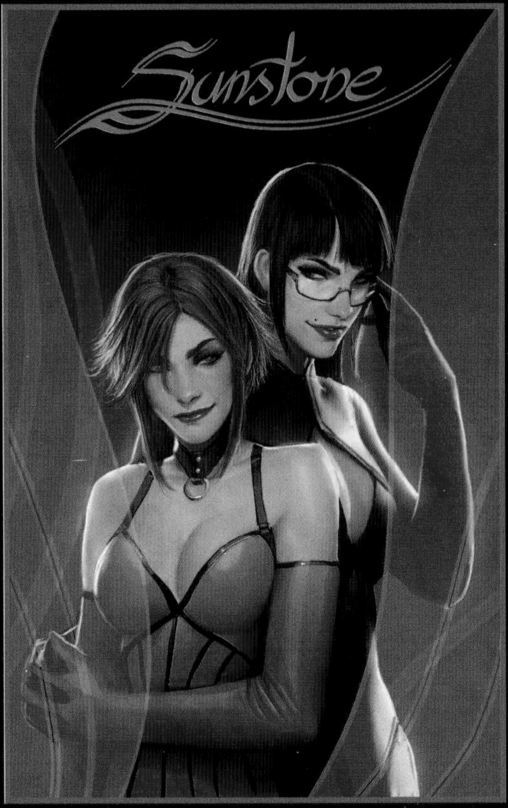
Sunstone

Volume 1

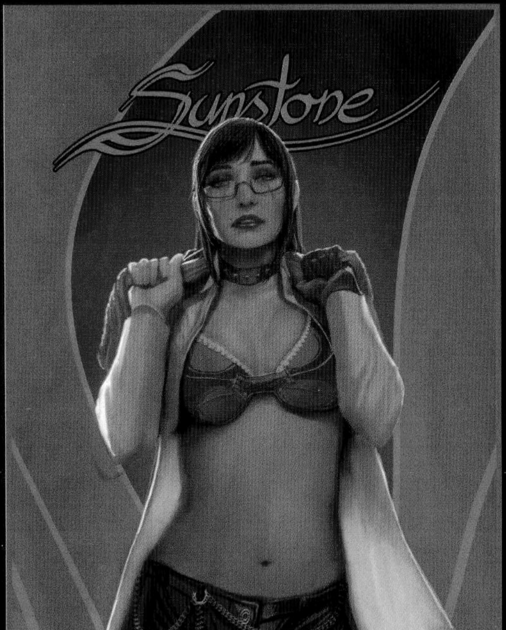
Sunstone

Volume 2

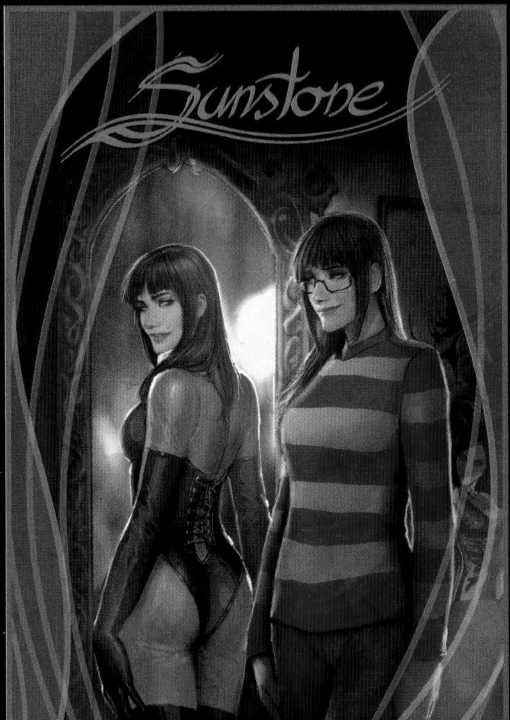
Sunstone

Volume 3

Available Now!

The Top Cow essentials checklist:

Aphrodite IX: Complete Series
(ISBN: 978-1-63215-368-5)

Artifacts Origins: First Born
(ISBN: 978-1-60706-506-7)

Broken Trinity, Volume 1
(ISBN: 978-1-60706-051-2)

Cyber Force: Rebirth, Volume 1
(ISBN: 978-1-60706-671-2)

The Darkness: Accursed, Volume 1
(ISBN: 978-1-58240-958-0)

The Darkness: Rebirth, Volume 1
(ISBN: 978-1-60706-585-2)

Death Vigil, Volume 1
(ISBN: 978-1-63215-278-7)

Impaler, Volume 1
(ISBN: 978-1-58240-757-9)

Postal, Volume 1
(ISBN: 978-1-63215-342-5)

Rising Stars Compendium
(ISBN: 978-1-63215-246-6)

Sunstone, Volume 1
(ISBN: 978-1-63215-212-1)

Think Tank, Volume 1
(ISBN: 978-1-60706-660-6)

Wanted
(ISBN: 978-1-58240-497-4)

Wildfire, Volume 1
(ISBN: 978-1-63215-024-0)

Witchblade: Redemption, Volume 1
(ISBN: 978-1-60706-193-9)

Witchblade: Rebirth, Volume 1
(ISBN: 978-1-60706-532-6)

Witchblade: Borne Again, Volume 1
(ISBN: 978-1-63215-025-7)

For more ISBN and ordering information on our latest collections go to:
www.topcow.com
Ask your retailer about our catalogue of collected editions,
digests, and hard covers or check the listings at:
Barnes and Noble, Amazon.com,
and other fine retailers.

To find your nearest comic shop go to:
www.comicshoplocator.com